The Complete Warrior's Mindset Collection (Vol. 7)

*Thus Spoke Zarathustra, Beyond Good and Evil &
Twilight of the Idols
— Nietzsche's Path to Self-Overcoming*

A Modern Translation

Adapted for the Contemporary Reader

Friedrich Nietzsche

Translated by Tim Zengerink

Table of Contents

Preface - Message to the Reader

What If You Could Help Rebuild the Greatest Library in Human History?

Thousands of years ago, the Library of Alexandria stood as the crown jewel of human achievement — a sanctuary where the collected wisdom of every known civilization was gathered, preserved, and shared freely.

And then, it was lost.

Through fire, conquest, and the slow erosion of time, humanity lost not just books — but ideas, dreams, discoveries, and stories that could have changed the world forever.

Today, the Library of Alexandria lives again — and you are invited to be a part of its restoration.

Our mission is simple yet profound:

To rebuild the greatest library the world has ever known, and to translate all timeless works into every language and dialect, so that no seeker of knowledge is ever left behind again.

By joining our movement to rebuild the modern Library of Alexandria, you become part of an unprecedented mission:

- **Unlimited Access to the Greatest Audiobooks & eBooks Ever Written:**

  Instantly explore thousands of legendary works—Plato, Shakespeare, Jane Austen, Leo Tolstoy, and countless more. All instantly available to read or listen, placing a complete literary universe at your fingertips.

- **Beautiful Paperback & Deluxe Editions at Printing Cost**

  Own any title as an elegant paperback, deluxe hardcover, or stunning collectible boxset—offered to you at true printing cost, delivered straight to your door. Build your personal Library of Alexandria, crafted for beauty, built for durability, and worthy of proud display.

- **Fresh Translations for Modern Readers—in Every Language & Dialect**

  Enjoy timeless masterpieces reimagined in clear, contemporary language—no more outdated phrases or obscure references. Alongside the original versions, we're tirelessly translating these classics into every language and dialect imaginable, ensuring accessibility and understanding across cultures and generations.

- **Join a Global Renaissance of Literature & Knowledge**

  You directly support expanding our library, publishing deluxe editions at true cost, translating works into all global languages, and bringing humanity's greatest stories to people everywhere. By joining today, you're not just preserving a legacy of masterpieces; you set in motion a powerful wave of literary accessibility.

Become a Torchbearer of Knowledge.

Join us for free now at **LibraryofAlexandria.com**

Together, we will ensure that the light of human wisdom never fades again.

With gratitude and a shared love of knowledge,
The Modern Library of Alexandria Team

Visit:

www.libraryofalexandria.com

Or scan the code below:

Introduction

Nietzsche's Warrior of the Spirit:
Overcoming, Revaluation, and the Will to Power

True warfare begins within. Before any sword is raised or battle joined, there is an inner conflict that precedes all outward victory: the struggle against mediocrity, conformity, resentment, and fear. In The Complete Warrior's Mindset Collection (Vol. 7), we enter the psychological, philosophical, and poetic battleground of Friedrich Nietzsche—one of the most provocative and enduring voices of self-mastery, radical strength, and existential confrontation.

This volume brings together three of Nietzsche's most transformative works: Thus Spoke Zarathustra, Beyond Good and Evil, and Twilight of the Idols. These are not books in the traditional sense. They are calls to arms. They seek not to inform, but to awaken—to destroy comfortable illusions, ignite the will to power, and guide the reader toward what Nietzsche called "self-overcoming."

Nietzsche is not a strategist in the military sense. His battlefield is the human soul, and his enemies are passive obedience, herd morality, and the life-denying values of traditional religion and philosophy. He believed that modern humanity had lost its way, becoming weak, resentful, and enslaved to inherited truths. His mission was to revalue all values—to break the old tablets and call forth a new type of human being: the Übermensch, or overman.

In these three texts, Nietzsche stages his philosophical revolution. Zarathustra offers a mythic narrative of personal transformation and prophetic rebirth. Beyond Good and Evil dismantles the illusions of traditional morality and exposes the psychological mechanisms of power. Twilight of the Idols hammers down the idols of Plato, Christianity, and morality itself, offering a new vision of strength, joy, and creative affirmation.

This introduction will explore Nietzsche's central themes, how each work contributes to the warrior's mindset, and how Nietzsche's philosophy challenges us to transcend comfort and become what we are. Nietzsche is not easy. He does not offer certainty, only fire. But for those willing to engage him, he offers one of the most powerful paths to inner clarity and outer courage ever written.

Zarathustra and the Myth of the Overman

Written in a lyrical, parable-like style, Thus Spoke Zarathustra (1883–1885) is Nietzsche's most ambitious and poetic work. It presents the teachings of Zarathustra, a prophet who descends from the mountains to bring a new message to humanity: that we must move beyond old gods, old morals, and old selves to give birth to something higher.

The central idea of Zarathustra is self-overcoming—the process by which individuals shed inherited values, confront their own weakness, and transform themselves into creators of meaning. Zarathustra's message is not merely philosophical—it is existential. He demands not only that we think differently, but that we live differently.

The book introduces some of Nietzsche's most famous concepts:

- The death of God, not as a religious doctrine, but as a cultural event marking the collapse of absolute truth.
- The Übermensch, the "overman" who creates his own values, dances with life's chaos, and lives with joyful responsibility.
- The doctrine of eternal recurrence, which challenges us to live as though we would repeat every moment forever.

Zarathustra himself is not a perfect guide. He struggles, fails, and retreats. Nietzsche uses him as a symbol of the difficulty of transformation. The path to the overman is not linear. It requires solitude, risk, suffering, and strength.

For the warrior-mind, Zarathustra is a training ground. It teaches that before you can command others, you must command yourself. That before you can lead, you must endure. That before you can act with power, you must break through the illusions that bind you. It is a book not of doctrine, but of challenge—and only those who rise to meet it can claim its rewards.

Beyond Good and Evil: Morality, Power, and the Courage to See

In Beyond Good and Evil (1886), Nietzsche turns from mythic poetry to aphoristic philosophy. Here he presents his critique of traditional morality more systematically, arguing that our so-called virtues—humility, meekness, compassion—are not universal truths, but the historical inventions of the weak.

He introduces the distinction between master morality and slave morality:

- Master morality arises from those who affirm life, assert power, and define good as strength, nobility, and vitality.
- Slave morality arises from the weak, who define good as meekness and evil as anything strong. It is reactive, born of ressentiment, a poisoned inversion of values.

Nietzsche argues that modern Europe, shaped by Christian morality and democratic idealism, has become dominated by slave morality. It praises safety over risk, equality over excellence, and guilt over joy. He sees philosophy itself as corrupted—no longer a quest for wisdom, but a disguise for the psychological needs of its creators.

What does Nietzsche propose instead? A new type of philosopher: the free spirit. This is a person who thinks dangerously, independently, and without the need for approval. The free spirit rejects herd values, laughs at sacred cows, and lives with intellectual nobility.

Beyond Good and Evil is a manual for such spirits. It teaches the warrior to question every assumption, to see behind every moral veil, and to understand power not as dominance, but as the ability to affirm life without illusion.

This is not a philosophy of cruelty. Nietzsche does not want a world of tyrants. He wants a world of creators—people strong enough to live without crutches, to will their own way into being, and to shape a culture worthy of admiration. For the warrior, it is a call to discernment, a reminder that ethics must be chosen, not inherited.

Twilight of the Idols: Hammering Down the False

Written in 1888, just before Nietzsche's collapse into madness, Twilight of the Idols is a furious, compact attack on everything Nietzsche saw as life-denying in Western culture. Subtitled "How to Philosophize with a Hammer," the book is Nietzsche's final declaration of war on the traditions he believed had poisoned vitality, strength, and joy.

He takes aim at:

- Socrates, for turning life into a problem to be solved rather than a force to be lived.
- Christianity, for teaching weakness, guilt, and the glorification of suffering.
- German philosophy, for obscuring truth behind abstractions and "moralistic" cowardice.

Nietzsche's hammer is not meant to destroy indiscriminately. He taps on the idols to test their hollowness. He wants to expose which values are decaying corpses, kept alive by habit and fear.

One of the central themes is anti-natural morality—Nietzsche's term for systems that deny instinct, repress desire, and make life itself a problem. He calls instead for a revaluation of all values. This is not a call to nihilism, but to rebirth. Nietzsche does not want nothing— he wants a new dawn.

Twilight of the Idols also contains one of Nietzsche's most important practical teachings: the idea of life affirmation. The highest sign of strength, he says, is not the ability to endure pain, but the ability to say "yes" to life in all its complexity. Even suffering, even chaos, must be embraced if we are to become whole.

For the warrior, this book is a sword. It teaches that not all tradition is sacred. That not all wisdom is wise. That to live fully, we must be willing to destroy illusions, confront falsehoods, and rebuild values from the ground up.

The Warrior of the Future: Nietzsche's Call to Greatness

In the synthesis of Zarathustra, Beyond Good and Evil, and Twilight of the Idols, Nietzsche offers a complete warrior philosophy—not of conquest over others, but of conquest over the self, and over the forces of cultural stagnation that limit human potential.

His path is not for everyone. It is difficult, dangerous, and lonely. But it is also liberating. It asks you to:

- Abandon inherited morality and build your own.
- Face suffering not with victimhood, but with artistic creation.
- Live with such intensity that every moment could be lived again.
- Break from the herd and take responsibility for shaping meaning.

Nietzsche does not give instructions. He offers provocations. He does not provide answers. He offers tools. He does not soothe. He sharpens.

For those on the warrior's path, Nietzsche's philosophy is essential. It develops the inner sight needed to avoid false virtue. It trains the will to affirm existence without excuse. It demands that we build our lives as we would build a sculpture: with discipline, passion, and the courage to strike away what is no longer true.

Welcome to The Complete Warrior's Mindset Collection (Vol. 7). May Nietzsche's fire illuminate your path—not with comfort, but with clarity, courage, and the strength to become who you truly are.

Thus Spoke Zarathustra

Friedrich Nietzsche

Introduction

"That which does not kill us makes us stronger."
~ Friedrich Nietzsche

Friedrich Wilhelm Nietzsche, one of the most influential and thought-provoking philosophers of the 19th century, questioned traditional beliefs and reshaped Western philosophy. His works explore the essence of human life, examining morality, religion, and the nature of power and knowledge. This collection gathers some of Nietzsche's most impactful writings, giving readers a full view of his revolutionary ideas.

In Thus Spoke Zarathustra, Nietzsche introduces the idea of the Übermensch and discusses the death of God and the concept of eternal return. Beyond Good and Evil challenges traditional moral values, while The Genealogy of Morals looks at the roots of guilt and punishment. The Will to Power, compiled from his notes after his death, presents Nietzsche's view that human actions are driven by a basic will to dominate.

Ecce Homo is a personal reflection on his life, and The Antichrist offers a strong critique of Christianity. In Twilight of the Idols, Nietzsche condenses his ideas into sharp, critical insights. Human, All Too Human and The Gay Science explore metaphysics, religion, and existentialism through aphorisms, while Daybreak questions moral values. Finally, The Birth of Tragedy shows Nietzsche's early thoughts on art, tragedy, and the conflict between reason and emotion.

Together, these writings create a deep picture of Nietzsche's philosophical journey, making this collection a valuable introduction to his transformative ideas.

Zarathustra's Prologue

When Zarathustra turned thirty, he left his home and the lake he grew up near, and went up into the mountains. There he enjoyed his spirit and solitude, and for ten years, he never grew tired of it. But finally, his heart changed. Rising one morning with the rosy dawn, he stood before the sun and spoke to it:

"You great star! What would your joy be if you had no one to shine for?

For ten years, you have climbed up to my cave: you would have grown tired of your light and the journey if not for me, my eagle, and my serpent.

Every morning, we awaited you, took in your overflow, and thanked you for it.

Look! I am tired of my wisdom, like a bee that has collected too much honey; I need hands to reach out and take it.

I want to give and share, so that the wise can become joyful again in their folly, and the poor can be happy in their wealth.

So, I must go down into the depths, just as you do in the evening when you sink below the sea and shine on the underworld, overflowing star!

I must go down, as people say, to those to whom I will descend.

Bless me, then, you calm eye, which can see even the greatest happiness without envy!

Bless the cup that is about to overflow, so that the water may pour out golden and carry your joy everywhere!

Look! This cup is about to empty itself again, and Zarathustra is going to be a man once more."

Thus began Zarathustra's descent.

Zarathustra went down the mountain alone, with no one meeting him. But when he entered the forest, an old man suddenly stood before him, who had left his simple hut to gather roots. And the old man spoke to Zarathustra:

"This wanderer is no stranger to me: he passed by many years ago. He was called Zarathustra; but he has changed.

Then, you carried your ashes up into the mountains; do you now want to carry your fire into the valleys? Aren't you afraid of the fate of an arsonist?

Yes, I recognize Zarathustra. His eyes are pure, and there's no bitterness around his mouth. Doesn't he walk like a dancer?

Zarathustra has changed; Zarathustra has become like a child; Zarathustra is awakened. But what will you do in the land of the sleepers?"

"You have lived in solitude as in the sea, and it has supported you. But now, will you go ashore? Will you carry your body again yourself?"

Zarathustra replied, "I love humanity."

"Why," asked the saint, "did I go into the forest and desert? Was it not because I loved people too much?

Now I love God; people, I do not love. Humanity is too flawed for me. Loving people would destroy me."

Zarathustra answered, "I didn't speak of love! I am bringing gifts to humanity."

"Give them nothing," said the saint. "Instead, share their burdens and carry them with them—that's what they'll appreciate most, if that suits you!

But if you must give them something, give only a small offering, and let them ask for it!"

"No," replied Zarathustra, "I don't give alms. I am not poor enough for that."

The saint laughed at Zarathustra and said, "Then make sure they accept your treasures! People don't trust hermits, and they don't believe we come with gifts.

Our footsteps sound too empty on their streets. And just as they think, when they hear a man walking before sunrise, 'Where goes the thief?'

Don't go to people; stay in the forest! Go to the animals! Why not be like me—a bear among bears, a bird among birds?"

"And what does the saint do in the forest?" asked Zarathustra.

The saint answered, "I make hymns and sing them; in making hymns, I laugh, weep, and mumble: that's how I praise God.

With singing, weeping, laughing, and mumbling, I praise the God who is my God. But what do you bring us as a gift?"

When Zarathustra heard these words, he bowed to the saint and said, "What do I have to give you! Let me hurry on before I take anything from you!" And so they parted, laughing like schoolboys.

When Zarathustra was alone, he said to himself, "Could it be possible! This old saint in the forest hasn't yet heard that God is dead!"

When Zarathustra arrived at the nearest town bordering the forest, he found a crowd gathered in the marketplace, for it had been announced that a tightrope walker would perform. And Zarathustra spoke to the people:

"I teach you the Superman. Humanity is something to be surpassed. What have you done to surpass humanity?

Every being up until now has created something beyond itself. And do you want to be the ebb of that great tide, and go back to the beast rather than rise beyond humanity?

What is the ape to humanity? A joke, a shame. And so shall humanity be to the Superman: a joke, a shame.

You have crawled your way from worm to human, and there's still much of the worm in you. You were once apes, and even now, humanity is more ape-like than any ape.

Even the wisest among you is only a mixture of plant and ghost. But do I ask you to become ghosts or plants?"

"Behold, I teach you the Superman!

The Superman is the meaning of the earth. Let your will declare: The Superman shall be the meaning of the earth!

I urge you, my brothers, stay true to the earth, and do not believe those who speak of hopes beyond this world! They are poisoners, whether they know it or not.

They are life's despisers, decayed and poisoned themselves, and the earth is weary of them—so cast them aside!

Once, blasphemy against God was the greatest sin; but God has died, and so have those blasphemers. Now, to curse the earth is the most dreadful sin, to place the heart of the unknowable above the meaning of the earth!

Once, the soul looked down upon the body, and this contempt was seen as the highest virtue. The soul wanted the body to be thin, pale, and starving. It thought it could free itself from the body and the earth that way.

Oh, but that soul was itself thin, pale, and starving—and cruelty was the joy of that soul!

But tell me, my brothers, what does your body say about your soul? Isn't your soul poor, polluted, and trapped in miserable self-satisfaction?

Truly, humanity is like a polluted stream. One must be an ocean to take in a polluted stream without becoming impure.

Behold, I teach you the Superman: he is that ocean; in him, your deepest contempt can be submerged.

What is the greatest experience you can have? It is the hour of profound contempt—the hour when even your happiness disgusts you, and so does your wisdom and virtue.

The hour when you say: 'What good is my happiness! It's nothing but poverty, pollution, and miserable self-satisfaction. But my happiness should justify life itself!'

The hour when you say: 'What good is my wisdom! Does it hunger for truth like a lion hungers for food? No—it's just poverty, pollution, and self-satisfaction!'

The hour when you say: 'What good is my virtue! It has not made me passionate. How tired I am of my good and my evil! It's all just poverty, pollution, and self-satisfaction!'

The hour when you say: 'What good is my justice! I do not see myself as fire and fuel. But the truly just are like fire and fuel!'

The hour when you say: 'What good is my pity! Isn't pity the cross that crucifies anyone who loves mankind? But my pity is no crucifixion.'

Have you ever spoken like this? Have you ever cried out like this? Oh, how I wish I had heard you cry out like this!

It's not your sin—it's your self-satisfaction that cries to the heavens; your very restraint in sinning cries to the heavens!

Where is the lightning to strike you down? Where is the madness that should infect you?

Behold, I teach you the Superman: he is that lightning, he is that madness!"

When Zarathustra had spoken, one of the crowd shouted, "We've heard enough about the tightrope walker; it's time to see him now!" And all the people laughed at Zarathustra. But the tightrope walker, thinking they were speaking to him, began his act.

Zarathustra, however, looked at the crowd with curiosity. Then he said:

"Humanity is a rope stretched between the animal and the Superman—a rope over an abyss.

It is a dangerous crossing, a risky journey, a perilous looking back, a trembling and hesitating.

What is great in humanity is that it is a bridge, not a destination. What is lovable in humanity is that it is an overcoming and a descent.

I love those who don't know how to live except as those who go down, for they are the ones who rise above.

I love the great despisers, for they are the great adorers, and arrows of longing for the far shore.

I love those who don't seek reasons beyond the stars to go down and make sacrifices, but who sacrifice themselves for the earth so that the world of the Superman may one day arrive.

I love those who live to understand, and seek to understand so that the Superman may one day live. In this way, they seek their own descent.

I love those who labor and create, building a home for the Superman and preparing the earth, the animals, and the plants for him. In this way, they seek their own descent.

I love those who love their virtue, for virtue is the will to descend and an arrow of longing.

I love those who keep no part of the spirit for themselves but want to be entirely the spirit of their virtue: they walk as spirits over the bridge.

I love those who make their virtue their purpose and fate, willing to live for it—or not to live at all.

I love those who do not desire too many virtues. One virtue is more virtuous than two because it is a stronger bond for one's destiny.

I love those whose souls are generous, who want no thanks and do not take anything back: for they always give and desire nothing for themselves.

I love those who feel ashamed when luck favors them, and who ask, 'Am I playing unfairly?'—for they are willing to fall.

I love those who scatter golden words before their actions, and who always do more than they promise: for they seek their own descent.

I love those who justify those who come after, and redeem those who came before: for they are willing to give themselves up in the present.

I love those who challenge their god, because they love their god: for they must fall through the wrath of their god.

I love those whose souls are deep, even when they suffer, and who can fall through the smallest of things: in this way, they cross the bridge willingly.

I love those whose souls are so full that they forget themselves, and everything fills them: in this way, everything becomes their descent.

I love those who are free in spirit and heart: thus, their head serves only their heart; and their heart leads them to descend.

I love all who are like heavy drops falling one by one from the dark cloud hanging over humanity: they are signs of the coming lightning, and they fall as its heralds.

Behold, I am a herald of the lightning, a heavy drop from the cloud: the lightning, however, is the Superman."

When Zarathustra had spoken these words, he looked again at the people and fell silent. "There they stand," he said to himself, "there they laugh; they do not understand me. I am not the voice for these ears."

"Must one first strike their ears, so they can learn to see with their eyes? Must one make noise like kettledrums or preach like a penitent? Or do they only believe the stammerer?

They are proud of something. What is it they call this thing that fills them with pride? They call it 'culture'; it sets them apart from the goatherds.

They don't want to hear about 'contempt' for themselves. So I will appeal to their pride.

I will speak to them of the most despicable thing: that is the last man!"

And Zarathustra spoke to the crowd:

"It is time for humanity to set a goal. It is time for humanity to plant the seed of its highest hope.

The soil is still rich enough for this. But one day that soil will be barren and lifeless, and no mighty tree will be able to grow in it anymore.

Alas! The time will come when humanity will no longer shoot its arrow of longing beyond itself—and the string of its bow will lose the sound of its flight!

I tell you: there must still be chaos within you to give birth to a dancing star. I tell you: you still have chaos within you.

Alas! The time will come when humanity will no longer give birth to any stars. Alas! The time of the most despicable man is coming, the one who can no longer despise himself.

Behold! I show you the last man.

'What is love? What is creation? What is longing? What is a star?'— so asks the last man, blinking.

The earth has become small, and on it hops the last man who makes everything small. His species is as indestructible as the flea; the last man lives the longest.

'We have discovered happiness,' say the last men, blinking.

They have left the lands where life is hard; they need warmth. People still love their neighbors and rub against each other—for warmth.

To feel ill or distrustful is seen as sinful: they walk carefully. It's foolish to stumble over stones or people!

A little poison now and then makes for pleasant dreams. And a lot of poison at the end makes for a gentle death.

People still work, for work is entertainment. But they are careful not to let it hurt them.

People no longer become poor or rich; both are too much trouble. Who still wants to rule? Who still wants to obey? Both are too much trouble.

No shepherd and one herd! Everyone wants the same; everyone is equal: anyone who feels differently voluntarily goes to the asylum.

'In the past, the whole world was mad,' say the cleverest among them, blinking.

They're sharp and know everything that has happened, so they can endlessly mock. People still argue, but quickly make up—otherwise it upsets their stomachs.

They have their little pleasures by day, and their little pleasures by night, but they take care of their health.

'We have discovered happiness,' say the last men, blinking."

And here Zarathustra's first speech ended, also called "The Prologue." For at this point, the crowd's laughter and shouts interrupted him. "Give us this last man, O Zarathustra," they cried, "make us these last men! Then we will give you the Superman!" And all the people cheered and smacked their lips.

But Zarathustra grew sad and said to himself:

"They do not understand me; I am not the voice for these ears."

"Perhaps I have lived too long in the mountains; perhaps I have listened too much to the streams and trees. Now I speak to these people as if they were goatherds.

My soul is calm and clear, like the mountains in the morning. But they think I am cold, a jester with terrible jokes.

They look at me and laugh, yet while they laugh, they hate me too. There is ice in their laughter."

Then something happened that silenced every mouth and fixed every eye. Meanwhile, the rope-dancer had begun his act: he had stepped out from a small door and was walking along a rope stretched between two towers, hanging above the marketplace and the crowd. When he was halfway across, the little door opened again, and a brightly dressed figure, like a clown, sprang out and hurried after him. "Move along, cripple!" he shouted, "move along, lazybones, intruder, pale-face!—or I'll nudge you with my heel! What are you doing here between the towers? You belong in the tower; you should be locked up! You're blocking the way for someone better than you!"—And with every word, he got closer and closer to the first man. But when he was just a step behind, the horrible thing happened that silenced every mouth and fixed every eye—he let out a scream like a demon and jumped over the man in his way. The first man, seeing his rival triumph, lost both his balance and his grip on the rope. He threw away his pole and fell downward, a whirl of flailing arms and legs, faster than the pole, into the depths. The marketplace and the crowd were like the sea as a storm arrives: they scattered in all directions, especially where the body was about to land.

Zarathustra, however, remained standing, and the body fell just beside him, badly injured and disfigured, but not yet dead. After a while, the injured man regained consciousness and saw Zarathustra kneeling beside him. "What are you doing here?" he said at last. "I knew long ago the devil would trip me up. Now he's dragging me to hell. Will you stop him?"

"On my honor, my friend," answered Zarathustra, "there is nothing of what you speak: there is no devil and no hell. Your soul will be dead even sooner than your body. So fear nothing more!"

The man looked up, doubtful. "If you speak the truth," he said, "then I lose nothing by losing my life. I am nothing more than an animal that was taught to dance through punishment and starvation."

"Not at all," said Zarathustra, "you made danger your calling, and there's nothing contemptible in that. Now you perish by your calling: therefore, I will bury you with my own hands."

After Zarathustra said this, the dying man did not answer, but he reached out his hand as if to find Zarathustra's in gratitude.

Evening fell, and the marketplace grew dark. Then the crowd dispersed, for even curiosity and fear grow weary. Zarathustra, however, still sat beside the dead man on the ground, deep in thought, forgetting the time. At last, night came, and a cold wind blew upon him, alone. Then Zarathustra stood up and said to his heart:

"Truly, Zarathustra has made a fine catch today! He has not caught a man but a corpse.

Somber is human life and still without meaning: even a clown can bring fate to it.

I want to teach people the purpose of their existence, which is the Superman, the lightning that comes from the dark cloud of man.

But I am still far from them, and my meaning does not speak to their understanding. To people, I am still something between a fool and a corpse.

The night is dark, and Zarathustra's path is dark. Come, cold and stiff companion! I will carry you to the place where I will bury you with my own hands."

When Zarathustra had spoken these words to himself, he lifted the corpse onto his shoulders and set off. Yet he had hardly gone a hundred steps when a man crept up and whispered in his ear—and it was none other than the buffoon from the tower. "Leave this town, O Zarathustra," he said, "there are too many here who hate you. The good and just despise you, calling you their enemy and critic; the orthodox believers see you as a threat to the crowd. You were fortunate to be laughed at, and indeed, you spoke like a jester. It was your good fortune to associate with the dead dog; by humiliating yourself, you saved your life today. Leave this town—or tomorrow I will jump over you, a living man over a dead one."

With that, the buffoon vanished, and Zarathustra continued through the dark streets.

At the town gate, he met the grave-diggers. They shone a torch on his face, and recognizing him, mocked him. "Look! Zarathustra is carrying away the dead dog. Zarathustra has become a grave-digger! Our hands are too clean for that kind of work. Will Zarathustra snatch a bite from the devil's plate? Good luck, then, to the feast! Unless the devil proves to be a better thief than Zarathustra—he might take them both, eat them both!" And they laughed, huddling together.

Zarathustra did not answer and continued on his way. After two hours of walking through forests and swamps, he had heard too much of the wolves' hungry howling, and he, too, began to feel hunger. So he stopped at a solitary house where a light was burning.

"Hunger strikes me," Zarathustra said, "like a thief. Among the forests and swamps, hunger attacks me late in the night.

"My hunger has strange moods. Often, it only comes after a meal, and all day it doesn't come at all—where has it been?"

With that, Zarathustra knocked on the door. An old man appeared, carrying a light, and asked, "Who comes to me and my restless sleep?"

"A living man and a dead one," replied Zarathustra. "Give me something to eat and drink, for I forgot to do so during the day. 'He who feeds the hungry refreshes his own soul,' says wisdom."

The old man withdrew, returning quickly with bread and wine. "This is a poor land for the hungry," he said, "which is why I live here.

Animal and man come to me, the hermit. But ask your companion to eat and drink as well—he looks wearier than you."

"My companion is dead," replied Zarathustra. "I doubt I can persuade him to eat."

"That doesn't concern me," said the old man bluntly. "Anyone who knocks at my door must take what I offer. Eat, and be on your way!"

Afterward, Zarathustra continued walking for another two hours, trusting in the path and the starlight, for he was a skilled night-walker and liked to gaze upon all that slept. But as morning dawned, he found himself in a thick forest, with no path in sight. So he placed the dead man in a hollow tree to shield him from the wolves, and then lay down on the ground and moss. He fell asleep immediately, tired in body but with a peaceful soul.

Zarathustra slept for a long time; not only did the rosy dawn pass over him, but also the entire morning. Finally, he opened his eyes and looked around, amazed at the stillness of the forest—and at himself. Then he rose quickly, like a sailor who suddenly sees land; he shouted with joy, for he had found a new truth. And he spoke to his heart:

"A light has dawned on me: I need companions—living ones, not dead companions and bodies that I carry with me wherever I go.

I need living companions who will follow me because they want to follow their own path—to the place where I am going. A light has dawned on me. Zarathustra is not meant to speak to the people but to companions! Zarathustra will not be a shepherd or a hound for the herd!

I have come to draw many away from the herd. The people and the herd must be angry with me; the herdsmen will call Zarathustra a thief.

I say 'herdsmen,' though they call themselves the good and just. I say 'herdsmen,' though they call themselves believers in true faith.

Look at the good and the just! Who do they hate most? The one who shatters their tables of values, the breaker of laws. But he is the creator.

Look at the believers of every belief! Who do they hate most? The one who shatters their tables of values, the law-breaker. But he is the creator.

The creator seeks companions, not corpses—not herds or believers, either. The creator seeks fellow creators—those who will carve new values onto new tablets.

The creator seeks companions and fellow reapers, for everything is ripe for harvest. But he lacks the hundred sickles he needs, so he plucks the ears of grain himself, growing frustrated.

The creator seeks companions who know how to sharpen their sickles. They will be called destroyers and haters of good and evil. But they are the reapers and rejoicers.

Zarathustra seeks fellow creators, fellow reapers, and fellow rejoicers. What does he have to do with herds, herdsmen, and corpses?

And you, my first companion, rest in peace! I buried you well in your hollow tree and hid you well from the wolves.

But I must part from you; the time has come. Between rosy dawns, a new truth has come to me.

I am not to be a herdsman, nor a grave-digger. I will not speak to the people anymore; I have spoken to the dead for the last time.

With creators, reapers, and rejoicers, I will keep company. I will show them the rainbow and all the steps leading to the Superman.

To those who dwell alone, I will sing my song; and to those who dwell in pairs; and to anyone who still has ears for what has not been heard, I will fill their hearts with my joy.

I am aiming for my goal, I am following my path. I will leap over the lazy and the slow. Let my progress be their decline!"

This is what Zarathustra said to his heart when the sun stood at noon. Then he looked up, for he heard the sharp cry of a bird above him. And behold! An eagle was gliding through the sky in wide circles, with a snake coiled around its neck—not as prey, but as a friend.

"They are my animals," said Zarathustra, rejoicing in his heart.

"The proudest animal under the sun and the wisest animal under the sun—they have come to see if Zarathustra still lives.

Do I still live?

Among men, I have found more danger than among animals; Zarathustra walks on dangerous paths. Let my animals lead me!"

When Zarathustra said this, he remembered the words of the saint in the forest. Then he sighed and spoke to his heart:

"I wish I were wiser! I wish I were wise from the heart, like my snake!

But I am asking for the impossible. So I ask my pride to stay with my wisdom always!

And if someday my wisdom leaves me—alas! It loves to fly away!—may my pride then stay with my foolishness!"

Thus began Zarathustra's journey downward.

Chapter 1
The Three Metamorphoses

I describe to you three transformations of the spirit: first, the spirit becomes a camel, then the camel becomes a lion, and finally, the lion becomes a child.

There are many heavy things for the spirit, the strong, burden-bearing spirit that honors reverence. It longs for weight—the heavy and the heaviest things.

"What is heavy?" asks the spirit that bears burdens, kneeling down like a camel, eager to be well-loaded.

"What is the heaviest thing, heroes?" asks the burden-bearing spirit, "so that I may take it upon me and rejoice in my strength."

Is it this: to humble oneself and let go of pride? To show one's own foolishness and mock one's own wisdom?

Or is it this: to abandon our cause at its moment of triumph? To climb high mountains just to test the spirit?

Or is it this: to feed on the acorns and grass of knowledge, and to suffer a hungry soul for the sake of truth?

Or is it this: to be ill and dismiss comforters, to make friends with those who cannot hear our pleas?

Or is it this: to wade into filthy waters when they contain the truth, and not shun the cold frogs and hot toads?

Or is it this: to love those who despise us, and to reach out to a ghost, even as it tries to scare us?

All these heaviest burdens, the load-bearing spirit takes upon itself. Like the camel that, once loaded, hurries into the desert, so the spirit heads into its wilderness.

But in the loneliest wilderness, the second transformation happens: here, the spirit becomes a lion; it seeks freedom and mastery in its own desert.

Here, it hunts down its last master and its last god, struggling for victory against the great dragon.

And what is this great dragon that the spirit no longer wants to call lord or god? It is called "Thou-shalt." But the spirit of the lion says, "I will."

"Thou-shalt" lies in its path, glittering with gold—a beast covered in scales, and on each scale, it shines, "Thou shalt!"

The values of a thousand years glitter on those scales, and the mightiest of all dragons speaks: "All values have already been created; I am the embodiment of all values. Verily, there shall be no more 'I will.'" Thus speaks the dragon.

But my friends, why is the lion needed by the spirit? Why isn't the burden-bearer, who renounces and shows reverence, enough?

To create new values—the lion cannot yet do this. But to create freedom for new creation—that is the strength of the lion.

To create freedom for itself and to say a holy "No" even to duty; for that, my friends, the lion is needed.

To take the right to create new values—this is the most difficult challenge for a burden-bearing, reverent spirit. For such a spirit, this act is both a fierce struggle and the work of a predator.

Once, it loved "Thou-shalt" as its holiest, but now it must find even the holiest things to be illusions and empty, so that it can win freedom from its love. The lion is needed for this victory.

But tell me, my friends, what can the child do that even the lion could not? Why must the lion still become a child?

The child is innocence, forgetfulness, a new beginning, a game, a self-propelled wheel, a first movement, a sacred "Yes."

Yes, for the game of creation, my friends, there must be a sacred "Yes" to life. The spirit now wills its own will, it wins its own world and its own destiny.

I have described to you three transformations of the spirit: how the spirit became a camel, the camel a lion, and the lion finally a child.

Thus spoke Zarathustra. And at that time, he stayed in the town called The Pied Cow.

Chapter 2
The Academic Chairs of Virtue

People praised a wise man to Zarathustra, calling him someone who could speak wisely about sleep and virtue. He was greatly respected and rewarded, and all the young people gathered before his chair. Zarathustra went to him and sat among the youths in front of his chair. And the wise man spoke:

"Respect and humility before sleep! That is the first rule! And stay away from all who sleep poorly and stay awake at night!

Even the thief is respectful before sleep; he always steals quietly through the night. But the night watchman is disrespectful; he blows his horn without shame.

It is no small art to sleep; to sleep well, one must stay awake all day.

You must overcome yourself ten times a day; this brings a healthy tiredness, like a poppy for the soul.

Ten times you must make peace with yourself; for overcoming brings bitterness, and those who are not at peace with themselves sleep poorly.

You must find ten truths during the day; otherwise, you'll seek truth during the night, leaving your soul hungry.

You must laugh ten times each day and be cheerful; otherwise, your stomach—the father of misery—will disturb you at night.

Few people realize this, but you need all the virtues to sleep well. Shall I bear false witness? Shall I commit adultery?

Shall I covet my neighbor's servant? Such things do not bring good sleep.

And even if you have all the virtues, there is still one thing more needed: to send those virtues to sleep at the right time.

They must not argue with each other, those good ladies! Nor should they argue over you, you poor soul!

Peace with God and your neighbor—that is what good sleep wants. And peace with your neighbor's demon, too! Otherwise, it will haunt you at night.

Honor the government and obey it, even the crooked government—that is what good sleep wants. How can I help it if power walks on crooked legs?

Whoever leads his sheep to the greenest pastures will always be the best shepherd to me; that suits good sleep.

I want neither many honors nor great treasures; they trouble the heart. But it's hard to sleep well without a good name and a small treasure.

A small company is better to me than a bad one, but they must come and go at the right time. That suits good sleep.

The humble also please me; they help sleep. Blessed are they, especially if one always gives in to them.

This is how the day passes for the virtuous. When night comes, I take care not to call for sleep. It dislikes being called—the lord of virtues, sleep!"

But I think about what I've done and thought during the day. Reflecting, as patient as a cow, I ask myself: What were my ten victories?

And what were the ten reconciliations, the ten truths, and the ten laughs that brought joy to my heart?

As I ponder, wrapped in forty thoughts, sleep suddenly overtakes me—unsummoned, the lord of virtues.

Sleep taps on my eyes, and they grow heavy. Sleep touches my mouth, and it falls open.

Truly, it comes on soft feet, the dearest of thieves, stealing my thoughts: I stand there, foolish, like this academic chair.

But I don't stand for long: I am already lying down—

When Zarathustra heard the wise man speak, he laughed to himself, for a light had dawned on him, and he said to his heart:

"This wise man seems like a fool with his forty thoughts, yet I believe he knows well how to sleep.

Happy is anyone who lives near this wise man! Such sleep is contagious—it spreads even through thick walls.

There is magic even in his academic chair. No wonder the youths sit before this preacher of virtue.

His wisdom is to stay awake in order to sleep well. And truly, if life had no purpose and I had to choose nonsense, this would be the most desirable nonsense for me too.

Now I understand what people once sought above all when they looked for teachers of virtue. They sought good sleep for themselves and virtues that would help them sleep well!

All those praised sages of the academic chairs—they valued wisdom as sleep without dreams; they knew no higher meaning in life.

Even now, there are still some like this preacher of virtue, though they are not always as honorable. But their time is past. They do not stand much longer; there they already lie.

Blessed are these drowsy ones, for soon they shall fall asleep."

Thus spoke Zarathustra.

Chapter 3

Backworldsmen

Once, like all those who look beyond this world, Zarathustra also cast his vision past humanity. The world seemed to me then to be the work of a suffering, tormented god.

The world seemed to me like the dream—and speech—of a god; colored mists before the eyes of a god dissatisfied with himself.

Good and evil, joy and sorrow, you and I—all seemed like colored mists to me before the eyes of the creator. The creator wanted to look away from himself—and so he made the world.

For someone suffering, it is intoxicating joy to look away from pain and forget oneself. The world once seemed to me like intoxicating joy and self-forgetfulness.

This world—eternally flawed, filled with contradiction and imperfection—seemed like intoxicating joy to its flawed creator; that is how the world once appeared to me.

Thus, once upon a time, I too cast my vision beyond humanity, like all those who look for something beyond. Beyond humanity, really?

Ah, my brothers, that god I created was a human creation and human madness, like all gods!

He was human, just a poor fragment of a man and his ego. Out of my own ashes and fire, that phantom came to me. And truly, it did not come from beyond!

What happened, my brothers? I surpassed myself, my own suffering; I carried my ashes up the mountain and made a brighter flame for myself. And behold! The phantom faded away from me!

Now, for me, the one who has healed, it would be pain and torment to believe in such phantoms again. It would be suffering and humiliation. That is what I say to those who look beyond this world.

It was suffering and helplessness that created all "other worlds"—and the brief madness of happiness that only the greatest sufferers know.

It was weariness, seeking one final leap, a leap of death—poor, ignorant weariness that no longer wanted to want anything—that created all gods and "other worlds."

Believe me, my brothers! It was the body that despaired of the body—it groped with the hands of a confused mind for the final walls.

Believe me, my brothers! It was the body that despaired of the earth—it heard the depths of existence speaking to it.

Then it tried to break through the final walls with its head—and not only with its head—into "another world."

But that "other world" is hidden from us, that dehumanized, inhuman world, a heavenly void. And the depths of existence do not speak to us, except as we are—humans.

Truly, proving the reality of existence is hard, and making it speak is even harder. Tell me, my brothers, isn't it true that the strangest of all things is the best proof?

Yes, this ego, with its contradictions and confusion, speaks most honestly about its existence—this creating, willing, evaluating ego that is the measure and value of all things.

And this most honest existence, the ego—it speaks of the body and still depends on the body, even when it dreams, raves, and flutters with broken wings.

The ego learns to speak more truthfully, and the more it learns, the more it finds respect and honor for the body and the earth.

My ego has taught me a new pride, and this I teach to humanity: no longer to bury one's head in the clouds of heavenly things, but to carry it high, as an earthly head that gives meaning to the earth!

I teach humanity a new will: to choose the path that humans have followed blindly and to embrace it—no longer to turn away from it like the sick and dying!

It was the sick and dying who despised the body and the earth, who invented the heavenly world and the redeeming blood-drops. Yet even those sweet and sad poisons were borrowed from the body and the earth!

They wanted to escape their misery, but the stars were too distant for them. So they sighed, "Oh, if only there were heavenly paths to sneak into another existence and find happiness!" And thus they invented their own detours and bloody potions.

Now they imagine themselves transported beyond the bounds of their body and this earth, these ungrateful ones. But what gave them the thrill and ecstasy of their escape? Their body and this earth.

Zarathustra is gentle with the sickly. Truly, he does not resent their ways of finding comfort or their ingratitude. May they become healed and victorious, and create stronger bodies for themselves!

Nor does Zarathustra resent a recovering soul who looks tenderly upon his old delusions and sneaks around his god's grave at midnight. But there remains illness and a weak frame even in his tears.

There have always been many sickly ones among those who yearn for God; they hate those who can see clearly and the newest virtue—uprightness.

They always look back to the dark ages, for then, indeed, delusion and faith were different. Raving reason was called "likeness to God," and doubt was a sin.

I know these "godlike" ones all too well: they demand belief and say that doubt is sin. I know too well what they truly believe in.

Not in other worlds or redeeming blood-drops: no, they believe most in their body; to them, their own body is the ultimate reality.

But it is a sickly thing to them, and they would gladly escape their skin. Therefore, they listen to the preachers of death and preach other worlds themselves.

Listen instead, my friends, to the voice of the healthy body; it speaks more truthfully and purely.

The healthy, square-built body speaks uprightly and clearly, and it speaks of the meaning of the earth.

Thus spoke Zarathustra.

Chapter 4
The Dispisers of the Body

To those who despise the body, I will speak my word. I don't wish for them to learn or to teach anew but simply to say goodbye to their bodies—and then be silent.

"I am body and soul," says the child. And why should we not speak like children?

But the awakened, the knowing one says: "I am entirely body and nothing more; and soul is just a name for something within the body."

The body is a great wisdom, a unity of many parts with a single purpose, a war and a peace, a flock and a shepherd.

Your small wisdom, which you call "spirit," is also an instrument of your body, my brother—a small tool and toy of your greater wisdom.

You say "I," and you are proud of that word. But the greater thing—which you do not want to believe in—is your body with its great wisdom; it doesn't say "I," but it does it.

What the senses feel, what the spirit perceives, never has an end in itself. But the senses and spirit want to convince you they are the end of all things: they are that vain.

Instruments and toys are the senses and spirit; behind them is still the Self. The Self sees through the eyes of the senses; it listens through the ears of the spirit.

The Self is always listening and seeking; it compares, controls, conquers, and destroys. It rules and is also the master of the ego.

Behind your thoughts and feelings, my brother, there is a powerful ruler, a wise unknown—called Self; it lives in your body; it is your body.

There is more wisdom in your body than in your greatest knowledge. And who can know why your body needs your highest wisdom?

Your Self laughs at your ego and its proud prancing. "What are these prancing and flights of thought to me?" it says to itself. "Just a path to my purpose. I am the guide of the ego and the prompt of its ideas."

The Self says to the ego: "Feel pain!" And so it suffers and thinks of how it may end the pain—and that is why it is meant to think.

The Self says to the ego: "Feel pleasure!" And so it rejoices and thinks of how it may feel joy again—and that is why it is meant to think.

To the despisers of the body, I will speak a word. Your contempt is born from your esteem. What is it that created esteeming and despising, worth and will?

The creative Self created esteem and contempt for itself; it created joy and sorrow. The creative body created spirit as a tool of its will.

Even in your foolishness and contempt, you serve your Self, you despisers of the body. I tell you, your very Self wishes to die and turns away from life.

Your Self can no longer do what it desires most:

to create beyond itself. That is what it desires above all; that is its passion.

But now it is too late for that—so your Self wishes to fall, you despisers of the body.

To fall—that is what your Self wishes, and that is why you have become despisers of the body. For you can no longer create beyond yourselves.

And so now you are angry with life and the earth. And an unconscious envy hides in the sideways glance of your contempt.

I do not follow your path, you despisers of the body! You are no bridges for me to the Superman!

Thus spoke Zarathustra.

Chapter 5
Joys and Passions

My brother, when you have a virtue, and it is truly your own, you share it with no one else.

Of course, you might want to give it a name and show affection for it; you might even want to playfully tug its ears and enjoy it.

But look! Then you would have its name in common with others, and with your virtue, you'd become one of the crowd, a part of the herd!

It is better to say, "Unspeakable and nameless is that which brings pain and sweetness to my soul and the hunger of my heart."

Let your virtue be too high for ordinary names, and if you must speak of it, do not be ashamed to stammer.

So speak and stammer: "This is my good, this I love, this pleases me fully, and only in this way do I desire the good.

Not as a god's law do I desire it, nor as human law or human need; it is not my guide to otherworldly realms or paradises.

It is an earthly virtue that I love; it has little prudence and even less daily wisdom.

But it built its nest beside me: so I love and cherish it—now it sits beside me on its golden eggs."

Thus you should stammer, and praise your virtue.

Once you had passions, and you called them evil. But now you have only virtues; they grew out of your passions.

You planted your highest aim into the heart of those passions, and then they became your virtues and your joys.

And even if you were of a hot-blooded, sensual, fanatic, or vengeful nature,

All your passions eventually became virtues, and all your devils became angels.

Once you kept wild dogs in your cellar; but at last, they turned into birds and delightful singers.

Out of your poisons, you brewed healing balm; from your sorrowful cow, you drew milk—and now you drink the sweet milk from her udder.

Nothing evil grows in you anymore, unless it is the evil that grows from the struggle between your virtues.

My brother, if you are fortunate, you will have only one virtue, and no more; this way, you can cross the bridge more easily.

It is noble to have many virtues, but it is a hard fate; many have gone into the wilderness and perished, worn down by being the battlefield of warring virtues.

My brother, are war and struggle evil? Evil may be necessary; necessary are the envy, mistrust, and rivalry among virtues.

Look! Each of your virtues covets the highest place; it wants all of your spirit to be its voice, all your strength to be its own, through anger, hatred, and love.

Each virtue is jealous of the others, and jealousy is a dreadful thing. Even virtues may fall to jealousy.

He who is surrounded by jealousy's flames eventually turns on himself, like a scorpion stinging with its poisoned tail.

Ah, my brother, have you never seen a virtue turn against itself, backstabbing in jealousy?

Humanity is something that must be overcome; so you should love your virtues, for they will be your downfall—

Thus spoke Zarathustra.

Chapter 6
The Pale Criminal

You judges and executioners, you do not intend to kill until the creature has bowed its head, do you? Look! The pale criminal has bowed his head; his eyes speak of deep contempt.

"My ego is something to be overcome: my ego is the great contempt for humanity," says that look in his eyes.

When he judged himself—that was his highest moment; do not let the exalted one fall back to his lower state!

For him who suffers from himself, there is no rescue except swift death.

Your killing, judges, should be out of pity, not revenge; and when you kill, make sure you justify life itself!

It is not enough to reconcile with the one you kill. Let your sorrow be love for the Superman; that way, you will justify your own survival!

Call him "enemy" but not "villain"; "sick" but not "wretch"; "fool" but not "sinner."

And you, red judge, if you spoke aloud all your thoughts, everyone would cry, "Away with the filth and venomous creature!"

But thought is one thing, the deed another, and the idea of the deed still another. The wheel of causality does not spin between them.

An idea made this pale man pale. He was ready for his deed when he did it, but he could not endure the thought of it afterward.

Now he sees himself as nothing but the doer of that one deed. I call this madness: the exception has become the rule for him.

Just as a chalk line hypnotizes a hen, the blow he struck hypnotized his weak mind. Madness after the deed, I call this.

Listen, judges! There is another kind of madness, and it comes before the deed. Ah! You have not looked deeply enough into his soul!

The red judge says, "Why did this man commit murder? He wanted to steal." But I tell you, his soul wanted blood, not loot; he thirsted for the thrill of the knife!

But his weak mind did not understand this madness, and it convinced him, "Why bother about blood? Can't you at least gain something from it? Or take revenge?"

And he listened to his weak mind; its words lay on him like lead. So, when he murdered, he stole as well. He did not want to be ashamed of his madness.

And now the weight of his guilt lies on him again, and his weak mind is numb, paralyzed, and dulled once more.

If only he could shake his head, his burden would fall away; but who will shake that head?

What is this man? A bundle of diseases that reach out into the world through his spirit, searching for something to seize.

What is this man? A coil of wild serpents, rarely at peace with each other—so they go out separately, hunting for prey in the world.

Look at that poor body! What it suffered and craved, the poor soul tried to interpret for itself—it saw it as murderous desire, a hunger for the thrill of the knife.

When someone turns sick, they are overtaken by what is now considered evil: they seek to cause pain with what has pained them. But there were other times, and a different sense of good and evil.

Once, doubt and the will to self were seen as evil. Then the sick one became a heretic or a sorcerer; as heretic or sorcerer, he suffered and sought to cause suffering.

But you won't let this enter your ears; you tell me it offends your good people. But what do your good people matter to me?

Many things about your good people disgust me, and it's not their evil. I wish they had a madness by which they would perish, like this pale criminal!

Truly, I wish their madness were called truth, or loyalty, or justice. But they hold onto their virtue only to live long, lost in their pitiful self-satisfaction.

I am railing alongside a rushing stream; whoever can hold onto me, let them hold! But I am not your crutch.—

Thus spoke Zarathustra.

Chapter 7
Reading and Writing

Of all that is written, I love only what a person has written with their blood. Write with blood, and you will find that blood is spirit.

It is not easy to understand another's deep struggles; I dislike idle readers.

He who truly knows the reader does nothing more for the reader. Give it another century of readers—and even the spirit itself will rot.

Allowing everyone to learn to read eventually ruins not only writing but also thinking.

Once, spirit was God; then it became man; and now it even becomes common.

He who writes in blood and proverbs does not want to be read, but learned by heart.

In the mountains, the shortest path is from peak to peak, but for that route, you must have long legs. Proverbs should be like peaks, and those spoken to should be big and tall.

Where the air is rare and pure, with danger close by and the spirit full of joyful mischief—there, things are well suited.

I want goblins around me, for I am brave. The courage that frightens away ghosts creates goblins for itself—it wants to laugh.

I no longer feel connected with you; even the cloud I see beneath me, the dark and heavy mass that I laugh at—that is your thundercloud.

You look upward when you long for elevation; I look downward because I am already elevated.

Who among you can laugh while feeling exalted?

He who climbs to the highest mountains laughs at all tragic plays and tragic realities.

Bold, free from worry, scornful, commanding—that's how wisdom wants us to be; she is a woman and always loves only a warrior.

You say to me, "Life is hard to bear." But why should you have your pride in the morning and your resignation at night?

Life is hard to bear; but don't pretend to be so delicate! We are all of us sturdy pack animals.

What do we have in common with the rosebud that trembles because a drop of dew has formed on it?

It's true we love life—not because we're used to living but because we're used to loving.

There is always some madness in love, but there is always some method in madness as well.

And to me, who values life, butterflies, soap bubbles, and whatever is like them among us seem to enjoy happiness the most.

Watching these light, foolish, pretty, lively little creatures flit about—this moves Zarathustra to tears and song.

I would only believe in a God who knew how to dance.

And when I saw my devil, I found him serious, intense, solemn, and deep. He was the spirit of gravity—through him, everything falls.

We do not kill with anger but with laughter. Come, let us kill the spirit of gravity!

I learned to walk; since then, I let myself run. I learned to fly; now I don't need a push to move from my spot.

Now I am light; now I fly; now I see myself beneath myself. Now, there dances a God within me.—

Thus spoke Zarathustra.

Chapter 8
The Tree on the Hill

Zarathustra noticed that a certain young man was avoiding him. One evening, as he walked alone over the hills surrounding the town called "The Pied Cow," he found the young man sitting against a tree, looking tiredly into the valley. Zarathustra took hold of the tree next to him and spoke:

"If I wanted to shake this tree with my hands, I would not be able to do it.

But the wind, which we cannot see, stirs it and bends it as it wishes. It is invisible forces that bend and trouble us the most."

The young man, startled, stood up and said, "I hear you, Zarathustra, and I was just thinking about you!" Zarathustra replied:

"Why does that frighten you?—But it is the same with people as it is with trees.

The more a person seeks to rise into the light, the more forcefully his roots push down into the darkness—into the depths, into what we call 'evil.'"

"Yes, into evil!" cried the young man. "How could you know what's in my soul?"

Zarathustra smiled and said, "Some souls one never finds unless one first imagines them."

"Yes, into evil!" the young man cried again.

"You spoke the truth, Zarathustra. I no longer trust myself since I tried to rise higher, and no one else trusts me either. Why is that?

I change too quickly: today contradicts my yesterday. I often skip steps as I climb, and for that, none of the steps forgives me.

Whenever I reach the heights, I find myself alone. No one speaks to me; the cold loneliness makes me shiver. What am I seeking up here?

My contempt and longing both grow stronger as I climb; the higher I go, the more I despise those who also climb. What are they looking for on the heights?

How ashamed I am of my own clumsy climbing! How I mock my own heavy breathing! How I hate those who fly! How tired I am on the heights!"

The young man fell silent. Zarathustra looked at the tree they stood beside and spoke:

"This tree stands here on the hill; it has grown tall, high above humans and animals.

If it wished to speak, it would find no one who could understand it; it has grown that high.

Now it waits and waits—but for what? It lives close to the clouds; perhaps it waits for the first lightning?"

When Zarathustra said this, the young man cried out with wild gestures, "Yes, Zarathustra, you speak the truth. I longed for my own destruction when I desired to reach the heights, and you are the lightning I was waiting for! Look what I have become since you appeared among us! My envy of you has destroyed me!" And with that, the young man wept bitterly. But Zarathustra put his arm around him and walked with him.

After they had walked together for a while, Zarathustra began to speak:

"It breaks my heart. Your eyes tell me of your danger even more than your words do.

You are not yet free; you still seek freedom. Your pursuit has left you exhausted and too restless.

You want to be on the open heights; your soul thirsts for the stars. But your darker urges also thirst for freedom.

Your wild impulses yearn for liberty; they bark with joy in their cellar when your spirit tries to open all prison doors.

You are still a prisoner—it seems to me—one who tries to invent freedom for himself. Ah, such prisoners become sharp-minded, but also deceitful and dangerous."

To purify himself is still necessary for the freed spirit. Much of the prison and the mold still remain in him; his vision must still become clear.

Yes, I know your danger. But by my love and hope, I urge you: do not throw away your love and hope!

You still feel noble, and others also still feel you are noble, though they bear grudges and cast dark looks. Know this: to everyone, a noble person stands in the way.

Even to the good, a noble person stands in the way; and even when they call him a good man, they only wish to set him aside.

The noble man would create something new, and a new virtue. The good man wants the old, and that the old should be preserved.

But it is not the danger of the noble man to turn into a good man; it is that he should become boastful, mocking, or destructive.

Ah! I have known noble ones who lost their highest hope. And then they scorned all high hopes.

Then they lived shamelessly in fleeting pleasures, with hardly an aim beyond the day.

"Spirit is also indulgence," they said. Then their spirit's wings broke, and now it creeps about, defiling where it gnaws.

Once, they dreamed of becoming heroes; but now they are sensualists. The hero has become a burden and a terror to them.

But by my love and hope, I urge you: do not throw away the hero in your soul! Keep your highest hope sacred!

Thus spoke Zarathustra.

Chapter 9

The Preachers of Death

There are preachers of death, and the earth is full of those to whom renouncing life must be preached.

The earth is full of the superfluous; life is marred by the many-too-many. May they be drawn out of this life by the promise of "eternal life"!

They are called "the yellow ones," or "the black ones"—the preachers of death. But I will show them to you in other colors as well.

There are the terrible ones who carry within themselves a beast of prey and have no choice but between lusts and self-harm. And even their lusts are a form of self-harm.

These terrible ones have not yet become human; may they preach renunciation of life, and then pass away themselves!

There are those who are spiritually consumptive: they are barely born when they begin to die and long for doctrines of weariness and renunciation.

They wish to be dead, and we should approve of their wish! Let us beware of waking these dead ones and damaging these living coffins!

They meet an invalid, or an old man, or a corpse—and immediately they say: "Life is disproven!"

But it is only they who are disproven, and their eyes, which see only one side of existence.

Wrapped in deep melancholy and hungry for little accidents that bring death, they wait and grit their teeth.

Or they grab at sweets and mock themselves for their childishness, clinging to their last straw of life, even as they mock their clinging.

Their wisdom says: "A fool is he who remains alive; but so far, we are all fools! And that is the most foolish thing about life!"

"Life is only suffering," say others, and they do not lie. Then make sure you cease! Make sure that life ceases that is only suffering!

And let this be the teaching of your virtue: "You shall kill yourself! You shall slip away from yourself!"—"Lust is sin," say some who preach death—"let us separate and have no children!"

"Giving birth is troublesome," say others—"why keep bearing children? We only bring forth the unfortunate!" And they, too, are preachers of death.

"Compassion is necessary," says a third group. "Take what I have! Take what I am! The less life binds me, the better!"

If they were truly compassionate, they would make their neighbors weary of life. To be wicked—that would be their truest goodness.

But they wish to be rid of life; what do they care if they bind others even more tightly with their chains and gifts!

And you, too, who find life to be hard labor and restlessness—are you not very tired of life? Are you not very ripe for the sermon of death?

All of you who love rough labor and the fast, the new, and the strange—you endure yourselves poorly; your diligence is an escape, a will to forget yourselves.

If you had more faith in life, you would devote yourselves less to the momentary. But for waiting, you do not have enough strength in you—nor even for idleness!

Everywhere sound the voices of those who preach death; the earth is full of those to whom death must be preached.

Or "eternal life"—it's all the same to me—if only they pass away quickly!—

Thus spoke Zarathustra.

Chapter 10
War and Warriors

My brothers in war! I love you from the depths of my heart. I am, and have always been, your opposite. And I am also your best enemy. So let me tell you the truth!

I know the hatred and envy within your hearts. You are not yet so great as to be free from hatred and envy. Then be great enough not to be ashamed of them!

And if you cannot be saints of knowledge, then, I ask of you, at least be its warriors. Warriors are the companions and forerunners of sainthood.

I see many soldiers; if only I could see many warriors! "Uniform" is what they call what you wear; may what you hide underneath not be uniform!

You should be the ones whose eyes are always searching for an enemy—your own enemy. And for some of you, hatred is born at first sight.

Seek out your enemy; wage your war, and do so for the sake of your thoughts! And if your thoughts fall in battle, let your integrity still shout triumph!

You should love peace as a means to new wars—and a brief peace more than a lasting one.

I do not advise you to work, but to fight. I do not advise you to peace, but to victory. Let your work be a battle; let your peace be a victory!

One can only be silent and sit peacefully when one has arrow and bow; otherwise, one prattles and quarrels. Let your peace be a victory!

You say it is the good cause that sanctifies even war? I tell you: it is the good war that sanctifies every cause.

War and courage have achieved greater things than charity. It is not your compassion, but your bravery, that has saved the suffering until now.

"What is good?" you ask. To be brave is good. Let little girls say, "Goodness is what's pretty and touching."

They call you heartless, but your heart is true, and I love the modesty of your goodwill. You are ashamed of your overflowing strength, while others are ashamed of their lack.

Are you ugly? Well then, my brothers, cloak yourselves in the sublime, the mantle of the ugly!

And when your soul becomes great, it also becomes proud, and in your greatness there is a touch of wickedness. I know you.

The proud man and the weakling meet in wickedness, but they misunderstand each other. I know you.

You should have enemies to hate, but not enemies to despise. You must be proud of your enemies; then their successes are also your successes.

Resistance is the mark of the slave. Let your distinction be obedience. Let your command itself be an act of obedience!

To the good warrior, "you shall" sounds sweeter than "I will." And everything dear to you, you should first have commanded to you.

Let your love of life be love for your highest hope, and let your highest hope be the highest thought of life!

Your highest thought, however, shall be commanded to you by me—and it is this: humanity is something that must be surpassed. So live your life of obedience and war! What does a long life matter? What warrior wishes to be spared?

I do not spare you; I love you from my very heart, my brothers in war!—

Thus spoke Zarathustra.

Chapter 11
The New Idol

Somewhere there are still peoples and herds, but not with us, my brothers: here, there are only states.

A state? What is that? Now, open your ears to me, for I will speak to you about the death of peoples.

A state is called the coldest of all cold monsters. Coldly it lies; and this lie slips from its mouth: "I, the state, am the people."

It is a lie! It was creators who formed peoples, draping them with faith and love: in this way, they served life.

It is destroyers who set traps for many and call it the state: they hang a sword and countless desires over them.

Wherever there is still a people, there the state is misunderstood but hated as the evil eye and as a sin against laws and customs.

This sign I give to you: every people speaks its own language of good and evil, which its neighbors do not understand. It has devised its language in its own laws and customs.

But the state lies in all languages of good and evil; whatever it says, it lies; whatever it owns, it has stolen. False is everything within it; with stolen teeth it bites, that biting one. Even its bowels are false.

A confusion of the language of good and evil: this sign I give to you as the mark of the state. Truly, this sign indicates the will to death! Verily, it calls to the preachers of death!

Far too many are born; the state was created for the superfluous ones!

See how it entices the many-too-many to itself! How it swallows them, chews them, and chews them again!

"On earth, nothing is greater than I: I am the guiding finger of God"—so roars the monster. And not only the long-eared and short-sighted fall to their knees!

Ah! even in your ears, you great souls, it whispers its gloomy lies! Ah! it finds out the rich hearts that willingly give of themselves!

Yes, it finds you out too, you conquerors of the old God! You grew weary of the struggle, and now your weariness serves the new idol!

Heroes and honorable ones, it wishes to place around itself, this new idol! Happily, it basks in the warmth of good consciences—the cold monster!

It will give you everything if you worship it, this new idol: thus it buys the gleam of your virtue and the shine of your proud eyes.

It seeks to attract the many-too-many through you. Yes, a hellish scheme has been devised here, a death-horse jingling with divine honors!

Yes, a mass dying has been devised here that calls itself life: truly, a hearty service for all preachers of death!

The state, I call it, where everyone drinks poison, both good and bad; the state, where everyone loses themselves, good and bad; the state, where everyone's slow suicide is called "life."

Just look at these superfluous ones! They steal the works of inventors and the wisdom of the wise. They call their theft "culture"—and everything becomes sickness and burden to them!

Just look at these superfluous ones! They are always sick; they spit out their bitterness and call it news. They devour each other and cannot even digest themselves.

Just look at these superfluous ones! They acquire wealth and become poorer by it. They seek power and above all, the lever of power: much money—these powerless ones!

See them climb, these nimble apes! They clamber over one another, and scramble into the muck of the abyss.

They all strive toward the throne; it is their madness—as if happiness sat on the throne! Often filth sits on the throne—and often the throne sits on filth.

They all seem like madmen to me, like climbing apes, too eager. Their idol stinks to me, the cold monster; and these idol worshipers, they too stink to me.

My brothers, will you suffocate in the fumes of their mouths and hungers? Better to break the windows and leap into the open air!

Get away from the stench! Withdraw from the idolatry of the superfluous!

Get away from the stench! Withdraw from the smoke of these human sacrifices!

The earth is still open to great souls. Many places are still empty for those who wander alone or in pairs, surrounded by the scent of the tranquil seas.

There is still an open, free life for great souls. Truly, he who owns little is so much the less possessed: blessed is modest poverty!

There, where the state ends—only there begins the human being who is not superfluous: there begins the song of the necessary ones, the single and irreplaceable melody.

There, where the state ends—look over there, my brothers! Don't you see it, the rainbow and the bridges to the Superman?—

Thus spoke Zarathustra.

Chapter 12
The Flies in the Market-Place

Flee, my friend, into your solitude! I see you overwhelmed by the noise of the so-called great men, and stung all over by the little ones.

The forest and rocks know well how to be silent with you. Be like the tree you love, the broad-branched one—it silently and attentively stretches over the sea.

Where solitude ends, there begins the marketplace; and where the marketplace begins, there also begins the noise of the grand actors and the buzzing of the poison-flies.

In the world, even the best things are worthless without those who represent them: these representatives, the people call great men.

The people understand little of what is truly great—that is, the act of creation itself. But they admire all who represent and perform great things. Around the creators of new values, the world revolves—invisibly. But around the actors revolve the people and the glory: such is the nature of things.

The actor has spirit, but little conscience of that spirit. He believes most in whatever makes him appear most convincing—to himself!

Tomorrow he has a new belief, and the day after, one newer still. He has sharp senses, like the people, and a fickle mood.

To "upset" means, for him, to "prove." To "drive mad" means, for him, to "convince." And to him, blood is the best of all arguments.

A truth that only glides into fine ears, he calls falsehood and nonsense. Truly, he believes only in gods that make a great noise in the world!

The marketplace is full of clattering buffoons—and the people glorify their great men! These are, to them, the rulers of the moment.

But the moment presses upon them; so they press upon you. And from you, too, they demand either a Yes or a No. Alas! would you place your chair between For and Against?

Do not envy those absolute and impatient ones, you lover of truth! Never has truth clung to the arm of an absolute one.

Return to your secure place on account of those abrupt ones; only in the marketplace does one get assailed with "Yes?" or "No?"

Slow is the experience of all deep fountains: they must wait long until they know what has fallen into their depths.

Away from the marketplace and fame, all that is great takes place: away from the marketplace and fame have the creators of new values always dwelt. Flee, my friend, into your solitude: I see you stung all over by poisonous flies. Flee there, where a strong, rough breeze blows!

Flee into your solitude! You have lived too close to the small and the pitiful. Flee from their invisible vengeance! They have nothing but vengeance toward you.

Raise your arm against them no longer! They are countless, and it is not your task to be a swatter of flies.

The small and pitiful are countless, and many a proud structure has been ruined by raindrops and weeds.

You are not made of stone; yet you have already been hollowed out by countless drops. You will break and shatter from the countless drops.

I see you exhausted by poisonous flies; I see you bleeding, torn in a hundred places; and your pride will not even let you complain.

They want blood from you in all innocence; blood is what their bloodless souls crave—and they sting you, therefore, in all innocence.

But you, profound one, you suffer too deeply even from small wounds; and before you have healed, the same poisonous worm crawls across your hand again.

You are too proud to kill these bloodsuckers. But take care that it does not become your fate to suffer all their poisonous injustice!

They buzz around you even with their praise: obtrusiveness is their form of praise. They want to get close to your skin and your blood.

They flatter you as one flatters a god or a devil; they whimper before you as before a god or a devil. What does it matter? They are nothing but flatterers and whimperers.

Often they even show themselves to you as agreeable.

But that has always been the cowardly's form of prudence. Yes! The cowardly are wise!

They think about you constantly with their narrow souls—you are always a source of suspicion to them! Whatever is thought about too much becomes suspect in the end.

They punish you for all your virtues. They pardon you in their innermost hearts only—for your errors.

Because you are gentle and upright, you say: "They are blameless for their small existence." But their narrow souls think: "All great existence is blameworthy."

Even when you are gentle toward them, they still feel despised by you; and they repay your kindness with secret malice.

Your silent pride is always distasteful to them; they rejoice when you are humble enough to become frivolous.

What we recognize in a person, we also provoke in them. Therefore, be cautious of the small ones!

In your presence, they feel small, and their baseness glows against you with invisible vengeance.

Did you not see how often they fell silent when you approached, and how their energy faded like the smoke from an extinguished fire?

Yes, my friend, you are the bad conscience of your neighbors; for they are unworthy of you. That is why they hate you and wish to drain your blood.

Your neighbors will always be poisonous flies; what is great in you—this alone makes them more poisonous, and ever more like flies.

Flee, my friend, into your solitude—go where a strong, rough wind blows. It is not your destiny to be a swatter of flies.—

Thus spoke Zarathustra.

Chapter 13

Chastity

I love the forest. It is bad to live in cities; there, there are too many of the lustful.

Is it not better to fall into the hands of a murderer than into the dreams of a lustful woman?

And just look at these men: their eyes reveal it—they know nothing better on earth than to lie with a woman.

Filth lies at the bottom of their souls; and alas if that filth still has spirit in it!

Would that you were perfect—at least like animals! But innocence belongs to animals.

Do I advise you to kill your instincts? I advise you to be innocent in your instincts.

Do I advise you to chastity? Chastity is a virtue for some, but for many, almost a vice.

These are continent, to be sure; but doggish lust peers enviously out from everything they do.

Even in the heights of their virtue and their cold spirit, this creature follows them with its discord.

And how well doggish lust can beg for a piece of spirit when it is denied a piece of flesh!

Do you love tragedies and all that breaks the heart? But I distrust your doggish lust.

You have too cruel eyes, and you gaze wantonly at those who suffer. Has your lust disguised itself and taken on the name of compassion?

And here is a parable for you: Not a few who meant to cast out their devil ended up running into the swine themselves.

To those for whom chastity is difficult, it should be discouraged, lest it become the road to hell—to filth and lust of the soul.

Do I speak of filthy things? That is not the worst thing I can do.

It is not when the truth is filthy, but when it is shallow, that the discerning one avoids its waters.

Truly, there are those who are chaste by nature; they are gentler at heart, and they laugh more freely and more often than you.

They laugh even at chastity, and ask, "What is chastity?

Is chastity not folly? But this folly came to us; we did not seek it out.

We offered that guest shelter and warmth; now it dwells with us—let it stay as long as it will!"

Thus spoke Zarathustra.

Chapter 14
The Friend

"One is always too many around me," thinks the hermit. "Always one more—eventually, that makes two!"

I and myself are always too deep in conversation; how could I bear it, if not for a friend?

The friend of a hermit is always the third one: the third one is the cork that keeps the conversation between the two from sinking into the depths.

Ah! There are too many depths for all hermits. That is why they long so much for a friend and for his elevation.

Our faith in others reveals that we want to have faith in ourselves. Our longing for a friend is our betrayer.

And often, with our love, we simply want to leap over our envy. Often, we attack and make enemies of ourselves to hide that we are vulnerable.

"Be at least my enemy!"—thus speaks true reverence, which does not dare to ask for friendship.

If one would have a friend, one must also be willing to wage war for him: and to wage war, one must be capable of being an enemy.

One should still honor the enemy within one's friend. Can you approach your friend and not go over to him?

In one's friend, one should have one's best enemy. You should be closest to him in your heart when you withstand him.

Would you wear no clothes before your friend? Is it out of honor to your friend that you show yourself as you truly are? But he wishes you to the devil for that!

He who makes no secret of himself shocks others: for good reason do you fear nakedness! Indeed, if you were gods, then you might be ashamed of clothing!

You cannot adorn yourself finely enough for your friend; for you should be to him an arrow and a longing for the Superman.

Have you ever seen your friend asleep—and observed how he looks? What does your friend's face usually show? It is your own face, in a rough and imperfect mirror.

Have you ever seen your friend asleep? Were you not alarmed to see your friend looking like that? Oh, my friend, man is something that must be surpassed.

In guessing and in silence, the friend should be a master: you should not wish to see everything. Your dreams will reveal to you what your friend does when awake.

Let your pity be intuitive: first, know if your friend desires pity. Perhaps he loves the unmoved gaze in you, and the look of eternity.

Let your pity for your friend be hidden under a hard shell; it should be tough enough to break a tooth. Thus, it will have delicacy and sweetness.

Are you pure air and solitude and bread and medicine to your friend? Many people cannot free themselves, but are nonetheless their friend's liberator.

Are you a slave? Then you cannot be a friend. Are you a tyrant? Then you cannot have friends.

Far too long have slave and tyrant been hidden in woman. For that reason, woman is not yet capable of friendship: she knows only love.

In woman's love, there is injustice and blindness to all she does not love. Even in a woman's conscious love, there is still always attack, lightning, and night, mixed with the light.

As yet, woman is not capable of friendship: women are still cats and birds—or, at best, cows.

As yet, woman is not capable of friendship. But tell me, you men, which of you is capable of friendship?

Oh, your poverty, you men, and your sparingness of soul! As much as you give to your friend, I would give even to my enemy and not become poorer for it.

There is comradeship: may there be friendship!

Thus spoke Zarathustra.

Chapter 15
The Thousand and One Goals

Zarathustra saw many lands and many peoples; thus, he discovered the good and bad of many peoples. Zarathustra found no greater power on earth than the forces of good and bad.

No people could survive without first creating values; but if a people wish to sustain themselves, they cannot value things as their neighbors do.

Much of what was considered good by one people was scorned and despised by another—so I found it. Many things called bad here were there adorned with purple honors.

Neighbors never understood each other; their souls were always in awe of each other's delusions and perceived wickedness.

A tablet of values hangs over every people. Look! It is the tablet of their triumphs; see, it is the voice of their Will to Power.

They call praiseworthy what they deem difficult; what is essential and tough they name good; and whatever offers relief in their darkest need, the unique and hardest of all—they honor as holy.

Whatever helps them to rule, to conquer, and to shine, inspiring fear and envy in their neighbors, they consider the highest and foremost thing, the measure and meaning of all else.

Truly, my brother, if you knew only a people's needs, its land, its sky, and its neighbors, you would understand the laws of its overcoming, and why it climbs that ladder to its hope.

"Always be the foremost and most outstanding among all others; love no one but your friend"—this thought stirred the soul of a Greek and guided him on his path to greatness.

"To speak the truth and be skilled with bow and arrow"—such seemed both appealing and difficult to the people from whom my name comes—a name both pleasing and challenging to me.

"To honor father and mother and to fulfill their will from the depths of the soul"—another people hung this tablet of triumph over themselves, and grew powerful and enduring because of it.

"To be faithful, and for fidelity's sake to risk honor and blood, even on dark and dangerous paths"—by teaching themselves this, another people mastered themselves, and in mastering, they grew pregnant with great hopes.

Indeed, humans gave themselves all their ideas of good and bad. They did not receive it, nor find it; it did not come to them as a voice from heaven.

Humans assigned values to things to sustain themselves—they created only the meaning of things, a human meaning! Thus, they call themselves "man," meaning the valuator.

To value is to create: hear it, you creators! Valuing itself is the treasure and jewel of all valued things.

Only through valuing is there value; and without it, the core of existence would be hollow. Hear it, you creators!

Change of values—that means change of those who create. Whoever must be a creator also must destroy.

At first, creators were entire peoples; only in later times did individuals emerge as creators. Truly, the individual is still the most recent creation.

Peoples once hung above themselves tablets of what was good. Love that wanted to rule and love that wanted to obey created such tablets for themselves.

Older is the pleasure found in the herd than the pleasure in the self; and as long as a good conscience belongs to the herd, the bad conscience only says, "self."

The cunning self, the loveless one, that seeks its own gain in the gain of many—is not the beginning of the herd, but its decline.

It has always been the loving ones and the creators who defined good and bad. The fire of love burns in the names of all virtues, as does the fire of wrath.

Zarathustra saw many lands and many peoples; no greater power did Zarathustra find on earth than the creations of the loving ones— "good" and "bad" are the names they have given.

Truly, a marvel is this power of praising and blaming. Tell me, my brothers, who will master it for me? Who will put a chain on the thousand necks of this beast?

There have been a thousand goals so far, for a thousand peoples. Only a chain for these thousand necks is still missing; there is still lacking a single goal. Humanity, as yet, has no goal.

But tell me, my brothers, if the goal of humanity is still missing, does that not mean—humanity itself is still missing?—

Thus spoke Zarathustra.

Chapter 16

Neighbour Love

You crowd around your neighbor, and you have noble words for it. But I say to you: your love for your neighbor is your poor love for yourselves.

You flee to your neighbor to escape from yourselves, and you would rather make a virtue of it; but I understand your "unselfishness."

The Thou is older than the I; the Thou has been sanctified, but the I has not yet: thus, man draws near to his neighbor.

Do I advise you to love your neighbor? Rather, I advise you to flee from your neighbor and to love what is farthest!

Higher than love of your neighbor is love for those furthest from you and for those yet to come; higher still than love for men is love for things and phantoms.

The phantom that runs ahead of you, my brother, is more beautiful than you; why not give it your flesh and bones? But you are afraid and run to your neighbor instead.

You cannot bear to be with yourselves, and you do not love yourselves enough; so you try to win your neighbor's love and seek to cover yourselves with his mistaken praise.

Would that you could not stand to be near any of those close to you or their neighbors; then you would have to create your friend, along with his overflowing heart, out of yourselves.

You summon a witness when you want to speak well of yourselves; and when you convince him to think well of you, you then believe it too.

Not only does he lie who speaks against his knowledge, but even more, he who speaks against his ignorance. Thus, you speak of yourselves in conversation, and deceive your neighbor about who you are.

So says the fool: "Association with people spoils one's character, especially when one has none."

One goes to his neighbor because he seeks himself, and another because he wishes to lose himself. Your poor love of yourselves makes solitude feel like a prison.

Those who are farthest from you pay for your love of those nearest; and when there are five of you together, a sixth must always die.

I do not love your gatherings either: I found too many actors there, and even the spectators often behaved like actors.

I do not teach you about the neighbor, but about the friend. Let the friend be your festival of the earth, a foretaste of the Superman.

I teach you the friend with an overflowing heart. But one must know how to be a sponge if one wishes to be loved by overflowing hearts.

I teach you the friend in whom the world stands complete, a capsule of the good—the creating friend, who always has a complete world to offer.

And as the world unrolls itself for him, so it rolls back together again for him in rings, as the growth of good through evil, as the growth of purpose from chance.

Let the future and the farthest be the purpose of your present; in your friend, you shall love the Superman as your purpose.

My brothers, I advise you not to love your neighbor—I advise you to love what is furthest!—

Thus spoke Zarathustra.

Chapter 17

The Way of the Creating One

Would you go into isolation, my brother? Would you seek the path to yourself? Wait a moment longer and listen to me.

"He who seeks may easily lose himself. All isolation is wrong," so says the herd. And long have you belonged to the herd.

The voice of the herd will still echo within you. And when you say, "I no longer share a conscience with you," it will sound like a complaint and a wound.

See, that very pain was born of the same conscience, and the last spark of that conscience still glows in your suffering.

But you wish to go by the way of your suffering, the path that leads to yourself? Then show me your strength and authority to do so!

Are you a new strength and a new authority? A primal motion? A self-rolling wheel? Can you also compel the stars to revolve around you?

Alas! There is much longing for loftiness! Many tremors of ambition! Show me that you are not one of the ambitious who thirst for height!

Alas! So many great thoughts are mere bellows; they inflate and leave things emptier than before.

Do you call yourself free? I want to hear of your guiding thought, not just that you escaped from a yoke.

Are you someone worthy of escaping a yoke? Many have thrown away their last value when they threw away their servitude.

Free from what? What does that matter to Zarathustra! But let your eyes make it clear to me: free for what?

Can you give yourself your own good and evil and set your will as a law over yourself? Can you be your own judge and avenger of your law?

Terrible is loneliness with the judge and avenger of one's own law. It is like a star cast into the empty space of the universe, into the icy breath of isolation.

Today, you still suffer from the crowd, you individual; today, you still hold your courage undiminished and your hopes.

But one day, solitude will tire you; one day, your pride will falter, and your courage will tremble. You will one day cry, "I am alone!"

One day, you will no longer see your height, and you will see your lowliness too closely; your sublimity itself will frighten you like a ghost. You will cry, "All is false!"

There are feelings that seek to kill the solitary; if they cannot succeed, they must die themselves! But are you capable of this—to be their murderer?

Have you ever known, my brother, the word "disdain"? And the agony of your justice in being just to those who disdain you?

Thou forcest many to think differently about thee; that, charge they heavily to thine account. Thou camest nigh unto them, and yet wenteth past: for that they never forgive thee.

Thou goest beyond them: but the higher thou risest, the smaller doth the eye of envy see thee. Most of all, however, is the flying one hated.

"How could ye be just unto me!"—must thou say—"I choose your injustice as my allotted portion."

Injustice and filth cast they at the lonesome one: but, my brother, if thou wouldst be a star, thou must shine for them none the less on that account!

And be on thy guard against the good and just! They would fain crucify those who devise their own virtue—they hate the lonesome ones.

Be on thy guard, also, against holy simplicity! All is unholy to it that is not simple; fain, likewise, would it play with the fire—of the fagot and the stake.

And be on thy guard, also, against the assaults of thy love! Too readily doth the recluse reach his hand to any one he meeteth him.

To many a one mayest thou not give thy hand, but only thy paw; and I want thy paw to have claws.

But the worst enemy thou canst meet, wilt thou thyself always be; thou waylayeth thyself in caverns and forests.

Thou lonesome one, thou goest the way to thyself! And past thyself and thy seven devils leadeth thy way!

A heretic wilt thou be to thyself, and a wizard and a soothsayer, and a fool, and a doubter, and a reprobate, and a villain.

Ready must thou be to burn thyself in thine own flame; how couldst thou become new if thou have not first become ashes!

Thou lonesome one, thou goest the way of the creating one: a God wilt thou create for thyself out of thy seven devils!

Thou lonesome one, thou goest the way of the loving one: thou lovest thyself, and on that account you despisest thyself, as only the loving ones despise.

To create, desireth the loving one, because he despiseth! What knoweth he of love who hath not bee obliged to despise just what he loved!

With thy love, go into thine isolation, my brother ,and with thy creating; and late only will justice limp after thee.

With my tears, go into thine isolation, my brother. I love him who seeketh to create beyond himself, and thus succumbeth.—

Thus spoke Zarathustra.

Chapter 18
Old and Young Women

Why do you sneak along so stealthily in the twilight, Zarathustra? And what are you hiding so carefully under your cloak?

Is it a treasure that has been given to you? Or a child that you've brought into the world? Or are you going on a thief's errand, you friend of evil?

"Indeed, my brother," said Zarathustra, "it is a treasure that has been given to me: it is a little truth that I carry.

But it is mischievous, like a young child; and if I don't hold its mouth, it screams too loudly."

As I went on my way alone today, at the hour when the sun dips low, I encountered an old woman, and she spoke to my soul, saying:

"Zarathustra has spoken much to us women, but he has never spoken about woman to us."

And I replied to her, "One should only speak of woman to men."

"Speak to me about woman, too," she said; "I am old enough to forget it soon."

And I humored the old woman, and I spoke to her as follows:

Everything in woman is a riddle, and everything in woman has one answer—it is called pregnancy.

Man is a means to an end for woman; the purpose is always the child. But what is woman to man?

The true man wants two different things: danger and distraction. That is why he desires woman, the most dangerous plaything.

Man should be trained for war, and woman for the warrior's relaxation: all else is folly.

Too sweet fruits—the warrior does not like these. That is why he likes woman;—even the sweetest woman has a bitter edge.

Woman understands children better than man, but man is more childlike than woman.

In the true man, a child is hidden: it wants to play. Rise up, women, and discover the child within man!

Let woman be a plaything, pure and radiant like a precious stone, lit with the virtues of a world yet to come.

Let the light of a star shine in your love! Let your hope be, "May I bear the Superman!"

In your love, let there be courage! With your love, you shall dare to face the one who makes you afraid!

In your love, let there be honor! Woman understands little else about honor. But let this be your honor: to always love more than you are loved, and never to be second.

Let man be wary of woman when she loves; for then she will make every sacrifice, and everything else will seem worthless to her.

Let man be wary of woman when she hates; for while man is merely evil in his innermost soul, woman can be petty.

Whom does woman hate most?—Thus spoke the iron to the magnet: "I hate you most because you attract but lack the strength to draw me to you."

The happiness of man is, "I will." The happiness of woman is, "He will."

"Behold! Now the world is perfect!"—thus thinks every woman when she obeys with all her love.

Woman must obey and find a depth within her surface. Woman's soul is surface—a shifting, stormy film on shallow water.

Man's soul, however, is deep, flowing in hidden caverns: woman senses its strength but cannot comprehend it.—

Then the old woman replied to me: "Many fine things has Zarathustra said, especially for those young enough for them.

How strange! Zarathustra knows little about women, yet he speaks the truth about them! Perhaps this is because, with women, nothing is impossible?

And now, take a little truth as thanks! I am old enough to give it!

Swaddle it and hold its mouth, or it will scream too loudly—this little truth."

"Give me your little truth, woman!" I said. And the old woman spoke thus:

"If you go to women, don't forget your whip!"—

Thus spoke Zarathustra.

Chapter 19
The Bite of the Adder

One day, Zarathustra had fallen asleep under a fig tree because of the heat, with his arm resting over his face. Suddenly, an adder came along and bit him on the neck, causing Zarathustra to cry out in pain. When he lifted his arm from his face, he looked at the serpent, which then recognized Zarathustra's eyes, wriggled awkwardly, and tried to slither away.

"Not so fast," said Zarathustra, "you haven't yet received my thanks! You woke me up at the right time; my journey is still long."

"Your journey is short," the adder replied sadly, "for my poison is deadly."

Zarathustra smiled. "When has a dragon ever died from a serpent's poison?" he said. "Take your poison back! You aren't wealthy enough to gift it to me."

Then the adder fell upon his neck again and licked his wound.

When Zarathustra once shared this story with his disciples, they asked him, "And what, O Zarathustra, is the moral of your story?" And Zarathustra replied:

The good and the just call me the destroyer of morality: my story is indeed immoral.

But when you have an enemy, do not repay evil with good, for that would embarrass him. Instead, show him he has done you some good.

And it is better to be angry than to embarrass anyone! And if someone curses you, I don't wish you to bless in return; rather, curse a little too!

And if a great injustice befalls you, then quickly do five small ones yourself. Wretched to see is he who bears injustice alone.

Did you know this? A shared injustice is half-justice. And he who can bear it should take the injustice upon himself!

A small revenge is kinder than no revenge at all. And if the punishment is not also a right and a privilege to the wrongdoer, I do not approve of your punishment.

It is nobler to admit you are wrong than to prove yourself right, especially if you are right. Only, you must be rich enough to do so.

I do not like your cold justice; there is always the executioner and his cold steel glancing from your judges' eyes.

Tell me: where can we find justice, which is love with open eyes?

Invent for me, then, a love that not only bears all punishment but also takes all guilt upon itself!

Invent for me the justice that pardons everyone—except the judges!

And would you hear one more thing? For the one who seeks to be just from the heart, even a lie becomes an act of kindness.

But how could I be just from the heart? How could I give everyone exactly what is theirs? Let this be enough for me: I give everyone a part of myself.

Lastly, my brethren, beware of doing wrong to any hermit. How could a hermit forget? How could he seek revenge?

A hermit is like a deep well. It is easy to toss a stone into it, but if that stone sinks to the bottom, tell me, who will retrieve it?

Guard against harming the hermit! And if you do, well, then you'd better kill him as well!—

Thus spoke Zarathustra.

Chapter 20
Child and Marriage

I have a question just for you, my brother: like a sounding weight, I cast this question into your soul to measure its depth.

You are young and desire a child and marriage. But I ask you: Are you truly a man worthy to desire a child?

Are you the victor, the self-master, the ruler of your desires, the master of your virtues? This is what I ask you.

Or is it the animal in you that speaks, or the need? Or loneliness? Or inner conflict?

I would have your victory and freedom long for a child. Living monuments you should build to your victory and liberation.

Beyond yourself you shall build. But first, you must build yourself, solid in body and soul.

Not only shall you continue yourself forward, but upward! For this, may the garden of marriage help you!

You shall create a higher body, a first movement, a freely rolling wheel—a creator you shall create.

Marriage: so I call the will of two to create one who is more than those who made it. The respect for each other as those who pursue this will is what I call marriage.

Let this be the meaning and truth of your marriage. But what the masses call marriage, those extra ones—ah, what should I call that?

Ah, the poverty of spirit in those two! Ah, the filth of spirit in those two! Ah, the pitiful self-satisfaction in those two!

They call it all marriage, and they say their marriages are made in heaven.

Well, I do not like that heaven of the extra ones! No, I do not like those animals tangled in heavenly traps!

Far from me also be the God who limps there to bless what he did not join together!

Don't laugh at such marriages! What child has not had a reason to weep over its parents?

This man seemed worthy and ready to understand the meaning of the earth; but when I saw his wife, the earth seemed like a home for fools to me.

Yes, I would wish the earth would tremble in fits when a saint and a goose marry each other.

One man went out seeking truth like a hero, and in the end got for himself a small, dressed-up lie: he calls it his marriage.

Another was reserved in his connections and chose carefully. But one day he ruined his company forever: he calls it his marriage.

Another sought a servant with the virtues of an angel. But suddenly he became the servant of a woman, and now he would also need to become an angel.

Careful—I have found that all buyers have sharp eyes. But even the sharpest among them buys his wife in a sack.

Many short follies—that is what you call love. And your marriage puts an end to your many short follies with one long mistake.

Your love for women, and woman's love for man—oh, if only it were sympathy for suffering and hidden gods! But usually, two animals simply land on each other.

But even your best love is only an enraptured imitation and a painful passion. It is a torch to light loftier paths for you.

Beyond yourselves you shall one day love! Then first, learn how to love. And for this, you had to drink the bitter cup of your love.

Bitterness is in the cup even of the best love; so it causes longing for the Superman; so it causes thirst in you, the creator!

Thirst in the creator, an arrow and longing for the Superman: tell me, my brother, is this your desire for marriage?

I call such a will holy, and such a marriage holy.—

Thus spoke Zarathustra.

Chapter 21
Voluntary Death

Many die too late, and some die too soon. Yet how strange it sounds: "Die at the right time!"

Die at the right time—that is Zarathustra's teaching.

But he who never lives at the right time, how could he ever die at the right time? Better if he had never been born!—Thus I advise the unnecessary ones.

But even the unnecessary make a big fuss about their death, and even the emptiest shell wants to be cracked.

Everyone sees dying as something significant; but death is not yet a celebration. People have yet to learn to create the most beautiful celebrations.

I show you a fulfilling death, one that serves as a spark and a promise to the living.

The fulfilling one dies triumphantly, surrounded by those who hope and promise.

This is how one should learn to die; and there should be no celebration where such a death does not bless the promises of the living!

To die this way is best; the next best is to die in battle, giving up a great soul.

But to the fighter, as to the victor, your sneaky death that comes grinning, like a thief yet arriving as master, is equally hateful.

I praise my death to you—the chosen death that comes because I want it.

And when will I want it?—One who has a purpose and an heir desires death at the right time for that purpose and for that heir.

And out of respect for that purpose and heir, he will hang no more withered garlands in the sanctuary of life.

Truly, I don't want to be like the rope-makers, who keep extending their rope and moving backward with each length.

Some also grow too old for their truths and triumphs; a toothless mouth no longer has a right to all truths.

And whoever desires fame must part from honor in time and practice the hard art of—leaving at the right moment.

One should stop being celebrated when one is at one's peak: those who want to be loved for a long time understand this.

There are sour apples, certainly, meant to wait until the last day of autumn: suddenly they ripen, turn yellow, and wither.

In some, the heart ages first; in others, the spirit. Some are gray in their youth, but those who bloom late stay young longer.

For many, life feels like a failure; a poisonous worm gnaws at their hearts. So, let them make sure their dying is a greater success.

Many never ripen; they decay even in summer. It's cowardice that keeps them clinging to their branches.

Far too many live, and they hang on their branches far too long. If only a storm would come and shake off all this decay and rot from the tree!

If only preachers of swift death would come! They'd be the perfect storms and shakers of the trees of life! But all I hear is preaching of slow death and patience with all that is "earthly."

Ah! You preach patience with what's earthly? It's the earth that has too much patience with you, you blasphemers!

Truly, that Hebrew whom the slow-death preachers honor died too soon—and it's been a disaster for many that he died so early.

He knew only sorrow, the sorrow of his people, and a hatred for the good and the just—the Hebrew Jesus: then he felt the longing for death.

If only he had stayed in the wilderness, far from the "good" and the "just"! Then maybe he would have learned to live and to love the earth—and even to laugh!

Believe me, my friends! He died too early; he would have renounced his teachings if he'd lived to my age! He was noble enough to renounce them!

But he was still immature. The young love immaturely, and they hate people and the earth immaturely too. Their spirits and their wings are still clumsy and cramped.

In man, there's more child than in youth, and less sorrow: he understands life and death better.

Free for death, and free in death; a holy Naysayer, when there's no longer time for Yes: that's how he understands life and death.

May your dying not bring blame upon humanity or the earth, my friends: that is what I ask from the sweetness of your souls.

In your dying, may your spirit and virtue still shine like the evening glow around the earth; otherwise, your dying was unfulfilling.

I want to die this way, so that you, my friends, might love the earth more for my sake; and I will become earth again, to find rest in her who bore me.

Truly, Zarathustra had a goal; he threw his ball. Now, my friends, be the heirs to my goal; to you, I throw the golden ball.

What I want most is to see you throw the golden ball, my friends! And so, I stay a little while on the earth—pardon me for it!

Chapter 22

The Bestowing Virtue

When Zarathustra had said goodbye to the town that held his heart, the town called "The Pied Cow," many people who called themselves his disciples followed him, keeping him company. When they came to a crossroads, Zarathustra told them he wanted to go alone from there, as he enjoyed solitude. However, his disciples presented him with a staff for his journey, one with a golden handle around which a serpent coiled, embracing the sun. Zarathustra felt joy for the staff and leaned on it, then spoke to his disciples:

Tell me, please: how did gold come to hold the highest value? Because it is rare, doesn't profit, shines brightly, and has a soft glow; it gives itself freely.

Gold only gained its highest value as a symbol of the highest virtue. Like gold, the glance of the giver shines. Its golden glow makes peace between the moon and the sun.

The highest virtue, too, is rare and unprofitable, radiant and soft in glow: it is a giving virtue, the highest virtue.

Truly, I understand you well, my disciples: like me, you strive for this giving virtue. What would you share with cats and wolves?

Your longing is to become sacrifices and gifts yourselves; therefore, you thirst to gather all riches in your souls.

Your souls crave endlessly for treasures and jewels because your virtue is insatiable in its desire to give.

You draw all things toward you, to flow into you, so that they can pour out again from your fountain as the gifts of your love.

Indeed, a giver of all value must such generous love become; but I call this healthy and holy self-interest.

There is another kind of self-interest, a poorer and hungrier kind, always seeking to steal—the self-interest of the sick, a selfishness born of weakness.

With a thief's eye, it looks at all that glitters; with the hunger of want, it measures those who have plenty; and it prowls around the tables of the givers.

This craving speaks of sickness and hidden decay; the thieving craving of this self-interest speaks of a sick body.

Tell me, my brother, what do we consider bad, and worst of all? Is it not decay? And we always suspect decay when a giving soul is absent.

Our path climbs upward, from species to greater kinds. But we are horrified by the decaying instinct that says, "All for myself."

Our spirit soars upward; it mirrors our body, like an ascent. The names of virtues are like symbols of that ascent.

Thus, the body moves through history, becoming and struggling. And the spirit—what is it to the body? It is the announcer of its battles and victories, its companion and echo.

All names of good and evil are merely symbols; they do not speak plainly, only hint. It is foolish to seek knowledge directly from them!

Listen, my brothers, to every moment when your spirit speaks in symbols: there lies the source of your virtue.

When your body rises and lifts you, it delights the spirit, making it a creator, a judge, a lover, a benefactor of all.

When your heart overflows like a river, blessing and threatening the lowlands—there lies the source of your virtue.

When you rise above praise and blame, and your will wishes to command all things with the tenderness of love—there lies the source of your virtue.

When you scorn comfort and refuse to rest near the weak and indulgent—there lies the source of your virtue.

When you are ruled by one purpose, and when constant change is essential to you—there lies the source of your virtue.

Truly, it is a new good and evil! Truly, it is a new, deep rumbling, the voice of a fresh spring!

This new virtue is power; it is a governing thought, with a subtle soul wrapped around it: a golden sun encircled by the serpent of wisdom.

Zarathustra paused for a moment and looked lovingly at his disciples. Then he continued, his voice changed:

Stay loyal to the earth, my brothers, with the strength of your virtue! Let your love and knowledge serve the meaning of the earth! This is my prayer and plea to you.

Do not let your virtue fly off, beating against the walls of eternity! Ah, so much virtue has flown away from earth!

Lead, as I do, the runaway virtue back to the earth—yes, back to body and life—so that it may give meaning to the earth, a human meaning!

A hundred times the spirit and virtue have flown away and strayed. Alas! All that error and confusion lives on in our bodies, becoming part of us.

A hundred times the spirit and virtue have tried and failed. Yes, humanity itself has been an attempt. Alas, so much ignorance and error have taken root in us!

Not only the wisdom of millennia—but also their madness—bursts forth in us. To inherit is dangerous.

We still struggle, step by step, with the giant, Chance, while nonsense has ruled over humanity thus far.

Let your spirit and virtue be devoted to the purpose of the earth, my brothers: let you be the ones to set the value of everything anew! Therefore, you must be fighters! Therefore, you must be creators!

The body purifies itself through wisdom; it rises by seeking knowledge; all impulses are hallowed in the discerning; to those who rise, the soul becomes joyful.

"Physician, heal yourself"—then you will heal your patient, too. Let his best cure be seeing with his own eyes one who has made himself whole.

A thousand paths remain untrodden; a thousand sources of health and hidden islands of life. Unexhausted and undiscovered is humanity and humanity's world.

Awake and listen, you who are lonely! Winds from the future are coming softly, and for those with keen ears, good news is in the air.

You who are alone today, who stand apart, one day you will become a people. From those who have chosen themselves will rise a chosen people—and from them, the Superman.

The earth shall become a place of healing! And already, a new fragrance fills the air, bringing hope and healing—a promise of something new!

When Zarathustra spoke these words, he paused, as if he had not yet spoken his last thought. He held his staff thoughtfully in his hand for a long time. Finally, he spoke again, his voice changed:

I now go alone, my disciples! You too must now go alone! That is my wish.

I advise you: leave me, and protect yourselves from Zarathustra! Better still: feel a bit ashamed of him! Maybe he has misled you.

A true thinker must be able not only to love his enemies but also to dislike his friends.

A teacher is not repaid well when a student only remains a student. Why won't you reach for my crown?

You honor me; but what if your honor collapses one day? Be careful not to let a statue fall on you!

You say you believe in Zarathustra? But what does Zarathustra matter? You are my followers, but what do followers matter? You had not yet found yourselves, so you found me. That is how all followers are, and that is why all belief is of little importance.

Now I tell you to lose me and find yourselves. Only when you all have turned away from me will I return to you.

With different eyes, my brothers, will I seek those who were lost; with a different love, I will love you then.

And once again, you will become my friends, children of a shared hope: then I will be with you for the third time, to celebrate the great noontime together.

And it is the great noontime when humanity stands midway between beast and Superman, celebrating its journey toward evening as its highest hope, for that hope is the start of a new morning.

Then will the one who descends bless himself for being one who rises higher; and the sun of his knowledge will be at its peak.

"All gods are dead: now we want the Superman to live." Let this be our final will at the great noontime!—

Thus spoke Zarathustra.

Chapter 23
The Child with the Mirror

After this, Zarathustra returned once more to the mountains, back to the solitude of his cave, and withdrew from people, waiting like a sower who has scattered his seed. Yet his soul grew restless and full of longing for those he loved, for he still had much to give them. This is the hardest thing of all: to close an open hand out of love, and stay humble as a giver.

Thus, months and years passed for the lonely one; his wisdom grew in the meantime, and its abundance brought him pain.

One morning, however, he awoke before the rosy dawn. After thinking for a long time on his bed, he finally spoke to his heart:

Why did I tremble in my dream, waking so suddenly? Did a child not come to me, holding a mirror?

"O Zarathustra," the child said to me, "look at yourself in this mirror!"

But when I looked into the mirror, I cried out, and my heart beat hard: for I did not see myself, but instead a devilish face twisted in mockery.

Yes, I understand the meaning and warning of this dream all too well: my teaching is in danger; weeds want to be seen as wheat!

My enemies have grown stronger and twisted the image of my teaching, so much that my dearest friends are ashamed of the gifts I gave them.

My friends are lost; the time has come for me to go and find my lost ones!

With these words, Zarathustra jumped up—not as one in anguish seeking relief, but rather like a seer or a singer filled with spirit. His eagle and serpent looked at him in wonder, for a sense of joy spread across his face like the dawn.

What has happened to me, my animals?—Zarathustra asked. Am I not changed? Has bliss not come upon me like a whirlwind?

My happiness is foolish, and foolish things it will speak—it's still too young, so be patient with it!

I am wounded by my happiness: let all those who suffer be my healers!

Now I can go back down to my friends, and to my enemies too! Zarathustra can speak and give again, and show his truest love to those he loves!

My restless love flows in streams—down toward both sunrise and sunset. Out of silent mountains and storms of suffering, my soul rushes down into the valleys.

Too long have I yearned and looked into the distance. Solitude has held me captive for too long; I've forgotten how to stay silent.

I have become all expression, like the noisy rush of a brook down from high rocks: I will hurl my words down into the valleys.

Let my love flow into untrodden streams! How could a river not finally reach the sea? Indeed, there is a lake within me, secluded and self-sufficient, but the current of my love carries even it, down—to the sea!

I walk new paths now; a new language comes to me. Like all creators, I have grown weary of the old tongues. My spirit no longer moves with worn-out shoes.

All speaking moves too slowly for me—I leap into your chariot, O storm! And even you will I drive forward with my rage!

I'll race across wide seas like a cry of joy, until I find the Happy Isles where my friends stay;—

And my enemies among them! How I love everyone now, as long as I can speak to them! Even my enemies are part of my happiness.

When I want to mount my wildest horse, my spear always helps me best; it's my ever-ready servant:

The spear I throw at my enemies! How grateful I am to my enemies, so I may finally hurl it!

My clouds have grown too heavy; between flashes of lightning, I'll cast down showers of hail into the depths.

My chest will heave with force; I'll blow my storm over the mountains—then comes my calm.

My happiness and freedom arrive like a storm! But my enemies will think it's the devil roaring over their heads.

Yes, my friends, you too will be startled by my fierce wisdom; perhaps you'll flee from it, along with my enemies.

Ah, if only I could draw you back with the tunes of a shepherd's flute! Ah, if only my lioness-like wisdom would learn to roar gently! We've already learned so much together!

My fierce wisdom became fruitful on the lonely mountains; she bore her youngest on the rough stones.

Now she runs foolishly in the dry wilderness, searching for soft grass—my old, wild wisdom!

On the soft grass of your hearts, my friends!—on your love, she wishes to rest her dearest one!—

Thus spoke Zarathustra.

Chapter 24

In the Happy Isles

The figs fall from the trees; they are good and sweet, and when they fall, their red skins burst open. I am like a north wind to ripe figs.

So, like figs, these teachings fall to you, my friends: take in their juice and sweetness! It is autumn all around, with a clear sky and afternoon light.

See how abundant everything is around us! And in the midst of this abundance, it's a joy to gaze out at distant seas.

People once said "God" when they looked at the distant seas; now, however, I have taught you to say "Superman."

God is a guess, but I don't want your guessing to go beyond your will to create.

Could you create a God?—Then, I ask you, be silent about all gods! But you could well create the Superman.

Perhaps not you yourselves, my friends, but you could transform yourselves into fathers and forefathers of the Superman. Let that be your highest act of creation!—

God is a guess, but let your guessing stay within what you can understand.

Could you imagine a God?—Let this be your Will to Truth: that everything be transformed into what can be understood by humans, seen by humans, and sensed by humans! Let your own discernment lead you to the end!

And what you have called "the world" should be something you create yourselves: your reason, your likeness, your will, and your love should shape it! And truly, for your happiness, you who seek understanding!

How would you endure life without that hope, you who seek understanding? You could not have been born into something beyond understanding, or into something senseless.

But to show you my heart completely, my friends: if there were gods, how could I bear not to be one myself! That's why there are no gods.

Yes, I have drawn this conclusion, but now it draws me as well.—

God is a guess, but who could taste all the bitterness of this guess without dying? Should the creator lose faith, and the eagle lose its flight into high places?

God is a thought; it bends all straight paths and makes everything that stands tremble. What? Would time be gone, and everything perishable just a lie?

Thinking this is dizzying and unsettling to human senses, even sickening to the stomach. Truly, I call it the sickness of vertigo to imagine such things.

I call it evil and unfriendly to humanity—all that teaching about the one, the whole, the unmoving, the self-sufficient, and the everlasting!

All that's "everlasting"—it's just a parable, and poets lie too much. But the best parables should speak of time and becoming: they should praise and justify all things that pass away!

Creating—that is the great rescue from suffering, and the relief of life. But for a creator to come forth, suffering itself is needed, and much transformation.

Yes, there must be much bitter dying in your lives, you creators! Thus you become defenders and justifiers of all that perishes.

For the creator to be the newborn child, he must also be willing to bear the child and endure the pains of giving birth.

Through a hundred souls I've journeyed, and through a hundred cradles and birth pangs. I've taken many farewells; I know the heartbreaking last moments.

But so my creating Will desires it, my fate. Or, to put it more plainly: it is just such a fate that my Will desires.

All feeling suffers and is imprisoned in me: but my will always comes to me as my liberator and comforter.

Willing brings freedom: that is the true teaching of will and freedom—so Zarathustra teaches you.

Not to will, not to value, not to create—ah, may such weakness always be far from me!

Even in understanding, I feel only the creative and growing joy of my will; and if my knowledge holds innocence, it is because it has the will to creation within it.

This will led me away from God and gods; for what would there be to create if there were gods?

But to man does it ever drive me anew, my fiery creative will; thus it drives the hammer to the stone.

Ah, you people, within the stone sleeps an image for me—the image of my visions! Ah, that it should sleep in the hardest, ugliest stone! Now my hammer strikes mercilessly against its prison. The fragments fly from the stone—what's that to me?

I will finish it: for a shadow came to me—the stillest and lightest of all things came to me once!

The beauty of the Superman came to me as a shadow. Ah, my brothers! What do the gods mean to me now?—

Thus spoke Zarathustra.

Chapter 25

The Pitiful

MY FRIENDS, there's a joke making the rounds about your friend: "Look at Zarathustra! Doesn't he walk among us as if we were animals?"

But it's better put this way: "The wise one walks among people as if among animals."

To the wise, man himself is like an animal with red cheeks.

How did that happen to him? Is it because he's had to feel shame so often?

O my friends! This is what the wise one says: shame, shame, shame—that is the story of mankind!

And so, the noble person instructs himself not to cause shame; he teaches himself modesty in the presence of all who suffer.

I don't care for those merciful ones who find joy in their pity: they lack too much modesty.

If I must be compassionate, I don't like to be called that; and if I am, I prefer to be so at a distance. I'd also rather cover my face and walk away than be recognized for it. I ask you to do the same, my friends!

May my path always lead me to those like you, who are free of suffering, with whom I can share hope, companionship, and sweetness!

I've done this and that for those in pain; but it always seemed I did better when I learned to enjoy myself more.

Since the dawn of humanity, man has not enjoyed himself enough: that alone, my brothers, is our original sin!

And as we learn to enjoy ourselves better, we learn best how not to harm others or bring them pain.

That's why I wash the hand that has helped the sufferer; that's why I cleanse my soul as well.

For in seeing the suffering suffer, I felt ashamed for his shame; and in helping him, I deeply hurt his pride.

Great debts do not bring gratitude but resentment; and when a small kindness is remembered too long, it turns into a nagging pain.

"Be cautious in accepting! Make acceptance a form of distinction!"—this is what I advise those who have nothing to give.

But I am a giver: I give willingly, as friend to friend. Strangers and the poor may pick for themselves the fruit from my tree—that causes less shame.

As for beggars, they should be done away with altogether! It's irritating to give to them, and it's irritating not to give to them.

And likewise, sinners and guilty consciences! Believe me, my friends: the sting of a guilty conscience teaches one to sting others. The worst, however, are petty thoughts. Better to have done wrong boldly than to think small-mindedly!

Of course, you may say: "The enjoyment of petty wrongs saves one from doing great wrongs." But here, one shouldn't aim to save.

The evil deed is like a sore: it itches, irritates, and breaks open—it speaks plainly.

"Look, I am a disease," says the evil deed; that's its honesty.

But the petty thought is like an infection: it creeps and hides, wanting to go unnoticed—until the whole body is rotted and wasted by the small infection.

To the person possessed by a demon, I would whisper: "Better for you to let your demon grow! Even for you, there is still a path to greatness!"

Ah, my brothers! We know a little too much about everyone! Many become clear to us, but we still cannot truly understand them.

It's hard to live among people because silence is so hard.

And we're often most unfair, not to those who offend us, but to those who mean nothing to us.

If you have a friend in pain, be a place of rest for his suffering, like a firm bed, a camp-bed: that will serve him best.

And if a friend wrongs you, say, "I forgive what you did to me; but that you did it to yourself—how could I forgive that?"

So speaks all great love: it goes beyond forgiveness and pity.

One should hold onto one's heart; for once it's let go, the mind quickly follows.

Ah, where in the world have there been greater follies than among the pitiful? And what in the world has caused more suffering than the follies of the pitiful?

Woe to all who love without a height above their pity!

Thus spoke the devil to me once: "Even God has his hell; it's his love for mankind."

And recently, I heard him say, "God is dead: he died of his pity for man."

So be warned against pity: it brings a heavy cloud to humanity! I know the signs of such weather!

But heed this as well: All great love is beyond pity; for it aims to create what it loves!

"I offer myself to my love, and my neighbor as I would myself"— such is the language of all creators.

And all creators are hard.

Thus spoke Zarathustra.

Chapter 26

The Priests

AND one day Zarathustra gave a signal to his followers and said:

"Here are priests: though they are my enemies, pass them peacefully, keeping your swords sheathed!

Among them, too, there are heroes; many of them have suffered too much—and so they wish to make others suffer.

They are bitter enemies: nothing is more vengeful than their gentleness. Anyone who touches them is easily tainted. But my blood is related to theirs, and I still wish to see my blood honored in theirs."

When they had passed, a pain struck Zarathustra; but he did not struggle with the pain for long before he began to speak:

My heart aches for these priests. They also go against my taste, but that doesn't matter much to me, as I am here among men.

But I suffer with them and have suffered like them: they are prisoners and bear the marks of bondage. The one they call "Savior" has shackled them.

They are bound by false values and foolish words! Oh, that someone would save them from their "Savior!"

Once, they thought they'd found solid ground when the sea tossed them about, but it was only a sleeping monster!

False values and foolish words: these are the most dangerous monsters for humans—their fate lies dormant in them for a long time, waiting.

But eventually, it awakens, devours, and swallows everything that has been built upon it.

Oh, look at those shrines the priests have made for themselves! Churches, they call these sweet-smelling caves of theirs!

Oh, the false light, the stale air! Where the soul cannot soar to its full height!

Yet their faith commands them: "On your knees, up the stairs, you sinners!"

I'd rather see a shameless person than the distorted eyes of their shame and submission.

Who created such caves and staircases of penitence? Was it not those who wanted to hide and felt ashamed under the clear sky? Only when sunlight shines through broken roofs and down upon red poppies growing among crumbling walls, will I open my heart again to the seats of this God.

They called God the force that opposed and afflicted them; indeed, there was much heroic spirit in their worship!

They knew no other way to love their God but by nailing people to the cross!

They thought they could live as corpses; they dressed their dead in black. Even in their words, I sense the dark staleness of burial places.

And anyone who lives near them lives close to dark pools, where toads croak their heavy, grave songs.

They would have to sing better songs for me to believe in their Savior! I'd want his followers to look more like people who had been saved!

I'd rather see them bare, for beauty alone should preach repentance. But who would be convinced by their disguised misery?

These saviors themselves did not come from freedom or freedom's seventh heaven! They themselves never walked the carpets of knowledge!

Their spirits were made up of flaws, but in every flaw, they placed their illusion, their plug, and called it "God."

In their pity, their spirit was drowned; and whenever they were overflowing with pity, a great folly would always rise to the surface.

With eagerness and loud shouts, they drove their flock across their narrow bridge, as if it were the only path to the future! But those shepherds were still part of the flock!

Those shepherds had small minds but vast souls. Yet, my brothers, even the widest souls have, so far, contained only small domains!

They wrote their journey in letters of blood, and their folly taught that truth is proven by blood.

But blood is the worst witness for truth; it stains the purest teaching, turning it into a distortion and hatred.

And if someone walks through fire for their teaching—what does that prove? It is far greater if one's teaching rises from one's own burning!

A heated heart and a cold mind—when these come together, they create the loud "Savior."

But truly, there have been greater people and those of nobler birth than those called "saviors" by the masses, these noisy preachers of rapture!

And if you wish to find the path to freedom, my brothers, you will need to be saved by someone greater than any of the "saviors"!

There has never yet been a Superman. I have seen both, the greatest and the smallest of men, stripped bare—

And still, they are far too alike. Even the greatest I found was— still all-too-human!

Thus spoke Zarathustra.

Chapter 27

The Virtuous

WITH thunder and heavenly fireworks one must speak to dull, sleepy senses.

But beauty speaks with a gentle voice; it reaches only the most alert souls. Today, my shield vibrated and laughed softly; it was the holy laughter and thrill of beauty.

Today, my beauty laughed at you, virtuous ones. And this is what it told me: "They want—to be paid, besides!"

You want to be paid, virtuous ones! You want a reward for virtue, heaven for earth, eternity for today?

And now you blame me for teaching there's no reward-giver, no paymaster? And indeed, I don't even teach that virtue is its own reward.

Ah! This is my sorrow: the ideas of reward and punishment have slipped into the heart of things—and now, even into the core of your souls, you virtuous ones!

But like the snout of a boar, my words will dig up the ground of your souls; you shall call me a plowshare.

All the hidden parts of your heart will be laid bare; and when you lie open and exposed in the sun, your falsehood will be separated from your truth.

For this is your truth: you are too pure for the filth of words like vengeance, punishment, reward, and retribution.

You love your virtue as a mother loves her child; but when has a mother ever wanted payment for her love?

Your virtue is your dearest Self. In you is the thirst of the ring: every ring struggles to return to itself and turns back on itself.

And like the star that shines its light, every act of your virtue travels on its way—and when will it stop traveling?

The light of your virtue continues on, even when its work is finished. Forgotten and gone, its light still lives and moves.

Your virtue is part of you, not some outer thing, a skin or a cloak. This is the truth from the core of your souls, virtuous ones!

But there are those for whom virtue means twisting under a whip—and you've listened to their cries for too long!

And others call virtue the laziness of their vices. When their hatred and jealousy relax, their "justice" awakens and rubs its sleepy eyes.

There are others drawn downwards—their demons pull them. But the deeper they sink, the more their eyes burn, and the more they long for their God.

Ah! Their cries have reached your ears too, virtuous ones: "What I am not, that—that is God to me, and virtue!"

And there are others who trudge heavily, creaking like carts dragging stones downhill. They talk much of dignity and virtue—their burden, they call virtue!

And some are like eight-day clocks wound up tight; they tick, wanting others to call their ticking—virtue.

Truly, I find my amusement in those kinds of people: whenever I find such clocks, I shall wind them up with my mockery, and they'll even whirr!

Then there are others, proud of their tiny bit of righteousness, and for that they do harm to all things, drowning the world in their own injustice.

Oh, how clumsily the word "virtue" comes from their mouths! And when they say, "I am just," it always sounds like, "I am just—revenged!"

They want to use their virtues to scratch out the eyes of their enemies; they lift themselves up only to push others down.

And there are those who sit in their swamp, saying from among the reeds, "Virtue—that's sitting quietly in the swamp.

We don't bite anyone, and we avoid anyone who bites; in all things, we take the opinion that's given to us."

Then there are those who love to strike a pose and think virtue is a kind of attitude.

Their knees are always worshiping, and their hands are constant praises of virtue, but their hearts know nothing of it.

And again, some say, "Virtue is necessary," but all they truly believe is that policemen are necessary.

And many who can't see men's heights call it virtue to see only their lowest parts; they name their critical eye virtue.

Some want to be uplifted, calling that virtue; others want to be knocked down—and call that virtue too.

So it goes—almost all believe they have a share in virtue; each one claims to be an authority on "good" and "evil."

But Zarathustra didn't come to tell these liars and fools, "What do you know of virtue? What could you know of virtue?"—

Instead, he came so that you, my friends, might grow weary of the old words you've learned from fools and liars:

That you might tire of words like "reward," "retribution," "punishment," "righteous vengeance."

That you might become weary of saying, "An action is good because it's unselfish."

Oh, my friends! Let your very Self be in your actions, as a mother is in her child: let that be your definition of virtue!

Yes, I've taken away a hundred definitions and your virtue's favorite playthings; and now you scold me, just as children scold.

They played by the sea—then a wave came and swept their toys into the deep; now they cry.

But the same wave will bring them new toys, spreading new, speckled shells before them!

Thus, they will be comforted; and like them, my friends, you too shall have your comforts—and your new, speckled shells!—

Thus spoke Zarathustra.

Chapter 28
The Rabble

LIFE is a well of joy, but where the crowds drink, every fountain becomes polluted.

I'm fond of all things pure, but I hate seeing the grinning mouths and the unclean thirst of the impure.

They peer into the fountain, and now their repulsive smiles rise up from the water to meet my gaze.

They have tainted the holy water with their lust; and when they call their filthy dreams "delight," they spoil the very meaning of the word.

The flame becomes angry when they press their damp hearts against it; even the spirit itself bubbles and smokes when the rabble approach.

In their hands, fruit becomes mushy and overripe; their gaze makes the fruit tree tremble, unsteady and withered at the top.

And many who have turned away from life did so only to escape the rabble: they couldn't bear to share the fountain, the flame, or the fruit with them.

Many who fled to the wilderness to thirst beside wild beasts simply couldn't stand sitting at the well with filthy camel drivers.

And some who have come like a storm, destroying fields of grain, merely wanted to jam their feet into the mouths of the rabble and silence them.

It's not the need for enmity, death, or torture that has choked me the most; I can accept that life itself requires these things.

But one question nearly suffocated me: What? Is the rabble also necessary for life?

Are poisoned fountains, foul fires, filthy dreams, and maggots in life's bread essential?

Not hatred, but disgust gnawed at my spirit. Oh, how often have I grown weary of spirit when I found that even the rabble have "spirit"!

I turned my back on rulers when I saw what they now call ruling: trading and bargaining for power—dealing with the rabble!

I lived among people whose language was strange to me, with my ears closed, so that the language of their trading remained foreign, and I would not hear their bargaining for power.

And with my nose held, I walked gloomily through all yesterdays and todays. Truly, how foully stink all the yesterdays and todays of the scribbling rabble!

Like a cripple who became deaf, blind, and silent—I lived this way for a long time, to avoid the power-hungry, the scribblers, and those chasing pleasure.

My spirit climbed painfully, step by step, finding refreshment in small offerings of joy, and life moved forward like a blind person with a cane.

What happened to me? How did I free myself from disgust? Who renewed my vision? How did I rise so high that no crowd sits at these wells?

Did my very disgust give me wings and the gift to sense pure fountains? I had to fly to the highest peak to find that spring of delight!

Oh, I have found it, my brothers! Here, on the highest peak, the spring of joy bubbles just for me! And there is a life at this well that none of the crowd drinks with me.

You flow almost too powerfully for me, fountain of joy! Often you empty my cup again just as I'm about to drink!

Yet I must learn to approach you more humbly; my heart still rushes toward you too violently.

My heart, in which my summer burns—my short, intense, melancholy, overjoyed summer—oh, how my summer heart longs for your coolness!

Gone is the lingering pain of my spring! Gone, the cruelty of my June snowflakes! I have become wholly summer, summer at noon!

A summer on the highest peak, with cold springs and blissful silence. Oh, come, my friends, that the silence may grow even more blissful!

This is our peak, our home: we live too high and steep here for the unclean and their thirst.

Just cast your pure eyes into my fountain of joy, my friends! How could it grow cloudy from your gaze? It will laugh back at you in its clarity.

We build our nest on the tree of the future; eagles shall bring food to us who are alone, carrying it in their beaks!

Truly, no food that the impure could share! To them, it would seem like fire, burning their mouths!

Truly, we have no dwelling prepared here for the impure! Our happiness would be an ice-cave for their bodies and their spirits!

Like strong winds, we live above them, neighbors to the eagles, the snow, the sun: such is the life of the strong winds.

And one day I will blow through them like a wind, my spirit stealing the breath from theirs—that is my future.

Truly, Zarathustra is a strong wind to all lowlands, and he gives this advice to his enemies, and to all who spit and spew: "Be careful not to spit against the wind!"

Thus spoke Zarathustra.

Chapter 29

The Tarantulas

Look, this is the tarantula's den! Do you want to see the tarantula itself? Here hangs its web: touch it, so that it trembles.

Here comes the tarantula eagerly: Welcome, tarantula! Black on your back is the triangle and symbol, and I also know what is in your soul. Revenge lies in your soul; wherever you bite, there appears a black scab. With revenge, your poison makes the soul dizzy!

So I speak to you in parables, you who make the soul spin, you preachers of equality! You are tarantulas to me, and secretly revengeful ones!

But I will soon expose your hiding places to the light; that is why I laugh in your face with the laughter of the heights.

Therefore, I tear at your web, so that your rage may lure you out of your den of lies, and that your revenge may leap out from behind your word "justice."

For to free mankind from revenge—that is, to me, the bridge to the highest hope, a rainbow after long storms.

But the tarantulas would have it differently. "Let it be true justice for the world to be filled with the storms of our vengeance"—this is how they speak to one another.

"Vengeance we shall use, and insult, against all who are not like us"—this is the pledge of the tarantula-hearts.

"And 'Will to Equality'—this shall henceforth be the name of virtue, and we will raise an outcry against all who have power!"

You preachers of equality, the tyrant-frenzy of impotence cries out in you for "equality": your hidden tyrant-longings hide themselves behind words of virtue!

Bitterness and suppressed envy—perhaps your fathers' bitterness and envy—break out in you now as flames and a frenzy of vengeance.

What the father kept hidden appears in the son; and often, I have found in the son the father's long-buried secret revealed.

They seem inspired, but it is not the heart that inspires them—it is vengeance. And when they become subtle and cold, it is not spirit, but envy, that makes them so.

Their jealousy leads them down paths of thought; and this is the sign of their jealousy—they always go too far, until their exhaustion forces them to rest on the cold snow. In all their lamentations, vengeance sounds; in all their praise, there is malice, and being a judge seems like bliss to them.

So I give you this counsel, my friends: Distrust all who are driven strongly to punish! They are people of low race and lineage; the hangman and the bloodhound peer from their faces.

Distrust all those who talk much about justice! Verily, in their souls, not only honey is missing.

And when they call themselves "the good and the just," remember, that only one thing is lacking for them to be Pharisees—power!

My friends, I do not want to be mixed up and confused with others. There are those who preach my doctrine of life but are, at the same time, preachers of equality and tarantulas.

They claim to speak for life, though they sit in their den like poison-spiders, withdrawn from life—because they wish to cause harm.

They wish to cause harm to those who hold power now: for with them, the preaching of death finds its true home.

If it were otherwise, then the tarantulas would teach otherwise: they were once the fiercest accusers of the world, the ones who burned heretics.

With these preachers of equality, I do not want to be mixed up or confused. For justice speaks to me thus: "Men are not equal."

And they shall not become so! What would my love for the Superman be if I spoke otherwise?

On a thousand bridges and piers, they shall crowd toward the future, and there will always be more conflict and inequality among them: thus does my great love make me speak!

They shall invent figures and phantoms to fight against; and with those figures and phantoms, they shall still engage in the ultimate battle!

Good and evil, rich and poor, high and low—all names of values: they shall be weapons and resounding signs, so that life must continuously strive to surpass itself!

Life will build itself upward with columns and stairs—life itself wants to gaze out to distant places and toward blissful beauty. For that, it needs elevation!

And because it requires elevation, it needs steps, different levels, and climbers! Life strives to rise and, in rising, to overcome itself.

Just look, my friends! Here, where the tarantula's den is, rises the ruins of an ancient temple—just look with enlightened eyes!

He who once raised his thoughts here in stone knew as well as the wisest about life's hidden meaning!

That there is struggle and inequality, even in beauty, and a battle for power and mastery: here, he teaches us this in the clearest parable.

How divinely do vault and arch here clash in their struggle: how they strive with light and shadow, the divinely battling ones.

So let us also be steadfast and beautiful as enemies, my friends! Let us strive divinely against one another!

But alas! The tarantula has bitten me, my old enemy! Divinely steadfast and beautiful, it has bitten my finger!

"Justice and punishment must be," it thinks. "No one shall sing of enmity here without a price!"

Yes, it has taken its revenge! And now, alas, it would make my soul dizzy with revenge as well!

So that I do not become dizzy, tie me fast, my friends, to this pillar! I would rather be a pillar-saint than a whirl of vengeance!

Zarathustra is no storm or cyclone, and if he is a dancer, he is certainly not a tarantula-dancer!—

Thus spoke Zarathustra.

Chapter 30
The Famous Wise Men

THE people have you served, and their superstitions—not the truth!—all you famous wise ones! And it's for that reason they've shown you respect.

And for that reason, too, they tolerated your lack of belief, because it amused them and gave them a diversion. This is how a master gives his slaves some freedom, even enjoying their boldness.

But the one who's hated by the people, as a wolf is hated by dogs, is the free spirit, the one who won't be bound, the one who doesn't worship, the one who lives in the wild.

To hunt him down, to drive him out—that was always called "justice" by the people. And they still send their fiercest dogs after him.

"For truth is wherever the people are! Woe, woe to those who search!"—this has echoed through all ages.

You wanted to justify the people's reverence for you; you called this "the Will to Truth," you famous wise ones!

And in your hearts, you've always thought, "I came from the people; from them came to me also the voice of God."

You have been as stubborn and crafty as donkeys, always as defenders of the people.

And many a powerful man who wanted to win favor with the people even harnessed a donkey—a famous wise man—at the front of his horses.

And now, you famous wise ones, I would like you to finally take off the lion's skin completely!

The skin of the beast of prey, the spotted skin, the wild mane of the explorer, the seeker, the conqueror!

Ah! For me to believe in your "conscientiousness," you would have to break your need to worship first.

Honest—that's what I call someone who goes into godless wildernesses and has broken the need to worship in his heart.

In the yellow sands, scorched by the sun, he gazes longingly at islands with fresh springs, where life rests under shady trees.

But his thirst doesn't make him want to be like those comfortable souls; for where there are oases, there are idols too.

Hungry, fierce, alone, and godforsaken—that is how the lion's will wants to be.

Free from the comfort of slaves, freed from gods and devotions, fearless and fearsome, grand and alone—that's the will of the conscientious.

In the wilderness, the conscientious have always dwelled, the free spirits, as lords of the wild; but in the cities live the well-fed, famous wise ones—the beasts of burden.

For they always pull, like donkeys—the people's carts!

Not that I scold them for it; they remain servants, harnessed ones, even if they shine in golden harnesses.

And often, they've been good servants, worthy of their pay. For, as virtue says, "If you must serve, then serve the one who benefits most from your work!

Let your master's spirit and virtue grow because of your service; in this way, you'll grow in spirit and virtue too!"

And truly, you famous wise ones, you servants of the people! You yourselves have grown with the people's spirit and virtue—and the people have grown with you! I say this in your honor.

Yet you remain "the people" to me, even with your virtues—the people with half-blind eyes, who do not know what spirit truly is!

Spirit is life cutting into life itself; it deepens its own knowledge through its own suffering—did you know that before?

And the spirit's joy is this: to be anointed and dedicated with tears as a sacrificial offering—did you know that before?

And the blindness of the blind man, his stumbling and searching, shall still testify to the power of the sun that he has tried to look upon—did you know that before?

And the discerning one will learn to build with mountains! It is a small thing for the spirit to remove mountains—did you know that before?

You only know the sparks of the spirit, but you do not see the anvil it strikes upon, nor the cruelty of its hammer!

You do not understand the spirit's pride! But even less could you bear the spirit's humility, if it ever chose to speak!

And you have never cast your spirit into an ice pit; you are not passionate enough for that! That's why you don't know the pleasure of its coldness.

In all things, you make too light of the spirit; you've often turned wisdom itself into a charity home, a hospital for bad poets.

You are not eagles, so you've never felt the happiness of the spirit's alarm. And he who is not a bird should not camp above abysses.

You seem lukewarm to me. But all deep knowledge flows cold. Ice-cold are the innermost wells of the spirit, refreshing for heated hands and handlers.

Respectable you stand there, stiff, with straight backs, you famous wise ones—no strong wind or force drives you forward.

Have you ever seen a sail crossing the sea, filled, rounded, trembling with the power of the wind?

Like that sail trembling with the force of the spirit, my wisdom crosses the sea—my wild wisdom!

But you servants of the people, you famous wise ones—how could you possibly sail with me!—

Thus spoke Zarathustra.

Chapter 31
The Night Song

It is night: now all the gushing fountains speak louder, and my soul is also a gushing fountain.

It is night: now only do all the songs of those who love truly awaken. And my soul is also the song of one who loves deeply.

There is something restless, something that cannot be soothed, within me; it longs to find expression. A deep desire for love stirs in me, speaking the language of love.

I am light—oh, how I wish I were night! But it is my loneliness to be surrounded by light!

Oh, how I wish I were dark and nocturnal! How gladly would I drink at the breasts of light!

And I would bless you, you twinkling stars and glow-worms up high—and I would rejoice in the gifts of your light.

But I live within my own light, drawing back into myself the flames that break out from me.

I do not know the joy of receiving, and I have often dreamt that stealing must be more blessed than receiving.

It is my poverty that my hand never stops giving; it is my envy that I see expectant eyes and the brightened nights of longing.

Oh, the sadness of all givers! Oh, the darkening of my sun! Oh, the craving to crave! Oh, the fierce hunger even in satisfaction!

They take from me: but do I truly touch their souls? There is a gap between giving and receiving, and this small gap must someday be bridged.

A hunger grows out of my beauty: I feel a desire to harm those I illuminate; I feel a longing to rob those I have blessed—thus I hunger for a touch of wickedness.

To withdraw my hand when another hand is already reaching for it; to hesitate like a waterfall that pauses even in its leap—this is how I hunger for wickedness!

Such revenge is thought of by my abundance, and such mischief wells up from my loneliness.

My joy in giving died from the giving; my virtue became weary of itself through its own abundance!

He who always gives is in danger of losing his modesty; he who always dispenses finds his hand and heart hardened by the act of giving.

My eyes no longer overflow with tears for the shame of those who plead; my hand has grown too hardened for the trembling of hands I fill.

Where have the tears of my eyes gone, and the tenderness of my heart? Oh, the loneliness of all who give! Oh, the silence of all who shine!

Many suns circle in the emptiness of space: to everything dark they speak with their light—but to me, they are silent.

Oh, this is the enmity of light toward one who shines: mercilessly, it pursues its path.

Unjust to the shining one in its innermost heart, cold even to the suns—that is how every sun travels.

Like a storm, the suns follow their paths; that is their journey. They follow their relentless will—that is their coldness.

Oh, only you, you dark, nightly ones, draw warmth from those who shine! Only you drink nourishment and refreshment from the udders of light!

Ah, there is ice around me; my hand burns from its chill! Ah, there is a thirst in me; it longs for the thirst within you!

It is night: oh, that I must be light! And long for the nightly! And for solitude!

It is night: now my longing bursts forth within me like a fountain—my soul yearns to speak.

It is night: now all the gushing fountains speak louder, and my soul is also a gushing fountain.

It is night: now all songs of those who love awaken, and my soul is also the song of one who loves deeply.

Thus sang Zarathustra.

Chapter 32
The Dance Song

One evening, Zarathustra and his disciples were walking through the forest, and as he searched for a well, he stumbled upon a green meadow, peacefully surrounded by trees and bushes, where maidens were dancing together. When the maidens recognized Zarathustra, they paused in their dance. Zarathustra, however, approached them with a friendly expression and spoke these words:

"Don't stop your dancing, lovely maidens! No joy-spoiler has come among you with an evil eye, no enemy of maidens.

I am God's advocate with the devil—though he is the spirit of gravity. How could I, you light-footed ones, be against divine dances? Or against maidens' feet with fine ankles?

Certainly, I am a forest and a night filled with dark trees; but those who are not afraid of my darkness will find rose-laden banks beneath my cypresses.

And they might even find the little god most beloved by maidens: resting by the well, lying still with his eyes closed.

He fell asleep in broad daylight, the little sluggard! Perhaps he chased butterflies too long?

Don't be angry, beautiful dancers, if I scold the little god a bit! Yes, he'll cry, certainly, and weep—but he's even laughable when he weeps!

With tears in his eyes, he'll ask you to dance; and I'll sing a song for his dance:

A dance-song, a satire on the spirit of gravity—my greatest, most powerful demon, the one who is said to be 'lord of the world.'"

And this is the song that Zarathustra sang while Cupid and the maidens danced together:

"Recently, I looked into your eyes, O Life! And there I seemed to sink into something unfathomable.

But you pulled me back with a golden hook; you laughed at me mockingly when I called you unfathomable.

'That's how all fish speak,' you said. 'Whatever they don't understand, they call unfathomable.

But I am only changeable, wild, and altogether a woman—and certainly not virtuous:

Even if men call me 'the profound one,' or 'the faithful one,' 'the eternal one,' 'the mysterious one.'"

But you men always project your own virtues onto us—alas, you virtuous ones!"

Thus laughed Life, the unbelievable one; yet I never believe her or her laughter when she speaks poorly of herself.

And when I spoke face-to-face with my wild Wisdom, she said to me in anger: "You desire, you crave, you love; for that reason alone do you praise Life!"

Then I nearly responded with indignation and told the truth to the angry one; for nothing can answer indignation better than truth spoken to one's own Wisdom.

For that is how it is between the three of us. In my heart, I love only Life—and truly, most when I despise her!

But that I am fond of Wisdom, and often overly so, is because she so strongly reminds me of Life!

She has her eyes, her laugh, even her golden angler's hook—can I be blamed that both resemble each other so?

And once, when Life asked me, "Who is this Wisdom then?" I replied eagerly: "Ah, yes! Wisdom!

One thirsts for her but is never satisfied, one peers through veils, grasps through nets.

Is she beautiful? How would I know! But even the oldest fish are still lured by her.

She is changeable and willful; I have often seen her bite her lip and comb her hair against the grain.

Maybe she is wicked and false, and altogether a woman; but when she speaks ill of herself, that's when she seduces the most."

When I had said this to Life, she laughed maliciously and closed her eyes. "Whom do you mean?" she asked. "Could it be me?

And if you were right—should you say such things to my face! But now, speak of your Wisdom, if you please!"

Ah, and now you have opened your eyes again, beloved Life! And into the unfathomable I seem to sink once more—

Thus sang Zarathustra. But when the dance was over and the maidens had gone, he grew sad.

"The sun has long set," he said at last, "the meadow is damp, and coolness comes from the forest.

An unknown presence surrounds me, gazing thoughtfully. What! Do you still live, Zarathustra?

Why? For what reason? How? Where? Is it not folly to live still?—

Ah, my friends, it is evening that asks me such questions. Forgive my sadness!

Evening has come—so forgive me that evening has come."

Thus sang Zarathustra.

Chapter 33
The Grave Song

Reflecting thus in my heart, I sailed across the sea.

Oh, you sights and memories of my youth! Oh, all those fleeting glimpses of love, those divine, passing glows! How could you vanish so quickly from me? Today, I think of you as my departed ones.

From you, my dearest lost ones, comes a sweet scent, stirring my heart and melting it. It stirs and opens the heart of this lonely wanderer.

I am still the richest, the one most envied—the most lonesome one! For I have possessed you, and you still possess me. Tell me, who else has ever received such rosy fruits from the tree of life as I have?

I am still the heir and legacy of your love, blossoming in memory of you, blooming with wild, untamed virtues, you dearest ones!

Ah, we were meant to remain close to each other, you kindly, strange wonders. You didn't come to me like timid birds, not at all; you came as those who trust, to one who trusts.

Yes, meant for faithfulness, as I am, and for timeless closeness; yet now I must call you by the name of faithlessness, you divine glances and fleeting lights—for I know no other name for you.

You left too soon, you fugitives. Yet you did not flee from me, nor did I from you; we are innocent of betrayal to each other.

They strangled you, my singing birds of hope, to hurt me! Yes, malice aimed its arrows at you, my dearest ones, to wound my heart!

And they struck! For you were always my most precious, my possession and my passion; because of that, you had to die young— far too young!

They aimed at my most sensitive place: at you, who are softer than down—or perhaps more like a smile that fades in a glance.

But this I say to my enemies: What is any mere killing compared to what you have done to me?

You have done me a worse wrong than killing; you took the irretrievable from me—thus I speak to you, my enemies!

You slew my visions and my dearest marvels of youth! You took my companions, the blessed spirits! To their memory, I lay down this wreath and this curse.

This curse on you, my enemies! Have you not shortened my eternity, like a sound fading in the cold night? It barely came to me as a divine flicker, like a passing light!

Thus once spoke my purity in a happy hour: "Let everything be divine to me."

Then you haunted me with dark phantoms; ah, where has that happy hour gone now?

"All my days shall be holy to me," once spoke the wisdom of my youth—yes, the words of joyful wisdom!

But then you, my enemies, stole my nights and sold them to sleepless torture; ah, where has that joyful wisdom gone now?

Once, I looked forward to good omens; then you led an owl-monster across my path—a dark sign. Ah, where did my gentle hopes flee then?

I had once vowed to abandon all hate; then you turned my closest ones into wounds. Ah, where did my noblest vow flee then?

Once I walked blind but blessed paths; then you cast filth on my way, and now I'm repulsed by the path I once walked.

When I achieved my hardest task and celebrated the triumph of my victories, you made those who loved me cry out that it was then I hurt them the most.

It was always your doing: you soured my best honey and disturbed the diligence of my finest bees.

To my charity, you sent the most shameless beggars; around my compassion, you gathered those beyond shame. Thus, you wounded my virtue's faith.

And when I offered my most sacred as a sacrifice, your "piety" placed its bulkier gifts beside it, so my offering suffocated in the smoke of your fat.

Once, I wished to dance as I had never danced before, to dance beyond all heavens. Then, you led my favorite musician astray.

Now he plays a mournful, somber tune; he wails like a sorrowful horn in my ear!

Murderous minstrel, instrument of harm, innocent tool! I was ready for my grandest dance, and you killed my joy with your sound!

Only in dance can I speak of the highest things in parable—and now my grandest parable remains unsaid, locked within my limbs!

Unspoken and unrealized has my highest hope remained! And with it, all the visions and comforts of my youth have perished!

How did I bear it? How did I survive and overcome such wounds? How did my soul rise again from those tombs?

Yes, something invincible, unburied lives within me—something that could break rocks: my Will. Silently it endures, unchanging through the years.

It will follow its path on my feet, my old Will; hard and unbreakable is its nature.

Only my heel remains invulnerable. There you live on, unchanged, most patient one! Always, you have shattered every tomb's restraint.

Within you, my youth's unfulfilled hopes still live; like life and youth, you sit here in hope on the golden ruins of graves.

Yes, you are still my destroyer of graves: Hail to you, my Will! And where there are graves, there are resurrections too.

Thus sang Zarathustra.

Chapter 34
Self-Overcoming

"Will to Truth," you call it, you wisest ones, this drive that moves you and makes you passionate.

I call it the will for all being to be thinkable, for that is your true will. You want to make all existence understandable, for you rightfully doubt it is already so.

Yet, everything shall shape itself to suit you, as your will desires. It shall become smooth, yielding to the spirit, mirroring and reflecting it.

This is your whole desire, you wisest ones—a Will to Power, even when you speak of good and evil or values.

You seek to create a world you can bow down to—such is your ultimate hope and ecstasy.

The ignorant masses are like a river carrying a boat along, and in that boat, there sit solemn, disguised values.

It's your will and values you've placed on the river of becoming. The beliefs of the people about good and evil reveal to me an old Will to Power.

It was you, you wisest ones, who seated such guests in this boat, gave them pompous and proud names—you and your ruling Will!

Now, the river must carry your boat forward, no matter how it foams and resists.

But it's not the river that threatens your good and evil's journey, you wisest ones; it's that Will itself—the inexhaustible, life-creating Will to Power.

To make you understand my gospel of good and evil, I'll share my gospel of life and of all living things.

I followed the living, walked both broad and narrow paths to grasp its nature.

With a hundred-faced mirror, I caught its glance, even when its mouth was shut, so its eyes could speak to me. And they spoke.

Wherever I found life, I heard the language of obedience—all living things are obedient things.

And this, too, I heard: anything that cannot obey itself is commanded. That's the nature of living things.

This third truth I learned—commanding is harder than obeying. Not just because the commander bears the weight of all who obey, a weight that can easily crush him.

Commanding seemed like both an attempt and a risk; and in commanding, the living thing risks itself.

Yes, even when it commands itself, it must bear the cost. It becomes judge, avenger, and victim of its own law.

How does this happen? I asked myself. What leads the living to obey and to command, even obeying in its command?

Listen now, you wisest ones! Test this carefully—have I reached into life's core and its roots?

Wherever I found a living thing, there I found a Will to Power; even in the servant's will, I found the will to be master.

The weaker serves the stronger—this serves his will, for he who would master still weaker beings will not give up that pleasure.

And as the lesser yields to the greater to gain power over the least of all, so do the greatest surrender and stake their lives for power.

The greatest must risk danger and gamble with death.

And where there is sacrifice, service, and loving looks, there is also the desire to be master. By secret paths, the weaker slip into the stronghold and the heart of the mightier—and there they steal power.

Life herself shared this secret with me. "Look," she said, "I am always meant to surpass myself.

You may call it the urge to create, or drive toward a goal, something higher, farther, more varied: but it is always the same secret.

I would rather perish than deny this one truth; and truly, where there is dying and decay, there Life sacrifices itself—for power!

That I must be a struggle, a becoming, a purpose, and an opposition—ah, whoever senses my will understands the winding paths it must follow!

Whatever I create and however deeply I love it, soon I must turn against it and against my love: so wills my will.

And even you, wise one, are just a step and a path for my will. Truly, my Will to Power walks even in your Will to Truth!

Whoever aimed for truth with the phrase, "Will to existence," missed the mark: that will does not exist!

For what is not yet cannot will, and what already exists—how could it still strive just to be?

Wherever there is life, there is will—not a Will to Life, but—so I teach you—a Will to Power!

The living hold many things higher than life itself; yet in this very valuing speaks the Will to Power!"

This is what Life once taught me; and with it, I reveal the mystery of your hearts, you wisest ones.

I say to you: good and evil that would endure forever do not exist! By its very nature, good and evil must continuously transform.

With your values and formulas of good and evil, you wield power, you who value; and that is your secret love, the sparkling, trembling, and overflowing of your souls.

But a greater power rises from your values, a new surpassing: by it, the egg cracks and the shell breaks.

And whoever must create in good and evil—truly, he must first be a destroyer, breaking values apart.

Thus, the greatest evil belongs to the greatest good; that, however, is the good that creates.

Let us speak of this, you wisest ones, even if it seems wrong. Silence is worse; all truths held back become toxic.

And let everything that can be broken by our truths be broken! There are still many houses left to build!

Thus spoke Zarathustra.

Chapter 35
The Sublime Ones

Calm lies the bottom of my sea: who would guess it hides strange monsters!

My depths are unmoved, yet they sparkle with swimming riddles and laughter.

Today I saw a lofty one, a solemn figure, a penitent of the spirit. Oh, how my soul laughed at his awkwardness!

He stood with a puffed-up chest, like someone drawing in a deep breath, and in silence.

He was draped in ugly truths, spoils from his hunt, and wore tattered garments; thorns clung to him—but I saw no rose.

He had not yet learned laughter and beauty. Gloomy, this hunter returned from the forest of knowledge.

From battles with wild beasts, he came back home, but an untamed beast still stared out from his seriousness—a beast he had not yet conquered!

Like a tiger, he stood, ready to leap; but I do not care for such strained souls—my taste is not for those who are too wrapped up in themselves.

And you say, friends, there is to be no dispute about taste? Yet all life is a debate over taste!

Taste: it is weight, and scales, and the weigher; and woe to every living being that would live without dispute about weight, scales, and the weigher!

When this lofty one tires of his high-mindedness, then will his beauty emerge—and only then will I find him savory.

Only when he turns away from himself will he leap beyond his own shadow—and, truly, into his sun.

He has spent far too long in the shade; the cheeks of the penitent of the spirit have grown pale; he nearly starved on his own expectations.

There is still contempt in his eyes, and disgust lingers at his lips. Though he rests now, he has not yet truly rested in the sunshine.

He should be like the ox, whose joy has the scent of the earth, not contempt for it.

I wish to see him like a white ox, snorting and lowing, guiding the plowshare—and his lowing should celebrate all things earthly!

His face is still shadowed; his own hand's shadow dances upon it. The purpose in his eyes is still veiled.

His deeds still cast shadows over him: his actions obscure the doer. He has not yet risen above what he has done.

I admire the strength of his shoulders, like those of an ox, but now I wish to see the eye of an angel too.

He must unlearn his hero's will; let him become not just lofty, but exalted—raised by the ether itself, one who wills nothing.

He has conquered monsters, he has solved riddles. But he should also redeem those monsters and riddles, transforming them into celestial children.

His wisdom has yet to learn to smile, to be free of jealousy; his rushing passion has yet to find calmness in beauty.

Let his longing end not in excess, but in beauty! Grace is the mark of the generous.

With his arm resting across his head: that is how the hero should find repose; that is how he should even conquer his own rest.

Yet for the hero, beauty is the hardest thing of all to attain. Beauty eludes all who seek it with intense will.

A slight shift, a little more or less: here, that small difference means everything.

To stand loose and relaxed, without a driven will—this is the hardest thing for you sublime ones.

When power descends gracefully into what is visible, I call that grace beauty.

From none do I desire beauty more than from you, mighty one: let goodness be your final triumph.

I attribute all evil to you, so I expect from you the good.

I have laughed at the weaklings who think they are virtuous just because they have feeble hands!

Your virtue should aim to be like the pillar: the higher it rises, the more beautiful and graceful it becomes—yet inwardly stronger and more sustaining.

Yes, one day, sublime one, you shall be beautiful and hold up a mirror to your own beauty.

Then your soul will throb with divine desires, and even your vanity will become worship!

For this is the soul's secret: only after the hero leaves it does the super-hero approach in dreams.

Thus spoke Zarathustra.

Chapter 36

The Land of Culture

I flew too far into the future, and a deep dread overtook me.

When I looked around, I found that time was my only companion.

So I flew back, faster and faster, toward home. Thus I arrived here, among you present-day people, in the land of culture.

I came with eyes open to see you, with a true longing in my heart.

But what happened? Even though I was frightened, I had to laugh! Never had my eyes seen such a wild array of colors!

I laughed and laughed, though my feet and heart still trembled. "This must be the home of all the paint pots," I said.

With faces and limbs covered in fifty patches, that's how I found you, present-day people!

And with fifty mirrors surrounding you, reflecting and repeating every shade and hue of your appearance!

Indeed, no better masks could you wear than your own faces! Who could possibly recognize you?

Written all over with symbols from the past, and then layered with fresh symbols— you've disguised yourselves so well from anyone trying to decipher you!

And who still believes you have reins to guide you? You look molded from colors and scraps glued together.

The shades of all eras and peoples peer through your layers; gestures and expressions speak with the voices of countless beliefs and customs.

If someone tried to strip off your veils, masks, and layers, there'd be hardly enough left to frighten the crows.

I myself am like that frightened crow who once saw you without your coverings and paint; I flew off when your bare bones glared at me.

I'd rather toil as a laborer in the underworld, among shadows of the past! Those in the netherworld are plumper and fuller than you!

This, yes, this, is the bitterness that churns within me: I can't bear you, clothed or naked, present-day people!

All that's foreign in the future, all that makes lost birds shiver, feels more familiar and welcoming than your so-called "reality."

For you say: "We are entirely real, without belief or superstition." You pride yourselves—alas, with nothing left to be proud of!

How could you possibly believe, you people of so many colors— you who are merely reflections of everything ever believed before!

You are walking contradictions of belief itself, disruptions of all thinking. Untrustworthy—that's what I call you, you so-called real ones!

All ages argue within your minds; and all the dreams and nonsense of past ages feel truer than your so-called awakeness!

You're barren, and that's why you lack belief. Those who needed to create have always had their dreams, their visions of stars, and believed deeply in believing.

You're like half-open doors where grave-diggers linger. And this is your reality: "Everything is worth letting perish."

Oh, how you look before me, you fruitless ones; how gaunt your frames! And many of you have certainly felt this emptiness.

Many have thought, "Did some god sneak up while I slept and steal enough from me to create a girl from it?"

"Amazing, how poor I am in spirit!" — that's the feeling many of you, present-day people, have confessed.

You truly make me laugh, you people of today—especially when you gaze in wonder at yourselves!

What a curse it would be if I couldn't laugh at your amazement, and had to swallow all that bitterness on your platters!

But as it is, I'll take you lightly, since I have heavier things to carry; and what harm if beetles and bugs land on my load?

It won't weigh me down! My true weariness won't come from you, people of today.

Ah, where shall I look now with my longing? From all mountains, I search for fatherlands and motherlands.

But nowhere have I found a home. I am a stranger in every city, ready to leave every gate.

Foreign and mocking are these people of today, whom my heart once led me to; I am estranged from all homelands, all family lands.

So, I love only the land of my children, that undiscovered country in the farthest sea. That's what I set my sails for, to seek and to seek.

To my children, I'll make amends for being my father's child; and to all the future—for this present-day!

Thus spoke Zarathustra.

Chapter 37

Immaculate Perception

Last night, when the moon rose, I thought it was about to give birth to a sun. It lay so broad and full on the horizon.

But it lied about being pregnant; sooner would I believe in the man in the moon than in a woman there.

Not much of a man is he, either—that timid wanderer of the night. He sneaks over rooftops with a guilty conscience.

He's greedy and envious, that monk in the moon, jealous of the earth and the joys of lovers.

No, I don't like him—that prowling tomcat on the roofs! I hate those who creep around half-closed windows!

He moves piously and silently across the starry carpet, but I distrust those who tread lightly, without even a jingle of spurs.

Every honest step has a sound, but the cat creeps over the ground. Look, the moon slinks like a cat, dishonestly.

This parable I speak for you, you sentimental pretenders, you so-called "pure observers"! I call you covetous ones!

You love the earth and the earthly—I've figured you out! But there's shame and guilt in your love; you're like the moon!

Your spirit was persuaded to despise the earthly, but not your body; it remains the strongest part of you!

And now your spirit is ashamed of serving your body and takes detours and lies to hide its own shame.

"That would be the highest thing for me," says your lying spirit to itself, "to gaze at life without desire, unlike a dog with its tongue hanging out.

"To be content just watching: with a dead will, free from the grip of selfishness—cold and ashy-gray, but with intoxicated moon-eyes!

"That would be my greatest joy," the deceived one deceives himself, "to love the earth as the moon does, and feel its beauty only with my eyes.

"And this I call pure perception: to want nothing more from things, but to lie before them as a mirror with a hundred faces."

Oh, you sentimental pretenders, you covetous ones! You lack innocence in your desire, and so you condemn desire itself!

You do not love the earth as creators, or as procreators, or as celebrators!

Where is innocence? It is where there's a will to create life. And for me, the purest will is in one who seeks to create beyond himself.

Where is beauty? Where I must will with all my strength; where I am ready to love and be lost, so an image does not remain just an image.

To love and to perish—these have always gone together. To will to love is to be ready for death. This I say to you, cowards!

But now your weakened gazing pretends to be "contemplation!" And what can be looked at with timid eyes, you call "beautiful!" Oh, you who dishonor noble words!

But it will be your curse, you so-called pure ones, you false discerners, that you will never give birth, even though you lie wide and full on the horizon!

You fill your mouths with noble words, wanting us to believe your hearts overflow. But who do you think you're fooling?

My words may be poor, clumsy, and stumbling. Happily, I'll gather up the crumbs that fall from your feasts.

Still, I can say the truth to pretenders. Yes, my leftover fish bones, shells, and thorny leaves will prick at the noses of pretenders!

Bad air surrounds you and your feasts—your hidden desires, lies, and secrets are thick in it!

Try believing in yourselves, in yourselves and your own insides! The one who does not believe in himself always lies.

You've hung a god's mask in front of yourselves, you "pure ones": a vile, coiling serpent is stuffed inside your holy disguise.

You truly deceive, you so-called contemplatives! Even Zarathustra once fell for your godlike appearances; he didn't suspect the snake hiding inside.

I once thought I saw a divine spirit in your games, you "pure discerners"! I never imagined there could be better arts than your arts!

Serpent filth and foul smells were hidden from me by distance, concealing the craftiness of the creeping lizard.

But I came close to you, and then came the daylight for me—and now it comes for you too. The moon's romance is over!

Look at it! Caught off guard and pale, standing there before the red dawn!

For she is coming now, glowing—her love for the earth is coming! Innocence and creative desire, that is the love of the sun!

See how she comes over the sea, eager! Can you feel the warmth and thirst of her love?

She wants to drink from the sea, to pull its depths up to her heights; now the sea itself rises with a thousand eager waves.

It wants to be kissed and pulled up by the sun's thirst; to become vapor, to rise, to light a path, to be light itself!

Like the sun, I love life and all deep seas.

And this is what knowledge means to me: all that is deep shall rise—to my height!

Chapter 38
Scholars

WHEN I lay asleep, a sheep came and nibbled at the ivy wreath on my head. It ate, and seemed to say, "Zarathustra is no longer a scholar."

It said this and wandered off, clumsy and proud. A child told me about it.

I like lying here where children play, next to the old wall, among thistles and red poppies.

To children, and to the thistles and poppies, I am still a scholar—innocent they are, even in their mischief.

But to the sheep, I am no longer a scholar. So fate wills it—blessings upon that!

For this is the truth: I have left the house of scholars, and I closed the door behind me.

Too long did my soul sit, hungry, at their table; I don't have their knack for investigating, like cracking open nuts.

I love freedom and fresh air; I would rather sleep on ox skins than on their honors and dignities.

I'm too fiery, too scorched by my own thoughts, which sometimes take my breath away. Then, I need to go outside, away from dusty rooms.

But they sit coolly in the shade. They prefer to be mere onlookers in everything, avoiding the sunny steps.

They are like people standing in the street, gawking at passersby; they wait and stare at thoughts others have already thought.

If someone shakes them up, they raise a cloud of dust like sacks of flour—without meaning to. But who would think their dust comes from grain and the golden delight of summer fields?

When they pose as wise, their little sayings and truths chill me; their wisdom often smells like it came from a swamp, and truly, I've even heard the frog's croak in it!

They are clever, with skillful fingers. What is my simplicity next to their complexity! They know all about threading, knitting, and weaving; that's how they make the stockings of the spirit!

Good clockworks they are; just be sure to wind them up right! Then they tell the time accurately and make a modest ticking sound.

They work like millstones and pestles; throw them some grain— they know how to grind it fine, turning it to white dust.

They keep a close watch on each other, never trusting too much. Clever in small tricks, they wait for those whose knowledge limps along—waiting like spiders.

I've seen them always handle their poison with care, putting on glass gloves.

They also know how to play with loaded dice, sweating from their eagerness to win at their own games.

We are strangers to each other, and I find their virtues even more distasteful than their lies and cheating.

When I lived among them, I lived above them, which made them resent me.

They don't want anyone walking above their heads, so they piled wood, earth, and rubbish between me and them to muffle my steps.

This way, the most learned hardly noticed me.

They stacked all of humankind's faults and failings between us—it's what they call a "false ceiling" in their houses.

But I still walk with my thoughts above their heads; and even if I step on my own errors, I'm still above them.

For men are not equal: so says justice. And what I will, they may not will!

Thus spoke Zarathustra.

Chapter 39
Poets

"Since I've come to understand the body better," Zarathustra said to one of his disciples, "the spirit has been merely a symbol to me; even the so-called 'imperishable' is just a parable."

"I've heard you say that before," replied the disciple, "and you added, 'But poets lie too much.' Why did you say that poets lie too much?"

"Why?" Zarathustra said, "You ask why? I'm not the kind who can be questioned about their Why.

Do you think my experiences are just from yesterday? Long ago, I lived through the reasons behind my opinions.

Would I have to be a barrel of memories to always carry my reasons with me?

Even keeping hold of my opinions is already too much; many of them fly away.

And sometimes I find a lost creature in my dovecote, one that doesn't belong to me and shivers when I touch it.

But what did Zarathustra once say to you? That poets lie too much?—Well, Zarathustra is also a poet.

Do you think he spoke the truth there? Why do you believe that?"

The disciple answered, "I believe in Zarathustra." But Zarathustra shook his head and smiled.

"Belief doesn't sanctify me," he said, "least of all belief in myself.

But suppose someone did say in all seriousness that poets lie too much—he would be right. We do lie too much.

We also know too little, and we are poor learners, which makes us have to lie.

And which one of us poets hasn't diluted our wine? Many poisonous mixtures have come from our cellars, many indescribable things have happened there.

And because we know so little, we're especially fond of the simple-minded, particularly when they're young women!

We even crave the tales that old women tell each other in the evenings. This we call the 'eternal feminine' within us.

And we pretend there's a secret path to knowledge, hidden from those who actually learn anything.

So we believe in the people and their so-called 'wisdom.'

This is what all poets believe: that anyone who lies in the grass or on lonely slopes and listens carefully will learn something about the mysteries between heaven and earth.

And if tender feelings come to them, poets always think that nature herself has fallen in love with them:

that she leans close to whisper secrets in their ear and flatter them with sweet words. They pride themselves on this above all others!

Ah, there are so many things between heaven and earth that only poets have dreamed of!

And especially above the heavens: for all gods are poetic inventions, poetic illusions!

We're always pulled upward—to the clouds. That's where we place our bright puppets and call them gods and superhumans.

Aren't these gods and superhumans light enough to sit in those airy seats?

Ah, how tired I am of everything that's passed off as reality but falls short! Ah, how weary I am of poets!

When Zarathustra said this, his disciple felt offended but stayed silent. Zarathustra was silent too, gazing inward as though looking into a distant future. At last, he sighed and spoke:

"I belong to today and to what has come before, yet there's something in me that belongs to tomorrow, and the days after, and what lies beyond.

I'm tired of poets, both old and new. They all seem shallow and superficial to me, like shallow seas.

They haven't thought deeply enough; that's why their feelings don't reach the depths.

Some thrill of pleasure, some sense of boredom: that's been the height of their contemplation.

Their harps play only ghostly tunes, as if they only half-feel the passion of true music.

They aren't pure enough for me: they muddy their water just to make it seem deep.

And they like to call themselves reconcilers, but to me, they're just mixers and go-betweens, half-and-half, impure!

Ah, I cast my net into their sea, hoping to catch good fish, but I always ended up with the head of some ancient god.

It was like the sea gave a stone to a hungry man. Maybe they even come from the sea themselves.

Yes, you can find pearls in them, which only makes them more like hard shells. And instead of a soul, I often found just salty slime.

They've also learned vanity from the sea. Isn't the sea the peacock of peacocks?

Even in front of the ugliest buffalo, it spreads out its tail and never tires of flaunting its silver and silk.

The buffalo looks on with scorn, close to the earth with its soul, even closer to the forest, and closest of all to the swamp.

What are beauty and sea and peacock-splendor to it! This parable I give to the poets.

Their spirit is the peacock of peacocks, and a sea of vanity!

The poet's spirit craves spectators—even if they're buffaloes!

But I have grown weary of this spirit, and I foresee the time when it will grow weary of itself.

Yes, I've seen poets change, turning their gaze toward themselves.

I've seen the penitents of the spirit emerge—they came from the poets."

Thus spoke Zarathustra.

Chapter 40
Great Events

There is an island in the sea—not far from Zarathustra's Blessed Isles—where a volcano constantly smokes. The people there, especially the old women, say the island stands like a rock before the gate to the underworld, and through the volcano itself runs a narrow path leading down to that gate.

Around the time Zarathustra stayed on the Blessed Isles, a ship anchored by the island with the smoking mountain, and the crew went ashore to hunt rabbits. Around noon, when the captain and his men gathered again, they suddenly saw someone approaching through the air, and a voice clearly said, "It's time! It's the highest time!" But as the figure flew past, like a shadow heading toward the volcano, they recognized it with great surprise as Zarathustra. They had all seen him before, except for the captain, and they loved him as people do— where both love and awe are mixed equally.

"Look!" said the old helmsman. "There goes Zarathustra to hell!"

Around the same time the sailors landed on the fire-isle, a rumor spread that Zarathustra had disappeared. When his friends were asked about it, they said he'd boarded a ship by night without telling anyone where he was going.

This caused some uneasiness. However, after three days, the crew's story added to this unease, and everyone began saying that the devil had taken Zarathustra. His disciples laughed at this, and one of them even said, "I'd sooner believe Zarathustra has taken the devil." But in their hearts, they were filled with worry and longing, so they were very joyful when, on the fifth day, Zarathustra appeared among them again.

And here is the story of Zarathustra's encounter with the fire-dog:

The earth, he said, has a skin, and this skin has diseases. One of these diseases, for example, is called "man."

And another of these diseases is called "the fire-dog." People have greatly deceived themselves about him and have allowed themselves to be deceived.

To uncover this mystery, I crossed the sea, and I've seen the truth laid bare, truly! Naked, up to my neck.

Now I know the truth about the fire-dog, and about all the spouting and rebellious devils that frighten people, not just the old women.

"Come up, fire-dog, out of your depths!" I shouted. "And confess how deep that depth really is! Where does what you snort up come from?

You drink a lot from the sea; your bitter tone gives that away! For a creature of the depths, you get your food much too close to the surface!

At most, I think of you as the earth's ventriloquist, and whenever I've heard rebellious, fiery devils speak, they've all been like you: bitter, deceitful, and shallow.

You know how to roar and darken things with ash! You are the best boasters, and you've learned well the art of making scum boil.

Wherever you are, there must always be scum, and plenty of spongy, hollow things nearby: all of it wants to be free.

'Freedom,' you all shout with great excitement. But I've unlearned believing in 'great events' just because there's a lot of noise and smoke around them.

And believe me, my friend Hullabaloo! The greatest events aren't loud; they happen in our quietest hours.

The world doesn't revolve around those who create new noise, but around those who create new values; it turns in silence.

And admit it! Little ever happens when your noise and smoke fade away. What if a city turned into a ruin, or a statue lay fallen in the mud?

And this I say also to those who topple statues: It's pure foolishness to throw salt into the sea and statues into the mud.

In the mud of your contempt lay the statue, but its nature is such that, out of scorn, it will rise again with new life and beauty!

With divine features, it will now stand again, alluring through its suffering; and truly, it will one day thank you for toppling it, you destroyers!

This advice I give to kings and churches, and to all who are weakened by age or virtue—let yourselves be toppled! So that you may come to life again, and that virtue may return to you!"

Thus I spoke before the fire-dog; then he interrupted me sulkily and asked, "Church? What is that?"

"Church?" I answered, "That's a kind of state, and indeed the most deceitful one. But stay calm, you deceitful dog! Surely, you know your own kind best!

The state, like you, is a deceitful dog; like you, it loves to speak with smoke and growls—to make people believe, like you, that it speaks from the heart of things.

For it strives in every way to be the most important thing on earth—the state; and people believe it to be."

When I said this, the fire-dog seemed crazed with jealousy. "What!" he cried, "the most important thing on earth? And people believe it?" So much vapor and awful noise came out of his throat that I thought he might choke on his fury and jealousy.

At last, he calmed down, and his heavy breathing slowed. As soon as he was quiet, I said with a laugh:

"You're angry, fire-dog, so I must be right about you!

And to hold my point, listen to the story of another fire-dog who truly speaks from the heart of the earth.

His breath exhales gold, and golden rain flows—this is what his heart desires. Ashes and smoke and scalding dregs mean nothing to him!

Laughter rises from him like a shimmering cloud; he despises your choking, your spewing, and your gut-wrenching!

The gold and the laughter—these he draws from the heart of the earth. Just so you know—the heart of the earth is gold."

When the fire-dog heard this, he couldn't bear to listen any longer. He slinked off, tail between his legs, muttered a feeble "bow-wow!" and crept back into his cave.

So told Zarathustra. But his disciples hardly listened to him, so eager were they to tell him about the sailors, the rabbits, and the flying man.

"What should I make of it?" said Zarathustra. "Am I really a ghost?

But maybe it was only my shadow. You must have heard something of the Wanderer and his Shadow?

One thing is certain: I must keep a tighter grip on it; otherwise, it may ruin my reputation."

Once more, Zarathustra shook his head in wonder. "What should I make of it?" he said again.

"Why did the ghost cry, 'It's time! It's the highest time!'

For what is it then—the highest time?"

Thus spoke Zarathustra.

Chapter 41
The Soothsayer

"AND I saw a great sadness come over humankind. The best among us grew tired of their efforts.

A new belief arose, and a doctrine came with it: 'All is empty, all is the same, all has been before!'

From all hills echoed the words: 'All is empty, all is the same, all has been before!'

Yes, we have harvested, but why have all our fruits turned rotten and brown? What was it that fell last night from the wicked moon?

Our efforts were in vain; our wine has become poisoned, and the evil eye has scorched our fields and hearts yellow.

We have all dried up; if fire falls on us, we crumble into dust like ashes. Even the fire itself has grown weary of us.

All our springs have dried up, even the sea has pulled back. The ground tries to open up, but the depth won't swallow us!

'Alas! Is there still a sea somewhere deep enough to drown in?' That's the cry we hear across the shallow swamps.

Even dying has become too tiresome for us; now we just stay awake and live on—in tombs."

Thus Zarathustra heard a soothsayer speak; the foreboding weighed on his heart and changed him. He went about sorrowfully and wearily, and he became like those the soothsayer had spoken of.

He said to his disciples, "A little while longer, and the long twilight will come. Alas, how will I keep my light through it!

So that it doesn't fade in this sadness! It must be a light for far-off worlds and the darkest nights!"

So Zarathustra walked around with a heavy heart, and for three days, he took no food or drink. He found no rest and lost his speech. At last, he fell into a deep sleep. His disciples sat around him, keeping vigil through the long nights, waiting anxiously to see if he would awaken, speak again, and recover from his sorrow.

And this is what Zarathustra said when he awoke; his voice, however, seemed distant to his disciples:

"Listen, I beg you, to the dream I dreamed, my friends, and help me uncover its meaning!

It is still a riddle to me, this dream; its meaning is hidden and locked up, not yet soaring free on open wings.

I dreamed I had renounced all life. I became a night watchman and guardian of graves, high up in the lonely mountain fortress of Death.

There, I guarded the coffins; the musty vaults were filled with those trophies of victory. From glass coffins, defeated life stared back at me."

The smell of dusty eternities filled the air, thick and stifling around my soul. Who could find a breath of fresh air in such a place?

Midnight brightness was ever present around me, with loneliness crouched beside it, and as a third companion, the stillness of death's final breath—my most haunting friend.

I carried keys, the rustiest of all keys, and I knew how to open the creakiest of gates with them.

Like an angry, bitter croak, the sound echoed down the long halls when the gates creaked open; that stubborn, unwilling bird cried out as if disturbed against its will.

But even more terrifying, more heart-gripping, was the silence that fell again, settling into an ominous quiet as I sat alone in that oppressive stillness.

Time slipped by like this, if time was even passing; who knows! But finally, something happened that woke me.

Three times a thunderous knocking shook the gates, three times the vaults resounded and echoed with a howl. Then I went to the gate.

"Alpa!" I cried. "Who carries ashes to the mountain? Alpa! Alpa! Who brings the ashes up the mountain?"

I pressed the key into the lock, pulled on the gate, and tried with all my might, but it barely budged.

Then, with a roaring gust, a fierce wind tore the gates apart, whistling and howling, and flung a black coffin toward me.

Amid the roaring, whistling, and piercing wind, the coffin burst open, releasing a thousand bursts of laughter.

A thousand mocking images of children, angels, owls, fools, and butterfly-like figures laughed and jeered at me.

It terrified me beyond measure; I was paralyzed, and I screamed in horror as I'd never screamed before.

But my own screaming woke me—and I came back to myself.

Thus, Zarathustra told his dream and then fell silent, for he didn't yet know what it meant. But the disciple he loved most quickly rose, took Zarathustra's hand, and said:

"Your own life shows us the meaning of this dream, O Zarathustra!

Are you not like that whistling wind that bursts open the gates of the fortress of Death?

Are you not like that coffin, full of colorful mischief and parodies of life?

Zarathustra, you enter all tombs with the laughter of a thousand children, laughing at night-watchmen, grave-keepers, and anyone else rattling sinister keys.

With your laughter, you'll terrify and humble them; fainting and recovering, you'll show your power over them.

And when the long twilight comes and the weariness of life sets in, you will not disappear from our skies, you defender of life!

You've shown us new stars, new glories of the night—truly, you've spread laughter over us like a canopy of many colors."

Now, children's laughter will forever flow from coffins; now, a strong wind will always blow victoriously upon all mortal weariness. You yourself are the promise and prophet of this!

In your dream, you saw your enemies—that was your hardest dream.

But just as you awoke from them and returned to yourself, so shall they awaken from themselves—and come to you!

So spoke the disciple, and then all the others crowded around Zarathustra, holding his hands and urging him to leave his sadness behind, to rise from his bed and rejoin them. Zarathustra, however, sat upright on his couch, looking at them with a distant gaze. He seemed like a man returning from a long journey to a foreign land, observing his disciples' faces as if he were seeing them for the first time, yet without recognizing them. But when they lifted him up and helped him to his feet, suddenly his eyes changed; he understood everything that had happened, stroked his beard, and spoke with a strong voice:

"Well! This has come at just the right time. But, my disciples, make sure we have a fine meal, and right away! This is how I intend to shake off the remnants of bad dreams!

And the soothsayer shall eat and drink beside me. Indeed, I'll even show him a sea where he can drown himself!"

Thus spoke Zarathustra. Then he looked long and steadily at the disciple who had interpreted his dream and shook his head.

Chapter 42
Redemption

When Zarathustra crossed the great bridge one day, a crowd of beggars and cripples gathered around him. A hunchback among them spoke to him, saying:

"Look, Zarathustra! Even the people are learning from you and starting to believe in your teachings. But if you want them to believe in you completely, there's still something missing—you need to convince us cripples first! Here you have a fine selection, and a real opportunity with more than one handle! You could make the blind see, the lame walk, and even take a bit off those who have too much behind them; that, I think, would be the right way to make us cripples believe in Zarathustra!"

But Zarathustra replied to him who had spoken:

"When you take a hunch from a hunchback, you also take away his spirit—that's what people say. And when you give eyes to a blind man, he suddenly sees all the ugliness in the world and curses the one who healed him. And if you make a lame man run, he's worse off than ever, for as soon as he can run, his vices will run away with him. That's what people teach about cripples. So, why shouldn't Zarathustra learn from the people, just as they learn from him?

It's a small matter to me since I've been among people to see one missing an eye, another an ear, and a third missing a leg, or to see those who have lost their tongue, or nose, or head. I've seen worse things, things so hideous I would neither like to speak of them all nor stay silent about some of them. I'm speaking of men who are missing everything except that they have too much of one thing—men who are nothing but a huge eye, or a huge mouth, or a huge belly, or something else exaggerated. I call such men reversed cripples.

When I first came out of my solitude and crossed this bridge, I couldn't trust my eyes. I looked again and again, and finally said, 'That's an ear! An ear as big as a person!' I looked closer, and there, underneath the ear, was something small, poor, and pitifully thin. And indeed, that huge ear was perched on a tiny stalk—the stalk was a man! If someone looked closely, they could even see a small, envious face and notice that a swollen little soul hung from that stalk. The people told me that the big ear wasn't just a man, but a great man, a genius. But I've never believed the people when they speak of great men, and I still believe it was a reversed cripple, someone with too little of everything and too much of one thing."

After Zarathustra spoke to the hunchback and those for whom the hunchback spoke, he turned to his disciples, deeply troubled, and said:

"My friends, I walk among people as if among the fragments and limbs of human beings! What troubles my eyes most is to see humanity shattered and scattered, like a battlefield or a butcher's yard.

And when I look back from the present to the past, I see the same thing: fragments, limbs, fearful accidents—but no whole men!

The present and the past on this earth—ah, my friends—that is my greatest sorrow. I would not know how to go on living if I could not see what is yet to come."

"A seer, a visionary, a creator, a glimpse of the future itself, and a bridge to that future—and yet, also, like a cripple on this bridge: all this is Zarathustra.

And you have often asked yourselves, 'Who is Zarathustra to us? What name should we give him?' And, like me, you have answered yourselves with more questions.

Is he a promise-giver? Or a fulfiller? A conqueror? Or an inheritor? A harvest? Or a plowshare? A healer? Or the one who's healed?

Is he a poet? Or an authentic soul? A liberator? Or an oppressor? A good person? Or a bad one?

I walk among people as pieces of the future—that future which I envision.

It is my deepest desire and purpose to bring together and unify what is fragmented, mysterious, and shaped by chance.

How could I bear to be human if humanity were not also capable of being the creator, the solver of riddles, and the redeemer of what seems like mere chance!

To redeem the past and transform every 'It was' into 'This is how I would have it be!'—that alone is what I call redemption.

The Will—this is the name of the liberator and bringer of joy: that is what I have taught you, my friends! But now understand this as well: the Will itself is still in chains.

The act of Willing brings freedom, but what can we call that which still keeps the liberator bound?

'It was': this is the name of the Will's grinding frustration, its deepest sorrow. Helpless before what has already happened, the Will is a bitter observer of all that has passed.

The Will cannot will itself backward in time; it cannot break time's grip and time's desire—that is the Will's most isolated struggle.

Willing brings freedom, so what does Willing itself create to release itself from this struggle and mock its own prison?

Ah, every prisoner becomes a fool! Foolishly, the trapped Will also betrays itself.

That time does not move backward—that is what it resents most. 'That which was': this is the rock it cannot roll.

And so, it rolls rocks out of resentment and bitterness, taking revenge on whatever, unlike itself, does not feel rage and bitterness.

This is how the Will, the liberator, turned into a tormentor; it takes revenge on everything that can suffer because it cannot go backward.

This alone is what revenge truly is: the Will's anger against time, and its hatred of 'It was.'

A great foolishness lives in our Will, and this foolishness became a curse upon all of humanity when it developed a spirit!

The spirit of revenge—this has been humanity's most profound contemplation; and wherever there was suffering, people said there must be punishment.

'Punishment'—this is what revenge calls itself. With a deceitful word, it pretends to have a clear conscience.

And because the one who wills also suffers, because he cannot will backward—Willing itself, and all life, came to be seen as a form of punishment!

Then cloud after cloud rolled over the spirit, until, in the end, madness preached: 'Everything perishes; therefore, everything deserves to perish!'

'And this is justice itself, the law of time—that it must devour its children': thus preached madness.

'All things are ordered according to justice and punishment. Oh, where is freedom from the endless changes and from the existence of punishment?' Thus preached madness.

'Is there any deliverance if there is eternal justice? Alas, the stone of "It was" cannot be rolled back: all punishments must also be eternal!' Thus preached madness.

'No deed can ever be erased: how could it be undone by punishment? This is what is eternal in the existence of punishment, that existence must also eternally repeat itself in action and guilt!'"

"Unless the Will eventually frees itself, and Willing becomes non-Willing—" but you know, my brothers, this fable of madness!

Away from those tales did I lead you when I taught you: "The Will is a creator."

All "It was" is a fragment, a mystery, a frightening chance—until the creating Will says to it: "But this is how I want it to be."

Until the creating Will says: "But this is how I will it! This is how I shall will it!"

But has it ever spoken thus? And when will this happen? Has the Will freed itself from its own folly?

Has the Will become its own deliverer and bringer of joy? Has it forgotten the spirit of revenge and all its gnashing of teeth?

And who has taught it to make peace with time and to aim for something higher than reconciliation?

Something greater than reconciliation must the Will will if it is truly the Will to Power—but how does this happen? Who has taught it to will backward, too?

—At that point, Zarathustra suddenly stopped, looking as if he were startled. With terror in his eyes, he stared at his disciples, his gaze piercing through their thoughts and hidden ideas. After a moment, though, he laughed, calming himself, and said:

"It's hard to live among people because keeping silent is so hard—especially for a chatterbox."

Thus spoke Zarathustra. The hunchback had been listening to the conversation, hiding his face, but when he heard Zarathustra laugh, he looked up curiously and asked slowly:

"But why does Zarathustra speak differently to us than to his disciples?"

Zarathustra replied, "Why is that surprising? With hunchbacks, one may well speak in a hunchbacked way!"

"Very well," said the hunchback, "and with students, one may well share tales out of school.

But why does Zarathustra speak differently to his students than to himself?"

Chapter 43
Manly Prudence

Not the height—it's the downward slope that's terrifying!

The slope, where the gaze falls downward, and the hand reaches upward. It's there that the heart grows dizzy from its double desire.

Ah, friends, do you sense my heart's double longing?

This, this is my descent and my danger: my gaze is fixed on the peak, while my hand wants to grasp and hold onto the depths!

My will clings to humanity; with chains, I tie myself to humanity, because I am drawn upwards to the Superman—that's where my other will wants to go.

So I live blindly among men, as if I don't know them: so my hand won't lose faith in stability.

I don't know you humans: this darkness and comfort often surround me.

I sit at the gate, waiting for any trickster, and I ask, "Who wishes to deceive me?"

This is my first wisdom of manhood: I allow myself to be deceived so I don't have to guard myself against deceivers.

Ah, if I guarded myself against people, how could people be the anchor to my ball? Too easily, I'd be pulled up and away!

This fate governs my destiny: I must be without foresight.

And anyone who doesn't want to waste away among people must learn to drink from all cups; and anyone who wants to stay clean among people must know how to wash himself even with dirty water.

So I often say to myself for comfort, "Courage! Cheer up, old heart! Some misfortune has failed to befall you: count that as your good fortune!"

This, though, is my other manly wisdom: I'm more patient with the vain than with the proud.

Isn't hurt vanity the mother of all tragedies? But where pride is wounded, something better than pride grows.

For life to be pleasing, the play must be well-performed; for that, it needs good actors.

I have found good actors among the vain: they act and want others to enjoy watching them—all their spirit lies in this desire.

They present themselves; they invent themselves. When I'm near them, I enjoy life—it lifts me from gloom.

That's why I'm patient with the vain; they are the doctors of my melancholy and keep me tied to people as though to a play.

And who understands the full depth of a vain man's modesty? I am kind to him and sympathetic because of his modesty.

He seeks from you his belief in himself; he feeds on your glances and devours praise from your hands.

He even believes your lies when you flatter him, for deep down his heart sighs, "What am I?"

And if true virtue is the virtue that doesn't know itself, then—well, the vain man is unaware of his modesty!

This is, however, my third manly wisdom: I'm not discouraged by the wicked, despite your fear of them.

I'm glad to see the marvels that the warm sun brings: tigers, palms, and rattlesnakes.

Among people, too, there's a fascinating offspring of the warm sun, and much that is marvelous in the wicked.

Honestly, just as your wisest ones didn't seem all that wise to me, I also found human wickedness to be less impressive than its reputation.

Often, I would shake my head and wonder, "Why are you still rattling, you rattlesnakes?"

There is still a future even for evil! And the warmest places on Earth are yet to be discovered by man.

How many things are now labeled the worst kind of evil, but are only twelve feet wide and last just three months! One day, however, bigger dragons will come into the world.

For the Superman to have a worthy opponent, a super-dragon fit for him, there still needs to be much warm sun over untouched rainforests!

Out of your wildcats must tigers emerge, and out of your poison-toads, crocodiles must grow: the best hunter should have a good hunt!

And truly, you who are good and just! There's much to laugh about in you, especially your fear of what has always been called "the devil."

Your souls are so far from anything great that you'd find the Superman frightening in his goodness!

And you wise ones, you would flee from the sunlight of the wisdom in which the Superman joyfully bathes his naked self!

You highest people I've encountered! This is what I doubt about you, and what makes me secretly laugh: I suspect you would call my Superman a devil!

Ah, I grew tired of those "highest" and "best" ones: from their "heights" I longed to rise even higher, to escape and go toward the Superman!

A dread seized me when I saw those best ones stripped bare; and then wings grew for me to fly away into distant futures.

Into even farther-off futures, into warmer, more southern lands than any artist has ever dreamed of—where gods feel embarrassed to wear any clothes!

But I want to see you in disguise, you neighbors and fellow men, dressed well, vain, and respectable as "the good and just."

And disguised, I will sit among you, too—so that I can misjudge you and myself: for that is my last manly wisdom.

Thus spoke Zarathustra.

Chapter 44
The Stillest Hour

What's happening to me, my friends? You see me troubled, pushed out, obeying against my will, ready to leave—oh, to leave you!

Yes, Zarathustra must go back to his solitude once more; but this time, the bear returns to his cave unwillingly, with no joy.

What's happening to me? Who commands this? Ah, it's my relentless mistress; she demanded it. Have I ever told you her name?

Yesterday, towards evening, my "still hour" spoke to me—that's the name of my frightening mistress.

And this is what happened—I must tell you everything so that your hearts won't harden against me, the one suddenly departing.

Do you know the terror of the one falling asleep?

He feels terror down to his toes because the ground seems to give way beneath him, and the dream begins.

I tell you this as a parable. Yesterday, during the still hour, the ground slipped from beneath me; the dream began.

The hour hand moved forward, the clock of my life took a breath—I'd never heard such silence around me, so silent it scared my heart.

Then a voice spoke to me without words: "You know it, Zarathustra?"

And I cried out in terror at this whisper, the blood drained from my face, but I stayed silent.

Then the voice spoke to me again, without words: "You know it, Zarathustra, but you won't say it!"

And finally, I replied, almost defiantly: "Yes, I know it, but I will not say it!"

Then the voice spoke to me again, without words: "You won't, Zarathustra? Is that true? Don't hide behind your defiance!"

And I wept and trembled like a child, saying: "Ah, I would indeed, but how could I? Just spare me this! It's beyond my power!"

Then the voice spoke to me again, without words: "What does it matter about you, Zarathustra! Speak your word, and perish!"

And I replied, "Ah, is it my word? Who am I? I am waiting for the one who is worthy; I'm not even worthy to perish by it."

Then the voice spoke to me again, without sound: "What does it matter about you? You are still not humble enough for me. Humility has the hardest skin."

And I replied, "What has my humility's skin not endured! I live at the foot of my own heights; no one has yet told me how high my summits are. But I know well my valleys."

Then the voice spoke again, without sound: "Oh, Zarathustra, he who removes mountains also removes valleys and plains."

And I replied, "My words have yet to move mountains, and what I have spoken has not reached mankind. I went to them, but I have not yet reached them."

Then the voice spoke again, without sound: "What do you know of this! The dew falls on the grass when the night is most silent."

And I replied, "They mocked me when I found and walked my own path; indeed, my feet trembled then.

And they said to me: 'You forgot the path before, and now you also forget how to walk!'"

Then the voice spoke again, without sound: "What does their mockery matter! You are one who has unlearned how to obey; now you must command!

Do you not know who is most needed by all? The one who commands great things.

To achieve great things is hard, but harder still is it to command great things.

This is your most unpardonable stubbornness: you have the power, yet you will not rule."

And I replied, "I lack the lion's voice for all commanding."

Then the voice spoke to me in a whisper: "It is the quiet words that bring the storm. Thoughts that come with the steps of doves move the world.

Oh, Zarathustra, you will go as the shadow of what is to come: that is how you will command, and lead from the front."

And I replied, "I am ashamed."

Then the voice spoke to me again, without sound: "You must still become like a child, without shame.

The pride of youth is still upon you; you became young late: but he who would become a child must overcome even his youth."

I pondered this for a long while, trembling. At last, I repeated what I had said at first. "I will not."

Then laughter surrounded me. Ah, how that laughter tore at my insides and cut into my heart!

And for the last time, the voice spoke: "Oh, Zarathustra, your fruits are ripe, but you are not yet ripe for your fruits!

So you must return again to solitude, for you must still become mellow."

And again there was laughter, and it faded; then it became silent around me, as with a doubled silence. I lay on the ground, and sweat poured from my limbs.

Now you have heard everything, and why I must go back into my solitude. I have kept nothing hidden from you, my friends.

But even this you have heard from me, who is still the most reserved of men—and always will be!

Ah, my friends! I feel I should say something more to you! I feel I should give you something more! Why do I not give it? Am I stingy?

When Zarathustra spoke these words, the weight of his sadness and the closeness of his departure from his friends overtook him, and he wept openly; no one knew how to comfort him. But in the night, he went away alone and left his friends.

Chapter 45
The Wanderer

Then, around midnight, Zarathustra began his journey over the island ridge, aiming to reach the other coast by morning to board a ship. There was a good harbor there where foreign ships often anchored, taking on passengers who wanted to cross from the Blessed Isles. As

Zarathustra climbed the mountain, he thought about his many solitary wanderings since his youth and about the countless mountains, ridges, and peaks he had already ascended.

"I am a wanderer and a mountain climber," he said to himself. "I don't love the plains, and it seems I can't stay in one place for long.

"Whatever comes to me now as fate and experience will involve wandering and climbing mountains. In the end, one only really experiences oneself.

"The time is past when anything truly new could happen to me; what could come now that isn't already part of me?

"It only returns, coming back home to me—my own self, parts of it that have been scattered for so long among events and circumstances.

"And I know something else: I am now at the base of my final peak, standing before the journey I've waited for the longest. Ah, now I face my hardest climb! I've begun my loneliest journey!

"But someone like me doesn't shy away from such a moment— the moment that tells him: Only now are you on the path to your greatness! Summit and abyss—both lie ahead of you now!

"You are on the way to your greatness: now what was once your greatest fear has become your last refuge!

"You are on the way to your greatness: let your courage come from the fact that there is no longer a path behind you!

"You are on the way to your greatness: no one can follow you here! Your own footsteps have erased the trail behind you, and over it stands written: Impossible.

"And if every ladder fails you now, then you must learn to climb using your own head—how else could you keep ascending?

"Upon your own head, and beyond your own heart! Now the gentlest part of you must become the strongest.

"He who has always indulged himself will eventually sicken from that indulgence. Praise to what makes us tough! I do not praise the land where milk and honey flow!

"To learn to look beyond oneself is essential to seeing many things. Every mountain climber needs that resilience.

"But one who is too eager to see everything up close, how could he ever see more than just the foreground of things?"

But you, O Zarathustra, want to see the depths of all things, and what lies beyond them: so you must climb even higher—up, up, until even the stars are beneath you!

Yes! To look down on myself, and even on my stars—that alone I would call my summit, the last summit that remains for me! Zarathustra said this to himself while climbing, strengthening his heart with stern words, for he was more troubled than ever before. When he reached the top of the mountain ridge, he saw the other sea stretched out before him. He stood still and was silent for a long time. The night was cold at this height, clear and full of stars.

I see my fate, he finally said, with sadness. Very well! I am ready. Now my final loneliness begins.

Ah, this dark, sorrowful sea below me! Ah, this somber night and its trials! Ah, fate and sea! Now, I must descend to you!

Here I am, standing before my highest mountain and my longest journey: which is why I must first go deeper than I have ever gone before:

Deeper down into pain than I ever rose—down into its darkest depths! So my fate wills. Very well! I am ready.

Where do the highest mountains come from? I once asked. And then I learned that they rise out of the sea.

That testimony is carved into their rocks and at the peaks of their summits. From the deepest depths, the highest rises to its height.

Thus spoke Zarathustra on the cold mountain ridge. But when he came near the sea, and finally stood alone among the cliffs, he felt tired from his journey and more eager than ever.

Everything is still asleep, he said; even the sea is asleep. Sleepily, its strange eye looks up at me.

But it breathes warmly—I feel it. And I feel that it dreams. It stirs dreamily on its hard pillows.

Listen! Listen! How it groans with dark memories! Or maybe dark expectations?

Ah, I share in your sorrow, you dusky creature, and I am angry with myself even for your sake.

Ah, that my hand is not strong enough! Gladly, yes, I would free you from these dark dreams!

And while Zarathustra spoke this way, he laughed at himself, bitterly and sadly. What? Zarathustra, he said, will you even sing comfort to the sea?

Ah, you gentle fool, Zarathustra, you too-trusting soul! But you have always been this way: always approaching confidently everything terrible.

You would try to caress every monster. A hint of warm breath, a bit of soft fur on its paw—and you are ready to love and soothe it.

Love is the greatest danger for someone utterly alone—to love anything, as long as it lives! Truly, my folly and my modesty in love are laughable!

Thus spoke Zarathustra, laughing again. Then, however, he thought of his abandoned friends—and as if he had wronged them by his thoughts, he reproached himself. And then it happened that the one who was laughing began to weep—Zarathustra wept bitterly, with both anger and longing.

Chapter 46
The Vision and the Riddle

When the sailors learned that Zarathustra was on board—along with a man who had come from the Blessed Isles—there was much curiosity and anticipation. But Zarathustra stayed silent for two days, feeling cold and deaf with sorrow, not responding to looks or questions. On the evening of the second day, however, he began to listen, though he still said nothing, for there was much to hear on board the ship, which had come from afar and was bound for even farther lands. Zarathustra liked all those who set out on distant journeys and preferred living with risk. And behold! As he listened, his own tongue was finally loosened, and the ice around his heart melted. Then he began to speak:

To you, the bold venturers and wanderers, and all who have set out with cunning sails on dangerous seas—

To you, the puzzle-lovers, the twilight-enjoyers, whose souls are drawn by flute songs to every deceitful gulf:

—For you hate to fumble for a thread with timid hands; and where you sense things, you hate to calculate—

To you alone I'll reveal the mystery I saw—a vision of the most lonesome one—

Gloomily I wandered recently in corpse-colored twilight—gloomily and sternly, with tight lips. Not just one sun had set for me.

A path climbed daringly among rocks, an evil, lonely path, which no grass or bush brightened, a mountain path, crunching under my daring footsteps.

Silently I marched over the mocking crunch of pebbles, trampling on stones that tried to slip away: thus did my foot press on upwards.

Upwards—despite the force that pulled me downward to the abyss, the spirit of gravity, my devil and greatest foe.

Upwards—though it clung to me, half-dwarf, half-mole, paralyzing and weighed down, dripping lead into my ear, and thoughts like drops of lead into my brain.

"O Zarathustra," it whispered mockingly, word by word, "you stone of wisdom! You hurled yourself high, but every thrown stone must—fall!

O Zarathustra, you stone of wisdom, you slingshot, you star-smasher! You flung yourself so high—yet every thrown stone—must fall!

You condemned yourself, and to your own stoning: O Zarathustra, far indeed did you fling your stone—but it will rebound upon you!"

Then the dwarf fell silent; and a long silence followed. But the silence weighed on me; and being with someone in such a way makes one feel lonelier than being truly alone!

I climbed, I climbed, I dreamed, I thought—but everything weighed on me. I felt like a sick person worn out by torture, who is awakened from his first sleep by an even worse dream.

But there is something within me that I call courage: it has always defeated any sadness. This courage finally made me stand still and say, "Dwarf! You or me!"—

For courage is the best killer—courage that attacks: for in every attack, there is the sound of victory. Man, however, is the most courageous creature: through this, he has conquered every other animal. With the sound of victory, he has conquered every kind of pain; yet human pain is the deepest pain.

Courage also kills the dizziness that comes from looking into the abyss; and where does man not find himself at the edge of an abyss! Isn't seeing itself—seeing abysses?

Courage is the best killer: courage also kills compassion. Compassion, however, is the deepest abyss: as deeply as man looks into life, so deeply does he look into suffering.

Courage is the best killer, courage that attacks: it even kills death itself; for it says, "Was that life? Well then! Once more!"

In such words, however, there is a great sound of triumph. He who has ears to hear, let him hear—

"Stop, dwarf!" I said. "It's either you or me! But I am the stronger of the two: you don't know my deepest thought! It—you couldn't endure!"

Then something happened that made me feel lighter: for the dwarf jumped from my shoulder, that prying little creature! It squatted on a rock in front of me. There was a gateway right where we stopped.

"Look at this gateway, dwarf!" I continued, "it has two faces. Two roads meet here, but no one has ever traveled to the end of either of them.

This long road behind us: it stretches back into eternity. And that long road ahead—that's another eternity.

They are opposites, these roads; they directly face each other— and here at this gateway is where they meet. The name of the gateway is written above: 'This Moment.'

But if one were to follow them further—and always further on, do you think, dwarf, that these roads would remain eternally opposed?"

"All straight paths lie," the dwarf muttered, contemptuously. "All truth is crooked; time itself is a circle."

"You spirit of gravity!" I said, angered, "don't take this lightly! Or I shall leave you right here where you squat, you little cripple—and I carried you high!"

"Observe," I continued, "This Moment! From this gateway, This Moment, there stretches an eternal road backward: behind us lies an eternity.

Must not everything that can happen, have already traveled down that road? Must not everything that can happen, have already happened, occurred, and passed by?

And if everything has already existed, what do you think, dwarf, about This Moment? Mustn't this gateway itself have already existed, too?

And aren't all things bound together in such a way that This Moment draws all coming things after it? So, doesn't it also draw itself?

For everything that can happen in all things must also travel down this long path forward—must it not also happen again?

And this slow spider crawling in the moonlight, this moonlight itself, and you and I here at this gateway whispering together about eternal things—haven't we all existed already?

And mustn't we all return and travel down that other path in front of us, that strange long path—mustn't we return forever?"

So I spoke, lowering my voice more and more, for I was afraid of my own thoughts and what might come after them. Then, suddenly, I heard a dog howl nearby.

Had I ever heard a dog howl like that? My thoughts went back. Yes! When I was a child, in my most distant childhood:

Then I heard a dog howl like that. And I saw it, too, its fur standing on end, its head raised, trembling in the silent midnight, when even dogs believe in ghosts:

So that it stirred my pity. For just then the full moon, silent as death, drifted over the house; it stood still, a glowing orb resting on the flat roof, as if on someone's property—

That's what had frightened the dog, for dogs believe in thieves and ghosts. And when I heard such howling again, it stirred my pity once more.

Where was the dwarf now? And the gateway? And the spider? And all the whispering? Had I dreamed? Had I woken up? Suddenly I was standing alone among rugged rocks, bathed in the most desolate moonlight.

But there lay a man! And there—the dog, leaping, bristling, whining—it saw me coming and howled again, then cried out. Had I ever heard a dog cry out like that for help?

And truly, what I saw was unlike anything I'd ever seen. I saw a young shepherd, writhing, choking, trembling, his face twisted, with a thick black serpent hanging out of his mouth.

Had I ever seen such loathing and horror on a face? Maybe he had fallen asleep? And then the serpent had slithered into his throat—and there it had sunk its fangs.

My hand reached for the serpent, tugged at it—uselessly! I couldn't pull the serpent out of his throat. Then I cried out, "Bite! Bite!

Bite its head off! Bite!"—so I shouted; my horror, my hatred, my disgust, my pity—all my good and my bad cried out in one voice.

You daring ones around me! You adventurers and explorers, and all of you who have sailed with clever sails on unknown seas! You who delight in mysteries!

Help me solve the enigma that I saw; interpret for me the vision of the most solitary one!

For it was a vision and a glimpse into the future—what did I see in that parable? And who must come someday?

Who is the shepherd into whose throat the serpent slithered? Who is the person into whose throat the heaviest and darkest will crawl?

But the shepherd bit as my cry urged him; he bit with a fierce bite! He spat out the serpent's head far away—and sprang up.

No longer a shepherd, no longer a mere man—he had transformed, a being surrounded by light, laughing! No human had ever laughed like he laughed!

Oh, my brothers, I heard a laughter that was not human—and now a thirst gnaws at me, a longing that can never be quenched.

My desire for that laughter gnaws at me: oh, how can I still bear to live! And how could I stand to die right now!-

Thus spoke Zarathustra.

Chapter 47
Involuntary Bliss

With such riddles and bitterness in his heart did Zarathustra sail over the sea. But after he had traveled for four days from the Blessed Isles and his friends, he overcame his pain—he accepted his fate again with a triumphant and steady heart. Then Zarathustra spoke like this to his exultant conscience:

I am alone again, and I welcome it, alone with the clear sky and the open sea; and once more it is afternoon around me.

It was in the afternoon that I first found my friends; it was in the afternoon, too, that I found them a second time—at the hour when all light grows quieter.

For whatever happiness is still moving between heaven and earth now seeks out a soul where it can rest: in happiness, all light grows quieter.

Oh, afternoon of my life! Once my happiness also descended into the valley to seek a resting place; there, it found those open, welcoming souls.

Oh, afternoon of my life! What did I not give up just to gain one thing: this living garden of my thoughts and the dawn of my highest hope!

The creator once sought companions and children of his hope; and behold, he found he could not have them unless he first created them himself.

So here I am in the middle of my work, going to my children and returning from them; for Zarathustra must make himself complete for the sake of his children.

For one loves only one's child and one's work with all one's heart; and when one has great love for oneself, it is a sign of something yet to be born—this I have found to be true.

Still my children are young, standing close together in their first spring, swayed by the same wind—the trees of my garden, planted in my best soil.

And indeed, where such trees grow side by side, there are Blessed Isles!

But one day I will separate them, setting each alone to learn solitude, defiance, and wisdom.

Bent and twisted yet with flexible strength, each shall stand by the sea, a living lighthouse of unconquerable life.

Out where the storms crash into the sea, and the mountain's edge drinks in water, each of them shall one day face their own watches of day and night, for their testing and recognition.

Each will be recognized and tested to see if they belong to my type and lineage: if they are masters of a long-lasting will, silent even in speech, giving in such a way that they take through giving—

So that one day they may become my companions, fellow creators and fellow enjoyers alongside Zarathustra—those who inscribe my will onto my law-tablets, completing all things more fully.

And for them, and for those like them, I must make myself perfect. Therefore, I turn away from happiness now and present myself to every hardship—for my final testing and recognition.

Indeed, it is time I went away; the wanderer's shadow, the long tedium, and the still hour—all have said to me, "It is the highest time!"

The word slipped to me through the keyhole and said, "Come!" The door swung open gently and said, "Go!"

But I lay bound by my love for my children; desire set this trap for me—the desire for love—that I should be caught by my children and lose myself in them.

To desire is now, for me, to lose myself. I possess you, my children! In this possession, all must be assurance, not longing.

But the sun of my love lay heavily on me, and Zarathustra stewed in his own warmth—then shadows and doubts swept over me.

I began to long for frost and winter: "Oh, that frost and winter might make me crack and shiver again!" I sighed—and then, a cold mist rose from me.

My past burst from its tomb; many buried pains awoke—they had only been sleeping, hidden in funeral clothes.

Everything around me spoke in signs: "It is time!" But I did not listen until at last my abyss stirred, and my thought bit me.

Oh, my abysmal thought, you who are my thought! When will I find the strength to hear you digging within me without trembling?

My heart pounds to my throat when I hear you burrowing! Even your silence threatens to choke me, you deep and mute one!

I've never dared to summon you; it has been enough just to carry you with me! I've not yet been strong enough for my final lion-like boldness and play.

You have always been formidable enough for me—but one day I shall find the strength and the lion's voice to call you forth!

When I overcome myself in that way, I will overcome myself in all that is greater; a victory will be the seal of my perfection!

Meanwhile, I sail along uncertain seas; chance flatters me, smooth-tongued chance; I look forward and back, yet see no end.

The hour of my final struggle has not yet come to me—or perhaps it's coming to me now? With seductive beauty, sea and life surround me, watching.

Oh, afternoon of my life! Oh, happiness before evening! Oh, safe harbor on the high seas! Oh, peace in uncertainty! How I distrust you all!

Distrustful am I of your seductive beauty! Like a lover, I distrust a smile that's too smooth.

As the jealous lover gently pushes his beloved away, so do I push this blissful hour from me.

Away with you, blissful hour! You bring me involuntary joy! Here I stand, ready for my deepest pain—how untimely you've come!

Away with you, blissful hour! Rather, stay with my children! Hurry and bless them with my happiness before nightfall!

Look, evening draws near: the sun sinks. Away, my happiness!—

Thus spoke Zarathustra. And he waited for misfortune all night long; but he waited in vain. The night stayed clear and calm, and happiness itself came closer and closer to him. In the early morning, however, Zarathustra laughed to himself and said mockingly: "Happiness chases after me. It's because I don't chase after women. But happiness is, after all, a woman."

Chapter 48

Before Sunrise

O HEAVEN above me, you pure, you deep heaven! You abyss of light! Gazing upon you, I tremble with divine desires.

To throw myself up to your height—that is my depth! To hide myself in your purity—that is my innocence!

The God hides his beauty: thus you hide your stars. You do not speak; this is how you reveal your wisdom to me.

Silent above the raging sea, you rose for me today; your love and your modesty reveal themselves to my stormy soul.

In coming to me, beautiful and veiled in beauty, in speaking to me in silence, clear in your wisdom—

Oh, how could I not sense the modesty of your soul! Before the sun, you came to me—the most lonesome one.

We have been friends from the beginning: grief, dread, and the ground are common to us; even the sun belongs to us both.

We do not speak to each other, for we know too much: we keep silent together, we share our knowledge with a smile.

Are you not the light of my fire? Do you not share the soul of my insight?

Together, we learned everything; together, we learned to rise beyond ourselves to ourselves and to smile uncloudedly—

To smile unclouded down from bright eyes and from miles of distance, while below us, restraint, purpose, and guilt stream like rain.

And when I wandered alone, what did my soul yearn for at night and in the winding paths? And when I climbed mountains, whom did I seek, if not you, on those heights?

And all my wandering and mountain-climbing—was it not only a necessity, just a makeshift for the awkward one? My whole will wants only to fly—to fly into you!

And what have I hated more than passing clouds, than whatever stains you? I have even hated my own hatred, because it stained you!

I loathe passing clouds—those sneaky beasts of prey; they steal from us what we share—the vast, boundless Yes, and the Amen.

These mediators and mixers—we loathe them—the passing clouds: those half-and-half creatures who have learned neither to bless nor to curse from the heart.

Rather would I sit in a tub under a closed-off sky; rather would I sit in the abyss without any sky than see you, my radiant heaven, stained with passing clouds!

And how often have I longed to pin them fast with sharp, golden threads of lightning, that I might beat the drum upon their bellies like thunder—

An angry drummer, because they rob me of your Yes and Amen! You heaven above me, you pure, you luminous heaven! You abyss of light! Because they rob you of my Yes and Amen.

For I would rather have noise and thunder and stormy gusts than this cautious, doubting cat-like calm; and among men do I hate most of all the soft-treaders, and half-and-half ones, and the doubting, hesitating, passing clouds.

And "he who cannot bless shall learn to curse!"—this clear teaching came to me from the pure heaven above; this star remains in my sky, even on the darkest nights.

I am a blesser and a Yes-sayer, as long as you are with me, you pure, luminous heaven! you abyss of light!—into all depths, I bring my benevolent Yes-saying.

A blesser I have become and a Yes-sayer; that is why I struggled and toiled, to one day free my hands for blessing.

This, then, is my blessing: to stand above everything as its own sky, its dome, its blue arch and eternal security: and blessed is he who blesses this way!

For all things are baptized in the fountain of eternity, beyond good and evil; good and evil themselves, however, are but fleeting shadows, damp burdens, and passing clouds.

It is a blessing, not a blasphemy, when I teach that "above all things is the heaven of chance, the heaven of innocence, the heaven of freedom, the heaven of playfulness."

"Of chance"—that is the oldest nobility in the world; that I restored to all things; I freed them from the shackles of purpose.

This freedom and celestial calm I placed like a blue arch above everything, when I taught that above and through them, no "eternal Will" wills.

This playfulness and light-heartedness I put in place of that Will, when I taught that "In everything, there is one impossibility— rationality!"

A touch of reason, perhaps, a hint of wisdom scattered from star to star—this spark is mingled in all things: for wisdom's sake, folly is mingled in all things!

A little wisdom may indeed be possible; but this blessed assurance I found in all things—that they would rather dance on the feet of chance.

O heaven above me! you pure, exalted heaven! This is your purity to me, that no eternal spider of reason spins webs here—That to me you are a dancing-floor for divine chances, a table of the gods for divine dice and dice-players!—

But are you blushing? Have I spoken things unspeakable? Did I offend when I meant to bless you?

Or is it the embarrassment of being with me that makes you blush? Do you bid me go and be silent because—day is coming?

The world is deep—deeper than day can comprehend. Not everything should be said in the presence of daylight. But day is coming; so let us part!

O heaven above me, you modest one! you radiant one! O you, my joy before sunrise! The day is coming; so let us part!—

Thus spoke Zarathustra.

Chapter 49
Virtue That Diminishes

WHEN Zarathustra was back on the continent, he didn't go straight to his mountains and cave but wandered around, asking questions and discovering things here and there. So he jokingly said of himself, "Look, a river winding back to its source!" He wanted to see what had changed among people during his absence: had they grown or shrunk? One time, seeing a row of new houses, he was amazed and said:

"What do these houses mean? No great soul built them as a reflection of itself!

Did some foolish child pull them from its toy box? I wish another child would put them back in!

And these rooms and chambers—do people actually live here? They look like they're made for silk dolls or delicate eaters, who maybe let others eat with them."

Zarathustra stopped, pondering. At last, he said sadly, "Everything has become smaller here!

Everywhere I see lower doorways: I can still go through, but—I must stoop!

Oh, when will I return home, where I won't have to stoop—where I won't have to bend down before the small ones!" And Zarathustra sighed, gazing into the distance.

That same day, he spoke about the virtue that makes things small.

As I pass through this people, I keep my eyes open: they don't forgive me for not envying their virtues.

They bite at me because I tell them that for small people, small virtues are needed—and because I struggle to understand that small people are even necessary!

I am still like a rooster in a strange barnyard, where even the hens peck at him. Yet I am not unfriendly to the hens because of it.

I'm courteous toward them, as with all small annoyances; being prickly toward what is small seems to me the wisdom of hedgehogs.

They all talk about me when they sit around their fires in the evening—they talk about me, but no one actually thinks of me!

This is a new stillness I've felt: their noise around me covers my thoughts like a mantle.

They call to each other, "What is this gloomy cloud planning to do to us? Let's make sure it doesn't bring us a plague!"

And recently, a woman grabbed her child who was approaching me: "Take the children away!" she cried. "Those eyes scorch children's souls."

They cough when I speak; they think coughing objects to strong winds—they have no idea of the joyfulness behind my spirited words!

"We don't have time for Zarathustra yet"—that's their excuse; but what does it matter if a time has "no time" for Zarathustra?

And if they were to praise me completely, how could I rest on their praise? Their praise feels like a belt of thorns: it scratches me even when I take it off.

This too I learned among them: the one who praises acts like he's giving something back, but really, he's hoping for more to be given to him!

Ask my feet if their flattery and luring songs please them! They don't care to march or stand still to such rhythm and tick-tock.

They would rather lure and praise me for small virtues; they would rather push my steps to the beat of small comforts.

I walk through these people with my eyes open; they have become smaller, and keep getting smaller—this is due to their idea of happiness and virtue.

They even limit their virtue—for the sake of comfort. Only moderate virtue fits well with comfort.

True, they also learn to move along, each in their way: but I call their progress a hobble—keeping them in the way of anyone who hurries.

Many of them shuffle forward, glancing back over their shoulders, with stiffened necks: those are the ones I like to run into.

Feet and eyes should not lie, nor mislead each other. But among small people, there is much deception.

Some want to act, but most are acted upon. Some are real, but most are just pretending.

Among them are actors without realizing it, and actors without intending it—the genuine are always few, especially genuine actors.

There is little manliness here; that's why their women make themselves more masculine. Only those man enough can protect the womanly in women.

The worst hypocrisy I found among them was that even those in command pretend to have the virtues of those who serve.

"I serve, you serve, we all serve"—this chant even their rulers sing, and alas! if the highest lord is nothing more than the highest servant!

Ah, my curious eyes even caught sight of their hypocrisy; I easily saw through all their buzzing joys, their fluttering around sunny windowpanes.

I see so much kindness, yet so much weakness. So much fairness and pity, yet so much weakness.

They are round, smooth, and considerate with each other, like grains of sand are round, smooth, and considerate with other grains of sand.

Modestly grasping a small happiness—that's what they call "submission"! And then, with modest looks, they seek out yet another small happiness.

Deep down, they mostly want one thing: that no one should harm them. So they try to anticipate everyone's needs and do good for everyone.

But that's cowardice, though they call it "virtue."

And when these small people happen to speak harshly, I hear only their frail voices—every little breeze makes them hoarse.

They are clever, yes, with virtues that have nimble fingers. But they lack fists: their fingers don't know how to turn into a fist.

To them, virtue is something that makes people modest and tame: by this, they've turned the wolf into a dog and man into his own best pet.

"We put our chair right in the middle," they say with a smirk, "and we sit as far from dying gladiators as we do from satisfied pigs."

But that is mediocrity, even if they call it moderation.

I pass through this crowd, letting fall many words; but they neither know how to take them nor keep them.

They wonder why I haven't come to condemn lust and vice; and indeed, I haven't come to warn against pickpockets either!

They're puzzled why I'm not there to sharpen their wisdom—as if they didn't already have enough know-it-alls, whose voices scratch my ears like chalk on slate!

And when I cry out, "Curse all the cowardly devils inside you, those who'd rather whimper and fold their hands and worship!"— they scream, "Zarathustra is godless!"

Especially their teachers of submission yell this. But I enjoy shouting in their ears: "Yes! I am Zarathustra, the godless!"

Those teachers of submission! Wherever there's anything small, sickly, or weak, there they crawl like lice; only my disgust stops me from crushing them.

Well, here's my sermon for their ears: I am Zarathustra, the godless, who says, "Who is more godless than I, that I might learn from him?"

I am Zarathustra, the godless: where is my equal? And all are my equals who give themselves their Will and free themselves from all submission.

I am Zarathustra, the godless! I cook every chance that comes to me in my pot. Only when it's fully cooked do I welcome it as my food.

Indeed, many a chance has come commanding me, but my Will spoke back to it even more commandingly—until it knelt before me in surrender.

-Imploring to find a home and heart with me, saying flatteringly: "See, O Zarathustra, how friend only comes to friend!"-

But why do I speak, when no one here has ears for me? So I will shout it out to all the winds:

You grow ever smaller, you little people! You crumble away, you comfortable ones! You will perish—

-By your many small virtues, by your many small omissions, and by your many small submissions!

Your soil is too tender, too soft! But for a tree to grow tall, it needs to wrap its roots firmly around hard rocks!

Even what you leave out weaves into the web of the future for all mankind; even your "nothing" is a web, and a spider that feeds on the blood of what's to come.

And when you take, you take like thieves, you little virtuous ones; but even among thieves, there's honor—they say, "Only steal when you can't take by force."

"It gives itself"—that's a doctrine of submission. But I say to you, you comfortable ones, that it takes to itself and will go on taking more and more from you!

Ah, that you would abandon your half-hearted will and decide for idleness as firmly as you decide for action!

Ah, if only you understood my words: "Always do as you will—but first, be those who truly can will.

Love your neighbor as yourselves—but first, be those who truly love themselves—

-Those who love with a great love, those who love with great disdain!" Thus speaks Zarathustra, the godless.

But why do I speak, when no one has my ears? It's still too early for me here.

I am my own forerunner among this people, my own cockcrow in the dark alleys.

But their hour will come! And my hour will come too! With each passing hour, they grow smaller, poorer, less fruitful—poor weeds! poor earth!

And soon they'll stand before me like dry grass in a plain, truly weary of themselves—and craving fire more than water!

O blessed hour of lightning! O mystery before midday! One day I will make them blazing fires and messengers with flaming tongues—

-Messengers with tongues of flame, shouting: It's coming, it's near, the great noontide!

Thus spoke Zarathustra.

Chapter 50
The Mount of Olives

WINTER, an unwelcome guest, is sitting here with me at home; my hands are blue from his chilly handshakes.

I respect this rough guest, but I'm happy to leave him alone. I gladly run from him; and when you run well, you can escape him!

With warm feet and warm thoughts, I head to the sunny corner of my olive grove, where the wind is calm.

There, I laugh at my stern guest and still appreciate him, for he clears my house of flies and quiets many little noises.

He doesn't tolerate even a gnat's buzzing or two of them; he makes the paths so empty that even the moonlight feels timid there at night.

He's a harsh guest—but I respect him and don't worship him as the delicate types do, who bow to the pot-bellied fire idol.

I'd rather a bit of teeth-chattering than worshipping an idol—that's just how I am. Especially, I hold a grudge against all those steaming, smoky fire idols.

Those I love, I love even more in winter than in summer; I find it even easier to mock my enemies and do so more heartily when winter's in my house.

Heartily, truly—even as I slip into bed. There, my hidden happiness still laughs and plays, and my sly dreams laugh too.

A creeper? Me? Never in my life did I creep before the powerful; and if I ever lied, it was out of love. That's why I'm glad, even in my winter bed.

A humble bed warms me more than a luxurious one, for I cherish my poverty. And in winter, it's most loyal to me.

Every day, I start with a bit of mischief: I mock the winter with a cold bath, which makes my stern housemate grumble.

I even like to tickle him with a little candlelight so that he finally lets the heavens emerge from their gray, ashy twilight.

For I'm especially mischievous in the morning: at that early hour when the pail rattles at the well and the horses neigh warmly in gray lanes—

I wait, almost impatiently, for the clear sky to finally dawn for me, the snow-bearded winter sky, the gray one, the white-headed—

The winter sky, the quiet winter sky, which often hides its own sun!

Did I perhaps learn this long, clear silence from it? Or did it learn it from me? Or did each of us create it for himself?

The origin of all good things is countless—the good, mischievous things come into being out of joy. How could they ever do so—just once?

A good, mischievous thing is also a long silence and to gaze out like the winter sky with a clear, round-eyed expression:

Like the winter sky, hiding one's sun and one's unyielding solar will: indeed, I've mastered this skill and this winter-like roguishness!

My favorite wickedness and art is making sure my silence doesn't give itself away by being silent.

With loud words and dice, I fool the somber onlookers: all those serious watchers, my will and purpose slip past them.

I made this long, clear silence so that no one could peer into my depth or my true intentions.

Many clever ones I found veiled their faces and muddied their water, so no one could see through it or beneath it.

But the even shrewder ones came to these, the cautious and perceptive; from them, they fished out their best-hidden secrets!

But to me, the clearest, the honest, the transparent, are the wisest silent ones: in them, their depths are so profound that even the clearest water can't reveal it.

You snow-bearded, silent winter sky, you round-eyed, white-headed one above me! Oh, you heavenly image of my soul and its playfulness!

And must I not hide myself as if I had swallowed gold—lest someone tear my soul apart to reach it?

Must I not stand tall, that they might overlook my long legs—all those envious and harmful ones around me?

Those dingy, fire-warmed, worn-out, greenish, mean-spirited souls—how could their envy bear my happiness!

Thus I show them only the ice and winter of my peaks—and not that my mountain wears all the solar belts around it!

They only hear the whistling of my winter storms and don't know I also travel across warm seas, like the heavy, longing winds from the south.

They feel sorry for my misfortunes and accidents—but my words say: "Let chance come to me: innocent as a little child!"

How could they bear my happiness if I didn't cover it with accidents, winter hardships, bear-skin hats, and veils of snowflakes?

If I didn't sympathize with their pity—the pity of those envious and injurious ones!

If I didn't sigh and chatter with cold before them and let them wrap me in their pity patiently!

This is the wise, humorous, good-willed desire of my soul: it hides neither its winters nor its icy storms; it hides not its cold sores, either.

For one person, solitude is an escape from the sick; for another, it's fleeing the company of the sick ones.

Let them hear me chatter and sigh in the winter cold, all those pitiful, narrow-eyed ones around me! With such sighs and chattering, I escape from their heated rooms.

Let them feel sorry for me, pity me for my frostbite: "At the ice of knowledge, he'll freeze to death!"—so they say sadly.

Meanwhile, I run with warm feet here and there on my olive mount: in the sunny corner of my olive mount, I sing and laugh at all their pity.

Thus Zarathustra sang.

Chapter 51
Passing By

Thus, slowly wandering through many people and various cities, Zarathustra returned by roundabout paths to his mountains and his cave. And behold, he unexpectedly came to the gate of the great city. Here, a foaming fool, with hands outstretched, jumped forward and blocked his path. It was the same fool the people called "the ape of Zarathustra" because he had learned something of Zarathustra's tone and manner of speaking, and perhaps also liked to borrow from his wisdom. And the fool spoke to Zarathustra:

"O Zarathustra, here lies the great city: here, you have nothing to gain and everything to lose.

Why would you wade through this muck? Have pity on your feet! Spit on the city gate instead, and—turn back!

Here is where hermits' thoughts go to ruin: here, great thoughts are boiled down and shrunk small.

Here, all noble sentiments rot: only hollow, rattling ideas are left to clatter around!

Can't you already smell the slaughterhouses and kitchens of the spirit? Doesn't the city reek with the stench of spirit being butchered?

Don't you see souls hanging like dirty, limp rags?—And they even make newspapers out of those rags!

Can't you hear how spirit has become nothing but a word game here? It vomits forth sickening word garbage—and they make newspapers out of that garbage too.

They chase after each other, not knowing why! They stir each other up, not knowing for what! They tinkle with cheap trinkets, they jingle with their gold.

They are cold, and seek warmth from distilled spirits; they are feverish, and seek coolness from icy drinks; they're all sick and wounded from public opinion.

All desires and vices make their home here; but here, too, are the virtuous ones, filled with appointed virtue:

Much appointed virtue with writer's fingers, sturdy seats for long sitting, and patient waiting bodies, with little stars on their chests and daughters padded and shapeless.

Here there's also a lot of piety, with plenty of devoted spit-licking and spit-licking devotion, before the God of Hosts.

'From on high,' the star and the gracious spit fall; every empty chest yearns for the favor.

The moon has its court, and the court has its starry-eyed calves: yet everything that comes from the court is prayed to by the beggarly masses, and all the virtue that can be appointed.

'I serve, you serve, we all serve,' so prays every virtue appointed to the prince: so that at last the earned star might rest on the skinny chest!

But the moon still revolves around all things earthly: so too does the prince revolve around what's most earthly of all—that, however, is the gold of the merchants."

The God of the Hosts of war is not the God of the golden bar; the prince proposes, but the shopman—disposes!

By all that is bright and strong and good in you, O Zarathustra! Spit on this city of shopkeepers and turn back!

Here, all blood flows putrid, lukewarm, and frothy through every vein: spit on the great city, this great slum where all the scum gathers and rises!

Spit on this city of cramped souls and narrow chests, of sharp eyes and sticky fingers—

—On the city of the shameless, the brazen, the writers and talkers who stir up the crowds, the fevered and over-ambitious—

Where all that is crippled, infamous, greedy, mistrustful, overly ripe, sickly-yellow, and rebellious festers dangerously—

—Spit on the great city and turn back!—

Here, however, Zarathustra interrupted the foaming fool, silencing him—

"Stop it right now!" called Zarathustra. "Your talk and your kind have disgusted me for too long!

Why did you stay by the swamp so long that you yourself had to become a frog and a toad?

Isn't there a foul, frothy, swamp-blood flowing in your own veins if you've learned to croak and curse this way?

Why didn't you go to the forest? Or till the ground? Isn't the sea full of green islands?

I despise your contempt; and when you warned me—why didn't you first warn yourself?

Only love will lift my contempt and my warning to flight like a bird; but not from the swamp!—

They call you my ape, you foaming fool: but I call you my grunting pig—by your grunting, you ruin even my praise of folly.

What first made you grunt? Because no one flattered you enough—so you sat beside this filth to have more to grunt about—

—To have an excuse for vengeance! For vengeance, you vain fool, is the reason for all your foaming; I've understood you well!

But your fool's words harm me, even when you're right! And even if Zarathustra's words were a hundred times justified, you would always do wrong with my words!"

Thus spoke Zarathustra. Then he looked upon the great city, sighed, and was silent for a long time. At last, he spoke again:

"I loathe this great city too, not only this fool. Here and there—there's nothing to improve, nothing to ruin.

Woe to this great city!—And I wish I could already see the pillar of fire that will consume it!

For such pillars of fire must come before the great noontide. But all this has its own time and fate. Yet I leave you with this parting advice, you fool: where one can no longer love, one should—pass by!"

Thus spoke Zarathustra, and he passed by the fool and the great city.

Chapter 52

The Apostates

Ah, has everything already withered and turned grey that recently stood green and full of color on this meadow? And how much honey of hope I carried from here to my beehives!

Those young hearts have already grown old—not truly old, but weary, ordinary, and comfortable. Now they claim: "We have become pious again."

Not long ago, I saw them stepping out at dawn with bold strides; but now their knowledge has grown weary, and they even criticize their own morning courage!

Many of them once lifted their legs like dancers, and the laughter of my wisdom beckoned to them. But then they reconsidered. Today, I see them bent down—crawling before the cross.

Once, they fluttered around light and freedom like gnats and young poets. A little older, a little colder, and already they've become mystics, mumblers, and soft-hearted souls.

Did their spirits fail because solitude swallowed me like a whale? Did their ears listen longingly, in vain, for my trumpet sounds and herald calls?

Ah! Only a few hearts have enduring courage and exuberance, and in them, the spirit remains steadfast. But the rest are cowards.

The rest—these are always the vast majority, the common people, the superfluous, the too-many—all of them are cowardly!

Whoever is like me will encounter experiences like mine on their path: their first companions will be corpses and fools.

Their second companions, though, will call themselves believers— a living crowd, with plenty of love, plenty of foolishness, and naive devotion.

But one who is like me must not bind his heart to those believers. Nor should he place faith in the springtimes and colorful meadows, knowing the fickle, faint-hearted nature of humanity!

If they could do differently, they would also want to do differently. The half-hearted ruin every whole. If the leaves wither and fall, why mourn?

Let them go and fall away, Zarathustra; do not lament! It's better even to blow among them with rustling winds—

Blow among those leaves, Zarathustra, so that all that is withered may flee from you even faster!

"We have become pious again"—so those who have fallen away confess. And some are still too timid to confess it openly. I look them in the eye, and before them, I say it to their faces, seeing the blush on their cheeks: You are the ones who pray again!

It is shameful to pray! Not for everyone, but for you, and for me, and for anyone with a conscience in their head. For you, it is shameful to pray!

You know it well: that faint-hearted devil in you, who would rather fold its arms, place its hands on its chest, and take the easy way out—that faint-hearted devil convinces you to believe, "There is a God!"

By doing so, you join the light-fearing type, those whom light never allows to rest; now you must push your head daily deeper into darkness and fog!

And you've chosen the hour well: for now, the night birds take flight. The hour has come for all light-fearing people, the evening hour, the hour of rest, though they do not truly "rest."

I hear it and smell it: their hour has come—their time for a hunt and a quiet procession, not a wild hunt, but a soft, lame, snuffling, gentle hunt, by those who walk softly and pray softly—

A hunt for easy prey among the naive: every heart-trap has been set once again! And each time I lift a curtain, a night-moth flies out.

Was it hiding there with another night-moth? I smell secret gatherings everywhere; wherever there are closets, there are new devotees and the atmosphere of worship.

They sit together long into the night, saying, "Let us become like little children again and say, 'Good God!'"—mouths and stomachs ruined by pious treats.

Or they spend long evenings watching a crafty, lurking spider on a cross, preaching prudence even to the spiders themselves, teaching that "under crosses, it's good for web-spinning!"

Or they sit all day by stagnant waters with their fishing poles and think themselves profound; but those who fish where there are no fish, I don't even call shallow!

Or they learn to strum the harp in a pious, cheerful way with a hymn-writer who'd rather charm his way into the hearts of young girls—he's grown tired of the praise from the older ones.

Or they learn to shudder with a half-crazed scholar who waits in darkened rooms for spirits to appear to him—while the spirit runs away entirely!

Or they listen to an old wandering piper, who has learned from the mournful winds how to make sad sounds; now he plays like the wind and preaches sadness with sad tunes.

And some have even become night-watchmen: they know now how to blow horns, and roam the night, waking old things long fallen asleep.

Five words about ancient things I heard last night at the garden wall—they came from these aged, sorrowful, withered night-watchmen.

"He doesn't care for his children like a father should: human fathers do this better!"

"He's too old! He doesn't care for his children anymore," said one of the night-watchmen.

"Does he even have children? No one can prove it unless he proves it himself! I've long wished he'd give us real proof for once."

"Proof? As if he's ever proven anything! Proving is hard for him; he just wants us to believe him."

"Yes! Yes! Belief keeps him going; belief in him. That's how it is with old folks! It's the same with us too!"

Thus the two old night-watchmen and light-fearers spoke to each other and blew their horns sorrowfully. So it happened last night at the garden wall.

As for me, my heart twisted with laughter and nearly broke; it didn't know where to turn and sank deep within me.

It'll be the death of me yet—to choke with laughter when I see drunken donkeys and hear night-watchmen doubting about God.

Hasn't the time long passed for such doubts? Who nowadays can wake up such ancient, light-fearing thoughts?

It's long been over for the old gods—and indeed, they had a good and joyful end!

They didn't "fade away" as people claim. No, they once laughed themselves to death!

It happened when the most ungodly thing was spoken by a god himself—the words: "There is but one God! You shall have no other gods before me!"

An old grumpy god, a jealous one, forgot himself and said that—

And all the other gods laughed, shook on their thrones, and shouted, "Isn't divinity about there being many gods, not just one?"

He who has ears, let him hear.

Thus spoke Zarathustra in the city he loved, nicknamed "The Pied Cow." From there, he had only two days' journey back to his cave and his animals; his heart, meanwhile, was filled with joy at the closeness of his return home.

Chapter 53
The Return Home

O Solitude! My home, my solitude! I have lived too wildly and far-off for too long to return to you without tears!

Now, scold me with a finger like a mother does; now smile at me like a mother smiles; now say simply: "Who was it that once rushed away from me like a whirlwind?

-Who, when departing, called out: 'Too long have I sat in solitude; there, I forgot how to be silent!' Have you remembered it now, at last?

O Zarathustra, I know everything about you; and I know you were lonelier among the crowd, you unique one, than you ever were with me!

Forsakenness is one thing, solitude is another: you've learned that now! And you've learned that among men, you will always feel wild and strange:

-Wild and strange, even when they love you, for, above all, they want to be treated gently!

Here, though, you are at home with yourself; here, you can say everything, let out all your motives; nothing here hides away in shame or holds back frozen feelings.

Here, everything comes close to listen to you and flatter you, for they want to ride on your back. On every metaphor, you ride toward every truth.

Here, you can speak honestly and openly to all things, and truly, it sounds like praise to them to be spoken to—directly!

But forsakenness is something else entirely. Do you remember, O Zarathustra? When your bird cried out above you, when you stood in the forest, uncertain, not knowing which way to go, standing beside a corpse—

-When you said, 'Let my animals lead me! I found it more dangerous among men than among animals'—that was forsakenness!

And do you remember, O Zarathustra? When you sat on your island, a well of wine, giving and granting among empty buckets, offering and distributing among the thirsty:

-Until at last, you sat alone, thirsty among the drunken, and cried out in the night: 'Is taking not more blessed than giving? And is stealing even more blessed than taking?'—That was forsakenness!

And do you remember, O Zarathustra? When your still hour came and forced you out of yourself, when it whispered wickedly: 'Speak and perish!'—

-When it made you sick of all your waiting and silence and drained your quiet courage: That was forsakenness!"

O solitude! My home, solitude! How blessedly and gently your voice speaks to me!

We do not question each other, we do not complain; together, we walk openly through open doors.

With you, everything is open and clear; even the hours seem to pass with lighter steps. For in darkness, time feels heavier than in light.

Here, all beings' words and secret cabinets open to me; here, all existence wants to become words, and all that is becoming wants to learn from me how to speak.

But down there—every word is in vain! There, forgetting and moving on are the highest wisdom: that, I have now learned!

One who wishes to understand everything in people must handle everything. But my hands are too clean for that.

I don't even like to breathe their air; alas! that I lived among their noise and foul breaths for so long!

O blessed stillness around me! O pure air around me! How from deep within, this stillness draws pure breath! How it listens, this blessed silence!

But down there—everything speaks, everything is misheard. If one announces wisdom with bells, the shopkeepers in the marketplace will drown it out with the jingling of pennies!

Everything down there talks; no one understands anymore. Everything sinks into shallow waters; nothing sinks deeply anymore.

Everything down there talks, nothing completes itself. Everything cackles, but who still sits quietly on the nest to hatch the eggs?

Everything down there talks, everything is over-talked. And what was too tough for time itself yesterday, today hangs chewed up and spit out from the mouths of the people.

Everything down there talks, everything is betrayed. What once was called the secret of profound souls now belongs to street performers and butterflies.

O human commotion, you strange thing! Noise of dark streets! Now you are behind me again—my greatest danger is behind me!

In indulging and pitying lay ever my greatest danger; and all human commotion wants to be indulged and tolerated.

Living with hidden truths, with a fool's hand and a befooled heart, and rich in small lies of pity—this is how I always lived among people.

I sat among them disguised, ready to misjudge myself so that I might endure them, willingly saying to myself: "You fool, you don't understand people!"

One unlearns people when one lives among them: there is too much foreground in everyone—what can far-seeing, far-reaching eyes accomplish there?

And, fool that I was, when they misjudged me, I indulged them more than myself, being habitually hard on myself, often even taking revenge on myself for indulging them.

Stung all over by poisonous flies, worn down like stone by countless drops of cruelty: thus I sat among them, still telling myself: "Everything petty is innocent in its pettiness!"

Especially did I find those who call themselves "the good" the most poisonous flies; they sting in all innocence, lie in all innocence—how could they ever be just towards me?

He who lives among the good learns to lie through pity. Pity creates stifling air for all free souls. For the stupidity of the good is bottomless.

To conceal myself and my abundance—that I learned down there; for in everyone I found a poverty of spirit. My pity's lie was that I knew in each person what they lacked in spirit.

I saw and sensed in everyone what was just enough spirit for them, and what was too much!

Their stiff wise men—I called them wise, not stiff—thus did I learn to soften my words.

The grave-diggers bury themselves in sickness. Beneath old rubbish lies foul air. One shouldn't stir the swamp. One should live on mountains.

With blessed nostrils I again breathe mountain freedom. Freed at last is my nose from the stench of all human noise!

Tickled by sharp breezes like sparkling wine, my soul sneezes—sneezes, and joyfully shouts: "Health to you!"

Thus spoke Zarathustra.

Chapter 54
The Three Evils

In my dream, in my last morning-dream, I stood today on a promontory—beyond the world; I held a pair of scales and weighed the world.

Alas, that the rosy dawn came too early for me: it glowed me awake, the jealous one! Jealous is she always of the glow of my morning-dream.

Weighable by one who has time, measurable by a good weigher, reachable by strong wings, divinable by divine nutcrackers: so did my dream find the world—

My dream, a bold sailor, half-ship, half-hurricane, silent as a butterfly, impatient as a falcon: how did it have the patience and leisure today for world-weighing!

Did my wisdom perhaps speak secretly to it—my laughing, fully awake day-wisdom, which mocks all "infinite worlds"? For it says,

"Where there is force, there becomes number the master: it has more force."

How confidently did my dream look upon this finite world—not newly, not old-fashionedly, not timidly, not pleadingly—

As if a large round apple offered itself to my hand, a ripe golden apple, with a cool, soft, velvety skin—so did the world present itself to me—

As if a tree nodded to me, a broad-branched, strong-willed tree, bending as a rest and foot-stool for weary travelers: so did the world stand on my promontory—

As if delicate hands brought a casket toward me—a casket open for the delight of modest, adoring eyes: so did the world present itself before me today—

Not enough of a riddle to scare human love from it, not enough of a solution to put human wisdom to sleep—a humanly good thing was the world to me today, though such bad things are often said about it!

How I thank my morning-dream for letting me weigh the world at today's dawn! As a humanly good thing did it come to me, this dream and heart-comforter!

And that I might do the same by day, and imitate and copy its best, I will now put the three worst things on the scales, and weigh them humanly well.

He who taught to bless also taught to curse: what are the three most cursed things in the world? These I will put on the scales.

Desire, passion for power, and selfishness—these three things have been most cursed and held in the worst, most mistaken repute—these three things I will weigh humanly well.

Well! Here is my promontory, and there is the sea—it rolls toward me, rough and loyal, like an old, faithful, hundred-headed dog-monster that I love!

Well! Here I will hold the scales above the rolling sea; and I choose a witness to look on—you, the solitary tree, you, the strong-scented, broad-arching tree that I love!

On what bridge does the present cross into the future? By what pull do the high stoop to the low? And what urges even the highest to still grow upward?

Now the scales stand balanced and still: three heavy questions I have thrown in; three heavy answers rest on the other side.

Pleasure: to all self-denying despisers of the body, a sting and a torment; cursed as "worldly" by all those who live for the next world, for it mocks and confounds all their errant, mistaken teachings.

Pleasure: to the common crowd, the slow fire that burns them; to all wormy wood, to all rotting rags, the prepared heat and stew pot.

Pleasure: to free hearts, a thing innocent and pure, the garden-happiness of earth, a stream of thanks from the future into the present.

Pleasure: to the withered, a sweet poison; to the lion-hearted, however, a grand elixir and the reverently preserved wine of wines.

Pleasure: the great symbol of a higher happiness and greatest hope. For many is marriage promised, and more than marriage—

To many who are more unknown to each other than man and woman: for who fully understands how unknown man and woman are to each other?

Pleasure—but I will set boundaries around my thoughts, and even around my words, lest swine and libertines break into my gardens!

Passion for power: the fierce scourge of the hardest of heart, the cruel trial reserved for the cruel themselves; the gloomy flame of living pyres.

Passion for power: the wicked gadfly that stings the most conceited people; the scoffer at all unreliable virtue; it rides on every steed and every pride.

Passion for power: the earthquake that breaks and shakes all that is rotten and hollow; the rolling, rumbling demolisher of whitewashed tombs; the flashing question mark beside premature answers.

Passion for power: before whose gaze humanity shrinks, crawls, and becomes lower than the serpent and the swine—until finally, from deep within, a cry of great contempt sounds.

Passion for power: the terrible teacher of great disdain, who preaches to the face of cities and empires, "Away with you!"—until a voice from within cries, "Away with me!"

Power's passion: yet it climbs alluringly even to the pure and solitary, up to self-satisfied heights, glowing like a love that paints purple dreams of happiness on earthly heavens.

Power's passion: but who would call it "passion" when a high place yearns to descend to power? There is nothing sick or diseased in such longing and descending!

That the solitary heights might not stay lonely and self-contained forever; that the mountains might reach the valleys and the mountain winds find the plains—

Oh, who could find the right name, the true honorific for such longing! "Giving virtue"—so did Zarathustra once name the unnamable.

And so it happened—yes, for the first time—that his words blessed a healthy, robust form of selfishness, the kind that springs from a powerful soul—

A powerful soul, with its high, triumphant body, a refreshing body around which everything becomes a mirror:

The flexible, persuasive body, the dancer, symbolizing the self-rejoicing soul. In such bodies and souls, this self-rejoicing calls itself "virtue."

Such self-rejoicing shields itself with words of good and bad as with sacred groves; it surrounds itself with the names of its happiness, banishing everything lowly.

It banishes all that is cowardly, saying, "Bad—that is cowardly!" To it, contemptible are the ever-cautious, the sighing, the complaining, and those who grasp at petty advantages.

It looks down on all bitter-sweet wisdom: for indeed, there is a kind of wisdom that grows in the dark, a nightshade wisdom, which forever sighs, "All is in vain!"

It sees shy distrust as low and scorns all who demand oaths over a handshake and look: also, all over-distrusting wisdom, for that is the way of timid souls.

Lower still does it rank the submissive, servile type, lying immediately on its back, ever yielding; there is even a wisdom that is submissive, fawning, pious, and obsequious.

Hateful to it, even loathsome, is anyone who never stands up for themselves, who swallows poisonous spittle and bad glances, the endlessly patient, endlessly tolerant, endlessly content type; that is the mark of a slave. Whether they bow down to gods and divine insults or to men and foolish human opinions, this blessed selfishness spits at all kinds of slaves!

"Bad"—that is its name for all that is broken in spirit, slavishly subservient, with downcast eyes, disheartened souls, and the false, fawning manner that kisses with broad, cowardly lips.

And counterfeit wisdom—that's what it calls all the wit that serves the slave-minded, the aged, and the weary, as well as the crafty, counterfeit, curious-minded foolishness of priests!

The counterfeit-wise, those priests, the world-weary, and the feminine, servile souls—oh, how their game has twisted and misused the idea of selfishness!

And this was supposed to be virtue, what they called virtue—to scorn and misuse selfishness! And "selfless"—yes, they wanted to be seen as "selfless," all those weary cowards and web-spinners!

But to all of them now comes a new day, a reckoning, the sword of judgment, the great noontide: then many things will be unveiled!

And he who declares the self wholesome and sacred, who blesses selfishness, indeed, he is the one who sees and speaks what he knows: "Look, it is coming, night is near, the great noontide!"

Thus spoke Zarathustra.

Chapter 55
The Spirit of Gravity

My mouthpiece—it belongs to the people: I speak too plainly, too warmly, for soft Angora rabbits. And my words sound stranger still to all the ink-fish and pen-foxes.

My hand—it's the hand of a fool: woe to all tables and walls, and anything that has space for a fool's sketches, a fool's scrawls!

My foot—it's a horse's foot; with it, I stomp and gallop over stick and stone, up and down the fields, lost in the joy of fast racing.

My stomach—surely it's an eagle's stomach? For it prefers lamb's meat. Certainly, it's a bird's stomach.

Nourished with simple things, ready and eager to fly—flying away, that's my nature now. Why shouldn't there be something of the bird in me?

Especially since I have such a fierce dislike for the spirit of gravity—that is bird-nature! Indeed, it's deeply hostile, passionately hostile, originally hostile! Oh, where has my hostility not flown, and misflown!

I could sing a song about it—and I will sing it, even if I'm alone in an empty house, singing to my own ears.

There are other singers, for sure, who only find their voices gentle, their hands eloquent, their eyes expressive, their hearts awake when the house is full. I'm not like them.

Whoever teaches mankind to fly will change all boundaries; to him, all boundaries will fly apart; he will christen the earth anew—as the "light body."

The ostrich runs faster than the swiftest horse, but it also buries its head deep in the heavy earth. It's the same with a person who cannot yet fly.

For him, life and earth are heavy, so insists the spirit of gravity! But anyone who wants to become light, who wants to be a bird, must learn to love themselves—that's what I teach.

Not, of course, with the love of the sick and the weak, for even self-love stinks among them!

One must learn to love oneself—this is what I teach—with a clean and healthy love: so one can endure being with oneself, and not wander aimlessly.

Such wandering calls itself "brotherly love"; through those words there has been, up to now, the best lying and pretending—especially by those who are a burden to everyone.

And truly, learning to love oneself is not a commandment for today and tomorrow. It is, instead, the finest, subtlest, most patient art of all.

For all possession is well hidden from its possessor, and of all treasure-pits, one's own is the last to be dug up—that's what the spirit of gravity does.

Almost from the cradle, we are burdened with heavy words and values: "good" and "evil"—this inheritance, they call it. And for its sake, we are excused for simply being alive.

And so, one lets little children come to them, to forbid them early from loving themselves—that's what the spirit of gravity commands.

And we—we carry what is given to us loyally, on strong shoulders, over rough mountains! And when we sweat, people say to us, "Yes, life is hard to bear!"

But it's man himself who is hard to bear! The reason is that he carries too many unnecessary things on his shoulders. Like a camel, he kneels down and lets himself be heavily loaded.

Especially the strong, load-bearing man, the one who reveres life. He takes on too many unnecessary heavy words and values—then life seems to him like a desert!

And truly! Many things of our own are hard to bear! Many things inside us are like oysters—slippery, unattractive, and hard to grasp.

So an elegant shell with fine decoration must advocate for them. But one must also learn this art: to have a shell, a good appearance, and a wise blindness!

And many things about man are deceiving because some shells are poor and pitiful, too much just shell. Many hidden qualities and strengths are never even noticed; the finest delicacies find no tasters!

Women know this, the finest among them: a little heavier, a little thinner—oh, how much fate rests in so little!

Man is hard to understand, and hardest of all to himself; often, the spirit deceives about the soul. So insists the spirit of gravity.

Yet, the person who has discovered himself says: This is my good and my evil. With that, he silences the mole and the dwarf who say, "Good for all, evil for all."

I don't care for those who call everything good and this world the best of all. I call those people the all-satisfied.

All-satisfaction that knows how to savor everything—that's not the best taste! I respect the firm, discerning tongues and stomachs that have learned to say "I" and "Yes" and "No."

But to chew and digest everything—that's true swine nature! To always say "Yea"—only the ass and others like it have mastered that!

Deep yellow and fiery red—that's what my taste desires—it blends blood with all colors. Yet, anyone who whitewashes his house shows me a whitewashed soul.

Some fall in love with mummies; others, with phantoms—both, equally hostile to all flesh and blood. Oh, how repulsive both are to my taste! For I love blood.

I would never live where everyone spits and spews—that is my taste now—I'd rather live among thieves and oath-breakers. No one carries gold in his mouth.

What disgusts me even more are all the flatterers; the most repulsive creature I found among humans, I named "parasite": it doesn't love, yet wants to live off love.

I call all those unhappy who have only one choice: either to become cruel beasts or cruel beast-tamers. Among such, I would never build my home.

I also call all those unhappy who must always wait—they are repulsive to my taste—all the toll-collectors, traders, kings, and other landholders and shopkeepers.

I learned to wait as well, and thoroughly—but only to wait for myself. And above all, I learned to stand, to walk, to run, to leap, to climb, and to dance.

This is my teaching: if someone wants to fly one day, he must first learn to stand, to walk, to run, to climb, and to dance—one does not simply fly into flying!

I used rope ladders to reach many windows, and with nimble legs I climbed high masts: sitting atop high masts of perception brought me no small joy—

—To flicker like a small flame on high masts: a small light, perhaps, but a great comfort to castaway sailors and the shipwrecked!

By many paths and wanderings, I arrived at my truth; I didn't reach the heights where my eyes roam into the distance by only one ladder.

And I asked directions only reluctantly—that was always against my taste! Instead, I questioned and tested the paths themselves.

My travels have been nothing but testing and questioning—and truly, one must also learn how to answer such questions! That, however, is my taste:

—Neither a good taste nor a bad taste, but my taste, of which I no longer feel shame or secrecy.

"This is my way—where is yours?" I answered those who asked me "the way." For the way—it does not exist!

Thus spoke Zarathustra.

Chapter 56
Old and New Tablets

Here I sit and wait, surrounded by old broken law tablets and new half-written ones. When will my hour come?

—The hour of my descent, my going down to men once more.

I wait for that hour now; for first, the signs must come to me that it is my hour—specifically, the laughing lion with the flock of doves.

In the meantime, I speak to myself as one with time on his hands. No one tells me anything new, so I tell myself my own story.

When I came to men, I found them resting on an old delusion: they all believed they had long known what was good and bad for men.

Talking about virtue seemed a worn-out matter to them; and whoever wanted to sleep well would talk of "good" and "bad" before going to bed.

I disturbed this slumber when I taught that no one yet knows what is truly good and bad—except the creator!

—It is the creator who sets man's goal, gives meaning and future to the earth: he alone makes anything good or bad.

And I urged them to topple their old academic seats and everywhere that old delusion had taken root; I urged them to laugh at their revered moralists, their saints, their poets, and their saviors.

I told them to laugh at their grim sages and at anyone who sat as a dark scarecrow on the tree of life.

I sat myself down on their grand grave-road, beside the corpses and vultures—and I laughed at all their bygone days and its mellow, rotting splendor.

Like a mad preacher, I called shame and scorn upon all their greatness and smallness. Oh, that their best is so very small! Oh, that their worst is so very small! Thus I laughed.

Thus did my wise longing, born in the mountains, cry and laugh within me; a wild wisdom, indeed!—my great, winged, rustling longing.

And often it carried me off, up, and away in laughter; then I flew, quivering like an arrow, in sun-drunk rapture:

—Out into distant futures no dream has yet seen, to warmer places than any sculptor has imagined, where gods dance and are ashamed of their clothing:

(For I speak in parables, pausing and stammering like poets do; and indeed, I am embarrassed that I must still be a poet!)

Where all existence seemed to me a dance of gods, a play of gods, with the world set free, unrestrained, and returning to itself:

—Like an eternal cycle of self-fleeing and rediscovery among many gods, a blessed self-contradicting, reconnecting, and rejoicing among gods:

Where all time seemed a joyful mockery of moments, where necessity was freedom itself, joyfully goaded by freedom;

Where I also encountered again my old devil and archenemy, the spirit of gravity, and all it created: constraint, law, necessity, consequence, purpose, will, good and evil:

For must there not be something to dance over, to dance beyond? Must there not, for the nimble, the nimblest,—be moles and clumsy dwarfs?

There it was also that I picked up along the path the word "Superman," and that man is something that must be surpassed.

—That man is a bridge and not an end goal—celebrating his noons and evenings as steps toward new rosy dawns:

—The word of Zarathustra on the great noontide, and all else I have hung over humanity like purple afterglows of evening.

I also made them see new stars and new nights; over cloud and day and night, I spread out laughter like a brightly colored canopy.

I taught them all my creative vision and longing: to unite what is fragmented in man, and to solve the riddle and master fearful chance;

—As composer, riddle-reader, and redeemer of chance, I taught them to create the future, and to redeem all that has been through creation.

To redeem humanity's past, and to transform every "It was" until the Will declares: "But thus I willed it! Thus shall I will it—"

—This I called redemption; this alone did I teach them to call redemption.

Now I await my redemption—that I may go to them one last time.

For once more will I go to humanity: among them shall my sun set; in my dying I shall give them my greatest gift!

From the sun, I learned this as it sets, the overflowing one: it pours its gold into the sea from boundless riches—

So that even the poorest fisherman rows with golden oars! I once saw this and wept without tiring as I beheld it.

Like the sun, Zarathustra too will go down: now he sits here and waits, surrounded by old broken law tablets and new ones, half-written.

Behold, here is a new tablet! But where are my brothers to carry it with me to the valley and into hearts of flesh?

This is my great love for those farthest away: do not be considerate of your neighbor! Humanity is something that must be overcome.

There are many ways and methods of overcoming—see to it! Only a fool believes that "humanity can also be skipped over."

Overcome yourself even in your neighbor; a right you can seize should not be passively granted to you!

What you do cannot be done to you in return. Behold, there is no repayment.

He who cannot command himself will obey. And there are many who can command themselves yet still lack self-obedience!

Thus desires the type of noble souls: they wish to have nothing for free, least of all life.

The rabble wants to live for free; we, however, to whom life has given itself—we are always considering how best to repay!

And verily, it is a noble saying: "What life promises us, we shall fulfill—to life!"

One should not wish to enjoy where one has contributed nothing to the enjoyment. And one should not even wish for enjoyment!

For enjoyment and innocence are the most bashful things; neither likes to be sought. One should possess them—but rather seek guilt and pain!

O my brothers, he who is a pioneer is always sacrificed. Now, however, we are pioneers!

We all bleed on hidden sacrificial altars; we all burn and broil in honor of ancient idols.

Our best is still young; this excites old tastes. Our flesh is tender, our skin only lambskin—how could we not excite old idol-priests!

Within us still dwells the old idol-priest, who broils our best for his feast. Ah, my brothers, how could pioneers not be sacrifices!

But this is how our kind desires it; I love those who do not wish to preserve themselves. I love those who are willing to descend with my whole heart—for they go beyond.

To be true—few can be! And those who can often choose not to! Least of all can the "good" be true.

Ah, those "good" ones! Good people rarely speak the truth. For to be good in spirit is a kind of malady.

They yield, those good ones, they surrender themselves; their heart repeats, their soul obeys: yet one who obeys does not listen to himself!

All that the good call evil must unite to allow one truth to be born. O my brothers, are you also bold enough, "evil" enough for this truth?

The daring venture, the prolonged doubt, the fierce "No," the cutting honesty—how rarely do these come together! Yet out of such seeds, truth is born!

Alongside a guilty conscience, all knowledge has thus far grown! Break, break, you insightful ones, the old law tablets!

When there are planks, gangways, and railings spanning the river, indeed, none believe the one who says, "All is in flux."

Even the simple-minded disagree. "What?" they say, "Everything in flux? Planks and railings still stand over the river!

"Above the river, all things remain stable, all values, bridges and foundations, all that is 'good' and 'evil'—all these are stable!"

But when the harsh winter comes, the tamer of streams, even the wisest begin to doubt; and it is not only the simple-minded who then say, "Shouldn't everything just…stand still?"

"Fundamentally, everything stands still"—such is a convenient winter doctrine, comfort for idle seasons, a warm notion for winter-sleepers and hearth-sitters.

"Fundamentally, everything stands still"—but the thawing wind defies this message!

The thawing wind—a fierce bull, but not a plowing bull—a raging beast that shatters the ice with furious horns! And the ice, in turn, shatters the pathways!

O my brothers, is not everything now in flux? Have not all railings and pathways fallen into the water? Who would still cling to "good" and "evil"?

"Woe to us! Rejoice with us! The thawing wind blows!"—this, my brothers, proclaim through all the streets!

There is an ancient illusion—it is called good and evil. Around prophets and astrologers, this illusion has long circled.

Once, people believed in soothsayers and astrologers; therefore, they believed, "Everything is fate: you must, for you have to!"

Then, people doubted the soothsayers and astrologers; therefore, they believed, "Everything is freedom: you can, for you wish!"

O my brothers, concerning the stars and the future, there has only been illusion so far, not knowledge. And so too with good and evil— only illusion, not knowledge!

"You shall not steal! You shall not kill!"—such commandments were once considered sacred; people knelt before them, lowered their heads, and even removed their shoes.

But I ask you: where have there ever been greater robbers and killers than those inspired by such "sacred" laws?

Is not all life itself filled with robbing and killing? And for those rules to be called sacred, was not truth itself killed?

Or was it a death sermon, calling sacred what contradicted life and dissuaded from living?——O my brothers, break up the old law-tablets for me!

I feel for all the past, for I see it abandoned—

—Abandoned to the whim, spirit, and madness of each passing generation, which reinterprets the past as its bridge!

A great potentate might come along, an artful prodigy, bending and stretching all of history to serve as his bridge, his herald, and his crowing rooster.

This, however, is the other danger and my other sympathy: those of the rabble, whose thoughts don't move past their grandfathers— yet for them, history ends there.

Thus, all of the past lies abandoned; for one day, the rabble might take control and drown all of history in shallow waters.

Therefore, O my brothers, a new nobility is needed to challenge the rule of both rabble and potentate and to inscribe the word "noble" on new law-tablets.

For many kinds of nobles are needed for a new nobility! Or, as I once said in parable: "That is divine—that there are gods, but no single God!"

O my brothers, I consecrate and point you toward a new nobility: you shall become the creators, cultivators, and sowers of the future—

—not a nobility that can be bought with trader's gold, for all that has a price is of little worth.

Let your honor henceforth not come from where you came, but from where you are going! Let your will and your forward-seeking feet—these be your new honor!

Not that you served a prince—what is a prince now?—nor that you became a buttress to that which merely wishes to stay standing.

Not that your family became courtly in the royal courts, learning to stand still in shallow waters, like flamingos in gaudy colors:

(for standing still is a skill among courtiers; and all courtiers believe blessedness after death means finally being allowed to sit!)

Nor that a "Holy Spirit" led your ancestors to promised lands, which I do not praise: for where the worst of all trees grew—the cross—there is nothing to praise!

And truly, wherever this "Holy Spirit" led its knights, there you'd find goats and geese, jesters and jesters' heads, leading the way!

O my brothers, let your nobility look forward, not backward! Be exiles from all lands of fathers and forefathers!

Let your children's land be the one you love: let this love be your new nobility—the undiscovered land in farthest seas! For this, I bid your sails search and search!

Make amends to your children for being the children of your fathers: in this way, redeem all the past! This new table do I set over you!

"Why live? All is in vain! To live is to thresh straw; to live is to burn oneself and never get warm."—

This ancient mumbling still passes for "wisdom"; because it is old and smells musty, it is more honored. Even mold ennobles.

Children might speak like this—they avoid fire because it burned them once! There is much childishness in old books of wisdom.

And whoever "threshes straw" endlessly, why should he complain about threshing? Such a fool should be silenced!

Such people sit at the table, bringing nothing with them, not even a good appetite—and then they complain, "All is vain!"

But, my brothers, eating and drinking well is no vain art! Break up the law-tablets of the never-joyous for me!

"To the clean, all things are clean"—so people say. But I say to you: To the swine, all things become swinish!

Thus do the visionaries and bowed-down ones preach (those with bowed hearts as well): "The world itself is a filthy monster."

These are all unclean spirits; especially those who find no peace or rest unless they see the world from the backside—the afterworldly!

I say it to them directly, though it sound harsh: the world resembles man in that it has a backside—this much is true!

There is indeed much filth in the world—this much is true! But that does not make the world a filthy monster!

There is wisdom in the fact that much in the world smells badly: for loathing itself gives wings and divining powers to find fountains!

Even in the best things, there is still something to loathe; and the best is always something that must be overcome.

O my brothers, there is much wisdom in the fact that there is much filth in the world!

Such sayings I have heard the pious afterworldly speak to their consciences, and truly, without malice or deceit—though nothing is more deceitful or malignant in this world!

"Let the world be as it is! Raise not a finger against it!"

"Let whoever wishes to choke, stab, skin, and scrape the people— raise not a finger against it! This way, they shall learn to renounce the world."

"And your own reason—stifle and choke it, for it is a reason of this world. Only then will you learn to renounce the world yourself!"

—Shatter, shatter, O my brothers, those old law-tablets of the pious! Tear apart the maxims of those who malign the world!—

"He who learns much unlearns all violent cravings"—so they whisper to each other in dark alleys.

"Wisdom wearies; nothing is worth the effort; you shall not crave!"—even this new tablet I found hanging in the public square.

Break up this new tablet for me, O my brothers! The weary-of-the-world ones hung it, the preachers of death, and the jailers—for lo, it is but another sermon on slavery:

They learned poorly, too quickly, and not the best; they ate badly, and now their stomachs are ruined.

Their spirit, truly, is a ruined stomach—it persuades them toward death! Verily, my brothers, the spirit is a stomach!

Life is a well of delight, but to him whose stomach is ruined, the father of affliction, every fountain tastes poisoned.

For the lion-willed, discernment is a delight! But he who has grown weary is only "willed"—and every wave plays with him.

And so it is with weak men: they lose themselves on their way, and their weariness eventually asks, "Why did we go on at all? Everything is indifferent!"

To them, it sounds pleasant when they hear this sermon: "Nothing is worth the effort! You shall not will!" Yet this is a sermon for slavery.

O my brothers, Zarathustra brings a fresh, blustering wind to all those weary of the way; many noses will he make sneeze yet!

Even through walls, my free breath blows into prisons and imprisoned spirits!

Willing liberates, for willing is creating—so I teach. And creating is all that you must learn!

Learn from me, too, the art of learning itself—learn it well! He who has ears, let him hear!

There stands the boat—there it goes over, perhaps into the vast unknown; but who wills to enter this "Perhaps"?

None of you wish to enter the death-boat! How, then, can you be weary of the world?

World-weary? And you haven't even left the earth! Eager have I always found you for the earth, still clinging to your own weariness of it!

That drooping lip of yours—it still holds a small worldly desire! And in your eye, is there not a faint glimmer of unforgotten earthly pleasure?

On this earth, there are many fine inventions—some useful, some pleasing—and for their sake, the earth is to be loved.

And many of these fine inventions are like a woman's embrace: useful and pleasant at once.

But you world-weary ones! You idlers of the earth! You should be beaten with stripes, until your limbs are sprightly again.

For if you are not sickly or decrepit, then you are sly loafers or pleasure-seeking cats. And if you will not run gaily once more, then you should—pass away!

Let no one attempt to cure the incurable: so teaches Zarathustra; therefore, you should pass away!

But more courage is needed to make an end than to make a new beginning—this, all doctors and poets know well.

O my brothers, there are law-tablets framed by weariness, and others by laziness, corrupt laziness: though they sound similar, they seek to be heard differently.

Look at this exhausted one! Just a hand's breadth from his goal, yet he lies down obstinately in the dust.

Weary, he yawns at the path, at the earth, at the goal, and at himself; he won't take another step—this brave one!

Now the sun shines on him, and dogs lick his sweat, but he lies there in his stubbornness, preferring to languish—

A hand's breadth from his goal, languishing! You would have to drag him to his heaven by his hair—this hero!

Better still, let him lie where he has fallen, so that sleep, the comforter, may come to him with cooling rain.

Let him lie there until he awakens on his own—until he casts off his weariness, and all that weariness taught him!

Only, my brothers, see to it that you keep the dogs away from him—the idle skulkers, and all the swarming vermin:

All the vermin of the "cultured" that feast on the sweat of every hero!

I form circles around me and set sacred boundaries; ever fewer ascend with me, ever higher mountains. I build a mountain range out of ever holier mountains.

But wherever you would ascend with me, O my brothers, be cautious lest a parasite should ascend with you!

A parasite: that is a reptile, a creeping, cringing reptile, that seeks to fatten itself on your weak and sore places.

And this is its art: it senses where aspiring souls are weary, in your trouble and dejection, in your tender modesty—it builds its loathsome nest there.

Where the strong grow weak, where the noble grow all-too-gentle, there it builds its loathsome nest; the parasite thrives where the great have small sore spots.

What is the highest species of being, and what is the lowest? The parasite is the lowest species; yet he who belongs to the highest species supports the most parasites.

For the soul that has the longest ladder, that can reach deepest down—how could it not support the most parasites upon it?

The most expansive soul, able to run, stray, and rove furthest within itself; the most necessary soul, that throws itself into chance out of sheer joy:

The soul in Being, that plunges into Becoming; the soul that possesses, that seeks to attain desire and longing;

The soul fleeing from itself, overtaking itself in the broadest circles; the wisest soul, to which even folly speaks sweetly;

The most self-loving soul, in which all things have their flow and counterflow, their ebb and tide—oh, how could the highest soul fail to carry the worst parasites?

O my brothers, am I cruel? But I say: Whatever falls, that shall one also push!

Everything of today—it falls, it decays. Who would preserve it? But I—I wish also to push it!

Do you know the delight that comes from rolling stones down precipitous slopes? See how these men of today roll into my depths!

A prelude am I to better players, O my brothers! An example! Do as I do!

And if you do not teach someone to fly, then I urge you—teach him to fall faster!

I love the brave; but it is not enough to be a swordsman. One must also know where to use swordsmanship!

And often it takes greater bravery to keep silent and pass by, reserving oneself for a worthier foe!

You should only have foes to hate, but not foes to despise: you must be proud of your foes. This I have already taught.

Go your own ways, and let the people go theirs—gloomy ways, indeed, on which not a single hope glints anymore!

Let the trader rule there, where all that still glitters is trader's gold. The age of kings is over: that which now calls itself the people is unworthy of kings.

See how these peoples now act like traders themselves: they pick out small advantages from all sorts of rubbish!

They lay traps for one another, they trick one another, and they call it "good neighborliness." O blessed distant time when a people could say, "I will be master over peoples!"

For, my brothers, the best should rule, and the best also wills to rule! And where the teaching is different, the best is absent.

If they received bread without labor, alas, what would they cry for? Their survival—that is their real entertainment; and they should find it hard!

Beasts of prey are what they are; in their "working," there is plundering; in their "earning," there is trickery! Therefore, they should have it hard!

They shall thus become better beasts of prey—subtler, cleverer, more human-like, for man is the best beast of prey.

Already man has robbed all animals of their virtues, which is why life has been hardest for man.

Only the birds are beyond him still. And if man should yet learn to fly, alas, how high would his greed soar!

Thus I would have man and woman: fit for war, the one; fit for motherhood, the other; yet both fit for dancing, with head and legs alike.

And lost be the day in which we have not danced a measure, and false be every truth that has not had laughter along with it!

As for arranging marriages: see that it is not a poor arrangement! Too hastily have you arranged them; hence follows marriage-breaking.

And better marriage-breaking than marriage-bending, marriage-lying! Thus spoke a woman to me: "Indeed, I broke the marriage, but first the marriage broke me!"

The poorly matched are always the most revengeful: they make everyone suffer for the fact that they no longer run singly.

On that account, I want the honest ones to say to one another, "We love each other; let us see to it that we maintain our love! Or shall our pledging be mere blundering?"

"Let us give ourselves a set term and a small marriage, that we may see if we are fit for the great marriage! It is a great matter always to be two."

Thus do I counsel all honest ones; and what would be my love for the Superman, and for all that is to come, if I should counsel otherwise?

Not only to propagate yourselves onward but upward—therefore, O my brothers, may the garden of marriage help you!

Whoever grows wise by learning about ancient origins will eventually seek out the sources of the future and new beginnings.

Oh, my friends, it won't be long before new people rise up, and fresh springs rush down into new depths.

For earthquakes—yes, they close up many wells and cause much suffering. But they also reveal inner powers and hidden things. Earthquakes bring new springs to the surface. In the quakes of ancient peoples, new springs burst forth.

And whoever shouts, "Look! Here is a well for all those who thirst, a heart for all who long, a will for many instruments!"—around him, people will gather; many will try to follow.

Who can lead, and who must follow—that is where attempts are made! Oh, what a long journey of seeking, solving, failing, learning, and trying again!

Human society: it is an attempt—that is my teaching—a long search. But it seeks a true leader!

It is an attempt, my friends! And not a "contract"! Tear up that word, please, tear up that word of the soft-hearted and half-hearted!

Oh, my friends! Where is the greatest threat to the future of humanity? Is it not with those who are good and just?

They are the ones who say and believe in their hearts, "We already know what's good and just, we possess it. Woe to those who still search for it!"

And whatever harm the wicked may do, the harm from the good is the most dangerous harm!

And whatever harm the world-haters may do, the harm from the good is the most dangerous harm!

Oh, my friends, long ago, someone looked into the hearts of the good and just and said, "They are like Pharisees." But people did not understand him.

The good and just could not see it; their spirit was trapped in their own sense of righteousness. The foolishness of the good is beyond understanding.

It's true, though: the good must be Pharisees—they have no choice!

The good must condemn anyone who creates his own virtues! That is the truth!

The second person who discovered their country—the land, the hearts, and the soil of the good and just—was the one who asked, "Whom do they hate most?"

They hate the creator the most, the one who breaks old laws and values, the one who challenges—them, they call the lawbreaker.

For the good—they cannot create; they are always the start of the end.

They condemn anyone who writes new values on new tablets. They sacrifice the future for themselves—they condemn the entire human future!

The good—they have always been the beginning of the end.

Oh, my friends, have you understood these words? And what I once said about the "last man"?

Where is the greatest danger to the future of humanity? Is it not with those who are good and just?

Break it up, break it up, I ask you, the good and just! Oh, my friends, have you understood these words?

You run from me? Are you scared? Do you shiver at this word?

Oh, my brothers, when I told you to break apart the good and the law-tablets of the good, it was then that I set humanity on its open seas.

And now comes the great fear, the vast outlook, the overwhelming sickness, the deep nausea, the true seasickness.

The good taught you false shores and false security; you were raised in the lies of the good. Everything has been twisted and warped by the good.

But the one who discovered the land of "man" also discovered the land of "man's future." Now, you shall be sailors for me—brave, steady sailors!

Prepare yourselves, my brothers, learn to keep yourselves afloat! The sea storms: many will try to lift themselves again by clinging to you.

The sea storms: everything is in the sea. Well then! Take heart, you old sailor souls!

What of the homeland! Our helm points to where our children's land is! That way, stormier than the sea, storms our great longing!

"Why so hard?" the charcoal asked the diamond one day. "Are we not close relatives?"

Why so soft? Oh, my brothers, I ask you this: are you not my brothers?

Why so soft, so yielding and obedient? Why so much denying and giving up in your hearts? Why is there so little destiny in your eyes?

And if you don't want to be forces of fate, if you aren't unyielding, then how can you one day triumph with me?

And if your hardness won't reflect, cut, and carve, how will you one day create with me?

Creators are hard. And it must feel like a blessing to press your hand on centuries as if they were wax.

A blessing to inscribe the will of centuries as if on brass—harder than brass, nobler than brass. Only the noblest is truly hard.

This new command, oh my brothers, I give to you: Become hard!

Oh, my Will! You who change with every need, my deepest need! Keep me from small victories!

You, destiny of my soul, whom I call fate! You within me! You above me! Protect and preserve me for one great fate!

And your ultimate strength, my Will, save it for your final moment—so that you may be unyielding in your victory! Ah, who has not been lost in victory?

Ah, whose eyes have not dimmed in that intoxicated twilight? Ah, whose feet have not stumbled and forgotten how to stand in victory!

So that I may be ready one day and ripened in the great noontime: ready and ripe like the glowing metal, the storm-bearing cloud, the full milk-udder:

Ready for myself and for my deepest Will: a bow eager for its arrow, an arrow eager for its star.

A star, ready and ripe at noon, glowing, pierced, blessed by the sun's fierce rays:

A sun itself, and an unbreakable sun-will, ready to be destroyed in victory!

Oh Will, you who change with every need, my deepest need! Spare me for one great victory!

Thus spoke Zarathustra.

Chapter 57
The Convalescent

One morning, not long after returning to his cave, Zarathustra jumped up from his bed like a madman, shouting in a terrible voice and acting as if someone still lay there who refused to get up. Zarathustra's voice was so intense that his animals approached him in fear, and all the nearby creatures fled from their caves and hiding places—flying, fluttering, creeping, or leaping, each according to its own way of moving. Zarathustra then spoke these words:

"Up, deep thought, from my depths! I am your rooster and morning dawn, you sluggish reptile—get up! Get up! My voice will crow you awake!

Unlock the chains from your ears: listen! I want to hear you! Get up! Get up! There is thunder enough to wake even the graves!

Rub the sleep and blindness from your eyes! Look at me with your eyes as well as your ears: my voice is a cure, even for those born blind.

And once you are awake, you shall stay awake. I don't wake great-grandmothers from their sleep just to tell them to sleep on!

You're stirring, stretching, gasping? Get up! Get up! No gasping—speak to me! Zarathustra is calling you, Zarathustra the godless!

I, Zarathustra, advocate for life, advocate for suffering, advocate for the cycle of life—I am calling you, my deepest thought!

Joy to me! You're coming—I hear you! My abyss speaks; I've brought my deepest depths into the light!

Joy to me! Come here! Give me your hand—ah, no, let it be! Oh! Disgust, disgust, disgust…oh, woe is me!"

But as soon as Zarathustra spoke these words, he collapsed as if dead, lying still for a long time. When he finally came to, he was pale and trembling, and he continued to lie there without eating or drinking. This state lasted seven days, and his animals stayed by his side day and night, with the eagle occasionally flying off to fetch food. It laid whatever it found on Zarathustra's bed, so that he was soon surrounded by yellow and red berries, grapes, rosy apples, fragrant herbs, and pine cones. Two lambs, which the eagle had stolen from shepherds, were even stretched out at his feet.

Finally, after seven days, Zarathustra sat up on his bed, took a rosy apple in his hand, smelled it, and found its scent pleasing. Then his animals sensed it was time to speak.

"O Zarathustra," they said, "you have been lying here with heavy eyes for seven days. Won't you stand on your feet again?

Step out of your cave; the world awaits you like a garden. The wind carries heavy fragrances searching for you, and all the brooks seem eager to follow you.

Everything longs for you since you have been alone for these seven days—step out of your cave! Everything wants to heal you!

Has some new knowledge come to you, a bitter, troubling knowledge? You lay like dough that had risen, and your soul swelled beyond all its bounds."

"O my animals," answered Zarathustra, "keep talking like this and let me listen! Your words are refreshing to me. Where there is talk, the world feels like a garden to me.

How wonderful it is that we have words and sounds; aren't words and sounds like rainbows and pretend bridges between things that are forever separate?

Each soul has its own world; to each soul, every other soul is like a distant land.

Even among those who are very similar, appearances can be delightfully deceptive: because even a small gap can be the hardest to cross.

For me—how could there be anything outside of me? There is no outside! But we forget this when we hear sounds; how lovely it is that we can forget!

Weren't names and sounds given to things so that people could find joy in them? Talking is a beautiful, silly thing; with it, people dance above everything. How lovely are all words and the lies of sounds! With sounds, our love dances across colorful rainbows."

"O Zarathustra," then said his animals, "for those who think as we do, everything seems to dance on its own: things come and reach out a hand, laugh, flee—and return again.

Everything goes, everything returns; the wheel of existence rolls forever. Everything dies, everything blooms again; the year of life runs on endlessly.

Everything breaks apart, everything comes back together; the house of existence rebuilds itself eternally. All things separate, all things greet each other again; the ring of existence remains forever true to itself.

Each moment begins existence, around every 'Here' rolls the ball to 'There.' The center is everywhere. The path of eternity is crooked."

"O you jokers and music-makers!" answered Zarathustra with a smile, "how well you know what must be completed in seven days—

And how that monster crept into my throat and nearly choked me! But I bit its head off and spit it out.

And you—you made a song about it? Now I'm lying here, still worn out from the biting and spitting, still sick from my own rescue.

And you saw it all? O my animals, are you also cruel? Did you enjoy watching my great suffering like people do? For man is a cruel creature.

On earth, he is happiest at tragedies, bullfights, and crucifixions; and when he invented hell, that was like creating his heaven on earth.

When the great man cries out, the little man immediately runs to him, tongue hanging out, eager for more. Yet he calls this his 'compassion.'

The little man, especially the poet—how passionately he blames life in his words! Listen to him, but don't miss the joy he takes in all his complaints.

These accusers of life—life overpowers them with just a look. 'Do you love me?' life asks with a smirk; 'Wait a bit, I don't have time for you right now.'

Man is a cruel creature toward himself, and in all who call themselves 'sinners,' 'cross-bearers,' or 'penitents,' don't overlook the strange pleasure they take in their suffering and accusations!

And I myself—do I want to be man's accuser because of this? Ah, my animals, here's the one thing I've learned so far: that for man, his own evil is necessary for his best—

That everything evil is the greatest strength and the hardest stone for the highest creator; and that man must become both better and more evil."

"I wasn't bound to this torment just to know that man is bad—I shouted out, like no one ever has:

'Ah, his evil is so small! Ah, his best is so small!'

The great disgust for humanity—it choked me and climbed into my throat. It was just as the soothsayer had predicted: 'Everything is the same, nothing matters, knowledge strangles.'

A long twilight limped before me, a deadly tired, deadly drunken sadness that spoke with a yawning mouth.

'He comes back forever, the man you're tired of, the small man,' yawned my sadness, dragging its foot and unable to sleep.

The human earth became a cave to me; its heart caved in. All living things turned into human dust, bones, and rotting past.

My sighing rested on all human graves, unable to rise again. My sighs and questions croaked and choked, gnawing and nagging day and night:

'Ah, man returns forever! The small man returns forever!'

I had once seen both of them bare—the greatest man and the small man—so alike, all too human, even the greatest!

All too small, even the greatest man! That was my disgust with humanity! And the eternal return of the small man! That was my disgust with all existence!

Ah, disgust! Disgust! Disgust!" Thus spoke Zarathustra, sighing and shuddering as he remembered his illness. Then his animals stopped him from speaking further.

"Don't say any more, you who are recovering!" his animals replied, "but go outside where the world waits for you like a garden.

Go out to the roses, the bees, and the flocks of doves! And especially to the songbirds, to learn singing from them!

For singing is for the recovering; the healthy ones may talk. And when the healthy also want songs, they want different songs than those who are recovering."

"O you jokers and music-boxes, be quiet!" replied Zarathustra, smiling at his animals. "You know too well what comfort I made for myself in those seven days!

That I have to sing once more—that comfort I made for myself, and this recovery. Do you want to make another tune out of it?"

"Don't speak further," his animals replied again. "Instead, you who are recovering, prepare yourself first a lyre, a new lyre! For look, O Zarathustra! For your new songs, you need new lyres."

"Sing and overflow with joy, O Zarathustra, heal your soul with new songs, so you can bear your great destiny, one that no one else has faced!

For we, your animals, know who you are and who you must become: you are the teacher of the eternal return—that is now your fate!

You must be the first to teach this truth—how could this great destiny not be both your greatest challenge and your greatest trial?

Yes, we know what you teach: that all things return endlessly, and we return with them, that we have already lived countless times, and all things with us.

You teach that there is a grand cycle of Becoming, a wondrous great year; like an hourglass, it must turn over and over again, to empty and refill.

So that all those years are alike, in both big and small ways, so that we ourselves, in every great year, repeat ourselves, both in the grand and the small.

And if you were to die now, O Zarathustra, we even know what you would say to yourself then—but your animals beg you not to die yet!

You would speak, not with fear, but rather with lightness and joy, as a heavy weight and worry would be lifted from you, you most patient one!

'Now I die and fade away,' you would say, 'and in a moment, I am nothing. Souls are just as mortal as bodies.

But the web of causes, in which I am entwined, will recreate me! I am part of the causes of the eternal return.

I will come again with this sun, with this earth, with this eagle, with this serpent—not to a new life, or a better life, or a different life:

—I return eternally to this same life, in all its greatness and smallness, to once again teach the eternal return of all things—

—To speak again the words of earth's great noon, of humankind's great noon, to proclaim once more the coming of the Superman.

I have spoken my word. My word is my end: so does my eternal destiny demand— as a prophet, I fade away!

The hour has come for the one going down to bless himself. Thus ends Zarathustra's descent.'"

When the animals had spoken these words, they fell silent and waited for Zarathustra to respond; but Zarathustra did not notice their silence. Instead, he lay quietly with his eyes closed as if sleeping, though he was not asleep; he was communing with his soul. Seeing him so silent, the serpent and the eagle respected the stillness around him and quietly withdrew.

Chapter 58

The Great Longing

O my soul, I taught you to speak of "today" as you would "once upon a time" or "in the past," and to dance freely across every place and moment.

O my soul, I freed you from all hidden corners, brushing away dust, spiders, and twilight from you.

O my soul, I washed away the small shames and narrow virtues, and urged you to stand bare under the sun's gaze.

With the storm called "spirit," I blew over your restless sea, scattering all clouds; I even defeated the force called "sin."

O my soul, I gave you the strength to say No like the storm, and Yes like the open sky: stay calm as the light, and walk boldly through storms of denial.

O my soul, I returned to you the freedom over all that is created and uncreated; who but you knows the thrill of what lies ahead?

O my soul, I taught you a contempt that doesn't destroy, the great, loving contempt that loves deepest where it scorns most.

O my soul, I showed you how to persuade even the ground beneath you to come to you, like the sun persuades the sea to rise to it.

O my soul, I removed from you all forms of submission and bowing, and gave you titles like "Change of Need" and "Fate."

O my soul, I gave you new names and colorful playthings, calling you "Fate," "Circle of Circles," "Cord of Time," and "Azure Bell."

O my soul, I let all wisdom flow into your domain to taste every new wine, and even the most ancient, potent wines of knowledge.

O my soul, I bathed you in every sun, every night, every silence, every longing: you grew strong, like a vine for me.

O my soul, now you stand rich and heavy with ripe, golden clusters of grapes, swelling and weighed down by your happiness, waiting in fullness but shy in your waiting.

O my soul, is there any soul more loving, more vast, more boundless than you? Where else could future and past come together so closely?

O my soul, I've given you everything, and my hands are empty now because of you—yet now! Now you look at me, smiling and a bit sorrowful, saying: "Which of us owes gratitude?

Does not the giver owe thanks because the receiver accepted? Is giving not a necessity? Is receiving not—pity?"

O my soul, I understand your sorrowful smile: your abundance itself reaches out with longing hands!

Your fullness looks out over the storming seas, searching and waiting; the longing of your overflowing heart shines from the bright heavens of your eyes!

And truly, O my soul! Who could see your smile and not feel moved to tears? Even the angels would weep, touched by the kindness of your smile.

Your kindness, your over-kindness—it chooses not to complain or cry. Yet, O my soul, your smile yearns for tears, and your quivering mouth for sobs.

"Isn't all weeping a form of complaint? And all complaining, a kind of accusation?" you tell yourself; so, O my soul, you'd rather smile than pour out your sorrow—

—rather than letting all your grief flow out in a flood of tears, all the sorrow of your fullness and the longing of the vine for the harvest and the vintager's knife!

But if you will not weep, if you hold back your purple sadness, then you must sing, O my soul!—Look, I smile as I say this to you: You must sing with a passionate song, until all seas calm to listen to your longing—

—until across those still seas glides the golden boat, the wonder of gold, around which all good, bad, and marvelous things play and dance:

—also many large and small creatures, and all with light, wondrous feet, so they can race along violet-blue paths—

—towards the golden wonder, the free-moving boat, and its master: he who is the vintager, waiting with his diamond blade for the harvest—

—your great deliverer, O my soul, the nameless one—who will one day be given names in future songs! And truly, your breath already carries the scent of those songs—

—you already glow and dream, you drink eagerly from every deep echoing well of comfort, your sadness already resting in the joy of songs to come!

O my soul, now I have given you everything, even my last possession, and now my hands are empty because of you: that I asked you to sing was my last gift to give!

That I asked you to sing—now say, tell me: which of us now owes thanks? Or better yet, sing to me, sing, O my soul! And let me be the one to thank you!

Thus spoke Zarathustra.

Chapter 59
The Second Dance Song

Into your eyes I looked recently, O Life: I saw gold glimmer in your dark eyes, and my heart stopped with joy:

I saw a golden boat glimmering on dark waters, sinking, drinking, flashing, a golden swing-boat!

You cast a playful, questioning, melting glance toward my dancing feet, a look tossed my way:

You moved your little hands twice with a playful rattle—and my feet took on a wild rhythm.

My heels rose high, my toes listened intently—they wanted to know you: doesn't a dancer listen through his toes?

I leapt toward you, but you slipped back from my reach; your flowing, flying locks waved toward me as you pulled away!

I sprang away from you and your snakelike tresses; you stood there half-turned, your eyes offering a soft invitation.

With mischievous glances, you teach me winding paths; my feet learn crafty moves along winding trails!

I fear you when you're close, I love you from afar; your escape draws me, your pursuit secures me—I would suffer anything for you!

For you, whose coolness stirs, whose hate misguides, whose flight binds, whose teasing begs:

Who wouldn't hate you, O great temptress, enchantress, searcher, capturer! Who wouldn't love you, you innocent, restless, wind-swift, childlike sinner!

Where are you pulling me now, you teasing, reckless one? Now you trick me with your flight; your sweet play both entices and frustrates!

I chase after you, following even the faintest of tracks. Where are you? Give me your hand! Or even just your finger!

Here are caves and shadows—we could get lost! Stop! Wait! Don't you see the owls and bats flitting about?

You bat! You owl! Are you trying to trick me? Where are we? Did you learn this barking and howling from the dogs?

You grin at me sweetly with your little white teeth; your mischievous eyes flash at me, your curly mane peeks out from below!

This is a wild dance over rocks and rough ground—I am the hunter—will you be my hound or my chamois?

Now beside me! Now swiftly, wickedly leaping! Now up! And over!—Alas! I fell as I overreached!

Oh, look at me here, humbled and asking for mercy! I'd gladly walk with you—to some lovelier place!

In paths of love, through gardens of bright flowers, calm and neat! Or along the lake, where golden fish dance and swim!

Are you tired now? Look up there—sheep and stripes of the sunset. Isn't it sweet to sleep to the shepherd's pipe?

You're so very weary? I'll carry you there; just let your arm fall. And if you're thirsty—I have something for you, though your lips may not care to drink it!

Ah, you sly, quick, sneaky serpent and lurking witch! Where did you go? But I feel your touch on my face, two spots itching, red blotches!

I'm truly tired of always being your shepherd. You witch, if I've sung to you all this time, now you'll cry for me!

To the rhythm of my whip, you'll dance and cry! I haven't forgotten my whip—no, not at all!

Then Life spoke back to me, keeping her lovely ears covered:

"O Zarathustra! Don't crack that whip so harshly! You know loud noise kills thought—and just now, I had such gentle thoughts.

We're both true wanderers, beyond good and evil, finding our own island and our green meadow—just the two of us! So we must be kind to each other!

And even if we don't love each other completely from the depths of our hearts—must we hold a grudge if our love isn't perfect?

I'm always friendly with you, even too friendly, you know it. And that's because I envy your Wisdom. Oh, that mad, old fool, Wisdom!

If your Wisdom ever left you, oh! my love for you would quickly leave as well."

Then Life looked thoughtfully around and behind and said quietly, "O Zarathustra, you're not faithful enough to me!

You don't love me as much as you claim; I know you're thinking of leaving me soon.

There's an old, heavy, echoing clock; it booms through the night up to your cave.

When you hear it chime midnight, you think to yourself, between the first and twelfth strikes—

You think, O Zarathustra, I know it—you're thinking of leaving me soon!"

"Yes," I replied slowly, "but you know it too"—and I whispered something in her ear, into her messy, yellow, wild locks.

"You know that, O Zarathustra? No one else knows that—"

We looked at each other, gazing over the green meadow where the cool evening was drifting, and we wept together. Then, in that moment, Life was dearer to me than all my Wisdom had ever been.

Thus spoke Zarathustra.
One!
O man! Take heed!
Two!
What does deep midnight's voice indeed say?
Three!
"I slept my sleep—
Four!
From the deepest dream I've woken and plead:
Five!
The world is deep,
Six!
And deeper than day itself can see.
Seven!
Deep is its sorrow—
Eight!
But joy is deeper still than grief could be.
Nine!
Sorrow says: Go away!
Ten!
But joy longs for eternity—
Eleven!
Yearns for profound eternity!"
Twelve!

Chapter 60
The Seven Seals
(or, The Yes and Amen Song)

If I am a diviner and filled with the spirit of prophecy, wandering on high mountain ridges between two seas—

Wandering between the past and future like a heavy cloud, avoiding the hot plains and all that is weary, unable to live or die—

Ready for the lightning within its dark core, ready for the redeeming flash, filled with lightnings that shout Yes! that laugh Yes! ready to release flashes of insight—

Blessed is he who holds such power! And truly, long must he wait like a heavy storm on the mountain, who will one day ignite the light of the future!

Oh, how could I not be passionate for Eternity and for the marriage ring of rings—the ring of eternal return?

Never yet have I found the woman with whom I'd want children, unless it be this woman I love: for I love you, O Eternity!

For I love you, O Eternity!

If ever my wrath has opened graves, moved boundaries, or cast shattered law-tablets into the depths—

If ever my scorn has scattered rotting words to the winds, and I've come like a broom to clear away cobwebs, like a cleansing wind through old charnel houses—

If ever I've sat rejoicing where old gods lie buried, blessing and loving the world, beside the graves of ancient world-condemners—

For even temples and graves of gods I love, as long as the sky peers through their broken roofs with pure eyes; gladly do I sit like grass and red poppies on ruined churches—

Oh, how could I not be passionate for Eternity and for the marriage ring of rings—the ring of eternal return?

Never yet have I found the woman with whom I'd want children, unless it be this woman I love: for I love you, O Eternity!

For I love you, O Eternity!

If ever I've felt the breath of creation, and the heavenly necessity that compels even chance to dance like stars—

If ever I've laughed with the laughter of the creative lightning, followed by the long thunder of deeds, rumbling yet obedient—

If ever I've played dice with the gods at the sacred table of the earth, so that the earth quaked and spewed fire—

For the earth is a divine table, trembling with fresh decrees and the gods' dice-casts:

Oh, how could I not be passionate for Eternity and for the marriage ring of rings—the ring of eternal return?

Never yet have I found the woman with whom I'd want children, unless it be this woman I love: for I love you, O Eternity!

For I love you, O Eternity!

If ever I've drunk deeply from the spicy and rich cup where all things are blended together:

If ever my hand has brought together the farthest and the closest, fire with spirit, joy with sorrow, and the harshest with the gentlest:

If I myself am a bit of the saving salt that makes everything blend perfectly in the mixture: -For there is a salt that unites good with evil; and even the worst has worth, as seasoning and as final, overflowing spice:

Oh, how could I not be passionate for Eternity, and for the marriage ring of rings—the ring of return?

Never yet have I found the woman with whom I'd want children, unless it's this woman I love: for I love you, O Eternity!

For I love you, O Eternity!

If I am drawn to the sea, and all that belongs to it, and love it most when it angrily opposes me:

If the joy of exploration is in me, driving sails toward the unknown, if the sailor's thrill is part of my thrill:

If ever my joy has shouted, "The shore has disappeared—now the last chain has fallen from me—

The boundless roars around me, far-off sparkles space and time for me—well! cheer up! old heart!"—

Oh, how could I not be passionate for Eternity, and for the marriage ring of rings—the ring of return?

Never yet have I found the woman with whom I'd want children, unless it's this woman I love: for I love you, O Eternity!

For I love you, O Eternity!

If my virtue is a dancer's virtue, and if I've often leaped with both feet into golden-green delight: If my wickedness is a laughing wickedness, feeling at home among roses and lily hedges:

Or is all evil present in laughter? But it is made pure and forgiven by its own joy:

And if my beginning and end is that all heavy things shall become light, all bodies become dancers, and every spirit a bird: truly, that is my beginning and my end!

Oh, how could I not be passionate for Eternity, and for the marriage ring of rings—the ring of return?

Never yet have I found the woman with whom I'd want children, unless it's this woman I love: for I love you, O Eternity!

For I love you, O Eternity!

If I have ever spread out a calm sky above me, and soared into my own heaven on my own wings:

If I have swum playfully in deep, glowing distances, and if the bird-like wisdom of my freedom has come to me:

Thus speaks this wisdom: "Look, there is no above and no below! Throw yourself around—outward, backward, you weightless one! Sing! Speak no more!

Aren't all words made for the heavy? Don't all words lie to those who are light? Sing! Speak no more!"

Oh, how could I not be passionate for Eternity, and for the marriage ring of rings—the ring of return?

Never yet have I found the woman with whom I'd want children, unless it's this woman I love: for I love you, O Eternity!

For I love you, O Eternity!

Chapter 61
The Honey Sacrifice

And again, months and years passed over Zarathustra's soul, but he barely noticed; however, his hair had turned white. One day, as he sat on a stone in front of his cave, gazing calmly into the distance—where one could see out over the sea and beyond winding chasms—his animals circled around him thoughtfully and eventually sat in front of him.

"O Zarathustra," they said, "are you perhaps looking out for your happiness?" "What does my happiness matter?" he replied. "I stopped striving for happiness long ago; I strive for my work." "O Zarathustra," his animals said again, "you say that like one who has had more than enough of good things. Don't you lie in a sky-blue lake of happiness?" "You jesters," Zarathustra answered, smiling, "how well you chose that comparison! But you also know my happiness is heavy, not like a flowing wave of water. It presses on me and won't leave me, more like molten pitch."

Then his animals again circled thoughtfully around him and settled back in front of him. "O Zarathustra," they said, "is that why you're becoming yellower and darker, though your hair is white and flaxen? Look, you sit in your pitch!" "What are you saying, my animals?" Zarathustra laughed. "I was exaggerating when I spoke of pitch. What happens to me happens to all fruits when they ripen. It's the honey in my veins that thickens my blood and quiets my soul." "So it is, O Zarathustra," answered his animals, drawing closer to him, "but won't you climb a high mountain today? The air is pure, and today one can see more of the world than ever." "Yes, my animals," he replied, "you advise me well and in line with my heart. I will climb a high mountain today! But make sure there is honey ready, yellow, white, good, ice-cool, golden honeycomb. For when I'm high up, I want to make a honey-sacrifice."

When Zarathustra reached the summit, he sent his animals back to the cave, leaving him alone. Then he laughed from deep within, looked around, and spoke aloud:

"That I spoke of sacrifices and honey-sacrifices, that was merely a trick in speech—a useful foolishness! Here on this peak, I can speak more freely than before mountain caves or around the domestic animals of hermits.

Sacrifice? I give away what is given to me, a spender with a thousand hands. How could I call that sacrificing?

And when I desired honey, I only wanted bait—sweet syrup and sticky nectar, which even makes the mouths of grumbling bears and strange, sulky birds water.

The best bait, just like hunters and fishermen need. For if the world is like a dark forest of animals and a playground for all wild hunters, then to me it seems, rather—and preferably—a deep, rich sea."

–A sea full of brightly colored fish and crabs that even the gods might envy, tempting them to become fishers themselves and cast their nets—so rich is the world, filled with amazing things, big and small!

Especially the human world, the sea of humanity—to it, I now cast my golden fishing rod and say: Open up, you human depths!

Open up, and send me your fish and shining crabs! With my best bait, I will lure the strangest human fish to me today!

I cast out my own happiness across every place, from east to west, to see if many human fish will take hold and be drawn to my happiness;

Until, nibbling at my sharp, hidden hooks, they'll have to rise to my height, these colorful creatures of the deep, as I become the craftiest fisher of humans.

For that is what I am from the heart and from the beginning—drawing, uplifting, training; a guide, a teacher, a mentor, who once wisely counseled himself: "Become what you are!"

So let people come to me now; for I still await the signs that my time to descend has come; I'm not yet ready to go down to be among people.

That's why I wait here, crafty and scornful on high mountains, neither impatient nor patient, but someone who has even forgotten patience—because I no longer "suffer."

My fate gives me time; maybe it has forgotten me? Or perhaps it sits behind a big stone, catching flies?

And truly, I'm in no hurry with my eternal fate, because it neither chases nor pressures me, but gives me time for laughter and play; and so, today, I climbed this high mountain to fish.

Has anyone ever caught fish on a high mountain? And if it's foolishness, what I'm doing here, it's still better than waiting down below, turning solemn and sickly—

Becoming a grumbling, wrathful preacher out of waiting, an angry voice on the mountain that shouts down to the valleys: "Listen, or I'll punish you with the wrath of God!"

Not that I hold any grudge against such angry voices; they are amusing enough to me! They have to be impatient now, those loud, echoing drums who must speak now or never!

But I and my fate—we don't speak to the Present, nor to the Never; we have patience and time and more than time for speaking. For one day it will come, and it cannot be missed.

What must come one day and not be missed? Our great Hazard, our great and distant human kingdom, the Zarathustra kingdom of a thousand years—

How far away is that "distance"? What does it matter to me? But for that reason, I am no less sure of it—I stand secure with both feet on this ground;

On an eternal ground, on hard, ancient rock, on this highest, firmest mountain ridge, where all winds come to meet, as to the storm's dividing point, asking: Where? and From where? and Where to?

Here, laugh, laugh, my hearty, healthy mischief! Cast down your shining laughter of scorn from these high mountains! Lure for me, with your glimmer, the finest human fish!

And whatever belongs to me in all the seas, whatever is truly mine in all things—fish that out for me, bring it up to me: for that, I wait, the boldest of all fishers.

Out! out! my fishing-hook! Down you go, baited with my happiness! Drip your sweetest drops, honey of my heart! Bite, fishing-hook, into the belly of all black sorrows!

Look out, look out, my eye! Oh, how many seas lie round about me, what dawning human futures! And above me—what rosy-red stillness! What unclouded silence!

Chapter 62
The Cry of Distress

The next day, Zarathustra sat once more on the stone in front of his cave while his animals roamed outside to bring back new food—and more honey, for Zarathustra had used up every last drop of his old supply. As he sat there, tracing the shadow of his figure on the ground with a stick, he was deep in thought—though not about himself or his shadow. Suddenly, he started and recoiled, for he saw another shadow beside his own. Looking around quickly, he saw the soothsayer standing beside him—the same one whom he'd once hosted, the prophet of great weariness, who had taught that "All is the same, nothing is worthwhile, life has no meaning, knowledge suffocates." But now, his face had changed, and when Zarathustra looked into his eyes, he felt a jolt in his heart: so much dark omen and ashy-gray lightning flashed across the soothsayer's face.

Sensing Zarathustra's reaction, the soothsayer wiped his face as if to erase its expression; Zarathustra did the same. After they both silently composed themselves, they extended their hands to each other as a sign that they wished to reconnect.

"Welcome here," said Zarathustra. "You prophet of great weariness. Your time as my tablemate and guest shall not be forgotten. Eat and drink with me again today, and pardon an old man who dares to be cheerful in your presence!"

"A cheerful old man?" replied the soothsayer, shaking his head. "Whoever you are, Zarathustra, or wish to be, you have stayed up here for too long—soon your vessel will no longer rest on dry land!"

"Do I rest on dry land, then?" asked Zarathustra with a laugh.

"The waves around your mountain," replied the soothsayer, "are rising and rising—the waves of distress and suffering. Soon, they will lift your vessel too and carry you away."

Zarathustra fell silent and looked thoughtful.

"Do you hear nothing yet?" continued the soothsayer. "Do you not hear the rushing and roaring from below?"

Once again, Zarathustra was silent and listened; then he heard a long, deep cry echoing from abyss to abyss, passed along by each as if no one wanted to hold on to it, so terrible did it sound.

"You ill-fated prophet," Zarathustra said at last, "that is a cry of distress—a human cry, perhaps from a dark sea. But what does human suffering mean to me? Do you know what my last temptation is, the sin that awaits me?"

"Pity!" exclaimed the soothsayer, his voice full of emotion, raising both hands. "O Zarathustra, I have come to tempt you into your last sin!"

Hardly had he spoken these words when the cry came again, louder, more frightening, and closer than before. "Do you hear it, Zarathustra?" called the soothsayer. "The cry concerns you—it calls for you: 'Come, come, come; it is time, it is the highest time!'"

Zarathustra was silent, troubled and shaken; finally, he asked hesitantly, "Who is it that calls for me?"

"But you know, surely," replied the soothsayer earnestly. "Why are you hiding from it? It is the higher man who cries for you!"

"The higher man?" Zarathustra cried, horrified. "What does he want? What does he want? The higher man! What is he doing here?" And he broke out in a sweat.

The soothsayer ignored Zarathustra's shock, continuing to listen intently to the depths. But when all fell silent again, he looked back and saw Zarathustra trembling.

"O Zarathustra," he said sorrowfully, "you don't look like one who is dizzy with joy. You'll have to dance, or else you'll stumble!

But even if you dance and leap with all your might, no one can say to me, 'Behold, here dances the last joyous man!'

Anyone who came to this height in search of him would be disappointed; he would find caves, yes, and hiding places for the concealed, but no rich veins of happiness, no treasure chambers, no new mines of gold."

Happiness—how could anyone find happiness among those who are buried alive, so alone and cut off? Must I still search for the last happiness on the Blessed Isles, far away across forgotten seas?

But all is the same; nothing matters; there's no point in seeking. There are no more Blessed Isles!"—

So sighed the soothsayer, but with that last sigh, Zarathustra became calm and confident again, like someone stepping from a dark abyss into the light. "No! No! Three times no!" he cried out in a strong voice, stroking his beard. "I know better than that! There are still Blessed Isles! Be silent, you sack of sorrow and sighs!

Stop splashing like a rain cloud in the morning! Look at me— drenched and dripping from your misery, soaked like a dog! Now I'm going to shake myself dry and walk away from you! Don't be surprised if I seem rude. This is my own court.

As for the 'higher man'—very well! I'll go seek him right now in those woods; that's where his cry came from. Maybe he's being attacked by some evil beast. He's on my land, so he'll be safe here! And believe me, there are plenty of evil beasts around me."

With that, Zarathustra turned to leave. Then the soothsayer called out, "O Zarathustra, you're a sly one! I know what you're doing—you just want to get rid of me! You'd rather run into the forest and set traps for wild animals!

But what good will that do you? By evening, I'll be back in your cave, sitting like a heavy, patient block, just waiting for you!"

"So be it!" Zarathustra shouted back as he walked away. "Whatever's in my cave is yours too, my guest! And if you find honey there, well, lick it up, you growling bear, and sweeten your spirit! Because tonight, we both want to be in good spirits—in good spirits and joyful, because another day has come to an end! And you'll even dance to my songs as my dancing bear.

Don't believe me? Shaking your head? Well, cheer up, old bear! I, too, am a soothsayer."

Thus spoke Zarathustra.

Chapter 63
Talk with the Kings

Zarathustra had not been traveling through the mountains and forests for even an hour when he suddenly encountered a strange procession. Right on the path he was descending, he saw two kings, crowned and dressed in purple sashes, their clothing as colorful as flamingo feathers. They were driving a burdened donkey ahead of them. "What are these kings doing in my territory?" Zarathustra wondered in surprise, hiding himself quickly behind some bushes. But as the kings approached, he spoke softly to himself, almost as if he were talking to no one at all: "Strange! So strange! I see two kings—but only one donkey!"

Hearing this, the two kings paused, exchanged smiles, and looked towards where the voice had come from, then glanced at each other. "We think the same things ourselves," said the king on the right, "but we do not say them aloud."

The king on the left shrugged and replied, "Perhaps that's just some goat-herd—or a hermit who's been in the wilderness too long. Not keeping company can also ruin one's manners."

"Manners?" replied the other king with irritation and bitterness. "What are we running away from if not 'manners'—our so-called 'good society'?

It would be far better to live among hermits and goat-herds than with our gilded, phony, over-powdered crowd, even if they do call themselves 'good society.'

Even if they call themselves 'nobility'—they're all fake and tainted, most of all in their blood, poisoned by old diseases and even worse treatments.

The people I prefer most right now are the hearty, tough peasants—rough, clever, stubborn, and resilient. They're the noblest sort these days.

The peasant is the best example right now; peasants should be the ones in charge! But instead, we're in a kingdom run by the rabble, and I refuse to put up with that. By rabble, I mean a mixture of everything—no order, just chaos.

The rabble—what a mess! Everything mixed together: saints with cheats, gentlemen with hucksters, every creature from Noah's ark thrown in.

'Good manners!' Everything with us is phony and foul. Nobody knows how to truly respect anything anymore—that's exactly why we're leaving. They're like overbearing dogs, putting gold leaf on palm leaves.

It sickens me that even we kings have become fake, dressing up in the faded costumes of our ancestors, posing for fools, for con men, and anyone scheming for power.

We're not the real leaders, yet we have to act like we are. We're fed up and disgusted with this charade.

We've left the rabble behind—all the loudmouths, the scribblers, the traders with their stench, the fidgeting for fame, the stale breath. It's revolting to live among them.

It's revolting to stand as leaders among the rabble! Ugh, the disgust! The revulsion! What do we kings even matter anymore?"

The king on the left replied, "Your old sickness is back, brother, your loathing has returned. But remember, someone is listening to us."

At that moment, Zarathustra, who had been listening closely, rose from his hiding spot and approached the kings, saying, "The one who hears you, who listens eagerly, is named Zarathustra. Yes, I am Zarathustra, the same who once said, 'What do kings matter now?' Forgive me, but I was delighted when I heard you say to each other, 'What does it matter about us kings!'

"But this is my domain—my land. What do you seek here? Perhaps you've found on your way what I seek: the higher man."

The kings thumped their chests in unison and replied, "You see right through us! With your words, you cut through the darkness in our hearts. You've seen our trouble, for we are searching for the higher man—someone greater than we are, even though we are kings. To him, we bring this donkey. For the highest man must be the highest ruler on earth.

"There is no greater misfortune in all of human fate than when the powerful on earth are not the greatest men. When that happens, everything becomes twisted and monstrous. And when those in power are more beast than human, even the people rise up, and in time, they start to say that their virtues are the only virtues."

"What have I just heard?" replied Zarathustra. "Such wisdom from kings! I am amazed, and I feel compelled to create a rhyme about this—even if it's not suited for all ears. I learned long ago not to cater to long ears. Very well, let's see!"

(At that moment, the donkey also decided to speak up, saying with a malicious tone, "Y-e-a.")

"Once, it was the first year of our Lord, And the Sybil cried, mad and untoward: 'How low we fall! Decline! Decline! Never has the world sunk so low this time! Rome is now a harlot's stew, Its Caesar a beast, and God—a Jew!'"

The kings were delighted by Zarathustra's rhymes. The king on the right said, "O Zarathustra, we're glad we came to see you! Your enemies painted a devilish picture of you in their stories—they showed us an image of you sneering and grimacing, so we feared you.

"But what could we do? Your words always pricked our hearts and ears. So at last, we said, 'What does it matter how he looks! We must hear him!' You, who teach, 'Love peace as a path to new wars, and cherish short peace over long peace!'

"Never had anyone spoken such words on war before. 'What is good? To be brave is good. A good war sanctifies every cause.' When you said that, it stirred the blood of our ancestors within us. It was like spring's first breath to old wine casks. When swords clashed like red-spotted serpents, our fathers felt alive. The sun during times of peace seemed pale and lukewarm to them, and long peace embarrassed them.

"Oh, how they sighed when they saw swords polished and dried up on the wall! They longed for war as a thirsty sword longs to drink blood, its metal gleaming with desire."

As the kings spoke, eagerly recalling the glory of their ancestors, Zarathustra felt a strong urge to laugh at their enthusiasm. For the kings he saw before him were clearly more peaceable and refined. But he restrained himself and said, "Well then! My cave lies that way, and today will be a long evening! But at this moment, a cry of distress urgently calls me away from you.

"It would honor my cave if kings chose to sit and wait there. But I must warn you—you may be waiting a long time!

"No matter! Where else does one learn the art of waiting as well as at court? And the main virtue left to kings today—what is it called, if not the ability to wait?"

Thus spoke Zarathustra.

Chapter 64
The Leech

And Zarathustra continued thoughtfully, descending further, through forests and across swampy grounds. As often happens to someone deep in thought on difficult matters, he accidentally stepped on a man lying in his path. Suddenly, he was hit in the face with a loud cry of pain, along with a couple of curses and several insults. Startled, Zarathustra instinctively raised his stick and struck the man he had stepped on. But immediately after, he regained his composure and felt amused by his own foolish reaction.

"Forgive me," he said to the man, who had now stood up, visibly furious, and was sitting on the ground, "forgive me, and listen first to a little story.

Imagine a wanderer, lost in thought about distant matters, walking down a lonely road and accidentally stepping on a sleeping dog lying in the sun. Both of them would jump up and snap at each other as if they were mortal enemies, both utterly startled—but isn't it possible that they could just as easily end up comforting each other, the lone traveler and the lonely dog? After all, aren't they both lonely?"

"Whoever you are," replied the man angrily, "your story hits too close, both with your foot and your words! Am I then supposed to be the dog?"

The man rose and pulled his bare arm out of the swamp, for he had been lying flat on the ground, hidden, like someone lying in wait for game by the swamp.

"But what are you doing?" Zarathustra asked, alarmed, for he saw blood streaming down the man's bare arm. "What has injured you? Has some wild animal bitten you, poor soul?"

The bleeding man, still angry, laughed and replied, "Why should it matter to you?" and was about to leave. "I belong here in these parts. Let anyone ask me what they will, but I don't answer fools."

"You're mistaken," Zarathustra said kindly, holding him back. "You're mistaken. This is not your land; it's my domain, and here, no one is harmed. Call me what you will—I am who I must be. I call myself Zarathustra.

"Look, up there is the path to my cave—it's not far. Wouldn't you rather treat your wounds in my home? It seems you've had a rough time: first, a beast bites you, then a man steps on you!"

When the man heard Zarathustra's name, his attitude changed completely. "What's happening?" he exclaimed. "Who else occupies my thoughts so deeply as this one man, Zarathustra, and one other creature that lives on blood—the leech?

"I came to this swamp for leeches, lying here like a fisherman with my arm outstretched, letting myself be bitten ten times already. But then, just as I was being bitten by the best leech yet, Zarathustra himself steps on me!

"Oh, what luck! What a miracle! Blessed be this day that drew me to the swamp! Blessed be the best and liveliest cupping-glass of all, Zarathustra, the great conscience-leech!"

The trodden one spoke in this way, and Zarathustra was pleased with his words and the refined, respectful way he expressed himself. "Who are you?" Zarathustra asked, extending his hand. "It seems there's much for us to clarify, yet I feel that a pure, clear day is dawning between us."

"I am a man of spiritual conscience," answered the man. "In matters of the spirit, no one is stricter, more exacting, or more rigorous than I—except the one from whom I learned it, Zarathustra himself.

Better to know nothing than to half-know many things! Better to be a fool on one's own terms than to be wise by the approval of others! I dig down to the foundation.

What does it matter if that foundation is large or small, whether it's a swamp or the sky? A handbreadth of ground is enough if it's solid!

A handbreadth of ground—there one can stand. In true knowledge, there's no great or small."

"So, you're an expert on leeches then?" asked Zarathustra. "And you examine the leech down to its very foundation, you man of conscience?"

"O Zarathustra," replied the man, "that would be an enormous task! How could I claim to do so?

But what I do know well, what I've mastered, is the brain of the leech. That's my world!

And it is a world, too! Forgive my pride in saying so, but in this I have no equal. That's why I said, 'Here I am at home.'

For so long I have studied this one thing—the brain of the leech—just to keep the slippery truth from slipping away! This is my domain!

I gave up everything else for this knowledge, let all else become unimportant; right next to what I know lies my vast ignorance.

My spiritual conscience demands this of me—that I know one thing fully and ignore all the rest. I cannot stand anything half-spiritual, hazy, or vague.

Where my honesty ends, I am blind—and I want to stay blind. But where I wish to know, I also want honesty—severe, exacting, narrow, relentless honesty.

Because you once said, O Zarathustra: 'Spirit is life that cuts into itself'—that's what drew me to your teaching. And truly, I've paid for my knowledge with my own blood!"

"Your evidence certainly supports it," Zarathustra interrupted, for blood was still dripping down the man's bare arm, where ten leeches had latched on.

"You strange fellow, how much I learn from this evidence—namely, from you! And there's much I might not be able to pour into your strict ears!

Well then! Here is where we part. But I hope to find you again. Up there is the path to my cave—tonight, you'll be my welcome guest!

I also want to make amends to your body for my stepping on you. I'll think on that. But for now, a cry of distress is calling me urgently away."

Thus spoke Zarathustra.

Chapter 65
The Magician

When Zarathustra rounded a rock, he saw, not far below on the same path, a man thrashing his limbs around like a madman before finally collapsing face-down on the ground. "Stop!" Zarathustra said to himself, "That must be the higher man; that terrible cry of distress came from him. I'll see if I can help him." So Zarathustra hurried to where the man lay, but he found only a trembling old man with a fixed, blank stare. Despite Zarathustra's efforts to lift him and help him to his feet, it was useless. The poor man seemed unaware that anyone was beside him; instead, he kept looking around with strange, frantic gestures, like someone abandoned and cut off from the whole world. Finally, after much trembling, convulsing, and curling up, he began to lament aloud:

Who warms me, who loves me still?
Bring me warm hands!
Bring comforting charcoal!
Here I lie, stretched out, shivering,
Like someone half-dead, cold, with feet warmed by another—
And shaken, ah! by strange fevers,
Shivering with sharp, ice-cold frost like arrows,
Hunted down by you, my imagination!
Unspeakable! Deep! Terrifying!
You hunter behind the clouds! Striking me with lightning,
You mocking eye that watches me in the darkness:
Here I lie,
Twisting, writhing, convulsing

In endless torment,
Struck
By you, cruel hunter,
You strange—God...
Strike deeper!
Once more, pierce through and tear my heart!
What does this torture mean,
With dull, blunted arrows?
Why do you look this way,
Never tired of human pain,
With those mischievous, divine flashes in your eyes?
You don't want to kill me,
But to torment, torment?
Why—torture me,
You playful, unfamiliar God?
Ha! Ha!
You sneak close
In midnight's dark hour?
What do you want?
Speak!
You crowd me, press me—
Ha! now far too close!
You hear me breathe,
You listen to my heart,
You jealous one!—Of what, I ask, are you jealous?
Off! Off!
Why the ladder?
Do you want to climb inside?
To crawl into my heart?
To slip into the innermost
Corners of my thoughts?
Shameless one! You unknown thief!
What do you want with your stealing?
What are you after with your listening?
Why do you torture me?

You torturer!
You—hangman-God!
Or should I, like a mastiff,
Roll before you?
And, cringing, enraptured, frenzied,
Wag my tail like a friendly dog?
In vain!
Spur me harder!
Cruel tormentor!
I'm not a dog—just your prey,
Cruel hunter!
Your proudest captive,
You thief hiding behind clouds…
Speak finally!
You, hidden in lightning! You unknown one! Speak!
What do you want from me, lurking in ambush?
What do you want, unfamiliar God?
What?
Ransom?
How much ransom? Demand a lot—that stirs my pride!
And be clear—my other pride needs that too!
Ha! Ha!
You want me? Me?
—All of me?...
Ha! Ha!
And you torture me, foolishly,
Killing my pride completely?
Give me love—who warms me now?
Who loves me still?
Bring me warm hands,
Bring me fiery coals,
Give warmth to the most alone,
To the ice (ah! seven-fold frozen ice
That only enemies,
Only foes, could make thirst).

Give, yield to me,
Cruel foe,
—Yourself!—
Away!
He's fled now, surely,
My final, only companion,
My greatest foe,
My unfamiliar—
My hangman-God!
—No!
Come back!
With all your great torments! To me, the last of the lonely,
Oh, come back!
All my hot tears flow
Their path to you!
And my last deep passion—
Flares up for you!
Oh, come back,
My unfamiliar God! My pain!
My final joy!

At this point, Zarathustra could hold back no longer. He took his staff and struck the lamenting man with all his might. "Enough of this!" he shouted with an angry laugh. "Stop it, you actor! You faker! You liar from the heart! I know you well! I'll give you a reason to move, you wicked magician—I know how to make things hot for people like you!"

"Enough, enough!" the old man cried, springing up from the ground. "No more, Zarathustra! I was only doing it for fun! This is part of my craft, my art. I wanted to test you by performing like this, and truly, you saw through me! But you, too, have given me quite a test yourself: you're hard, wise Zarathustra! Hard, with your 'truths'— your staff forced this truth out of me!"

"Don't flatter yourself," Zarathustra replied, still angry and frowning. "You performer from the heart! You're false; how can you talk of truth? You vain peacock, you sea of pride! What were you even trying to show me, you wicked magician? Who was I supposed to believe in when you wailed like that?"

"I was playing the penitent in spirit," the old man explained. "That's who I was supposed to be. After all, you're the one who came up with that idea—a poet and magician who turns his spirit against himself, becoming someone who freezes to death by his own faulty knowledge and conscience. And admit it, Zarathustra—it took you quite a while to realize it was all an act! You believed my distress when you held my head in your hands. I even heard you say, 'We loved him too little, loved him too little!' I was thrilled with wicked glee because I fooled you so well."

"You may have deceived those subtler than I," Zarathustra answered sternly. "But I don't guard myself against deceivers; I must live without caution—that's my fate. You, however, must always deceive—I know that much about you! You have to keep things ambiguous, layered, always twisting words and meanings. Even now, your confession isn't quite true, nor entirely false enough for me! You're a bad counterfeiter; you wouldn't even show yourself honestly to your own doctor if you were laid bare."

Zarathustra continued, "You even tried to cover up your lie when you said, 'I did it only for amusement!' But there was more to it than that—there was some seriousness, too. You are something of a 'penitent in spirit.' I see you clearly: you've enchanted the whole world, yet for yourself, there's no magic left. You're disenchanted with yourself. Disgust is your only remaining truth. There's no longer any real word in you—only your mouth is genuine, because it reeks of that disgust."

"Who are you, then?" cried the old magician, his voice defiant. "Who dares speak to me like this, the greatest man alive?" A flash of green lit up in his eye as he glared at Zarathustra. But then he softened and said, sadly, "Oh, Zarathustra, I'm tired of it all. I'm sick of my tricks. I'm not great. Why keep pretending? But you know it well—I sought greatness. I wanted to appear as a great man, and I convinced many people of it. But the lie was too much for me. It's crushed me. Oh, Zarathustra, everything in me is a lie, except for one thing—that I am broken. My breaking is real."

"It does you credit," Zarathustra replied solemnly, looking downward, "that you sought greatness, but it also reveals the truth about you: you are not great."

"You're an old, bad magician," said Zarathustra, "but the best and most honest thing I respect about you is that you're tired of yourself and admitted it: 'I am not great.' That's what I honor in you, a rare moment of true honesty, a glimpse of a 'penitent-in-spirit.' In that instant, just for a flash, you were genuine. But tell me, why are you here, wandering through my forests and rocks? And if you're crossing my path, what is it you're testing me for?"

This Zarathustra said with eyes gleaming. The old magician was silent for a while before finally responding, "Testing you? No, I'm only searching. O Zarathustra, I'm looking for someone genuine, someone real and direct, a man of absolute honesty, a vessel of wisdom, a seeker of knowledge, a truly great man! Don't you understand, Zarathustra? I'm searching for Zarathustra himself."

There was a long silence between them. Zarathustra fell deep into thought, even closing his eyes. When he finally returned to the moment, he took the magician's hand and, with great courtesy and caution, said, "Alright, follow the path up ahead. There is Zarathustra's cave. There, you may search for the one you wish to find. And if you need help, seek advice from my animals—my eagle and my serpent—they will aid your search. My cave is large, after all.

"As for me, I have yet to see a truly great man. Today, even the sharpest eyes overlook what is truly great; it's the age of the common rabble. I've seen many inflate themselves, and people cry out, 'Look, a great man!' But what's the use of such bluster? Eventually, the wind escapes. The frog that puffs itself up too long will burst, and what's left? Only air. It's a fun pastime to prick such swollen bellies— remember that, boys!

"Our times belong to the popular crowd; who even knows what's truly great or small? Only fools could look for greatness today—and only fools would find it. Are you really seeking great men, you strange fool? Who taught you that? And is now really the time for it? Ah, you poor seeker, why are you tempting me?"

With that, Zarathustra felt comforted in his heart and went on his way, laughing.

Chapter 66
Out of Service

Not long after Zarathustra had freed himself from the magician, he noticed another figure sitting along the path he was traveling. This figure was a tall, dark-clad man with a pale, thin face, whose presence deeply saddened him. "Alas," he said to himself, "there sits sorrow in disguise; he looks like one of those priests. What are they doing in my domain? What! I just escaped that magician, and now another sorcerer blocks my path—some holy spellbinder, a somber miracle-worker by God's grace, some anointed bearer of gloom! May the devil take him! But the devil never shows up on time; he's always late, that cursed little club-footed dwarf!"

With these thoughts, Zarathustra cursed impatiently, wondering how he might pass by the dark figure without drawing attention. But as it happened, the man had already noticed him and, as though suddenly struck by good fortune, stood up and approached Zarathustra directly.

"Whoever you may be, traveler," he said, "help a lost soul, a seeker, an old man who may soon find himself in trouble! This place is strange and wild to me; I've even heard beasts howling. And the one who could have sheltered me is no longer here.

"I was looking for a pious man, a saint and hermit who, alone in these woods, had not yet heard what the whole world now knows."

"What does the world know now?" asked Zarathustra. "Perhaps that the old God, in whom everyone once believed, is no longer alive?"

"You have said it," the old man answered sorrowfully. "And I served that old God until his last hour. Now, though, I am out of service, without a master and still not free. I no longer feel joy, even for a single hour—except in memories. So I climbed these mountains to have one last festival for myself, as an old pope and church father should—a festival of holy memories and sacred rites. For you see, I am the last pope!

"But now, the most pious man, the saint in the forest, the one who constantly praised his God with singing and muttering, is dead. When I reached his cabin, he was nowhere to be found. Instead, I found two wolves there, howling over his death. All the animals loved him, so I left quickly.

"Did I come all this way through these forests and mountains for nothing? My heart told me then to seek out another—the most faithful of all those who do not believe in God. My heart told me to seek Zarathustra."

So spoke the old man, gazing keenly at the one standing before him. Zarathustra, in turn, took the old pope's hand, looking at it for a long time in admiration.

"Look at this!" said Zarathustra, "What a noble and long hand! This is the hand of someone who has blessed others for a lifetime. And now, it holds on to the one you sought—me, Zarathustra."

When Zarathustra had walked around a rock, he spotted a figure sitting further down the same path. It was a man, tall and dressed in black, with a thin, pale face, and his sight brought Zarathustra deep sadness. "Oh," he thought, "there sits a sorrowful soul, and he looks like a priest. What does he want here in my domain?

What's this? I barely escaped that magician, and now another sorcerer has appeared—another mystic, perhaps, who meddles with prayers and dark magic. May the devil have him! But the devil always shows up late, that cursed little cripple!"

With these words, Zarathustra's irritation grew, and he wondered how he might sneak past the man without drawing attention. But it turned out otherwise, for the man had already seen him and, looking pleased, got to his feet and walked toward Zarathustra.

"Traveler, whoever you may be," he began, "please help a lost soul, a seeker, an old man who may come to ruin here! This place is strange and wild to me; I've even heard the howls of beasts, and the one I sought for refuge—he is no more.

"I came looking for a holy man, a saint and hermit who, alone in the woods, hadn't yet heard what everyone now knows."

"What is it that everyone knows now?" asked Zarathustra. "Perhaps that the old God in whom all once believed is no longer alive?"

"You've said it," the old man replied sorrowfully. "And I served that old God until his very last hour. Now I am without a master, though I am not free. I am not happy, even for a moment, except in my memories. That is why I climbed these mountains, hoping to have one last celebration for myself, as is proper for an old pope and church father—a festival of holy memories and sacred rituals. For I am the last pope!

"But the most pious man, the saint in the forest who never ceased praising his God with songs and murmurs, is now dead. When I arrived at his hut, he was gone, and I found two wolves inside, howling over his death. The animals loved him, so I quickly departed.

"Did I travel through these woods and mountains all for nothing? My heart told me to seek someone else, someone holy but who no longer believes in God. My heart told me to find Zarathustra."

So spoke the old man, gazing keenly at the one before him. Zarathustra took the old pope's hand and looked at it for a long moment in admiration.

"Look here, venerable one," said Zarathustra, "what a fine and long hand! This is the hand of someone who has given blessings all his life. And now it holds fast to the one you've sought—me, Zarathustra.

Chapter 67
The Ugliest Man

"AND again did Zarathustra's feet carry him through mountains and forests, and his eyes searched tirelessly, but nowhere did he find the one he sought—the deeply troubled and crying soul. Along the way, however, his heart swelled with joy and gratitude. 'What gifts this day has granted me,' he said, 'to make up for its rough start! What strange people I've met! I'll be pondering their words for a long time, like chewing good grain; my teeth will grind and crush until their words turn to milk and flow into my soul.'

But then the path bent around a rock, and suddenly the landscape changed. Zarathustra entered a realm of death. Black and red cliffs loomed high above, lifeless, without grass, trees, or the songs of birds. This valley, avoided by all animals—even predators—was where a type of thick, green snake came to die when it grew old. Because of this, the shepherds called the valley "Serpent-death."

Zarathustra was pulled into dark memories, for he felt as though he had once stood in this valley before. A heavy sadness settled over him, slowing his steps until he finally stood still. Then, opening his eyes, he saw something sitting by the path—a shape that was vaguely human but hardly so, something indescribable. A wave of shame overtook Zarathustra, as if he had intruded upon something he should not see. Blushing deeply, he looked away and lifted his foot to leave this cursed place. But then the dead silence of the wilderness broke.

From the ground rose a sound, bubbling and rattling, like water struggling through blocked pipes at night. At last, it turned into a human voice and spoke:

'Zarathustra! Zarathustra! Solve my riddle! Tell me, tell me, what is revenge upon the witness? I lure you back; here is slippery ice! Watch yourself—don't let your pride slip and fall! You think yourself wise, proud Zarathustra! Then crack this hard nut of a riddle—figure me out! Tell me, who am I?'

When Zarathustra heard these words, what do you think happened in his soul? Compassion swept over him, and he fell suddenly, like an oak tree that has long withstood many woodcutters—heavily and abruptly, to the terror even of those trying to fell it. But he quickly rose again, his face stern.

'I know you well,' he said in a steely voice, 'you are the murderer of God! Let me go. You couldn't bear the gaze of the One who saw you, who saw right through you, you ugliest of men. You took revenge upon that witness!'

So spoke Zarathustra, and he turned to leave. But the strange figure clutched the edge of his robe and, struggling for words, began to speak again, gurgling and stammering. At last, he managed to say, 'Wait—don't go. I understand now what struck you down like an axe: Hail to you, Zarathustra, for standing tall again! You understand, I know it well, the feeling of the one who killed him—the murderer of God. Wait! Sit with me a while; it's not for nothing. Where else could I go but to you? Sit down! Don't look at me, though! Honor my ugliness this way.

They pursue me; you are my last refuge. Not with hate, not with jailers; oh, such persecution I could mock and even take pride in! Have not the best successes always come to those who are well-persecuted? And those who persecute eagerly learn humility—once they're left behind! But it's their pity—

'It's their pity I flee from, and I flee to you. O Zarathustra, protect me, you, my last refuge, the only one who understands me."

You understood how the man who killed him must feel. Stay! And if you must go, don't go the way I came. That path is dangerous. Are you angry because I've used so many words? Because I've already tried to guide you? But know this: I am the ugliest of men, and I also have the biggest, heaviest feet. Wherever I go, the way is dark and doomed. I walk paths of ruin and death.

But you passed me in silence; you even blushed—I saw it clearly, and in that moment, I recognized you as Zarathustra. Anyone else would have tossed me pity in a look or a word. But I am not lowly enough to need pity—that much, you understood. I am too rich for that, rich in what is great, terrible, ugliest, and unspeakable! Your shame, Zarathustra, honored me!

It was hard for me to escape from the crowd of the pitiful, to find the only one who teaches today that pity is intrusive—you, Zarathustra! Whether pity is divine or human, it insults dignity. Sometimes refusing to help is more noble than rushing to give aid. Yet people today call pity "virtue," especially small-minded people who have no respect for great tragedy, great ugliness, or great failure.

I look over them all like a dog looks over a flock of sheep, petty, harmless, well-meaning, gray people. I view them as a heron glances back at shallow pools, with a turned head, scornful of the small waves and shallow desires and spirits below.

For too long we believed that the small-minded were right. So we gave them power, and now they claim that only what they call "good" is truly good. And "truth" now means what the preacher, who came from among them, said about himself: "I am the truth." That shameless one has made the petty people proud; he taught them one big error when he said, "I am the truth."

Was anyone ever given a kinder answer than what you said, Zarathustra? You passed by him and said, "No! No! Three times, no!"

You warned against his error, against pity—first to do so, even though it was only you and your kind who understood. You were ashamed of the shame of the great sufferer, and when you said, "Pity casts a heavy shadow; beware, people!" you were wise.

When you teach that all creators are tough, that all great love is beyond pity, Zarathustra, you seem to know the signs of the times! Yet you warn yourself about pity! Many are on their way to you—suffering, doubting, despairing, drowning, freezing. I even warn you against myself. You have understood me, my deepest and worst riddle, what I have done. I know the blow that can strike you down.

But he had to die. He saw everything—he saw into people's depths and darkness, all the hidden shame and ugliness. His pity knew no limits; he probed into my dirtiest corners. This nosiest, most meddling, overly-pitying one had to die. He saw everything about me, and I could not let that witness live without revenge.

The God who sees everything and sees man for what he is—that God had to die! Man cannot stand having a witness like that live."

So spoke the ugliest man. Zarathustra stood up, preparing to go on, feeling a chill deep inside.

"You strange being," he said, "you warned me against your path. For that, I thank you. Look, up there is Zarathustra's cave. It is large and deep, with many hidden places where even the most secretive can find shelter. And nearby, there are a hundred nooks and crannies for creeping, fluttering, and hopping creatures.

Outcast, you who cast yourself out—you can't live among people and their pity? Then do as I do! You'll also learn from me, for only the doer truly learns. And first, speak with my animals! The proudest and the wisest—they may be the best guides for us both!"

So Zarathustra spoke and walked on, even more slowly and thoughtfully than before, asking himself many things, unsure of what to answer.

"How poor man truly is," he thought, "how ugly, how weary, how full of hidden shame! They tell me that man loves himself. Ah, how great that love must be, with so much contempt against it! Even this man has loved himself, even as he despised himself—he is a great lover, I think, and a great despiser. I have never met anyone who despised himself so completely: and even that is a kind of greatness. Could this be the higher man whose cry I heard? I admire those who truly despise themselves. Man is something that must be overcome."

Chapter 68
The Voluntary Beggar

When Zarathustra left the ugliest man, he felt a chill and a sense of loneliness. A deep coldness filled his spirit, making even his limbs feel numb. But as he continued on, wandering up hills and down slopes, sometimes passing green meadows and other times crossing over rough stone paths—perhaps where an eager brook once flowed—he suddenly felt a new warmth and energy inside him.

"What's happening to me?" he wondered. "Something warm and alive is stirring around me; it must be nearby. I feel less alone; unseen companions, maybe even brothers, seem to roam around me, and their warm breath touches my soul."

As he looked around to find the source of this comfort, he spotted a group of cows standing together on a small hill. Their closeness and scent had warmed his heart. The cows seemed to be listening attentively to a speaker, paying no attention to Zarathustra as he approached. When he got closer, he realized he was hearing a human voice among the cows. It seemed they were all facing this speaker as though listening to him.

Zarathustra quickly ran up and gently moved the animals aside, worried that someone might be hurt and that the pity of the cows wouldn't be enough to help. But he was mistaken. There, sitting on the ground, was a peaceful man speaking softly to the cows, trying to reassure them not to fear him. His eyes radiated kindness, and he seemed like a gentle Preacher-on-the-Mount. Zarathustra called out in surprise, "What are you doing here?"

"What am I doing here?" replied the man. "The same as you, mischief-maker—seeking happiness on earth. For that reason, I decided to learn from these cows. I've already been talking to them all morning, and they were just about to answer me. Why did you disturb them?

"Unless we change and become like cows, we won't enter the kingdom of heaven. There's something we need to learn from them: how to ruminate. Truly, if a man gains the whole world but doesn't learn how to ruminate, what good does it do him? He won't escape his own suffering.

"That great suffering, which we now call disgust—who doesn't feel their heart, mouth, and eyes filled with disgust these days? Even you! But look at these cows!"

With that, the Preacher-on-the-Mount turned his gaze from the cows and looked at Zarathustra. Then his expression changed. "Who am I speaking to?" he cried, suddenly alarmed, leaping up from the ground. "This is the man without disgust! This is Zarathustra himself, the one who has overcome great disgust. This is the eye, this is the mouth, this is the heart of Zarathustra himself!"

As he spoke, he took Zarathustra's hands and kissed them with tears in his eyes, as though a precious gift had unexpectedly fallen to him from heaven. The cows watched the scene with wonder.

"Please, don't talk about me, kind stranger," Zarathustra said, gently holding back his own feelings. "Tell me about yourself first! Aren't you the voluntary beggar who once gave up great riches? The one who felt ashamed of wealth and left it behind to share his abundance and his heart with the poorest? But they didn't accept you."

"They didn't accept me," the voluntary beggar replied, "You know this well. So, at last, I came to the animals—and to these cows."

"Then you learned," Zarathustra interrupted, "how much harder it is to give properly than to take properly, and that giving well is an art—the last, most refined art of kindness."

"Especially now," answered the voluntary beggar. "Today, when everything low has become rebellious, exclusive, and haughty in its ways—like the rabble. The time has come, you know, for the long, dark, slow revolt of the masses and slaves: it keeps spreading!

"Now the lower classes mock at any small acts of kindness or charity; and the overly rich had better beware! People these days are like bloated bottles with narrow necks; it doesn't take much to want to break their necks.

"I saw greed, bitter envy, spiteful revenge, and rabble-pride all around me. It's no longer true that the poor are blessed. The kingdom of heaven, it seems, belongs with the cows."

"And why doesn't it belong to the rich?" asked Zarathustra, teasing as he held back the cows that were sniffing curiously at the gentle one.

"Why do you tempt me?" the man replied. "You know the answer better than I. What drove me to the poorest, Zarathustra? Wasn't it my disgust with the richest?

"With the greedy ones, whose eyes are cold and whose minds are rotten, who pull profit from any garbage they find—that rabble that reeks to the heavens.

"That gilded, phony rabble, whose fathers were thieves, vultures, or rag-pickers, with wives who were compliant, lewd, and forgetful—they're all not far from being harlots.

"Rabble at the top, rabble at the bottom! What are 'rich' and 'poor' today? I forgot the difference and kept going further and further until I found these cows."

Thus spoke the gentle one, puffing and sweating as he spoke, and the cows looked on, curious. Zarathustra kept watching his face with a smile, shaking his head silently as the man spoke with such sternness.

"You go too hard on yourself, Preacher-on-the-Mount, when you speak so harshly. Neither your mouth nor your eyes were made for such severity.

"Nor, I think, was your stomach. All this anger, hatred, and ranting doesn't sit well with you. You prefer gentler things; you're not a butcher.

"You seem more like a plant-eater to me, a root-man. Maybe you grind grain. But certainly, you avoid earthly pleasures, and I'd guess you like honey."

"You understand me well," answered the voluntary beggar, his heart lightened. "I love honey; I also grind corn, because I've sought out what is sweet and brings pure breath.

"I've also found things that take a long time—a day's work, a mouth's work, for gentle idlers and slow-goers.

"But those cows have taken it even further: they invented ruminating and lying in the sun. They avoid all heavy thoughts that weigh down the heart."

"Well!" said Zarathustra. "Then you should see my animals—my eagle and my serpent. There's nothing like them on earth right now.

"Look, there's the path to my cave. Stay there tonight as my guest, and talk with my animals about the happiness of animals.

"I'll join you when I return, but for now, a call of distress draws me away from you. And if you find new honey there, ice-cold golden-comb honey, enjoy it!

"But now, say goodbye to your cows, strange one, kind one, even though it may be hard for you. They are your warmest friends and teachers."

"Except for one whom I hold even dearer," the voluntary beggar replied. "You yourself are good, Zarathustra—better even than a cow!"

"Away, away with you, you wicked flatterer!" cried Zarathustra, laughing. "Why do you spoil me with such praise and flattery-honey?

"Away, away from me!" he called again, playfully waving his stick at the affectionate beggar, who quickly scampered off.

Chapter 69
The Shadow

Barely had the voluntary beggar hurried off and Zarathustra was alone again when he heard a new voice behind him calling, "Wait! Zarathustra! Stop! It's me, Zarathustra, your shadow!" But Zarathustra didn't wait; a sudden irritation crept over him at the crowd in his mountains. "Where's my solitude gone?" he muttered.

"It's all becoming too much for me; these mountains are swarming with people; my kingdom is no longer of this world. I need new mountains.

"My shadow is calling me? What does it matter about my shadow! Let it follow me! I'll just run away from it."

So Zarathustra spoke to himself and ran on. But the one behind him kept following, so there were three runners in a row: first, the voluntary beggar, then Zarathustra, and lastly, his shadow. They hadn't been running long when Zarathustra realized his own foolishness and shook off his irritation and annoyance in a single motion.

"What!" he said, "haven't ridiculous things always happened to us old hermits and saints?

"My foolishness has only grown here in the mountains! Now I hear six old fools' feet rattling along, one after another!

"But should Zarathustra really be scared of his shadow? Besides, I think my shadow has longer legs than I do."

So Zarathustra spoke, laughing from his eyes and his insides, and he stopped abruptly, turning quickly—and almost knocked his shadow-follower to the ground, for he had been following so closely behind and looked so frail. When Zarathustra looked at him closely, he was startled, for the shadow appeared so thin, dark, hollow, and worn out.

"Who are you?" asked Zarathustra sharply. "What are you doing here? And why do you call yourself my shadow? I don't find you very agreeable."

"Forgive me," answered the shadow, "that it's me; and if I'm not pleasing to you—well, Zarathustra! I admire you for that and your good taste.

"I am a wanderer who's trailed after you for a long time; always moving, but without a purpose, without a home. I'm nearly the eternal Wandering Jew, though I'm neither eternal nor Jewish.

"What? Must I be forever on the road? Blown by every wind, unsettled, drifting? O earth, you're too round for me!

"I've sat on every surface, fallen asleep like weary dust on mirrors and windowpanes. Everything takes from me; nothing gives back; I'm thinning out—practically just a shadow.

"But I've followed you the longest, Zarathustra; and though I hid myself from you, I was still your best shadow: wherever you sat, I sat too.

"With you, I wandered into the farthest, coldest worlds, like a ghost willingly haunting winter roofs and snow.

"With you, I pushed into all forbidden, worst, and furthest places. And if I have any virtue, it's that I feared no prohibition.

"With you, I toppled all the things my heart once respected. I threw down all boundaries and statues, pursued the most dangerous desires, even past every crime.

"With you, I unlearned my belief in words, values, and famous names. When the devil sheds his skin, doesn't his name fall off too? It's just another layer. Perhaps the devil himself is merely—skin.

'Nothing is true; everything is allowed': that's what I told myself. Into the coldest waters, I dove headfirst. Ah, how often did I end up standing there naked on that account, like a red crab!"

Ah, where have all my goodness, my shame, and my faith in the good gone! Ah, where is the naive innocence I once had, the innocence of the good and their noble lies!

Too often I followed right behind truth's heels, only to get kicked in the face. Sometimes I meant to lie, and behold—only then did I strike at the truth.

Too much has become clear to me, and now I no longer care. Nothing I love is alive anymore—how could I still love myself?

"To live as I choose, or not to live at all"—that's what I want; that's what the holiest want too. But, alas! Do I still have any desires?

Do I still have a goal? A harbor toward which my sails are set?

A good wind? Ah, only the one who knows where he's sailing knows what winds are good and fair for him.

What remains for me? A weary, indifferent heart; a wavering will; fluttering wings; a broken backbone.

This search for my home, O Zarathustra, do you know it has become my homesickness; it's eating me up.

"Where is my home?" I ask and search, and I've searched, but I haven't found it. O eternal everywhere, O eternal nowhere, O eternally in vain!"

So spoke the shadow, and Zarathustra's face grew longer as he listened. "You really are my shadow!" he said at last, with sadness.

"Your danger is no small thing, you free spirit, you wanderer! You've had a rough day; take care that an even rougher night doesn't find you!

To such restless souls as you, even a prison can start to look like a blessing. Have you ever noticed how soundly captured criminals sleep? They sleep peacefully; they savor their newfound security.

Beware that in the end you aren't caught in a narrow belief, a rigid, harsh delusion! Right now, everything that's narrow and firm seems to tempt you.

You've lost your goal. Ah, how will you get past and forget that loss? For in losing your goal, you've also lost your way!

You poor wanderer, you tired butterfly! Do you want rest and a home this evening? Then go up to my cave!

The way to my cave is there. But now I'll hurry away from you once again. It's as if a shadow already lies upon me.

I need to run alone so that it may become bright around me again. So I'll keep my legs merry for a long while yet. This evening, though, there will be—dancing with me!"

So spoke Zarathustra.

Chapter 70
At Noontide

And Zarathustra ran and ran, but he met no one else and was alone, always returning to himself; he enjoyed and savored his solitude, thinking good thoughts for hours. Around noon, however, when the sun stood directly over him, he came upon an old, twisted tree wrapped tightly by a vine's warm embrace, so entwined it was hidden within. Clusters of yellow grapes hung before the wanderer. He felt tempted to quench his thirst by taking a bunch of grapes. But as he reached out his hand, he felt a stronger desire to lie down beneath the tree, to rest at this perfect hour and sleep.

So Zarathustra did; and as soon as he lay down on the earth in the stillness of the colorful grass, he forgot his little thirst and fell asleep. For, as Zarathustra's aphorism says: "One thing is more necessary than another." His eyes, however, remained open, never tiring of watching and admiring the tree and the loving vine. Falling asleep, Zarathustra spoke to his heart:

"Hush! Hush! Has the world not now become perfect? What has happened to me?

As a gentle breeze dances softly across a still sea, feather-light, so does sleep dance over me.

It does not close my eyes, but leaves my soul awake. It is light, so feather-light.

It persuades me in ways I cannot describe, touching me deep inside with a gentle hand, pressing me down. Yes, it presses me so that my soul stretches out—

How long and weary it feels, my strange soul! Has a Sabbath evening come to it now, right at noon? Has it wandered for too long among good, ripe things?

It stretches longer, even longer! It lies still, my strange soul. It has tasted too many good things; a golden sadness weighs on it, curling its mouth.

Like a ship pulling into the calmest harbor: now it draws close to the shore, tired of long voyages and uncertain seas. Isn't the shore more faithful?

Just as a ship clings to the coast, draws close to land: now a spider's thread ties it to shore. No stronger rope is needed here.

Like that tired ship in the calmest harbor, so I now lie close to the earth, faithful, trusting, waiting, bound to it by the lightest threads.

O happiness! O happiness! Will you perhaps sing, O my soul? You lie here in the grass. But this is the quiet, solemn hour when no shepherd plays his pipe.

Be careful! Hot noon sleeps on the fields. Do not sing! Hush! The world is perfect.

Do not sing, prairie-bird, my soul! Don't even whisper! Look—hush! The old noon sleeps, its mouth moving: is it sipping a drop of happiness right now—

An old brown drop of golden happiness, like golden wine? Something flits across it; its happiness laughs. That's how a god laughs. Hush!

'How little it takes for happiness!' So I once said and thought myself wise. But that was blasphemy, I now realize. Wise fools speak better.

The smallest thing, the gentlest thing, the lightest thing—a lizard's rustle, a breath, a whisk, a glance—small things bring the best happiness. Hush!"

What has happened to me? Listen! Has time slipped away? Am I falling? Haven't I already fallen—listen!—into the well of eternity?

What's going on with me? Hush! It pierces me—oh!—right to the heart! To the heart! Oh, break open, break open, my heart, after such happiness, after such a piercing feeling!

What? Hasn't the world just now become perfect? Round and ripe? Oh, the golden circle—where is it flying? Let me chase it! Quickly!

Hush—" (And here Zarathustra stretched himself and realized he was asleep.)

"Get up!" he said to himself, "you sleepyhead! You noontime dreamer! Come on, up, you old legs! It's time and more than time; there are still many good miles waiting for you to cover—

Now you've slept enough; for how long, though? A half-eternity! Well, up now, my old heart! After such a sleep, how long can you stay awake?"

(But then he fell back into sleep, and his soul resisted, defending itself, lying back down.) "Leave me alone! Hush! Hasn't the world just now become perfect? Oh, the golden, round ball!"

"Get up," said Zarathustra, "you little thief, you sluggard! What! Still stretching, yawning, sighing, falling into deep wells?

Who are you, then, oh my soul?" (And here he felt a sudden fright, as a sunbeam shot down from the sky onto his face.)

"Oh, heaven above me," he said, sighing and sitting up, "do you watch me? Do you listen to my strange soul?

When will you drink up this drop of dew that has fallen on all earthly things—when will you drink this strange soul—

When, you well of eternity! you joyful, terrifying, noontime abyss! When will you take my soul back into you?"

Thus spoke Zarathustra, rising from his resting place beside the tree, as if awakening from a strange stupor. And behold! The sun still stood directly above his head. From this, one could rightly conclude that Zarathustra had not slept for long.

□

Chapter 71
The Greeting

It was late in the afternoon when Zarathustra, after hours of wandering and searching without success, finally returned to his cave. But just as he reached it, standing only about twenty paces away, something happened that he least expected: he heard once again the loud cry of distress. And incredibly, this time the cry came from inside his own cave. It was a long, layered, peculiar sound, and Zarathustra could clearly tell that it was made up of many voices, though from afar it might have sounded like the cry from a single mouth.

Zarathustra rushed forward to his cave, and what a sight awaited him after that strange chorus! There they all sat—the ones he had met throughout the day: the king on the right and the king on the left, the old magician, the pope, the voluntary beggar, the shadow, the intellectually conscientious one, the sorrowful soothsayer, and the ass. The ugliest man had even set a crown upon his head and draped two purple sashes around himself, for like all who are unattractive, he enjoyed disguising himself to appear noble. In the middle of this sorrowful gathering stood Zarathustra's eagle, ruffled and uneasy, having been made to answer for more than its pride could bear, while the wise serpent hung around its neck.

Zarathustra looked upon all this with great astonishment; then he inspected each guest with courteous curiosity, reading their souls and marveling again. Meanwhile, the group had risen from their seats, waiting respectfully for Zarathustra to speak. Zarathustra spoke to them:

"You desperate souls! You strange ones! Was it your cry of distress that I heard? Now I understand where to find the one I sought all day in vain: the higher man—he is in my own cave! But why am I surprised? Have I not lured him here with offerings of honey and the playful calls of my happiness?

It seems, however, that you do not mix well together; you make each other's hearts uneasy. Is this why you cried out when you gathered here? There's someone still missing, someone who can make you all laugh again—a good-natured fool, a dancer, a wild spirit, a playful old joker. What do you think?

Forgive me, you despairing ones, for speaking so lightly before you, words unworthy of such guests! But you don't realize what makes my heart light—it's you and your presence! Forgive me! For anyone who sees a soul in despair feels courage rise in themselves. To comfort someone in despair makes anyone think themselves strong enough.

You've given me this strength, my honorable guests! Such a gift! And it's only fair I give you something in return. This is my realm and my domain; what is mine, however, shall be yours tonight. My animals shall serve you, and my cave will be your resting place.

In my home, no one will despair. Here, everyone is protected from their wild beasts. And that's the first gift I offer you: safety. The second gift, however, is my little finger. And when you have that, then take the whole hand, yes, and my heart with it! Welcome here—welcome, my guests!"

Thus spoke Zarathustra, laughing with warmth and mischief. His guests bowed again in silence and reverence. Then, the king on the right spoke on behalf of them all:

"O Zarathustra, by the way you extended your hand and your greeting, we recognize you as Zarathustra. You have humbled yourself before us, almost too much—enough to move our reverence.

But who could humble himself as you have, with such pride? It lifts us as well; it refreshes our eyes and hearts. Just to see this, we would gladly climb even higher mountains than this, for we came as eager witnesses, wanting to see what brightens dull eyes."

And look! Now all our cries of distress are behind us. Our hearts and minds are open and filled with joy. There's little holding our spirits back from being carefree.

Nothing grows more beautifully on earth than a strong, noble will, Zarathustra; it's the most glorious growth. A whole landscape finds refreshment near such a tree. I compare you to the pine, Zarathustra, tall, silent, hardy, and alone, with the finest, most supple wood.

In the end, though, it reaches out with strong green branches, questioning the wind, the storm, and all that lives high above. It answers back with power, commanding like a conqueror! Oh, who wouldn't want to climb high mountains to witness such a tree?

Even those who are gloomy and weak find themselves renewed by your presence, Zarathustra; those who waver find steadiness, and even their hearts are healed. Today, many eyes turn toward you and your mountain; a deep longing has awakened, and people are beginning to ask, "Who is Zarathustra?"

All who have heard your song and tasted your honey, the hidden ones, the lone dwellers, and those who live only for each other, have all asked in their hearts: "Is Zarathustra still alive? If he isn't, then life no longer seems worth living. Everything feels indifferent, useless—unless we can live alongside Zarathustra!"

"Where is he?" many wonder. "Has his solitude swallowed him up, or should we go to him ourselves?"

Now, it seems even solitude cannot hold itself together; it's cracking open like a grave that can no longer contain its dead. Everywhere, we see people returning to life.

The waves of longing are rising around your mountain, Zarathustra. And however high you are, many will rise to meet you. Your boat will not stay much longer on dry land.

And the fact that we, the despairing ones, are here in your cave, no longer despairing, is only a sign that better ones are on their way to you.

Yes, the last trace of God among men—those with great longing, great disgust, great weariness. All who are unwilling to live without learning to hope once more—all these are on their way to you, Zarathustra, to find the great hope.

So spoke the king on the right, reaching to take Zarathustra's hand to kiss it, but Zarathustra withdrew, stepping back in alarm, as though to escape. After a brief moment, though, he returned to his guests, gazing at them with clear, examining eyes, and said:

"My guests, my higher men, I will speak directly to you. It is not for you that I have been waiting here in these mountains."

("'Directly?' Good heavens!" muttered the king on the left to himself. "He doesn't understand the good Westerners, this sage from the East! But I suppose he means 'bluntly.' Well, that's not the worst style these days!")

"You all may indeed be higher men," Zarathustra continued, "but you're neither high enough nor strong enough for me.

You see, for me, and for the relentless will that lies silent within me but will not stay silent forever, you are not enough. If you are part of me, it's not as my right arm.

For those who stand on uncertain, frail legs seek leniency, even if they don't realize it, or perhaps try to hide it from themselves.

But I am not lenient with my arms or my legs, and I am certainly not lenient with my warriors. So how could you be ready for my battles?

I would ruin all my victories with you. Many of you would fall just from hearing the loud beating of my drums."

Moreover, you are not beautiful or noble enough for me. I need clear, flawless mirrors for my teachings; with you, even my own image appears distorted.

You carry heavy burdens—memories and mischievous doubts—and there are hidden flaws within you. Even if you are high and of a higher type, much in you is crooked and unshaped. There is no craftsman in the world who could forge you straight and true for me.

You are only bridges—may higher ones cross over on you! You are steps, so do not blame him who climbs higher, reaching greater heights!

One day, from your kind, there may rise a true son and perfect heir for me, but that time is distant. You yourselves are not the ones meant for my legacy and name.

I do not wait here in these mountains for you; you will not be with me when I descend for the last time. You have come to me only as a sign that higher ones are on their way to me—

Not men of great longing, or loathing, or even satiety, and not those who are remnants of God;

No! No! Three times No! I wait for others here in these mountains and will not lift my foot to descend without them;

For stronger ones, higher ones, more triumphant, joyful ones; for those built solidly in body and soul: lions who laugh must come!

Oh, my guests, my strange ones—have you heard nothing of my children, that they are on their way to me?

Won't you speak to me of my gardens, of my Blessed Isles, of my new beautiful race—why do you say nothing of these?

This is the gift I ask of your love, that you speak to me of my children. For them, I am rich; for them, I became poor. What haven't I given up?

What wouldn't I give to have this one thing—these children, this living growth, these life-trees of my will and my highest hope!"

Thus spoke Zarathustra, and then suddenly stopped, as his deep longing came over him. He closed his eyes and his mouth, moved by his heart's emotion. All his guests fell silent too and stood still, taken aback, except for the old soothsayer, who made signs with his hands and gestures.

Chapter 72
The Last Supper

At this moment, the soothsayer interrupted Zarathustra's greeting with urgency, pressing forward as if he had no time to lose. He grabbed Zarathustra's hand and exclaimed, "But Zarathustra! One thing is always more necessary than another—you say that yourself. And right now, there's one thing I need above all else.

A word at the right moment. Didn't you invite me to your table? And here we are, many of us who have traveled far. Do you mean to feed us only with speeches? We've all been thinking about freezing, drowning, suffocating, and other dangers to our bodies, but no one here has considered my danger—namely, starving to death!"

(When Zarathustra's animals heard this, they ran away in terror, realizing that everything they had gathered that day would hardly be enough to satisfy just the soothsayer alone.)

"Also dying of thirst," the soothsayer continued. "And though I hear water trickling like words of wisdom—flowing freely and endlessly—I want wine! Not everyone is born to drink only water like Zarathustra. Water is hardly suitable for the weary and dried-up; we deserve wine. It alone gives instant vigor and brings health!"

As the soothsayer spoke about wine, the silent king on the left finally spoke. "We thought ahead," he said, "my brother the king on the right and I. We brought plenty of wine—an entire load of it on the back of an ass. So, the only thing missing is bread."

"Bread?" replied Zarathustra with a laugh. "Bread is exactly what hermits don't have. But man does not live by bread alone! I also have two good lambs, and we'll roast them quickly and season them with sage—just the way I like it. And we have plenty of roots and fruits, fit even for the fussy and refined, along with nuts and other riddles to crack.

We'll soon have a fine feast, but anyone who wants to eat with us must also lend a hand, even the kings. With Zarathustra, even a king can become a cook."

This suggestion pleased them all, except the voluntary beggar, who objected to the idea of meat, wine, and spices.

"Listen to Zarathustra, the glutton!" he said, laughing. "Does one really go into caves and high mountains for such feasts? Now I understand why he once taught, 'Blessed be moderate poverty!' and why he'd like to do away with beggars."

"Cheer up," replied Zarathustra. "Follow your own ways, my friend: grind your grain, drink your water, praise your cooking, so long as it brings you joy! I am only a law to my own people, not to everyone. But those who belong to me must be strong in body and light in step,

Ready to fight and to feast, not sullen, not idle dreamers, but eager for the hardest tasks as well as the feast—healthy and sound. The best belongs to mine and me, and if it's not given to us, we take it—the best food, the clearest skies, the strongest thoughts, and the fairest women!"

Zarathustra's words made the king on the right exclaim, "How strange! Has anyone ever heard such reasonable things come from a wise man? It's amazing for a wise man to be sensible as well, and not a fool."

So spoke the king on the right in wonder; but the ass, with a disagreeable tone, brayed, "Yea," to his remark. Thus began that lengthy meal, known as "The Supper" in the history books, during which the higher man was the only topic of conversation.

At this moment, the soothsayer interrupted Zarathustra's greeting to his guests. He stepped forward as if he couldn't wait, grabbed Zarathustra's hand, and said, "But Zarathustra!

One thing is more necessary than another, as you often say yourself; well, one thing is more necessary to me right now than anything else.

A word at the right moment: didn't you invite me to your table? And here are many who have traveled far to be here. Surely, you don't plan to feed us only with speeches?

Besides, all of you have been too concerned with freezing, drowning, suffocating, and other physical dangers. Yet none of you has considered my danger — which is dying of hunger."

(As the soothsayer spoke, Zarathustra's animals, hearing his words, fled in fright. They realized that all they had gathered during the day wouldn't be nearly enough to satisfy even this one soothsayer.)

"And of thirst too," the soothsayer added. "Though I hear water splashing here, like words of wisdom — in abundance and tirelessly — I need wine!

Not everyone is naturally suited to drinking water, like Zarathustra. Water doesn't revive the weary and withered; we deserve wine. Only wine brings immediate strength and restored energy!"

Just as the soothsayer expressed his craving for wine, the king on the left — usually the quiet one — finally spoke up. "We've taken care of that," he said. "About the wine, I, along with my brother the king on the right, brought plenty — a whole load of it, enough to fill an entire donkey. All that's missing is the bread."

"Bread," said Zarathustra, laughing, "is precisely what hermits don't have. But man doesn't live by bread alone; he also lives by the flesh of good lambs, of which I happen to have two.

We'll slaughter them quickly and cook them well with sage: that's how I like it. And we have roots and fruits too, good enough for the choosy and refined, along with nuts and other things to crack.

So, in a short while, we'll have a fine meal. But anyone who wants to eat with us will have to pitch in, even the kings. For with Zarathustra, even a king may become a cook."

This suggestion pleased everyone's hearts, except the voluntary beggar, who objected to the meat, wine, and spices.

"Just listen to this glutton Zarathustra!" he joked. "Do people come to caves and high mountains to prepare such feasts?

Now I understand what he once taught us: 'Blessed be modest poverty!' And why he wishes to do away with beggars."

"Cheer up," Zarathustra replied, "as I am. Stick with your ways, you fine one: grind your grain, drink your water, and praise your cooking, as long as it makes you happy!

I'm only a rule for my own people; I'm not a rule for everyone. But anyone who belongs to me must be strong of bone and light on their feet,

joyful in battle and feasting, not sluggish or sleepy, ready for the hardest tasks as much as for the feasts, healthy and hearty.

The best belongs to me and mine; and if it's not given to us, we take it ourselves: the finest food, the clearest skies, the most powerful thoughts, the fairest women!"

So Zarathustra spoke, and the king on the right replied, "How strange! Have you ever heard such sensible words from a wise man?

And truly, it's the strangest thing in a wise man, if in addition to wisdom, he's also sensible, and not an ass."

That's what the king on the right said in wonder, and the ass, though not pleased, brayed "Y-A" to his remark. And this was how that long meal began, which, in the history books, is called "The Supper." During it, the only topic of discussion was the higher man.

Chapter 73
The Higher Man

When I first came to men, I made the mistake of a hermit—a great mistake. I appeared in the marketplace. And when I spoke to everyone, I spoke to no one. By evening, my companions were tightrope walkers and corpses, and I was nearly a corpse myself.

But with the new morning came a new truth: I learned to say, "What do I care for the marketplace, for the rabble, for their noise and their endless processions!"

You higher men, learn this from me: No one in the marketplace believes in higher men. But if you must speak there, so be it. The rabble, however, only blinks and says, "We are all equal."

"You higher men,"—so says the rabble, "there are no higher men; we are all equal. Man is man, and before God, we are all equal!"

Before God! But now, that God has died. Before the rabble, though, we will not be equal. You higher men, leave the marketplace!

Before God! But now this God has died! You higher men, this God was your greatest danger. Only now that he lies in the grave have you risen again. Only now does the great noontide arrive, only now does the higher man become—master!

Do you understand this, my brothers? Are you frightened? Does your heart falter? Do you feel the abyss open before you? Does the hellhound howl at you here?

Then take courage, you higher men! For only now is the mountain of humanity's future beginning to labor. God has died; now we desire the Superman to live.

Today, many ask, "How will humanity survive?" Zarathustra, however, is the first and only one to ask, "How is man to be surpassed?"

I care about the Superman; that is all that matters to me—not man: not the neighbor, not the poorest, not the weakest, nor even the best.

O my brothers, what I can love in man is that he is a transition and a decline. And there is much in you that makes me love and hope.

In your contempt, you higher men, lies my hope. For those who despise greatly are those who revere greatly.

In your despair, there is much to honor, for you have not learned to submit or to practice petty politics.

Today, however, the petty people have become masters: they preach submission, humility, policy, diligence, consideration, and an endless list of petty virtues.

The weak, the servile, and especially the rabble—this is what now seeks to rule over all of humanity's destiny. O disgust! Disgust! Disgust!

They endlessly ask, "How can humanity survive best, longest, and most comfortably?" And by that, they have become today's masters.

These masters of today—overcome them, O my brothers—these petty people: they are the greatest threat to the Superman!

Overcome the petty virtues, the petty politics, the small-mindedness, the ant-hill concerns, the pitiful contentment, the "happiness of the greatest number"!

Better to despair than to submit! And truly, I love you because you don't know how to live today, you higher men! For that is how you live best!

Are you brave, my brothers? Do you have the courage of hermits and eagles, which not even a god sees anymore?

I do not call mules, the blind, or the drunk courageous. True courage belongs to those who know fear but conquer it; who see the abyss and look into it with pride.

Those who look at the abyss with eagle eyes—who seize it with eagle claws—have true courage.

"Man is evil," all the wise ones told me, to console me. Ah, if only that were still true today! For evil is man's best strength.

"Man must become better and worse," that is what I teach. The worst in man is necessary for the Superman's best.

It may have suited the preacher of the petty people to suffer and bear humanity's sins. But I, I rejoice in great sin as my great consolation.

Such things are not meant for long ears. Every word is not suited for every mouth. These are fine, distant matters, beyond the reach of sheep's hooves!

You higher men, do you think I am here to fix what you have broken?

Or to make softer beds for you sufferers? Or to show you lost, wandering, climbing ones, new and easier paths?

No! No! Three times No! Always more, always better men of your kind must fall—because you must always face harder trials. Only in this way—only in this way—can man grow high enough to reach where the lightning strikes him: high enough for the lightning!

My soul and my seeking go out towards the few, the long, the distant; what do your countless little, brief sufferings matter to me? You don't yet suffer enough for me! For you suffer from yourselves, not yet from mankind. If you claim otherwise, you would be lying! None of you suffers from what I have suffered.

It's not enough for me that the lightning does no harm. I don't want to deflect it—I want it to learn to work for me. My wisdom has gathered for long like a cloud; it grows quieter, darker. So does all wisdom that one day will bear lightnings.

I will not be light to the men of today, nor will I be called light. I will blind them—lightning of my wisdom! Put out their eyes!

Do not desire beyond your power; there's a deceitfulness in those who desire beyond their power. Especially when they crave great things! For they create distrust of great things, these sly impostors and actors—until, at last, they become false even towards themselves, like squint-eyed masks painted with glowing words, fake virtues, and shining false acts.

Be cautious, you higher men! For nothing is more precious to me, and rarer, than honesty.

Today, honesty belongs to the rabble. The rabble does not know what is great and small, what is straight and what is honest. It is innocently crooked; it always lies.

Have a healthy mistrust, you higher men, you bold-hearted ones, you open-hearted ones! And keep your reasons hidden! For today belongs to the rabble. What the rabble once learned to believe without reasons, who could convince them otherwise with reasons?

In the marketplace, people are persuaded with gestures. But reasons make the rabble suspicious.

And when truth has once won there, ask yourself with a wise distrust: "What strong error has fought for it?"

Beware also of the learned! They resent you because they create nothing! They have cold, lifeless eyes, before which every bird is stripped bare.

Such people boast of never lying; but being unable to lie is still far from loving the truth. Be on your guard! Freedom from fever is still far from knowledge! I do not trust cooled-down spirits. One who cannot lie does not know what truth is.

If you want to rise high, use your own legs! Don't be carried up on other people's backs or heads!

Have you mounted a horse, racing up to your goal? Well, friend! But remember that your lame foot rides along with you!

When you reach your goal, when you dismount, right there at the height, you higher man—you will stumble!

You creators, you higher men! Each one bears only his own child. Don't let yourselves be deceived or burdened with false goals! Who is your neighbor, anyway? Even if you act "for your neighbor"—you do not create for him!

Forget, I urge you, this "for." You creators, let your virtue have nothing to do with "for" and "because." Close your ears to these false little words.

"For one's neighbor" is the virtue only of the small-minded: for them, it's all about "like helps like" and "you scratch my back, I'll scratch yours"—they lack the right and the strength for self-seeking!

In your self-seeking, creators, there's the foresight and anticipation of the one who bears life within! What no one's eye has yet seen—the fruit of your labor—this is what shelters, preserves, and nourishes your whole love.

Where your whole love resides, namely, with your creation, there lies all your virtue! Your work, your will, is your "neighbor"—don't let false values distract you!

Creators, you higher men! Whoever is in labor suffers; yet after birth, one is unclean.

Ask women: no one gives birth for pleasure. The pain makes hens and poets cluck.

Creators, within you lies much that is unclean. This comes from the necessity of being mothers.

A new child! Oh, how much new filth has also entered the world! Go aside! Whoever has given birth must cleanse his soul!

Do not aim for virtue beyond your strength! Seek nothing in yourself that contradicts possibility!

Walk in the path where the virtue of your fathers has already walked! How will you rise higher unless your fathers' will rises within you?

Yet anyone wishing to be a firstling must take care not to become a lastling! And where the flaws of your fathers exist, don't try to stand as saints!

If one's fathers were given to women, strong wine, and rich meat—how could he demand chastity of himself?

It would be folly! Indeed, for such a person, being the husband of one, two, or even three wives seems quite a feat.

And if he founded monasteries with signs reading "The Path to Holiness," I would still say, "What's the use? It's just a new foolishness!"

He has made for himself a house of penance and refuge—fine, if it helps him! But I wouldn't believe in it.

In solitude, what grows is what anyone brings into it—including the brute in one's nature. For many, solitude is unsuitable.

Has there ever been anything filthier on earth than the saints of the wilderness? Around them, not only was the devil loose but also the swine.

Shy, ashamed, awkward, like a tiger whose leap has failed—this is how I've often seen you, higher men, shrink away. A throw you made had failed.

But what does it matter, you gamblers! You haven't yet learned to play and mock as one must play and mock! Are we not always seated at the great table of jest and play?

And if great things have failed you, does that mean you yourselves have failed? And if you yourselves have failed, does it mean humanity has failed? If humanity, however, has failed—well then! Never mind!

The higher the type, the less often does success occur. You higher men, have you not all—been failures?

Be cheerful; what does it matter? How much is still possible! Learn to laugh at yourselves as you ought to laugh!

What wonder that you have failed and only half-succeeded, you half-broken ones! Does not humanity's future strive and struggle within you?

The furthest reaches, the deepest thoughts, and the highest powers of man—don't all of these surge together in you? It's no wonder that many a vessel shatters from holding so much! Learn to laugh at yourselves, as you truly should! You higher men, so much is still possible!

And indeed, so much has already been achieved! This earth is so rich in small, good, perfect things, in well-made things! Surround yourselves with small, good, perfect things, you higher men. Their golden ripeness heals the heart. The perfect teaches us to hope.

What has been the greatest sin here on earth so far? Was it not the saying of one who declared: "Woe to those who laugh now!" Didn't he find anything on earth to laugh about? Then he searched poorly. Even a child finds reasons to laugh.

He simply didn't love enough; otherwise, he would have loved us too, we who laugh! But instead, he hated and condemned us; he promised us weeping and gnashing of teeth.

Must we curse when we don't love? That seems like poor taste to me. Yet he did it, this absolute one. He was born from the crowd.

And he didn't love enough; otherwise, he would have raged less when people did not love him. True love doesn't seek love; it seeks something greater.

Avoid all such absolute ones! They are a poor, sickly type, a common type; they look at life with resentment, and they have a gloomy outlook on this earth.

Stay away from them! They carry heavy burdens and sultry hearts—they don't know how to dance. How could life be light to them?

All good things come slowly to their goal, like cats arching their backs and purring as they near their happiness. All good things laugh.

You can tell if someone walks on their own path by how they step: watch how I walk! But one who nears his goal dances.

And truly, I am not a statue yet; I don't stand stiff, dull, and stony, like a pillar. I love to move swiftly.

And though there are muddy places and heavy burdens on this earth, one with light feet can cross even the mud and dance as if on polished ice.

Lift up your hearts, my brothers, high, higher! And don't forget your legs! Lift your legs, you good dancers—better yet, try standing on your heads!

This crown of laughter, this garland of roses—I put this crown on myself; I alone blessed my laughter. I have found no one today strong enough for this.

Zarathustra, the dancer, Zarathustra, the light-hearted one, who waves his wings, ready to take flight, calling to all birds, a blissfully light-hearted soul—Zarathustra the prophet, Zarathustra the joyful one, not impatient, not absolute, one who loves leaps and side-leaps. I crowned myself!

Lift up your hearts, my brothers, high, higher! And don't forget your legs! Lift up your legs, you good dancers—better yet, stand on your heads!

There are also heavy creatures who find happiness, the clumsy from the start. They try awkwardly, like an elephant trying to stand on its head.

But better to be foolish with joy than foolish with sorrow, better to dance awkwardly than limp along sadly. So learn, please, my wisdom, you higher men: even the worst thing has two good sides—

Even the worst thing has good dancing legs. So learn, I pray you, you higher men, to find your footing!

So, I beg you, unlearn the sighing and sorrow, and all the sadness of the crowd! Oh, how gloomy the fools of the masses seem to me today! Today, however, belongs to the crowd.

Be like the wind when it bursts out of its mountain caves: it will dance to its own music, and the seas tremble and leap beneath its steps.

Blessed be that wild, ungovernable spirit that gives wings to donkeys and draws milk from lionesses—a spirit that blows like a hurricane through everything present and every crowd,

That spirit, hostile to prickly minds and dull thinkers, and to all the withered and lifeless—it dances upon marshes and misfortunes as if they were meadows!

It despises the sickly dogs of the masses and all the sullen, miserable sorts—blessed be this spirit of freedom, the laughing storm, that blows dust into the eyes of all the melancholy!

You higher men, the worst in you is that none of you have learned to dance as you should—to dance beyond yourselves! So what if you have stumbled!

There is still so much possible! So learn to laugh beyond yourselves! Lift your hearts, you joyful dancers, high! Higher! And don't forget the joy of laughter!

This crown of laughter, this garland of roses: I toss it to you, my brothers! Laughing, I have blessed it. You higher men, learn, I beg you—to laugh!

Chapter 74

The Song of Melancholy

When Zarathustra spoke these words, he stood close to the entrance of his cave. But with his last words, he slipped away from his guests and went into the open air for a moment.

"O pure scents around me!" he cried. "O blessed stillness around me! But where are my animals? Here, here, my eagle and my serpent! Tell me, my animals: all these higher men—do they perhaps not smell so good? O pure scents around me! Now, only now, do I realize how much I love you, my animals."

And Zarathustra said once more, "I love you, my animals!" The eagle and the serpent came close to him when he said this and looked up at him. The three of them stood together in silence, breathing in and tasting the fresh air around them. For the air here outside was fresher than in the company of the higher men.

But Zarathustra had barely left the cave when the old magician got up, looked around craftily, and said, "He's gone! And already, you higher men—let me flatter you with this pleasant name, as he himself does—already my deceptive and magical spirit begins to stir, my melancholy devil. It is an enemy to this Zarathustra right to its core. Forgive it for that! Now it wants to make its plea to you; this is its hour, and I struggle in vain with this wicked spirit.

"To all of you, whatever titles you may prefer—whether you call yourselves 'free spirits,' 'the conscientious,' 'penitents of the spirit,' 'the liberated,' or 'the great seekers'—to all of you who, like me, suffer from the great disgust, to whom the old god has died, and no new god yet lies in cradles and swaddling clothes—to all of you, my evil spirit, this magic-devil of mine, is favorable.

"I know you, you higher men; I know him, too—I know this fiend I love against my will, this Zarathustra. Often, he seems to me like the lovely mask of a saint, like a strange new disguise my evil spirit, this melancholy devil, delights in. I love Zarathustra, or so it often feels to me, for the sake of my own evil spirit.

"But now it attacks me and overwhelms me, this spirit of melancholy, this twilight devil. And truly, you higher men, it has a desire—it longs—open your eyes! It longs to come forth bare, whether man or woman, I cannot yet tell; but it comes, it compels me—alas! Open your minds!

"Day is ending; evening comes to all things, even to the best of things. Look now and listen, you higher men, to what devil—man or woman—this spirit of evening melancholy is!"

So spoke the old magician, glancing about with cunning, and then he picked up his harp.

In the clear evening air,
When the gentle dewdrops
Fall quietly to the earth, unseen and unheard-
For the dew walks softly, like all things kind and gentle-:
Do you remember, oh, burning heart,
How you once thirsted
For heaven's gentle tears and refreshing drops of dew,

Longing and weary,
While on yellow grass paths,
Harsh, western sunbeams
Played through the shadowed trees around you,
Blinding you with their bright, stinging glow?
"Are you a seeker of truth? Really, you?" - they mocked -
"No! Just a poet!
A sly creature, creeping and hiding,
That you have to lie,
That knowingly, intentionally, you lie:
Driven by desire,
Masked in colors,
Hiding yourself,
Chasing your own desires-
A seeker of truth?
No! Just a fool! Just a poet!
Just a jester,
Shouting in confusion from behind a fool's mask,
Walking on made-up bridges of words,
On colorful rainbow paths,
Between false heavens,
And false earth,
Wandering around us, floating above us,-
Just a fool! Just a poet!
A seeker of truth?
Not still, rigid, smooth, and cold,
Like an image,
A godlike statue,
Placed in front of temples,
As the guardian of a god's doorway:
No! He opposes all such statues of truth,
Feeling more at home in every wilderness than at temples,
With playful, cat-like ease,
Leaping through every window
Every wild forest sniffing,

Greedily and eagerly sniffing,
So that in those wild woods,
Among the fierce, colorful creatures,
You should roam, sinful and bright,
With lips longing and smacking,
Joyfully mocking, joyfully wild, joyfully bloodthirsty,
Sneaking, hiding, lying—wandering:—
Or like eagles, who gaze intently,
Far down the cliffs,
Down into their depths:——
Oh, how they dive now,
Down below, into it,
Whirling deeper and deeper into the dark!—
Then,
Suddenly,
With precise aim,
With a trembling flight,
They dive on lambs,
Headfirst, driven by hunger,
Longing for the lambs,
Fierce against all lamb-spirits,
Raging and fierce against anything
That looks like sheep, or has soft lamb eyes, or curly wool,
—Gray, with that kind, lamb-like look!
Just like that,
With eagle's hunger, panther's drive,
Are the poet's desires,
Are your own desires, taking on countless forms.
You fool! You poet!
You who look upon all humankind—
Like God, like sheep—:
The god to tear apart within mankind,
Just like sheep within mankind,
And laughing as you tear-
That, that is your own joy!

A joy like the panther's and eagle's!
A joy like the poet's and fool's!
In the clear evening air,
When the moon's sickle,
Green, between the purple glow,
Creeps out, jealous:
-An enemy of day,
With every secret step,
Gently cutting down
The rosy garlands of light,
Until they sink
Down into the night, fading, fallen into the dusk:-
One day I, too, had sunk
From my own crazy truth,
From my burning, daylight dreams,
Tired of the day, sick of sunlight,
Sank downward, toward the evening, toward the shadows:
Scorched and thirsty,
By one lonely truth.
Do you remember, oh, burning heart,
How you thirsted then?-
That I should be banned
From all truth!
Just a fool! Just a poet!

Chapter 75

Science

Thus the magician sang; and everyone there, without realizing it, was drawn in like birds caught in the net, into the spell of his artful and sad longing. Only the spiritually cautious one was not caught: he immediately seized the harp from the magician and called out: "Air! Let fresh air in! Let Zarathustra in! You're making this cave stuffy and poisonous, you wicked old magician!

You seducer, you deceiver, drawing people to strange desires and deserts. And how terrible that people like you should speak and make such a fuss about the truth!

Alas, for all free spirits who don't protect themselves against such magicians! Their freedom is as good as gone: you lure and tempt them back into prisons,-

-You old, sad devil, your laments are a trap: you're like those who talk of purity, while secretly urging indulgence!

So spoke the cautious one; but the old magician only looked around, relishing his success, and for that reason tolerated the annoyance the cautious one caused him. "Be silent!" he said softly, "good songs need to echo; after good songs, one should remain silent for a long time.

This is what everyone here does, these higher men. But you, perhaps you understood very little of my song? There is little of the magic spirit in you.

"You flatter me," replied the cautious one, "by setting me apart from yourself; very well! But the rest of you, what do I see? You all still sit here, with longing eyes-:

You free spirits, where has your freedom gone! You seem to me almost like people who have watched wicked dancers too long: even your souls are dancing!

In you, you higher men, there must be more of what the magician calls his evil spirit of trickery and deceit:- we are indeed different.

And truly, we have spoken and thought together for long enough before Zarathustra returned to his cave for me not to know that we are different.

We seek different things even here, high up, you and I. For I seek more security; for that reason, I have come to Zarathustra. For he is still the most steadfast tower and the strongest will-

-Today, when everything wavers, when all the earth shakes. But you, when I see what sort of looks you give, it almost seems to me that you seek more insecurity,

-More horror, more danger, more earthquakes. You desire (so it almost seems to me- forgive my boldness, you higher men)-

-You desire the worst and most dangerous life, which frightens me the most,- the life of wild animals, of forests, caves, steep mountains, and twisting ravines.

And it's not those who lead you out of danger whom you admire most, but those who lead you off the path, the misguiders. But if that longing of yours is truly real, it still seems impossible to me.

Because fear—that is the oldest and most basic feeling in humanity; fear explains everything, original sin and original virtue alike. My virtue, too, grew from fear, that is: Knowledge.

Fear of wild beasts—that is the oldest and deepest fear in man, including the beast he hides and fears within himself:- Zarathustra calls it 'the beast inside.'

Such an ancient, long-lasting fear, which has finally become refined, spiritual, and intellectual—today, I think it's called Knowledge."-

So spoke the cautious one; but Zarathustra, who had just come back into his cave and had overheard and understood the last part of this conversation, threw a handful of roses at the cautious one, and laughed at his "truths." "Why!" he exclaimed, "what did I just hear? It seems to me, either you are a fool, or I am one: and quickly and quietly, I'll turn your 'truth' upside down."

For fear—is rare among us. Courage, however, and adventure, and delight in the unknown, in the untried—courage, to me, is the entire early history of humanity.

The wildest and most courageous animals he envied and stole all their strengths from: only in this way did he become—human.

This courage, finally becoming subtle, spiritual, and intellectual, this human courage, with the wings of an eagle and the wisdom of a serpent: this, it seems to me, is called today—"

"Zarathustra!" they all cried in unison, as if with one voice, and suddenly burst into loud laughter; yet it was as if a heavy cloud rose up from them. Even the magician laughed, and said knowingly: "Well! My evil spirit has left!

Didn't I warn you about it when I said it was a deceiver, a lying and tricky spirit?

Especially when it shows itself bare. But what can I do about its tricks! Did I create it and the world?

Well! Let us be kind again, and in good spirits! And though Zarathustra looks at me with a harsh gaze—look at him! he dislikes me—:

—Before night falls, he will once again learn to love and praise me; he cannot go long without such foolishness.

He—loves his enemies: he knows this art better than anyone I have known. But he takes his revenge for it—on his friends!"

Thus spoke the old magician, and the higher men applauded him; so Zarathustra went around, mischievously and warmly shaking hands with his friends,—like one who must make up and apologize to everyone for something. But when he had come to the door of his cave, behold, he suddenly longed for the fresh air outside, for his animals,—and wished to slip away.

Chapter 76

Among Daughters of the Desert

"Don't go!" said the wanderer who called himself Zarathustra's shadow, "stay with us—otherwise the old gloomy sadness might fall upon us again.

That old magician has given us his worst for our own good, and look! The good, devout pope there has tears in his eyes, and he's drifting again on the sea of sorrow.

Those kings may still put on a brave face for us—at that, they've learned best from us all! But if no one were watching, I'd bet they too would slip back into that bad game,-

-The bad game of drifting clouds, of damp melancholy, of hidden skies, of stolen sunlight, of wailing autumn winds,

-The bad game of our cries and shouts for help! Stay with us, O Zarathustra! Here there's much hidden sorrow wanting to speak, much evening, many clouds, much heavy air!

You have fed us strong food for men, and powerful words: don't let the weak, womanly spirits come back to trouble us at dessert!

Only you make the air around you strong and clear. Have I ever found air as good anywhere on earth as with you in your cave?

I've traveled many lands; my nose has learned to test and evaluate many types of air: but here, my nostrils take their greatest delight!

Unless it be—unless it be—do forgive an old memory! Forgive me an old after-dinner song I once wrote among the daughters of the desert:-

For with them there was also such good, clear, Eastern air; there I felt furthest from the cloudy, damp, and melancholy Old-Europe!

Back then, I loved those Eastern maidens and those other blue skies of heaven, over which no clouds or thoughts hung.

You wouldn't believe how charmingly they sat there, when they weren't dancing, deep but without thoughts, like little secrets, like ribboned riddles, like dessert nuts—

Bright-colored and foreign, indeed! but without clouds: riddles that can be solved. To please such maidens, I once wrote an after-dinner psalm."

So spoke the wanderer who called himself Zarathustra's shadow; and before anyone answered, he had taken up the harp of the old magician, crossed his legs, and looked around calmly and wisely—yet he slowly, questioningly breathed in the air through his nostrils, like someone in a new land tasting unfamiliar air. Then he began to sing with a sort of deep roar:

The deserts grow: woe to him who tries to hide them!
—Ha!
Solemnly!
Indeed, quite solemnly!
A worthy beginning!
In the African style, solemnly!
Worthy of a lion,
Or perhaps a virtuous howling monkey—
—But it doesn't mean much to you,
You friendly damsels dearly loved,
Before whom, for the first time,
A European like me,
Is now seated under palm trees. Selah.
Wonderful, truly!
Here I sit now,
The desert close, and yet I am
Still so far from the desert,
In no way deserted at all:
Instead, I've been swallowed whole
By this little oasis—:
—It opened up, yawning wide,
Its loveliest mouth, sweet-smelling
Of all small mouths:
Then down I fell,
Right down, right through—into the midst of you,
You friendly damsels dearly loved! Selah.
Hail! Hail! to this whale, fish-like,
If it's made things so nice

For its guest's pleasure—(you surely understand,
My learned reference?)
Hail to its belly,
If it ever had
Such a lovely oasis-belly
As this one: though, I have my doubts,
—For I come from Old-Europe,
Where one doubts more eagerly than any
Old married woman.
May the Lord make it better!
Amen!
Here I sit now,
In this small oasis,
Like a date indeed,
Brown, quite sweet, golden and ripe,
For the rounded mouth of a maiden in longing,
But even more so for young, maiden-like,
Ice-cold and snow-white, sharp
Front teeth: and for these, without a doubt,
The hearts of all fiery dates pine. Selah.
Like those south-fruits just mentioned,
Similar, all-too-similar,
I lie here; surrounded by little
Flying insects
Sniffing around and playing,
And also by smaller,
More foolish, more guilty
Wishes and fantasies,
Encircled by you,
You quiet, most perceptive
Maiden-kittens,
Dudu and Suleika,
-Round like sphinxes, to capture much feeling
In a single word:
(Forgive me, O God,

For such sinful speech!)
-I sit here sniffing the best of air,
Paradise air, truly,
Clear and uplifting, gold-flecked air,
As fine an air as ever
Fell down from the moon-
Was it by chance,
Or did it come by proud design,
As the ancient poets say?
But as a doubter, I'm now calling it
Into question: indeed, this is what I bring
Out of Europe,
Where one doubts more eagerly than any
Old married woman.
May the Lord make it better!
Amen.
Here I am drinking this finest air,
With nostrils flared like goblets,
Free of future, free of memories,
Thus I sit here, you
Friendly damsels dearly loved,
And gaze at the palm tree there,
How it, like a dancing girl,
Bows and bends, bouncing on its haunches,
-One does, too, if one watches it long enough!-
Like a dancer, who, it seems to me,
Has stood too long, too dangerously persistent,
Always, always, on just one leg?
-Then it seems she forgot, as it seems to me,
The other leg?
For I, at least, have searched in vain
For that missing
Counterpart jewel
—Namely, the other leg—
In the holy surroundings,

Near her most precious, most delicate,
Fluttering, flickering skirt.
Yes, if you, beautiful friendly ones,
Would believe me entirely:
She has, alas, lost it!
Hu! Hu! Hu! Hu! Hu!
It's gone!
Gone forever!
The other leg!
Oh, pity for that most lovely other leg!
Where does it now linger, abandoned and weeping?
The most lonesome leg?
Perhaps trembling in fear before a
Furious, yellow, blond, curly
Lion-like monster? Or perhaps even
Gnawed away, chewed to bits—
Most unfortunate, sorrowful! sorrowful! chewed to bits! Selah.
Oh, don't weep,
Gentle spirits!
Don't cry, you
Date-fruit spirits! Milk-breasted!
Sweetwood-hearted
Little purses!
Weep no more,
Pale Dudu!
Be brave, Suleika! Bold! Bold!
—Or should there perhaps be
Something strengthening, something heartening,
Most fitting here?
Some uplifting words?
A solemn encouragement?—
Ha! Now rise! honor!
Moral honor! European honor!
Blow again, keep going,
Bellows of virtue!

Ha!
Once more your roaring,
Your moral roar!
Like a virtuous lion
Roaring near the daughters of deserts!
—For virtue's mighty howl,
You dearest maidens,
Is greater than any
European zeal, European hot-hunger!
And here I stand,
As a European,
I can't be otherwise, God help me!
Amen!
The deserts grow: woe to him who tries to hide them!

Chapter 77

The Awakening

After the song of the wanderer and shadow, the cave was suddenly filled with noise and laughter: all the gathered guests spoke at once, and even the ass, encouraged by them, no longer stayed silent. A small feeling of distaste and scorn for his visitors came over Zarathustra, though he rejoiced in their happiness. For he took it as a sign of their recovery. So he slipped outside into the open air and spoke to his animals.

"Where has their misery gone now?" he said, and already felt his own slight disgust fade. "With me, it seems, they have unlearned their cries of misery!

—Though, alas! not yet their whining." And Zarathustra covered his ears, for just then the braying of the ass mixed oddly with the loud cheers of those higher men.

"They are happy," he began again, "and who knows? maybe at their host's expense; and if they've learned to laugh from me, it's still not my laughter they've learned.

But what does that matter! They are older people: they recover in their own way, they laugh in their own way; my ears have already endured worse and haven't turned sour.

Today is a victory: he is already retreating, he flees—the spirit of gravity, my old arch-enemy! How well this day is ending, a day that began so badly and darkly!

And it is ending. Evening is already coming: over the sea it rides here, the good rider! How it bobs, the blessed one, the homeward-bound one, in its purple saddles!

The sky shines bright over there, the world lies deep. Oh, all of you strange ones who came to me, it's already been worth it to have lived with me!"

Thus spoke Zarathustra. And again, the shouts and laughter of the higher men echoed from the cave: then he began again:

"They're taking the bait, they're biting; their enemy, the spirit of gravity, is leaving them too. Now they're learning to laugh at themselves—am I hearing this right?

My strong food is working, my hearty sayings are taking effect: and truly, I didn't feed them with puffed-up vegetables! But with warrior's food, conqueror's food: I stirred up new desires.

New hopes are moving in their arms and legs, their hearts are growing. They're finding new words; soon, their spirits will breathe freely.

Such food may not be right for children, or even for wistful young and old girls. They need to be fed differently; I'm not their healer or teacher.

The disgust is leaving these higher men; well! That's my victory. In my realm, they grow sure of themselves; all their stupid shame fades; they're letting things out.

They're pouring out their hearts, good times are returning to them, they're celebrating and reflecting—they're becoming grateful.

That, I take as the best sign: they're becoming grateful. It won't be long before they create festivals and put up memorials to their old joys.

They are recovering!" Thus Zarathustra spoke joyfully to himself and gazed outward; his animals pressed up to him, honoring his happiness and his silence.

All of a sudden, Zarathustra's ear was startled: for the cave, which had been filled with noise and laughter, became suddenly silent as death;—his nose, however, detected a sweet-smelling vapor and the scent of incense, as if from burning pine cones.

"What's going on? What are they up to?" he asked himself, and crept up to the entrance, so he could secretly observe his guests. But wonder upon wonder! What was he forced to see with his own eyes!

"They've all become pious again, they're praying, they've gone mad!" he exclaimed, astonished beyond words. And indeed! all these higher men—the two kings, the retired pope, the wicked magician, the voluntary beggar, the wanderer and shadow, the old soothsayer, the spiritually conscientious one, and the ugliest man—they were all on their knees like children and devout old women, worshiping the ass.

And just then, the ugliest man began to gurgle and snort, as though something inexpressible inside him was struggling to come out; but when he finally found words, behold! it was a strange, reverent litany in praise of the adored and incense-scented ass. And the litany went like this:

Amen! And glory and honor and wisdom and thanks and praise and strength be to our God, from everlasting to everlasting!

—The ass, however, here brayed you-A.

He has carried our burdens, he has taken on the form of a servant, he is patient of heart and never says No; and he who loves his God disciplines him.

—The ass, however, here brayed you-A.

He speaks not, except that he always says Yes to the world he created: in this way, he praises his world. It is his wisdom not to speak: in this way, he is rarely proven wrong.

—The ass, however, here brayed you-A.

Through the world, he walks ungracefully. Gray is his favorite color in which he wraps his virtue. If he has a spirit, he hides it; everyone, however, believes in his long ears.

—The ass, however, here brayed you-A.

What hidden wisdom it is to wear long ears, to say only Yes and never No! Has he not made the world in his own image, that is, as foolish as possible?

—The ass, however, here brayed you-A.

You walk both straight and crooked paths; you care little for what seems straight or crooked to us humans. Your realm is beyond good and evil. It is your innocence not to know what innocence is.

—The ass, however, here brayed you-A.

Look! how you reject no one, neither beggars nor kings. You let little children come to you, and when the naughty boys tease you, you simply say you-A.

—The ass, however, here brayed you-A.

You love she-asses and fresh figs, you're no food snob. A thistle delights your heart when you happen to be hungry. In this, there is the wisdom of a God.

—The ass, however, here brayed you-A.

Chapter 78

The Ass Festival

At this point in the litany, Zarathustra could no longer hold back; he himself shouted you-A, even louder than the ass, and sprang into the midst of his maddened guests. "What on earth are you doing, you grown-up children?" he exclaimed, pulling the praying ones up from the ground. "Alas, if anyone other than Zarathustra had seen you:

Everyone would think you the worst blasphemers or the most foolish old women, with your new belief!

And you, old pope, how can you bring yourself to worship an ass as though it were God?"—

"O Zarathustra," answered the pope, "forgive me, but in matters of divinity, I'm more enlightened even than you. And it is fitting that it should be so.

Better to worship God in this form than in no form at all! Think on this saying, my exalted friend: you'll quickly see that there's wisdom in it.

The one who said 'God is a Spirit'—made the greatest leap toward unbelief ever taken on earth: that saying isn't easily undone!

My old heart leaps with joy because there's still something left to worship on earth. Forgive it, O Zarathustra, for the sake of an old, pious pontiff's heart!"—

"And you," said Zarathustra to the wanderer and shadow, "you call yourself a free spirit? And yet here you practice such idolatry and worship?

This is worse, truly, than with your bad brown girls, you terrible new believer!"

"It's sad enough," replied the wanderer and shadow, "you're right: but what can I do about it! The old god lives again, O Zarathustra, you can say what you want.

The ugliest man is to blame for all of it; he's revived him. And if he says he once killed him, well, the death of gods is always just a matter of opinion."

"And you," said Zarathustra, "you wicked old magician, what did you do! Who could believe in you anymore in this age of freedom, when you believe in such holy donkey-worship?

It was a foolish thing you did; how could you, a clever man, do something so foolish?"

"O Zarathustra," answered the shrewd magician, "you're right, it was a foolish thing—and it repulsed me, too."

"And you," said Zarathustra, turning to the spiritually conscientious one, "think about it and put your finger to your nose! Doesn't any of this go against your conscience? Isn't your spirit too pure for all this praying and the incense of these worshippers?"

"There's something in this," said the spiritually conscientious one, putting his finger to his nose. "There's something in this scene that actually feels good for my conscience.

Perhaps I dare not believe in God, yet surely, God seems most worthy of belief in this form.

God is said to be eternal, according to the testimony of the most pious; one who has so much time, takes time. As slow and as dull as possible: such a one could still go far.

And one who has too much spirit might well become infatuated with stupidity and folly. Think of yourself, O Zarathustra!

Even you—truly!—even you might become an ass from an overflow of wisdom.

Do not the true sages often walk the most crooked paths? The evidence proves it, O Zarathustra—your own evidence!"

"And you yourself, finally," said Zarathustra, turning to the ugliest man, who was still lying on the ground, stretching his arm up to the ass (for he was giving it wine to drink). "Tell me, you peculiar creature, what have you been doing!

You seem changed to me; your eyes are glowing, and a mantle of the sublime covers your ugliness. What did you do?

Is it true what they say, that you have reawakened him? And why? Was he not killed and disposed of for good reason?

You seem awakened yourself; what did you do? Why did you turn back? Why did you get converted? Speak, you peculiar one!"

"O Zarathustra," answered the ugliest man, "you are a rogue!

Whether he still lives, or lives again, or is completely dead—who of us knows best? I ask you.

But one thing I know—something I once learned from you, O Zarathustra: he who wants to kill most completely, laughs.

'Not by wrath, but by laughter does one kill'—that's what you once said, O Zarathustra, you hidden one, you wrathless destroyer, you dangerous saint—you are a rogue!"

Then it happened that Zarathustra, astonished by such roguish answers, jumped back to the door of his cave, and turning to all his guests, cried out in a loud voice:

"O you jesters, all of you, you fools! Why do you pretend and disguise yourselves before me!

How your hearts leaped with joy and wickedness, because you had finally become like little children again—yes, pious—

—Because you finally did again what children do—praying, folding your hands, and saying 'dear God'!

But now, please, leave this nursery, my own cave, where today all this childishness has been played out. Calm down here outside, your hot childlike excitement and heart-tumult!

Truly: except you become as little children, you shall not enter that kingdom of heaven." (And Zarathustra pointed upward with his hands.)

"But we don't want to enter the kingdom of heaven at all: we've become men—and so we want the kingdom of earth."

And Zarathustra began to speak again. "O my new friends," he said, "you strange ones, you higher men, how well you please me now—

—Since you have become joyful once again! You have all, truly, blossomed forth: it seems to me that new festivals are needed for such flowers as you.

—A little bold nonsense, a bit of divine service, an ass-festival, some old joyful Zarathustra folly, some loud bluster to set your spirits aglow. Remember this night and this ass-festival, you higher men! You created it while with me, and I take it as a good sign—such things only the recovering create!

And if you celebrate it again, this ass-festival, do it out of love for yourselves, and also out of love for me! And in remembrance of me!"

Thus spoke Zarathustra.

Chapter 79
The Drunken Song

Meanwhile, one by one, they went out into the open air, into the cool, contemplative night; Zarathustra himself, however, led the ugliest man by the hand, so he could show him his night-world—the great, round moon and the silver waterfalls near his cave. There they finally stood still beside one another—all of them older people, yet with comforted, brave hearts, astonished within themselves that it was so well with them on earth; and the mystery of the night drew nearer and nearer to their hearts. And once again, Zarathustra thought to himself, "Oh, how well they please me now, these higher men!"—but he did not say it aloud, for he respected their happiness and their silence.

Then something happened, the most astonishing event on this astonishingly long day: the ugliest man began once more, and for the last time, to gurgle and snort, and when he finally found the words, behold! Out of his mouth came a question, blunt and clear, a good, deep, straightforward question that moved the hearts of all who heard him.

"My friends, all of you," said the ugliest man, "what do you think? For the sake of this day—I am, for the first time, content to have lived my whole life.

And saying so much still doesn't seem enough. It's worth living on earth: one day, one festival with Zarathustra, has taught me to love the earth.

'Was that—life?' I will say to death. 'Well then! Once more!'

My friends, what do you think? Will you not, like me, say to death: 'Was that—life? For the sake of Zarathustra, well then! Once more!'"

Thus spoke the ugliest man; it was not far from midnight. And what happened then, do you think? As soon as the higher men heard his question, they suddenly became aware of their transformation and recovery, and of the one who caused it: then they rushed to Zarathustra, thanking, honoring, embracing him, and kissing his hands, each in his own way, so that some laughed and some wept. The old soothsayer even danced with delight; and though, as some say, he may have been full of sweet wine, he was certainly even fuller of sweet life, having cast aside all weariness. There are even some who claim that the ass danced as well, for the ugliest man had, after all, given it wine to drink earlier. Perhaps it happened, perhaps not; but even if the ass didn't dance that night, still, greater and rarer wonders took place than a dancing ass would have been. In short, as Zarathustra's saying goes: "What does it matter!"

When this happened with the ugliest man, Zarathustra stood there as if drunk: his gaze was dulled, his speech faltered, and his steps wavered. And who could guess what thoughts were moving through Zarathustra's soul? Apparently, however, his spirit had withdrawn and wandered far away, as though "walking along high mountain ridges," as it is written, "between two seas,

—Wandering between the past and the future like a heavy cloud." Slowly, however, as the higher men held him in their arms, he came back to himself, resisting the crowd of those honoring and caring for him with his hands; yet he said nothing. All at once, he quickly turned his head, as though he heard something; then he laid his finger on his lips and said, "Come!"

Immediately, a deep silence and mystery filled the air around them; from the depths below, the sound of a clock bell slowly rose. Zarathustra listened, as did the higher men; then he laid his finger to his lips a second time and said again, "Come! Come! Midnight is near!"—and his voice had changed. But he still hadn't moved from his spot. Then it grew even quieter and more mysterious, and everything listened—even the ass, Zarathustra's noble animals, the eagle and the serpent, the cave of Zarathustra, the great cool moon, and the night itself. Zarathustra, however, laid his hand on his lips a third time, and said:

Come! Come! Come! Let us now wander! The hour has come: let us wander into the night!

You higher men, it's nearly midnight; so I will whisper something to you, just as that old clock-bell whispers to me—

—As mysteriously, as fearfully, and as warmly as that midnight bell speaks to me, which has seen more than one man's life:

—It has counted the painful throbbings of your fathers' hearts—ah! ah! how it sighs! how it laughs in its sleep! The old, deep, deep midnight!

Hush! Hush! Now there are things heard that cannot be heard by day; now, in the cool air, when even the tumult in your hearts has grown still—

—Now it speaks, now it's heard, now it slips into the wakeful, nocturnal souls: ah! ah! how midnight sighs! how it laughs in its sleep!

—Do you not hear how it speaks to you, mysterious, fearsome, and warm, the old, deep, deep midnight?

O man, take heed!

Woe to me! Where has the time gone? Have I fallen into deep wells? The world sleeps—

Ah! Ah! The dog howls, the moon shines. I'd rather die, rather die, than tell you what my midnight heart is thinking now.

I have already died. It's all over. Spider, why do you spin around me? Do you want blood? Ah! Ah! The dew falls, the hour approaches—

The hour when I freeze and shiver, when it asks and asks and asks: "Who has the courage for it?

—Who will be the master of the world? Who will say: Thus shall you flow, great and small streams!"

The hour is coming: O man, you higher man, take heed! This is a message for fine ears, for your ears—what does the voice of deep midnight say?

It carries me away; my soul dances. Day's work! Day's work! Who will be the master of the world?

The moon is cool, the wind is still. Ah! Ah! Have you flown high enough already? You've danced, but remember, a leg is not a wing.

You good dancers, all the delight is over now; wine has turned to dregs, every cup is brittle, the graves murmur.

You haven't flown high enough: now the graves murmur, "Release the dead! Why is it still night? Doesn't the moon make us drunk?"

You higher men, free the graves, awaken the corpses! Ah, why does the worm still burrow? The hour is approaching—

—The clock bell tolls, the heart still trembles, the woodworm still burrows, the heartworm. Ah! Ah! The world is deep!

Sweet lyre! Sweet lyre! I love your tune, your drunken, wild tune! How long, how far, your sound has reached me, from the distance, from the ponds of love!

You old clock-bell, you sweet lyre! Every pain has torn your heart—father's pain, forefathers' pain; your voice has ripened,

—Ripened like golden autumn and afternoon, like my hermit's heart—now you say: The world itself has ripened, the grape turns brown,

—Now it wants to die, to die of happiness. You higher men, don't you feel it? There rises up a mysterious scent,

—A fragrance, a scent of eternity, a rosy-blessed, brown, golden-wine scent of ancient happiness.

—Of drunken, midnight-death happiness, which sings: the world is deep, and deeper than the day can understand!

Leave me alone! Leave me alone! I am too pure for you. Do not touch me! Has my world not just now become perfect?

My skin is too pure for your hands. Leave me alone, you dull, clumsy, foolish day! Is not midnight brighter?

The purest are to be the masters of the world, the most unknown, the strongest, the midnight-souls, brighter and deeper than any day.

O day, do you grope for me? Do you seek my happiness? Am I rich for you, lonely, a treasure-pit, a golden chamber?

O world, do you want me? Am I worldly to you? Am I spiritual for you? Am I divine for you? But day and world, you are too coarse—

—Find cleverer hands, grasp at deeper happiness, deeper sorrow; grasp for a god, but not for me:

—My sorrow, my joy is deep, strange day, but I am not a god, nor a god's torment. Deep is its woe.

God's woe is deeper, strange world! Grasp at God's woe, not at me! What am I? A drunken sweet lyre—

—A midnight lyre, a bell-frog that no one understands, but must still speak before the deaf, you higher men! For you do not understand me!

Gone! Gone! O youth! O noon! O afternoon! Now evening and night and midnight have come— the dog howls, the wind:

—Is the wind not a dog? It whines, it barks, it howls. Ah! Ah! How she sighs! How she laughs, how she wheezes and pants, this midnight!

How she speaks soberly now, this drunken poetess! Has she perhaps outdrunk her drunkenness? Has she become over-awake? Does she brood?

—She broods over her woe in a dream, the old, deep midnight— and over her joy even more. For joy, though woe be deep, is still deeper than grief can be.

You grapevine! Why do you praise me? Have I not pruned you? I am cruel; you bleed—what does your praise mean for my drunken cruelty?

"Whatever is perfected, everything mature—wants to die!" so you say. Blessed, blessed be the vintner's knife! But everything unripe wants to live—alas!

Woe says: "Go! Go away, you woe!" But everything that suffers wants to live, so it can become ripe and full of life and longing,

—Longing for the further, the higher, the brighter. "I want heirs," says everything that suffers. "I want children; I do not want myself"—

But joy wants no heirs, no children—joy wants itself, it wants eternity, it wants recurrence, it wants everything eternally the same.

Woe says: "Break, bleed, you heart! Wander, you leg! Fly, you wing! Forward! Upward! you pain!" Well then! Cheer up, O my old heart! Woe says: "Go!"

You higher men, what do you think? Am I a soothsayer? A dreamer? A drunkard? A dream-reader? A midnight bell?

Or a drop of dew? Or a fume and fragrance of eternity? Don't you hear it? Don't you smell it? Just now my world has become perfect; midnight is also midday—

Pain is also joy, curse is also blessing, night is also sun—go away, or you will learn that a sage is also a fool.

Did you ever say Yes to one joy? O my friends, then you also said Yes to all woe. All things are interlinked, entwined, and in love with each other—

—Did you ever once wish for time to return; did you ever say: "You please me, happiness! Instant! Moment!"—then you wanted all to come back again!

—All anew, all eternal, all interwoven, interlinked, in love—Oh, then you loved the world,—

—You eternal ones, you love it eternally and forever; and even to woe, you say: Go! but come back! For all joy wants—eternity!

All joy desires the eternity of all things; it wants honey, it wants dregs, it wants drunken midnight, it wants graves, it wants the comfort of grave-tears, it wants golden evening-red—

—What does joy not want! It thirsts more, it hungers more, it's fiercer, more mysterious, than all woe; it wants itself, it bites into itself, the ring's will twists within it,—

—It wants love, it wants hate; it's overflowing, it gives, it throws itself away, it begs for someone to take from it, it thanks the taker, it would rather be hated,—

—So rich is joy that it thirsts for woe, for hell, for hate, for shame, for the lame, for the world—for this world, oh, you know it well!

You higher men, it longs for you, this joy, this unstoppable, blessed joy—it longs for your woe, you failures! All eternal joy longs for failures.

For all joys want themselves; therefore, they also want grief! O happiness, O pain! Oh, break, you heart! You higher men, learn this, that joys desire eternity.

—Joys desire the eternity of all things; they desire deep, profound eternity!

Have you learned my song now? Have you guessed what it would say? Well! Cheer up! You higher men, now sing my roundelay!

Now sing the song yourselves, the song called "Once more," the meaning of which is "To all eternity!"—sing, you higher men, Zarathustra's roundelay!

O man! Take heed!
What says deep midnight's voice indeed?
"I slept my sleep—,
"From deepest dream I've woken, and plead:—
"The world is deep,
"And deeper than the day could see.
"Deep is its woe—,
"But joy deeper still than grief can be:
"Woe says: Go!
"But all joy wants eternity—,
"—Wants deep, profound eternity!"

Chapter 80
The Sign

In the morning, however, after that night, Zarathustra sprang up from his couch; and, having girded his loins, he stepped out of his cave glowing and strong, like a morning sun emerging from dark mountains.

"You great star," he spoke, as he had spoken once before, "you deep eye of happiness, what would all your happiness be if you didn't have those for whom you shine!

And if they stayed in their chambers while you're already awake, coming to give and share, how would your proud modesty reproach them for it!

Well! They still sleep, these higher men, while I am awake; they are not my true companions! Not for them do I wait here in my mountains.

I want to be at my work, at my day; but they don't understand the signs of my morning, my step is not their call to awaken.

They still sleep in my cave; their dreams still drink from my drunken songs. They still lack the listening ear, the obedient ear in their limbs."

This is what Zarathustra said to his heart as the sun rose. Then he looked questioningly above, for he heard the sharp cry of his eagle overhead. "Good!" he called upward. "This pleases me; it's fitting. My animals are awake, for I am awake.

My eagle is awake, and like me, it honors the sun. It grasps at the new light with eagle talons. You are my true animals; I love you.

But I still lack my true men!"

Thus spoke Zarathustra; then suddenly he became aware that he was surrounded and fluttered about, as if by countless birds. The sound of so many wings, and the gathering around his head, was so overwhelming that he closed his eyes. And truly, it seemed as if a cloud descended upon him, like a cloud of arrows raining down on a new enemy. But behold, it was a cloud of love, showered upon a new friend.

"What is happening to me?" wondered Zarathustra in his astonished heart, and he slowly sat down on the large stone near the entrance to his cave. While he reached out with his hands, around him, above him, and below him, to ward off the gentle birds, something even stranger happened: his hand unknowingly sank into a mass of thick, warm, shaggy fur; and at the same moment, he heard a roar—a long, soft lion's roar.

"The sign has come," said Zarathustra, and a change came over his heart. And indeed, when he looked clearly before him, there lay a powerful yellow animal at his feet, resting its head on his knee, unwilling to leave him out of love, behaving like a dog reunited with its old master. The doves were no less eager with their affection than the lion; and whenever a dove flitted over its nose, the lion shook its head, puzzled yet amused.

When all this was happening, Zarathustra spoke only a single word: "My children are near, my children"—then he fell completely silent. His heart, however, was loosened, and tears dropped from his eyes onto his hands. He took no further notice of anything, remaining still, without brushing the animals away. The doves flew back and forth, perching on his shoulders, caressing his white hair, never tiring of their gentleness and joy. The strong lion, meanwhile, licked the tears that fell on Zarathustra's hands, shyly roaring and growling. This was how the animals acted.

This went on for a long time, or perhaps only a short time; for truly, there is no time on earth for such things. Meanwhile, however, the higher men had awakened in Zarathustra's cave and prepared for a procession to greet Zarathustra, giving him their morning welcome; for they had realized upon waking that he was no longer with them. When they reached the cave's entrance and their footsteps echoed before them, the lion jumped in alarm. It suddenly turned away from

Zarathustra, roaring wildly, and sprang toward the cave. When the higher men heard the lion's roar, they cried out as one voice, fled in panic, and vanished instantly.

Zarathustra, stunned and feeling strange, rose from his seat, looked around him, and stood there astonished, questioning his heart, reflecting, and realizing he was alone. "What did I hear?" he said at last, slowly. "What just happened to me?" But soon he remembered everything, and all that had taken place between yesterday and today became clear. "Here is the stone," he said, stroking his beard, "where I sat yesterday morning; and here the soothsayer came to me, and here I first heard the cry I just heard again—the great cry of distress.

Oh, you higher men, it was your distress that the old soothsayer foretold to me yesterday morning—

—He wanted to seduce and tempt me to your distress: 'O Zarathustra,' he said, 'I come to lure you to your final sin.'

To my final sin?" cried Zarathustra, laughing angrily at his own words. "What could be reserved for me as my final sin?"

And once more, Zarathustra fell into deep thought, sitting down on the large stone and pondering. Suddenly, he sprang up, exclaiming, "Compassion! Compassion with the higher men!" His face turned stern and unmoving like brass. "Well! That—has had its time!

My suffering and my compassion—what do they matter! Do I seek happiness, then? I seek only my work!

Good! The lion has come, my children are near, Zarathustra has grown ripe, my hour has come—

This is my morning, my day begins: arise now, arise, you great noontide!"

Thus spoke Zarathustra, and he left his cave, glowing and strong, like a morning sun emerging from dark mountains.

Beyond Good and Evil

Friedrich Nietzsche

Introduction

UPPOSING that Truth is a woman--what then? Is there not ground for suspecting that all philosophers, in so far as they have been dogmatists, have failed to understand women--that the terrible seriousness and clumsy importunity with which they have usually paid their addresses to Truth, have been unskilled and unseemly methods for winning a woman? Certainly she has never allowed herself to be won; and at present every kind of dogma stands with sad and discouraged mien--IF, indeed, it stands at all! For there are scoffers who maintain that it has fallen, that all dogma lies on the ground--nay more, that it is at its last gasp. But to speak seriously, there are good grounds for hoping that all dogmatizing in philosophy, whatever solemn, whatever conclusive and decided airs it has assumed, may have been only a noble puerilism and tyronism; and probably the time is at hand when it will be once and again understood WHAT has actually sufficed for the basis of such imposing and absolute philosophical edifices as the dogmatists have hitherto reared: perhaps some popular superstition of immemorial time (such as the soul-superstition, which, in the form of subject- and ego-superstition, has not yet ceased doing mischief): perhaps some play upon words, a deception on the part of grammar, or an audacious generalization of very restricted, very personal, very human--all-too-human facts. The philosophy of the dogmatists, it is to be hoped, was only a promise for thousands of years afterwards, as was astrology in still earlier times, in the service of which probably more labour, gold, acuteness, and patience have been spent than on any actual science hitherto: we owe to it, and to its "super- terrestrial" pretensions in Asia and Egypt, the grand style of architecture. It seems that in order to inscribe themselves upon the heart of humanity with everlasting claims, all great things have first to wander about the earth as enormous and awe-inspiring caricatures: dogmatic philosophy has been a caricature of this kind--for instance, the Vedanta doctrine in Asia, and Platonism in Europe. Let us not be ungrateful to it, although it must certainly be confessed that the worst, the most tiresome, and the most dangerous of errors hitherto has been a dogmatist error--namely, Plato's invention of Pure Spirit and the Good in Itself. But now when it has been surmounted, when Europe, rid of this nightmare, can again draw breath freely and at least enjoy a healthier--sleep, we, WHOSE DUTY IS WAKEFULNESS ITSELF, are the heirs of all the strength which the struggle against this error has fostered. It amounted to the very inversion of truth, and the denial of the PERSPECTIVE--the fundamental condition--of life, to speak of Spirit and the Good as Plato spoke of them; indeed one might ask, as a physician: "How did such a malady attack that finest product of antiquity, Plato? Had the wicked Socrates really corrupted him? Was Socrates after all a corrupter of youths, and deserved his hemlock?" But the struggle against Plato, or--to speak plainer, and for the "people"--the struggle against the ecclesiastical oppression of millenniums of Christianity (FOR CHRISTIANITY IS PLATONISM FOR THE "PEOPLE"), produced in Europe a magnificent tension of soul, such as had not existed anywhere previously; with such a tensely strained bow one can now aim at the furthest goals. As a matter of fact, the European feels this tension as a state of distress, and twice attempts have been made in grand style to unbend the bow: once by means of Jesuitism, and the second time by means of democratic enlightenment--which, with the aid of liberty of the press and newspaper-reading, might, in fact, bring it about that the spirit would not so easily find itself in "distress"! (The Germans invented gunpowder-all credit to them! but they again made things square--they invented printing.) But we, who are neither Jesuits, nor democrats, nor even sufficiently Germans, we GOOD EUROPEANS, and free, VERY free spirits--we have it still, all the distress of spirit and all the tension of its bow! And perhaps also the arrow, the duty, and, who knows? THE GOAL TO AIM AT.

Chapter 1
On the Prejudices of Philosophers

The Will to Truth, which is to tempt us to many a hazardous enterprise, the famous Truthfulness of which all philosophers have hitherto spoken with respect, what questions has this Will to Truth not laid before us! What strange, perplexing, questionable questions! It is already a long story; yet it seems as if it were hardly commenced. Is it any wonder if we at last grow distrustful, lose patience, and turn impatiently away? That this Sphinx teaches us at last to ask questions ourselves? WHO is it really that puts questions to us here? WHAT really is this "Will to Truth" in us? In fact we made a long halt at the question as to the origin of this Will--until at last we came to an absolute standstill before a yet more fundamental question. We inquired about the VALUE of this Will. Granted that we want the truth: WHY NOT RATHER untruth? And uncertainty? Even ignorance? The problem of the value of truth presented itself before us--or was it we who presented ourselves before the problem? Which of us is the Oedipus here? Which the Sphinx? It would seem to be a rendezvous of questions and notes of interrogation. And could it be believed that it at last seems to us as if the problem had never been propounded before, as if we were the first to discern it, get a sight of it, and RISK RAISING it? For there is risk in raising it, perhaps there is no greater risk.

"HOW COULD anything originate out of its opposite? For example, truth out of error? or the Will to Truth out of the will to deception? or the generous deed out of selfishness? or the pure sun-bright vision of the wise man out of covetousness? Such genesis is impossible; whoever dreams of it is a fool, nay, worse than a fool; things of the highest value must have a different origin, an origin of THEIR own--in this transitory, seductive, illusory, paltry world, in this turmoil of delusion and cupidity, they cannot have their source. But rather in the lap of Being, in the intransitory, in the concealed God, in the 'Thing-in-itself-- THERE must be their source, and nowhere else!"--This mode of reasoning discloses the typical prejudice by which metaphysicians of all times can be recognized, this mode of valuation is at the back of all their logical procedure; through this "belief" of theirs, they exert themselves for their "knowledge," for something that is in the end solemnly christened "the Truth." The fundamental belief of metaphysicians is THE BELIEF IN ANTITHESES OF VALUES. It never occurred even to the wariest of them to doubt here on the very threshold (where doubt, however, was most necessary); though they had made a solemn vow, "DE OMNIBUS DUBITANDUM." For it may be doubted, firstly, whether antitheses exist at all; and secondly, whether the popular valuations and antitheses of value upon which metaphysicians have set their seal, are not perhaps merely superficial estimates, merely provisional perspectives, besides being probably made from some corner, perhaps from below--"frog perspectives," as it were, to borrow an expression current among painters. In spite of all the value which may belong to the true, the positive, and the unselfish, it might be possible that a higher and more fundamental value for life generally should be assigned to pretence, to the will to delusion, to selfishness, and cupidity. It might even be possible that WHAT constitutes the value of those good and respected things, consists precisely in their being insidiously related, knotted, and crocheted to these evil and apparently opposed things-- perhaps even in being essentially identical with them. Perhaps! But who wishes to concern himself with such dangerous "Perhapses"! For that investigation one must await the advent of a new order of philosophers, such as will have other tastes and inclinations, the reverse of those hitherto prevalent--philosophers of the dangerous "Perhaps" in every sense of the term. And to speak in all seriousness, I see such new philosophers beginning to appear.

Having kept a sharp eye on philosophers, and having read between their lines long enough, I now say to myself that the greater part of conscious thinking must be counted among the Instinctive functions, and it is so even in the case of philosophical thinking; one has here to learn anew, as one learned anew about heredity and "innateness." As little as the act of birth comes into consideration in the whole process and procedure of heredity, just as little is "being-conscious" OPPOSED to the instinctive in any decisive sense; the greater part of the conscious thinking of a philosopher is secretly influenced by his instincts, and forced into definite channels. And behind all logic and its seeming sovereignty of movement, there are valuations, or to speak more plainly, physiological demands, for the maintenance of a definite mode of life For example, that the certain is worth more than the uncertain, that illusion is less valuable than "truth" such valuations, in spite of their regulative importance for US, might notwithstanding be only superficial valuations, special kinds of maiserie, such as may be necessary for the maintenance of beings such as ourselves. Supposing, in effect, that man is not just the "measure of things."

The falseness of an opinion is not for us any objection to it: it is here, perhaps, that our new language sounds most strangely. The question is, how far an opinion is life-furthering, life- preserving, species-preserving, perhaps species-rearing, and we are fundamentally inclined to maintain that the falsest opinions (to which the synthetic judgments a priori belong), are the most indispensable to us, that without a recognition of logical fictions, without a comparison of reality with the purely IMAGINED world of the absolute and immutable, without a constant counterfeiting of the world by means of numbers, man could not live--that the renunciation of false opinions would be a renunciation of life, a negation of life. TO RECOGNISE UNTRUTH AS A CONDITION OF LIFE; that is certainly to impugn the traditional ideas of value in a dangerous manner, and a philosophy which ventures to do so, has thereby alone placed itself beyond good and evil.

That which causes philosophers to be regarded half- distrustfully and half-mockingly, is not the oft-repeated discovery how innocent they are--how often and easily they make mistakes and lose their way, in short, how childish and childlike they are,--but that there is not enough honest dealing with them, whereas they all raise a loud and virtuous outcry when the problem of truthfulness is even hinted at in the remotest manner. They all pose as though their real opinions had been discovered and attained through the self-evolving of a cold, pure, divinely indifferent dialectic (in contrast to all sorts of mystics, who, fairer and foolisher, talk of "inspiration"), whereas, in fact, a prejudiced proposition, idea, or "suggestion," which is generally their heart's desire abstracted and refined, is defended by them with arguments sought out after the event. They are all advocates who do not wish to be regarded as such, generally astute defenders, also, of their prejudices, which they dub "truths,"-- and VERY far from having the conscience which bravely admits this to itself, very far from having the good taste of the courage which goes so far as to let this be understood, perhaps to warn friend or foe, or in cheerful confidence and self-ridicule. The spectacle of the Tartuffery of old Kant, equally stiff and decent, with which he entices us into the dialectic by-ways that lead (more correctly mislead) to his "categorical imperative"-- makes us fastidious ones smile, we who find no small amusement in spying out the subtle tricks of old moralists and ethical preachers. Or, still more so, the hocus-pocus in mathematical form, by means of which Spinoza has, as it were, clad his philosophy in mail and mask-- in fact, the "love of HIS wisdom," to translate the term fairly and squarely--in order thereby to strike terror at once into the heart of the assailant who should dare to cast a glance on that invincible maiden, that Pallas Athene:--how much of personal timidity and vulnerability does this masquerade of a sickly recluse betray!

It has gradually become clear to me what every great philosophy up till now has consisted of--namely, the confession of its originator, and a species of involuntary and unconscious auto-biography; and moreover that the moral (or immoral) purpose in every philosophy has constituted the true vital germ out of which the entire plant has always grown. Indeed, to understand how the abstrusest metaphysical assertions of a philosopher have been arrived at, it is always well (and wise) to first ask oneself: "What morality do they (or does he) aim at?" Accordingly, I do not believe that an "impulse to knowledge" is the father of philosophy; but that another impulse, here as elsewhere, has only made use of knowledge (and mistaken knowledge!) as an instrument. But whoever considers the fundamental impulses of man with a view to determining how far they may have here acted as INSPIRING GENII (or as demons and cobolds), will find that they have all practiced philosophy at one time or another, and that each one of them would have been only too glad to look upon itself as the ultimate end of existence and the legitimate LORD over all the other impulses. For every impulse is imperious, and as SUCH, attempts to philosophize. To be sure, in the case of scholars, in the case of really scientific men, it may be otherwise--"better," if you will; there there may really be such a thing as an "impulse to knowledge," some kind of small, independent clock-work, which, when well wound up, works away industriously to that end, WITHOUT the rest of the scholarly impulses taking any material part therein. The actual "interests" of the scholar, therefore, are generally in quite another direction--in the family, perhaps, or in money-making, or in politics; it is, in fact, almost indifferent at what point of research his little machine is placed, and whether the hopeful young worker becomes a good philologist, a mushroom specialist, or a chemist; he is not CHARACTERISED by becoming this or that. In the philosopher, on the contrary, there is absolutely nothing impersonal; and above all, his morality furnishes a decided and decisive testimony as to WHO HE IS,--that is to say, in what order the deepest impulses of his nature stand to each other.

How malicious philosophers can be! I know of nothing more stinging than the joke Epicurus took the liberty of making on Plato and the Platonists; he called them Dionysiokolakes. In its original sense, and on the face of it, the word signifies "Flatterers of Dionysius"--consequently, tyrants' accessories and lick-spittles; besides this, however, it is as much as to say, "They are all ACTORS, there is nothing genuine about them" (for Dionysiokolax was a popular name for an actor). And the latter is really the malignant reproach that Epicurus cast upon Plato: he was annoyed by the grandiose manner, the mise en scene style of which Plato and his scholars were masters--of which Epicurus was not a master! He, the old school-teacher of Samos, who sat concealed in his little garden at Athens, and wrote three hundred books, perhaps out of rage and ambitious envy of Plato, who knows! Greece took a hundred years to find out who the garden-god Epicurus really was. Did she ever find out?

There is a point in every philosophy at which the "conviction" of the philosopher appears on the scene; or, to put it in the words of an ancient mystery:

Adventavit asinus, Pulcher et fortissimus.

You desire to LIVE "according to Nature"? Oh, you noble Stoics, what fraud of words! Imagine to yourselves a being like Nature, boundlessly extravagant, boundlessly indifferent, without purpose or consideration, without pity or justice, at once fruitful and barren and uncertain: imagine to yourselves INDIFFERENCE as a power--how COULD you live in accordance with such indifference? To live--is not that just endeavouring to be otherwise than this Nature? Is not living valuing, preferring, being unjust, being limited, endeavouring to be different? And granted that your imperative, "living according to Nature," means actually the same as "living according to life"--how could you do DIFFERENTLY? Why should you make a principle out of what you yourselves are, and must be? In reality, however, it is quite otherwise with you: while you pretend to read with rapture the canon of your law in Nature, you want something quite the contrary, you extraordinary stage-players and self-deluders! In your pride you wish to dictate your morals and ideals to Nature, to Nature herself, and to incorporate them therein; you insist that it shall be Nature "according to the Stoa," and would like everything to be made after your own image, as a vast, eternal glorification and generalism of Stoicism! With all your love for truth, you have forced yourselves so long, so persistently, and with such hypnotic rigidity to see Nature FALSELY, that is to say, Stoically, that you are no longer able to see it otherwise-- and to crown all, some unfathomable superciliousness gives you the

Bedlamite hope that BECAUSE you are able to tyrannize over yourselves--Stoicism is self-tyranny--Nature will also allow herself to be tyrannized over: is not the Stoic a PART of Nature? . . . But this is an old and everlasting story: what happened in old times with the Stoics still happens today, as soon as ever a philosophy begins to believe in itself. It always creates the world in its own image; it cannot do otherwise; philosophy is this tyrannical impulse itself, the most spiritual Will to Power, the will to "creation of the world," the will to the causa prima.

The eagerness and subtlety, I should even say craftiness, with which the problem of "the real and the apparent world" is dealt with at present throughout Europe, furnishes food for thought and attention; and he who hears only a "Will to Truth" in the background, and nothing else, cannot certainly boast of the sharpest ears. In rare and isolated cases, it may really have happened that such a Will to Truth--a certain extravagant and adventurous pluck, a metaphysician's ambition of the forlorn hope--has participated therein: that which in the end always prefers a handful of "certainty" to a whole cartload of beautiful possibilities; there may even be puritanical fanatics of conscience, who prefer to put their last trust in a sure nothing, rather than in an uncertain something. But that is Nihilism, and the sign of a despairing, mortally wearied soul, notwithstanding the courageous bearing such a virtue may display. It seems, however, to be otherwise with stronger and livelier thinkers who are still eager for life. In that they side AGAINST appearance, and speak superciliously of "perspective," in that they rank the credibility of their own bodies about as low as the credibility of the ocular evidence that "the earth stands still," and thus, apparently, allowing with complacency their securest possession to escape (for what does one at present believe in more firmly than in one's body?),--who knows if they are not really trying to win back something which was formerly an even securer possession, something of the old domain of the faith of former times, perhaps the "immortal soul," perhaps "the old God," in short, ideas by which they could live better, that is to say, more vigorously and more joyously, than by "modern ideas"? There is DISTRUST of these modern ideas in this mode of looking at things, a disbelief in all that has been constructed yesterday and today; there is perhaps some slight admixture of satiety and scorn, which can no longer endure the BRIC-A-BRAC of ideas of the most varied origin, such as so-called Positivism at present throws on the market; a disgust of the more refined taste at the village-fair motleyness and patchiness of all these reality-philosophasters, in whom there is nothing either new or true, except this motleyness. Therein it seems to me that we should agree with those skeptical anti-realists and knowledge-microscopists of the present day; their instinct, which repels them from MODERN reality, is unrefuted . . . what do their retrograde by-paths concern us! The main thing about them is NOT that they wish to go "back," but that they wish to get AWAY therefrom. A little MORE strength, swing, courage, and artistic power, and they would be OFF--and not back!

It seems to me that there is everywhere an attempt at present to divert attention from the actual influence which Kant exercised on German philosophy, and especially to ignore prudently the value which he set upon himself. Kant was first and foremost proud of his Table of Categories; with it in his hand he said: "This is the most difficult thing that could ever be undertaken on behalf of metaphysics." Let us only understand this "could be"! He was proud of having DISCOVERED a new faculty in man, the faculty of synthetic judgment a priori. Granting that he deceived himself in this matter; the development and rapid flourishing of German philosophy depended nevertheless on his pride, and on the eager rivalry of the younger generation to discover if possible something--at all events "new faculties"--of which to be still prouder!--But let us reflect for a moment--it is high time to do so. "How are synthetic judgments a priori POSSIBLE?" Kant asks himself--and what is really his answer? "BY MEANS OF A MEANS (faculty)"--but unfortunately not in five words, but so circumstantially, imposingly, and with such display of German profundity and verbal flourishes, that one altogether loses sight of the comical niaiserie allemande involved in such an answer.

People were beside themselves with delight over this new faculty, and the jubilation reached its climax when Kant further discovered a moral faculty in man--for at that time Germans were still moral, not yet dabbling in the "Politics of hard fact." Then came the honeymoon of German philosophy. All the young theologians of the Tubingen institution went immediately into the groves--all seeking for "faculties." And what did they not find--in that innocent, rich, and still youthful period of the German spirit, to which Romanticism, the malicious fairy, piped and sang, when one could not yet distinguish between "finding" and "inventing"! Above all a faculty for the "transcendental"; Schelling christened it, intellectual intuition, and thereby gratified the most earnest longings of the naturally pious-inclined Germans. One can do no greater wrong to the whole of this exuberant and eccentric movement (which was really youthfulness, notwithstanding that it disguised itself so boldly, in hoary and senile conceptions), than to take it seriously, or even treat it with moral indignation. Enough, however--the world grew older, and the dream vanished. A time came when people rubbed their foreheads, and they still rub them today. People had been dreaming, and first and foremost--old Kant. "By means of a means (faculty)"--he had said, or at least meant to say. But, is that--an answer? An explanation? Or is it not rather merely a repetition of the question? How does opium induce sleep? "By means of a means (faculty), "namely the virtus dormitiva, replies the doctor in Moliere,

Quia est in eo virtus dormitiva,

Cujus est natura sensus assoupire.

But such replies belong to the realm of comedy, and it is high time to replace the Kantian question, "How are synthetic judgments a PRIORI possible?" by another question, "Why is belief in such judgments necessary?"--in effect, it is high time that we should understand that such judgments must be believed to be true, for the sake of the preservation of creatures like ourselves; though they still might naturally be false judgments! Or, more plainly spoken, and roughly and readily--synthetic judgments a priori should not "be possible" at all; we have no right to them; in our mouths they are nothing but false judgments. Only, of course, the belief in their truth is necessary, as plausible belief and ocular evidence belonging to the perspective view of life. And finally, to call to mind the enormous influence which "German philosophy"--I hope you understand its right to inverted commas (goosefeet)?--has exercised throughout the whole of Europe, there is no doubt that a certain VIRTUS DORMITIVA had a share in it; thanks to German philosophy, it was a delight to the noble idlers, the virtuous, the mystics, the artiste, the three-fourths Christians, and the political obscurantists of all nations, to find an antidote to the still overwhelming sensualism which overflowed from the last century into this, in short--"sensus assoupire." . . .

As regards materialistic atomism, it is one of the best- refuted theories that have been advanced, and in Europe there is now perhaps no one in the learned world so unscholarly as to attach serious signification to it, except for convenient everyday use (as an abbreviation of the means of expression)-- thanks chiefly to the Pole Boscovich: he and the Pole Copernicus have hitherto been the greatest and most successful opponents of ocular evidence. For while Copernicus has persuaded us to believe, contrary to all the senses, that the earth does NOT stand fast, Boscovich has taught us to abjure the belief in the last thing that "stood fast" of the earth--the belief in "substance," in "matter," in the earth-residuum, and particle- atom: it is the greatest triumph over the senses that has hitherto been gained on earth. One must, however, go still further, and also declare war, relentless war to the knife, against the "atomistic requirements" which still lead a dangerous after-life in places where no one suspects them, like the more celebrated "metaphysical requirements": one must also above all give the finishing stroke to that other and more portentous atomism which Christianity has taught best and longest, the SOUL-ATOMISM. Let it be permitted to designate by this expression the belief which regards the soul as something indestructible, eternal, indivisible, as a monad, as an atomon: this belief ought to be expelled from science! Between ourselves, it is not at all necessary to get rid of "the soul" thereby, and thus renounce one of the oldest and most venerated hypotheses--as happens frequently to the clumsiness of naturalists, who can hardly touch on the soul without immediately losing it. But the way is open for new acceptations and refinements of the soul-hypothesis; and such conceptions as "mortal soul," and "soul of subjective multiplicity," and "soul as social structure of the instincts and passions," want henceforth to have legitimate rights in science. In that the NEW psychologist is about to put an end to the superstitions which have hitherto flourished with almost tropical luxuriance around the idea of the soul, he is really, as it were, thrusting himself into a new desert and a new distrust--it is possible that the older psychologists had a merrier and more comfortable time of it; eventually, however, he finds that precisely thereby he is also condemned to INVENT-- and, who knows? perhaps to DISCOVER the new.

Psychologists should bethink themselves before putting down the instinct of self-preservation as the cardinal instinct of an organic being. A living thing seeks above all to DISCHARGE its strength--life itself is WILL TO POWER; self-preservation is only one of the indirect and most frequent RESULTS thereof. In short, here, as everywhere else, let us beware of SUPERFLUOUS teleological principles!--one of which is the instinct of self- preservation (we owe it to Spinoza's inconsistency). It is thus, in effect, that method ordains, which must be essentially economy of principles.

It is perhaps just dawning on five or six minds that natural philosophy is only a world-exposition and world-arrangement (according to us, if I may say so!) and NOT a world-explanation; but in so far as it is based on belief in the senses, it is regarded as more, and for a long time to come must be regarded as more--namely, as an explanation. It has eyes and fingers of its own, it has ocular evidence and palpableness of its own: this operates fascinatingly, persuasively, and CONVINCINGLY upon an age with fundamentally plebeian tastes--in fact, it follows instinctively the canon of truth of eternal popular sensualism. What is clear, what is "explained"? Only that which can be seen and felt--one must pursue every problem thus far. Obversely, however, the charm of the Platonic mode of thought, which was an ARISTOCRATIC mode, consisted precisely in RESISTANCE to obvious sense-evidence--perhaps among men who enjoyed even stronger and more fastidious senses than our contemporaries, but who knew how to find a higher triumph in remaining masters of them: and this by means of pale, cold, grey conceptional networks which they threw over the motley whirl of the senses--the mob of the senses, as Plato said. In this overcoming of the world, and interpreting of the world in the manner of Plato, there was an ENJOYMENT different from that which the physicists of today offer us--and likewise the Darwinists and anti-teleologists among the physiological workers, with their principle of the "smallest possible effort," and the greatest possible blunder. "Where there is nothing more to see or to grasp, there is also nothing more for men to do"-- that is certainly an imperative different from the Platonic one, but it may notwithstanding be the right imperative for a hardy, laborious race of machinists and bridge- builders of the future, who have nothing but ROUGH work to perform.

To study physiology with a clear conscience, one must insist on the fact that the sense-organs are not phenomena in the sense of the idealistic philosophy; as such they certainly could not be causes! Sensualism, therefore, at least as regulative hypothesis, if not as heuristic principle. What? And others say even that the external world is the work of our organs? But then our body, as a part of this external world, would be the work of our organs! But then our organs themselves would be the work of our organs! It seems to me that this is a complete REDUCTIO AD ABSURDUM, if the conception CAUSA SUI is something fundamentally absurd. Consequently, the external world is NOT the work of our organs--?

There are still harmless self-observers who believe that there are "immediate certainties"; for instance, "I think," or as the superstition of Schopenhauer puts it, "I will"; as though cognition here got hold of its object purely and simply as "the thing in itself," without any falsification taking place either on the part of the subject or the object. I would repeat it, however, a hundred times, that "immediate certainty," as well as "absolute knowledge" and the "thing in itself," involve a CONTRADICTIO IN ADJECTO; we really ought to free ourselves from the misleading significance of words! The people on their part may think that cognition is knowing all about things, but the philosopher must say to himself: "When I analyze the process that is expressed in the sentence, 'I think,' I find a whole series of daring assertions, the argumentative proof of which would be difficult, perhaps impossible: for instance, that it is _I_ who think, that there must necessarily be something that thinks, that thinking is an activity and operation on the part of a being who is thought of as a cause, that there is an 'ego,' and finally, that it is already determined what is to be designated by thinking--that I KNOW what thinking is. For if I had not already decided within myself what it is, by what standard could I determine whether that which is just happening is not perhaps 'willing' or 'feeling'? In short, the assertion 'I think,' assumes that I COMPARE my state at the present moment with other states of myself which I know, in order to determine what it is; on account of this retrospective connection with further 'knowledge,' it has, at any rate, no immediate certainty for me."--In place of the "immediate certainty" in which the people may believe in the special case, the philosopher thus finds a series of metaphysical questions presented to him, veritable conscience questions of the intellect, to wit: "Whence did I get the notion of 'thinking'? Why do I believe in cause and effect? What gives me the right to speak of an 'ego,' and even of an 'ego' as cause, and finally of an 'ego' as cause of thought?" He who ventures to answer these metaphysical questions at once by an appeal to a sort of INTUITIVE perception, like the person who says, "I think, and know that this, at least, is true, actual, and certain"--will encounter a smile and two notes of interrogation in a philosopher nowadays. "Sir," the philosopher will perhaps give him to understand, "it is improbable that you are not mistaken, but why should it be the truth?"

With regard to the superstitions of logicians, I shall never tire of emphasizing a small, terse fact, which is unwillingly recognized by these credulous minds--namely, that a thought comes when "it" wishes, and not when "I" wish; so that it is a PERVERSION of the facts of the case to say that the subject "I" is the condition of the predicate "think." ONE thinks; but that this "one" is precisely the famous old "ego," is, to put it mildly, only a supposition, an assertion, and assuredly not an "immediate certainty." After all, one has even gone too far with this "one thinks"--even the "one" contains an INTERPRETATION of the process, and does not belong to the process itself. One infers here according to the usual grammatical formula--"To think is an activity; every activity requires an agency that is active; consequently" . . . It was pretty much on the same lines that the older atomism sought, besides the operating "power," the material particle wherein it resides and out of which it operates--the atom. More rigorous minds, however, learnt at last to get along without this "earth-residuum," and perhaps some day we shall accustom ourselves, even from the logician's point of view, to get along without the little "one" (to which the worthy old "ego" has refined itself).

It is certainly not the least charm of a theory that it is refutable; it is precisely thereby that it attracts the more subtle minds. It seems that the hundred-times-refuted theory of the "free will" owes its persistence to this charm alone; some one is always appearing who feels himself strong enough to refute it.

Philosophers are accustomed to speak of the will as though it were the best-known thing in the world; indeed, Schopenhauer has given us to understand that the will alone is really known to us, absolutely and completely known, without deduction or addition. But it again and again seems to me that in this case Schopenhauer also only did what philosophers are in the habit of doing-he seems to have adopted a POPULAR PREJUDICE and exaggerated it. Willing-seems to me to be above all something COMPLICATED, something that is a unity only in name--and it is precisely in a name that popular prejudice lurks, which has got the mastery over the inadequate precautions of philosophers in all ages. So let us for once be more cautious, let us be "unphilosophical": let us say that in all willing there is firstly a plurality of sensations, namely, the sensation of the condition "AWAY FROM WHICH we go," the sensation of the condition "TOWARDS WHICH we go," the sensation of this "FROM" and "TOWARDS" itself, and then besides, an accompanying muscular sensation, which, even without our putting in motion "arms and legs," commences its action by force of habit, directly we "will" anything. Therefore, just as sensations (and indeed many kinds of sensations) are to be recognized as ingredients of the will, so, in the second place, thinking is also to be recognized; in every act of the will there is a ruling thought;--and let us not imagine it possible to sever this thought from the "willing," as if the will would then remain over! In the third place, the will is not only a complex of sensation and thinking, but it is above all an EMOTION, and in fact the emotion of the command. That which is termed "freedom of the will" is essentially the emotion of supremacy in respect to him who must obey: "I am free, 'he' must obey"--this consciousness is inherent in every will; and equally so the straining of the attention, the straight look which fixes itself exclusively on one thing, the unconditional judgment that "this and nothing else is necessary now," the inward certainty that obedience will be rendered--and whatever else pertains to the position of the commander. A man who WILLS commands something within himself which renders obedience, or which he believes renders obedience. But now let us notice what is the strangest thing about the will,--this affair so extremely complex, for which the people have only one name. Inasmuch as in the given circumstances we are at the same time the commanding AND the obeying parties, and as the obeying party we know the sensations of constraint, impulsion, pressure, resistance, and motion, which usually commence immediately after the act of will; inasmuch as, on the other hand, we are accustomed to disregard this duality, and to deceive ourselves about it by means of the synthetic term "I": a whole series of erroneous conclusions, and consequently of false judgments about the will itself, has become attached to the act of willing--to such a degree that he who wills believes firmly that willing SUFFICES for action. Since in the majority of cases there has only been exercise of will when the effect of the command-- consequently obedience, and therefore action--was to be EXPECTED, the APPEARANCE has translated itself into the sentiment, as if there were a NECESSITY OF EFFECT; in a word, he who wills believes with a fair amount of certainty that will and action are somehow one; he ascribes the success, the carrying out of the willing, to the will itself, and thereby enjoys an increase of the sensation of power which accompanies all success. "Freedom of Will"--that is the expression for the complex state of delight of the person exercising volition, who commands and at the same time identifies himself with the executor of the order-- who, as such, enjoys also the triumph over obstacles, but thinks within himself that it was really his own will that overcame them. In this way the person exercising volition adds the feelings of delight of his successful executive instruments, the useful "underwills" or under-souls--indeed, our body is but a social structure composed of many souls--to his feelings of delight as commander. L'EFFET C'EST MOI. what happens here is what happens in every well-constructed and happy commonwealth, namely, that the governing class identifies itself with the successes of the commonwealth. In all willing it is absolutely a question of commanding and obeying, on the basis, as already said, of a social structure composed of many "souls", on which account a philosopher should claim the right to include willing- as-such within the sphere of morals--regarded as the doctrine of the relations of supremacy under which the phenomenon of "life" manifests itself.

That the separate philosophical ideas arc not anything optional or autonomously evolving, but grow up in connection and relationship with each other, that, however suddenly and arbitrarily they seem to appear in the history of thought, they nevertheless belong just as much to a system as the collective members of the fauna of a Continent--is betrayed in the end by the circumstance: how unfailingly the most diverse philosophers always fill in again a definite fundamental scheme of POSSIBLE philosophies. Under an invisible spell, they always revolve once more in the same orbit, however independent of each other they may feel themselves with their critical or systematic wills, something within them leads them, something impels them in definite order the one after the other--to wit, the innate methodology and relationship of their ideas. Their thinking is, in fact, far less a discovery than a re-recognizing, a remembering, a return and a home-coming to a far-off, ancient common-household of the soul, out of which those ideas formerly grew: philosophizing is so far a kind of atavism of the highest order. The wonderful family resemblance of all Indian, Greek, and German philosophizing is easily enough explained. In fact, where there is affinity of language, owing to the common philosophy of grammar--I mean owing to the unconscious domination and guidance of similar grammatical functions--it cannot but be that everything is prepared at the outset for a similar development and succession of philosophical systems, just as the way seems barred against certain other possibilities of world- interpretation. It is highly probable that philosophers within the domain of the Ural-Altaic languages (where the conception of the subject is least developed) look otherwise "into the world," and will be found on paths of thought different from those of the Indo-Germans and Mussulmans, the spell of certain grammatical functions is ultimately also the spell of PHYSIOLOGICAL valuations and racial conditions.--So much by way of rejecting Locke's superficiality with regard to the origin of ideas.

The CAUSA SUI is the best self-contradiction that has yet been conceived, it is a sort of logical violation and unnaturalness; but the extravagant pride of man has managed to entangle itself profoundly and frightfully with this very folly. The desire for "freedom of will" in the superlative, metaphysical sense, such as still holds sway, unfortunately, in the minds of the half-educated, the desire to bear the entire and ultimate responsibility for one's actions oneself, and to absolve God, the world, ancestors, chance, and society therefrom, involves nothing less than to be precisely this CAUSA SUI, and, with more than Munchausen daring, to pull oneself up into existence by the hair, out of the slough of nothingness. If any one should find out in this manner the crass stupidity of the celebrated conception of "free will" and put it out of his head altogether, I beg of him to carry his "enlightenment" a step further, and also put out of his head the contrary of this monstrous conception of "free will": I mean "non-free will," which is tantamount to a misuse of cause and effect. One should not wrongly MATERIALISE "cause" and "effect," as the natural philosophers do (and whoever like them naturalize in thinking at present), according to the prevailing mechanical doltishness which makes the cause press and push until it "effects" its end; one should use "cause" and "effect" only as pure CONCEPTIONS, that is to say, as conventional fictions for the purpose of designation and mutual understanding,--NOT for explanation. In "being-in-itself" there is nothing of "casual- connection," of "necessity," or of "psychological non-freedom"; there the effect does NOT follow the cause, there "law" does not obtain. It is WE alone who have devised cause, sequence, reciprocity, relativity, constraint, number, law, freedom, motive, and purpose; and when we interpret and intermix this symbol-world, as "being-in-itself," with things, we act once more as we have always acted--MYTHOLOGICALLY. The "non-free will" is mythology; in real life it is only a question of STRONG and WEAK wills.--It is almost always a symptom of what is lacking in himself, when a thinker, in every "causal-connection" and "psychological necessity," manifests something of compulsion, indigence, obsequiousness, oppression, and non-freedom; it is suspicious to have such feelings--the person betrays himself. And in general, if I have observed correctly, the "non-freedom of the will" is regarded as a problem from two entirely opposite standpoints, but always in a profoundly PERSONAL manner: some will not give up their "responsibility," their belief in THEMSELVES, the personal right to THEIR merits, at any price (the vain races belong to this class); others on the contrary, do not wish to be answerable for anything, or blamed for anything, and owing to an inward self-contempt, seek to GET OUT OF THE BUSINESS, no matter how. The latter, when they write books, are in the habit at present of taking the side of criminals; a sort of socialistic sympathy is their favourite disguise. And as a matter of fact, the fatalism of the weak-willed embellishes itself surprisingly when it can pose as "la religion de la souffrance humaine"; that is ITS "good taste."

Let me be pardoned, as an old philologist who cannot desist from the mischief of putting his finger on bad modes of interpretation, but "Nature's conformity to law," of which you physicists talk so proudly, as though--why, it exists only owing to your interpretation and bad "philology." It is no matter of fact, no "text," but rather just a naively humanitarian adjustment and perversion of meaning, with which you make abundant concessions to the democratic instincts of the modern soul! "Everywhere equality before the law--Nature is not different in that respect, nor better than we": a fine instance of secret motive, in which the vulgar antagonism to everything privileged and autocratic-- likewise a second and more refined atheism--is once more disguised. "Ni dieu, ni maitre"--that, also, is what you want; and therefore "Cheers for natural law!"-- is it not so? But, as has been said, that is interpretation, not text; and somebody might come along, who, with opposite intentions and modes of interpretation, could read out of the same "Nature," and with regard to the same phenomena, just the tyrannically inconsiderate and relentless enforcement of the claims of power--an interpreter who should so place the unexceptionalness and unconditionalness of all "Will to Power" before your eyes, that almost every word, and the word "tyranny" itself, would eventually seem unsuitable, or like a weakening and softening metaphor--as being too human; and who should, nevertheless, end by asserting the same about this world as you do, namely, that it has a "necessary" and "calculable" course, NOT, however, because laws obtain in it, but because they are absolutely LACKING, and every power effects its ultimate consequences every moment. Granted that this also is only interpretation--and you will be eager enough to make this objection?- -well, so much the better.

All psychology hitherto has run aground on moral prejudices and timidities, it has not dared to launch out into the depths. In so far as it is allowable to recognize in that which has hitherto been written, evidence of that which has hitherto been kept silent, it seems as if nobody had yet harboured the notion of psychology as the Morphology and DEVELOPMENT-DOCTRINE OF THE WILL TO POWER, as I conceive of it. The power of moral prejudices has penetrated deeply into the most intellectual world, the world apparently most indifferent and unprejudiced, and has obviously operated in an injurious, obstructive, blinding, and distorting manner. A proper physio-psychology has to contend with unconscious antagonism in the heart of the investigator, it has "the heart" against it even a doctrine of the reciprocal conditionalness of the "good" and the "bad" impulses, causes (as refined immorality) distress and aversion in a still strong and manly conscience--still more so, a doctrine of the derivation of all good impulses from bad ones. If, however, a person should regard even the emotions of hatred, envy, covetousness, and imperiousness as life-conditioning emotions, as factors which must be present, fundamentally and essentially, in the general economy of life (which must, therefore, be further developed if life is to be further developed), he will suffer from such a view of things as from sea-sickness. And yet this hypothesis is far from being the strangest and most painful in this immense and almost new domain of dangerous knowledge, and there are in fact a hundred good reasons why every one should keep away from it who CAN do so! On the other hand, if one has once drifted hither with one's bark, well! very good! now let us set our teeth firmly! let us open our eyes and keep our hand fast on the helm! We sail away right OVER morality, we crush out, we destroy perhaps the remains of our own morality by daring to make our voyage thither--but what do WE matter. Never yet did a PROFOUNDER world of insight reveal itself to daring travelers and adventurers, and the psychologist who thus "makes a sacrifice"-- it is not the sacrifizio dell' intelletto, on the contrary!--will at least be entitled to demand in return that psychology shall once more be recognized as the queen of the sciences, for whose service and equipment the other sciences exist. For psychology is once more the path to the fundamental problems.

Chapter 2
The Free Spirit

O sancta simplicitas! In what strange simplification and falsification man lives! One can never cease wondering when once one has got eyes for beholding this marvel! How we have made everything around us clear and free and easy and simple! how we have been able to give our senses a passport to everything superficial, our thoughts a godlike desire for wanton pranks and wrong inferences!--how from the beginning, we have contrived to retain our ignorance in order to enjoy an almost inconceivable freedom, thoughtlessness, imprudence, heartiness, and gaiety--in order to enjoy life! And only on this solidified, granitelike foundation of ignorance could knowledge rear itself hitherto, the will to knowledge on the foundation of a far more powerful will, the will to ignorance, to the uncertain, to the untrue! Not as its opposite, but--as its refinement! It is to be hoped, indeed, that LANGUAGE, here as elsewhere, will not get over its awkwardness, and that it will continue to talk of opposites where there are only degrees and many refinements of gradation; it is equally to be hoped that the incarnated Tartuffery of morals, which now belongs to our unconquerable "flesh and blood," will turn the words round in the mouths of us discerning ones. Here and there we understand it, and laugh at the way in which precisely the best knowledge seeks most to retain us in this SIMPLIFIED, thoroughly artificial, suitably imagined, and suitably falsified world: at the way in which, whether it will or not, it loves error, because, as living itself, it loves life!

After such a cheerful commencement, a serious word would fain be heard; it appeals to the most serious minds. Take care, ye philosophers and friends of knowledge, and beware of martyrdom! Of suffering "for the truth's sake"! even in your own defense! It spoils all the innocence and fine neutrality of your conscience; it makes you headstrong against objections and red rags; it stupefies, animalizes, and brutalizes, when in the struggle with danger, slander, suspicion, expulsion, and even worse consequences of enmity, ye have at last to play your last card as protectors of truth upon earth--as though "the Truth" were such an innocent and incompetent creature as to require protectors! and you of all people, ye knights of the sorrowful countenance, Messrs Loafers and Cobweb-spinners of the spirit! Finally, ye know sufficiently well that it cannot be of any consequence if YE just carry your point; ye know that hitherto no philosopher has carried his point, and that there might be a more laudable truthfulness in every little interrogative mark which you place after your special words and favourite doctrines (and occasionally after yourselves) than in all the solemn pantomime and trumping games before accusers and law-courts! Rather go out of the way! Flee into concealment! And have your masks and your ruses, that ye may be mistaken for what you are, or somewhat feared! And pray, don't forget the garden, the garden with golden trellis-work! And have people around you who are as a garden--or as music on the waters at eventide, when already the day becomes a memory. Choose the GOOD solitude, the free, wanton, lightsome solitude, which also gives you the right still to remain good in any sense whatsoever! How poisonous, how crafty, how bad, does every long war make one, which cannot be waged openly by means of force! How PERSONAL does a long fear make one, a long watching of enemies, of possible enemies! These pariahs of society, these long-pursued, badly-persecuted ones--also the compulsory recluses, the Spinozas or Giordano Brunos--always become in the end, even under the most intellectual masquerade, and perhaps without being themselves aware of it, refined vengeance-seekers and poison-Brewers (just lay bare the foundation of Spinoza's ethics and theology!), not to speak of the stupidity of moral indignation, which is the unfailing sign in a philosopher that the sense of philosophical humour has left him. The martyrdom of the philosopher, his "sacrifice for the sake of truth," forces into the light whatever of the agitator and actor lurks in him; and if one has hitherto contemplated him only with artistic curiosity, with regard to many a philosopher it is easy to understand the dangerous desire to see him also in his deterioration (deteriorated into a "martyr," into a stage-and- tribune-bawler). Only, that it is necessary with such a desire to be clear WHAT spectacle one will see in any case--merely a satyric play, merely an epilogue farce, merely the continued proof that the long, real tragedy IS AT AN END, supposing that every philosophy has been a long tragedy in its origin.

Every select man strives instinctively for a citadel and a privacy, where he is FREE from the crowd, the many, the majority-- where he may forget "men who are the rule," as their exception;-- exclusive only of the case in which he is pushed straight to such men by a still stronger instinct, as a discerner in the great and exceptional sense. Whoever, in intercourse with men, does not occasionally glisten in all the green and grey colours of distress, owing to disgust, satiety, sympathy, gloominess, and solitariness, is assuredly not a man of elevated tastes; supposing, however, that he does not voluntarily take all this burden and disgust upon himself, that he persistently avoids it, and remains, as I said, quietly and proudly hidden in his citadel, one thing is then certain: he was not made, he was not predestined for knowledge. For as such, he would one day have to say to himself: "The devil take my good taste! but 'the rule' is more interesting than the exception--than myself, the exception!" And he would go DOWN, and above all, he would go "inside." The long and serious study of the AVERAGE man--and consequently much disguise, self-overcoming, familiarity, and bad intercourse (all intercourse is bad intercourse except with one's equals):--that constitutes a necessary part of the life-history of every philosopher; perhaps the most disagreeable, odious, and disappointing part. If he is fortunate, however, as a favourite child of knowledge should be, he will meet with suitable auxiliaries who will shorten and lighten his task; I mean so- called cynics, those who simply recognize the animal, the commonplace and "the rule" in themselves, and at the same time have so much spirituality and ticklishness as to make them talk of themselves and their like BEFORE WITNESSES--sometimes they wallow, even in books, as on their own dung-hill. Cynicism is the only form in which base souls approach what is called honesty; and the higher man must open his ears to all the coarser or finer cynicism, and congratulate himself when the clown becomes shameless right before him, or the scientific satyr speaks out. There are even cases where enchantment mixes with the disgust-- namely, where by a freak of nature, genius is bound to some such indiscreet billy-goat and ape, as in the case of the Abbe Galiani, the profoundest, acutest, and perhaps also filthiest man of his century--he was far profounder than Voltaire, and consequently also, a good deal more silent. It happens more frequently, as has been hinted, that a scientific head is placed on an ape's body, a fine exceptional understanding in a base soul, an occurrence by no means rare, especially among doctors and moral physiologists. And whenever anyone speaks without bitterness, or rather quite innocently, of man as a belly with two requirements, and a head with one; whenever any one sees, seeks, and WANTS to see only hunger, sexual instinct, and vanity as the real and only motives of human actions; in short, when any one speaks "badly"--and not even "ill"--of man, then ought the lover of knowledge to hearken attentively and diligently; he ought, in general, to have an open ear wherever there is talk without indignation. For the indignant man, and he who perpetually tears and lacerates himself with his own teeth (or, in place of himself, the world, God, or society), may indeed, morally speaking, stand higher than the laughing and self- satisfied satyr, but in every other sense he is the more ordinary, more indifferent, and less instructive case. And no one is such a LIAR as the indignant man.

It is difficult to be understood, especially when one thinks and lives gangasrotogati [Footnote: Like the river Ganges: presto.] among those only who think and live otherwise--namely, kurmagati [Footnote: Like the tortoise: lento.], or at best "froglike," mandeikagati [Footnote: Like the frog: staccato.] (I do everything to be "difficultly understood" myself!)--and one should be heartily grateful for the good will to some refinement of interpretation. As regards "the good friends," however, who are always too easy-going, and think that as friends they have a right to ease, one does well at the very first to grant them a play-ground and romping-place for misunderstanding--one can thus laugh still; or get rid of them altogether, these good friends-- and laugh then also!

What is most difficult to render from one language into another is the TEMPO of its style, which has its basis in the character of the race, or to speak more physiologically, in the average TEMPO of the assimilation of its nutriment. There are honestly meant translations, which, as involuntary vulgarizations, are almost falsifications of the original, merely because its lively and merry TEMPO (which overleaps and obviates all dangers in word and expression) could not also be rendered. A German is almost incapacitated for PRESTO in his language; consequently also, as may be reasonably inferred, for many of the most delightful and daring NUANCES of free, free-spirited thought. And just as the buffoon and satyr are foreign to him in body and conscience, so Aristophanes and Petronius are untranslatable for him. Everything ponderous, viscous, and pompously clumsy, all long-winded and wearying species of style, are developed in profuse variety among Germans--pardon me for stating the fact that even Goethe's prose, in its mixture of stiffness and elegance, is no exception, as a reflection of the "good old time" to which it belongs, and as an expression of German taste at a time when there was still a "German taste," which was a rococo-taste in moribus et artibus. Lessing is an exception, owing to his histrionic nature, which understood much, and was versed in many things; he who was not the translator of Bayle to no purpose, who took refuge willingly in the shadow of Diderot and Voltaire, and still more willingly among the Roman comedy-writers--Lessing loved also free-spiritism in the TEMPO, and flight out of Germany. But how could the German language, even in the prose of Lessing, imitate the TEMPO of Machiavelli, who in his "Principe" makes us breathe the dry, fine air of Florence, and cannot help presenting the most serious events in a boisterous allegrissimo, perhaps not without a malicious artistic sense of the contrast he ventures to present--long, heavy, difficult, dangerous thoughts, and a TEMPO of the gallop, and of the best, wantonest humour? Finally, who would venture on a German translation of Petronius, who, more than any great musician hitherto, was a master of PRESTO in invention, ideas, and words? What matter in the end about the swamps of the sick, evil world, or of the "ancient world," when like him, one has the feet of a wind, the rush, the breath, the emancipating scorn of a wind, which makes everything healthy, by making everything RUN! And with regard to Aristophanes--that transfiguring, complementary genius, for whose sake one PARDONS all Hellenism for having existed, provided one has understood in its full profundity ALL that there requires pardon and transfiguration; there is nothing that has caused me to meditate more on PLATO'S secrecy and sphinx-like nature, than the happily preserved petit fait that under the pillow of his death-bed there was found no "Bible," nor anything Egyptian, Pythagorean, or Platonic--but a book of Aristophanes. How could even Plato have endured life--a Greek life which he repudiated--without an Aristophanes!

It is the business of the very few to be independent; it is a privilege of the strong. And whoever attempts it, even with the best right, but without being OBLIGED to do so, proves that he is probably not only strong, but also daring beyond measure. He enters into a labyrinth, he multiplies a thousandfold the dangers which life in itself already brings with it; not the least of which is that no one can see how and where he loses his way, becomes isolated, and is torn piecemeal by some minotaur of conscience. Supposing such a one comes to grief, it is so far from the comprehension of men that they neither feel it, nor sympathize with it. And he cannot any longer go back! He cannot even go back again to the sympathy of men!

Our deepest insights must--and should--appear as follies, and under certain circumstances as crimes, when they come unauthorizedly to the ears of those who are not disposed and predestined for them. The exoteric and the esoteric, as they were formerly distinguished by philosophers--among the Indians, as among the Greeks, Persians, and Mussulmans, in short, wherever people believed in gradations of rank and NOT in equality and equal rights--are not so much in contradistinction to one another in respect to the exoteric class, standing without, and viewing, estimating, measuring, and judging from the outside, and not from the inside; the more essential distinction is that the class in question views things from below upwards--while the esoteric class views things FROM ABOVE DOWNWARDS. There are heights of the soul from which tragedy itself no longer appears to operate tragically; and if all the woe in the world were taken together, who would dare to decide whether the sight of it would NECESSARILY seduce and constrain to sympathy, and thus to a doubling of the woe? . . . That which serves the higher class of men for nourishment or refreshment, must be almost poison to an entirely different and lower order of human beings. The virtues of the common man would perhaps mean vice and weakness in a philosopher; it might be possible for a highly developed man, supposing him to degenerate and go to ruin, to acquire qualities thereby alone, for the sake of which he would have to be honoured as a saint in the lower world into which he had sunk. There are books which have an inverse value for the soul and the health according as the inferior soul and the lower vitality, or the higher and more powerful, make use of them. In the former case they are dangerous, disturbing, unsettling books, in the latter case they are herald-calls which summon the bravest to THEIR bravery. Books for the general reader are always ill-smelling books, the odour of paltry people clings to them. Where the populace eat and drink, and even where they reverence, it is accustomed to stink. One should not go into churches if one wishes to breathe PURE air.

In our youthful years we still venerate and despise without the art of NUANCE, which is the best gain of life, and we have rightly to do hard penance for having fallen upon men and things with Yea and Nay. Everything is so arranged that the worst of all tastes, THE TASTE FOR THE UNCONDITIONAL, is cruelly befooled and abused, until a man learns to introduce a little art into his sentiments, and prefers to try conclusions with the artificial, as do the real artists of life. The angry and reverent spirit peculiar to youth appears to allow itself no peace, until it has suitably falsified men and things, to be able to vent its passion upon them: youth in itself even, is something falsifying and deceptive. Later on, when the young soul, tortured by continual disillusions, finally turns suspiciously against itself--still ardent and savage even in its suspicion and remorse of conscience: how it upbraids itself, how impatiently it tears itself, how it revenges itself for its long self-blinding, as though it had been a voluntary blindness! In this transition one punishes oneself by distrust of one's sentiments; one tortures one's enthusiasm with doubt, one feels even the good conscience to be a danger, as if it were the self-concealment and lassitude of a more refined uprightness; and above all, one espouses upon principle the cause AGAINST "youth."--A decade later, and one comprehends that all this was also still--youth!

Throughout the longest period of human history--one calls it the prehistoric period--the value or non-value of an action was inferred from its CONSEQUENCES; the action in itself was not taken into consideration, any more than its origin; but pretty much as in China at present, where the distinction or disgrace of a child redounds to its parents, the retro-operating power of success or failure was what induced men to think well or ill of an action. Let us call this period the PRE-MORAL period of mankind; the imperative, "Know thyself!" was then still unknown. --In the last ten thousand years, on the other hand, on certain large portions of the earth, one has gradually got so far, that one no longer lets the consequences of an action, but its origin, decide with regard to its worth: a great achievement as a whole, an important refinement of vision and of criterion, the unconscious effect of the supremacy of aristocratic values and of the belief in "origin," the mark of a period which may be designated in the narrower sense as the MORAL one: the first attempt at self-knowledge is thereby made. Instead of the consequences, the origin-- what an inversion of perspective! And assuredly an inversion effected only after long struggle and wavering! To be sure, an ominous new superstition, a peculiar narrowness of interpretation, attained supremacy precisely thereby: the origin of an action was interpreted in the most definite sense possible, as origin out of an INTENTION; people were agreed in the belief that the value of an action lay in the value of its intention. The intention as the sole origin and antecedent history of an action: under the influence of this prejudice moral praise and blame have been bestowed, and men have judged and even philosophized almost up to the present day.--Is it not possible, however, that the necessity may now have arisen of again making up our minds with regard to the reversing and fundamental shifting of values, owing to a new self-consciousness and acuteness in man--is it not possible that we may be standing on the threshold of a period which to begin with, would be distinguished negatively as ULTRA-MORAL: nowadays when, at least among us immoralists, the suspicion arises that the decisive value of an action lies precisely in that which is NOT INTENTIONAL, and that all its intentionalness, all that is seen, sensible, or "sensed" in it, belongs to its surface or skin-- which, like every skin, betrays something, but CONCEALS still more? In short, we believe that the intention is only a sign or symptom, which first requires an explanation--a sign, moreover, which has too many interpretations, and consequently hardly any meaning in itself alone: that morality, in the sense in which it has been understood hitherto, as intention-morality, has been a prejudice, perhaps a prematureness or preliminariness, probably something of the same rank as astrology and alchemy, but in any case something which must be surmounted. The surmounting of morality, in a certain sense even the self-mounting of morality-- let that be the name for the long-secret labour which has been reserved for the most refined, the most upright, and also the most wicked consciences of today, as the living touchstones of the soul.

It cannot be helped: the sentiment of surrender, of sacrifice for one's neighbour, and all self-renunciation-morality, must be mercilessly called to account, and brought to judgment; just as the aesthetics of "disinterested contemplation," under which the emasculation of art nowadays seeks insidiously enough to create itself a good conscience. There is far too much witchery and sugar in the sentiments "for others" and "NOT for myself," for one not needing to be doubly distrustful here, and for one asking promptly: "Are they not perhaps--DECEPTIONS?"--That they PLEASE-- him who has them, and him who enjoys their fruit, and also the mere spectator--

that is still no argument in their FAVOUR, but just calls for caution. Let us therefore be cautious!

At whatever standpoint of philosophy one may place oneself nowadays, seen from every position, the ERRONEOUSNESS of the world in which we think we live is the surest and most certain thing our eyes can light upon: we find proof after proof thereof, which would fain allure us into surmises concerning a deceptive principle in the "nature of things." He, however, who makes thinking itself, and consequently "the spirit," responsible for the falseness of the world-- an honourable exit, which every conscious or unconscious advocatus dei avails himself of--he who regards this world, including space, time, form, and movement, as falsely DEDUCED, would have at least good reason in the end to become distrustful also of all thinking; has it not hitherto been playing upon us the worst of scurvy tricks? and what guarantee would it give that it would not continue to do what it has always been doing? In all seriousness, the innocence of thinkers has something touching and respect-inspiring in it, which even nowadays permits them to wait upon consciousness with the request that it will give them HONEST answers: for example, whether it be "real" or not, and why it keeps the outer world so resolutely at a distance, and other questions of the same description. The belief in "immediate certainties" is a MORAL NAIVETE which does honour to us philosophers; but--we have now to cease being "MERELY moral" men! Apart from morality, such belief is a folly which does little honour to us! If in middle-class life an ever- ready distrust is regarded as the sign of a "bad character," and consequently as an imprudence, here among us, beyond the middle- class world and its Yeas and Nays, what should prevent our being imprudent and saying: the philosopher has at length a RIGHT to "bad character," as the being who has hitherto been most befooled on earth--he is now under OBLIGATION to distrustfulness, to the wickedest squinting out of every abyss of suspicion.--Forgive me the joke of this gloomy grimace and turn of expression; for I myself have long ago learned to think and estimate differently with regard to deceiving and being deceived, and I keep at least a couple of pokes in the ribs ready for the blind rage with which philosophers struggle against being deceived. Why NOT? It is nothing more than a moral prejudice that truth is worth more than semblance; it is, in fact, the worst proved supposition in the world. So much must be conceded: there could have been no life at all except upon the basis of perspective estimates and semblances; and if, with the virtuous enthusiasm and stupidity of many philosophers, one wished to do away altogether with the "seeming world"--well, granted that YOU could do that,--at least nothing of your "truth" would thereby remain! Indeed, what is it that forces us in general to the supposition that there is an essential opposition of "true" and "false"? Is it not enough to suppose degrees of seemingness, and as it were lighter and darker shades and tones of semblance-- different valeurs, as the painters say? Why might not the world WHICH CONCERNS US--be a fiction? And to any one who suggested: "But to a fiction belongs an originator?"--might it not be bluntly replied: WHY? May not this "belong" also belong to the fiction? Is it not at length permitted to be a little ironical towards the subject, just as towards the predicate and object? Might not the philosopher elevate himself above faith in grammar? All respect to governesses, but is it not time that philosophy should renounce governess-faith?

O Voltaire! O humanity! O idiocy! There is something ticklish in "the truth," and in the SEARCH for the truth; and if man goes about it too humanely--"il ne cherche le vrai que pour faire le bien"--I wager he finds nothing!

Supposing that nothing else is "given" as real but our world of desires and passions, that we cannot sink or rise to any other "reality" but just that of our impulses--for thinking is only a relation of these impulses to one another:--are we not permitted to make the attempt and to ask the question whether this which is "given" does not SUFFICE, by means of our counterparts, for the understanding even of the so-called mechanical (or "material") world? I do not mean as an illusion, a "semblance," a "representation" (in the Berkeleyan and Schopenhauerian sense), but as possessing the same degree of reality as our emotions themselves--as a more primitive form of the world of emotions, in which everything still lies locked in a mighty unity, which afterwards branches off and develops itself in organic processes (naturally also, refines and debilitates)--as a kind of instinctive life in which all organic functions, including self- regulation, assimilation, nutrition, secretion, and change of matter, are still synthetically united with one another--as a PRIMARY FORM of life?--In the end, it is not only permitted to make this attempt, it is commanded by the conscience of LOGICAL METHOD. Not to assume several kinds of causality, so long as the attempt to get along with a single one has not been pushed to its furthest extent (to absurdity, if I may be allowed to say so): that is a morality of method which one may not repudiate nowadays--it follows "from its definition," as mathematicians say. The question is ultimately whether we really recognize the will as OPERATING, whether we believe in the causality of the will; if we do so--and fundamentally our belief IN THIS is just our belief in causality itself--we MUST make the attempt to posit hypothetically the causality of the will as the only causality. "Will" can naturally only operate on "will"--and not on "matter" (not on "nerves," for instance): in short, the hypothesis must be hazarded, whether will does not operate on will wherever "effects" are recognized--and whether all mechanical action, inasmuch as a power operates therein, is not just the power of will, the effect of will. Granted, finally, that we succeeded in explaining our entire instinctive life as the development and ramification of one fundamental form of will--namely, the Will to Power, as my thesis puts it; granted that all organic functions could be traced back to this Will to Power, and that the solution of the problem of generation and nutrition--it is one problem-- could also be found therein: one would thus have acquired the right to define ALL active force unequivocally as WILL TO POWER. The world seen from within, the world defined and designated according to its "intelligible character"--it would simply be "Will to Power," and nothing else.

"What? Does not that mean in popular language: God is disproved, but not the devil?"--On the contrary! On the contrary, my friends! And who the devil also compels you to speak popularly!

As happened finally in all the enlightenment of modern times with the French Revolution (that terrible farce, quite superfluous when judged close at hand, into which, however, the noble and visionary spectators of all Europe have interpreted from a distance their own indignation and enthusiasm so long and passionately, UNTIL THE TEXT HAS DISAPPEARED UNDER THE INTERPRETATION), so a noble posterity might once more misunderstand the whole of the past, and perhaps only thereby make ITS aspect endurable.--Or rather, has not this already happened? Have not we ourselves been--that "noble posterity"? And, in so far as we now comprehend this, is it not--thereby already past?

Nobody will very readily regard a doctrine as true merely because it makes people happy or virtuous--excepting, perhaps, the amiable "Idealists," who are enthusiastic about the good, true, and beautiful, and let all kinds of motley, coarse, and good-natured desirabilities swim about promiscuously in their pond. Happiness and virtue are no arguments. It is willingly forgotten, however, even on the part of thoughtful minds, that to make unhappy and to make bad are just as little counter- arguments. A thing could be TRUE, although it were in the highest degree injurious and dangerous; indeed, the fundamental constitution of existence might be such that one succumbed by a full knowledge of it--so that the strength of a mind might be measured by the amount of "truth" it could endure--or to speak more plainly, by the extent to which it REQUIRED truth attenuated, veiled, sweetened, damped, and falsified. But there is no doubt that for the discovery of certain PORTIONS of truth the wicked and unfortunate are more favourably situated and have a greater likelihood of success; not to speak of the wicked who are happy--a species about whom moralists are silent. Perhaps severity and craft are more favourable conditions for the development of strong, independent spirits and philosophers than the gentle, refined, yielding good-nature, and habit of taking things easily, which are prized, and rightly prized in a learned man. Presupposing always, to begin with, that the term "philosopher" be not confined to the philosopher who writes books, or even introduces HIS philosophy into books!--Stendhal furnishes a last feature of the portrait of the free-spirited philosopher, which for the sake of German taste I will not omit to underline--for it is OPPOSED to German taste. "Pour etre bon philosophe," says this last great psychologist, "il faut etre sec, clair, sans illusion. Un banquier, qui a fait fortune, a une partie du caractere requis pour faire des decouvertes en philosophie, c'est-a-dire pour voir clair dans ce qui est."

Everything that is profound loves the mask: the profoundest things have a hatred even of figure and likeness. Should not the CONTRARY only be the right disguise for the shame of a God to go about in? A question worth asking!--it would be strange if some mystic has not already ventured on the same kind of thing. There are proceedings of such a delicate nature that it is well to overwhelm them with coarseness and make them unrecognizable; there are actions of love and of an extravagant magnanimity after which nothing can be wiser than to take a stick and thrash the witness soundly: one thereby obscures his recollection. Many a one is able to obscure and abuse his own memory, in order at least to have vengeance on this sole party in the secret: shame is inventive. They are not the worst things of which one is most ashamed: there is not only deceit behind a mask--there is so much goodness in craft. I could imagine that a man with something costly and fragile to conceal, would roll through life clumsily and rotundly like an old, green, heavily-hooped wine-cask: the refinement of his shame requiring it to be so. A man who has depths in his shame meets his destiny and his delicate decisions upon paths which few ever reach, and with regard to the existence of which his nearest and most intimate friends may be ignorant; his mortal danger conceals itself from their eyes, and equally so his regained security. Such a hidden nature, which instinctively employs speech for silence and concealment, and is inexhaustible in evasion of communication, DESIRES and insists that a mask of himself shall occupy his place in the hearts and heads of his friends; and supposing he does not desire it, his eyes will some day be opened to the fact that there is nevertheless a mask of him there--and that it is well to be so. Every profound spirit needs a mask; nay, more, around every profound spirit there continually grows a mask, owing to the constantly false, that is to say, SUPERFICIAL interpretation of every word he utters, every step he takes, every sign of life he manifests.

One must subject oneself to one's own tests that one is destined for independence and command, and do so at the right time. One must not avoid one's tests, although they constitute perhaps the most dangerous game one can play, and are in the end tests made only before ourselves and before no other judge. Not to cleave to any person, be it even the dearest--every person is a prison and also a recess. Not to cleave to a fatherland, be it even the most suffering and necessitous--it is even less difficult to detach one's heart from a victorious fatherland. Not to cleave to a sympathy, be it even for higher men, into whose peculiar torture and helplessness chance has given us an insight. Not to cleave to a science, though it tempt one with the most valuable discoveries, apparently specially reserved for us. Not to cleave to one's own liberation, to the voluptuous distance and remoteness of the bird, which always flies further aloft in order always to see more under it--the danger of the flier. Not to cleave to our own virtues, nor become as a whole a victim to any of our specialties, to our "hospitality" for instance, which is the danger of dangers for highly developed and wealthy souls, who deal prodigally, almost indifferently with themselves, and push the virtue of liberality so far that it becomes a vice. One must know how TO CONSERVE ONESELF--the best test of independence.

A new order of philosophers is appearing; I shall venture to baptize them by a name not without danger. As far as I understand them, as far as they allow themselves to be understood--for it is their nature to WISH to remain something of a puzzle--these philosophers of the future might rightly, perhaps also wrongly, claim to be designated as "tempters." This name itself is after all only an attempt, or, if it be preferred, a temptation.

Will they be new friends of "truth," these coming philosophers? Very probably, for all philosophers hitherto have loved their truths. But assuredly they will not be dogmatists. It must be contrary to their pride, and also contrary to their taste, that their truth should still be truth for every one--that which has hitherto been the secret wish and ultimate purpose of all dogmatic efforts. "My opinion is MY opinion: another person has not easily a right to it"--such a philosopher of the future will say, perhaps. One must renounce the bad taste of wishing to agree with many people. "Good" is no longer good when one's neighbour takes it into his mouth. And how could there be a "common good"! The expression contradicts itself; that which can be common is always of small value. In the end things must be as they are and have always been--the great things remain for the great, the abysses for the profound, the delicacies and thrills for the refined, and, to sum up shortly, everything rare for the rare.

Need I say expressly after all this that they will be free, VERY free spirits, these philosophers of the future--as certainly also they will not be merely free spirits, but something more, higher, greater, and fundamentally different, which does not wish to be misunderstood and mistaken? But while I say this, I feel under OBLIGATION almost as much to them as to ourselves (we free spirits who are their heralds and forerunners), to sweep away from ourselves altogether a stupid old prejudice and misunderstanding, which, like a fog, has too long made the conception of "free spirit" obscure. In every country of Europe, and the same in America, there is at present something which makes an abuse of this name a very narrow, prepossessed, enchained class of spirits, who desire almost the opposite of what our intentions and instincts prompt--not to mention that in respect to the NEW philosophers who are appearing, they must still more be closed windows and bolted doors. Briefly and regrettably, they belong to the LEVELLERS, these wrongly named "free spirits"--as glib-tongued and scribe-fingered slaves of the democratic taste and its "modern ideas" all of them men without solitude, without personal solitude, blunt honest fellows to whom neither courage nor honourable conduct ought to be denied, only, they are not free, and are ludicrously superficial, especially in their innate partiality for seeing the cause of almost ALL human misery and failure in the old forms in which society has hitherto existed--a notion which happily inverts the truth entirely! What they would fain attain with all their strength, is the universal, green-meadow happiness of the herd, together with security, safety, comfort, and alleviation of life for every one, their two most frequently chanted songs and doctrines are called "Equality of Rights" and "Sympathy with All Sufferers"--and suffering itself is looked upon by them as something which must be DONE AWAY WITH. We opposite ones, however, who have opened our eye and conscience to the question how and where the plant "man" has hitherto grown most vigorously, believe that this has always taken place under the opposite conditions, that for this end the dangerousness of his situation had to be increased enormously, his inventive faculty and dissembling power (his "spirit") had to develop into subtlety and daring under long oppression and compulsion, and his Will to Life had to be increased to the unconditioned Will to Power--we believe that severity, violence, slavery, danger in the street and in the heart, secrecy, stoicism, tempter's art and devilry of every kind,--that everything wicked, terrible, tyrannical, predatory, and serpentine in man, serves as well for the elevation of the human species as its opposite--we do not even say enough when we only say THIS MUCH, and in any case we find ourselves here, both with our speech and our silence, at the OTHER extreme of all modern ideology and gregarious desirability, as their anti-podes perhaps? What wonder that we "free spirits" are not exactly the most communicative spirits? that we do not wish to betray in every respect WHAT a spirit can free itself from, and WHERE perhaps it will then be driven? And as to the import of the dangerous formula, "Beyond Good and Evil," with which we at least avoid confusion, we ARE something else than "libres-penseurs," "liben pensatori" "free-thinkers," and whatever these honest advocates of "modern ideas" like to call themselves. Having been at home, or at least guests, in many realms of the spirit, having escaped again and again from the gloomy, agreeable nooks in which preferences and prejudices, youth, origin, the accident of men and books, or even the weariness of travel seemed to confine us, full of malice against the seductions of dependency which he concealed in honours, money, positions, or exaltation of the senses, grateful even for distress and the vicissitudes of illness, because they always free us from some rule, and its "prejudice," grateful to the God, devil, sheep, and worm in us, inquisitive to a fault, investigators to the point of cruelty, with unhesitating fingers for the intangible, with teeth and stomachs for the most indigestible, ready for any business that requires sagacity and acute senses, ready for every adventure, owing to an excess of "free will", with anterior and posterior souls, into the ultimate intentions of which it is difficult to pry, with foregrounds and backgrounds to the end of which no foot may run, hidden ones under the mantles of light, appropriators, although we resemble heirs and spendthrifts, arrangers and collectors from morning till night, misers of our wealth and our full-crammed drawers, economical in learning and forgetting, inventive in scheming, sometimes proud of tables of categories, sometimes pedants, sometimes night-owls of work even in full day, yea, if necessary, even scarecrows--and it is necessary nowadays, that is to say, inasmuch as we are the born, sworn, jealous friends of SOLITUDE, of our own profoundest midnight and midday solitude--such kind of men are we, we free spirits! And perhaps ye are also something of the same kind, ye coming ones? ye NEW philosophers?

Chapter 3
What is Religious

The human soul and its limits, the range of man's inner experiences hitherto attained, the heights, depths, and distances of these experiences, the entire history of the soul UP TO THE PRESENT TIME, and its still unexhausted possibilities: this is the preordained hunting-domain for a born psychologist and lover of a "big hunt". But how often must he say despairingly to himself: "A single individual! alas, only a single individual! and this great forest, this virgin forest!" So he would like to have some hundreds of hunting assistants, and fine trained hounds, that he could send into the history of the human soul, to drive HIS game together. In vain: again and again he experiences, profoundly and bitterly, how difficult it is to find assistants and dogs for all the things that directly excite his curiosity. The evil of sending scholars into new and dangerous hunting-domains, where courage, sagacity, and subtlety in every sense are required, is that they are no longer serviceable just when the "BIG hunt," and also the great danger commences,--it is precisely then that they lose their keen eye and nose. In order, for instance, to divine and determine what sort of history the problem of KNOWLEDGE AND CONSCIENCE has hitherto had in the souls of homines religiosi, a person would perhaps himself have to possess as profound, as bruised, as immense an experience as the intellectual conscience of Pascal; and then he would still require that wide-spread heaven of clear, wicked spirituality, which, from above, would be able to oversee, arrange, and effectively formulize this mass of dangerous and painful experiences.--But who could do me this service! And who would have time to wait for such servants!--they evidently appear too rarely, they are so improbable at all times! Eventually one must do everything ONESELF in order to know something; which means that one has MUCH to do!--But a curiosity like mine is once for all the most agreeable of vices--pardon me! I mean to say that the love of truth has its reward in heaven, and already upon earth.

Faith, such as early Christianity desired, and not infrequently achieved in the midst of a skeptical and southernly free-spirited world, which had centuries of struggle between philosophical schools behind it and in it, counting besides the education in tolerance which the Imperium Romanum gave--this faith is NOT that sincere, austere slave-faith by which perhaps a Luther or a Cromwell, or some other northern barbarian of the spirit remained attached to his God and Christianity, it is much rather the faith of Pascal, which resembles in a terrible manner a continuous suicide of reason--a tough, long-lived, worm-like reason, which is not to be slain at once and with a single blow. The Christian faith from the beginning, is sacrifice the sacrifice of all freedom, all pride, all self-confidence of spirit, it is at the same time subjection, self-derision, and self-mutilation. There is cruelty and religious Phoenicianism in this faith, which is adapted to a tender, many-sided, and very fastidious conscience, it takes for granted that the subjection of the spirit is indescribably PAINFUL, that all the past and all the habits of such a spirit resist the absurdissimum, in the form of which "faith" comes to it. Modern men, with their obtuseness as regards all Christian nomenclature, have no longer the sense for the terribly superlative conception which was implied to an antique taste by the paradox of the formula, "God on the Cross". Hitherto there had never and nowhere been such boldness in inversion, nor anything at once so dreadful, questioning, and questionable as this formula: it promised a transvaluation of all ancient values--It was the Orient, the PROFOUND Orient, it was the Oriental slave who thus took revenge on Rome and its noble, light-minded toleration, on the Roman "Catholicism" of non-faith, and it was always not the faith, but the freedom from the faith, the half-stoical and smiling indifference to the seriousness of the faith, which made the slaves indignant at their masters and revolt against them. "Enlightenment" causes revolt, for the slave desires the unconditioned, he understands nothing but the tyrannous, even in morals, he loves as he hates, without NUANCE, to the very depths, to the point of pain, to the point of sickness--his many HIDDEN sufferings make him revolt against the noble taste which seems to DENY suffering. The skepticism with regard to suffering, fundamentally only an attitude of aristocratic morality, was not the least of the causes, also, of the last great slave-insurrection which began with the French Revolution.

Wherever the religious neurosis has appeared on the earth so far, we find it connected with three dangerous prescriptions as to regimen: solitude, fasting, and sexual abstinence--but without its being possible to determine with certainty which is cause and which is effect, or IF any relation at all of cause and effect exists there. This latter doubt is justified by the fact that one of the most regular symptoms among savage as well as among civilized peoples is the most sudden and excessive sensuality, which then with equal suddenness transforms into penitential paroxysms, world-renunciation, and will-renunciation, both symptoms perhaps explainable as disguised epilepsy? But nowhere is it MORE obligatory to put aside explanations around no other type has there grown such a mass of absurdity and superstition, no other type seems to have been more interesting to men and even to philosophers--perhaps it is time to become just a little indifferent here, to learn caution, or, better still, to look AWAY, TO GO AWAY--Yet in the background of the most recent philosophy, that of Schopenhauer, we find almost as the problem in itself, this terrible note of interrogation of the religious crisis and awakening. How is the negation of will POSSIBLE? how is the saint possible?--that seems to have been the very question with which Schopenhauer made a start and became a philosopher. And thus it was a genuine Schopenhauerian consequence, that his most convinced adherent (perhaps also his last, as far as Germany is concerned), namely, Richard Wagner, should bring his own life- work to an end just here, and should finally put that terrible and eternal type upon the stage as Kundry, type vecu, and as it loved and lived, at the very time that the mad-doctors in almost all European countries had an opportunity to study the type close at hand, wherever the religious neurosis--or as I call it, "the religious mood"--made its latest epidemical outbreak and display as the "Salvation Army"--If it be a question, however, as to what has been so extremely interesting to men of all sorts in all ages, and even to philosophers, in the whole phenomenon of the saint, it is undoubtedly the appearance of the miraculous therein--namely, the immediate SUCCESSION OF OPPOSITES, of states of the soul regarded as morally antithetical: it was believed here to be self-evident that a "bad man" was all at once turned into a "saint," a good man. The hitherto existing psychology was wrecked at this point, is it not possible it may have happened principally because psychology had placed itself under the dominion of morals, because it BELIEVED in oppositions of moral values, and saw, read, and INTERPRETED these oppositions into the text and facts of the case? What? "Miracle" only an error of interpretation? A lack of philology?

It seems that the Latin races are far more deeply attached to their Catholicism than we Northerners are to Christianity generally, and that consequently unbelief in Catholic countries means something quite different from what it does among Protestants--namely, a sort of revolt against the spirit of the race, while with us it is rather a return to the spirit (or non- spirit) of the race.

We Northerners undoubtedly derive our origin from barbarous races, even as regards our talents for religion--we have POOR talents for it. One may make an exception in the case of the Celts, who have theretofore furnished also the best soil for Christian infection in the North: the Christian ideal blossomed forth in France as much as ever the pale sun of the north would allow it. How strangely pious for our taste are still these later French skeptics, whenever there is any Celtic blood in their origin! How Catholic, how un-German does Auguste Comte's Sociology seem to us, with the Roman logic of its instincts! How Jesuitical, that amiable and shrewd cicerone of Port Royal, Sainte-Beuve, in spite of all his hostility to Jesuits! And even Ernest Renan: how inaccessible to us Northerners does the language of such a Renan appear, in whom every instant the merest touch of religious thrill throws his refined voluptuous and comfortably couching soul off its balance! Let us repeat after him these fine sentences--and what wickedness and haughtiness is immediately aroused by way of answer in our probably less beautiful but harder souls, that is to say, in our more German souls!--"DISONS DONC HARDIMENT QUE LA RELIGION EST UN PRODUIT DE L'HOMME NORMAL, QUE L'HOMME EST LE PLUS DANS LE VRAI QUANT IL EST LE PLUS RELIGIEUX ET LE PLUS ASSURE D'UNE DESTINEE INFINIE. . . . C'EST QUAND IL EST BON QU'IL VEUT QUE LA VIRTU CORRESPONDE A UN ORDER ETERNAL, C'EST QUAND IL CONTEMPLE LES CHOSES D'UNE MANIERE DESINTERESSEE QU'IL TROUVE LA MORT REVOLTANTE

ET ABSURDE. COMMENT NE PAS SUPPOSER QUE C'EST DANS CES MOMENTS-LA, QUE L'HOMME VOIT LE MIEUX?" . . . These sentences are so extremely ANTIPODAL to my ears and habits of thought, that in my first impulse of rage on finding them, I wrote on the margin, "LA NIAISERIE RELIGIEUSE PAR EXCELLENCE!"--until in my later rage I even took a fancy to them, these sentences with their truth absolutely inverted! It is so nice and such a distinction to have one's own antipodes!

That which is so astonishing in the religious life of the ancient Greeks is the irrestrainable stream of GRATITUDE which it pours forth--it is a very superior kind of man who takes SUCH an attitude towards nature and life.--Later on, when the populace got the upper hand in Greece, FEAR became rampant also in religion; and Christianity was preparing itself.

The passion for God: there are churlish, honest-hearted, and importunate kinds of it, like that of Luther--the whole of Protestantism lacks the southern DELICATEZZA. There is an Oriental exaltation of the mind in it, like that of an undeservedly favoured or elevated slave, as in the case of St. Augustine, for instance, who lacks in an offensive manner, all nobility in bearing and desires. There is a feminine tenderness and sensuality in it, which modestly and unconsciously longs for a UNIO MYSTICA ET PHYSICA, as in the case of Madame de Guyon. In many cases it appears, curiously enough, as the disguise of a girl's or youth's puberty; here and there even as the hysteria of an old maid, also as her last ambition. The Church has frequently canonized the woman in such a case.

The mightiest men have hitherto always bowed reverently before the saint, as the enigma of self-subjugation and utter voluntary privation--why did they thus bow? They divined in him-- and as it were behind the questionableness of his frail and wretched appearance--the superior force which wished to test itself by such a subjugation; the strength of will, in which they recognized their own strength and love of power, and knew how to honour it: they honoured something in themselves when they honoured the saint. In addition to this, the contemplation of the saint suggested to them a suspicion: such an enormity of self- negation and anti-naturalness will not have been coveted for nothing--they have said, inquiringly. There is perhaps a reason for it, some very great danger, about which the ascetic might wish to be more accurately informed through his secret interlocutors and visitors? In a word, the mighty ones of the world learned to have a new fear before him, they divined a new power, a strange, still unconquered enemy:--it was the "Will to Power" which obliged them to halt before the saint. They had to question him.

In the Jewish "Old Testament," the book of divine justice, there are men, things, and sayings on such an immense scale, that Greek and Indian literature has nothing to compare with it. One stands with fear and reverence before those stupendous remains of what man was formerly, and one has sad thoughts about old Asia and its little out-pushed peninsula Europe, which would like, by all means, to figure before Asia as the "Progress of Mankind." To be sure, he who is himself only a slender, tame house-animal, and knows only the wants of a house-animal (like our cultured people of today, including the Christians of "cultured" Christianity), need neither be amazed nor even sad amid those ruins--the taste for the Old Testament is a touchstone with respect to "great" and "small": perhaps he will find that the New Testament, the book of grace, still appeals more to his heart (there is much of the odour of the genuine, tender, stupid beadsman and petty soul in it). To have bound up this New Testament (a kind of ROCOCO of taste in every respect) along with the Old Testament into one book, as the "Bible," as "The Book in Itself," is perhaps the greatest audacity and "sin against the Spirit" which literary Europe has upon its conscience.

Why Atheism nowadays? "The father" in God is thoroughly refuted; equally so "the judge," "the rewarder." Also his "free will": he does not hear--and even if he did, he would not know how to help. The worst is that he seems incapable of communicating himself clearly; is he uncertain?--This is what I have made out (by questioning and listening at a variety of conversations) to be the cause of the decline of European theism; it appears to me that though the religious instinct is in vigorous growth,--it rejects the theistic satisfaction with profound distrust.

What does all modern philosophy mainly do? Since Descartes--and indeed more in defiance of him than on the basis of his procedure--an ATTENTAT has been made on the part of all philosophers on the old conception of the soul, under the guise of a criticism of the subject and predicate conception--that is to say, an ATTENTAT on the fundamental presupposition of Christian doctrine. Modern philosophy, as epistemological skepticism, is secretly or openly ANTI-CHRISTIAN, although (for keener ears, be it said) by no means anti-religious. Formerly, in effect, one believed in "the soul" as one believed in grammar and the grammatical subject: one said, "I" is the condition, "think" is the predicate and is conditioned--to think is an activity for which one MUST suppose a subject as cause. The attempt was then made, with marvelous tenacity and subtlety, to see if one could not get out of this net,--to see if the opposite was not perhaps true: "think" the condition, and "I" the conditioned; "I," therefore, only a synthesis which has been MADE by thinking itself. KANT really wished to prove that, starting from the subject, the subject could not be proved--nor the object either: the possibility of an APPARENT EXISTENCE of the subject, and therefore of "the soul," may not always have been strange to him,--the thought which once had an immense power on earth as the Vedanta philosophy.

There is a great ladder of religious cruelty, with many rounds; but three of these are the most important. Once on a time men sacrificed human beings to their God, and perhaps just those they loved the best--to this category belong the firstling sacrifices of all primitive religions, and also the sacrifice of the Emperor Tiberius in the Mithra-Grotto on the Island of Capri, that most terrible of all Roman anachronisms. Then, during the moral epoch of mankind, they sacrificed to their God the strongest instincts they possessed, their "nature"; THIS festal joy shines in the cruel glances of ascetics and "anti-natural" fanatics. Finally, what still remained to be sacrificed? Was it not necessary in the end for men to sacrifice everything comforting, holy, healing, all hope, all faith in hidden harmonies, in future blessedness and justice? Was it not necessary to sacrifice God himself, and out of cruelty to themselves to worship stone, stupidity, gravity, fate, nothingness? To sacrifice God for nothingness--this paradoxical mystery of the ultimate cruelty has been reserved for the rising generation; we all know something thereof already.

Whoever, like myself, prompted by some enigmatical desire, has long endeavoured to go to the bottom of the question of pessimism and free it from the half-Christian, half-German narrowness and stupidity in which it has finally presented itself to this century, namely, in the form of Schopenhauer's philosophy; whoever, with an Asiatic and super-Asiatic eye, has actually looked inside, and into the most world-renouncing of all possible modes of thought--beyond good and evil, and no longer like Buddha and Schopenhauer, under the dominion and delusion of morality,--whoever has done this, has perhaps just thereby, without really desiring it, opened his eyes to behold the opposite ideal: the ideal of the most world-approving, exuberant, and vivacious man, who has not only learnt to compromise and arrange with that which was and is, but wishes to have it again AS IT WAS AND IS, for all eternity, insatiably calling out de capo, not only to himself, but to the whole piece and play; and not only the play, but actually to him who requires the play--and makes it necessary; because he always requires himself anew--and makes himself necessary.--What? And this would not be--circulus vitiosus deus?

The distance, and as it were the space around man, grows with the strength of his intellectual vision and insight: his world becomes profounder; new stars, new enigmas, and notions are ever coming into view. Perhaps everything on which the intellectual eye has exercised its acuteness and profundity has just been an occasion for its exercise, something of a game, something for children and childish minds. Perhaps the most solemn conceptions that have caused the most fighting and suffering, the conceptions "God" and "sin," will one day seem to us of no more importance than a child's plaything or a child's pain seems to an old man;-- and perhaps another plaything and another pain will then be necessary once more for "the old man"-- always childish enough, an eternal child!

Has it been observed to what extent outward idleness, or semi-idleness, is necessary to a real religious life (alike for its favourite microscopic labour of self-examination, and for its soft placidity called "prayer," the state of perpetual readiness for the "coming of God"), I mean the idleness with a good conscience, the idleness of olden times and of blood, to which the aristocratic sentiment that work is DISHONOURING--that it vulgarizes body and soul--is not quite unfamiliar? And that consequently the modern, noisy, time-engrossing, conceited, foolishly proud laboriousness educates and prepares for "unbelief" more than anything else? Among these, for instance, who are at present living apart from religion in Germany, I find "free-thinkers" of diversified species and origin, but above all a majority of those in whom laboriousness from generation to generation has dissolved the religious instincts; so that they no longer know what purpose religions serve, and only note their existence in the world with a kind of dull astonishment. They feel themselves already fully occupied, these good people, be it by their business or by their pleasures, not to mention the "Fatherland," and the newspapers, and their "family duties"; it seems that they have no time whatever left for religion; and above all, it is not obvious to them whether it is a question of a new business or a new pleasure--for it is impossible, they say to themselves, that people should go to church merely to spoil their tempers. They are by no means enemies of religious customs; should certain circumstances, State affairs perhaps, require their participation in such customs, they do what is required, as so many things are done--with a patient and unassuming seriousness, and without much curiosity or discomfort;--they live too much apart and outside to feel even the necessity for a FOR or AGAINST in such matters. Among those indifferent persons may be reckoned nowadays the majority of German Protestants of the middle classes, especially in the great laborious centres of trade and commerce; also the majority of laborious scholars, and the entire University personnel (with the exception of the theologians, whose existence and possibility there always gives psychologists new and more subtle puzzles to solve). On the part of pious, or merely church-going people, there is seldom any idea of HOW MUCH good-will, one might say arbitrary will, is now necessary for a German scholar to take the problem of religion seriously; his whole profession (and as I have said, his whole workmanlike laboriousness, to which he is compelled by his modern conscience) inclines him to a lofty and almost charitable serenity as regards religion, with which is occasionally mingled a slight disdain for the "uncleanliness" of spirit which he takes for granted wherever any one still professes to belong to the Church. It is only with the help of history (NOT through his own personal experience, therefore) that the scholar succeeds in bringing himself to a respectful seriousness, and to a certain timid deference in presence of religions; but even when his sentiments have reached the stage of gratitude towards them, he has not personally advanced one step nearer to that which still maintains itself as Church or as piety; perhaps even the contrary. The practical indifference to religious matters in the midst of which he has been born and brought up, usually sublimates itself in his case into circumspection and cleanliness, which shuns contact with religious men and things; and it may be just the depth of his tolerance and humanity which prompts him to avoid the delicate trouble which tolerance itself brings with it.--Every age has its own divine type of naivete, for the discovery of which other ages may envy it: and how much naivete--adorable, childlike, and boundlessly foolish naivete is involved in this belief of the scholar in his superiority, in the good conscience of his tolerance, in the unsuspecting, simple certainty with which his instinct treats the religious man as a lower and less valuable type, beyond, before, and ABOVE which he himself has developed-- he, the little arrogant dwarf and mob-man, the sedulously alert, head-and-hand drudge of "ideas," of "modern ideas"!

Whoever has seen deeply into the world has doubtless divined what wisdom there is in the fact that men are superficial. It is their preservative instinct which teaches them to be flighty, lightsome, and false. Here and there one finds a passionate and exaggerated adoration of "pure forms" in philosophers as well as in artists: it is not to be doubted that whoever has NEED of the cult of the superficial to that extent, has at one time or another made an unlucky dive BENEATH it. Perhaps there is even an order of rank with respect to those burnt children, the born artists who find the enjoyment of life only in trying to FALSIFY its image (as if taking wearisome revenge on it), one might guess to what degree life has disgusted them, by the extent to which they wish to see its image falsified, attenuated, ultrified, and deified,--one might reckon the homines religiosi among the artists, as their HIGHEST rank. It is the profound, suspicious fear of an incurable pessimism which compels whole centuries to fasten their teeth into a religious interpretation of existence: the fear of the instinct which divines that truth might be attained TOO soon, before man has become strong enough, hard enough, artist enough. . . . Piety, the "Life in God," regarded in this light, would appear as the most elaborate and ultimate product of the FEAR of truth, as artist-adoration and artist- intoxication in presence of the most logical of all falsifications, as the will to the inversion of truth, to untruth at any price. Perhaps there has hitherto been no more effective means of beautifying man than piety, by means of it man can become so artful, so superficial, so iridescent, and so good, that his appearance no longer offends.

To love mankind FOR GOD'S SAKE--this has so far been the noblest and remotest sentiment to which mankind has attained. That love to mankind, without any redeeming intention in the background, is only an ADDITIONAL folly and brutishness, that the inclination to this love has first to get its proportion, its delicacy, its gram of salt and sprinkling of ambergris from a higher inclination--whoever first perceived and "experienced" this, however his tongue may have stammered as it attempted to express such a delicate matter, let him for all time be holy and respected, as the man who has so far flown highest and gone astray in the finest fashion!

The philosopher, as WE free spirits understand him--as the man of the greatest responsibility, who has the conscience for the general development of mankind,--will use religion for his disciplining and educating work, just as he will use the contemporary political and economic conditions. The selecting and disciplining influence-- destructive, as well as creative and fashioning--which can be exercised by means of religion is manifold and varied, according to the sort of people placed under its spell and protection. For those who are strong and independent, destined and trained to command, in whom the judgment and skill of a ruling race is incorporated, religion is an additional means for overcoming resistance in the exercise of authority--as a bond which binds rulers and subjects in common, betraying and surrendering to the former the conscience of the latter, their inmost heart, which would fain escape obedience. And in the case of the unique natures of noble origin, if by virtue of superior spirituality they should incline to a more retired and contemplative life, reserving to themselves only the more refined forms of government (over chosen disciples or members of an order), religion itself may be used as a means for obtaining peace from the noise and trouble of managing GROSSER affairs, and for securing immunity from the UNAVOIDABLE filth of all political agitation. The Brahmins, for instance, understood this fact. With the help of a religious organization, they secured to themselves the power of nominating kings for the people, while their sentiments prompted them to keep apart and outside, as men with a higher and super-regal mission. At the same time religion gives inducement and opportunity to some of the subjects to qualify themselves for future ruling and commanding the slowly ascending ranks and classes, in which, through fortunate marriage customs, volitional power and delight in self-control are on the increase. To them religion offers sufficient incentives and temptations to aspire to higher intellectuality, and to experience the sentiments of authoritative self-control, of silence, and of solitude.

Asceticism and Puritanism are almost indispensable means of educating and ennobling a race which seeks to rise above its hereditary baseness and work itself upwards to future supremacy. And finally, to ordinary men, to the majority of the people, who exist for service and general utility, and are only so far entitled to exist, religion gives invaluable contentedness with their lot and condition, peace of heart, ennoblement of obedience, additional social happiness and sympathy, with something of transfiguration and embellishment, something of justification of all the commonplaceness, all the meanness, all the semi-animal poverty of their souls. Religion, together with the religious significance of life, sheds sunshine over such perpetually harassed men, and makes even their own aspect endurable to them, it operates upon them as the Epicurean philosophy usually operates upon sufferers of a higher order, in a refreshing and refining manner, almost TURNING suffering TO ACCOUNT, and in the end even hallowing and vindicating it. There is perhaps nothing so admirable in Christianity and Buddhism as their art of teaching even the lowest to elevate themselves by piety to a seemingly higher order of things, and thereby to retain their satisfaction with the actual world in which they find it difficult enough to live--this very difficulty being necessary.

To be sure--to make also the bad counter-reckoning against such religions, and to bring to light their secret dangers--the cost is always excessive and terrible when religions do NOT operate as an educational and disciplinary medium in the hands of the philosopher, but rule voluntarily and PARAMOUNTLY, when they wish to be the final end, and not a means along with other means. Among men, as among all other animals, there is a surplus of defective, diseased, degenerating, infirm, and necessarily suffering individuals; the successful cases, among men also, are always the exception; and in view of the fact that man is THE ANIMAL NOT YET PROPERLY ADAPTED TO HIS ENVIRONMENT, the rare exception. But worse still. The higher the type a man represents, the greater is the improbability that he will SUCCEED; the accidental, the law of irrationality in the general constitution of mankind, manifests itself most terribly in its destructive effect on the higher orders of men, the conditions of whose lives are delicate, diverse, and difficult to determine. What, then, is the attitude of the two greatest religions above-mentioned to the SURPLUS of failures in life? They endeavour to preserve and keep alive whatever can be preserved; in fact, as the religions FOR SUFFERERS, they take the part of these upon principle; they are always in favour of those who suffer from life as from a disease, and they would fain treat every other experience of life as false and impossible. However highly we may esteem this indulgent and preservative care (inasmuch as in applying to others, it has applied, and applies also to the highest and usually the most suffering type of man), the hitherto PARAMOUNT religions--to give a general appreciation of them--are among the principal causes which have kept the type of "man" upon a lower level--they have preserved too much THAT WHICH SHOULD HAVE PERISHED. One has to thank them for invaluable services; and who is sufficiently rich in gratitude not to feel poor at the contemplation of all that the "spiritual men" of Christianity have done for Europe hitherto! But when they had given comfort to the sufferers, courage to the oppressed and despairing, a staff and support to the helpless, and when they had allured from society into convents and spiritual penitentiaries the broken-hearted and distracted: what else had they to do in order to work systematically in that fashion, and with a good conscience, for the preservation of all the sick and suffering, which means, in deed and in truth, to work for the DETERIORATION OF THE EUROPEAN RACE? To REVERSE all estimates of value--THAT is what they had to do! And to shatter the strong, to spoil great hopes, to cast suspicion on the delight in beauty, to break down everything autonomous, manly, conquering, and imperious--all instincts which are natural to the highest and most successful type of "man"-- into uncertainty, distress of conscience, and self-destruction; forsooth, to invert all love of the earthly and of supremacy over the earth, into hatred of the earth and earthly things--THAT is the task the Church imposed on itself, and was obliged to impose, until, according to its standard of value, "unworldliness," "unsensuousness," and "higher man" fused into one sentiment. If one could observe the strangely painful, equally coarse and refined comedy of European Christianity with the derisive and impartial eye of an Epicurean god, I should think one would never cease marvelling and laughing; does it not actually seem that some single will has ruled over Europe for eighteen centuries in order to make a SUBLIME ABORTION of man? He, however, who, with opposite requirements (no longer Epicurean) and with some divine hammer in his hand, could approach this almost voluntary degeneration and stunting of mankind, as exemplified in the European Christian (Pascal, for instance), would he not have to cry aloud with rage, pity, and horror: "Oh, you bunglers, presumptuous pitiful bunglers, what have you done! Was that a work for your hands? How you have hacked and botched my finest stone! What have you presumed to do!"--I should say that Christianity has hitherto been the most portentous of presumptions. Men, not great enough, nor hard enough, to be entitled as artists to take part in fashioning MAN; men, not sufficiently strong and far-sighted to ALLOW, with sublime self-constraint, the obvious law of the thousandfold failures and perishings to prevail; men, not sufficiently noble to see the radically different grades of rank and intervals of rank that separate man from man:--SUCH men, with their "equality before God," have hitherto swayed the destiny of Europe; until at last a dwarfed, almost ludicrous species has been produced, a gregarious animal, something obliging, sickly, mediocre, the European of the present day.

Chapter 4

Apophthegms and Interludes

He who is thouroughly a teacher takes all things seriously only in relation to his pupils--even himself.

"Knowledge for its own sake" -- that is the last snare laid by morality: we are thereby completely entangled in morals once more.

The charm of knowledge would be small, were it not so much shame has to be overcome on the way to it.

We are most dishonourable towards our God: he is not PERMITTED to sin.

The tendency of a person to degrade himself, to allow himself to be robbed, deceived, and exploited might be the diffidence of a God among men.

Love to one only is a barbarity, for it is exercised at the expense of all others. Love to God also!

"I did that," says my memory. "I could not have done that," says my pride, and remains inexorable. Eventually--the memory yields.

One has regarded life carelessly, if one has failed to see the hand that--kills with leniency.

If a man has character, he has also his typical experience, which always recurs.

THE SAGE AS ASTRONOMER.--So long as thou feelest the stars as an "above thee," thou lackest the eye of the discerning one.

It is not the strength, but the duration of great sentiments that makes those high among mankind.

He who attains his ideal, precisely thereby surpasses it.

Many a peacock hides his tail from every eye--and calls it his pride.

A man of genius is unbearable, unless he possess at least two things besides: gratitude and purity.

The degree and nature of a person's gender extends to the highest altitudes of their spirit.

Under peaceful conditions the militant man attacks himself.

With his principles a man seeks either to tyrranize, or justify, or honour, or reproach, or conceal his habits: two men with the same principles probably seek fundamentally different ends therewith.

He who despises himself, does still esteem himself as a despiser.

A soul which knows that it is loved, but does not itself love, betrays its sediment: its dregs come up.

A thing that is explained ceases to concern us--What did the God mean who gave the advice, "Know thyself!" Did it perhaps imply "Cease to be concerned about thyself! become objective!"-- And Socrates?--And the "scientific man"?

It is terrible to die of thirst at sea. Is it necessary that you should so salt your truth that it will no longer--quench the thirst?

"Sympathy for all"--would be harshness and tyranny for THEE, my good neighbour.

INSTINCT--When the house is on fire one forgets even the dinner--Yes, but one recovers it from among the ashes.

Woman learns how to hate in proportion as she--forgets how to charm.

The same emotions are in man and woman, but in different TEMPO: therefore man and woman never cease to misunderstand one another.

In the background of all their personal vanity, women themselves have still their impersonal scorn--for "woman".

FETTERED HEART, FREE SPIRIT--When one firmly fetters one's heart and keeps it prisoner, one can allow one's spirit many liberties: I said this once before. But people do not believe it when I say so, unless they know it already.

One begins to distrust very clever persons when they become embarrassed.

Dreadful experiences raise the question whether he who experiences them is not something dreadful also.

Heavy, melancholy men turn lighter, and come temporarily to their surface, precisely by that which makes others heavy--by hatred and love.

So cold, so icy, that one burns one's finger at the touch of him! Every hand that lays hold of him shrinks back!--And for that very reason many think him red-hot.

Who has not, at one time or another--sacrificed himself for the sake of his good name?

In affability there is no hatred of men, but precisely on that account a great deal too much contempt of men.

The maturity of man--that means, to have reacquired the seriousness that one had as a child at play.

To be ashamed of one's immorality is a step on the ladder at the end of which one is ashamed also of one's morality.

One should part from life as Ulysses parted from Nausicaa-- blessing it more than in love with it.

What? A great man? I always see merely the play-actor of his own ideal.

When we train our conscience, it imminently kisses us, by biting.

THE DISAPPOINTED ONE SPEAKS--"I listened for reverberations and I heard only praise".

We all feign to ourselves that we are simpler than we are: we thereby relax ourselves away from our fellows.

Today a discerning one might easily wish to regard himself as the animalization of God.

Discovering reciprocal love should really disenchant the lover with regard to the beloved. "What! She is modest enough to love even you? Or stupid enough? Or--or---"

THE DANGER IN HAPPINESS.--"Everything now turns out best for me, I now love every fate:--who would like to be my fate?"

Not their love of humanity, but the impotence of their love, prevents the Christians of today--burning us.

The pia fraus is still more repugnant to the taste (the "piety") of the free spirit (the "pious man of knowledge") than the impia fraus. Hence the profound lack of judgment, in comparison with the Church, characteristic of the type "free spirit"--as ITS non-freedom.

By means of music the very passions enjoy themselves.

A sign of strong character, when once the resolution has been taken, to shut the ear even to the best counter-arguments. Occasionally, therefore, a will to stupidity.

There is no such thing as moral phenomena, but only a moral interpretation of phenomena.

The criminal is often enough not equal to his deed: he extenuates and maligns it.

The advocates of a criminal are seldom artists enough to turn the beautiful terribleness of the deed to the advantage of the doer.

Our vanity is most difficult to wound just when our pride has been wounded.

To him who feels himself preordained to contemplation and not to belief, all believers are too noisy and obtrusive; he guards against them.

"You want to prepossess him in your favour? Then you must be embarrassed before him."

The immense expectation with regard to sexual love, and the coyness in this expectation, spoils all the perspectives of women at the outset.

Where there is neither love nor hatred in the game, woman's play is mediocre.

The great epochs of our life are at the points when we gain courage to rebaptize our badness as the best in us.

The will to overcome an emotion, is ultimately only the will of another, or of several other, emotions.

There is an innocence of admiration: it is possessed by him to whom it has not yet occurred that he himself may be admired some day.

Our loathing of dirt may be so great as to prevent our cleaning ourselves--"justifying" ourselves.

Sensuality often forces the growth of love too much, so that its root remains weak, and is easily torn up.

It is a curious thing that God learned Greek when he wished to turn author--and that he did not learn it better.

To rejoice on account of praise is in many cases merely politeness of heart--and the very opposite of vanity of spirit.

Even concubinage has been corrupted--by marriage.

He who exults at the stake, does not triumph over pain, but because of the fact that he does not feel pain where he expected it. A parable.

When we have to change an opinion about any one, we charge heavily to his account the inconvenience he thereby causes us.

A nation is a detour of nature to arrive at six or seven great men.--Yes, and then to get round them.

In the eyes of all true women science is hostile to the sense of shame. They feel as if one wished to peep under their skin with it--or worse still! under their dress and finery.

The more abstract the truth you wish to teach, the more must you allure the senses to it.

The devil has the most extensive perspectives for God; on that account he keeps so far away from him:--the devil, in effect, as the oldest friend of knowledge.

What a person IS begins to betray itself when his talent decreases,--when he ceases to show what he CAN do. Talent is also an adornment; an adornment is also a concealment.

The sexes deceive themselves about each other: the reason is that in reality they honour and love only themselves (or their own ideal, to express it more agreeably). Thus man wishes woman to be peaceable: but in fact woman is ESSENTIALLY unpeaceable, like the cat, however well she may have assumed the peaceable demeanour.

One is punished best for one's virtues.

He who cannot find the way to HIS ideal, lives more frivolously and shamelessly than the man without an ideal.

From the senses originate all trustworthiness, all good conscience, all evidence of truth.

Pharisaism is not a deterioration of the good man; a considerable part of it is rather an essential condition of being good.

The one seeks an accoucheur for his thoughts, the other seeks some one whom he can assist: a good conversation thus originates.

In intercourse with scholars and artists one readily makes mistakes of opposite kinds: in a remarkable scholar one not infrequently finds a mediocre man; and often, even in a mediocre artist, one finds a very remarkable man.

We do the same when awake as when dreaming: we only invent and imagine him with whom we have intercourse--and forget it immediately.

In revenge and in love woman is more barbarous than man.

ADVICE AS A RIDDLE.--"If the band is not to break, bite it first--secure to make!"

The belly is the reason why man does not so readily take himself for a God.

The chastest utterance I ever heard: "Dans le veritable amour c'est I l'ame qui enveloppe le corps."

Our vanity would like what we do best to pass precisely for what is most difficult to us.--Concerning the origin of many systems of morals.

When a woman has scholarly inclinations there is generally something wrong with her sexual nature. Barrenness itself conduces to a certain virility of taste; man, indeed, if I may say so, is "the barren animal."

Comparing man and woman generally, one may say that woman would not have the genius for adornment, if she had not the instinct for the SECONDARY role.

He who fights with monsters should be careful lest he thereby become a monster. And if thou gaze long into an abyss, the abyss will also gaze into thee.

From old Florentine novels--moreover, from life: Buona femmina e mala femmina vuol bastone.--Sacchetti, Nov. 86.

To seduce their neighbour to a favourable opinion, and afterwards to believe implicitly in this opinion of their neighbour--who can do this conjuring trick so well as women?

That which an age considers evil is usually an unseasonable echo of what was formerly considered good--the atavism of an old ideal.

Around the hero everything becomes a tragedy; around the demigod everything becomes a satyr-play; and around God everything becomes--what? perhaps a "world"?

It is not enough to possess a talent: one must also have your permission to possess it;--eh, my friends?

"Where there is the tree of knowledge, there is always Paradise": so say the most ancient and the most modern serpents.

What is done out of love always takes place beyond good and evil.

Objection, evasion, joyous distrust, and love of irony are signs of health; everything absolute belongs to pathology.

The sense of the tragic increases and declines with sensuousness.

Insanity in individuals is something rare--but in groups, parties, nations, and epochs it is the rule.

The thought of suicide is a great consolation: by means of it one gets successfully through many a bad night.

Not only our reason, but also our conscience, truckles to our strongest impulse--the tyrant in us.

One MUST repay good and ill; but why just to the person who did us good or ill?

One no longer loves one's knowledge sufficiently after one has communicated it.

Poets act shamelessly towards their experiences: they exploit them.

"Our fellow-creature is not our neighbour, but our neighbour's neighbour":--so thinks every nation.

Love brings to light the noble and hidden qualities of a lover--his rare and exceptional traits: it is thus liable to be deceptive as to his normal character.

Jesus said to his Jews: "The law was for servants;--love God as I love him, as his Son! What have we Sons of God to do with morals!"

IN SIGHT OF EVERY PARTY.--A shepherd has always need of a bell-wether--or he has himself to be a wether occasionally.

One may indeed lie with the mouth; but with the accompanying grimace one nevertheless tells the truth.

To vigorous men intimacy is a matter of shame--and something precious.

Christianity gave Eros poison to drink; he did not die of it, certainly, but degenerated to Vice.

To talk much about oneself may also be a means of concealing oneself.

In praise there is more obtrusiveness than in blame.

Pity has an almost ludicrous effect on a man of knowledge, like tender hands on a Cyclops.

One occasionally embraces some one or other, out of love to mankind (because one cannot embrace all); but this is what one must never confess to the individual.

One does not hate as long as one disesteems, but only when one esteems equal or superior.

Ye Utilitarians--ye, too, love the UTILE only as a VEHICLE for your inclinations,--ye, too, really find the noise of its wheels insupportable!

One loves ultimately one's desires, not the thing desired.

The vanity of others is only counter to our taste when it is counter to our vanity.

With regard to what "truthfulness" is, perhaps nobody has ever been sufficiently truthful.

One does not believe in the follies of clever men: what a forfeiture of the rights of man!

The consequences of our actions seize us by the forelock, very indifferent to the fact that we have meanwhile "reformed."

There is an innocence in lying which is the sign of good faith in a cause.

It is inhuman to bless when one is being cursed.

The familiarity of superiors embitters one, because it may not be returned.

"I am affected, not because you have deceived me, but because I can no longer believe in you."

There is a haughtiness of kindness which has the appearance of wickedness.

"I dislike him."--Why?--"I am not a match for him."--Did any one ever answer so?

Chapter 5
The Natural History of Morals

The moral sentiment in Europe at present is perhaps as subtle, belated, diverse, sensitive, and refined, as the "Science of Morals" belonging thereto is recent, initial, awkward, and coarse-fingered:--an interesting contrast, which sometimes becomes incarnate and obvious in the very person of a moralist. Indeed, the expression, "Science of Morals" is, in respect to what is designated thereby, far too presumptuous and counter to GOOD taste,--which is always a foretaste of more modest expressions. One ought to avow with the utmost fairness WHAT is still necessary here for a long time, WHAT is alone proper for the present: namely, the collection of material, the comprehensive survey and classification of an immense domain of delicate sentiments of worth, and distinctions of worth, which live, grow, propagate, and perish--and perhaps attempts to give a clear idea of the recurring and more common forms of these living crystallizations--as preparation for a THEORY OF TYPES of morality. To be sure, people have not hitherto been so modest. All the philosophers, with a pedantic and ridiculous seriousness, demanded of themselves something very much higher, more pretentious, and ceremonious, when they concerned themselves with morality as a science: they wanted to GIVE A BASIC to morality-- and every philosopher hitherto has believed that he has given it a basis; morality itself, however, has been regarded as something "given." How far from their awkward pride was the seemingly insignificant problem--left in dust and decay--of a description of forms of morality, notwithstanding that the finest hands and senses could hardly be fine enough for it! It was precisely owing to moral philosophers' knowing the moral facts imperfectly, in an arbitrary epitome, or an accidental abridgement--perhaps as the morality of their environment, their position, their church, their Zeitgeist, their climate and zone--it was precisely because they were badly instructed with regard to nations, eras, and past ages, and were by no means eager to know about these matters, that they did not even come in sight of the real problems of morals--problems which only disclose themselves by a comparison of MANY kinds of morality. In every "Science of Morals" hitherto, strange as it may sound, the problem of morality itself has been OMITTED: there has been no suspicion that there was anything problematic there! That which philosophers called "giving a basis to morality," and endeavoured to realize, has, when seen in a right light, proved merely a learned form of good FAITH in prevailing morality, a new means of its EXPRESSION, consequently just a matter-of-fact within the sphere of a definite morality, yea, in its ultimate motive, a sort of denial that it is LAWFUL for this morality to be called in question--and in any case the reverse of the testing, analyzing, doubting, and vivisecting of this very faith. Hear, for instance, with what innocence--almost worthy of honour--Schopenhauer represents his own task, and draw your conclusions concerning the scientificness of a "Science" whose latest master still talks in the strain of children and old wives: "The principle," he says (page 136 of the Grundprobleme der Ethik), [Footnote: Pages 54-55 of Schopenhauer's Basis of Morality, translated by Arthur B. Bullock, M.A. (1903).] "the axiom about the purport of which all moralists are PRACTICALLY agreed: neminem laede, immo omnes quantum potes juva--is REALLY the proposition which all moral teachers strive to establish, . . . the REAL basis of ethics which has been sought, like the philosopher's stone, for centuries."--The difficulty of establishing the proposition referred to may indeed be great--it is well known that Schopenhauer also was unsuccessful in his efforts; and whoever has thoroughly realized how absurdly false and sentimental this proposition is, in a world whose essence is Will to Power, may be reminded that Schopenhauer, although a pessimist, ACTUALLY--played the flute . . . daily after dinner: one may read about the matter in his biography. A question by the way: a pessimist, a repudiator of God and of the world, who MAKES A HALT at morality--who assents to morality, and plays the flute to laede-neminem morals, what? Is that really--a pessimist?

Apart from the value of such assertions as "there is a categorical imperative in us," one can always ask: What does such an assertion indicate about him who makes it? There are systems of morals which are meant to justify their author in the eyes of other people; other systems of morals are meant to tranquilize him, and make him self-satisfied; with other systems he wants to crucify and humble himself, with others he wishes to take revenge, with others to conceal himself, with others to glorify himself and gave superiority and distinction,-- this system of morals helps its author to forget, that system makes him, or something of him, forgotten, many a moralist would like to exercise power and creative arbitrariness over mankind, many another, perhaps, Kant especially, gives us to understand by his morals that "what is estimable in me, is that I know how to obey--and with you it SHALL not be otherwise than with me!" In short, systems of morals are only a SIGN-LANGUAGE OF THE EMOTIONS.

In contrast to laisser-aller, every system of morals is a sort of tyranny against "nature" and also against "reason", that is, however, no objection, unless one should again decree by some system of morals, that all kinds of tyranny and unreasonableness are unlawful What is essential and invaluable in every system of morals, is that it is a long constraint. In order to understand Stoicism, or Port Royal, or Puritanism, one should remember the constraint under which every language has attained to strength and freedom--the metrical constraint, the tyranny of rhyme and rhythm. How much trouble have the poets and orators of every nation given themselves!--not excepting some of the prose writers of today, in whose ear dwells an inexorable conscientiousness-- "for the sake of a folly," as utilitarian bunglers say, and thereby deem themselves wise--"from submission to arbitrary laws," as the anarchists say, and thereby fancy themselves "free," even free-spirited. The singular fact remains, however, that everything of the nature of freedom, elegance, boldness, dance, and masterly certainty, which exists or has existed, whether it be in thought itself, or in administration, or in speaking and persuading, in art just as in conduct, has only developed by means of the tyranny of such arbitrary law, and in all seriousness, it is not at all improbable that precisely this is "nature" and "natural"--and not laisser-aller! Every artist knows how different from the state of letting himself go, is his "most natural" condition, the free arranging, locating, disposing, and constructing in the moments of "inspiration"--and how strictly and delicately he then obeys a thousand laws, which, by their very rigidness and precision, defy all formulation by means of ideas (even the most stable idea has, in comparison therewith, something floating, manifold, and ambiguous in it). The essential thing "in heaven and in earth" is, apparently (to repeat it once more), that there should be long OBEDIENCE in the same direction, there thereby results, and has always resulted in the long run, something which has made life worth living; for instance, virtue, art, music, dancing, reason, spirituality--anything whatever that is transfiguring, refined, foolish, or divine. The long bondage of the spirit, the distrustful constraint in the communicability of ideas, the discipline which the thinker imposed on himself to think in accordance with the rules of a church or a court, or conformable to Aristotelian premises, the persistent spiritual will to interpret everything that happened according to a Christian scheme, and in every occurrence to rediscover and justify the Christian God:--all this violence, arbitrariness, severity, dreadfulness, and unreasonableness, has proved itself the disciplinary means whereby the European spirit has attained its strength, its remorseless curiosity and subtle mobility; granted also that much irrecoverable strength and spirit had to be stifled, suffocated, and spoilt in the process (for here, as everywhere, "nature" shows herself as she is, in all her extravagant and INDIFFERENT magnificence, which is shocking, but nevertheless noble). That for centuries European thinkers only thought in order to prove something-nowadays, on the contrary, we are suspicious of every thinker who "wishes to prove something"--that it was always settled beforehand what WAS TO BE the result of their strictest thinking, as it was perhaps in the Asiatic astrology of former times, or as it is still at the present day in the innocent, Christian-moral explanation of immediate personal events "for the glory of God," or "for the good of the soul":--this tyranny, this arbitrariness, this severe and magnificent stupidity, has EDUCATED the spirit; slavery, both in the coarser and the finer sense, is apparently an indispensable means even of spiritual education and discipline. One may look at every system of morals in this light: it is "nature" therein which teaches to hate the laisser-aller, the too great freedom, and implants the need for limited horizons, for immediate duties--it teaches the NARROWING OF PERSPECTIVES, and thus, in a certain sense, that stupidity is a condition of life and development. "Thou must obey some one, and for a long time; OTHERWISE thou wilt come to grief, and lose all respect for thyself"--this seems to me to be the moral imperative of nature, which is certainly neither "categorical," as old Kant wished (consequently the "otherwise"), nor does it address itself to the individual (what does nature care for the individual!), but to nations, races, ages, and ranks; above all, however, to the animal "man" generally, to MANKIND.

Industrious races find it a great hardship to be idle: it was a master stroke of ENGLISH instinct to hallow and begloom Sunday to such an extent that the Englishman unconsciously hankers for his week-- and work-day again:--as a kind of cleverly devised, cleverly intercalated FAST, such as is also frequently found in the ancient world (although, as is appropriate in southern nations, not precisely with respect to work). Many kinds of fasts are necessary; and wherever powerful influences and habits prevail, legislators have to see that intercalary days are appointed, on which such impulses are fettered, and learn to hunger anew. Viewed from a higher standpoint, whole generations and epochs, when they show themselves infected with any moral fanaticism, seem like those intercalated periods of restraint and fasting, during which an impulse learns to humble and submit itself--at the same time also to PURIFY and SHARPEN itself; certain philosophical sects likewise admit of a similar interpretation (for instance, the Stoa, in the midst of Hellenic culture, with the atmosphere rank and overcharged with Aphrodisiacal odours).--Here also is a hint for the explanation of the paradox, why it was precisely in the most Christian period of European history, and in general only under the pressure of Christian sentiments, that the sexual impulse sublimated into love (amour-passion).

There is something in the morality of Plato which does not really belong to Plato, but which only appears in his philosophy, one might say, in spite of him: namely, Socratism, for which he himself was too noble. "No one desires to injure himself, hence all evil is done unwittingly. The evil man inflicts injury on himself; he would not do so, however, if he knew that evil is evil. The evil man, therefore, is only evil through error; if one free him from error one will necessarily make him--good."--This mode of reasoning savours of the POPULACE, who perceive only the unpleasant consequences of evil-doing, and practically judge that "it is STUPID to do wrong"; while they accept "good" as identical with "useful and pleasant," without further thought. As regards every system of utilitarianism, one may at once assume that it has the same origin, and follow the scent: one will seldom err.-- Plato did all he could to interpret something refined and noble into the tenets of his teacher, and above all to interpret himself into them--he, the most daring of all interpreters, who lifted the entire Socrates out of the street, as a popular theme and song, to exhibit him in endless and impossible modifications --namely, in all his own disguises and multiplicities. In jest, and in Homeric language as well, what is the Platonic Socrates, if not-- πρόσθε Πλάτων ὀπιθέν τε Πλάτων μέσση τε Χίμαιρα.

The old theological problem of "Faith" and "Knowledge," or more plainly, of instinct and reason--the question whether, in respect to the valuation of things, instinct deserves more authority than rationality, which wants to appreciate and act according to motives, according to a "Why," that is to say, in conformity to purpose and utility--it is always the old moral problem that first appeared in the person of Socrates, and had divided men's minds long before Christianity. Socrates himself, following, of course, the taste of his talent--that of a surpassing dialectician--took first the side of reason; and, in fact, what did he do all his life but laugh at the awkward incapacity of the noble Athenians, who were men of instinct, like all noble men, and could never give satisfactory answers concerning the motives of their actions? In the end, however, though silently and secretly, he laughed also at himself: with his finer conscience and introspection, he found in himself the same difficulty and incapacity. "But why"--he said to himself-- "should one on that account separate oneself from the instincts! One must set them right, and the reason ALSO--one must follow the instincts, but at the same time persuade the reason to support them with good arguments." This was the real FALSENESS of that great and mysterious ironist; he brought his conscience up to the point that he was satisfied with a kind of self-outwitting: in fact, he perceived the irrationality in the moral judgment.-- Plato, more innocent in such matters, and without the craftiness of the plebeian, wished to prove to himself, at the expenditure of all his strength--the greatest strength a philosopher had ever expended--that reason and instinct lead spontaneously to one goal, to the good, to "God"; and since Plato, all theologians and philosophers have followed the same path--which means that in matters of morality, instinct (or as Christians call it, "Faith," or as I call it, "the herd") has hitherto triumphed. Unless one should make an exception in the case of Descartes, the father of rationalism (and consequently the grandfather of the Revolution), who recognized only the authority of reason: but reason is only a tool, and Descartes was superficial.

Whoever has followed the history of a single science, finds in its development a clue to the understanding of the oldest and commonest processes of all "knowledge and cognizance": there, as here, the premature hypotheses, the fictions, the good stupid will to "belief," and the lack of distrust and patience are first developed--our senses learn late, and never learn completely, to be subtle, reliable, and cautious organs of knowledge. Our eyes find it easier on a given occasion to produce a picture already often produced, than to seize upon the divergence and novelty of an impression: the latter requires more force, more "morality." It is difficult and painful for the ear to listen to anything new; we hear strange music badly. When we hear another language spoken, we involuntarily attempt to form the sounds into words with which we are more familiar and conversant--it was thus, for example, that the Germans modified the spoken word ARCUBALISTA into ARMBRUST (cross-bow). Our senses are also hostile and averse to the new; and generally, even in the "simplest" processes of sensation, the emotions DOMINATE--such as fear, love, hatred, and the passive emotion of indolence.--As little as a reader nowadays reads all the single words (not to speak of syllables) of a page --he rather takes about five out of every twenty words at random, and "guesses" the probably appropriate sense to them--just as little do we see a tree correctly and completely in respect to its leaves, branches, colour, and shape; we find it so much easier to fancy the chance of a tree. Even in the midst of the most remarkable experiences, we still do just the same; we fabricate the greater part of the experience, and can hardly be made to contemplate any event, EXCEPT as "inventors" thereof. All this goes to prove that from our fundamental nature and from remote ages we have been--ACCUSTOMED TO LYING. Or, to express it more politely and hypocritically, in short, more pleasantly--one is much more of an artist than one is aware of.--In an animated conversation, I often see the face of the person with whom I am speaking so clearly and sharply defined before me, according to the thought he expresses, or which I believe to be evoked in his mind, that the degree of distinctness far exceeds the STRENGTH of my visual faculty--the delicacy of the play of the muscles and of the expression of the eyes MUST therefore be imagined by me. Probably the person put on quite a different expression, or none at all.

Quidquid luce fuit, tenebris agit: but also contrariwise. What we experience in dreams, provided we experience it often, pertains at last just as much to the general belongings of our soul as anything "actually" experienced; by virtue thereof we are richer or poorer, we have a requirement more or less, and finally, in broad daylight, and even in the brightest moments of our waking life, we are ruled to some extent by the nature of our dreams. Supposing that someone has often flown in his dreams, and that at last, as soon as he dreams, he is conscious of the power and art of flying as his privilege and his peculiarly enviable happiness; such a person, who believes that on the slightest impulse, he can actualize all sorts of curves and angles, who knows the sensation of a certain divine levity, an "upwards" without effort or constraint, a "downwards" without descending or lowering- -without TROUBLE!--how could the man with such dream-experiences and dream-habits fail to find "happiness" differently coloured and defined, even in his waking hours! How could he fail-- to long DIFFERENTLY for happiness? "Flight," such as is described by poets, must, when compared with his own "flying," be far too earthly, muscular, violent, far too "troublesome" for him.

The difference among men does not manifest itself only in the difference of their lists of desirable things--in their regarding different good things as worth striving for, and being disagreed as to the greater or less value, the order of rank, of the commonly recognized desirable things:--it manifests itself much more in what they regard as actually HAVING and POSSESSING a desirable thing. As regards a woman, for instance, the control over her body and her sexual gratification serves as an amply sufficient sign of ownership and possession to the more modest man; another with a more suspicious and ambitious thirst for possession, sees the "questionableness," the mere apparentness of such ownership, and wishes to have finer tests in order to know especially whether the woman not only gives herself to him, but also gives up for his sake what she has or would like to have- - only THEN does he look upon her as "possessed." A third, however, has not even here got to the limit of his distrust and his desire for possession: he asks himself whether the woman, when she gives up everything for him, does not perhaps do so for a phantom of him; he wishes first to be thoroughly, indeed, profoundly well known; in order to be loved at all he ventures to let himself be found out. Only then does he feel the beloved one fully in his possession, when she no longer deceives herself about him, when she loves him just as much for the sake of his devilry and concealed insatiability, as for his goodness, patience, and spirituality. One man would like to possess a nation, and he finds all the higher arts of Cagliostro and Catalina suitable for his purpose. Another, with a more refined thirst for possession, says to himself: "One may not deceive where one desires to possess"--he is irritated and impatient at the idea that a mask of him should rule in the hearts of the people: "I must, therefore, MAKE myself known, and first of all learn to know myself!" Among helpful and charitable people, one almost always finds the awkward craftiness which first gets up suitably him who has to be helped, as though, for instance, he should "merit" help, seek just THEIR help, and would show himself deeply grateful, attached, and subservient to them for all help. With these conceits, they take control of the needy as a property, just as in general they are charitable and helpful out of a desire for property. One finds them jealous when they are crossed or forestalled in their charity. Parents involuntarily make something like themselves out of their children--they call that "education"; no mother doubts at the bottom of her heart that the child she has borne is thereby her property, no father hesitates about his right to HIS OWN ideas and notions of worth. Indeed, in former times fathers deemed it right to use their discretion concerning the life or death of the newly born (as among the ancient Germans). And like the father, so also do the teacher, the class, the priest, and the prince still see in every new individual an unobjectionable opportunity for a new possession. The consequence is . . .

The Jews--a people "born for slavery," as Tacitus and the whole ancient world say of them; "the chosen people among the nations," as they themselves say and believe--the Jews performed the miracle of the inversion of valuations, by means of which life on earth obtained a new and dangerous charm for a couple of millenniums. Their prophets fused into one the expressions "rich," "godless," "wicked," "violent," "sensual," and for the first time coined the word "world" as a term of reproach. In this inversion of valuations (in which is also included the use of the word "poor" as synonymous with "saint" and "friend") the significance of the Jewish people is to be found; it is with THEM that the SLAVE-INSURRECTION IN MORALS commences.

It is to be INFERRED that there are countless dark bodies near the sun--such as we shall never see. Among ourselves, this is an allegory; and the psychologist of morals reads the whole star-writing merely as an allegorical and symbolic language in which much may be unexpressed.

The beast of prey and the man of prey (for instance, Caesar Borgia) are fundamentally misunderstood, "nature" is misunderstood, so long as one seeks a "morbidness" in the constitution of these healthiest of all tropical monsters and growths, or even an innate "hell" in them-- as almost all moralists have done hitherto. Does it not seem that there is a hatred of the virgin forest and of the tropics among moralists? And that the "tropical man" must be discredited at all costs, whether as disease and deterioration of mankind, or as his own hell and self-torture? And why? In favour of the "temperate zones"? In favour of the temperate men? The "moral"? The mediocre?--This for the chapter: "Morals as Timidity."

All the systems of morals which address themselves with a view to their "happiness," as it is called--what else are they but suggestions for behaviour adapted to the degree of DANGER from themselves in which the individuals live; recipes for their passions, their good and bad propensities, insofar as such have the Will to Power and would like to play the master; small and great expediencies and elaborations, permeated with the musty odour of old family medicines and old-wife wisdom; all of them grotesque and absurd in their form--because they address themselves to "all," because they generalize where generalization is not authorized; all of them speaking unconditionally, and taking themselves unconditionally; all of them flavoured not merely with one grain of salt, but rather endurable only, and sometimes even seductive, when they are over-spiced and begin to smell dangerously, especially of "the other world." That is all of little value when estimated intellectually, and is far from being "science," much less "wisdom"; but, repeated once more, and three times repeated, it is expediency, expediency, expediency, mixed with stupidity, stupidity, stupidity--whether it be the indifference and statuesque coldness towards the heated folly of the emotions, which the Stoics advised and fostered; or the no- more-laughing and no-more-weeping of Spinoza, the destruction of the emotions by their analysis and vivisection, which he recommended so naively; or the lowering of the emotions to an innocent mean at which they may be satisfied, the Aristotelianism of morals; or even morality as the enjoyment of the emotions in a voluntary attenuation and spiritualization by the symbolism of art, perhaps as music, or as love of God, and of mankind for God's sake--for in religion the passions are once more enfranchised, provided that . . . ; or, finally, even the complaisant and wanton surrender to the emotions, as has been taught by Hafis and Goethe, the bold letting-go of the reins, the spiritual and corporeal licentia morum in the exceptional cases of wise old codgers and drunkards, with whom it "no longer has much danger." --This also for the chapter: "Morals as Timidity."

Inasmuch as in all ages, as long as mankind has existed, there have also been human herds (family alliances, communities, tribes, peoples, states, churches), and always a great number who obey in proportion to the small number who command--in view, therefore, of the fact that obedience has been most practiced and fostered among mankind hitherto, one may reasonably suppose that, generally speaking, the need thereof is now innate in every one, as a kind of FORMAL CONSCIENCE which gives the command "Thou shalt unconditionally do something, unconditionally refrain from something", in short, "Thou shalt". This need tries to satisfy itself and to fill its form with a content, according to its strength, impatience, and eagerness, it at once seizes as an omnivorous appetite with little selection, and accepts whatever is shouted into its ear by all sorts of commanders--parents, teachers, laws, class prejudices, or public opinion. The extraordinary limitation of human development, the hesitation, protractedness, frequent retrogression, and turning thereof, is attributable to the fact that the herd-instinct of obedience is transmitted best, and at the cost of the art of command. If one imagine this instinct increasing to its greatest extent, commanders and independent individuals will finally be lacking altogether, or they will suffer inwardly from a bad conscience, and will have to impose a deception on themselves in the first place in order to be able to command just as if they also were only obeying. This condition of things actually exists in Europe at present--I call it the moral hypocrisy of the commanding class. They know no other way of protecting themselves from their bad conscience than by playing the role of executors of older and higher orders (of predecessors, of the constitution, of justice, of the law, or of God himself), or they even justify themselves by maxims from the current opinions of the herd, as "first servants of their people," or "instruments of the public weal". On the other hand, the gregarious European man nowadays assumes an air as if he were the only kind of man that is allowable, he glorifies his qualities, such as public spirit, kindness, deference, industry, temperance, modesty, indulgence, sympathy, by virtue of which he is gentle, endurable, and useful to the herd, as the peculiarly human virtues. In cases, however, where it is believed that the leader and bell-wether cannot be dispensed with, attempt after attempt is made nowadays to replace commanders by the summing together of clever gregarious men all representative constitutions, for example, are of this origin. In spite of all, what a blessing, what a deliverance from a weight becoming unendurable, is the appearance of an absolute ruler for these gregarious Europeans--of this fact the effect of the appearance of Napoleon was the last great proof the history of the influence of Napoleon is almost the history of the higher happiness to which the entire century has attained in its worthiest individuals and periods.

The man of an age of dissolution which mixes the races with one another, who has the inheritance of a diversified descent in his body--that is to say, contrary, and often not only contrary, instincts and standards of value, which struggle with one another and are seldom at peace--such a man of late culture and broken lights, will, on an average, be a weak man. His fundamental desire is that the war which is IN HIM should come to an end; happiness appears to him in the character of a soothing medicine and mode of thought (for instance, Epicurean or Christian); it is above all things the happiness of repose, of undisturbedness, of repletion, of final unity--it is the "Sabbath of Sabbaths," to use the expression of the holy rhetorician, St. Augustine, who was himself such a man.--Should, however, the contrariety and conflict in such natures operate as an ADDITIONAL incentive and stimulus to life--and if, on the other hand, in addition to their powerful and irreconcilable instincts, they have also inherited and indoctrinated into them a proper mastery and subtlety for carrying on the conflict with themselves (that is to say, the faculty of self-control and self-deception), there then arise those marvelously incomprehensible and inexplicable beings, those enigmatical men, predestined for conquering and circumventing others, the finest examples of which are Alcibiades and Caesar (with whom I should like to associate the FIRST of Europeans according to my taste, the Hohenstaufen, Frederick the Second), and among artists, perhaps Leonardo da Vinci. They appear precisely in the same periods when that weaker type, with its longing for repose, comes to the front; the two types are complementary to each other, and spring from the same causes.

As long as the utility which determines moral estimates is only gregarious utility, as long as the preservation of the community is only kept in view, and the immoral is sought precisely and exclusively in what seems dangerous to the maintenance of the community, there can be no "morality of love to one's neighbour." Granted even that there is already a little constant exercise of consideration, sympathy, fairness, gentleness, and mutual assistance, granted that even in this condition of society all those instincts are already active which are latterly distinguished by honourable names as "virtues," and eventually almost coincide with the conception "morality": in that period they do not as yet belong to the domain of moral valuations--they are still ULTRA-MORAL. A sympathetic action, for instance, is neither called good nor bad, moral nor immoral, in the best period of the Romans; and should it be praised, a sort of resentful disdain is compatible with this praise, even at the best, directly the sympathetic action is compared with one which contributes to the welfare of the whole, to the RES PUBLICA. After all, "love to our neighbour" is always a secondary matter, partly conventional and arbitrarily manifested in relation to our FEAR OF OUR NEIGHBOUR. After the fabric of society seems on the whole established and secured against external dangers, it is this fear of our neighbour which again creates new perspectives of moral valuation. Certain strong and dangerous instincts, such as the love of enterprise, foolhardiness, revengefulness, astuteness, rapacity, and love of power, which up till then had not only to be honoured from the point of view of general utility--under other names, of course, than those here given--but had to be fostered and cultivated (because they were perpetually required in the common danger against the common enemies), are now felt in their dangerousness to be doubly strong--when the outlets for them are lacking--and are gradually branded as immoral and given over to calumny. The contrary instincts and inclinations now attain to moral honour, the gregarious instinct gradually draws its conclusions. How much or how little dangerousness to the community or to equality is contained in an opinion, a condition, an emotion, a disposition, or an endowment-- that is now the moral perspective, here again fear is the mother of morals. It is by the loftiest and strongest instincts, when they break out passionately and carry the individual far above and beyond the average, and the low level of the gregarious conscience, that the self-reliance of the community is destroyed, its belief in itself, its backbone, as it were, breaks, consequently these very instincts will be most branded and defamed. The lofty independent spirituality, the will to stand alone, and even the cogent reason, are felt to be dangers, everything that elevates the individual above the herd, and is a source of fear to the neighbour, is henceforth called EVIL, the tolerant, unassuming, self-adapting, self-equalizing disposition, the MEDIOCRITY of desires, attains to moral distinction and honour. Finally, under very peaceful circumstances, there is always less opportunity and necessity for training the feelings to severity and rigour, and now every form of severity, even in justice, begins to disturb the conscience, a lofty and rigorous nobleness and self-responsibility almost offends, and awakens distrust, "the lamb," and still more "the sheep," wins respect. There is a point of diseased mellowness and effeminacy in the history of society, at which society itself takes the part of him who injures it, the part of the CRIMINAL, and does so, in fact, seriously and honestly. To punish, appears to it to be somehow unfair--it is certain that the idea of "punishment" and "the obligation to punish" are then painful and alarming to people. "Is it not sufficient if the criminal be rendered HARMLESS? Why should we still punish? Punishment itself is terrible!"--with these questions gregarious morality, the morality of fear, draws its ultimate conclusion. If one could at all do away with danger, the cause of fear, one would have done away with this morality at the same time, it would no longer be necessary, it WOULD NOT CONSIDER ITSELF any longer necessary!--Whoever examines the conscience of the present-day European, will always elicit the same imperative from its thousand moral folds and hidden recesses, the imperative of the timidity of the herd "we wish that some time or other there may be NOTHING MORE TO FEAR!" Some time or other--the will and the way THERETO is nowadays called "progress" all over Europe.

Let us at once say again what we have already said a hundred times, for people's ears nowadays are unwilling to hear such truths--OUR truths. We know well enough how offensive it sounds when any one plainly, and without metaphor, counts man among the animals, but it will be accounted to us almost a CRIME, that it is precisely in respect to men of "modern ideas" that we have constantly applied the terms "herd," "herd-instincts," and such like expressions. What avail is it? We cannot do otherwise, for it is precisely here that our new insight is. We have found that in all the principal moral judgments, Europe has become unanimous, including likewise the countries where European influence prevails in Europe people evidently KNOW what Socrates thought he did not know, and what the famous serpent of old once promised to teach--they "know" today what is good and evil. It must then sound hard and be distasteful to the ear, when we always insist that that which here thinks it knows, that which here glorifies itself with praise and blame, and calls itself good, is the instinct of the herding human animal, the instinct which has come and is ever coming more and more to the front, to preponderance and supremacy over other instincts, according to the increasing physiological approximation and resemblance of which it is the symptom. MORALITY IN EUROPE AT PRESENT IS HERDING-ANIMAL MORALITY, and therefore, as we understand the matter, only one kind of human morality, beside which, before which, and after which many other moralities, and above all HIGHER moralities, are or should be possible. Against such a "possibility," against such a "should be," however, this morality defends itself with all its strength, it says obstinately and inexorably "I am morality itself and nothing else is morality!" Indeed, with the help of a religion which has humoured and flattered the sublimest desires of the herding-animal, things have reached such a point that we always find a more visible expression of this morality even in political and social arrangements: the DEMOCRATIC movement is the inheritance of the Christian movement. That its TEMPO, however, is much too slow and sleepy for the more impatient ones, for those who are sick and distracted by the herding-instinct, is indicated by the increasingly furious howling, and always less disguised teeth- gnashing of the anarchist dogs, who are now roving through the highways of European culture. Apparently in opposition to the peacefully industrious democrats and Revolution-ideologues, and still more so to the awkward philosophasters and fraternity- visionaries who call themselves Socialists and want a "free society," those are really at one with them all in their thorough and instinctive hostility to every form of society other than that of the AUTONOMOUS herd (to the extent even of repudiating the notions "master" and "servant"--ni dieu ni maitre, says a socialist formula); at one in their tenacious opposition to every special claim, every special right and privilege (this means ultimately opposition to EVERY right, for when all are equal, no one needs "rights" any longer); at one in their distrust of punitive justice (as though it were a violation of the weak, unfair to the NECESSARY consequences of all former society); but equally at one in their religion of sympathy, in their compassion for all that feels, lives, and suffers (down to the very animals, up even to "God"--the extravagance of "sympathy for God" belongs to a democratic age); altogether at one in the cry and impatience of their sympathy, in their deadly hatred of suffering generally, in their almost feminine incapacity for witnessing it or ALLOWING it; at one in their involuntary beglooming and heart-softening, under the spell of which Europe seems to be threatened with a new Buddhism; at one in their belief in the morality of MUTUAL sympathy, as though it were morality in itself, the climax, the ATTAINED climax of mankind, the sole hope of the future, the consolation of the present, the great discharge from all the obligations of the past; altogether at one in their belief in the community as the DELIVERER, in the herd, and therefore in "themselves."

We, who hold a different belief--we, who regard the democratic movement, not only as a degenerating form of political organization, but as equivalent to a degenerating, a waning type of man, as involving his mediocrising and depreciation: where have WE to fix our hopes? In NEW PHILOSOPHERS--there is no other alternative: in minds strong and original enough to initiate opposite estimates of value, to transvalue and invert "eternal valuations"; in forerunners, in men of the future, who in the present shall fix the constraints and fasten the knots which will compel millenniums to take NEW paths. To teach man the future of humanity as his WILL, as depending on human will, and to make preparation for vast hazardous enterprises and collective attempts in rearing and educating, in order thereby to put an end to the frightful rule of folly and chance which has hitherto gone by the name of "history" (the folly of the "greatest number" is only its last form)--for that purpose a new type of philosopher and commander will some time or other be needed, at the very idea of which everything that has existed in the way of occult, terrible, and benevolent beings might look pale and dwarfed. The image of such leaders hovers before OUR eyes:--is it lawful for me to say it aloud, ye free spirits? The conditions which one would partly have to create and partly utilize for their genesis; the presumptive methods and tests by virtue of which a soul should grow up to such an elevation and power as to feel a CONSTRAINT to these tasks; a transvaluation of values, under the new pressure and hammer of which a conscience should be steeled and a heart transformed into brass, so as to bear the weight of such responsibility; and on the other hand the necessity for such leaders, the dreadful danger that they might be lacking, or miscarry and degenerate:--these are OUR real anxieties and glooms, ye know it well, ye free spirits! these are the heavy distant thoughts and storms which sweep across the heaven of OUR life. There are few pains so grievous as to have seen, divined, or experienced how an exceptional man has missed his way and deteriorated; but he who has the rare eye for the universal danger of "man" himself DETERIORATING, he who like us has recognized the extraordinary fortuitousness which has hitherto played its game in respect to the future of mankind--a game in which neither the hand, nor even a "finger of God" has participated!--he who divines the fate that is hidden under the idiotic unwariness and blind confidence of "modern ideas," and still more under the whole of Christo-European morality-suffers from an anguish with which no other is to be compared. He sees at a glance all that could still BE MADE OUT OF MAN through a favourable accumulation and augmentation of human powers and arrangements; he knows with all the knowledge of his conviction how unexhausted man still is for the greatest possibilities, and how often in the past the type man has stood in presence of mysterious decisions and new paths:--he knows still better from his painfulest recollections on what wretched obstacles promising developments of the highest rank have hitherto usually gone to pieces, broken down, sunk, and become contemptible. The UNIVERSAL DEGENERACY OF MANKIND to the level of the "man of the future"--as idealized by the socialistic fools and shallow-pates--this degeneracy and dwarfing of man to an absolutely gregarious animal (or as they call it, to a man of "free society"), this brutalizing of man into a pigmy with equal rights and claims, is undoubtedly POSSIBLE! He who has thought out this possibility to its ultimate conclusion knows ANOTHER loathing unknown to the rest of mankind--and perhaps also a new MISSION!

Chapter 6
We Scholars

At the risk that moralizing may also reveal itself here as that which it has always been--namely, resolutely MONTRER SES PLAIES, according to Balzac--I would venture to protest against an improper and injurious alteration of rank, which quite unnoticed, and as if with the best conscience, threatens nowadays to establish itself in the relations of science and philosophy. I mean to say that one must have the right out of one's own EXPERIENCE--experience, as it seems to me, always implies unfortunate experience?--to treat of such an important question of rank, so as not to speak of colour like the blind, or AGAINST science like women and artists ("Ah! this dreadful science!" sigh their instinct and their shame, "it always FINDS THINGS OUT!"). The declaration of independence of the scientific man, his emancipation from philosophy, is one of the subtler after-effects of democratic organization and disorganization: the self-glorification and self-conceitedness of the learned man is now everywhere in full bloom, and in its best springtime--which does not mean to imply that in this case self-praise smells sweet. Here also the instinct of the populace cries, "Freedom from all masters!" and after science has, with the happiest results, resisted theology, whose "hand-maid" it had been too long, it now proposes in its wantonness and indiscretion to lay down laws for philosophy, and in its turn to play the "master"--what am I saying! to play the PHILOSOPHER on its own account. My memory-- the memory of a scientific man, if you please!--teems with the naivetes of insolence which I have heard about philosophy and philosophers from young naturalists and old physicians (not to mention the most cultured and most conceited of all learned men, the philologists and schoolmasters, who are both the one and the other by profession). On one occasion it was the specialist and the Jack Horner who instinctively stood on the defensive against all synthetic tasks and capabilities; at another time it was the industrious worker who had got a scent of OTIUM and refined luxuriousness in the internal economy of the philosopher, and felt himself aggrieved and belittled thereby. On another occasion it was the colour-blindness of the utilitarian, who sees nothing in philosophy but a series of REFUTED systems, and an extravagant expenditure which "does nobody any good". At another time the fear of disguised mysticism and of the boundary-adjustment of knowledge became conspicuous, at another time the disregard of individual philosophers, which had involuntarily extended to disregard of philosophy generally. In fine, I found most frequently, behind the proud disdain of philosophy in young scholars, the evil after-effect of some particular philosopher, to whom on the whole obedience had been foresworn, without, however, the spell of his scornful estimates of other philosophers having been got rid of--the result being a general ill-will to all philosophy. (Such seems to me, for instance, the after-effect of Schopenhauer on the most modern Germany: by his unintelligent rage against Hegel, he has succeeded in severing the whole of the last generation of Germans from its connection with German culture, which culture, all things considered, has been an elevation and a divining refinement of the HISTORICAL SENSE, but precisely at this point Schopenhauer himself was poor, irreceptive, and un-German to the extent of ingeniousness.) On the whole, speaking generally, it may just have been the humanness, all-too-humanness of the modern philosophers themselves, in short, their contemptibleness, which has injured most radically the reverence for philosophy and opened the doors to the instinct of the populace. Let it but be acknowledged to what an extent our modern world diverges from the whole style of the world of Heraclitus, Plato, Empedocles, and whatever else all the royal and magnificent anchorites of the spirit were called, and with what justice an honest man of science MAY feel himself of a better family and origin, in view of such representatives of philosophy, who, owing to the fashion of the present day, are just as much aloft as they are down below--in Germany, for instance, the two lions of Berlin, the anarchist Eugen Duhring and the amalgamist Eduard von Hartmann. It is especially the sight of those hotch-potch philosophers, who call themselves "realists," or "positivists," which is calculated to implant a dangerous distrust in the soul of a young and ambitious scholar those philosophers, at the best, are themselves but scholars and specialists, that is very evident! All of them are persons who have been vanquished and BROUGHT BACK AGAIN under the dominion of science, who at one time or another claimed more from themselves, without having a right to the "more" and its responsibility--and who now, creditably, rancorously, and vindictively, represent in word and deed, DISBELIEF in the master-task and supremacy of philosophy After all, how could it be otherwise? Science flourishes nowadays and has the good conscience clearly visible on its countenance, while that to which the entire modern philosophy has gradually sunk, the remnant of philosophy of the present day, excites distrust and displeasure, if not scorn and pity Philosophy reduced to a "theory of knowledge," no more in fact than a diffident science of epochs and doctrine of forbearance a philosophy that never even gets beyond the threshold, and rigorously DENIES itself the right to enter--that is philosophy in its last throes, an end, an agony, something that awakens pity. How could such a philosophy--RULE!

The dangers that beset the evolution of the philosopher are, in fact, so manifold nowadays, that one might doubt whether this fruit could still come to maturity. The extent and towering structure of the sciences have increased enormously, and therewith also the probability that the philosopher will grow tired even as a learner, or will attach himself somewhere and "specialize" so that he will no longer attain to his elevation, that is to say, to his superspection, his circumspection, and his DESPECTION. Or he gets aloft too late, when the best of his maturity and strength is past, or when he is impaired, coarsened, and deteriorated, so that his view, his general estimate of things, is no longer of much importance. It is perhaps just the refinement of his intellectual conscience that makes him hesitate and linger on the way, he dreads the temptation to become a dilettante, a millepede, a milleantenna, he knows too well that as a discerner, one who has lost his self-respect no longer commands, no longer LEADS, unless he should aspire to become a great play-actor, a philosophical Cagliostro and spiritual rat- catcher--in short, a misleader. This is in the last instance a question of taste, if it has not really been a question of conscience. To double once more the philosopher's difficulties, there is also the fact that he demands from himself a verdict, a Yea or Nay, not concerning science, but concerning life and the worth of life--he learns unwillingly to believe that it is his right and even his duty to obtain this verdict, and he has to seek his way to the right and the belief only through the most extensive (perhaps disturbing and destroying) experiences, often hesitating, doubting, and dumbfounded. In fact, the philosopher has long been mistaken and confused by the multitude, either with the scientific man and ideal scholar, or with the religiously elevated, desensualized, desecularized visionary and God-intoxicated man; and even yet when one hears anybody praised, because he lives "wisely," or "as a philosopher," it hardly means anything more than "prudently and apart." Wisdom: that seems to the populace to be a kind of flight, a means and artifice for withdrawing successfully from a bad game; but the GENUINE philosopher--does it not seem so to US, my friends?--lives "unphilosophically" and "unwisely," above all, IMPRUDENTLY, and feels the obligation and burden of a hundred attempts and temptations of life--he risks HIMSELF constantly, he plays THIS bad game.

In relation to the genius, that is to say, a being who either ENGENDERS or PRODUCES--both words understood in their fullest sense--the man of learning, the scientific average man, has always something of the old maid about him; for, like her, he is not conversant with the two principal functions of man. To both, of course, to the scholar and to the old maid, one concedes respectability, as if by way of indemnification--in these cases one emphasizes the respectability--and yet, in the compulsion of this concession, one has the same admixture of vexation. Let us examine more closely: what is the scientific man? Firstly, a commonplace type of man, with commonplace virtues: that is to say, a non-ruling, non-authoritative, and non-self-sufficient type of man; he possesses industry, patient adaptableness to rank and file, equability and moderation in capacity and requirement; he has the instinct for people like himself, and for that which they require--for instance: the portion of independence and green meadow without which there is no rest from labour, the claim to honour and consideration (which first and foremost presupposes recognition and recognisability), the sunshine of a good name, the perpetual ratification of his value and usefulness, with which the inward DISTRUST which lies at the bottom of the heart of all dependent men and gregarious animals, has again and again to be overcome. The learned man, as is appropriate, has also maladies and faults of an ignoble kind: he is full of petty envy, and has a lynx-eye for the weak points in those natures to whose elevations he cannot attain. He is confiding, yet only as one who lets himself go, but does not FLOW; and precisely before the man of the great current he stands all the colder and more reserved-- his eye is then like a smooth and irresponsive lake, which is no longer moved by rapture or sympathy. The worst and most dangerous thing of which a scholar is capable results from the instinct of mediocrity of his type, from the Jesuitism of mediocrity, which labours instinctively for the destruction of the exceptional man, and endeavours to break--or still better, to relax--every bent bow To relax, of course, with consideration, and naturally with an indulgent hand--to RELAX with confiding sympathy that is the real art of Jesuitism, which has always understood how to introduce itself as the religion of sympathy.

However gratefully one may welcome the OBJECTIVE spirit-- and who has not been sick to death of all subjectivity and its confounded IPSISIMOSITY!--in the end, however, one must learn caution even with regard to one's gratitude, and put a stop to the exaggeration with which the unselfing and depersonalizing of the spirit has recently been celebrated, as if it were the goal in itself, as if it were salvation and glorification--as is especially accustomed to happen in the pessimist school, which has also in its turn good reasons for paying the highest honours to "disinterested knowledge" The objective man, who no longer curses and scolds like the pessimist, the IDEAL man of learning in whom the scientific instinct blossoms forth fully after a thousand complete and partial failures, is assuredly one of the most costly instruments that exist, but his place is in the hand of one who is more powerful He is only an instrument, we may say, he is a MIRROR--he is no "purpose in himself" The objective man is in truth a mirror accustomed to prostration before everything that wants to be known, with such desires only as knowing or "reflecting" implies--he waits until something comes, and then expands himself sensitively, so that even the light footsteps and gliding-past of spiritual beings may not be lost on his surface and film Whatever "personality" he still possesses seems to him accidental, arbitrary, or still oftener, disturbing, so much has he come to regard himself as the passage and reflection of outside forms and events He calls up the recollection of "himself" with an effort, and not infrequently wrongly, he readily confounds himself with other persons, he makes mistakes with regard to his own needs, and here only is he unrefined and negligent Perhaps he is troubled about the health, or the pettiness and confined atmosphere of wife and friend, or the lack of companions and society--indeed, he sets himself to reflect on his suffering, but in vain! His thoughts already rove away to the MORE GENERAL case, and tomorrow he knows as little as he knew yesterday how to help himself He does not now take himself seriously and devote time to himself he is serene, NOT from lack of trouble, but from lack of capacity for grasping and dealing with HIS trouble The habitual complaisance with respect to all objects and experiences, the radiant and impartial hospitality with which he receives everything that comes his way, his habit of inconsiderate good-nature, of dangerous indifference as to Yea and Nay: alas! there are enough of cases in which he has to atone for these virtues of his!--and as man generally, he becomes far too easily the CAPUT MORTUUM of such virtues. Should one wish love or hatred from him--I mean love and hatred as God, woman, and animal understand them--he will do what he can, and furnish what he can. But one must not be surprised if it should not be much--if he should show himself just at this point to be false, fragile, questionable, and deteriorated. His love is constrained, his hatred is artificial, and rather UNN TOUR DE FORCE, a slight ostentation and exaggeration. He is only genuine so far as he can be objective; only in his serene totality is he still "nature" and "natural." His mirroring and eternally self-polishing soul no longer knows how to affirm, no longer how to deny; he does not command; neither does he destroy. "JE NE MEPRISE PRESQUE RIEN"-- he says, with Leibniz: let us not overlook nor undervalue the PRESQUE! Neither is he a model man; he does not go in advance of any one, nor after, either; he places himself generally too far off to have any reason for espousing the cause of either good or evil. If he has been so long confounded with the PHILOSOPHER, with the Caesarian trainer and dictator of civilization, he has had far too much honour, and what is more essential in him has been overlooked--he is an instrument, something of a slave, though certainly the sublimest sort of slave, but nothing in himself--PRESQUE RIEN! The objective man is an instrument, a costly, easily injured, easily tarnished measuring instrument and mirroring apparatus, which is to be taken care of and respected; but he is no goal, not outgoing nor upgoing, no complementary man in whom the REST of existence justifies itself, no termination-- and still less a commencement, an engendering, or primary cause, nothing hardy, powerful, self-centred, that wants to be master; but rather only a soft, inflated, delicate, movable potter's- form, that must wait for some kind of content and frame to "shape" itself thereto--for the most part a man without frame and content, a "selfless" man. Consequently, also, nothing for women, IN PARENTHESI.

When a philosopher nowadays makes known that he is not a skeptic--I hope that has been gathered from the foregoing description of the objective spirit?--people all hear it impatiently; they regard him on that account with some apprehension, they would like to ask so many, many questions . . . indeed among timid hearers, of whom there are now so many, he is henceforth said to be dangerous. With his repudiation of skepticism, it seems to them as if they heard some evil-threatening sound in the distance, as if a new kind of explosive were being tried somewhere, a dynamite of the spirit, perhaps a newly discovered Russian NIHILINE, a pessimism BONAE VOLUNTATIS, that not only denies, means denial, but-dreadful thought! PRACTISES denial. Against this kind of "good-will"--a will to the veritable, actual negation of life--there is, as is generally acknowledged nowadays, no better soporific and sedative than skepticism, the mild, pleasing, lulling poppy of skepticism; and Hamlet himself is now prescribed by the doctors of the day as an antidote to the "spirit," and its underground noises. "Are not our ears already full of bad sounds?" say the skeptics, as lovers of repose, and almost as a kind of safety police; "this subterranean Nay is terrible! Be still, ye pessimistic moles!" The skeptic, in effect, that delicate creature, is far too easily frightened; his conscience is schooled so as to start at every Nay, and even at that sharp, decided Yea, and feels something like a bite thereby. Yea! and Nay!--they seem to him opposed to morality; he loves, on the contrary, to make a festival to his virtue by a noble aloofness, while perhaps he says with Montaigne: "What do I know?" Or with Socrates: "I know that I know nothing." Or: "Here I do not trust myself, no door is open to me." Or: "Even if the door were open, why should I enter immediately?" Or: "What is the use of any hasty hypotheses? It might quite well be in good taste to make no hypotheses at all. Are you absolutely obliged to straighten at once what is crooked? to stuff every hole with some kind of oakum? Is there not time enough for that? Has not the time leisure? Oh, ye demons, can ye not at all WAIT? The uncertain also has its charms, the Sphinx, too, is a Circe, and Circe, too, was a philosopher."--Thus does a skeptic console himself; and in truth he needs some consolation. For skepticism is the most spiritual expression of a certain many-sided physiological temperament, which in ordinary language is called nervous debility and sickliness; it arises whenever races or classes which have been long separated, decisively and suddenly blend with one another. In the new generation, which has inherited as it were different standards and valuations in its blood, everything is disquiet, derangement, doubt, and tentativeness; the best powers operate restrictively, the very virtues prevent each other growing and becoming strong, equilibrium, ballast, and perpendicular stability are lacking in body and soul. That, however, which is most diseased and degenerated in such nondescripts is the WILL; they are no longer familiar with independence of decision, or the courageous feeling of pleasure in willing--they are doubtful of the "freedom of the will" even in their dreams Our present-day Europe, the scene of a senseless, precipitate attempt at a radical blending of classes, and CONSEQUENTLY of races, is therefore skeptical in all its heights and depths, sometimes exhibiting the mobile skepticism which springs impatiently and wantonly from branch to branch, sometimes with gloomy aspect, like a cloud over-charged with interrogative signs--and often sick unto death of its will! Paralysis of will, where do we not find this cripple sitting nowadays! And yet how bedecked oftentimes' How seductively ornamented! There are the finest gala dresses and disguises for this disease, and that, for instance, most of what places itself nowadays in the show-cases as "objectiveness," "the scientific spirit," "L'ART POUR L'ART," and "pure voluntary knowledge," is only decked-out skepticism and paralysis of will--I am ready to answer for this diagnosis of the European disease--The disease of the will is diffused unequally over Europe, it is worst and most varied where civilization has longest prevailed, it decreases according as "the barbarian" still--or again--asserts his claims under the loose drapery of Western culture It is therefore in the France of today, as can be readily disclosed and comprehended, that the will is most infirm, and France, which has always had a masterly aptitude for converting even the portentous crises of its spirit into something charming and seductive, now manifests emphatically its intellectual ascendancy over Europe, by being the school and exhibition of all the charms of skepticism The power to will and to persist, moreover, in a resolution, is already somewhat stronger in Germany, and again in the North of Germany it is stronger than in Central Germany, it is considerably stronger in England, Spain, and Corsica, associated with phlegm in the former and with hard skulls in the latter--not to mention Italy, which is too young yet to know what it wants, and must first show whether it can exercise will, but it is strongest and most surprising of all in that immense middle empire where Europe as it were flows back to Asia--namely, in Russia There the power to will has been long stored up and accumulated, there the will--uncertain whether to be negative or affirmative--waits threateningly to be discharged (to borrow their pet phrase from our physicists) Perhaps not only Indian wars and complications in Asia would be necessary to free Europe from its greatest danger, but also internal subversion, the shattering of the empire into small states, and above all the introduction of parliamentary imbecility, together with the obligation of every one to read his newspaper at breakfast I do not say this as one who desires it, in my heart I should rather prefer the contrary--I mean such an increase in the threatening attitude of Russia, that Europe would have to make up its mind to become equally threatening--namely, TO ACQUIRE ONE WILL, by means of a new caste to rule over the Continent, a persistent, dreadful will of its own, that can set its aims thousands of years ahead; so that the long spun-out comedy of its petty-statism, and its dynastic as well as its democratic many-willed-ness, might finally be brought to a close. The time for petty politics is past; the next century will bring the struggle for the dominion of the world--the COMPULSION to great politics.

As to how far the new warlike age on which we Europeans have evidently entered may perhaps favour the growth of another and stronger kind of skepticism, I should like to express myself preliminarily merely by a parable, which the lovers of German history will already understand. That unscrupulous enthusiast for big, handsome grenadiers (who, as King of Prussia, brought into being a military and skeptical genius--and therewith, in reality, the new and now triumphantly emerged type of German), the problematic, crazy father of Frederick the Great, had on one point the very knack and lucky grasp of the genius: he knew what was then lacking in Germany, the want of which was a hundred times more alarming and serious than any lack of culture and social form--his ill-will to the young Frederick resulted from the anxiety of a profound instinct. MEN WERE LACKING; and he suspected, to his bitterest regret, that his own son was not man enough. There, however, he deceived himself; but who would not have deceived himself in his place? He saw his son lapsed to atheism, to the ESPRIT, to the pleasant frivolity of clever Frenchmen--he saw in the background the great bloodsucker, the spider skepticism; he suspected the incurable wretchedness of a heart no longer hard enough either for evil or good, and of a broken will that no longer commands, is no longer ABLE to command. Meanwhile, however, there grew up in his son that new kind of harder and more dangerous skepticism--who knows TO WHAT EXTENT it was encouraged just by his father's hatred and the icy melancholy of a will condemned to solitude?--the skepticism of daring manliness, which is closely related to the genius for war and conquest, and made its first entrance into Germany in the person of the great Frederick. This skepticism despises and nevertheless grasps; it undermines and takes possession; it does not believe, but it does not thereby lose itself; it gives the spirit a dangerous liberty, but it keeps strict guard over the heart. It is the GERMAN form of skepticism, which, as a continued Fredericianism, risen to the highest spirituality, has kept Europe for a considerable time under the dominion of the German spirit and its critical and historical distrust Owing to the insuperably strong and tough masculine character of the great German philologists and historical critics (who, rightly estimated, were also all of them artists of destruction and dissolution), a NEW conception of the German spirit gradually established itself--in spite of all Romanticism in music and philosophy--in which the leaning towards masculine skepticism was decidedly prominent whether, for instance, as fearlessness of gaze, as courage and sternness of the dissecting hand, or as resolute will to dangerous voyages of discovery, to spiritualized North Pole expeditions under barren and dangerous skies. There may be good grounds for it when warm-blooded and superficial humanitarians cross themselves before this spirit, CET ESPRIT FATALISTE, IRONIQUE, MEPHISTOPHELIQUE, as Michelet calls it, not without a shudder. But if one would realize how characteristic is this fear of the "man" in the German spirit which awakened Europe out of its "dogmatic slumber," let us call to mind the former conception which had to be overcome by this new one--and that it is not so very long ago that a masculinized woman could dare, with unbridled presumption, to recommend the Germans to the interest of Europe as gentle, goodhearted, weak-willed, and poetical fools. Finally, let us only understand profoundly enough Napoleon's astonishment when he saw Goethe it reveals what had been regarded for centuries as the "German spirit" "VOILA UN HOMME!"--that was as much as to say "But this is a MAN! And I only expected to see a German!"

Supposing, then, that in the picture of the philosophers of the future, some trait suggests the question whether they must not perhaps be skeptics in the last-mentioned sense, something in them would only be designated thereby--and not they themselves. With equal right they might call themselves critics, and assuredly they will be men of experiments. By the name with which I ventured to baptize them, I have already expressly emphasized their attempting and their love of attempting is this because, as critics in body and soul, they will love to make use of experiments in a new, and perhaps wider and more dangerous sense? In their passion for knowledge, will they have to go further in daring and painful attempts than the sensitive and pampered taste of a democratic century can approve of?--There is no doubt these coming ones will be least able to dispense with the serious and not unscrupulous qualities which distinguish the critic from the skeptic I mean the certainty as to standards of worth, the conscious employment of a unity of method, the wary courage, the standing-alone, and the capacity for self-responsibility, indeed, they will avow among themselves a DELIGHT in denial and dissection, and a certain considerate cruelty, which knows how to handle the knife surely and deftly, even when the heart bleeds They will be STERNER (and perhaps not always towards themselves only) than humane people may desire, they will not deal with the "truth" in order that it may "please" them, or "elevate" and "inspire" them--they will rather have little faith in "TRUTH" bringing with it such revels for the feelings. They will smile, those rigourous spirits, when any one says in their presence "That thought elevates me, why should it not be true?" or "That work enchants me, why should it not be beautiful?" or "That artist enlarges me, why should he not be great?" Perhaps they will not only have a smile, but a genuine disgust for all that is thus rapturous, idealistic, feminine, and hermaphroditic, and if any one could look into their inmost hearts, he would not easily find therein the intention to reconcile "Christian sentiments" with "antique taste," or even with "modern parliamentarism" (the kind of reconciliation necessarily found even among philosophers in our very uncertain and consequently very conciliatory century). Critical discipline, and every habit that conduces to purity and rigour in intellectual matters, will not only be demanded from themselves by these philosophers of the future, they may even make a display thereof as their special adornment-- nevertheless they will not want to be called critics on that account. It will seem to them no small indignity to philosophy to have it decreed, as is so welcome nowadays, that "philosophy itself is criticism and critical science--and nothing else whatever!" Though this estimate of philosophy may enjoy the approval of all the Positivists of France and Germany (and possibly it even flattered the heart and taste of KANT: let us call to mind the titles of his principal works), our new philosophers will say, notwithstanding, that critics are instruments of the philosopher, and just on that account, as instruments, they are far from being philosophers themselves! Even the great Chinaman of Konigsberg was only a great critic.

I insist upon it that people finally cease confounding philosophical workers, and in general scientific men, with philosophers--that precisely here one should strictly give "each his own," and not give those far too much, these far too little. It may be necessary for the education of the real philosopher that he himself should have once stood upon all those steps upon which his servants, the scientific workers of philosophy, remain standing, and MUST remain standing he himself must perhaps have been critic, and dogmatist, and historian, and besides, poet, and collector, and traveler, and riddle-reader, and moralist, and seer, and "free spirit," and almost everything, in order to traverse the whole range of human values and estimations, and that he may BE ABLE with a variety of eyes and consciences to look from a height to any distance, from a depth up to any height, from a nook into any expanse. But all these are only preliminary conditions for his task; this task itself demands something else--it requires him TO CREATE VALUES. The philosophical workers, after the excellent pattern of Kant and Hegel, have to fix and formalize some great existing body of valuations--that is to say, former DETERMINATIONS OF VALUE, creations of value, which have become prevalent, and are for a time called "truths"--whether in the domain of the LOGICAL, the POLITICAL (moral), or the ARTISTIC. It is for these investigators to make whatever has happened and been esteemed hitherto, conspicuous, conceivable, intelligible, and manageable, to shorten everything long, even "time" itself, and to SUBJUGATE the entire past: an immense and wonderful task, in the carrying out of which all refined pride, all tenacious will, can surely find satisfaction. THE REAL PHILOSOPHERS, HOWEVER, ARE COMMANDERS AND LAW-GIVERS; they say: "Thus SHALL it be!" They determine first the Whither and the Why of mankind, and thereby set aside the previous labour of all philosophical workers, and all subjugators of the past--they grasp at the future with a creative hand, and whatever is and was, becomes for them thereby a means, an instrument, and a hammer. Their "knowing" is CREATING, their creating is a law-giving, their will to truth is-- WILL TO POWER. --Are there at present such philosophers? Have there ever been such philosophers? MUST there not be such philosophers some day? . . .

412

It is always more obvious to me that the philosopher, as a man INDISPENSABLE for the morrow and the day after the morrow, has ever found himself, and HAS BEEN OBLIGED to find himself, in contradiction to the day in which he lives; his enemy has always been the ideal of his day. Hitherto all those extraordinary furtherers of humanity whom one calls philosophers--who rarely regarded themselves as lovers of wisdom, but rather as disagreeable fools and dangerous interrogators--have found their mission, their hard, involuntary, imperative mission (in the end, however, the greatness of their mission), in being the bad conscience of their age. In putting the vivisector's knife to the breast of the very VIRTUES OF THEIR AGE, they have betrayed their own secret; it has been for the sake of a NEW greatness of man, a new untrodden path to his aggrandizement. They have always disclosed how much hypocrisy, indolence, self-indulgence, and self-neglect, how much falsehood was concealed under the most venerated types of contemporary morality, how much virtue was OUTLIVED, they have always said "We must remove hence to where YOU are least at home" In the face of a world of "modern ideas," which would like to confine every one in a corner, in a "specialty," a philosopher, if there could be philosophers nowadays, would be compelled to place the greatness of man, the conception of "greatness," precisely in his comprehensiveness and multifariousness, in his all-roundness, he would even determine worth and rank according to the amount and variety of that which a man could bear and take upon himself, according to the EXTENT to which a man could stretch his responsibility Nowadays the taste and virtue of the age weaken and attenuate the will, nothing is so adapted to the spirit of the age as weakness of will consequently, in the ideal of the philosopher, strength of will, sternness, and capacity for prolonged resolution, must specially be included in the conception of "greatness", with as good a right as the opposite doctrine, with its ideal of a silly, renouncing, humble, selfless humanity, was suited to an opposite age--such as the sixteenth century, which suffered from its accumulated energy of will, and from the wildest torrents and floods of selfishness In the time of Socrates, among men only of worn-out instincts, old conservative Athenians who let themselves go--"for the sake of happiness," as they said, for the sake of pleasure, as their conduct indicated--and who had continually on their lips the old pompous words to which they had long forfeited the right by the life they led, IRONY was perhaps necessary for greatness of soul, the wicked Socratic assurance of the old physician and plebeian, who cut ruthlessly into his own flesh, as into the flesh and heart of the "noble," with a look that said plainly enough "Do not dissemble before me! here--we are equal!" At present, on the contrary, when throughout Europe the herding- animal alone attains to honours, and dispenses honours, when "equality of right" can too readily be transformed into equality in wrong--I mean to say into general war against everything rare, strange, and privileged, against the higher man, the higher soul, the higher duty, the higher responsibility, the creative plenipotence and lordliness--at present it belongs to the conception of "greatness" to be noble, to wish to be apart, to be capable of being different, to stand alone, to have to live by personal initiative, and the philosopher will betray something of his own ideal when he asserts "He shall be the greatest who can be the most solitary, the most concealed, the most divergent, the man beyond good and evil, the master of his virtues, and of super-abundance of will; precisely this shall be called GREATNESS: as diversified as can be entire, as ample as can be full." And to ask once more the question: Is greatness POSSIBLE-- nowadays?

It is difficult to learn what a philosopher is, because it cannot be taught: one must "know" it by experience--or one should have the pride NOT to know it. The fact that at present people all talk of things of which they CANNOT have any experience, is true more especially and unfortunately as concerns the philosopher and philosophical matters:--the very few know them, are permitted to know them, and all popular ideas about them are false. Thus, for instance, the truly philosophical combination of a bold, exuberant spirituality which runs at presto pace, and a dialectic rigour and necessity which makes no false step, is unknown to most thinkers and scholars from their own experience, and therefore, should any one speak of it in their presence, it is incredible to them. They conceive of every necessity as troublesome, as a painful compulsory obedience and state of constraint; thinking itself is regarded by them as something slow and hesitating, almost as a trouble, and often enough as "worthy of the SWEAT of the noble"--but not at all as something easy and divine, closely related to dancing and exuberance! "To think" and to take a matter "seriously," "arduously"--that is one and the same thing to them; such only has been their "experience."-- Artists have here perhaps a finer intuition; they who know only too well that precisely when they no longer do anything "arbitrarily," and everything of necessity, their feeling of freedom, of subtlety, of power, of creatively fixing, disposing, and shaping, reaches its climax--in short, that necessity and "freedom of will" are then the same thing with them. There is, in fine, a gradation of rank in psychical states, to which the gradation of rank in the problems corresponds; and the highest problems repel ruthlessly every one who ventures too near them, without being predestined for their solution by the loftiness and power of his spirituality. Of what use is it for nimble, everyday intellects, or clumsy, honest mechanics and empiricists to press, in their plebeian ambition, close to such problems, and as it were into this "holy of holies"--as so often happens nowadays! But coarse feet must never tread upon such carpets: this is provided for in the primary law of things; the doors remain closed to those intruders, though they may dash and break their heads thereon. People have always to be born to a high station, or, more definitely, they have to be BRED for it: a person has only a right to philosophy--taking the word in its higher significance--in virtue of his descent; the ancestors, the "blood," decide here also. Many generations must have prepared the way for the coming of the philosopher; each of his virtues must have been separately acquired, nurtured, transmitted, and embodied; not only the bold, easy, delicate course and current of his thoughts, but above all the readiness for great responsibilities, the majesty of ruling glance and contemning look, the feeling of separation from the multitude with their duties and virtues, the kindly patronage and defense of whatever is misunderstood and calumniated, be it God or devil, the delight and practice of supreme justice, the art of commanding, the amplitude of will, the lingering eye which rarely admires, rarely looks up, rarely loves. . . .

Chapter 7
Our Virtues

OUR Virtues?--It is probable that we, too, have still our virtues, althoughnaturally they are not those sincere and massive virtues on account of which we hold our grandfathers in esteem and also at a little distance from us. We Europeans of the day after tomorrow, we firstlings of the twentieth century--with all our dangerous curiosity, our multifariousness and art of disguising, our mellow and seemingly sweetened cruelty in sense and spirit--we shall presumably, IF we must have virtues, have those only which have come to agreement with our most secret and heartfelt inclinations, with our most ardent requirements: well, then, let us look for them in our labyrinths!--where, as we know, so many things lose themselves, so many things get quite lost! And is there anything finer than to SEARCH for one's own virtues? Is it not almost to BELIEVE in one's own virtues? But this "believing in one's own virtues"--is it not practically the same as what was formerly called one's "good conscience," that long, respectable pigtail of an idea, which our grandfathers used to hang behind their heads, and often enough also behind their understandings? It seems, therefore, that however little we may imagine ourselves to be old-fashioned and grandfatherly respectable in other respects, in one thing we are nevertheless the worthy grandchildren of our grandfathers, we last Europeans with good consciences: we also still wear their pigtail.--Ah! if you only knew how soon, so very soon--it will be different!

As in the stellar firmament there are sometimes two suns which determine the path of one planet, and in certain cases suns of different colours shine around a single planet, now with red light, now with green, and then simultaneously illumine and flood it with motley colours: so we modern men, owing to the complicated mechanism of our "firmament," are determined by DIFFERENT moralities; our actions shine alternately in different colours, and are seldom unequivocal--and there are often cases, also, in which our actions are MOTLEY-COLOURED.

To love one's enemies? I think that has been well learnt: it takes place thousands of times at present on a large and small scale; indeed, at times the higher and sublimer thing takes place:--we learn to DESPISE when we love, and precisely when we love best; all of it, however, unconsciously, without noise, without ostentation, with the shame and secrecy of goodness, which forbids the utterance of the pompous word and the formula of virtue. Morality as attitude--is opposed to our taste nowadays. This is ALSO an advance, as it was an advance in our fathers that religion as an attitude finally became opposed to their taste, including the enmity and Voltairean bitterness against religion (and all that formerly belonged to freethinker-pantomime). It is the music in our conscience, the dance in our spirit, to which Puritan litanies, moral sermons, and goody- goodness won't chime.

Let us be careful in dealing with those who attach great importance to being credited with moral tact and subtlety in moral discernment! They never forgive us if they have once made a mistake BEFORE us (or even with REGARD to us)--they inevitably become our instinctive calumniators and detractors, even when they still remain our "friends."--Blessed are the forgetful: for they "get the better" even of their blunders.

The psychologists of France--and where else are there still psychologists nowadays?--have never yet exhausted their bitter and manifold enjoyment of the betise bourgeoise, just as though . . . in short, they betray something thereby. Flaubert, for instance, the honest citizen of Rouen, neither saw, heard, nor tasted anything else in the end; it was his mode of self-torment and refined cruelty. As this is growing wearisome, I would now recommend for a change something else for a pleasure--namely, the unconscious astuteness with which good, fat, honest mediocrity always behaves towards loftier spirits and the tasks they have to perform, the subtle, barbed, Jesuitical astuteness, which is a thousand times subtler than the taste and understanding of the middle-class in its best moments--subtler even than the understanding of its victims:--a repeated proof that "instinct" is the most intelligent of all kinds of intelligence which have hitherto been discovered. In short, you psychologists, study the philosophy of the "rule" in its struggle with the "exception": there you have a spectacle fit for Gods and godlike malignity! Or, in plainer words, practise vivisection on "good people," on the "homo bonae voluntatis," ON YOURSELVES!

The practice of judging and condemning morally, is the favourite revenge of the intellectually shallow on those who are less so, it is also a kind of indemnity for their being badly endowed by nature, and finally, it is an opportunity for acquiring spirit and BECOMING subtle--malice spiritualises. They are glad in their inmost heart that there is a standard according to which those who are over-endowed with intellectual goods and privileges, are equal to them, they contend for the "equality of all before God," and almost NEED the belief in God for this purpose. It is among them that the most powerful antagonists of atheism are found. If any one were to say to them "A lofty spirituality is beyond all comparison with the honesty and respectability of a merely moral man"--it would make them furious, I shall take care not to say so. I would rather flatter them with my theory that lofty spirituality itself exists only as the ultimate product of moral qualities, that it is a synthesis of all qualities attributed to the "merely moral" man, after they have been acquired singly through long training and practice, perhaps during a whole series of generations, that lofty spirituality is precisely the spiritualising of justice, and the beneficent severity which knows that it is authorized to maintain GRADATIONS OF RANK in the world, even among things--and not only among men.

Now that the praise of the "disinterested person" is so popular one must--probably not without some danger--get an idea of WHAT people actually take an interest in, and what are the things generally which fundamentally and profoundly concern ordinary men-- including the cultured, even the learned, and perhaps philosophers also, if appearances do not deceive. The fact thereby becomes obvious that the greater part of what interests and charms higher natures, and more refined and fastidious tastes, seems absolutely "uninteresting" to the average man--if, notwithstanding, he perceive devotion to these interests, he calls it desinteresse, and wonders how it is possible to act "disinterestedly." There have been philosophers who could give this popular astonishment a seductive and mystical, other-worldly expression (perhaps because they did not know the higher nature by experience?), instead of stating the naked and candidly reasonable truth that "disinterested" action is very interesting and "interested" action, provided that. . . "And love?"--What! Even an action for love's sake shall be "unegoistic"? But you fools--! "And the praise of the self-sacrificer?"--But whoever has really offered sacrifice knows that he wanted and obtained something for it--perhaps something from himself for something from himself; that he relinquished here in order to have more there, perhaps in general to be more, or even feel himself "more." But this is a realm of questions and answers in which a more fastidious spirit does not like to stay: for here truth has to stifle her yawns so much when she is obliged to answer. And after all, truth is a woman; one must not use force with her.

"It sometimes happens," said a moralistic pedant and trifle- retailer, "that I honour and respect an unselfish man: not, however, because he is unselfish, but because I think he has a right to be useful to another man at his own expense. In short, the question is always who HE is, and who THE OTHER is. For instance, in a person created and destined for command, self- denial and modest retirement, instead of being virtues, would be the waste of virtues: so it seems to me. Every system of unegoistic morality which takes itself unconditionally and appeals to every one, not only sins against good taste, but is also an incentive to sins of omission, an ADDITIONAL seduction under the mask of philanthropy--and precisely a seduction and injury to the higher, rarer, and more privileged types of men. Moral systems must be compelled first of all to bow before the GRADATIONS OF RANK; their presumption must be driven home to their conscience--until they thoroughly understand at last that it is IMMORAL to say that 'what is right for one is proper for another.'"--So said my moralistic pedant and bonhomme. Did he perhaps deserve to be laughed at when he thus exhorted systems of morals to practise morality? But one should not be too much in the right if one wishes to have the laughers on ONE'S OWN side; a grain of wrong pertains even to good taste.

Wherever sympathy (fellow-suffering) is preached nowadays-- and, if I gather rightly, no other religion is any longer preached--let the psychologist have his ears open through all the vanity, through all the noise which is natural to these preachers (as to all preachers), he will hear a hoarse, groaning, genuine note of SELF-CONTEMPT. It belongs to the overshadowing and uglifying of Europe, which has been on the increase for a century (the first symptoms of which are already specified documentarily in a thoughtful letter of Galiani to Madame d'Epinay)--IF IT IS NOT REALLY THE CAUSE THEREOF! The man of "modern ideas," the conceited ape, is excessively dissatisfied with himself-this is perfectly certain. He suffers, and his vanity wants him only "to suffer with his fellows."

The hybrid European--a tolerably ugly plebeian, taken all in all--absolutely requires a costume: he needs history as a storeroom of costumes. To be sure, he notices that none of the costumes fit him properly--he changes and changes. Let us look at the nineteenth century with respect to these hasty preferences and changes in its masquerades of style, and also with respect to its moments of desperation on account of "nothing suiting" us. It is in vain to get ourselves up as romantic, or classical, or Christian, or Florentine, or barocco, or "national," in moribus et artibus: it does not "clothe us"! But the "spirit," especially the "historical spirit," profits even by this desperation: once and again a new sample of the past or of the foreign is tested, put on, taken off, packed up, and above all studied--we are the first studious age in puncto of "costumes," I mean as concerns morals, articles of belief, artistic tastes, and religions; we are prepared as no other age has ever been for a carnival in the grand style, for the most spiritual festival--laughter and arrogance, for the transcendental height of supreme folly and Aristophanic ridicule of the world. Perhaps we are still discovering the domain of our invention just here, the domain where even we can still be original, probably as parodists of the world's history and as God's Merry-Andrews,--perhaps, though nothing else of the present have a future, our laughter itself may have a future!

The historical sense (or the capacity for divining quickly the order of rank of the valuations according to which a people, a community, or an individual has lived, the "divining instinct" for the relationships of these valuations, for the relation of the authority of the valuations to the authority of the operating forces),--this historical sense, which we Europeans claim as our specialty, has come to us in the train of the enchanting and mad semi-barbarity into which Europe has been plunged by the democratic mingling of classes and races--it is only the nineteenth century that has recognized this faculty as its sixth sense. Owing to this mingling, the past of every form and mode of life, and of cultures which were formerly closely contiguous and superimposed on one another, flows forth into us "modern souls"; our instincts now run back in all directions, we ourselves are a kind of chaos: in the end, as we have said, the spirit perceives its advantage therein. By means of our semi-barbarity in body and in desire, we have secret access everywhere, such as a noble age never had; we have access above all to the labyrinth of imperfect civilizations, and to every form of semi-barbarity that has at any time existed on earth; and in so far as the most considerable part of human civilization hitherto has just been semi-barbarity, the "historical sense" implies almost the sense and instinct for everything, the taste and tongue for everything: whereby it immediately proves itself to be an IGNOBLE sense. For instance, we enjoy Homer once more: it is perhaps our happiest acquisition that we know how to appreciate Homer, whom men of distinguished culture (as the French of the seventeenth century, like Saint- Evremond, who reproached him for his ESPRIT VASTE, and even Voltaire, the last echo of the century) cannot and could not so easily appropriate-- whom they scarcely permitted themselves to enjoy. The very decided Yea and Nay of their palate, their promptly ready disgust, their hesitating reluctance with regard to everything strange, their horror of the bad taste even of lively curiosity, and in general the averseness of every distinguished and self-sufficing culture to avow a new desire, a dissatisfaction with its own condition, or an admiration of what is strange: all this determines and disposes them unfavourably even towards the best things of the world which are not their property or could not become their prey--and no faculty is more unintelligible to such men than just this historical sense, with its truckling, plebeian curiosity. The case is not different with Shakespeare, that marvelous Spanish-Moorish-Saxon synthesis of taste, over whom an ancient Athenian of the circle of Eschylus would have half-killed himself with laughter or irritation: but we--accept precisely this wild motleyness, this medley of the most delicate, the most coarse, and the most artificial, with a secret confidence and cordiality; we enjoy it as a refinement of art reserved expressly for us, and allow ourselves to be as little disturbed by the repulsive fumes and the proximity of the English populace in which Shakespeare's art and taste lives, as perhaps on the Chiaja of Naples, where, with all our senses awake, we go our way, enchanted and voluntarily, in spite of the drain-odour of the lower quarters of the town. That as men of the "historical sense" we have our virtues, is not to be disputed:-- we are unpretentious, unselfish, modest, brave, habituated to self-control and self-renunciation, very grateful, very patient, very complaisant--but with all this we are perhaps not very "tasteful." Let us finally confess it, that what is most difficult for us men of the "historical sense" to grasp, feel, taste, and love, what finds us fundamentally prejudiced and almost hostile, is precisely the perfection and ultimate maturity in every culture and art, the essentially noble in works and men, their moment of smooth sea and halcyon self-sufficiency, the goldenness and coldness which all things show that have perfected themselves. Perhaps our great virtue of the historical sense is in necessary contrast to GOOD taste, at least to the very bad taste; and we can only evoke in ourselves imperfectly, hesitatingly, and with compulsion the small, short, and happy godsends and glorifications of human life as they shine here and there: those moments and marvelous experiences when a great power has voluntarily come to a halt before the boundless and infinite,--when a super-abundance of refined delight has been enjoyed by a sudden checking and petrifying, by standing firmly and planting oneself fixedly on still trembling ground. PROPORTIONATENESS is strange to us, let us confess it to ourselves; our itching is really the itching for the infinite, the immeasurable. Like the rider on his forward panting horse, we let the reins fall before the infinite, we modern men, we semi- barbarians--and are only in OUR highest bliss when we-- ARE IN MOST DANGER.

Whether it be hedonism, pessimism, utilitarianism, or eudaemonism, all those modes of thinking which measure the worth of things according to PLEASURE and PAIN, that is, according to accompanying circumstances and secondary considerations, are plausible modes of thought and naivetes, which every one conscious of CREATIVE powers and an artist's conscience will look down upon with scorn, though not without sympathy. Sympathy for you!--to be sure, that is not sympathy as you understand it: it is not sympathy for social "distress," for "society" with its sick and misfortuned, for the hereditarily vicious and defective who lie on the ground around us; still less is it sympathy for the grumbling, vexed, revolutionary slave-classes who strive after power--they call it "freedom." OUR sympathy is a loftier and further-sighted sympathy:--we see how MAN dwarfs himself, how YOU dwarf him! and there are moments when we view YOUR sympathy with an indescribable anguish, when we resist it,-- when we regard your seriousness as more dangerous than any kind of levity. You want, if possible--and there is not a more foolish "if possible" --TO DO AWAY WITH SUFFERING; and we?--it really seems that WE would rather have it increased and made worse than it has ever been! Well-being, as you understand it--is certainly not a goal; it seems to us an END; a condition which at once renders man ludicrous and contemptible--and makes his destruction DESIRABLE! The discipline of suffering, of GREAT suffering--know ye not that it is only THIS discipline that has produced all the elevations of humanity hitherto? The tension of soul in misfortune which communicates to it its energy, its shuddering in view of rack and ruin, its inventiveness and bravery in undergoing, enduring, interpreting, and exploiting misfortune, and whatever depth, mystery, disguise, spirit, artifice, or greatness has been bestowed upon the soul--has it not been bestowed through suffering, through the discipline of great suffering? In man CREATURE and CREATOR are united: in man there is not only matter, shred, excess, clay, mire, folly, chaos; but there is also the creator, the sculptor, the hardness of the hammer, the divinity of the spectator, and the seventh day--do ye understand this contrast? And that YOUR sympathy for the "creature in man" applies to that which has to be fashioned, bruised, forged, stretched, roasted, annealed, refined--to that which must necessarily SUFFER, and IS MEANT to suffer? And our sympathy--do ye not understand what our REVERSE sympathy applies to, when it resists your sympathy as the worst of all pampering and enervation?--So it is sympathy AGAINST sympathy!--But to repeat it once more, there are higher problems than the problems of pleasure and pain and sympathy; and all systems of philosophy which deal only with these are naivetes.

WE IMMORALISTS.-This world with which WE are concerned, in which we have to fear and love, this almost invisible, inaudible world of delicate command and delicate obedience, a world of "almost" in every respect, captious, insidious, sharp, and tender--yes, it is well protected from clumsy spectators and familiar curiosity! We are woven into a strong net and garment of duties, and CANNOT disengage ourselves--precisely here, we are "men of duty," even we! Occasionally, it is true, we dance in our "chains" and betwixt our "swords"; it is none the less true that more often we gnash our teeth under the circumstances, and are impatient at the secret hardship of our lot. But do what we will, fools and appearances say of us: "These are men WITHOUT duty,"-- we have always fools and appearances against us!

Honesty, granting that it is the virtue of which we cannot rid ourselves, we free spirits--well, we will labour at it with all our perversity and love, and not tire of "perfecting" ourselves in OUR virtue, which alone remains: may its glance some day overspread like a gilded, blue, mocking twilight this aging civilization with its dull gloomy seriousness! And if, nevertheless, our honesty should one day grow weary, and sigh, and stretch its limbs, and find us too hard, and would fain have it pleasanter, easier, and gentler, like an agreeable vice, let us remain HARD, we latest Stoics, and let us send to its help whatever devilry we have in us:--our disgust at the clumsy and undefined, our "NITIMUR IN VETITUM," our love of adventure, our sharpened and fastidious curiosity, our most subtle, disguised, intellectual Will to Power and universal conquest, which rambles and roves avidiously around all the realms of the future--let us go with all our "devils" to the help of our "God"! It is probable that people will misunderstand and mistake us on that account: what does it matter! They will say: "Their 'honesty'--that is their devilry, and nothing else!" What does it matter! And even if they were right--have not all Gods hitherto been such sanctified, re-baptized devils? And after all, what do we know of ourselves? And what the spirit that leads us wants TO BE CALLED? (It is a question of names.) And how many spirits we harbour? Our honesty, we free spirits--let us be careful lest it become our vanity, our ornament and ostentation, our limitation, our stupidity! Every virtue inclines to stupidity, every stupidity to virtue; "stupid to the point of sanctity," they say in Russia,-- let us be careful lest out of pure honesty we eventually become saints and bores! Is not life a hundred times too short for us-- to bore ourselves? One would have to believe in eternal life in order to . . .

I hope to be forgiven for discovering that all moral philosophy hitherto has been tedious and has belonged to the soporific appliances--and that "virtue," in my opinion, has been MORE injured by the TEDIOUSNESS of its advocates than by anything else; at the same time, however, I would not wish to overlook their general usefulness. It is desirable that as few people as possible should reflect upon morals, and consequently it is very desirable that morals should not some day become interesting! But let us not be afraid! Things still remain today as they have always been: I see no one in Europe who has (or DISCLOSES) an idea of the fact that philosophizing concerning morals might be conducted in a dangerous, captious, and ensnaring manner--that CALAMITY might be involved therein. Observe, for example, the indefatigable, inevitable English utilitarians: how ponderously and respectably they stalk on, stalk along (a Homeric metaphor expresses it better) in the footsteps of Bentham, just as he had already stalked in the footsteps of the respectable Helvetius! (no, he was not a dangerous man, Helvetius, CE SENATEUR POCOCURANTE, to use an expression of Galiani). No new thought, nothing of the nature of a finer turning or better expression of an old thought, not even a proper history of what has been previously thought on the subject: an IMPOSSIBLE literature, taking it all in all, unless one knows how to leaven it with some mischief. In effect, the old English vice called CANT, which is MORAL TARTUFFISM, has insinuated itself also into these moralists (whom one must certainly read with an eye to their motives if one MUST read them), concealed this time under the new form of the scientific spirit; moreover, there is not absent from them a secret struggle with the pangs of conscience, from which a race of former Puritans must naturally suffer, in all their scientific tinkering with morals. (Is not a moralist the opposite of a Puritan? That is to say, as a thinker who regards morality as questionable, as worthy of interrogation, in short, as a problem? Is moralizing not-immoral?) In the end, they all want English morality to be recognized as authoritative, inasmuch as mankind, or the "general utility," or "the happiness of the greatest number,"--no! the happiness of ENGLAND, will be best served thereby. They would like, by all means, to convince themselves that the striving after English happiness, I mean after COMFORT and FASHION (and in the highest instance, a seat in Parliament), is at the same time the true path of virtue; in fact, that in so far as there has been virtue in the world hitherto, it has just consisted in such striving. Not one of those ponderous, conscience-stricken herding-animals (who undertake to advocate the cause of egoism as conducive to the general welfare) wants to have any knowledge or inkling of the facts that the "general welfare" is no ideal, no goal, no notion that can be at all grasped, but is only a nostrum,--that what is fair to one MAY NOT at all be fair to another, that the requirement of one morality for all is really a detriment to higher men, in short, that there is a DISTINCTION OF RANK between man and man, and consequently between morality and morality. They are an unassuming and fundamentally mediocre species of men, these utilitarian Englishmen, and, as already remarked, in so far as they are tedious, one cannot think highly enough of their utility. One ought even to ENCOURAGE them, as has been partially attempted in the following rhymes:

Hail, ye worthies, barrow-wheeling,
"Longer--better," aye revealing,
Stiffer aye in head and knee;
Unenraptured, never jesting,
Mediocre everlasting,
SANS GENIE ET SANS ESPRIT!

In these later ages, which may be proud of their humanity, there still remains so much fear, so much SUPERSTITION of the fear, of the "cruel wild beast," the mastering of which constitutes the very pride of these humaner ages--that even obvious truths, as if by the agreement of centuries, have long remained unuttered, because they have the appearance of helping the finally slain wild beast back to life again. I perhaps risk something when I allow such a truth to escape; let others capture it again and give it so much "milk of pious sentiment" [FOOTNOTE: An expression from Schiller's William Tell, Act IV, Scene 3.] to drink, that it will lie down quiet and forgotten, in its old corner.--One ought to learn anew about cruelty, and open one's eyes; one ought at last to learn impatience, in order that such immodest gross errors--as, for instance, have been fostered by ancient and modern philosophers with regard to tragedy--may no longer wander about virtuously and boldly. Almost everything that we call "higher culture" is based upon the spiritualising and intensifying of CRUELTY--this is my thesis; the "wild beast" has not been slain at all, it lives, it flourishes, it has only been-- transfigured. That which constitutes the painful delight of tragedy is cruelty; that which operates agreeably in so-called tragic sympathy, and at the basis even of everything sublime, up to the highest and most delicate thrills of metaphysics, obtains its sweetness solely from the intermingled ingredient of cruelty. What the Roman enjoys in the arena, the Christian in the ecstasies of the cross, the Spaniard at the sight of the faggot and stake, or of the bull-fight, the present-day Japanese who presses his way to the tragedy, the workman of the Parisian suburbs who has a homesickness for bloody revolutions, the Wagnerienne who, with unhinged will, "undergoes" the performance of "Tristan and Isolde"--what all these enjoy, and strive with mysterious ardour to drink in, is the philtre of the great Circe "cruelty." Here, to be sure, we must put aside entirely the blundering psychology of former times, which could only teach with regard to cruelty that it originated at the sight of the suffering of OTHERS: there is an abundant, super-abundant enjoyment even in one's own suffering, in causing one's own suffering--and wherever man has allowed himself to be persuaded to self-denial in the RELIGIOUS sense, or to self-mutilation, as among the Phoenicians and ascetics, or in general, to desensualisation, decarnalisation, and contrition, to Puritanical repentance-spasms, to vivisection of conscience and to Pascal- like SACRIFIZIA DELL' INTELLETO, he is secretly allured and impelled forwards by his cruelty, by the dangerous thrill of cruelty TOWARDS HIMSELF.-- Finally, let us consider that even the seeker of knowledge operates as an artist and glorifier of cruelty, in that he compels his spirit to perceive AGAINST its own inclination, and often enough against the wishes of his heart:--he forces it to say Nay, where he would like to affirm, love, and adore; indeed, every instance of taking a thing profoundly and fundamentally, is a violation, an intentional injuring of the fundamental will of the spirit, which instinctively aims at appearance and superficiality,--even in every desire for knowledge there is a drop of cruelty.

Perhaps what I have said here about a "fundamental will of the spirit" may not be understood without further details; I may be allowed a word of explanation.--That imperious something which is popularly called "the spirit," wishes to be master internally and externally, and to feel itself master; it has the will of a multiplicity for a simplicity, a binding, taming, imperious, and essentially ruling will. Its requirements and capacities here, are the same as those assigned by physiologists to everything that lives, grows, and multiplies. The power of the spirit to appropriate foreign elements reveals itself in a strong tendency to assimilate the new to the old, to simplify the manifold, to overlook or repudiate the absolutely contradictory; just as it arbitrarily re-underlines, makes prominent, and falsifies for itself certain traits and lines in the foreign elements, in every portion of the "outside world." Its object thereby is the incorporation of new "experiences," the assortment of new things in the old arrangements--in short, growth; or more properly, the FEELING of growth, the feeling of increased power--is its object. This same will has at its service an apparently opposed impulse of the spirit, a suddenly adopted preference of ignorance, of arbitrary shutting out, a closing of windows, an inner denial of this or that, a prohibition to approach, a sort of defensive attitude against much that is knowable, a contentment with obscurity, with the shutting-in horizon, an acceptance and approval of ignorance: as that which is all necessary according to the degree of its appropriating power, its "digestive power," to speak figuratively (and in fact "the spirit" resembles a stomach more than anything else). Here also belong an occasional propensity of the spirit to let itself be deceived (perhaps with a waggish suspicion that it is NOT so and so, but is only allowed to pass as such), a delight in uncertainty and ambiguity, an exulting enjoyment of arbitrary, out-of-the-way narrowness and mystery, of the too-near, of the foreground, of the magnified, the diminished, the misshapen, the beautified--an enjoyment of the arbitrariness of all these manifestations of power. Finally, in this connection, there is the not unscrupulous readiness of the spirit to deceive other spirits and dissemble before them-- the constant pressing and straining of a creating, shaping, changeable power: the spirit enjoys therein its craftiness and its variety of disguises, it enjoys also its feeling of security therein--it is precisely by its Protean arts that it is best protected and concealed!--COUNTER TO this propensity for appearance, for simplification, for a disguise, for a cloak, in short, for an outside--for every outside is a cloak--there operates the sublime tendency of the man of knowledge, which takes, and INSISTS on taking things profoundly, variously, and thoroughly; as a kind of cruelty of the intellectual conscience and taste, which every courageous thinker will acknowledge in himself, provided, as it ought to be, that he has sharpened and hardened his eye sufficiently long for introspection, and is accustomed to severe discipline and even severe words. He will say: "There is something cruel in the tendency of my spirit": let the virtuous and amiable try to convince him that it is not so! In fact, it would sound nicer, if, instead of our cruelty, perhaps our "extravagant honesty" were talked about, whispered about, and glorified--we free, VERY free spirits--and some day perhaps SUCH will actually be our--posthumous glory! Meanwhile-- for there is plenty of time until then--we should be least inclined to deck ourselves out in such florid and fringed moral verbiage; our whole former work has just made us sick of this taste and its sprightly exuberance. They are beautiful, glistening, jingling, festive words: honesty, love of truth, love of wisdom, sacrifice for knowledge, heroism of the truthful-- there is something in them that makes one's heart swell with pride. But we anchorites and marmots have long ago persuaded ourselves in all the secrecy of an anchorite's conscience, that this worthy parade of verbiage also belongs to the old false adornment, frippery, and gold-dust of unconscious human vanity, and that even under such flattering colour and repainting, the terrible original text HOMO NATURA must again be recognized. In effect, to translate man back again into nature; to master the many vain and visionary interpretations and subordinate meanings which have hitherto been scratched and daubed over the eternal original text, HOMO NATURA; to bring it about that man shall henceforth stand before man as he now, hardened by the discipline of science, stands before the OTHER forms of nature, with fearless Oedipus-eyes, and stopped Ulysses-ears, deaf to the enticements of old metaphysical bird-catchers, who have piped to him far too long: "Thou art more! thou art higher! thou hast a different origin!"--this may be a strange and foolish task, but that it is a TASK, who can deny! Why did we choose it, this foolish task? Or, to put the question differently: "Why knowledge at all?" Every one will ask us about this. And thus pressed, we, who have asked ourselves the question a hundred times, have not found and cannot find any better answer. . . .

Learning alters us, it does what all nourishment does that does not merely "conserve"--as the physiologist knows. But at the bottom of our souls, quite "down below," there is certainly something unteachable, a granite of spiritual fate, of predetermined decision and answer to predetermined, chosen questions. In each cardinal problem there speaks an unchangeable "I am this"; a thinker cannot learn anew about man and woman, for instance, but can only learn fully--he can only follow to the end what is "fixed" about them in himself. Occasionally we find certain solutions of problems which make strong beliefs for us; perhaps they are henceforth called "convictions." Later on--one sees in them only footsteps to self-knowledge, guide-posts to the problem which we ourselves ARE--or more correctly to the great stupidity which we embody, our spiritual fate, the UNTEACHABLE in us, quite "down below."--In view of this liberal compliment which I have just paid myself, permission will perhaps be more readily allowed me to utter some truths about "woman as she is," provided that it is known at the outset how literally they are merely--MY truths.

Woman wishes to be independent, and therefore she begins to enlighten men about "woman as she is"--THIS is one of the worst developments of the general UGLIFYING of Europe. For what must these clumsy attempts of feminine scientificality and self- exposure bring to light! Woman has so much cause for shame; in woman there is so much pedantry, superficiality, schoolmasterliness, petty presumption, unbridledness, and indiscretion concealed--study only woman's behaviour towards children!--which has really been best restrained and dominated hitherto by the FEAR of man. Alas, if ever the "eternally tedious in woman"--she has plenty of it!--is allowed to venture forth! if she begins radically and on principle to unlearn her wisdom and art-of charming, of playing, of frightening away sorrow, of alleviating and taking easily; if she forgets her delicate aptitude for agreeable desires! Female voices are already raised, which, by Saint Aristophanes! make one afraid:--with medical explicitness it is stated in a threatening manner what woman first and last REQUIRES from man. Is it not in the very worst taste that woman thus sets herself up to be scientific? Enlightenment hitherto has fortunately been men's affair, men's gift-we remained therewith "among ourselves"; and in the end, in view of all that women write about "woman," we may well have considerable doubt as to whether woman really DESIRES enlightenment about herself--and CAN desire it. If woman does not thereby seek a new ORNAMENT for herself--I believe ornamentation belongs to the eternally feminine?--why, then, she wishes to make herself feared: perhaps she thereby wishes to get the mastery. But she does not want truth--what does woman care for truth? From the very first, nothing is more foreign, more repugnant, or more hostile to woman than truth--her great art is falsehood, her chief concern is appearance and beauty. Let us confess it, we men: we honour and love this very art and this very instinct in woman: we who have the hard task, and for our recreation gladly seek the company of beings under whose hands, glances, and delicate follies, our seriousness, our gravity, and profundity appear almost like follies to us. Finally, I ask the question: Did a woman herself ever acknowledge profundity in a woman's mind, or justice in a woman's heart? And is it not true that on the whole "woman" has hitherto been most despised by woman herself, and not at all by us?--We men desire that woman should not continue to compromise herself by enlightening us; just as it was man's care and the consideration for woman, when the church decreed: mulier taceat in ecclesia. It was to the benefit of woman when Napoleon gave the too eloquent Madame de Stael to understand: mulier taceat in politicis!--and in my opinion, he is a true friend of woman who calls out to women today: mulier taceat de mulierel.

It betrays corruption of the instincts--apart from the fact that it betrays bad taste--when a woman refers to Madame Roland, or Madame de Stael, or Monsieur George Sand, as though something were proved thereby in favour of "woman as she is." Among men, these are the three comical women as they are--nothing more!--and just the best involuntary counter-arguments against feminine emancipation and autonomy.

Stupidity in the kitchen; woman as cook; the terrible thoughtlessness with which the feeding of the family and the master of the house is managed! Woman does not understand what food means, and she insists on being cook! If woman had been a thinking creature, she should certainly, as cook for thousands of years, have discovered the most important physiological facts, and should likewise have got possession of the healing art! Through bad female cooks-- through the entire lack of reason in the kitchen--the development of mankind has been longest retarded and most interfered with: even today matters are very little better. A word to High School girls.

There are turns and casts of fancy, there are sentences, little handfuls of words, in which a whole culture, a whole society suddenly crystallises itself. Among these is the incidental remark of Madame de Lambert to her son: "MON AMI, NE VOUS PERMETTEZ JAMAIS QUE DES FOLIES, QUI VOUS FERONT GRAND PLAISIR"--the motherliest and wisest remark, by the way, that was ever addressed to a son.

I have no doubt that every noble woman will oppose what Dante and Goethe believed about woman--the former when he sang, "ELLA GUARDAVA SUSO, ED IO IN LEI," and the latter when he interpreted it, "the eternally feminine draws us ALOFT"; for THIS is just what she believes of the eternally masculine.

SEVEN APOPHTHEGMS FOR WOMEN
How the longest ennui flees, When a man comes to our knees!
Age, alas! and science staid, Furnish even weak virtue aid.
Sombre garb and silence meet: Dress for every dame--discreet.
Whom I thank when in my bliss? God!--and my good tailoress!
Young, a flower-decked cavern home; Old, a dragon thence doth roam.
Noble title, leg that's fine, Man as well: Oh, were HE mine!
Speech in brief and sense in mass--Slippery for the jenny-ass!

Woman has hitherto been treated by men like birds, which, losing their way, have come down among them from an elevation: as something delicate, fragile, wild, strange, sweet, and animating- -but as something also which must be cooped up to prevent it flying away.

To be mistaken in the fundamental problem of "man and woman," to deny here the profoundest antagonism and the necessity for an eternally hostile tension, to dream here perhaps of equal rights, equal training, equal claims and obligations: that is a TYPICAL sign of shallow-mindedness; and a thinker who has proved himself shallow at this dangerous spot--shallow in instinct!--may generally be regarded as suspicious, nay more, as betrayed, as discovered; he will probably prove too "short" for all fundamental questions of life, future as well as present, and will be unable to descend into ANY of the depths. On the other hand, a man who has depth of spirit as well as of desires, and has also the depth of benevolence which is capable of severity and harshness, and easily confounded with them, can only think of woman as ORIENTALS do: he must conceive of her as a possession, as confinable property, as a being predestined for service and accomplishing her mission therein--he must take his stand in this matter upon the immense rationality of Asia, upon the superiority of the instinct of Asia, as the Greeks did formerly; those best heirs and scholars of Asia--who, as is well known, with their INCREASING culture and amplitude of power, from Homer to the time of Pericles, became gradually STRICTER towards woman, in short, more Oriental. HOW necessary, HOW logical, even HOW humanely desirable this was, let us consider for ourselves!

The weaker sex has in no previous age been treated with so much respect by men as at present--this belongs to the tendency and fundamental taste of democracy, in the same way as disrespectfulness to old age--what wonder is it that abuse should be immediately made of this respect? They want more, they learn to make claims, the tribute of respect is at last felt to be well-nigh galling; rivalry for rights, indeed actual strife itself, would be preferred: in a word, woman is losing modesty. And let us immediately add that she is also losing taste. She is unlearning to FEAR man: but the woman who "unlearns to fear" sacrifices her most womanly instincts. That woman should venture forward when the fear-inspiring quality in man--or more definitely, the MAN in man--is no longer either desired or fully developed, is reasonable enough and also intelligible enough; what is more difficult to understand is that precisely thereby-- woman deteriorates. This is what is happening nowadays: let us not deceive ourselves about it! Wherever the industrial spirit has triumphed over the military and aristocratic spirit, woman strives for the economic and legal independence of a clerk: "woman as clerkess" is inscribed on the portal of the modern society which is in course of formation. While she thus appropriates new rights, aspires to be "master," and inscribes "progress" of woman on her flags and banners, the very opposite realises itself with terrible obviousness: WOMAN RETROGRADES. Since the French Revolution the influence of woman in Europe has DECLINED in proportion as she has increased her rights and claims; and the "emancipation of woman," insofar as it is desired and demanded by women themselves (and not only by masculine shallow-pates), thus proves to be a remarkable symptom of the increased weakening and deadening of the most womanly instincts. There is STUPIDITY in this movement, an almost masculine stupidity, of which a well-reared woman--who is always a sensible woman--might be heartily ashamed. To lose the intuition as to the ground upon which she can most surely achieve victory; to neglect exercise in the use of her proper weapons; to let-herself-go before man, perhaps even "to the book," where formerly she kept herself in control and in refined, artful humility; to neutralize with her virtuous audacity man's faith in a VEILED, fundamentally different ideal in woman, something eternally, necessarily feminine; to emphatically and loquaciously dissuade man from the idea that woman must be preserved, cared for, protected, and indulged, like some delicate, strangely wild, and often pleasant domestic animal; the clumsy and indignant collection of everything of the nature of servitude and bondage which the position of woman in the hitherto existing order of society has entailed and still entails (as though slavery were a counter- argument, and not rather a condition of every higher culture, of every elevation of culture):--what does all this betoken, if not a disintegration of womanly instincts, a defeminising? Certainly, there are enough of idiotic friends and corrupters of woman among the learned asses of the masculine sex, who advise woman to defeminize herself in this manner, and to imitate all the stupidities from which "man" in Europe, European "manliness," suffers,--who would like to lower woman to "general culture," indeed even to newspaper reading and meddling with politics. Here and there they wish even to make women into free spirits and literary workers: as though a woman without piety would not be something perfectly obnoxious or ludicrous to a profound and godless man;--almost everywhere her nerves are being ruined by the most morbid and dangerous kind of music (our latest German music), and she is daily being made more hysterical and more incapable of fulfilling her first and last function, that of bearing robust children. They wish to "cultivate" her in general still more, and intend, as they say, to make the "weaker sex" STRONG by culture: as if history did not teach in the most emphatic manner that the "cultivating" of mankind and his weakening--that is to say, the weakening, dissipating, and languishing of his FORCE OF WILL--have always kept pace with one another, and that the most powerful and influential women in the world (and lastly, the mother of Napoleon) had just to thank their force of will--

and not their schoolmasters--for their power and ascendancy over men. That which inspires respect in woman, and often enough fear also, is her NATURE, which is more "natural" than that of man, her genuine, carnivora-like, cunning flexibility, her tiger-claws beneath the glove, her NAIVETE in egoism, her untrainableness and innate wildness, the incomprehensibleness, extent, and deviation of her desires and virtues. That which, in spite of fear, excites one's sympathy for the dangerous and beautiful cat, "woman," is that she seems more afflicted, more vulnerable, more necessitous of love, and more condemned to disillusionment than any other creature. Fear and sympathy it is with these feelings that man has hitherto stood in the presence of woman, always with one foot already in tragedy, which rends while it delights--What? And all that is now to be at an end? And the DISENCHANTMENT of woman is in progress? The tediousness of woman is slowly evolving? Oh Europe! Europe! We know the horned animal which was always most attractive to thee, from which danger is ever again threatening thee! Thy old fable might once more become "history"--an immense stupidity might once again overmaster thee and carry thee away! And no God concealed beneath it--no! only an "idea," a "modern idea"!

Chapter 8
Peoples and Fatherlands

I HEARD, once again for the first time, Richard Wagner's overture to the Mastersinger: it is a piece of magnificent, gorgeous, heavy, latter-day art, which has the pride to presuppose two centuries of music as still living, in order that it may be understood:--it is an honour to Germans that such a pride did not miscalculate! What flavours and forces, what seasons and climes do we not find mingled in it! It impresses us at one time as ancient, at another time as foreign, bitter, and too modern, it is as arbitrary as it is pompously traditional, it is not infrequently roguish, still oftener rough and coarse--it has fire and courage, and at the same time the loose, dun- coloured skin of fruits which ripen too late. It flows broad and full: and suddenly there is a moment of inexplicable hesitation, like a gap that opens between cause and effect, an oppression that makes us dream, almost a nightmare; but already it broadens and widens anew, the old stream of delight-the most manifold delight,--of old and new happiness; including ESPECIALLY the joy of the artist in himself, which he refuses to conceal, his astonished, happy cognizance of his mastery of the expedients here employed, the new, newly acquired, imperfectly tested expedients of art which he apparently betrays to us. All in all, however, no beauty, no South, nothing of the delicate southern clearness of the sky, nothing of grace, no dance, hardly a will to logic; a certain clumsiness even, which is also emphasized, as though the artist wished to say to us: "It is part of my intention"; a cumbersome drapery, something arbitrarily barbaric and ceremonious, a flirting of learned and venerable conceits and witticisms; something German in the best and worst sense of the word, something in the German style, manifold, formless, and inexhaustible; a certain German potency and super-plenitude of soul, which is not afraid to hide itself under the RAFFINEMENTS of decadence--which, perhaps, feels itself most at ease there; a real, genuine token of the German soul, which is at the same time young and aged, too ripe and yet still too rich in futurity. This kind of music expresses best what I think of the Germans: they belong to the day before yesterday and the day after tomorrow-- THEY HAVE AS YET NO TODAY.

We "good Europeans," we also have hours when we allow ourselves a warm-hearted patriotism, a plunge and relapse into old loves and narrow views--I have just given an example of it-- hours of national excitement, of patriotic anguish, and all other sorts of old-fashioned floods of sentiment. Duller spirits may perhaps only get done with what confines its operations in us to hours and plays itself out in hours--in a considerable time: some in half a year, others in half a lifetime, according to the speed and strength with which they digest and "change their material." Indeed, I could think of sluggish, hesitating races, which even in our rapidly moving Europe, would require half a century ere they could surmount such atavistic attacks of patriotism and soil-attachment, and return once more to reason, that is to say, to "good Europeanism." And while digressing on this possibility, I happen to become an ear-witness of a conversation between two old patriots--they were evidently both hard of hearing and consequently spoke all the louder. "HE has as much, and knows as much, philosophy as a peasant or a corps-student," said the one-- "he is still innocent. But what does that matter nowadays! It is the age of the masses: they lie on their belly before everything that is massive. And so also in politicis. A statesman who rears up for them a new Tower of Babel, some monstrosity of empire and power, they call 'great'--what does it matter that we more prudent and conservative ones do not meanwhile give up the old belief that it is only the great thought that gives greatness to an action or affair. Supposing a statesman were to bring his people into the position of being obliged henceforth to practise 'high politics,' for which they were by nature badly endowed and prepared, so that they would have to sacrifice their old and reliable virtues, out of love to a new and doubtful mediocrity;-- supposing a statesman were to condemn his people generally to 'practise politics,' when they have hitherto had something better to do and think about, and when in the depths of their souls they have been unable to free themselves from a prudent loathing of the restlessness, emptiness, and noisy wranglings of the essentially politics-practising nations;--supposing such a statesman were to stimulate the slumbering passions and avidities of his people, were to make a stigma out of their former diffidence and delight in aloofness, an offence out of their exoticism and hidden permanency, were to depreciate their most radical proclivities, subvert their consciences, make their minds narrow, and their tastes 'national'--what! a statesman who should do all this, which his people would have to do penance for throughout their whole future, if they had a future, such a statesman would be GREAT, would he?"--"Undoubtedly!" replied the other old patriot vehemently, "otherwise he COULD NOT have done it! It was mad perhaps to wish such a thing! But perhaps everything great has been just as mad at its commencement!"-- "Misuse of words!" cried his interlocutor, contradictorily-- "strong! strong! Strong and mad! NOT great!"--The old men had obviously become heated as they thus shouted their "truths" in each other's faces, but I, in my happiness and apartness, considered how soon a stronger one may become master of the strong, and also that there is a compensation for the intellectual superficialising of a nation--namely, in the deepening of another.

Whether we call it "civilization," or "humanising," or "progress," which now distinguishes the European, whether we call it simply, without praise or blame, by the political formula the DEMOCRATIC movement in Europe--behind all the moral and political foregrounds pointed to by such formulas, an immense PHYSIOLOGICAL PROCESS goes on, which is ever extending the process of the assimilation of Europeans, their increasing detachment from the conditions under which, climatically and hereditarily, united races originate, their increasing independence of every definite milieu, that for centuries would fain inscribe itself with equal demands on soul and body,--that is to say, the slow emergence of an essentially SUPER-NATIONAL and nomadic species of man, who possesses, physiologically speaking, a maximum of the art and power of adaptation as his typical distinction. This process of the EVOLVING EUROPEAN, which can be retarded in its TEMPO by great relapses, but will perhaps just gain and grow thereby in vehemence and depth--the still-raging storm and stress of "national sentiment" pertains to it, and also the anarchism which is appearing at present--this process will probably arrive at results on which its naive propagators and panegyrists, the apostles of "modern ideas," would least care to reckon. The same new conditions under which on an average a levelling and mediocrising of man will take place--a useful, industrious, variously serviceable, and clever gregarious man--are in the highest degree suitable to give rise to exceptional men of the most dangerous and attractive qualities. For, while the capacity for adaptation, which is every day trying changing conditions, and begins a new work with every generation, almost with every decade, makes the POWERFULNESS of the type impossible; while the collective impression of such future Europeans will probably be that of numerous, talkative, weak-willed, and very handy workmen who REQUIRE a master, a commander, as they require their daily bread; while, therefore, the democratising of Europe will tend to the production of a type prepared for SLAVERY in the most subtle sense of the term: the STRONG man will necessarily in individual and exceptional cases, become stronger and richer than he has perhaps ever been before--owing to the unprejudicedness of his schooling, owing to the immense variety of practice, art, and disguise. I meant to say that the democratising of Europe is at the same time an involuntary arrangement for the rearing of TYRANTS--taking the word in all its meanings, even in its most spiritual sense.

I hear with pleasure that our sun is moving rapidly towards the constellation Hercules: and I hope that the men on this earth will do like the sun. And we foremost, we good Europeans!

There was a time when it was customary to call Germans "deep" by way of distinction; but now that the most successful type of new Germanism is covetous of quite other honours, and perhaps misses "smartness" in all that has depth, it is almost opportune and patriotic to doubt whether we did not formerly deceive ourselves with that commendation: in short, whether German depth is not at bottom something different and worse--and something from which, thank God, we are on the point of successfully ridding ourselves. Let us try, then, to relearn with regard to German depth; the only thing necessary for the purpose is a little vivisection of the German soul.--The German soul is above all manifold, varied in its source, aggregated and super- imposed, rather than actually built: this is owing to its origin. A German who would embolden himself to assert: "Two souls, alas, dwell in my breast," would make a bad guess at the truth, or, more correctly, he would come far short of the truth about the number of souls. As a people made up of the most extraordinary mixing and mingling of races, perhaps even with a preponderance of the pre-Aryan element as the "people of the centre" in every sense of the term, the Germans are more intangible, more ample, more contradictory, more unknown, more incalculable, more surprising, and even more terrifying than other peoples are to themselves:--they escape DEFINITION, and are thereby alone the despair of the French. It IS characteristic of the Germans that the question: "What is German?" never dies out among them. Kotzebue certainly knew his Germans well enough: "We are known," they cried jubilantly to him--but Sand also thought he knew them. Jean Paul knew what he was doing when he declared himself incensed at Fichte's lying but patriotic flatteries and exaggerations,--but it is probable that Goethe thought differently about Germans from Jean Paul, even though he acknowledged him to be right with regard to Fichte. It is a question what Goethe really thought about the Germans?--But about many things around him he never spoke explicitly, and all his life he knew how to keep an astute silence--probably he had good reason for it. It is certain that it was not the "Wars of Independence" that made him look up more joyfully, any more than it was the French Revolution,--the event on account of which he RECONSTRUCTED his "Faust," and indeed the whole problem of "man," was the appearance of Napoleon. There are words of Goethe in which he condemns with impatient severity, as from a foreign land, that which Germans take a pride in, he once defined the famous German turn of mind as "Indulgence towards its own and others' weaknesses." Was he wrong? it is characteristic of Germans that one is seldom entirely wrong about them. The German soul has passages and galleries in it, there are caves, hiding- places, and dungeons therein, its disorder has much of the charm of the mysterious, the German is well acquainted with the bypaths to chaos. And as everything loves its symbol, so the German loves the clouds and all that is obscure, evolving, crepuscular, damp, and shrouded, it seems to him that everything uncertain, undeveloped, self-displacing, and growing is "deep". The German himself does not EXIST, he is BECOMING, he is "developing himself". "Development" is therefore the essentially German discovery and hit in the great domain of philosophical formulas,-- a ruling idea, which, together with German beer and German music, is labouring to Germanise all Europe. Foreigners are astonished and attracted by the riddles which the conflicting nature at the basis of the German soul propounds to them (riddles which Hegel systematised and Richard Wagner has in the end set to music). "Good-natured and spiteful"--such a juxtaposition, preposterous in the case of every other people, is unfortunately only too often justified in Germany one has only to live for a while among Swabians to know this! The clumsiness of the German scholar and his social distastefulness agree alarmingly well with his physical rope-dancing and nimble boldness, of which all the Gods have learnt to be afraid. If any one wishes to see the "German soul" demonstrated ad oculos, let him only look at German taste, at German arts and manners what boorish indifference to "taste"! How the noblest and the commonest stand there in juxtaposition! How disorderly and how rich is the whole constitution of this soul! The German DRAGS at his soul, he drags at everything he experiences. He digests his events badly; he never gets "done" with them; and German depth is often only a difficult, hesitating "digestion." And just as all chronic invalids, all dyspeptics like what is convenient, so the German loves "frankness" and "honesty"; it is so CONVENIENT to be frank and honest!--This confidingness, this complaisance, this showing-the-cards of German HONESTY, is probably the most dangerous and most successful disguise which the German is up to nowadays: it is his proper Mephistophelean art; with this he can "still achieve much"! The German lets himself go, and thereby gazes with faithful, blue, empty German eyes--and other countries immediately confound him with his dressing-gown!--I meant to say that, let "German depth" be what it will--among ourselves alone we perhaps take the liberty to laugh at it--we shall do well to continue henceforth to honour its appearance and good name, and not barter away too cheaply our old reputation as a people of depth for Prussian "smartness," and Berlin wit and sand. It is wise for a people to pose, and LET itself be regarded, as profound, clumsy, good-natured, honest, and foolish: it might even be--profound to do so! Finally, we should do honour to our name--we are not called the "TIUSCHE VOLK" (deceptive people) for nothing. . . .

The "good old" time is past, it sang itself out in Mozart-- how happy are WE that his ROCOCO still speaks to us, that his "good company," his tender enthusiasm, his childish delight in the Chinese and its flourishes, his courtesy of heart, his longing for the elegant, the amorous, the tripping, the tearful, and his belief in the South, can still appeal to SOMETHING LEFT in us! Ah, some time or other it will be over with it!--but who can doubt that it will be over still sooner with the intelligence and taste for Beethoven! For he was only the last echo of a break and transition in style, and NOT, like Mozart, the last echo of a great European taste which had existed for centuries. Beethoven is the intermediate event between an old mellow soul that is constantly breaking down, and a future over-young soul that is always COMING; there is spread over his music the twilight of eternal loss and eternal extravagant hope,--the same light in which Europe was bathed when it dreamed with Rousseau, when it danced round the Tree of Liberty of the Revolution, and finally almost fell down in adoration before Napoleon. But how rapidly does THIS very sentiment now pale, how difficult nowadays is even the APPREHENSION of this sentiment, how strangely does the language of Rousseau, Schiller, Shelley, and Byron sound to our ear, in whom COLLECTIVELY the same fate of Europe was able to SPEAK, which knew how to SING in Beethoven!--Whatever German music came afterwards, belongs to Romanticism, that is to say, to a movement which, historically considered, was still shorter, more fleeting, and more superficial than that great interlude, the transition of Europe from Rousseau to Napoleon, and to the rise of democracy. Weber--but what do WE care nowadays for "Freischutz" and "Oberon"! Or Marschner's "Hans Heiling" and "Vampyre"! Or even Wagner's "Tannhauser"! That is extinct, although not yet forgotten music. This whole music of Romanticism, besides, was not noble enough, was not musical enough, to maintain its position anywhere but in the theatre and before the masses; from the beginning it was second-rate music, which was little thought of by genuine musicians. It was different with Felix Mendelssohn, that halcyon master, who, on account of his lighter, purer, happier soul, quickly acquired admiration, and was equally quickly forgotten: as the beautiful EPISODE of German music. But with regard to Robert Schumann, who took things seriously, and has been taken seriously from the first--he was the last that founded a school,--do we not now regard it as a satisfaction, a relief, a deliverance, that this very Romanticism of Schumann's has been surmounted? Schumann, fleeing into the "Saxon Switzerland" of his soul, with a half Werther-like, half Jean-Paul-like nature (assuredly not like Beethoven! assuredly not like Byron!)--his MANFRED music is a mistake and a misunderstanding to the extent of injustice; Schumann, with his taste, which was fundamentally a PETTY taste (that is to say, a dangerous propensity--doubly dangerous among Germans--for quiet lyricism and intoxication of the feelings), going constantly apart, timidly withdrawing and retiring, a noble weakling who revelled in nothing but anonymous joy and sorrow, from the beginning a sort of girl and NOLI ME TANGERE--this Schumann was already merely a GERMAN event in music, and no longer a European event, as Beethoven had been, as in a still greater degree Mozart had been; with Schumann German music was threatened with its greatest danger, that of LOSING THE VOICE FOR THE SOUL OF EUROPE and sinking into a merely national affair.

What a torture are books written in German to a reader who has a THIRD ear! How indignantly he stands beside the slowly turning swamp of sounds without tune and rhythms without dance, which Germans call a "book"! And even the German who READS books! How lazily, how reluctantly, how badly he reads! How many Germans know, and consider it obligatory to know, that there is ART in every good sentence--art which must be divined, if the sentence is to be understood! If there is a misunderstanding about its TEMPO, for instance, the sentence itself is misunderstood! That one must not be doubtful about the rhythm-determining syllables, that one should feel the breaking of the too-rigid symmetry as intentional and as a charm, that one should lend a fine and patient ear to every STACCATO and every RUBATO, that one should divine the sense in the sequence of the vowels and diphthongs, and how delicately and richly they can be tinted and retinted in the order of their arrangement--who among book-reading Germans is complaisant enough to recognize such duties and requirements, and to listen to so much art and intention in language? After all, one just "has no ear for it"; and so the most marked contrasts of style are not heard, and the most delicate artistry is as it were SQUANDERED on the deaf.--These were my thoughts when I noticed how clumsily and unintuitively two masters in the art of prose- writing have been confounded: one, whose words drop down hesitatingly and coldly, as from the roof of a damp cave--he counts on their dull sound and echo; and another who manipulates his language like a flexible sword, and from his arm down into his toes feels the dangerous bliss of the quivering, over-sharp blade, which wishes to bite, hiss, and cut.

How little the German style has to do with harmony and with the ear, is shown by the fact that precisely our good musicians themselves write badly. The German does not read aloud, he does not read for the ear, but only with his eyes; he has put his ears away in the drawer for the time. In antiquity when a man read-- which was seldom enough--he read something to himself, and in a loud voice; they were surprised when any one read silently, and sought secretly the reason of it. In a loud voice: that is to say, with all the swellings, inflections, and variations of key and changes of TEMPO, in which the ancient PUBLIC world took delight. The laws of the written style were then the same as those of the spoken style; and these laws depended partly on the surprising development and refined requirements of the ear and larynx; partly on the strength, endurance, and power of the ancient lungs. In the ancient sense, a period is above all a physiological whole, inasmuch as it is comprised in one breath. Such periods as occur in Demosthenes and Cicero, swelling twice and sinking twice, and all in one breath, were pleasures to the men of ANTIQUITY, who knew by their own schooling how to appreciate the virtue therein, the rareness and the difficulty in the deliverance of such a period;--WE have really no right to the BIG period, we modern men, who are short of breath in every sense! Those ancients, indeed, were all of them dilettanti in speaking, consequently connoisseurs, consequently critics--they thus brought their orators to the highest pitch; in the same manner as in the last century, when all Italian ladies and gentlemen knew how to sing, the virtuosoship of song (and with it also the art of melody) reached its elevation. In Germany, however (until quite recently when a kind of platform eloquence began shyly and awkwardly enough to flutter its young wings), there was properly speaking only one kind of public and APPROXIMATELY artistical discourse--that delivered from the pulpit. The preacher was the only one in Germany who knew the weight of a syllable or a word, in what manner a sentence strikes, springs, rushes, flows, and comes to a close; he alone had a conscience in his ears, often enough a bad conscience: for reasons are not lacking why proficiency in oratory should be especially seldom attained by a German, or almost always too late. The masterpiece of German prose is therefore with good reason the masterpiece of its greatest preacher: the BIBLE has hitherto been the best German book. Compared with Luther's Bible, almost everything else is merely "literature"--something which has not grown in Germany, and therefore has not taken and does not take root in German hearts, as the Bible has done.

There are two kinds of geniuses: one which above all engenders and seeks to engender, and another which willingly lets itself be fructified and brings forth. And similarly, among the gifted nations, there are those on whom the woman's problem of pregnancy has devolved, and the secret task of forming, maturing, and perfecting-- the Greeks, for instance, were a nation of this kind, and so are the French; and others which have to fructify and become the cause of new modes of life--like the Jews, the Romans, and, in all modesty be it asked: like the Germans?-- nations tortured and enraptured by unknown fevers and irresistibly forced out of themselves, amorous and longing for foreign races (for such as "let themselves be fructified"), and withal imperious, like everything conscious of being full of generative force, and consequently empowered "by the grace of God." These two kinds of geniuses seek each other like man and woman; but they also misunderstand each other--like man and woman.

Every nation has its own "Tartuffery," and calls that its virtue.--One does not know--cannot know, the best that is in one.

What Europe owes to the Jews?--Many things, good and bad, and above all one thing of the nature both of the best and the worst: the grand style in morality, the fearfulness and majesty of infinite demands, of infinite significations, the whole Romanticism and sublimity of moral questionableness--and consequently just the most attractive, ensnaring, and exquisite element in those iridescences and allurements to life, in the aftersheen of which the sky of our European culture, its evening sky, now glows--perhaps glows out. For this, we artists among the spectators and philosophers, are--grateful to the Jews.

It must be taken into the bargain, if various clouds and disturbances--in short, slight attacks of stupidity--pass over the spirit of a people that suffers and WANTS to suffer from national nervous fever and political ambition: for instance, among present-day Germans there is alternately the anti-French folly, the anti-Semitic folly, the anti-Polish folly, the Christian-romantic folly, the Wagnerian folly, the Teutonic folly, the Prussian folly (just look at those poor historians, the Sybels and Treitschkes, and their closely bandaged heads), and whatever else these little obscurations of the German spirit and conscience may be called. May it be forgiven me that I, too, when on a short daring sojourn on very infected ground, did not remain wholly exempt from the disease, but like every one else, began to entertain thoughts about matters which did not concern me--the first symptom of political infection. About the Jews, for instance, listen to the following:--I have never yet met a German who was favourably inclined to the Jews; and however decided the repudiation of actual anti-Semitism may be on the part of all prudent and political men, this prudence and policy is not perhaps directed against the nature of the sentiment itself, but only against its dangerous excess, and especially against the distasteful and infamous expression of this excess of sentiment; --on this point we must not deceive ourselves. That Germany has amply SUFFICIENT Jews, that the German stomach, the German blood, has difficulty (and will long have difficulty) in disposing only of this quantity of "Jew"--as the Italian, the Frenchman, and the Englishman have done by means of a stronger digestion:--that is the unmistakable declaration and language of a general instinct, to which one must listen and according to which one must act. "Let no more Jews come in! And shut the doors, especially towards the East (also towards Austria)!"--thus commands the instinct of a people whose nature is still feeble and uncertain, so that it could be easily wiped out, easily extinguished, by a stronger race. The Jews, however, are beyond all doubt the strongest, toughest, and purest race at present living in Europe, they know how to succeed even under the worst conditions (in fact better than under favourable ones), by means of virtues of some sort, which one would like nowadays to label as vices--owing above all to a resolute faith which does not need to be ashamed before "modern ideas", they alter only, WHEN they do alter, in the same way that the Russian Empire makes its conquest--as an empire that has plenty of time and is not of yesterday--namely, according to the principle, "as slowly as possible"! A thinker who has the future of Europe at heart, will, in all his perspectives concerning the future, calculate upon the Jews, as he will calculate upon the Russians, as above all the surest and likeliest factors in the great play and battle of forces. That which is at present called a "nation" in Europe, and is really rather a RES FACTA than NATA (indeed, sometimes confusingly similar to a RES FICTA ET PICTA), is in every case something evolving, young, easily displaced, and not yet a race, much less such a race AERE PERENNUS, as the Jews are such "nations" should most carefully avoid all hotheaded rivalry and hostility! It is certain that the Jews, if they desired--or if they were driven to it, as the anti-Semites seem to wish--COULD now have the ascendancy, nay, literally the supremacy, over Europe, that they are NOT working and planning for that end is equally certain. Meanwhile, they rather wish and desire, even somewhat importunely, to be insorbed and absorbed by Europe, they long to be finally settled, authorized, and respected somewhere, and wish to put an end to the nomadic life, to the "wandering Jew",--and one should certainly take account of this impulse and tendency, and MAKE ADVANCES to it (it possibly betokens a mitigation of the Jewish instincts) for which purpose it would perhaps be useful and fair to banish the anti-Semitic bawlers out of the country. One should make advances with all prudence, and with selection, pretty much as the English nobility do It stands to reason that the more powerful and strongly marked types of new Germanism could enter into relation with the Jews with the least hesitation, for instance, the nobleman officer from the Prussian border it would be interesting in many ways to see whether the genius for money and patience (and especially some intellect and intellectuality--sadly lacking in the place referred to) could not in addition be annexed and trained to the hereditary art of commanding and obeying--for both of which the country in question has now a classic reputation But here it is expedient to break off my festal discourse and my sprightly Teutonomania for I have already reached my SERIOUS TOPIC, the "European problem," as I understand it, the rearing of a new ruling caste for Europe.

They are not a philosophical race--the English: Bacon represents an ATTACK on the philosophical spirit generally, Hobbes, Hume, and Locke, an abasement, and a depreciation of the idea of a "philosopher" for more than a century. It was AGAINST Hume that Kant uprose and raised himself; it was Locke of whom Schelling RIGHTLY said, "JE MEPRISE LOCKE"; in the struggle against the English mechanical stultification of the world, Hegel and Schopenhauer (along with Goethe) were of one accord; the two hostile brother-geniuses in philosophy, who pushed in different directions towards the opposite poles of German thought, and thereby wronged each other as only brothers will do.--What is lacking in England, and has always been lacking, that half-actor and rhetorician knew well enough, the absurd muddle-head, Carlyle, who sought to conceal under passionate grimaces what he knew about himself: namely, what was LACKING in Carlyle--real POWER of intellect, real DEPTH of intellectual perception, in short, philosophy. It is characteristic of such an unphilosophical race to hold on firmly to Christianity--they NEED its discipline for "moralizing" and humanizing. The Englishman, more gloomy, sensual, headstrong, and brutal than the German--is for that very reason, as the baser of the two, also the most pious: he has all the MORE NEED of Christianity. To finer nostrils, this English Christianity itself has still a characteristic English taint of spleen and alcoholic excess, for which, owing to good reasons, it is used as an antidote--the finer poison to neutralize the coarser: a finer form of poisoning is in fact a step in advance with coarse-mannered people, a step towards spiritualization. The English coarseness and rustic demureness is still most satisfactorily disguised by Christian pantomime, and by praying and psalm-singing (or, more correctly, it is thereby explained and differently expressed); and for the herd of drunkards and rakes who formerly learned moral grunting under the influence of Methodism (and more recently as the "Salvation Army"), a penitential fit may really be the relatively highest manifestation of "humanity" to which they can be elevated: so much may reasonably be admitted. That, however, which offends even in the humanest Englishman is his lack of music, to speak figuratively (and also literally): he has neither rhythm nor dance in the movements of his soul and body; indeed, not even the desire for rhythm and dance, for "music." Listen to him speaking; look at the most beautiful Englishwoman WALKING--in no country on earth are there more beautiful doves and swans; finally, listen to them singing! But I ask too much . . .

There are truths which are best recognized by mediocre minds, because they are best adapted for them, there are truths which only possess charms and seductive power for mediocre spirits:--one is pushed to this probably unpleasant conclusion, now that the influence of respectable but mediocre Englishmen--I may mention Darwin, John Stuart Mill, and Herbert Spencer--begins to gain the ascendancy in the middle-class region of European taste. Indeed, who could doubt that it is a useful thing for SUCH minds to have the ascendancy for a time? It would be an error to consider the highly developed and independently soaring minds as specially qualified for determining and collecting many little common facts, and deducing conclusions from them; as exceptions, they are rather from the first in no very favourable position towards those who are "the rules." After all, they have more to do than merely to perceive:--in effect, they have to BE something new, they have to SIGNIFY something new, they have to REPRESENT new values! The gulf between knowledge and capacity is perhaps greater, and also more mysterious, than one thinks: the capable man in the grand style, the creator, will possibly have to be an ignorant person;--while on the other hand, for scientific discoveries like those of Darwin, a certain narrowness, aridity, and industrious carefulness (in short, something English) may not be unfavourable for arriving at them.--Finally, let it not be forgotten that the English, with their profound mediocrity, brought about once before a general depression of European intelligence.

What is called "modern ideas," or "the ideas of the eighteenth century," or "French ideas"--that, consequently, against which the GERMAN mind rose up with profound disgust--is of English origin, there is no doubt about it. The French were only the apes and actors of these ideas, their best soldiers, and likewise, alas! their first and profoundest VICTIMS; for owing to the diabolical Anglomania of "modern ideas," the AME FRANCAIS has in the end become so thin and emaciated, that at present one recalls its sixteenth and seventeenth centuries, its profound, passionate strength, its inventive excellency, almost with disbelief. One must, however, maintain this verdict of historical justice in a determined manner, and defend it against present prejudices and appearances: the European NOBLESSE--of sentiment, taste, and manners, taking the word in every high sense--is the work and invention of FRANCE; the European ignobleness, the plebeianism of modern ideas--is ENGLAND'S work and invention.

Even at present France is still the seat of the most intellectual and refined culture of Europe, it is still the high school of taste; but one must know how to find this "France of taste." He who belongs to it keeps himself well concealed:--they may be a small number in whom it lives and is embodied, besides perhaps being men who do not stand upon the strongest legs, in part fatalists, hypochondriacs, invalids, in part persons over- indulged, over-refined, such as have the AMBITION to conceal themselves.

They have all something in common: they keep their ears closed in presence of the delirious folly and noisy spouting of the democratic BOURGEOIS. In fact, a besotted and brutalized France at present sprawls in the foreground--it recently celebrated a veritable orgy of bad taste, and at the same time of self- admiration, at the funeral of Victor Hugo. There is also something else common to them: a predilection to resist intellectual Germanizing--and a still greater inability to do so! In this France of intellect, which is also a France of pessimism, Schopenhauer has perhaps become more at home, and more indigenous than he has ever been in Germany; not to speak of Heinrich Heine, who has long ago been re-incarnated in the more refined and fastidious lyrists of Paris; or of Hegel, who at present, in the form of Taine--the FIRST of living historians--exercises an almost tyrannical influence. As regards Richard Wagner, however, the more French music learns to adapt itself to the actual needs of the AME MODERNE, the more will it "Wagnerite"; one can safely predict that beforehand,--it is already taking place sufficiently! There are, however, three things which the French can still boast of with pride as their heritage and possession, and as indelible tokens of their ancient intellectual superiority in Europe, in spite of all voluntary or involuntary Germanizing and vulgarizing of taste. FIRSTLY, the capacity for artistic emotion, for devotion to "form," for which the expression, L'ART POUR L'ART, along with numerous others, has been invented:--such capacity has not been lacking in France for three centuries; and owing to its reverence for the "small number," it has again and again made a sort of chamber music of literature possible, which is sought for in vain elsewhere in Europe.--The SECOND thing whereby the French can lay claim to a superiority over Europe is their ancient, many-sided, MORALISTIC culture, owing to which one finds on an average, even in the petty ROMANCIERS of the newspapers and chance BOULEVARDIERS DE PARIS, a psychological sensitiveness and curiosity, of which, for example, one has no conception (to say nothing of the thing itself!) in Germany. The Germans lack a couple of centuries of the moralistic work requisite thereto, which, as we have said, France has not grudged: those who call the Germans "naive" on that account give them commendation for a defect. (As the opposite of the German inexperience and innocence IN VOLUPTATE PSYCHOLOGICA, which is not too remotely associated with the tediousness of German intercourse,--and as the most successful expression of genuine French curiosity and inventive talent in this domain of delicate thrills, Henri Beyle may be noted; that remarkable anticipatory and forerunning man, who, with a Napoleonic TEMPO, traversed HIS Europe, in fact, several centuries of the European soul, as a surveyor and discoverer thereof:--it has required two generations to OVERTAKE him one way or other, to divine long afterwards some of the riddles that perplexed and enraptured him--this strange Epicurean and man of interrogation, the last great psychologist of France).--There is yet a THIRD claim to superiority: in the French character there is a successful half-way synthesis of the North and South, which makes them comprehend many things, and enjoins upon them other things, which an Englishman can never comprehend. Their temperament, turned alternately to and from the South, in which from time to time the Provencal and Ligurian blood froths over, preserves them from the dreadful, northern grey-in-grey, from sunless conceptual-spectrism and from poverty of blood--our GERMAN infirmity of taste, for the excessive prevalence of which at the present moment, blood and iron, that is to say "high politics," has with great resolution been prescribed (according to a dangerous healing art, which bids me wait and wait, but not yet hope).--There is also still in France a pre-understanding and ready welcome for those rarer and rarely gratified men, who are too comprehensive to find satisfaction in any kind of fatherlandism, and know how to love the South when in the North and the North when in the South--the born Midlanders, the "good

Europeans." For them BIZET has made music, this latest genius, who has seen a new beauty and seduction,--who has discovered a piece of the SOUTH IN MUSIC.

I hold that many precautions should be taken against German music. Suppose a person loves the South as I love it--as a great school of recovery for the most spiritual and the most sensuous ills, as a boundless solar profusion and effulgence which o'erspreads a sovereign existence believing in itself--well, such a person will learn to be somewhat on his guard against German music, because, in injuring his taste anew, it will also injure his health anew. Such a Southerner, a Southerner not by origin but by BELIEF, if he should dream of the future of music, must also dream of it being freed from the influence of the North; and must have in his ears the prelude to a deeper, mightier, and perhaps more perverse and mysterious music, a super-German music, which does not fade, pale, and die away, as all German music does, at the sight of the blue, wanton sea and the Mediterranean clearness of sky--a super-European music, which holds its own even in presence of the brown sunsets of the desert, whose soul is akin to the palm-tree, and can be at home and can roam with big, beautiful, lonely beasts of prey . . . I could imagine a music of which the rarest charm would be that it knew nothing more of good and evil; only that here and there perhaps some sailor's home-sickness, some golden shadows and tender weaknesses might sweep lightly over it; an art which, from the far distance, would see the colours of a sinking and almost incomprehensible MORAL world fleeing towards it, and would be hospitable enough and profound enough to receive such belated fugitives.

Owing to the morbid estrangement which the nationality-craze has induced and still induces among the nations of Europe, owing also to the short-sighted and hasty-handed politicians, who with the help of this craze, are at present in power, and do not suspect to what extent the disintegrating policy they pursue must necessarily be only an interlude policy--owing to all this and much else that is altogether unmentionable at present, the most unmistakable signs that EUROPE

WISHES TO BE ONE, are now overlooked, or arbitrarily and falsely misinterpreted. With all the more profound and large-minded men of this century, the real general tendency of the mysterious labour of their souls was to prepare the way for that new SYNTHESIS, and tentatively to anticipate the European of the future; only in their simulations, or in their weaker moments, in old age perhaps, did they belong to the "fatherlands"--they only rested from themselves when they became "patriots." I think of such men as Napoleon, Goethe, Beethoven, Stendhal, Heinrich Heine, Schopenhauer: it must not be taken amiss if I also count Richard Wagner among them, about whom one must not let oneself be deceived by his own misunderstandings (geniuses like him have seldom the right to understand themselves), still less, of course, by the unseemly noise with which he is now resisted and opposed in France: the fact remains, nevertheless, that Richard Wagner and the LATER FRENCH ROMANTICISM of the forties, are most closely and intimately related to one another. They are akin, fundamentally akin, in all the heights and depths of their requirements; it is Europe, the ONE Europe, whose soul presses urgently and longingly, outwards and upwards, in their multifarious and boisterous art--whither? into a new light? towards a new sun? But who would attempt to express accurately what all these masters of new modes of speech could not express distinctly? It is certain that the same storm and stress tormented them, that they SOUGHT in the same manner, these last great seekers! All of them steeped in literature to their eyes and ears--the first artists of universal literary culture--for the most part even themselves writers, poets, intermediaries and blenders of the arts and the senses (Wagner, as musician is reckoned among painters, as poet among musicians, as artist generally among actors); all of them fanatics for EXPRESSION "at any cost"--I specially mention Delacroix, the nearest related to Wagner; all of them great discoverers in the realm of the sublime, also of the loathsome and dreadful, still greater discoverers in effect, in display, in the art of the show-shop; all of them talented far beyond their genius, out and out VIRTUOSI, with mysterious accesses to all that seduces, allures, constrains, and upsets; born enemies of logic and of the straight line, hankering after the strange, the exotic, the monstrous, the crooked, and the self-contradictory; as men, Tantaluses of the will, plebeian parvenus, who knew themselves to be incapable of a noble TEMPO or of a LENTO in life and action-- think of Balzac, for instance,-- unrestrained workers, almost destroying themselves by work; antinomians and rebels in manners, ambitious and insatiable, without equilibrium and enjoyment; all of them finally shattering and sinking down at the Christian cross (and with right and reason, for who of them would have been sufficiently profound and sufficiently original for an ANTI- CHRISTIAN philosophy?);--on the whole, a boldly daring, splendidly overbearing, high-flying, and aloft-up-dragging class of higher men, who had first to teach their century-and it is the century of the MASSES--the conception "higher man." . . . Let the German friends of Richard Wagner advise together as to whether there is anything purely German in the Wagnerian art, or whether its distinction does not consist precisely in coming from SUPER- GERMAN sources and impulses: in which connection it may not be underrated how indispensable Paris was to the development of his type, which the strength of his instincts made him long to visit at the most decisive time--and how the whole style of his proceedings, of his self-apostolate, could only perfect itself in sight of the French socialistic original. On a more subtle comparison it will perhaps be found, to the honour of Richard Wagner's German nature, that he has acted in everything with more strength, daring, severity, and elevation than a nineteenth- century Frenchman could have done--owing to the circumstance that we Germans are as yet nearer to barbarism than the French;-- perhaps even the most remarkable creation of Richard Wagner is not only at present, but for ever inaccessible, incomprehensible, and inimitable to the whole latter-day Latin race: the figure of Siegfried, that VERY FREE man, who is probably far too free, too hard, too cheerful, too healthy, too ANTI-CATHOLIC for the taste of old and mellow civilized nations. He may even have been a sin against Romanticism, this anti-Latin Siegfried: well, Wagner atoned amply for this sin in his old sad days, when--anticipating a taste which has meanwhile passed into politics--he began, with the religious vehemence peculiar to him, to preach, at least, THE WAY TO ROME, if not to walk therein.--That these last words may not be misunderstood, I will call to my aid a few powerful rhymes, which will even betray to less delicate ears what I mean --what I mean COUNTER TO the "last Wagner" and his Parsifal music:-

--Is this our mode?--From German heart came this vexed ululating? From German body, this self-lacerating? Is ours this priestly hand-dilation, This incense-fuming exaltation? Is ours this faltering, falling, shambling, This quite uncertain ding-dong- dangling? This sly nun-ogling, Ave-hour-bell ringing, This wholly false enraptured heaven-o'erspringing?--Is this our mode?--Think well!--ye still wait for admission--For what ye hear is ROME-- ROME'S FAITH BY INTUITION!

Chapter 9
What is Noble?

EVERY elevation of the type "man," has hitherto been the work of an aristocratic society and so it will always be--a society believing in a long scale of gradations of rank and differences of worth among human beings, and requiring slavery in some form or other. Without the PATHOS OF DISTANCE, such as grows out of the incarnated difference of classes, out of the constant out-looking and down-looking of the ruling caste on subordinates and instruments, and out of their equally constant practice of obeying and commanding, of keeping down and keeping at a distance--that other more mysterious pathos could never have arisen, the longing for an ever new widening of distance within the soul itself, the formation of ever higher, rarer, further, more extended, more comprehensive states, in short, just the elevation of the type "man," the continued "self-surmounting of man," to use a moral formula in a supermoral sense. To be sure, one must not resign oneself to any humanitarian illusions about the history of the origin of an aristocratic society (that is to say, of the preliminary condition for the elevation of the type "man"): the truth is hard. Let us acknowledge unprejudicedly how every higher civilization hitherto has ORIGINATED! Men with a still natural nature, barbarians in every terrible sense of the word, men of prey, still in possession of unbroken strength of will and desire for power, threw themselves upon weaker, more moral, more peaceful races (perhaps trading or cattle-rearing communities), or upon old mellow civilizations in which the final vital force was flickering out in brilliant fireworks of wit and depravity. At the commencement, the noble caste was always the barbarian caste: their superiority did not consist first of all in their physical, but in their psychical power--they were more COMPLETE men (which at every point also implies the same as "more complete beasts").

Corruption--as the indication that anarchy threatens to break out among the instincts, and that the foundation of the emotions, called "life," is convulsed--is something radically different according to the organization in which it manifests itself. When, for instance, an aristocracy like that of France at the beginning of the Revolution, flung away its privileges with sublime disgust and sacrificed itself to an excess of its moral sentiments, it was corruption:--it was really only the closing act of the corruption which had existed for centuries, by virtue of which that aristocracy had abdicated step by step its lordly prerogatives and lowered itself to a FUNCTION of royalty (in the end even to its decoration and parade-dress). The essential thing, however, in a good and healthy aristocracy is that it should not regard itself as a function either of the kingship or the commonwealth, but as the SIGNIFICANCE and highest justification thereof--that it should therefore accept with a good conscience the sacrifice of a legion of individuals, who, FOR ITS SAKE, must be suppressed and reduced to imperfect men, to slaves and instruments. Its fundamental belief must be precisely that society is NOT allowed to exist for its own sake, but only as a foundation and scaffolding, by means of which a select class of beings may be able to elevate themselves to their higher duties, and in general to a higher EXISTENCE: like those sun- seeking climbing plants in Java--they are called Sipo Matador,-- which encircle an oak so long and so often with their arms, until at last, high above it, but supported by it, they can unfold their tops in the open light, and exhibit their happiness.

To refrain mutually from injury, from violence, from exploitation, and put one's will on a par with that of others: this may result in a certain rough sense in good conduct among individuals when the necessary conditions are given (namely, the actual similarity of the individuals in amount of force and degree of worth, and their co-relation within one organization). As soon, however, as one wished to take this principle more generally, and if possible even as the FUNDAMENTAL PRINCIPLE OF SOCIETY, it would immediately disclose what it really is--namely, a Will to the DENIAL of life, a principle of dissolution and decay. Here one must think profoundly to the very basis and resist all sentimental weakness: life itself is ESSENTIALLY appropriation, injury, conquest of the strange and weak, suppression, severity, obtrusion of peculiar forms, incorporation, and at the least, putting it mildest, exploitation;--but why should one for ever use precisely these words on which for ages a disparaging purpose has been stamped? Even the organization within which, as was previously supposed, the individuals treat each other as equal--it takes place in every healthy aristocracy--must itself, if it be a living and not a dying organization, do all that towards other bodies, which the individuals within it refrain from doing to each other it will have to be the incarnated Will to Power, it will endeavour to grow, to gain ground, attract to itself and acquire ascendancy-- not owing to any morality or immorality, but because it LIVES, and because life IS precisely Will to Power. On no point, however, is the ordinary consciousness of Europeans more unwilling to be corrected than on this matter, people now rave everywhere, even under the guise of science, about coming conditions of society in which "the exploiting character" is to be absent--that sounds to my ears as if they promised to invent a mode of life which should refrain from all organic functions. "Exploitation" does not belong to a depraved, or imperfect and primitive society it belongs to the nature of the living being as a primary organic function, it is a consequence of the intrinsic Will to Power, which is precisely the Will to Life--Granting that as a theory this is a novelty--as a reality it is the FUNDAMENTAL FACT of all history let us be so far honest towards ourselves!

In a tour through the many finer and coarser moralities which have hitherto prevailed or still prevail on the earth, I found certain traits recurring regularly together, and connected with one another, until finally two primary types revealed themselves to me, and a radical distinction was brought to light. There is MASTER-MORALITY and SLAVE-MORALITY,--I would at once add, however, that in all higher and mixed civilizations, there are also attempts at the reconciliation of the two moralities, but one finds still oftener the confusion and mutual misunderstanding of them, indeed sometimes their close juxtaposition--even in the same man, within one soul. The distinctions of moral values have either originated in a ruling caste, pleasantly conscious of being different from the ruled--or among the ruled class, the slaves and dependents of all sorts. In the first case, when it is the rulers who determine the conception "good," it is the exalted, proud disposition which is regarded as the distinguishing feature, and that which determines the order of rank. The noble type of man separates from himself the beings in whom the opposite of this exalted, proud disposition displays itself he despises them. Let it at once be noted that in this first kind of morality the antithesis "good" and "bad" means practically the same as "noble" and "despicable",-- the antithesis "good" and "EVIL" is of a different origin. The cowardly, the timid, the insignificant, and those thinking merely of narrow utility are despised; moreover, also, the distrustful, with their constrained glances, the self- abasing, the dog-like kind of men who let themselves be abused, the mendicant flatterers, and above all the liars:--it is a fundamental belief of all aristocrats that the common people are untruthful. "We truthful ones"--the nobility in ancient Greece called themselves. It is obvious that everywhere the designations of moral value were at first applied to MEN; and were only derivatively and at a later period applied to ACTIONS; it is a gross mistake, therefore, when historians of morals start with questions like, "Why have sympathetic actions been praised?" The noble type of man regards HIMSELF as a determiner of values; he does not require to be approved of; he passes the judgment: "What is injurious to me is injurious in itself;" he knows that it is he himself only who confers honour on things; he is a CREATOR OF VALUES. He honours whatever he recognizes in himself: such morality equals self-glorification. In the foreground there is the feeling of plenitude, of power, which seeks to overflow, the happiness of high tension, the consciousness of a wealth which would fain give and bestow:--the noble man also helps the unfortunate, but not--or scarcely--out of pity, but rather from an impulse generated by the super-abundance of power. The noble man honours in himself the powerful one, him also who has power over himself, who knows how to speak and how to keep silence, who takes pleasure in subjecting himself to severity and hardness, and has reverence for all that is severe and hard. "Wotan placed a hard heart in my breast," says an old Scandinavian Saga: it is thus rightly expressed from the soul of a proud Viking. Such a type of man is even proud of not being made for sympathy; the hero of the Saga therefore adds warningly: "He who has not a hard heart when young, will never have one." The noble and brave who think thus are the furthest removed from the morality which sees precisely in sympathy, or in acting for the good of others, or in DESINTERESSEMENT, the characteristic of the moral; faith in oneself, pride in oneself, a radical enmity and irony towards "selflessness," belong as definitely to noble morality, as do a careless scorn and precaution in presence of sympathy and the "warm heart."--It is the powerful who KNOW how to honour, it is their art, their domain for invention. The profound reverence for age and for tradition--all law rests on this double reverence,-- the belief and prejudice in favour of ancestors and unfavourable to newcomers, is typical in the morality of the powerful; and if, reversely, men of "modern ideas" believe almost instinctively in "progress" and the "future," and are more and more lacking in respect for old age, the ignoble origin of these "ideas" has complacently betrayed itself thereby. A morality of the ruling class, however, is more especially foreign and irritating to present-day taste in the sternness of its principle that one has duties only to one's equals; that one may act towards beings of a lower rank, towards all that is foreign, just as seems good to one, or "as the heart desires," and in any case "beyond good and evil": it is here that sympathy and similar sentiments can have a place. The ability and obligation to exercise prolonged gratitude and prolonged revenge--both only within the circle of equals,-- artfulness in retaliation, RAFFINEMENT of the idea in friendship, a certain necessity to have enemies (as outlets for the emotions of envy, quarrelsomeness, arrogance--in fact, in order to be a good FRIEND): all these are typical characteristics of the noble morality, which, as has been pointed out, is not the morality of "modern ideas," and is therefore at present difficult to realize, and also to unearth and disclose.--It is otherwise with the second type of morality, SLAVE-MORALITY. Supposing that the abused, the oppressed, the suffering, the unemancipated, the weary, and those uncertain of themselves should moralize, what will be the common element in their moral estimates? Probably a pessimistic suspicion with regard to the entire situation of man will find expression, perhaps a condemnation of man, together with his situation. The slave has an unfavourable eye for the virtues of the powerful; he has a skepticism and distrust, a REFINEMENT of distrust of everything "good" that is there honoured--he would fain persuade himself that the very happiness there is not genuine. On the other hand, THOSE qualities which serve to alleviate the existence of sufferers are brought into prominence and flooded with light; it is here that sympathy, the kind, helping hand, the warm heart, patience, diligence, humility, and friendliness attain to honour; for here these are the most useful qualities, and almost the only means of supporting the burden of existence. Slave-morality is essentially the morality of utility. Here is the seat of the origin of the famous antithesis "good" and "evil":--power and dangerousness are assumed to reside in the evil, a certain dreadfulness, subtlety, and strength, which do not admit of being despised. According to slave-morality, therefore, the "evil" man arouses fear; according to master-morality, it is precisely the "good" man who arouses fear and seeks to arouse it, while the bad man is regarded as the despicable being. The contrast attains its maximum when, in accordance with the logical consequences of slave-morality, a shade of depreciation--it may be slight and well-intentioned--at last attaches itself to the "good" man of this morality; because, according to the servile mode of thought, the good man must in any case be the SAFE man: he is good-natured, easily deceived, perhaps a little stupid, un bonhomme. Everywhere that slave- morality gains the ascendancy, language shows a tendency to approximate the significations of the words "good" and "stupid."--A last fundamental difference: the desire for FREEDOM, the instinct for happiness and the refinements of the feeling of liberty belong as necessarily to slave-morals and morality, as artifice and enthusiasm in reverence and devotion are the regular symptoms of an aristocratic mode of thinking and estimating.-- Hence we can understand without further detail why love AS A PASSION--it is our European specialty--must absolutely be of noble origin; as is well known, its invention is due to the Provencal poet-cavaliers, those brilliant, ingenious men of the "gai saber," to whom Europe owes so much, and almost owes itself.

Vanity is one of the things which are perhaps most difficult for a noble man to understand: he will be tempted to deny it, where another kind of man thinks he sees it self-evidently. The problem for him is to represent to his mind beings who seek to arouse a good opinion of themselves which they themselves do not possess--and consequently also do not "deserve,"--and who yet BELIEVE in this good opinion afterwards. This seems to him on the one hand such bad taste and so self-disrespectful, and on the other hand so grotesquely unreasonable, that he would like to consider vanity an exception, and is doubtful about it in most cases when it is spoken of. He will say, for instance: "I may be mistaken about my value, and on the other hand may nevertheless demand that my value should be acknowledged by others precisely as I rate it:--that, however, is not vanity (but self-conceit, or, in most cases, that which is called 'humility,' and also 'modesty')." Or he will even say: "For many reasons I can delight in the good opinion of others, perhaps because I love and honour them, and rejoice in all their joys, perhaps also because their good opinion endorses and strengthens my belief in my own good opinion, perhaps because the good opinion of others, even in cases where I do not share it, is useful to me, or gives promise of usefulness:--all this, however, is not vanity." The man of noble character must first bring it home forcibly to his mind, especially with the aid of history, that, from time immemorial, in all social strata in any way dependent, the ordinary man WAS only that which he PASSED FOR:--not being at all accustomed to fix values, he did not assign even to himself any other value than that which his master assigned to him (it is the peculiar RIGHT OF MASTERS to create values). It may be looked upon as the result of an extraordinary atavism, that the ordinary man, even at present, is still always WAITING for an opinion about himself, and then instinctively submitting himself to it; yet by no means only to a "good" opinion, but also to a bad and unjust one (think, for instance, of the greater part of the self- appreciations and self-depreciations which believing women learn from their confessors, and which in general the believing Christian learns from his Church). In fact, conformably to the slow rise of the democratic social order (and its cause, the blending of the blood of masters and slaves), the originally noble and rare impulse of the masters to assign a value to themselves and to "think well" of themselves, will now be more and more encouraged and extended; but it has at all times an older, ampler, and more radically ingrained propensity opposed to it--and in the phenomenon of "vanity" this older propensity overmasters the younger. The vain person rejoices over EVERY good opinion which he hears about himself (quite apart from the point of view of its usefulness, and equally regardless of its truth or falsehood), just as he suffers from every bad opinion: for he subjects himself to both, he feels himself subjected to both, by that oldest instinct of subjection which breaks forth in him.--It is "the slave" in the vain man's blood, the remains of the slave's craftiness-- and how much of the "slave" is still left in woman, for instance!-- which seeks to SEDUCE to good opinions of itself; it is the slave, too, who immediately afterwards falls prostrate himself before these opinions, as though he had not called them forth.--And to repeat it again: vanity is an atavism.

A SPECIES originates, and a type becomes established and strong in the long struggle with essentially constant UNFAVOURABLE conditions. On the other hand, it is known by the experience of breeders that species which receive super-abundant nourishment, and in general a surplus of protection and care, immediately tend in the most marked way to develop variations, and are fertile in prodigies and monstrosities (also in monstrous vices). Now look at an aristocratic commonwealth, say an ancient Greek polis, or Venice, as a voluntary or involuntary contrivance for the purpose of REARING human beings; there are there men beside one another, thrown upon their own resources, who want to make their species prevail, chiefly because they MUST prevail, or else run the terrible danger of being exterminated. The favour, the super-abundance, the protection are there lacking under which variations are fostered; the species needs itself as species, as something which, precisely by virtue of its hardness, its uniformity, and simplicity of structure, can in general prevail and make itself permanent in constant struggle with its neighbours, or with rebellious or rebellion-threatening vassals. The most varied experience teaches it what are the qualities to which it principally owes the fact that it still exists, in spite of all Gods and men, and has hitherto been victorious: these qualities it calls virtues, and these virtues alone it develops to maturity. It does so with severity, indeed it desires severity; every aristocratic morality is intolerant in the education of youth, in the control of women, in the marriage customs, in the relations of old and young, in the penal laws (which have an eye only for the degenerating): it counts intolerance itself among the virtues, under the name of "justice." A type with few, but very marked features, a species of severe, warlike, wisely silent, reserved, and reticent men (and as such, with the most delicate sensibility for the charm and nuances of society) is thus established, unaffected by the vicissitudes of generations; the constant struggle with uniform UNFAVOURABLE conditions is, as already remarked, the cause of a type becoming stable and hard. Finally, however, a happy state of things results, the enormous tension is relaxed; there are perhaps no more enemies among the neighbouring peoples, and the means of life, even of the enjoyment of life, are present in superabundance. With one stroke the bond and constraint of the old discipline severs: it is no longer regarded as necessary, as a condition of existence--if it would continue, it can only do so as a form of LUXURY, as an archaizing TASTE. Variations, whether they be deviations (into the higher, finer, and rarer), or deteriorations and monstrosities, appear suddenly on the scene in the greatest exuberance and splendour; the individual dares to be individual and detach himself. At this turning-point of history there manifest themselves, side by side, and often mixed and entangled together, a magnificent, manifold, virgin-forest-like up-growth and up-striving, a kind of TROPICAL TEMPO in the rivalry of growth, and an extraordinary decay and self- destruction, owing to the savagely opposing and seemingly exploding egoisms, which strive with one another "for sun and light," and can no longer assign any limit, restraint, or forbearance for themselves by means of the hitherto existing morality. It was this morality itself which piled up the strength so enormously, which bent the bow in so threatening a manner:--it is now "out of date," it is getting "out of date." The dangerous and disquieting point has been reached when the greater, more manifold, more comprehensive life IS LIVED BEYOND the old morality; the "individual" stands out, and is obliged to have recourse to his own law-giving, his own arts and artifices for self-preservation, self-elevation, and self-deliverance. Nothing but new "Whys," nothing but new "Hows," no common formulas any longer, misunderstanding and disregard in league with each other, decay, deterioration, and the loftiest desires frightfully entangled, the genius of the race overflowing from all the cornucopias of good and bad, a portentous simultaneousness of Spring and Autumn, full of new charms and mysteries peculiar to the fresh, still inexhausted, still unwearied corruption. Danger is again present, the mother of morality, great danger; this time shifted into the individual, into the neighbour and friend, into the street, into their own child, into their own heart, into all the most personal and secret recesses of their desires and volitions. What will the moral philosophers who appear at this time have to preach? They discover, these sharp onlookers and loafers, that the end is quickly approaching, that everything around them decays and produces decay, that nothing will endure until the day after tomorrow, except one species of man, the incurably MEDIOCRE. The mediocre alone have a prospect of continuing and propagating themselves--they will be the men of the future, the sole survivors; "be like them! become mediocre!" is now the only morality which has still a significance, which still obtains a hearing.--But it is difficult to preach this morality of mediocrity! it can never avow what it is and what it desires! it has to talk of moderation and dignity and duty and brotherly love--it will have difficulty IN CONCEALING ITS IRONY!

There is an INSTINCT FOR RANK, which more than anything else is already the sign of a HIGH rank; there is a DELIGHT in the NUANCES of reverence which leads one to infer noble origin and habits. The refinement, goodness, and loftiness of a soul are put to a perilous test when something passes by that is of the highest rank, but is not yet protected by the awe of authority from obtrusive touches and incivilities: something that goes its way like a living touchstone, undistinguished, undiscovered, and tentative, perhaps voluntarily veiled and disguised. He whose task and practice it is to investigate souls, will avail himself of many varieties of this very art to determine the ultimate value of a soul, the unalterable, innate order of rank to which it belongs: he will test it by its INSTINCT FOR REVERENCE. DIFFERENCE ENGENDRE HAINE: the vulgarity of many a nature spurts up suddenly like dirty water, when any holy vessel, any jewel from closed shrines, any book bearing the marks of great destiny, is brought before it; while on the other hand, there is an involuntary silence, a hesitation of the eye, a cessation of all gestures, by which it is indicated that a soul FEELS the nearness of what is worthiest of respect. The way in which, on the whole, the reverence for the BIBLE has hitherto been maintained in Europe, is perhaps the best example of discipline and refinement of manners which Europe owes to Christianity: books of such profoundness and supreme significance require for their protection an external tyranny of authority, in order to acquire the PERIOD of thousands of years which is necessary to exhaust and unriddle them. Much has been achieved when the sentiment has been at last instilled into the masses (the shallow-pates and the boobies of every kind) that they are not allowed to touch everything, that there are holy experiences before which they must take off their shoes and keep away the unclean hand--it is almost their highest advance towards humanity. On the contrary, in the so-called cultured classes, the believers in "modern ideas," nothing is perhaps so repulsive as their lack of shame, the easy insolence of eye and hand with which they touch, taste, and finger everything; and it is possible that even yet there is more RELATIVE nobility of taste, and more tact for reverence among the people, among the lower classes of the people, especially among peasants, than among the newspaper-reading DEMIMONDE of intellect, the cultured class.

It cannot be effaced from a man's soul what his ancestors have preferably and most constantly done: whether they were perhaps diligent economizers attached to a desk and a cash-box, modest and citizen-like in their desires, modest also in their virtues; or whether they were accustomed to commanding from morning till night, fond of rude pleasures and probably of still ruder duties and responsibilities; or whether, finally, at one time or another, they have sacrificed old privileges of birth and possession, in order to live wholly for their faith--for their "God,"--as men of an inexorable and sensitive conscience, which blushes at every compromise. It is quite impossible for a man NOT to have the qualities and predilections of his parents and ancestors in his constitution, whatever appearances may suggest to the contrary. This is the problem of race. Granted that one knows something of the parents, it is admissible to draw a conclusion about the child: any kind of offensive incontinence, any kind of sordid envy, or of clumsy self-vaunting--the three things which together have constituted the genuine plebeian type in all times--such must pass over to the child, as surely as bad blood; and with the help of the best education and culture one will only succeed in DECEIVING with regard to such heredity.--And what else does education and culture try to do nowadays! In our very democratic, or rather, very plebeian age, "education" and "culture" MUST be essentially the art of deceiving-- deceiving with regard to origin, with regard to the inherited plebeianism in body and soul. An educator who nowadays preached truthfulness above everything else, and called out constantly to his pupils: "Be true! Be natural! Show yourselves as you are!"--even such a virtuous and sincere ass would learn in a short time to have recourse to the FURCA of Horace, NATURAM EXPELLERE: with what results? "Plebeianism" USQUE RECURRET. [FOOTNOTE: Horace's "Epistles," I. x. 24.]

At the risk of displeasing innocent ears, I submit that egoism belongs to the essence of a noble soul, I mean the unalterable belief that to a being such as "we," other beings must naturally be in subjection, and have to sacrifice themselves. The noble soul accepts the fact of his egoism without question, and also without consciousness of harshness, constraint, or arbitrariness therein, but rather as something that may have its basis in the primary law of things:--if he sought a designation for it he would say: "It is justice itself." He acknowledges under certain circumstances, which made him hesitate at first, that there are other equally privileged ones; as soon as he has settled this question of rank, he moves among those equals and equally privileged ones with the same assurance, as regards modesty and delicate respect, which he enjoys in intercourse with himself--in accordance with an innate heavenly mechanism which all the stars understand. It is an ADDITIONAL instance of his egoism, this artfulness and self-limitation in intercourse with his equals--every star is a similar egoist; he honours HIMSELF in them, and in the rights which he concedes to them, he has no doubt that the exchange of honours and rights, as the ESSENCE of all intercourse, belongs also to the natural condition of things. The noble soul gives as he takes, prompted by the passionate and sensitive instinct of requital, which is at the root of his nature. The notion of "favour" has, INTER PARES, neither significance nor good repute; there may be a sublime way of letting gifts as it were light upon one from above, and of drinking them thirstily like dew-drops; but for those arts and displays the noble soul has no aptitude. His egoism hinders him here: in general, he looks "aloft" unwillingly--he looks either FORWARD, horizontally and deliberately, or downwards--HE KNOWS THAT HE IS ON A HEIGHT.

"One can only truly esteem him who does not LOOK OUT FOR himself."--Goethe to Rath Schlosser.

The Chinese have a proverb which mothers even teach their children: "SIAO-SIN" ("MAKE THY HEART SMALL"). This is the essentially fundamental tendency in latter-day civilizations. I have no doubt that an ancient Greek, also, would first of all remark the self-dwarfing in us Europeans of today--in this respect alone we should immediately be "distasteful" to him.

What, after all, is ignobleness?--Words are vocal symbols for ideas; ideas, however, are more or less definite mental symbols for frequently returning and concurring sensations, for groups of sensations. It is not sufficient to use the same words in order to understand one another: we must also employ the same words for the same kind of internal experiences, we must in the end have experiences IN COMMON. On this account the people of one nation understand one another better than those belonging to different nations, even when they use the same language; or rather, when people have lived long together under similar conditions (of climate, soil, danger, requirement, toil) there ORIGINATES therefrom an entity that "understands itself"--namely, a nation. In all souls a like number of frequently recurring experiences have gained the upper hand over those occurring more rarely: about these matters people understand one another rapidly and always more rapidly--the history of language is the history of a process of abbreviation; on the basis of this quick comprehension people always unite closer and closer. The greater the danger, the greater is the need of agreeing quickly and readily about what is necessary; not to misunderstand one another in danger--that is what cannot at all be dispensed with in intercourse. Also in all loves and friendships one has the experience that nothing of the kind continues when the discovery has been made that in using the same words, one of the two parties has feelings, thoughts, intuitions, wishes, or fears different from those of the other. (The fear of the "eternal misunderstanding": that is the good genius which so often keeps persons of different sexes from too hasty attachments, to which sense and heart prompt them-- and NOT some Schopenhauerian "genius of the species"!) Whichever groups of sensations within a soul awaken most readily, begin to speak, and give the word of command--these decide as to the general order of rank of its values, and determine ultimately its list of desirable things. A man's estimates of value betray something of the STRUCTURE of his soul, and wherein it sees its conditions of life, its intrinsic needs. Supposing now that necessity has from all time drawn together only such men as could express similar requirements and similar experiences by similar symbols, it results on the whole that the easy COMMUNICABILITY of need, which implies ultimately the undergoing only of average and COMMON experiences, must have been the most potent of all the forces which have hitherto operated upon mankind. The more similar, the more ordinary people, have always had and are still having the advantage; the more select, more refined, more unique, and difficultly comprehensible, are liable to stand alone; they succumb to accidents in their isolation, and seldom propagate themselves. One must appeal to immense opposing forces, in order to thwart this natural, all-too-natural PROGRESSUS IN SIMILE, the evolution of man to the similar, the ordinary, the average, the gregarious --to the IGNOBLE!--

The more a psychologist--a born, an unavoidable psychologist and soul-diviner--turns his attention to the more select cases and individuals, the greater is his danger of being suffocated by sympathy: he NEEDS sternness and cheerfulness more than any other man. For the corruption, the ruination of higher men, of the more unusually constituted souls, is in fact, the rule: it is dreadful to have such a rule always before one's eyes. The manifold torment of the psychologist who has discovered this ruination, who discovers once, and then discovers ALMOST repeatedly throughout all history, this universal inner "desperateness" of higher men, this eternal "too late!" in every sense--may perhaps one day be the cause of his turning with bitterness against his own lot, and of his making an attempt at self-destruction-- of his "going to ruin" himself. One may perceive in almost every psychologist a tell-tale inclination for delightful intercourse with commonplace and well-ordered men; the fact is thereby disclosed that he always requires healing, that he needs a sort of flight and forgetfulness, away from what his insight and incisiveness--from what his "business"--has laid upon his conscience. The fear of his memory is peculiar to him. He is easily silenced by the judgment of others; he hears with unmoved countenance how people honour, admire, love, and glorify, where he has PERCEIVED--or he even conceals his silence by expressly assenting to some plausible opinion. Perhaps the paradox of his situation becomes so dreadful that, precisely where he has learnt GREAT SYMPATHY, together with great CONTEMPT, the multitude, the educated, and the visionaries, have on their part learnt great reverence--reverence for "great men" and marvelous animals, for the sake of whom one blesses and honours the fatherland, the earth, the dignity of mankind, and one's own self, to whom one points the young, and in view of whom one educates them. And who knows but in all great instances hitherto just the same happened: that the multitude worshipped a God, and that the "God" was only a poor sacrificial animal! SUCCESS has always been the greatest liar--and the "work" itself is a success; the great statesman, the conqueror, the discoverer, are disguised in their creations until they are unrecognizable; the "work" of the artist, of the philosopher, only invents him who has created it, is REPUTED to have created it; the "great men," as they are reverenced, are poor little fictions composed afterwards; in the world of historical values spurious coinage PREVAILS. Those great poets, for example, such as Byron, Musset, Poe, Leopardi, Kleist, Gogol (I do not venture to mention much greater names, but I have them in my mind), as they now appear, and were perhaps obliged to be: men of the moment, enthusiastic, sensuous, and childish, light- minded and impulsive in their trust and distrust; with souls in which usually some flaw has to be concealed; often taking revenge with their works for an internal defilement, often seeking forgetfulness in their soaring from a too true memory, often lost in the mud and almost in love with it, until they become like the Will-o'-the-Wisps around the swamps, and PRETEND TO BE stars- -the people then call them idealists,--often struggling with protracted disgust, with an ever-reappearing phantom of disbelief, which makes them cold, and obliges them to languish for GLORIA and devour "faith as it is" out of the hands of intoxicated adulators:--what a TORMENT these great artists are and the so-called higher men in general, to him who has once found them out! It is thus conceivable that it is just from woman--who is clairvoyant in the world of suffering, and also unfortunately eager to help and save to an extent far beyond her powers--that THEY have learnt so readily those outbreaks of boundless devoted SYMPATHY, which the multitude, above all the reverent multitude, do not understand, and overwhelm with prying and self-gratifying interpretations. This sympathizing invariably deceives itself as to its power; woman would like to believe that love can do EVERYTHING--it is the SUPERSTITION peculiar to her. Alas, he who knows the heart finds out how poor, helpless, pretentious, and blundering even the best and deepest love is--he finds that it rather DESTROYS than saves!--It is possible that under the holy fable and travesty of the life of Jesus there is hidden one of the most painful cases of the martyrdom of KNOWLEDGE ABOUT LOVE: the martyrdom of the most innocent and most craving heart, that never had enough of any human love, that DEMANDED love, that demanded inexorably and frantically to be loved and nothing else, with terrible outbursts against those who refused him their love; the story of a poor soul insatiated and insatiable in love, that had to invent hell to send thither those who WOULD NOT love him--and that at last, enlightened about human love, had to invent a God who is entire love, entire CAPACITY for love--who takes pity on human love, because it is so paltry, so ignorant! He who has such sentiments, he who has such KNOWLEDGE about love--SEEKS for death!--But why should one deal with such painful matters? Provided, of course, that one is not obliged to do so.

The intellectual haughtiness and loathing of every man who has suffered deeply--it almost determines the order of rank HOW deeply men can suffer--the chilling certainty, with which he is thoroughly imbued and coloured, that by virtue of his suffering he KNOWS MORE than the shrewdest and wisest can ever know, that he has been familiar with, and "at home" in, many distant, dreadful worlds of which "YOU know nothing"!--this silent intellectual haughtiness of the sufferer, this pride of the elect of knowledge, of the "initiated," of the almost sacrificed, finds all forms of disguise necessary to protect itself from contact with officious and sympathizing hands, and in general from all that is not its equal in suffering. Profound suffering makes noble: it separates.--One of the most refined forms of disguise is Epicurism, along with a certain ostentatious boldness of taste, which takes suffering lightly, and puts itself on the defensive against all that is sorrowful and profound. They are "gay men" who make use of gaiety, because they are misunderstood on account of it--they WISH to be misunderstood. There are "scientific minds" who make use of science, because it gives a gay appearance, and because scientificness leads to the conclusion that a person is superficial--they WISH to mislead to a false conclusion. There are free insolent minds which would fain conceal and deny that they are broken, proud, incurable hearts (the cynicism of Hamlet--the case of Galiani); and occasionally folly itself is the mask of an unfortunate OVER- ASSURED knowledge.--From which it follows that it is the part of a more refined humanity to have reverence "for the mask," and not to make use of psychology and curiosity in the wrong place.

That which separates two men most profoundly is a different sense and grade of purity. What does it matter about all their honesty and reciprocal usefulness, what does it matter about all their mutual good-will: the fact still remains--they "cannot smell each other!" The highest instinct for purity places him who is affected with it in the most extraordinary and dangerous isolation, as a saint: for it is just holiness--the highest spiritualization of the instinct in question. Any kind of cognizance of an indescribable excess in the joy of the bath, any kind of ardour or thirst which perpetually impels the soul out of night into the morning, and out of gloom, out of "affliction" into clearness, brightness, depth, and refinement:--just as much as such a tendency DISTINGUISHES--it is a noble tendency--it also SEPARATES.--The pity of the saint is pity for the FILTH of the human, all-too-human. And there are grades and heights where pity itself is regarded by him as impurity, as filth.

Signs of nobility: never to think of lowering our duties to the rank of duties for everybody; to be unwilling to renounce or to share our responsibilities; to count our prerogatives, and the exercise of them, among our DUTIES.

A man who strives after great things, looks upon every one whom he encounters on his way either as a means of advance, or a delay and hindrance--or as a temporary resting-place. His peculiar lofty BOUNTY to his fellow-men is only possible when he attains his elevation and dominates. Impatience, and the consciousness of being always condemned to comedy up to that time--for even strife is a comedy, and conceals the end, as every means does--spoil all intercourse for him; this kind of man is acquainted with solitude, and what is most poisonous in it.

THE PROBLEM OF THOSE WHO WAIT.--Happy chances are necessary, and many incalculable elements, in order that a higher man in whom the solution of a problem is dormant, may yet take action, or "break forth," as one might say--at the right moment. On an average it DOES NOT happen; and in all corners of the earth there are waiting ones sitting who hardly know to what extent they are waiting, and still less that they wait in vain. Occasionally, too, the waking call comes too late--the chance which gives "permission" to take action--when their best youth, and strength for action have been used up in sitting still; and how many a one, just as he "sprang up," has found with horror that his limbs are benumbed and his spirits are now too heavy! "It is too late," he has said to himself--and has become self-distrustful and henceforth for ever useless.--In the domain of genius, may not the "Raphael without hands" (taking the expression in its widest sense) perhaps not be the exception, but the rule?-- Perhaps genius is by no means so rare: but rather the five hundred HANDS which it requires in order to tyrannize over the χαιϱοζ, "the right time"--in order to take chance by the forelock!

He who does not WISH to see the height of a man, looks all the more sharply at what is low in him, and in the foreground-- and thereby betrays himself.

In all kinds of injury and loss the lower and coarser soul is better off than the nobler soul: the dangers of the latter must be greater, the probability that it will come to grief and perish is in fact immense, considering the multiplicity of the conditions of its existence.--In a lizard a finger grows again which has been lost; not so in man.--

It is too bad! Always the old story! When a man has finished building his house, he finds that he has learnt unawares something which he OUGHT absolutely to have known before he-- began to build. The eternal, fatal "Too late!" The melancholia of everything COMPLETED!--

Wanderer, who art thou? I see thee follow thy path without scorn, without love, with unfathomable eyes, wet and sad as a plummet which has returned to the light insatiated out of every depth--what did it seek down there?--with a bosom that never sighs, with lips that conceal their loathing, with a hand which only slowly grasps: who art thou? what hast thou done? Rest thee here: this place has hospitality for every one--refresh thyself! And whoever thou art, what is it that now pleases thee? What will serve to refresh thee? Only name it, whatever I have I offer thee! "To refresh me? To refresh me? Oh, thou prying one, what sayest thou! But give me, I pray thee---" What? what? Speak out! "Another mask! A second mask!"

Men of profound sadness betray themselves when they are happy: they have a mode of seizing upon happiness as though they would choke and strangle it, out of jealousy--ah, they know only too well that it will flee from them!

"Bad! Bad! What? Does he not--go back?" Yes! But you misunderstand him when you complain about it. He goes back like every one who is about to make a great spring.

"Will people believe it of me? But I insist that they believe it of me: I have always thought very unsatisfactorily of myself and about myself, only in very rare cases, only compulsorily, always without delight in 'the subject,' ready to digress from 'myself,' and always without faith in the result, owing to an unconquerable distrust of the POSSIBILITY of self- knowledge, which has led me so far as to feel a CONTRADICTIO IN ADJECTO even in the idea of 'direct knowledge' which theorists allow themselves:--this matter of fact is almost the most certain thing I know about myself. There must be a sort of repugnance in me to BELIEVE anything definite about myself.--Is there perhaps some enigma therein? Probably; but fortunately nothing for my own teeth.--Perhaps it betrays the species to which I belong?--but not to myself, as is sufficiently agreeable to me."

"But what has happened to you?"--"I do not know," he said, hesitatingly; "perhaps the Harpies have flown over my table."--It sometimes happens nowadays that a gentle, sober, retiring man becomes suddenly mad, breaks the plates, upsets the table, shrieks, raves, and shocks everybody--and finally withdraws, ashamed, and raging at himself--whither? for what purpose? To famish apart? To suffocate with his memories?--To him who has the desires of a lofty and dainty soul, and only seldom finds his table laid and his food prepared, the danger will always be great--nowadays, however, it is extraordinarily so. Thrown into the midst of a noisy and plebeian age, with which he does not like to eat out of the same dish, he may readily perish of hunger and thirst--or, should he nevertheless finally "fall to," of sudden nausea.--We have probably all sat at tables to which we did not belong; and precisely the most spiritual of us, who are most difficult to nourish, know the dangerous DYSPEPSIA which originates from a sudden insight and disillusionment about our food and our messmates--the AFTER-DINNER NAUSEA.

If one wishes to praise at all, it is a delicate and at the same time a noble self-control, to praise only where one DOES NOT agree-- otherwise in fact one would praise oneself, which is contrary to good taste:--a self-control, to be sure, which offers excellent opportunity and provocation to constant MISUNDERSTANDING. To be able to allow oneself this veritable luxury of taste and morality, one must not live among intellectual imbeciles, but rather among men whose misunderstandings and mistakes amuse by their refinement--or one will have to pay dearly for it!--"He praises me, THEREFORE he acknowledges me to be right"--this asinine method of inference spoils half of the life of us recluses, for it brings the asses into our neighbourhood and friendship.

To live in a vast and proud tranquility; always beyond . . . To have, or not to have, one's emotions, one's For and Against, according to choice; to lower oneself to them for hours; to SEAT oneself on them as upon horses, and often as upon asses:--for one must know how to make use of their stupidity as well as of their fire. To conserve one's three hundred foregrounds; also one's black spectacles: for there are circumstances when nobody must look into our eyes, still less into our "motives." And to choose for company that roguish and cheerful vice, politeness. And to remain master of one's four virtues, courage, insight, sympathy, and solitude. For solitude is a virtue with us, as a sublime bent and bias to purity, which divines that in the contact of man and man--"in society"--it must be unavoidably impure. All society makes one somehow, somewhere, or sometime--"commonplace."

The greatest events and thoughts--the greatest thoughts, however, are the greatest events--are longest in being comprehended: the generations which are contemporary with them do not

EXPERIENCE such events--they live past them. Something happens there as in the realm of stars. The light of the furthest stars is longest in reaching man; and before it has arrived man DENIES--that there are stars there. "How many centuries does a mind require to be understood?"--that is also a standard, one also makes a gradation of rank and an etiquette therewith, such as is necessary for mind and for star.

"Here is the prospect free, the mind exalted." [FOOTNOTE: Goethe's "Faust," Part II, Act V. The words of Dr. Marianus.]-- But there is a reverse kind of man, who is also upon a height, and has also a free prospect--but looks DOWNWARDS.

What is noble? What does the word "noble" still mean for us nowadays? How does the noble man betray himself, how is he recognized under this heavy overcast sky of the commencing plebeianism, by which everything is rendered opaque and leaden?-- It is not his actions which establish his claim--actions are always ambiguous, always inscrutable; neither is it his "works." One finds nowadays among artists and scholars plenty of those who betray by their works that a profound longing for nobleness impels them; but this very NEED of nobleness is radically different from the needs of the noble soul itself, and is in fact the eloquent and dangerous sign of the lack thereof. It is not the works, but the BELIEF which is here decisive and determines the order of rank--to employ once more an old religious formula with a new and deeper meaning--it is some fundamental certainty which a noble soul has about itself, something which is not to be sought, is not to be found, and perhaps, also, is not to be lost.--THE NOBLE SOUL HAS REVERENCE FOR ITSELF.--

There are men who are unavoidably intellectual, let them turn and twist themselves as they will, and hold their hands before their treacherous eyes--as though the hand were not a betrayer; it always comes out at last that they have something which they hide--namely, intellect. One of the subtlest means of deceiving, at least as long as possible, and of successfully representing oneself to be stupider than one really is--which in everyday life is often as desirable as an umbrella,--is called ENTHUSIASM, including what belongs to it, for instance, virtue. For as Galiani said, who was obliged to know it: VERTU EST ENTHOUSIASME.

In the writings of a recluse one always hears something of the echo of the wilderness, something of the murmuring tones and timid vigilance of solitude; in his strongest words, even in his cry itself, there sounds a new and more dangerous kind of silence, of concealment. He who has sat day and night, from year's end to year's end, alone with his soul in familiar discord and discourse, he who has become a cave-bear, or a treasure- seeker, or a treasure-guardian and dragon in his cave--it may be a labyrinth, but can also be a gold-mine--his ideas themselves eventually acquire a twilight-colour of their own, and an odour, as much of the depth as of the mould, something uncommunicative and repulsive, which blows chilly upon every passerby. The recluse does not believe that a philosopher--supposing that a philosopher has always in the first place been a recluse--ever expressed his actual and ultimate opinions in books: are not books written precisely to hide what is in us?--indeed, he will doubt whether a philosopher CAN have "ultimate and actual" opinions at all; whether behind every cave in him there is not, and must necessarily be, a still deeper cave: an ampler, stranger, richer world beyond the surface, an abyss behind every bottom, beneath every "foundation." Every philosophy is a foreground philosophy--this is a recluse's verdict: "There is something arbitrary in the fact that the PHILOSOPHER came to a stand here, took a retrospect, and looked around; that he HERE laid his spade aside and did not dig any deeper--there is also something suspicious in it." Every philosophy also CONCEALS a philosophy; every opinion is also a LURKING-PLACE, every word is also a MASK.

Every deep thinker is more afraid of being understood than of being misunderstood. The latter perhaps wounds his vanity; but the former wounds his heart, his sympathy, which always says: "Ah, why would you also have as hard a time of it as I have?"

Man, a COMPLEX, mendacious, artful, and inscrutable animal, uncanny to the other animals by his artifice and sagacity, rather than by his strength, has invented the good conscience in order finally to enjoy his soul as something SIMPLE; and the whole of morality is a long, audacious falsification, by virtue of which generally enjoyment at the sight of the soul becomes possible. From this point of view there is perhaps much more in the conception of "art" than is generally believed.

A philosopher: that is a man who constantly experiences, sees, hears, suspects, hopes, and dreams extraordinary things; who is struck by his own thoughts as if they came from the outside, from above and below, as a species of events and lightning-flashes PECULIAR TO HIM; who is perhaps himself a storm pregnant with new lightnings; a portentous man, around whom there is always rumbling and mumbling and gaping and something uncanny going on. A philosopher: alas, a being who often runs away from himself, is often afraid of himself--but whose curiosity always makes him "come to himself" again.

A man who says: "I like that, I take it for my own, and mean to guard and protect it from every one"; a man who can conduct a case, carry out a resolution, remain true to an opinion, keep hold of a woman, punish and overthrow insolence; a man who has his indignation and his sword, and to whom the weak, the suffering, the oppressed, and even the animals willingly submit and naturally belong; in short, a man who is a MASTER by nature-- when such a man has sympathy, well! THAT sympathy has value! But of what account is the sympathy of those who suffer! Or of those even who preach sympathy! There is nowadays, throughout almost the whole of Europe, a sickly irritability and sensitiveness towards pain, and also a repulsive irrestrainableness in complaining, an effeminizing, which, with the aid of religion and philosophical nonsense, seeks to deck itself out as something superior--there is a regular cult of suffering. The UNMANLINESS of that which is called "sympathy" by such groups of visionaries, is always, I believe, the first thing that strikes the eye.-- One must resolutely and radically taboo this latest form of bad taste; and finally I wish people to put the good amulet, "GAI SABER" ("gay science," in ordinary language), on heart and neck, as a protection against it.

THE OLYMPIAN VICE.--Despite the philosopher who, as a genuine Englishman, tried to bring laughter into bad repute in all thinking minds--"Laughing is a bad infirmity of human nature, which every thinking mind will strive to overcome" (Hobbes),--I would even allow myself to rank philosophers according to the quality of their laughing--up to those who are capable of GOLDEN laughter. And supposing that Gods also philosophize, which I am strongly inclined to believe, owing to many reasons--I have no doubt that they also know how to laugh thereby in an overman-like and new fashion--and at the expense of all serious things! Gods are fond of ridicule: it seems that they cannot refrain from laughter even in holy matters.

The genius of the heart, as that great mysterious one possesses it, the tempter-god and born rat-catcher of consciences, whose voice can descend into the nether-world of every soul, who neither speaks a word nor casts a glance in which there may not be some motive or touch of allurement, to whose perfection it pertains that he knows how to appear,--not as he is, but in a guise which acts as an ADDITIONAL constraint on his followers to press ever closer to him, to follow him more cordially and thoroughly;--the genius of the heart, which imposes silence and attention on everything loud and self-conceited, which smoothes rough souls and makes them taste a new longing--to lie placid as a mirror, that the deep heavens may be reflected in them;--the genius of the heart, which teaches the clumsy and too hasty hand to hesitate, and to grasp more delicately; which scents the hidden and forgotten treasure, the drop of goodness and sweet spirituality under thick dark ice, and is a divining- rod for every grain of gold, long buried and imprisoned in mud and sand; the genius of the heart, from contact with which every one goes away richer; not favoured or surprised, not as though gratified and oppressed by the good things of others; but richer in himself, newer than before, broken up, blown upon, and sounded by a thawing wind; more uncertain, perhaps, more delicate, more fragile, more bruised, but full of hopes which as yet lack names, full of a new will and current, full of a new ill-will and counter-current . . . but what am I doing, my friends? Of whom am I talking to you? Have I forgotten myself so far that I have not even told you his name? Unless it be that you have already divined of your own accord who this questionable God and spirit is, that wishes to be PRAISED in such a manner? For, as it happens to every one who from childhood onward has always been on his legs, and in foreign lands, I have also encountered on my path many strange and dangerous spirits; above all, however, and again and again, the one of whom I have just spoken: in fact, no less a personage than the God DIONYSUS, the great equivocator and tempter, to whom, as you know, I once offered in all secrecy and reverence my first-fruits--the last, as it seems to me, who has offered a SACRIFICE to him, for I have found no one who could understand what I was then doing. In the meantime, however, I have learned much, far too much, about the philosophy of this God, and, as I said, from mouth to mouth--I, the last disciple and initiate of the God Dionysus: and perhaps I might at last begin to give you, my friends, as far as I am allowed, a little taste of this philosophy? In a hushed voice, as is but seemly: for it has to do with much that is secret, new, strange, wonderful, and uncanny. The very fact that Dionysus is a philosopher, and that therefore Gods also philosophize, seems to me a novelty which is not unensnaring, and might perhaps arouse suspicion precisely among philosophers;-- among you, my friends, there is less to be said against it, except that it comes too late and not at the right time; for, as it has been disclosed to me, you are loth nowadays to believe in God and gods. It may happen, too, that in the frankness of my story I must go further than is agreeable to the strict usages of your ears? Certainly the God in question went further, very much further, in such dialogues, and was always many paces ahead of me . . . Indeed, if it were allowed, I should have to give him, according to human usage, fine ceremonious tides of lustre and merit, I should have to extol his courage as investigator and discoverer, his fearless honesty, truthfulness, and love of wisdom. But such a God does not know what to do with all that respectable trumpery and pomp. "Keep that," he would say, "for thyself and those like thee, and whoever else require it! I--have no reason to cover my nakedness!" One suspects that this kind of divinity and philosopher perhaps lacks shame?--He once said: "Under certain circumstances I love mankind"--and referred thereby to Ariadne, who was present; "in my opinion man is an agreeable, brave, inventive animal, that has not his equal upon earth, he makes his way even through all labyrinths. I like man, and often think how I can still further advance him, and make him stronger, more evil, and more profound."--"Stronger, more evil, and more profound?" I asked in horror. "Yes," he said again, "stronger, more evil, and more profound; also more beautiful"--and thereby the tempter-god smiled with his halcyon smile, as though he had just paid some charming compliment. One here sees at once that it is not only shame that this divinity lacks;--and in general there are good grounds for supposing that in some things the Gods could all of them come to us men for instruction. We men are--more human.--

Alas! what are you, after all, my written and painted thoughts! Not long ago you were so variegated, young and malicious, so full of thorns and secret spices, that you made me sneeze and laugh--and now? You have already doffed your novelty, and some of you, I fear, are ready to become truths, so immortal do they look, so pathetically honest, so tedious! And was it ever otherwise? What then do we write and paint, we mandarins with Chinese brush, we immortalisers of things which LEND themselves to writing, what are we alone capable of painting? Alas, only that which is just about to fade and begins to lose its odour! Alas, only exhausted and departing storms and belated yellow sentiments! Alas, only birds strayed and fatigued by flight, which now let themselves be captured with the hand--with OUR hand! We immortalize what cannot live and fly much longer, things only which are exhausted and mellow! And it is only for your AFTERNOON, you, my written and painted thoughts, for which alone I have colours, many colours, perhaps, many variegated softenings, and fifty yellows and browns and greens and reds;-- but nobody will divine thereby how ye looked in your morning, you sudden sparks and marvels of my solitude, you, my old, beloved-- EVIL thoughts!

Aftersong - 'From the Heights'

MIDDAY of Life! Oh, season of delight!
My summer's park!
Uneaseful joy to look, to lurk, to hark–
I peer for friends, am ready day and night,–
Where linger ye, my friends? The time is right!
Is not the glacier's grey today for you
Rose-garlanded?
The brooklet seeks you, wind, cloud, with longing thread
And thrust themselves yet higher to the blue,
To spy for you from farthest eagle's view
My table was spread out for you on high–
Who dwelleth so
Star-near, so near the grisly pit below?–
My realm–what realm hath wider boundary?
My honey–who hath sipped its fragrancy?
Friends, ye are there! Woe me,–yet I am not
He whom ye seek?
Ye stare and stop–better your wrath could speak!
I am not I? Hand, gait, face, changed? And what
I am, to you my friends, now am I not?
Am I an other? Strange am I to Me?
Yet from Me sprung?
A wrestler, by himself too oft self-wrung?
Hindering too oft my own self's potency,
Wounded and hampered by self-victory?
I sought where-so the wind blows keenest. There
I learned to dwell

Where no man dwells, on lonesome ice-lorn fell,
And unlearned Man and God and curse and prayer?
Became a ghost haunting the glaciers bare?
Ye, my old friends! Look! Ye turn pale, filled o'er
With love and fear!
Go! Yet not in wrath. Ye could ne'er live here.
Here in the farthest realm of ice and scaur,
A huntsman must one be, like chamois soar.
An evil huntsman was I? See how taut
My bow was bent!
Strongest was he by whom such bolt were sent—
Woe now! That arrow is with peril fraught,
Perilous as none.—Have yon safe home ye sought!
Ye go! Thou didst endure enough, oh, heart;—
Strong was thy hope;
Unto new friends thy portals widely ope,
Let old ones be. Bid memory depart!
Wast thou young then, now—better young thou art!
What linked us once together, one hope's tie—
(Who now doth con
Those lines, now fading, Love once wrote thereon?)—
Is like a parchment, which the hand is shy
To touch—like crackling leaves, all seared, all dry.
Oh! Friends no more! They are—what name for those?—
Friends' phantom-flight
Knocking at my heart's window-pane at night,
Gazing on me, that speaks "We were" and goes,—
Oh, withered words, once fragrant as the rose!
Pinings of youth that might not understand!
For which I pined,
Which I deemed changed with me, kin of my kind:
But they grew old, and thus were doomed and banned:
None but new kith are native of my land!
Midday of life! My second youth's delight!
My summer's park!

Unrestful joy to long, to lurk, to hark!
I peer for friends!—am ready day and night,
For my new friends. Come! Come! The time is right!
This song is done,—the sweet sad cry of rue
Sang out its end;
A wizard wrought it, he the timely friend,
The midday-friend,—no, do not ask me who;
At midday 'twas, when one became as two.
We keep our Feast of Feasts, sure of our bourne,
Our aims self-same:
The Guest of Guests, friend Zarathustra, came!
The world now laughs, the grisly veil was torn,
And Light and Dark were one that wedding-morn.

Twilight of the Idols

Friedrich Nietzsche

Prologue

To stay cheerful while dealing with a grim and extremely serious task is no small artistic skill. Yet, what could be more essential than cheerfulness? Nothing is ever truly successful unless vibrant energy has helped create it. Only extra strength proves real power. A rethinking of all values—a question so dark and massive that it even casts a shadow over the one who raises it—is a task so heavy with consequence that anyone who takes it on must occasionally step into the sunlight to shake off a seriousness that becomes overwhelming, unbearably so. This goal justifies any method, and every event along the way becomes an unexpected benefit. Above all, war. War has always been the ultimate strategy for those who have delved too deeply into their own thoughts or grown too profound; a wound provokes the strength to heal.

For many years, I've lived by a saying, though I'll keep its origin a secret from curious scholars: "The spirit grows, virtue flourishes through a wound."

At other times, another way to recover, one I prefer even more, is to question idols. There are more idols than truths in the world, and this is why I have such a "sharp eye" for this world. It is also why I have such a "sharp ear." To ask questions of these idols with a hammer, and maybe hear that familiar hollow sound that comes from something empty—what joy this brings to someone who listens carefully, even with a mind attuned to what isn't spoken. For an old psychologist and Pied Piper like me, even the things that wish to remain silent cannot help but reveal themselves.

This book, as its title suggests, is mainly a kind of relaxation, a flash of light, a playful escape for a psychologist in his free time. But could it also be a new kind of battle? Are we once again questioning new idols? This small work is a bold declaration of war. As for questioning idols, this time, it isn't just the idols of the present day but the eternal ones that are struck with a hammer, as though they were tuning forks.

These idols are certainly the oldest, the most self-assured, and the most puffed-up. None are more hollow. Yet this doesn't change the fact that they are believed in more than any others. They are never even called idols—at least, not the most revered ones among them.

Chapter 1
Maxims – And Missiles

Idleness is the root of all psychology. What? Does that mean psychology is a kind of vice? Even the bravest among us rarely has the courage to face what they truly know. Aristotle said that to live alone, a person must be either an animal or a god. But there's a third option missing: one must be both—a philosopher.

"All truth is simple."—Isn't that a double lie? Sometimes, I choose to remain blind to certain things. Wisdom places limits even on knowledge. A person recovers best from their extraordinary nature—from their intellect—by letting their instincts take over for a while.

So which is it? Is humanity just a mistake made by God? Or is God simply a mistake made by humanity?

From life's school of war: That which doesn't kill me makes me stronger.

Help yourself, and others will help you too. This is the true meaning of loving your neighbor.

A person should never be ashamed of their actions. Once a deed is done, they shouldn't disown it. Feelings of guilt are indecent.

Can a donkey be tragic? To be crushed under a burden it can neither carry nor throw off—isn't this the fate of a philosopher?

If someone knows why they exist, they can figure out how to live. Happiness isn't the goal of life; only the English make that their aim.

Man created woman—out of what? Out of a rib taken from his god, from his "ideal."

What are you searching for? Do you wish to multiply yourself tenfold, a hundredfold? Are you seeking followers? Look for zeros, not people!

Those of us who belong to the future, like myself, are harder to understand than those who mirror their time, but we're treated with more respect. Simply put: we are never fully understood— that's why we have authority.

On women: "Truth? Oh, you don't understand truth! Isn't it an insult to all our sense of modesty?"

There is an artist after my own heart, humble in his needs. He only desires two things: his bread and his art—panem et Circem.

Those who cannot impose their will onto the world at least give it some meaning. They believe there's already a will within it. (This is the essence of faith.)

What? You chose virtue and a heart full of passion, yet you still glance enviously at the rewards of the shameless? But by choosing virtue, you've renounced all "advantages"... (this belongs nailed to the door of an anti-Semite).

The perfect woman writes literature as if it were a minor vice, a passing experiment, all the while looking around to see if anyone is noticing—and hoping that someone does.

One should only choose situations where fake virtues are unnecessary, where, like a tightrope walker on their rope, one must either fall, stand firm, or find a way out.

"Evil men have no songs."—How, then, do the Russians have songs?

"German intellect"—for eighteen years this phrase has been a contradiction in terms.

When a man tries to find the origins of everything, he becomes like a crab. The historian always looks backward; eventually, he even starts believing backward.

Feeling content keeps a person from catching a cold. Has a woman who knew she was well-dressed ever gotten sick?—No, not even if she was barely covered by rags.

I distrust anyone who builds elaborate systems and avoid them. The desire to create a system shows a lack of honesty.

Man thinks women are profound—why? Because he can never fully understand them. Women are not even shallow.

When a woman has masculine virtues, she can make you want to run away.

When she doesn't have any masculine virtues, she runs away herself.

"How often conscience used to sting in the past! It must have had strong teeth back then! But today, what's gone wrong?"—A question for the dentist.

Mistakes made in haste rarely come alone. The first time, a person always overdoes things. Because of that, they make a second mistake, where they end up doing too little.

When a worm is stepped on, it curls up. This shows its caution—it lowers the chances of being stepped on again. In moral terms, this is called humility.

There is a kind of hatred for lies and deceit that comes from a sharp sense of humor. There is also the same hatred, but born from cowardice—the fear of lying because it's forbidden by divine law. Too cowardly to lie...

What tiny things bring happiness! The sound of bagpipes. Life without music would be a mistake. The German even imagines God as a singer.

"One can only think and write while sitting" (G. Flaubert). Now I've got you, you nihilist! Living a sedentary life is the true sin against the Holy Spirit. Only the thoughts that come to you while walking have any real worth.

Sometimes, we psychologists are like restless horses, growing uneasy as we see our own shadow rise and fall before us. A psychologist must look away from himself if he wants to see anything clearly.

Do we immoralists harm virtue in any way? No more than anarchists harm royalty. In fact, only after being shot at have princes returned to their thrones with greater strength. The moral of the story: morality must be tested by attack.

Are you rushing ahead?—Are you doing so as a leader or as an exception? Or perhaps you're just running away?... This is the first question of conscience.

Are you authentic, or are you just acting? Are you the real thing or merely a representative of it? Or, worse, are you just a copy of an actor?... This is the second question of conscience.

The disappointed man says: "I searched for great men, but all I found were imitators of their ideals."

Are you someone who observes from the sidelines, or someone who lends a hand? Or are you someone who looks away or even turns their back? This is the third question of conscience.

Do you want to follow, lead, or walk your own path alone? A person must know what they desire—and that they truly desire something. This is the fourth question of conscience.

They were merely rungs on my ladder, steps I used to climb higher. For that purpose, I had to move past them. But they thought I wanted to stop and rest on them.

Does it matter whether others agree that I'm right? I am far too right. And the one who laughs best today will also laugh last.

The formula for my happiness: a Yes, a No, a straight path, and a goal.

Chapter 2
The Problem of Socrates

Throughout history, the wisest minds have always agreed on one thing: life is not good. No matter the time or place, their words have been the same— filled with doubt, sadness, weariness, and even hostility toward life. Even Socrates, in his final moments, said: "To live is to be sick for a long time. I owe a cock to the god Æsculapius." Even Socrates had had enough of life. But what does that mean? What does it suggest? In the past, people would have said—and it was said loudly, especially by the Pessimists—"Surely there must be some truth in this! The agreement of the wisest proves it." Should we say the same thing today? Can we?

Instead, we now respond: "Surely there must be some sickness here." These so-called great thinkers of every age need to be examined more closely! Could it be that they all shared something physically or mentally fragile, something decadent? Is it possible that wisdom comes to earth like a crow drawn to the faint smell of decay?

This bold and disrespectful thought—that these great thinkers were actually signs of decline—first came to me in connection with a case where both scholarly and common opinions stood firmly against my own view. I came to see Socrates and Plato as symptoms of a culture in collapse, as tools of the disintegration of Greece, as fake Greeks, even anti-Greek (this was my argument in The Birth of Tragedy, 1872). The agreement of these sages— the consensus sapientium, as I increasingly realized—was not evidence that they were right about life. Instead, it suggested that they all shared some underlying physical or mental weakness that made them take the same negative stance toward life. Their judgments about life, whether positive or negative, are not true in themselves. Their value lies only in what they reveal about their creators. Such judgments are symptoms, and nothing more. In themselves, these opinions about life are meaningless.

You must grasp this critical idea: the value of life cannot be measured. A living person cannot judge it because they are too involved—they are part of the conflict, not a neutral observer. A dead person cannot judge it either, for obvious reasons. For a philosopher to see life's value as a problem suggests something is flawed in their perspective. It raises a question about their wisdom—or even their lack of wisdom.

Could it be that all these so-called great thinkers were not only signs of decline but also not wise at all? Let us now return to the case of Socrates.

Judging by his origins, Socrates came from the lowest social class—Socrates was part of the common mob. You know, and can still observe in the descriptions of him, how remarkably ugly he was. In Greek society, where beauty was highly valued, ugliness was not only an objection but often taken as evidence of deeper flaws. Was Socrates truly Greek? Ugliness often reflects a thwarted or disrupted development, or perhaps one stunted by mixed influences. In other cases, it signals a degenerative decline. Anthropologists who study criminals say that the typical criminal is often ugly: monstrum in fronte, monstrum in animo—a monster in appearance, a monster in spirit. Does that mean the criminal is a degenerate? Was Socrates, then, a typical criminal?

This idea wouldn't conflict with the infamous judgment made about Socrates by a physiognomist, which deeply upset his friends. While passing through Athens, a foreigner skilled in reading faces told Socrates directly that he was a monster and that his body harbored every kind of vice and passion. Socrates simply replied: "You know me, sir!"

Not only do Socrates' wild and chaotic instincts point to degeneracy, but so do his extreme reliance on logic and the peculiar malice that seemed tied to his disfigured features. We must also not forget his auditory hallucinations, which he religiously interpreted as "the demon of Socrates." Everything about him was excessive, exaggerated, almost comical—a caricature. His nature was also secretive, filled with hidden motives and underlying currents. I attempt to understand the strange personality behind the Socratic equation: Reason = Virtue = Happiness. This is perhaps the strangest formula ever devised, and it fundamentally contradicted the instincts of the earlier Greeks.

With Socrates, Greek taste shifted toward dialectics. What happened as a result? First, the refined and noble taste of earlier Greek culture was overthrown. Dialectics allowed the common crowd to rise to prominence. Before Socrates, the art of argument was avoided in polite society; it was considered improper and even disgraceful. Young men were warned against indulging in it. Arguing and constantly explaining oneself were seen as suspicious behaviors. Honest people, like honest things, don't need to constantly justify themselves. It was considered poor form to put everything on display. Anything that required proof was seen as having little inherent value.

In societies where authority was respected, where people gave commands rather than explanations, the dialectician was viewed as a kind of jester. People laughed at him and didn't take him seriously. Yet Socrates, a master of dialectics, managed to make people take him seriously. How did this happen? What was going on?

A person resorts to dialectics only when they have no other options available. People know that using it creates suspicion and that it's not particularly persuasive. Nothing is more easily overturned than the effect of a dialectical argument—this is clear from the experience of any debate or discussion. Dialectics can only be a last resort, the weapon of someone who has no other tools left. One must be desperate to demand their rights this way; otherwise, they wouldn't need to rely on it. This is why the Jews became skilled in dialectics. Reynard the Fox was a dialectician. But what about Socrates—was he one too?

Is Socratic irony a form of rebellion, a weapon of resentment from the common people? Did Socrates, oppressed and suffering, enjoy his inherent cruelty by inflicting sharp attacks through his arguments? Was he taking revenge on the noblemen he managed to charm? As a dialectician, a person wields a ruthless weapon; they can dominate and even humiliate their opponents. By defeating someone in debate, the dialectician undermines them; their victory is always a compromise. The dialectician forces their opponent to prove they're not a fool, which often provokes anger and renders them defenseless. A dialectician paralyzes their opponent's thinking. Could dialectics, for Socrates, have been a form of revenge?

I have explained why Socrates could repel people; now it's just as important to understand why he was so captivating. One reason is that he invented a new kind of Agon, a competitive struggle, becoming the first master of verbal combat in Athens' elite circles. He charmed others by appealing to the Greek love of competition—he transformed intellectual debate into a new kind of contest between men and youths. Socrates also had an intense and magnetic personality, one deeply rooted in eroticism.

But Socrates saw even further. He understood his noble Athenian peers better than they understood themselves. He recognized that his situation—his unusual inner conflict—was not unique. The same kind of decline was quietly spreading everywhere: ancient Athens was dying. Socrates realized that the entire world needed him—his method, his remedy, and his unique technique for self-discipline and survival. Everywhere, instincts were in chaos; everywhere, people were teetering on the edge of excess. The monstrum in animo—the monster within—had become a widespread threat. "Instincts must be tamed," he thought. "We need to find a counterforce, a ruler stronger than they are."

When the physiognomist unmasked Socrates, calling him a volcano of evil desires, Socrates, the great Master of Irony, uttered a few revealing words that explain his nature. "That is true," he admitted, "but I overcame them all."

How did Socrates manage to master himself? His case was, at its core, simply the most extreme and visible example of a widespread crisis. It was a time when no one could control themselves, and instincts constantly clashed with one another. As the clearest example of this disorder, Socrates fascinated people. His shocking ugliness made him impossible to ignore, and his ability to present himself as a solution—a cure for this state— made him even more compelling.

When a man feels compelled, as Socrates did, to turn reason into a tyrant, it is a clear sign that something else is attempting to seize control. In Socrates' case, reason was seen as a savior. Neither Socrates nor his followers had the freedom to choose whether to be rational—they had no choice. At that time, being rational was mandatory, a last resort. The intensity with which all of Greek thought embraced reason reveals the severity of their situation: humanity was at a critical crossroads. The options were stark— either perish or cling desperately to excessive rationality.

The moral focus of Greek philosophy from Plato onward, and its reverence for dialectics, stemmed from a pathological state. The equation Reason =

Virtue = Happiness essentially meant: we must follow Socrates' example and constantly confront our dark passions with the light of reason. We must prioritize cleverness, precision, and clarity above all else. To yield to instinct or the unconscious was seen as a descent into chaos.

I have now explained why Socrates was so captivating: he appeared as a healer, a savior. But should we examine the flaws in his faith in "reason at any cost"? It was an illusion, a self- deception among philosophers and moralists, to believe they could free themselves from decline simply by fighting against it. This approach cannot lead to liberation. The tools they used, the path they chose as a solution, were themselves symptoms of the very degeneration they sought to overcome. They only altered the form of the problem—they did not eliminate it. Socrates was a misunderstanding. The entire morality of "improvement," including that of Christianity, was also a misunderstanding.

The brightest light of reason—this insistence on clarity, coldness, caution, and conscious control—opposed to instinct and detached from it, was itself a disease, simply a different kind of sickness. It was not a path back to "virtue," "health," or "happiness." To be forced to fight against one's instincts is the very definition of degeneration. As long as life is ascending, happiness is synonymous with instinct.

Did Socrates, the most intelligent of self-deceivers, understand this? Did he admit it to himself at the end, in his brave acceptance of death? Socrates wanted to die. It wasn't Athens that gave him the hemlock—it was his own hand. He pushed Athens to hand him the poisoned cup. "Socrates is not a doctor," he may have whispered to himself. "Only death can heal this. Socrates himself has simply been sick for a very long time."

Chapter 3
"Reason" In Philosophy

You ask me what defines the peculiarities of philosophers? For example, their lack of a sense of history, their disdain for the idea of change, and their obsession with preserving things like the ancient Egyptians did. They believe they honor something by removing it from its history, placing it "under the aspect of eternity"—essentially turning it into a mummy. For thousands of years, philosophers have dealt with mummified ideas; nothing alive has ever emerged from their work. These worshippers of concepts kill and preserve things when they idolize them—they endanger the life of everything they claim to revere. To them, death, change, aging, and even growth and creation are flaws, even arguments against life itself. What is, they claim, cannot change; and what changes, they insist, is not real.

All philosophers believe—desperately—in the idea of Being. But because they cannot grasp it, they search for reasons why this understanding is denied to them. "There must be some illusion, some trick, preventing us from knowing the true nature of Being," they say. "Where is this deceiver?" Then, triumphantly, they declare: "We've found it—it's sensuality!" The senses, they argue, are immoral in other ways and deceive us about the true world. The moral they draw is this: we must rid ourselves of the illusion brought by the senses, of change, of history, of lies. For them, history is nothing but belief in the senses, belief in falsehood. Their conclusion: we must reject everything the senses tell us. We must reject humanity and everything connected to it. Let us become philosophers—mummies, believers in monotony, grave-diggers! Above all, they cry, let us cast aside the body, this miserable obsession of the senses. The body, they claim, is infected with every flaw of logic and is neither real nor possible, even though it has the audacity to pretend otherwise.

With great respect, I make an exception for Heraclitus. While other philosophers dismissed the senses because they revealed variety and change, Heraclitus dismissed them because they seemed to show permanence and unity. Yet even Heraclitus was unfair to the senses. The senses do not lie, as the Eleatics thought, nor as Heraclitus believed. They don't lie at all. It is our interpretation of what the senses reveal that introduces falsehood—the lies of unity, matter, substance, and permanence. Reason is the source of these distortions. As long as the senses show us a world of change and impermanence, they are truthful. Heraclitus was entirely correct, however, in saying that the idea of Being is an empty illusion. The "apparent" world is the only world that exists; the so-called "true world" is nothing but a false add-on to it.

What delicate instruments our senses are! Take the human nose, for example—no philosopher has ever spoken of it with the reverence and gratitude it deserves. Yet, for now, it is the most finely tuned instrument we have. It can detect even the tiniest changes in motion, subtleties that even a spectroscope cannot measure. Our scientific achievements today reach as far as we have trusted our senses, sharpened them, enhanced them, and followed their evidence to its limits. What lies beyond that is incomplete and not yet science—it is metaphysics, theology, psychology, epistemology, or abstract systems like logic and mathematics. In all of these fields, reality is not even considered, not even as a problem, just as the broader value of these symbolic conventions like logic is not questioned.

Another strange trait of philosophers is just as dangerous. They confuse the last things with the first. They take what appears last—unfortunately, as it often shouldn't appear at all—"the highest concept," the most general, emptiest, and vaguest shadow of reality, and place it at the beginning, treating it as the origin. This, too, reflects their habit of reverence: the highest thing must not have arisen from anything lower, it must not have grown or developed at all. Their moral: anything of the highest rank must be causa sui—its own cause. If something derives from something else, it loses value and becomes suspect.

All the so-called higher values—like Being, the Absolute, Goodness, Truth, and Perfection—are assumed to be of the highest rank. They cannot have evolved; they must be self- caused. Moreover, these concepts must be alike, never in conflict with one another. And so they arrive at their grand concept of "God," the final, most diluted, and emptiest thing, which they declare to be the first cause, the ens r ealissimum, the ultimate reality. Imagine humanity taking the mental cobwebs spun by these diseased minds seriously! And yet, humanity has paid a high price for doing so.

Let us contrast this with how we approach the problem of error and deception in things (and notice, I politely say "we"). In the past, people saw change and evolution as proof that the world was deceptive, that something was leading us astray. Today, however, we understand that the real source of error lies in our rational thinking. Whenever we insist on unity, identity, permanence, substance, cause, materiality, or Being, we are driven into error— despite knowing from careful study that the error lies here.

This is similar to how people once believed their eyes deceived them about the sun's motion. In this case, it isn't our eyes but our language that keeps reinforcing these mistaken concepts. Language was developed in a time when human psychology was still very primitive. If we look at the origins of language metaphysics—that is, reasoning itself—we find it rooted in a kind of fetishism. Language imposes the idea of a doer behind every deed; it assumes that willpower is a cause and that the self, the "ego," is a kind of Being or substance. This faith in the ego as a substance is then projected onto the world, creating the concept of "things." From the ego alone comes the idea of Being.

At the root of all this is a grave mistake: the belief that the will is something active, a force. Now we know it's just a word. Much later, in a far more enlightened world, philosophers marveled at how certain and reliable these categories of reason seemed. They concluded that these concepts could not have come from experience since experience actually contradicts them. Where, then, do they come from? In both India and Greece, people made the same mistake: "We must have lived in a higher world once," they thought, "because we possess reason!" But the truth is, we came from a much simpler and less developed state.

Nothing has been more convincing than the error of Being, as first proposed by the Eleatics. Their concept of Being is supported by every word and sentence we speak! Even those who opposed the Eleatics fell into the trap of their idea, such as Democritus with his theory of the atom. "Reason" in language—what an old and cunning deceiver it is! I suspect we will never rid ourselves of the idea of God as long as we believe in grammar.

To make this important and novel perspective clear, I will summarize it in four points to simplify understanding and encourage discussion.

Proposition One. The arguments claiming this world is only "apparent" actually support its reality. No other kind of reality can be proven.

Proposition Two. The qualities people attribute to the "true Being" of things are actually qualities of nonexistence. The "true world" was constructed by denying the real world, and it is indeed an illusion—a moral and optical trick.

Proposition Three. Imagining another world makes no sense unless there is a deep, instinctual urge to slander, diminish, and distrust this life. In that case, this imaginary "better" world is just an act of revenge against the life we live.

Proposition Four. Dividing the world into a "true" and "apparent" world, whether in Christianity or Kant's philosophy (which is essentially Christianity in disguise), is a sign of decline and a symptom of decaying life. The fact that an artist values appearances more than reality does not contradict this. For the artist, "appearance" is reality, but in a refined, intensified, and improved form. The tragic artist is not a pessimist—they affirm even the most troubling and terrifying aspects of life. They are Dionysian.

Chapter 4
How The "True World"
Ultimately Became a Fable the History of An
Error

The true world is reachable by the wise, the virtuous, and the devout. They live in it—they are it.

(This earliest version of the idea was relatively simple, clever, and convincing. It was essentially a rewording of "I, Plato, am the truth.")

The true world, though unattainable for now, is promised to the wise, the virtuous, and the devout—especially to the sinner who repents.

(The idea evolves: it becomes subtler, more deceptive, more elusive. It takes on a new form—it becomes feminine, it becomes Christian.)

The true world is beyond reach. It cannot be proven or promised, but merely thinking about it provides comfort, obligation, and direction.

(This is essentially the same old sun, but seen through a haze of doubt and skepticism. The idea becomes lofty, pale, northern—Königsbergian.)

The true world—is it unattainable? In any case, it is unattained. And because it is unattained, it is also unknown. As something unknown, it can no longer comfort, save, or command. How could the unknown demand anything of us?

(The first light of dawn. Reason begins to stir and stretch. The cockcrow of positivism.)

The "true world"—an idea that no longer has any use, that no longer demands anything—a pointless, unnecessary idea, now discarded: let us get rid of it!

(The brightness of morning; breakfast; the return of common sense and joy.

Plato blushes in shame, and all free spirits celebrate wildly.)

We have abolished the true world. What remains? The apparent world, perhaps? Certainly not! By getting rid of the true world, we have also done away with the world of appearances!

(Noon; the time of the shortest shadows; the end of the longest mistake; the height of humanity. Thus Spoke Zarathustra begins.)

Chapter 5
Morality as The Enemy of Nature

There is a time when all passions are destructive, dragging people down with their reckless force. But there comes a much later time when passions merge with the spirit and refine themselves—they become "spiritualized." In the past, because of the inherent foolishness of passion, people waged war against it. They committed themselves to eradicating it. All ancient moralists agreed on this point: "Il faut tuer les passions"—passions must be killed. The most famous version of this idea is found in the New Testament, in the Sermon on the Mount, where, let's be clear, things are hardly viewed from an elevated perspective. It says there, for example, about sexuality: "If your eye offends you, pluck it out." Thankfully, no Christian truly follows this advice.

Destroying passions and desires simply because of their foolishness or to avoid the unpleasant outcomes of their excess now seems to us like an even greater form of foolishness. We no longer admire dentists who pull teeth just so they won't ache again. On the other hand, it's fair to say that the soil from which Christianity grew could never have allowed for the idea of "spiritualizing passion" to take root. Everyone knows the early Church waged war on intelligence in favor of the "poor in spirit." Under those conditions, how could passions have been fought intelligently? The Church combats passion through methods of removal and suppression. Its solution, its "remedy," is castration. It never asks, "How can desire be refined, elevated, or even sanctified?"

Throughout history, the Church's discipline has always focused on eradicating passions entirely—on destroying sensuality, pride, the thirst for power, the desire for wealth, and even the urge for revenge. But attacking passions at their roots is the same as attacking life at its source. The Church's approach is fundamentally hostile to life itself.

The same methods—castration and eradication—are instinctively chosen to battle passions by those who are too weak-willed or degenerate to impose some form of moderation. These are the kinds of people who, metaphorically (or even literally), need La Trappe or some extreme declaration of war against their desires, a vast gulf separating them from temptation. Only degenerates need such drastic methods. A weak will—or, more precisely, an inability to resist reacting to stimuli—is itself a form of degeneration.

A radical and absolute hatred of sensuality is always a suspicious sign. It gives good reason to doubt the overall health of the person who takes such an extreme stance. Moreover, this hatred reaches its peak only when such people no longer have the strength of character to commit to the ultimate remedy—to renounce their inner "Satan."

Consider the history of priests, philosophers, and even artists. The most venomous attacks on the senses have not come from those who are impotent or naturally ascetic, but from those who found it necessary to become ascetics. These were people whose inner struggles forced them into extreme positions, and their attacks on sensuality reflect their personal battles more than any genuine wisdom.

The spiritualization of sensuality is called love: this represents a great victory over Christianity. Another triumph is the spiritualization of hostility. This means we are beginning to deeply understand the value of having enemies. In short, we now act and think in the exact opposite way from how we once did. Throughout history, the Church sought to destroy its enemies. But we, the immoralists and Antichrists, see an advantage in the Church's survival. Even in politics, hostility has become more refined—more cautious, thoughtful, and restrained. Nearly every political party now sees its self-interest in ensuring its opposition doesn't collapse. The same is true in global politics.

A new creation—such as the new Empire—needs enemies more than friends. It only becomes necessary as a contrast to what opposes it; it defines itself through opposition. We approach our inner conflicts in much the same way. Here too, we have spiritualized enmity and come to understand its value. A person is productive only when they are rich in opposing instincts; they stay youthful only so long as their soul resists comfort and rejects the yearning for peace.

The "peace of the soul," which Christianity holds as its highest goal, has become entirely foreign to us. Nothing could make us less envious than the moral complacency and contentment of a clean conscience—the happiness of a "moral cow." A man who renounces conflict also renounces a life of grandeur.

Of course, in many cases, what people call "peace of the soul" is really something else, disguised and unable to name itself honestly. Let me, without hesitation or bias, suggest a few examples.

"Peace of the soul" could be the radiant glow of abundant animal energy within the realm of morality or religion. Or it might be the first sign of fatigue, the shadow cast by the evening, as all evenings cast shadows. Or it could be a signal of humid air and southern winds on the horizon. Perhaps it is an unconscious gratitude for good digestion, sometimes mistaken for "brotherly love." It could also be the calmness of someone recovering from illness, savoring every flavor of life anew and waiting patiently. Or it might follow the satisfaction of a powerful passion, the comfort of an unfamiliar fullness.

"Peace of the soul" might be the weariness of our will, desires, and vices as they grow old. Or it could be laziness, dressed up by vanity in the clothes of morality. Sometimes, it's the relief that follows the end of long periods of uncertainty, even if that end is marked by terrible certainty. It might also be the expression of mastery during a creative effort, the deep, steady breathing of someone who has achieved true freedom of will.

Who knows? Perhaps even The Twilight of the Idols is nothing more than a form of "peace of the soul."

Let me lay down a principle: all natural morality—that is, every healthy morality—is guided by the instinct for life. It fulfills one of life's fundamental laws by creating definite rules like "you shall" or "you shall not," and in doing so, it clears obstacles from the path of life. In contrast, morality that opposes nature—which describes almost every morality that has been taught, praised, and preached so far—is aimed directly against life's instincts. It secretly or openly condemns these very instincts. When it says, "God sees into the heart of man," it denies the deepest and most vital desires of life, turning God into life's enemy. The saint, whom God supposedly favors, is nothing more than an ideal eunuch. Life ends where the "Kingdom of God" begins.

If you understand the wickedness of this rebellion against life, which Christian morality has made almost sacred, you also see its emptiness, its falseness, and its absurdity. For any condemnation of life by a living being is merely a symptom of a specific kind of life. The question of whether such a condemnation is right or wrong doesn't even arise. To even approach the question of life's value, one would need to be outside life itself and yet know it as completely as everyone who has ever lived. This makes the question entirely inaccessible to us.

When we speak of values, we do so under the influence and perspective of life itself. Life urges us to create values; life evaluates through us. This means that even morality that opposes life—one that sees God as the rejection and condemnation of life—is still an evaluation of life. But what kind of life does it reflect? I have already answered: it is the perspective of declining, weakened, exhausted, and doomed life. Morality, as it has been understood up to now—as Schopenhauer put it in his idea of

"The Denial of the Will to Life"—is the instinct of degeneration turned into a command. It says, "Perish!" It is the death sentence pronounced by those already marked for death.

Now, consider how absurdly simple it is for someone to say, "Man should be like this or that!" Reality shows us a wondrous abundance of types, an endless variety of forms and transformations. Yet the first petty moralist who comes along declares, "No! Man should be different!" This self-righteous fool even imagines he knows what man should be like. He draws his own face on the wall and proclaims: "Behold the man!"

Even when the moralist addresses an individual and says, "You should be this way or that way!" he still makes a fool of himself. The individual, with their past and future, is part of fate—a law, a necessity added to the universe. To say to someone, "Change yourself," is the same as demanding that the entire world change, even retroactively. These moralists have been consistent in their madness—they wanted man to be different, to be virtuous, to reflect their own image. In doing so, they denied the world itself. This is no small form of insanity! Nor is it a humble kind of arrogance!

Morality, when it condemns for the sake of condemnation itself—without any regard for life's goals, needs, or motives—is a specific kind of error. It is a degenerative quirk that has caused immeasurable harm, and no one should feel pity for it. We, the immoralists, on the other hand, have opened our hearts to understanding, acceptance, and affirmation. We do not reject life lightly; instead, we take pride in saying "yes" to things.

Our vision has widened to include the economy of life—a system that knows how to use even what priests and moralists reject. It finds value even in what the sanctimonious or the sickly-minded condemn. It turns the so-called repulsive elements—priests, bigots, and the "virtuous"—to its own advantage. What is that advantage? We, the immoralists, are the living answer to that question.

Chapter 6
The Four Great Errors

The error of confusing cause and effect—there is no more dangerous mistake than mistaking the effect for the cause.

I call this mistake the fundamental perversion of reason. Yet, this error has been one of humanity's oldest habits, and one that persists even today. In some parts of the world, it has even been elevated to sacred status, taking the form of "religion" and "morality." Every principle put forth by religion and morality is built upon this very error. Priests and moral lawgivers have been the most enthusiastic promoters of this distortion of reason.

Take, for example, the famous book by Cornaro, in which he promotes a strict, modest diet as the key to a long, happy, and virtuous life. This book, widely read and still reprinted in large numbers, has likely caused more harm and shortened more lives than almost any other well-intentioned work—except, of course, the Bible. Why? Because it confuses cause and effect. Cornaro believed his longevity was caused by his restricted diet. However, the truth is that his unique physiology, marked by an unusually slow rate of molecular change and low energy expenditure, was the actual cause of his meager diet. His constitution didn't allow him to eat much—if he had eaten more, he would have fallen ill.

For most people, especially those with a different metabolism, such a diet would be disastrous. A modern scholar, for example, whose nervous energy is rapidly consumed, would waste away on Cornaro's diet. Crede exper to— trust someone who knows from experience.

The same confusion of cause and effect lies at the heart of every religion and morality. Their central message is always: "Do this and avoid that, and you will be happy. Otherwise—" This "otherwise" is an unspoken threat. Every moral or religious imperative repeats this same formula. I call this the original sin of reason—immortal unreason.

But in my hands, this principle is turned on its head. This is the first example of my "transvaluation of all values." A well-constituted person, one who is a masterpiece of nature, instinctively performs certain actions and avoids others. Such a person embodies the natural order and harmony their body expresses. Their virtue is not a cause but an effect of their excellent constitution. Their longevity and ability to have many children are not rewards for their virtue; rather, these qualities result from their robust and healthy nature. This is the true basis of what I call Cornarism.

In contrast, the Church and traditional morality assert, "A race or a people perishes because of vice and luxury." My reinstated reason says the opposite: when a people are already in decline, when they are physically degenerating, vice and luxury naturally emerge. These are not the causes of their downfall but symptoms of their exhaustion. Their declining energy leads them to crave stronger and more frequent stimuli, which is typical of all weakened natures.

Consider a young man who becomes pale and sickly. His friends may blame an illness, but I say the illness itself is merely a symptom of his already weakened state, the result of hereditary exhaustion. Similarly, when a political party makes a fatal mistake, the common view is that the mistake leads to its demise. But my superior understanding of politics says: a party capable of making such errors is already in its death throes. It has lost its instinctual certainty.

Every error, in any context, is the consequence of a degeneration of instincts and a disintegration of the will. This is the essence of what we call "evil." Everything truly valuable arises from instinct and is therefore effortless, necessary, and free. Strain and effort are objections to value. The divine is characterized not by struggle but by lightness—the god has light feet, unlike the hero who battles against obstacles.

The error of false causality also runs deep. Throughout history, humans have believed they understood causality. But where did this belief come from? What gave us such confidence in causality? It came from what we call the "inner facts of consciousness." Yet not one of these so-called facts has ever been proven.

We assumed we were the causes of our own actions, that our will was an undeniable proof of causality. We believed that all the motives for our actions could be found in our consciousness, as if they were sitting there waiting to be uncovered. Without these motives, we thought, we wouldn't be free or responsible. Finally, we believed that thoughts themselves were caused by the ego, the "self."

But now, we have come to our senses. Today, we know none of this is true. The "inner world" is a collection of illusions. The will doesn't cause anything; it doesn't explain anything. It merely accompanies processes and sometimes isn't even present. What we call "motive" is another falsehood, a surface ripple that often conceals the deeper causes of action rather than revealing them. As for the ego, it is now nothing more than a myth, a fiction, an empty word.

What's the result of all this? There are no such things as spiritual causes. The entire foundation of popular experience—our belief that the world is built on causes and effects, wills and spirits—has collapsed. Humanity blissfully projected its own inner illusions onto the world, turning it into a vast system of agents and actions. Man imagined his ego as the root of all things and built the concept of "Being" upon this illusion.

Even the concept of the atom, cherished by physicists, still carries remnants of this old psychological error. And the metaphysicians' notion of the "thing-in- itself" is the ultimate example of this confusion—a disgraceful relic of primitive thinking.

The greatest error of all has been to regard the spirit as a cause, to mistake it for reality, and to use it as a measure of the real. This error was even elevated to the status of a deity—it was called God.

The Error of Imaginary Causes

Starting in the realm of dreams, we often ascribe causes to sensations after the fact. Take, for instance, the sound of a distant cannon shot in a dream. We frequently weave a story around such sensations, turning them into little dramas where we ourselves are the central figures. The sensation lingers, echoing and intensifying, until our instinct for causality demands an explanation. But instead of recognizing the sensation as random, we interpret it as something meaningful—a direct result of a fabricated cause. In dreams, this often leads to a reversal of the natural order of events: the sensation, which should be the starting point, is made the result of the imagined cause. The cannon shot is explained as though it were caused by events that supposedly happened earlier in the dream.

What occurs here? Ideas associated with a particular sensory state are misinterpreted as the cause of that state. This same process happens when we are awake. Many of our general sensations— like tension, pressure, obstacles, or explosions in the interplay of our bodily systems, particularly in the sympathetic nervous system— trigger the instinct to search for a cause. We need an explanation for why we feel good or bad, ill or well. It is not enough for us to simply recognize that we feel a certain way. We only become fully conscious of the feeling when we have assigned it a cause.

Memory plays a key role in this process, unconsciously recalling past states that were similar, along with the causal interpretations we previously attached to them. However, memory rarely retrieves the actual causes. Instead, it presents familiar interpretations. The belief that our thoughts or conscious processes are the causes of these sensations stems from the way memory works. This mechanism leads us to accept a fixed interpretation of causes, one that often hinders or entirely blocks us from investigating the real causes of our sensations.

The Psychological Explanation

Why do we trace the unfamiliar back to the familiar? Because doing so brings relief, comfort, and a sense of control. The unfamiliar provokes fear, anxiety, and unease. Our most basic instinct is to eliminate these uncomfortable feelings. Thus, our first principle becomes: any explanation is better than none at all. Since our goal is simply to free ourselves from troubling ideas, we are not overly picky about the explanations we adopt. The first explanation that makes the unfamiliar seem familiar gives us such comfort that we readily accept it as true.

This process relies on the "proof" of happiness or relief to determine truth. In this way, the instinct for causality is closely tied to feelings of fear and the need to alleviate it. Whenever possible, the question "why?" doesn't just seek any cause but rather a particular kind of cause—one that comforts, liberates, and reassures us.

The easiest way to achieve this is by attributing causes to something we already know, something familiar and stored in memory. The new, unfamiliar factor is excluded from consideration as a possible cause. We prefer explanations that remove the sensation of strangeness, novelty, or unpredictability. Over time, a particular way of explaining causes becomes dominant, solidifies into a system, and eventually crowds out alternative explanations.

For example, a banker instinctively attributes everything to business, a Christian sees sin behind every event, and a young woman interprets everything through the lens of her love life.

The Domain of Morality and Religion as Imaginary Causes

The entire realm of morality and religion can be categorized under the heading of "imaginary causes." Consider how unpleasant sensations are explained in these frameworks. Such sensations are often attributed to malevolent external forces, like evil spirits. For example, the hysteria of women in the past was frequently interpreted as possession by witches. Similarly, feelings of guilt or sinfulness are seen as evidence of moral failings, yet they are often just symptoms of physiological imbalances. People have always found reasons to be dissatisfied with themselves, projecting these feelings onto moral or religious explanations.

Religions often go further, interpreting unpleasant sensations as punishment for wrongdoing, as if suffering proves guilt or sinfulness. Schopenhauer took this idea to its extreme, claiming that all great suffering reveals what we deserve, as it could not happen without a reason rooted in guilt. In this way, morality and religion turn life's natural challenges into accusations and condemnations.

Even physiological conditions like exhaustion or illness are interpreted through this lens. The passions and bodily senses are blamed as causes, and their effects are deemed deserved punishments for indulging in sinful behavior. This moralization of suffering twists natural occurrences into a system of guilt and penalty.

Similarly, pleasant sensations are explained through imaginary causes. They are attributed to faith, good deeds, or divine favor. A "good conscience," for instance, may simply be the result of good digestion, yet it is often interpreted as a reward for moral virtue. Even successful outcomes of endeavors are misattributed; a hypochondriac or someone like Pascal, for example, would not feel general happiness simply because of a fortunate result.

Religious virtues like faith, love, and hope are also misinterpretations. The feelings of strength and abundance that underpin these states are mistaken for their causes. A person trusts in God because they feel strong and peaceful, not the other way around.

Morality and Religion as Psychology of Error

At their core, morality and religion belong to the psychology of error. They consistently confuse cause and effect. They mistake feelings of pleasure or pain for their supposed causes and interpret them through a lens of moral or religious belief. They turn subjective states of consciousness into explanations, obscuring the true causes behind these sensations.

In every case, morality and religion invert the relationship between cause and effect, making them systems of misinterpretation. Truth is conflated with the effects of what is believed to be true, and the underlying processes that produce sensations are hidden behind a false dialect of moral and religious explanations. These systems are not rooted in reality but are deeply embedded in the errors of human psychology.

The Error of Free Will

Today, we have no patience for the concept of "free will." We know too well what it really is: the most audacious theological trick ever devised to make humanity "responsible" in a theological sense—that is, to make humanity dependent on theologians. Let me explain the psychology behind how this sense of responsibility is instilled.

Whenever people assign responsibility to someone, it is driven by the instinct for punishment and judgment. The innocence of Becoming—the natural unfolding of events—is destroyed the moment any state of affairs is attributed to a will, intentions, or deliberate actions. The doctrine of the will was invented primarily as a tool for punishment, specifically to assign guilt.

The entire foundation of ancient psychology, or the psychology of the will, arose because its creators—the priests who ruled early societies—sought to justify their power to punish. They wanted to grant themselves, or their gods, the right to judge and condemn. To make this possible, humanity had to be considered "free," so that individuals could be judged and held guilty. Consequently, every action was framed as voluntary, and the origin of every action was imagined to lie in conscious choice. This fraud became the foundation of psychology: the deliberate falsification of human nature to serve the interests of power and control.

Now, we are moving in the opposite direction. We immoralists are working tirelessly to eliminate the concepts of guilt and punishment from the world. We aim to cleanse psychology, history, nature, and all social customs and institutions of these poisonous ideas. Our most determined adversaries in this effort are the theologians, who still cling to the notion of a "moral order of things." They continue to pollute the innocence of Becoming with the concepts of punishment and guilt. Christianity, in this regard, is nothing more than the metaphysics of the executioner.

What, then, can our teaching be? It is this: No one gives a person their qualities—not God, not society, not parents, not ancestors, and certainly not the person themselves. This nonsensical notion, which has been perpetuated for centuries, was called "intelligible freedom" by Kant and perhaps even earlier by Plato. But it is utterly refuted here.

No one is responsible for their existence, for being the way they are, or for the circumstances in which they find themselves. A person's existence is inextricably linked to the entire chain of events that has been and will be. It is not the product of an intention, a will, or an aim. There is no striving for some "ideal man," "ideal happiness," or "ideal morality." To think otherwise is absurd.

The concept of "purpose" is something we invented—it does not exist in reality. There is no purpose driving existence. Each individual is a necessary part of the whole, a fragment of fate, inseparably bound to the totality of existence. No one can judge, measure, or condemn an individual's existence because to do so would mean judging, measuring, and condemning the entirety of existence. But there is nothing outside the whole to serve as a basis for such judgment.

The liberation we offer is this: no one can be made responsible. Existence cannot be traced to a causa prima—a first cause. The world is not an entity driven by a central consciousness, a divine spirit, or a purpose. This realization restores the innocence of Becoming. It frees the world from the burden of guilt and condemnation.

The concept of "God" has been the greatest obstacle to accepting existence as it is. For centuries, God has been used to justify the idea of ultimate responsibility, judgment, and guilt. But we deny God. We deny responsibility in God. Only by doing so can we truly save the world. This denial restores the innocence of existence and frees us from the chains of metaphysical guilt. This is the great liberation.

Chapter 7
The "Improvers" Of Mankind

You are familiar with my demand upon philosophers: that they rise above the notions of Good and Evil, leaving behind the illusion of moral judgment. This demand arises from a perspective I was the first to articulate—that there are no moral facts. Moral judgment, like religious judgment, believes in unrealities, in things that do not exist. Morality is merely an interpretation of certain phenomena—or, more accurately, a misinterpretation.

Moral judgment belongs to a stage of ignorance, a time when the very idea of reality, the distinction between what is real and imagined, had not yet emerged. At this stage, "truth" was applied to a multitude of things we now consider imaginary. For this reason, moral judgment should never be taken literally. On its own, it is nonsense. However, as a system of signs, it is invaluable to those who understand it. It offers insight into the cultural and psychological conditions of societies that lacked the knowledge to understand themselves. Morality, in essence, is a kind of language, a symptomatology. To make use of it, one must already grasp what it signifies.

Let me offer a preliminary example. Throughout history, certain individuals have sought to "improve" humanity—a goal that has always been closely tied to morality. But beneath this single word, vastly different tendencies are concealed. The "improvement" of humanity has sometimes meant the taming of the wild animal in man, while at other times it has meant the cultivation of a specific type of human being. These two approaches are fundamentally distinct, though both are described as moral.

Take the taming of an animal as an example. To call this process an "improvement" seems almost laughable to modern ears. Anyone who has observed a menagerie knows that animals are not improved there—they are weakened. Their natural power and danger are subdued through fear, pain, and deprivation, transforming them into sick, broken creatures. The same holds true for humanity under the influence of the priestly "improvers."

Consider the Middle Ages, when the Church acted as a menagerie for humanity. The Church hunted down the most vital and noble individuals—the "blond beasts," such as the Germans—and set about "improving" them. But what did this "improved" person look like after the process? He became a shadow of himself, a distorted caricature of humanity. Lured into monasteries, stripped of his instincts, and imprisoned behind oppressive concepts of sin and guilt, he was rendered sick and wretched, filled with self- hatred and suspicion of all that is strong and joyful in life. In short, he became a Christian.

From a physiological standpoint, this "improvement" was no different than what one does to an animal: weakening it by making it sick. The Church understood this strategy well. It ruined man, drained his strength, and then claimed to have made him better.

Now, let us consider a very different example of morality: the deliberate cultivation of a particular type of humanity. The most striking example of this is found in Indian morality as laid out in the Law of Manu. This text describes the structured breeding of four distinct castes: priests, warriors, merchants and farmers, and finally servants (the Sudras). Here, we are no longer dealing with the taming of wild animals. To conceive of such a system presupposes a level of mildness and rationality far beyond that of the lion-tamer.

Emerging from the Christian atmosphere of prisons and hospitals, one can breathe more freely in the world of Manu. Here, the goal is not to break humanity but to cultivate it. The vision is vast, orderly, and noble. By comparison, the New Testament reeks of pettiness and decay. Yet even this grand system had to confront challenges, particularly from those who did not fit into its carefully crafted structure—the "non-caste" people, the Chandala.

For the Chandala, the morality of Manu was as harsh as the Church's morality was to the strong. Unable to assimilate these "mixed" people into the system, Indian morality sought to render them weak and harmless by making them sick. This was a struggle against the sheer numbers of the Chandala, whose very existence threatened the structure of the caste system.

Some of the measures taken against the Chandala are repugnant to modern sensibilities. For instance, the Avadana- Sastra decrees that their diet should consist solely of garlic and onions; they were forbidden access to grains, clean water, or fire. Their drinking water had to be drawn from ditches and animal tracks, and they were prohibited from washing themselves or their clothing. Chandala women were barred from assisting one another during childbirth, and Sudra women were forbidden from helping them as well.

Such sanitary regulations had predictable results: deadly epidemics and venereal diseases ravaged the Chandala population. In response, the Law of the K nife—circumcision for males and genital mutilation for females—was introduced. Manu himself described the Chandala as the offspring of adultery, incest, and crime. Their clothing was to be made from rags taken from corpses, their utensils from broken pottery, and their jewelry from old iron. They were to worship malevolent spirits, wander endlessly, and were even forbidden to write using their right hand or in the direction reserved for virtuous people.

This is the logical outcome of a morality focused on breeding: the deliberate dehumanization of those who threaten the system. The Chandala were treated as the living embodiment of chaos, their suffering justified as the necessary cost of order.

The stark contrast between these two examples—the Christian taming of man and the Indian cultivation of castes—reveals the true diversity hidden within the concept of morality. While both systems aimed to "improve" humanity, their methods and goals were fundamentally different. The Christian moralist sought to weaken and break the strong, while the Indian lawgiver aimed to build a structured and lasting society. Yet both relied on the same principle: to make the undesirable elements weak and subservient, even at the cost of their health and humanity.

These regulations are profoundly revealing: they offer a glimpse into the primal and unfiltered humanity of the Aryans. From them, we see that the concept of "pure blood" is far from innocent—it carries with it a profound and often ruthless seriousness. At the same time, these regulations help us identify the people in whom a deep-seated hatred of this Aryan humanity—the Chandala hatred—has been immortalized. Among these people, this hatred was transformed into both religion and genius.

From this perspective, the gospels are invaluable historical documents, and the Book of Enoch is even more significant. Christianity, having sprung from Jewish roots and comprehensible only in the context of this heritage, represents the exact opposite of the morality of breeding, race, and privilege. Christianity is, at its core, an anti-Aryan religion. It is the transvaluation of all Aryan values— a complete reversal. It is the triumph of Chandala values, the gospel of the poor, the lowly, and the oppressed.

Christianity embodies the general uprising of the downtrodden— the miserable, the failed, and the broken—against the concept of "race." It is the eternal revenge of the Chandala, disguised as the "religion of love."

When comparing the morality of breeding to the morality of taming, we see that the methods employed by each are equally ruthless. Both rely on a deep commitment to immorality in order to enforce their respective visions of morality. One could even propose a principle: to create morality, one must possess an absolute will to immorality.

This paradoxical principle forms the basis of a profound and perplexing problem that I have studied for years: the psychology of those who claim to "improve" humanity. This problem first presented itself to me in the form of a seemingly trivial yet deeply significant phenomenon known as the pia fraus— the "pious fraud." This concept, the shared legacy of all philosophers and priests who have sought to improve mankind, opened the door to my exploration of this issue.

Figures like Manu, Plato, Confucius, and the teachers of Judaism and Christianity have all relied on the pia fraus. None of them ever doubted their right to deceive. Moreover, they never questioned their right to many other tools of manipulation and control.

To summarize this idea in a formula: every method ever used to make humanity "moral" has been, at its core, thoroughly immoral.

Chapter 8
Things the Germans Lack

Among Germans today, it is not enough to simply possess intellect; one must actively claim it, assert it, even lay hold of it.

Perhaps I know the Germans well enough to tell them a few uncomfortable truths. Modern Germany possesses a vast reserve of inherited and cultivated abilities, so vast that it could afford to spend this accumulated wealth liberally for some time. However, what has emerged in modern Germany is not a superior culture, nor refined taste, nor noble instincts for beauty. Instead, it is a set of virtues— admirable, yes, but also heavily pragmatic—more robust and "manly" than those of other European nations.

Germany still demonstrates a remarkable level of good spirits and self- respect, along with strength in human relationships and a reliable sense of mutual obligations. There is an abundance of industriousness and perseverance, paired with an inherited sobriety that seems to require stimulation rather than restraint. It is worth noting that Germans still know how to obey without feeling that obedience diminishes them, and they maintain respect for their opponents rather than despising them.

You can see that I wish to be fair to the Germans; it is my intention not to betray my commitment to balance, even when critiquing them. But fairness requires me to voice my objections as well. Achieving a position of power comes at a cost, for power inevitably stultifies.

Once upon a time, the Germans were known as a nation of thinkers. But do they truly think anymore? Today, Germans seem bored by intellect, mistrustful of it. Politics has consumed the seriousness once reserved for intellectual pursuits. The rallying cry, "Ger many, Ger many above all," seems to have delivered a fatal blow to German philosophy. Abroad, people ask me, "Are there still German philosophers? Are there still German poets? Are there any good German books?" I feel ashamed, though I muster the courage to answer, even in my moments of despair, "Yes, Bismarck!"

But could I dare to reveal what books are actually being read in Germany today? The curse of mediocrity dominates.

What could German intellect have become? Who has not lamented this question! For nearly a thousand years, this nation has deliberately dulled its own edge. Nowhere else have Europe's two great narcotics—alcohol and Christianity—been so excessively and destructively consumed as in Germany. To these, a third opiate has been added, one that could alone have sufficed to extinguish the spark of intellectual daring: music. German music—ponderous, bloated, and stifling—has completed the paralysis of German thought. How much sluggishness, heaviness, dampness, lethargy, and beer-fueled languor are entangled in German intellect!

How can it be that young men who dedicate their lives to intellectual pursuits lack the most basic instinct for intellectual self-preservation and drink beer? The alcoholism of academic youth doesn't prevent them from becoming scholars—after all, one can be a great scholar without being truly intelligent. But in every other respect, this is a disaster. What kind of intellectual softness, what kind of dull degeneration, comes from beer?

I once pointed out an infamous example of this kind of intellectual degeneration: the decline of David Strauss, once a leading German free spirit, who devolved into the author of a pedestrian gospel and a "New Faith." His intellect succumbed not just to mediocrity but to the very spirit he himself had celebrated—"the dear old brown liquor," to which he remained faithful to the end.

This kind of degeneration—soft, indulgent, and self-defeating— offers a troubling reflection of the broader intellectual culture in Germany, one that undermines the potential for brilliance with a relentless embrace of comfort, conformity, and the narcotics of religion, alcohol, and art.

I have spoken about the state of German intellect, noting that it has become coarser and shallower. But is that enough? In truth, what concerns me far more is the steady and alarming decline of German seriousness, depth, and passion in intellectual matters. It is not just intellect that has diminished; even the emotional force— what we might call the pathos—behind intellectual pursuits has been transformed.

When I occasionally encounter German universities, I am struck by the atmosphere that prevails there. What barrenness! What smug, tepid intellectuality! These institutions have grown content with mediocrity, and the once-earnest German intellectual spirit now feels lukewarm, drained of vitality.

Some might point to German science as a counterargument to my observations. Such a claim would only prove they have misunderstood me and failed to grasp even a single page of my writings. For seventeen years, I have devoted myself to exposing the dehumanizing and de-intellectualizing effects of modern scientific pursuits. The rigid, mechanical labor demanded by the vast scope of modern sciences has left individuals shackled, unable to cultivate the fuller, richer, and deeper natures that once thrived in intellectual endeavors.

Our age suffers from an overabundance of shallow dilettantes and fragmented personalities—half-formed individuals who flit aimlessly through life. The universities, though unintentionally, have become factories for producing this kind of intellectual decay, training people whose instincts for genuine intellectuality have withered. And this problem is not confined to Germany. All of Europe is beginning to recognize this trend. Large-scale politics, the realm in which Germany has invested so much, fools no one. Germany is becoming, ever more clearly, the flatland of Europe, a place devoid of the peaks of culture and thought.

I am still searching for a German with whom I could engage in the kind of seriousness that defines my way of thinking. And even more elusive is a German with whom I could share genuine cheerfulness. The Twilight of the Idols— what man today could grasp the kind of seriousness from which a philosopher recovers in such a work? Of all things, our cheerfulness is the most misunderstood.

Now let us shift our focus slightly. It is not just that German culture is visibly in decline; there are also clear reasons behind this fall. No one, whether an individual or a nation, can expend more energy than they possess. If your resources of reason, seriousness, will, and self-discipline are poured entirely into pursuits such as political power, economics, large-scale commerce, parliamentary systems, or military ambitions, then you cannot also spend them on culture.

Culture and the state are fundamentally opposed to one another. Let no one be misled: the idea of a "culture-state" is a modern illusion. One thrives at the expense of the other. Throughout history, every great period of culture coincided with political decline. That which is culturally great is always unpolitical, even anti-political.

Consider Goethe. His heart swelled with hope at the rise of Napoleon, a figure of cultural vitality, but it closed at the thought of the "Wars of Liberation," which signaled Germany's move toward becoming a political power. Similarly, when Germany emerged as a dominant force in global politics, France rose anew as a cultural powerhouse. Even now, much of Europe's intellectual seriousness and passion have migrated to Paris. Questions of pessimism, the works of Wagner, and other psychological and artistic debates are approached in France with a level of subtlety and depth that Germany seems incapable of matching.

In matters that truly define culture—those that demand intellectual and artistic earnestness—the Germans are no longer relevant. This shift marks a profound displacement of Europe's intellectual center of gravity. In the history of European culture, the rise of the German Empire signifies not progress but a retreat from cultural significance.

I challenge you to name a single German thinker today who can stand alongside the great figures of Europe's intellectual past. Where is the modern equivalent of Goethe, Hegel, Heinrich Heine, or Schopenhauer? The absence of any contemporary German philosopher worthy of comparison with such minds is an ever-growing marvel—and a deeply troubling one.

The entire higher educational system in Germany has lost sight of everything that truly matters—both the ultimate goals and the means to achieve them. People seem to have forgotten that education itself is the goal, the process of cultivation an end in itself—not "the Empire" or any other external objective. They forget that education demands true educators, not merely public- school teachers or university scholars. What is needed are educators who are themselves cultivated, superior, and noble minds—individuals who can demonstrate their worth at every moment of their lives through their words and their actions. These are individuals who are ripe and refined products of culture.

Instead, Germany is plagued by an abundance of learned louts— "superior wet-nurses"—foisted upon its youth by public schools and universities. These are not educators in the true sense, but mere functionaries. What Germany lacks, with few exceptions, is the very foundation of education: genuine educators. And without educators, there can be no culture. This deficit has led to the decline of German culture.

One of those rare exceptions, and a man I deeply respect, is my friend Jacob Burckhardt of Bâle. It is to him, above all, that Bâle owes its position as a center of true human culture. He stands as a shining example of what an educator should be.

What, then, do Germany's higher schools actually achieve? They ruthlessly and rapidly train vast numbers of young men to become useful and exploitable servants of the state. This process prioritizes utility over cultivation, treating education as a means to an end rather than an end in itself. The very concept of "higher education" contradicts the idea of catering to the masses. True higher education can only concern the exceptional few; it is a privilege reserved for those capable of appreciating and embodying it.

Great and beautiful things cannot belong to the masses. As the Latin phrase goes, pulchrum est paucorum hominum—the beautiful is for the few. This democratization of education— this attempt to make cultivation "general" and common—is one of the root causes of Germany's cultural decline. When higher education is treated as a universal right rather than a privilege, it inevitably deteriorates in quality.

Another factor undermining German education is the influence of the military profession. The privileges associated with military careers drive far too many people into the higher schools, flooding the system and degrading its standards. In modern Germany, no parent has the freedom to provide their children with a noble education. The teachers, curricula, and goals of the higher schools are all built on a fundamentally mediocre foundation.

Everywhere one looks, haste reigns supreme. It is as if something vital would be lost if a young man were not "finished" by the age of twenty-three, or if he were unable to answer the all-important question: "What career should I choose?" But the superior individual, the one truly capable of higher culture, does not think in terms of "careers." Such a person feels called to something higher and cannot simply conform to the idea of a "calling" imposed by society.

The superior individual takes their time—they must take their time. For such a person, the idea of being "finished" is absurd. In the realm of higher culture, a man of thirty is still a beginner, still a child.

Meanwhile, our overcrowded public schools and the mass production of mediocre teachers are nothing short of a scandal. While some may present serious motives for defending this state of affairs—

like the professors at Heidelberg recently did—there can be no legitimate reasons to support it. The rush to "complete" education and the focus on quantity over quality are destroying the very foundation of culture.

Germany's educational system is not cultivating exceptional individuals; it is churning out uniform, functional tools for the state. This is a betrayal of what education should be and a clear indication of the decline of German intellectual and cultural life.

To remain true to my affirmative nature—a nature that deals with contradictions and criticism only reluctantly and as a secondary matter—I will begin by stating the three essential goals for which we require educators. People must learn to see, they must learn to think, and they must learn to speak and write. These three abilities are the foundation of a noble culture.

To learn to see means to train the eye in calmness, patience, and the ability to let things present themselves. It involves postponing judgment and approaching every individual case from all possible angles. This is the first and most essential preparation for intellectual development. One must not react immediately to stimuli; one must cultivate the instincts of restraint and isolation. To learn to see, as I understand it, is closely related to what is popularly referred to as "strength of will." Its core is the ability not to want to see immediately, to defer decisions, and to resist impulses.

All lack of intellectuality and all vulgarity stem from the inability to resist stimuli. Such people feel compelled to respond to every impulse and indulge every reaction. In many cases, this immediate response is a sign of decline, a symptom of exhaustion or morbidity. Most of what common language calls "vices" is simply the physiological inability to refrain from reacting.

To illustrate what it means to have learned to see, consider a person who has undergone this training. As a learner, this individual will likely become cautious, slow, and resistant. With a calm and almost hostile skepticism, they will allow strange and unfamiliar things to approach them but will refrain from immediately engaging or forming judgments. They will withdraw their hand, metaphorically speaking, as the new comes near, watching and observing instead.

In contrast, to be perpetually open, to have the "doors of one's soul" flung wide for every trivial fact, to constantly lie in submission before the flood of external impressions—this is what modern people call "objectivity." But such objectivity is in poor taste; it is vulgar and cheap. It is the intellectual equivalent of being at the mercy of every passing whim, ready to leap into others' souls and experiences without discernment or control.

As for learning to think—our schools have long since abandoned any understanding of this process. Even at the universities, among scholars of philosophy, the discipline of logic is withering away, both as a theory and as a practical skill. Look into any German book, and you will find no trace of the understanding that thinking has a technique, a structure, and a discipline. There is no recognition that thinking must be learned, much like dancing must be learned. Thinking, like dancing, demands practice and a will to mastery.

Who among the Germans today knows, from experience, the subtle joy— the delicate shudder—that comes when intellectual movements are as graceful as light footfalls? Instead, intellectual clumsiness abounds. Awkward postures of the mind and a heavy-handed approach to grasping ideas are so distinctly German that outside of Germany, they are mistakenly equated with the German spirit itself. The German mind has no "fingers" for fine nuances.

The Germans' tolerance for their philosophers, particularly for Kant—the most malformed and crippled figure in the realm of ideas—speaks volumes about their lack of elegance. Kant is a testament to their coarse intellectual habits and their inability to recognize intellectual grace.

In truth, no noble education can exclude dancing in all its forms. This includes dancing with one's feet, but also with ideas, with words, and, above all, with the pen. Writing is, in its highest form, a kind of intellectual dance, requiring rhythm, precision, and lightness. Yet at this point, I must acknowledge that these thoughts will likely remain utterly incomprehensible to most German readers.

Chapter 9

Skirmishes in A War with The Age

My Impossible People.—Seneca, the showman of virtue, performing like a bullfighter in the ring of morals. Rousseau, the preacher of returning to nature, lost in his own unpolished, raw state. Schiller, the trumpet of morality, blasting his tunes from Säckingen with little depth behind the noise. Dante, the scavenger who writes poetry over the graves he haunts. Kant, whose moral preaching is nothing more than a cleverly disguised form of empty rhetoric. Victor Hugo, a beacon on the vast sea of nonsense, shining brightly but without direction. Liszt, master of chasing not only after musical greatness but also after women. George Sand, overflowing with creativity, like a cow with an endless supply of beautiful milk. Michelet, all fire and passion, but dressed casually in the everyday garb of enthusiasm. Carlyle, the voice of pessimism, but one born of a poorly digested meal rather than deep reflection. John Stuart Mill, whose clarity is so sharp it feels almost offensive. The brothers Goncourt, two literary warriors battling Homer with their pens, their drama set to Offenbach's music.

Zola, who finds inspiration in the repulsive and thrives in the stench of decay.

Renan. Theology personified, corrupted by the original sin of Christianity. His thoughts are tainted with the contradictions of faith. Even when Renan dares to take a stance, to say "yes" or "no" on a major issue, he almost always misses the point entirely. He tries to combine science with nobility, seemingly unaware that science is inherently democratic and cannot be aligned with his aristocratic ideals. He dreams of an intellectual aristocracy, yet at the same time, he bows down to the gospel of humility and grovels before it. What good is his modern free-spiritedness, his wit, his irony, and his intellectual acrobatics, if deep inside he remains tied to the faith of a Christian, a Catholic, and even a priest?

Renan's strength, much like that of a Jesuit or a confessor, lies in his ability to seduce. His intellect has the same unctuous, self- satisfied tone as a parson. Like all priests, he becomes dangerous when he loves, because his love distorts the truth. He has a rare talent for worshipping dangerous ideas in such a way that they appear benign. But his intellect, rather than invigorating, weakens and softens. For France, already suffering from a broken will and diminishing strength, Renan is one more calamity—a soothing voice at a time when sharp clarity and decisiveness are needed.

Sainte-Beuve. There is nothing manly about him. He is filled with petty malice toward all strong and noble spirits. He drifts aimlessly, subtle yet spiteful, always restless and curious. He listens at keyholes, gathering whispers, but never facing things head-on. At heart, he is more like a woman, full of revenge and sensuality. As a psychologist, he is a genius of slander, endlessly creative in his ability to add a touch of poison even to his praise. His instincts are plebeian, closely aligned with the resentful spirit of Rousseau. This makes him a Romanticist, for beneath all Romanticism lies Rousseau's vengeful nature, grumbling and restless.

Sainte-Beuve is a restrained revolutionary, his actions kept in check by fear. He flinches before strength, whether it comes in the form of public opinion, the Academy, the court, or even the cloistered thinkers of Port Royal. He is filled with bitterness toward all that is great, toward everything that has confidence in itself. He is enough of a poet, enough of a sensualist, to recognize power when he sees it, but he writhes under its weight like a worm being trodden upon.

As a critic, Sainte-Beuve lacks a foundation—no standard of judgment, no clear principles, no backbone. While he speaks with the versatility of a worldly libertine, chattering endlessly about countless subjects, he lacks the courage to own his own libertinism. As a historian, he has no philosophical depth, no ability to see history as a coherent whole. This lack of vision leads him to avoid making judgments, opting instead for a mask of "objectivity" in matters of importance.

Yet when it comes to things that demand subtlety and refined taste, Sainte- Beuve finds his footing. Here, he dares to embrace his true nature, enjoying his own personality and even achieving mastery. In this sense, he is a precursor to Baudelaire, though without Baudelaire's courage to push boundaries.

"The Imitation of Christ." This is a book I cannot even touch without feeling physically repulsed. It reeks of the "eternally feminine," a cloying sweetness that can only appeal to French sensibilities or to Wagnerites. Its saintly musings on love are delivered in a tone so saccharine that even the most worldly Parisian women might find themselves intrigued.

I have been told that Auguste Comte, the clever Jesuit disguised as a man of science, took inspiration from this book in his attempt to lead his countrymen back to Rome by way of science. I can believe it. This is the essence of the "religion of the heart"—a sentimental, deceptive path back to the old faith, cloaked in modern rhetoric. It is as much a symbol of decline as it is of misplaced devotion.

G. Eliot.—They have let go of the Christian God, yet they cling even harder to Christian morality. This is a very English way of thinking, and while it might seem strange, one can hardly blame moral women like George Eliot for following it. In England, even the smallest step away from theology must be balanced by an extreme embrace of morality. It's their way of making amends, their form of penance. Anyone who begins to stray from religious belief feels compelled to prove their virtue by becoming a moral fanatic.

We, however, are different. When we abandon Christian faith, we also give up any claim to Christian morality. This connection might not be obvious to everyone, but it must be emphasized repeatedly, especially to counter the shallow thinkers so common in England.

Christianity is not a loose collection of values; it is a complete system, a worldview where every part supports the whole. If you remove its central pillar—the belief in God—the entire structure collapses. What remains is empty, lifeless, and without meaning.

Christianity assumes that humans cannot know what is good or bad for themselves. It teaches that only God knows these things. Christian morality, therefore, is not a product of human reasoning but a divine command. It is immune to criticism because it rests entirely on the belief that God is the ultimate truth. Without God, Christian morality loses its foundation and cannot stand on its own.

The English, however, seem to believe otherwise. They think they can intuitively know what is good or evil without needing Christianity to guide them. But this belief only shows how deeply Christian values still shape their thinking. Their moral standards remain rooted in Christian teachings, even when they deny the religion itself. This is not evidence of independence; it is proof of how strong Christianity's influence remains. The English no longer recognize the origins of their morality, nor do they realize how fragile it is without its theological base. For them, morality is not a question to be examined—it is simply assumed, a problem they have yet to confront.

George Sand.—I recently read the first Lettres d'un Voyageur, and like everything influenced by Rousseau, it felt artificial, exaggerated, and insincere. The style reminded me of cheap wallpaper—bright, decorative, but ultimately shallow. The writing seems overly concerned with appearing noble and generous, yet lacks any genuine depth. What struck me most was Sand's affected masculinity, which came across as forced and unconvincing, like the awkward swagger of a poorly mannered schoolboy.

And how cold she must have been beneath this performance! She seemed like a machine, wound up and ready to produce her work, writing not out of passion but out of routine. This coldness is not unique to her; it is the hallmark of Romanticists like Hugo and Balzac, whose writing often feels detached from true feeling. Sand's self-satisfaction is evident in her prolific output, as if she took pride in her ability to churn out words endlessly. There was something undeniably German in her style—not in the good sense, but in the clumsy, heavy-handed way that marks the decline of true French taste. And yet Renan adores her!

A Moral for Psychologists.—Never engage in psychology just for the sake of observing. Observing for its own sake leads to a distorted view of things, to exaggeration, and to a forced perspective. Experiencing something intentionally, with the purpose of analyzing it, is not helpful. When in the middle of an experience, a person should not turn their attention inward to observe themselves. In such moments, even the clearest vision becomes clouded—it turns into the "evil eye." A true psychologist avoids observing for the sake of observation. The same is true for a true artist. A born painter, for instance, does not work directly "from nature." Instead, they rely on their instinct, their internal lens, to filter and shape their perception of reality. For them, only the general idea, the final impression, reaches conscious thought. They do not bother with the painstaking process of building conclusions from small, particular details.

But what happens when someone approaches this differently? Take, for example, the Parisian novelists who practice "note-book psychology," recording every detail, large or small, that catches their attention. Such people are constantly spying on life, collecting observations like trinkets to carry home at the end of each day. The result? A chaotic mess, at best resembling a mosaic of unrelated fragments. Their work is restless and garish, more like a patchwork quilt than a coherent picture. The Goncourts are the worst offenders in this regard. They cannot write three sentences without causing pain to anyone with an eye for psychology or aesthetics.

From an artistic perspective, nature is no model to imitate. Nature exaggerates, distorts, and leaves gaps—it is full of accidents. To study "from nature" is, in my view, a bad sign. It shows submission, weakness, and a kind of fatalism. This slavish worship of trivial facts is beneath a true artist. The ability to see "what is" belongs to a different kind of intellect altogether—one that is practical and matter-of-fact, not artistic. An artist must know who they are and what their purpose is, rather than bowing before the randomness of nature.

To make art possible—that is, to create an aesthetic way of acting and seeing—a certain physiological state must come first: ecstasy. Without this heightened state of being, art simply cannot exist. Ecstasy heightens the sensitivity of the whole body and mind, making them more receptive and powerful. Many kinds of ecstasy can lead to art, no matter how they arise. Sexual excitement, for example, is the oldest and most fundamental form of ecstasy. Similarly, ecstasy can come from powerful desires, intense passions, the energy of celebration, the thrill of a battle, the bravery of a daring act, the joy of victory, or the rush of destruction. Even seasonal changes, such as the vibrancy of spring, or the use of drugs can trigger this state. Another form of ecstasy arises from a strong surge of willpower, when one feels driven and overflowing with determination.

At its core, ecstasy creates a feeling of increased strength and abundance. In this state, a person projects their inner wealth onto the world around them. They impose their energy onto things, forcing them to reflect their own richness and power. This act of projecting oneself onto the world is called idealizing. Contrary to popular belief, idealizing does not mean removing details or simplifying things. Instead, it emphasizes the main characteristics so powerfully that lesser details fade away.

In this state of abundance, a person enriches everything they encounter. Whatever they see or desire appears to them as larger, stronger, and more alive. They transform objects and ideas until these reflect their own strength and perfection. This drive to transform things into something beautiful is what we call art. Through art, a person celebrates themselves as a reflection of perfection, even in things they are not.

It is also possible to imagine the opposite of this artistic state—an anti- artistic condition. In such a state, a person drains energy from everything around them. Instead of enriching and enhancing, they weaken and impoverish. These individuals lack vitality and draw from others to sustain themselves. History is full of such anti-artists—individuals like Pascal, whose Christian faith exemplifies this draining tendency. A true Christian, by nature, cannot also be an artist. Even suggesting otherwise by pointing to figures like Raphael misses the point entirely. Raphael affirmed life, celebrated beauty, and said "yes" to the world, which means he was not a Christian in the true sense.

The terms Apollonian and Dionysian, which I introduced to aesthetics, represent two opposing forms of ecstasy. Apollonian ecstasy sharpens vision, giving the eye a heightened ability to see and understand. This type of ecstasy inspires painters, sculptors, and epic poets, who are fundamentally visionaries. On the other hand, Dionysian ecstasy awakens the entire system of passions, intensifying them and causing them to pour out in a flood of expression. This state drives transformation and imitation, releasing all forms of mimicry and artistic display at once. The Dionysian artist is incredibly sensitive to every emotion and suggestion. They instinctively grasp and communicate emotions, transforming themselves into whatever role or passion they encounter. Music, as we understand it today, is a surviving fragment of this broader Dionysian expression—a remnant of a once richer form of emotional discharge. For music to become its own art form, many other senses, such as the sense of touch and movement, had to be partially suppressed. Rhythm, however, still appeals to our physical senses to some extent, linking music to its Dionysian roots.

Actors, mimes, dancers, musicians, and lyricists all share a common foundation in their instincts. Over time, however, they have specialized, developing their own distinct fields of art, even to the point of becoming opposites. Among these, lyricists remained closely connected to musicians for the longest period, while actors were similarly linked to dancers. Architects, however, represent something different. Their art is born not from

Dionysian or Apollonian ecstasy but from the overwhelming will to create. Architecture expresses human pride, triumph over nature, and the will to power in physical form. Great men have always inspired architects, who in turn translate this power into structures that symbolize strength and security. Architecture becomes a language of power, speaking through form. It can persuade, command, or simply exist with quiet confidence. True grandeur in architecture reflects power that is self-assured, needing no validation, unconcerned with opposition, and relying only on itself.

Recently, I read about Thomas Carlyle's life, a mix of unintended comedy and moral posturing. Carlyle was a man of dramatic words and gestures, forever in search of a strong faith that he could not find. This unfulfilled longing makes him a quintessential Romantic. The desire for strong faith, however, is not a sign of having it but rather the opposite. A person with true faith can afford the luxury of doubt and skepticism because their foundation is firm. Carlyle's loud proclamations of reverence for those with strong faith, combined with his anger at those who lacked it, reveal his inner turmoil. He needed noise—both literal and figurative—to distract himself from his doubts.

Carlyle's defining trait was his persistent dishonesty with himself. This quality makes him fascinating, though it also explains why he was so admired in England. Honesty, as the English understand it, often overlaps with hypocrisy, and Carlyle fits this mold perfectly. At heart, he was an atheist who stubbornly refused to admit it, making his struggle with faith all the more dramatic and emblematic of the English spirit.

Emerson is far more enlightened, versatile, and refined than Carlyle, and most importantly, he is happier. He lives instinctively, enjoying the best parts of life while discarding what he finds unpleasant. Compared to Carlyle, Emerson has better taste and a lighter, more joyous intellectuality. Carlyle, who admired him greatly, complained that Emerson "does not give us enough to chew." While this criticism may be true, it hardly counts as a flaw—it is simply a reflection of Emerson's different approach. Emerson's cheerfulness shields him from the heaviness of life. He does not burden himself with excessive seriousness, and he approaches existence with a kind of perpetual youthfulness, blissfully unaware of his age or the weight of time. He might have described himself, in Lope de Vega's words, as someone who constantly succeeds himself, always renewing and reimagining his life. His mind naturally seeks reasons to be content, even grateful, and he often approaches a carefree joyfulness akin to the bourgeois simplicity of a man returning from a romantic escapade, satisfied with life's fleeting pleasures.

The "struggle for existence," a centerpiece of Darwinian thought, strikes me as more of an assumption than an established fact. It does happen, but it is the exception, not the rule. Life's general state is not one of scarcity and competition but one of abundance, extravagance, and even absurd excess. Where struggle does occur, it is more often a struggle for power than for mere survival. The idea of nature as fundamentally Malthusian is misleading. Even if the struggle for existence does take place, its outcomes are often the opposite of what Darwin and his followers might hope. Instead of favoring the strong, the exceptional, and the privileged, it often benefits the weak, simply because they are the majority and frequently more cunning. Darwin overlooked the role of intellect—an oversight that seems distinctly English. The weak are often more intelligent, driven by necessity to develop cleverness and adaptability. By contrast, the strong, having less need for such traits, may grow complacent and neglect their intellect, letting it atrophy. Intellect, after all, demands caution, patience, and subtlety—qualities the powerful may disdain in favor of brute strength.

Those who study humanity deeply often have ulterior motives. A politician, for instance, uses his understanding of people to gain power or advantage. But what of the so-called disinterested observer, the one who claims to seek no personal benefit? A closer look often reveals a darker purpose: the desire to feel superior, to distance oneself from humanity, to no longer belong. This kind of person despises mankind, even if they claim objectivity and fairness. By contrast, the more "self-serving" politician may actually be more humane, for at least he sees himself as part of the same world as those he studies.

The German approach to intellect and psychology leaves much to be desired, as evidenced by certain cultural missteps. Consider, for example, the pairing of names like Goethe and Schiller, or worse, Schiller and Goethe, as if they were equals. Has no one yet recognized the vast gulf between them? And then there are other egregious pairings, such as Schopenhauer and Hartmann. Such thoughtless associations reflect a lack of discernment and an inability to appreciate true intellectual refinement.

The most intelligent and courageous individuals often endure the greatest tragedies because they confront life's most daunting challenges. Yet, paradoxically, these struggles lead them to honor life all the more, for it forces them to grapple with its fiercest adversaries. In this way, their suffering becomes a testament to their strength and their profound engagement with existence.

In today's world, genuine hypocrisy has become increasingly rare. Hypocrisy requires a strong belief, a faith so deeply held that one is willing to outwardly adopt another, contradictory stance while maintaining one's inner conviction. Such duality thrives only in an era of fervent faith, where abandoning one's belief is unthinkable. Modern culture, however, allows for a multiplicity of beliefs, making hypocrisy almost obsolete. People no longer feel the need to maintain a façade; instead, they adopt multiple convictions and live comfortably with them, ensuring these beliefs never truly conflict or demand consistency.

This tolerance for contradictions is both a sign of our age and a symptom of its weaknesses. Modern individuals avoid compromising themselves by avoiding consistency. They cultivate convenience rather than conviction, preferring a life free of challenges or demands on their integrity. Even vices, once expressions of strong will, have degenerated into virtues in this climate of comfort and ease. The few hypocrites I've encountered are mere imitations of the real thing, like actors playing a role. They lack the depth and complexity of true hypocrisy, reduced instead to shallow performances in a world that no longer requires or even understands the profound struggles of belief and deceit.

Beautiful and Ugly:—Our sense of the beautiful is deeply relative, tightly bound to the limitations of human perception and context. To try and separate beauty from the joy humans derive from their surroundings, especially other humans, would be to sever it from its grounding altogether. "Beauty in itself" is nothing more than an abstract phrase, a hollow idea without true substance or universal agreement. In perceiving beauty, humans essentially declare themselves as the measure of perfection. At times, in exceptional circumstances, they even idolize themselves as that ultimate standard. This impulse stems from the most basic instinct of survival and self-preservation. Even the loftiest ideas of beauty are, at their core, expressions of humanity's need to affirm and expand itself.

Man views the world as brimming with beauty, failing to recognize that he is the source of this projection. The beauty he perceives is merely a reflection of himself, a human imprint upon the world. Alas, it is not a universal beauty, but rather one that is all-too-human. In truth, man mirrors himself in everything he beholds, deeming things beautiful because they resonate with his own image.

The judgment of beauty is thus the vanity of the human species, an echo of its own self-love. A skeptic might wonder, "Is the world genuinely beautiful because man finds it so?" Perhaps not. Perhaps all man has done is to humanize the world, to imprint it with his desires and perceptions. Yet, there is no definitive proof that man is the ultimate standard of beauty. What if, in the eyes of a more refined judge of taste, mankind appeared peculiar, comical, or arbitrary? Imagine Dionysus teasing Ariadne about her ears during a philosophical conversation, playfully suggesting, "Why are they not a little longer?" The joke may contain a deeper truth.

From this perspective, nothing in itself is beautiful; it is man alone who declares beauty. Aesthetic sensibility begins with this innocent assumption, the first axiom of aesthetics. Alongside it stands a second principle: nothing is truly ugly except the degenerate man. Together, these principles define the bounds of aesthetic judgment. From a physiological standpoint, ugliness weakens and demoralizes. It reminds humanity of fragility, decay, and the loss of vitality. In the presence of ugliness, man's strength diminishes, as if the sight itself drains him of energy. This reaction, measurable even by a dynamometer, reveals a deep instinctual response: ugliness signals something threatening, something that disrupts the will to power.

When a man feels a sudden drop in confidence or courage, it often stems from encountering something that he perceives as ugly. This reaction emerges from deep within his instincts, stored with countless associations between appearances and their inferred meanings. Ugliness is perceived as a symptom of decline and degeneration. Anything that even faintly suggests a deterioration of the human type—be it physical exhaustion, aging, stiffness, or the crudeness of decomposition—is judged as ugly. Colors, smells, and forms associated with decay, even when abstracted into mere symbols, provoke the same visceral rejection.

This response is not simply distaste; it is hatred, a primal and profound aversion. What is it that man hates in ugliness? He hates the signs of decline in his own kind. This hatred is rooted in the deepest instincts of survival, resonating with the need to preserve the strength and vitality of his type. It is a hatred tinged with horror and caution, expressing a far-sighted instinct for the preservation of life. This reaction is not shallow; it is the most profound hatred man possesses, one that is etched into the very fabric of his being.

It is this hatred of decline, this refusal to accept degeneration, that gives art its depth. Art draws from the profound tension between man's yearning for beauty and his rejection of what threatens his sense of vitality and perfection. In this way, art is more than an expression of the beautiful; it is an affirmation of life, shaped by man's most primal fears and desires.

Schopenhauer, the last German thinker of significance, stands alongside figures like Goethe, Hegel, and Heinrich Heine as a European, not merely a national, event. For a psychologist, he is a fascinating case of the highest order. His work represents a cunning and skillful effort to turn the most life-affirming aspects of human existence—such as art, heroism, genius, beauty, deep compassion, the pursuit of truth, and even the grandeur of tragedy—into arguments for a nihilistic rejection of life. In this, Schopenhauer engages in what could be called one of history's greatest intellectual forgeries, rivaled only by Christianity. He reinterpreted all the noble affirmations of life as if they were but expressions of the denial of the "will to live" or as steps leading inevitably toward that denial.

When scrutinized more closely, Schopenhauer appears as an inheritor of the Christian worldview, repackaged for a secular age. Unlike Christianity, which outright rejects many aspects of human culture, Schopenhauer found a way to nihilistically "approve" of them. To him, these elements of culture—art, beauty, and even human striving—were not ends in themselves but tools to draw the soul toward "salvation," mere appetizers to stimulate a hunger for deliverance from life itself.

Take, for example, his view of beauty. Schopenhauer speaks of beauty with a sorrowful intensity, valuing it as a bridge to something beyond, a fleeting liberation from the burdens of the "will to live." He sees beauty as a temporary escape, particularly from the "burning core" of the will—sexuality. To him, beauty negates the reproductive instinct, offering a glimpse of salvation. Singular saint, indeed! But someone challenges this notion— Nature herself. Why does Nature create beauty in sound, color, fragrance, and rhythm if not to affirm life and reproduction? Why does beauty compel and captivate?

Schopenhauer's own idol, Plato, offers a striking contradiction to his thesis.

Plato, whom Schopenhauer venerates as a divine authority, takes an entirely different view. For Plato, beauty is not a denial of life; it is an irresistible lure toward creation and procreation. Beauty inspires both the lowest sensual desires and the highest intellectual pursuits. With a Greek innocence utterly foreign to the Christian mindset, Plato claims that without the beauty of young men in Athens, there would have been no Platonic philosophy. It was their radiance that stirred the philosopher's soul, igniting a passion that refused to rest until it had planted the seeds of great ideas in such captivating soil. Plato himself, then, was a singular saint of a different kind—one for whom the aesthetic and the erotic were deeply intertwined.

This reveals a starkly different approach to philosophy in Athens, where it was pursued openly, even playfully. Unlike the cloistered, abstract cogitations of later thinkers such as Spinoza with his intellectual love of God, Platonic philosophy was an extension of the Greek tradition of competitive games, agon, infused with an erotic dimension. Plato's philosophy was, in many ways, an elevated and spiritualized form of the Greek gymnastic competitions, with dialectics becoming a new art form born of this philosophic eroticism.

In defense of Plato and against Schopenhauer's austere view, it is worth noting that much of the higher culture and literature of classical France also flourished on the fertile ground of sexual interests. Whether in gallantry, the passions, sexual rivalry, or the role of women, these themes pervade French culture and cannot be overlooked. The sensual and the intellectual intertwined seamlessly, revealing that higher culture, far from denying life, often springs from its most vibrant and primal energies.

The idea of l'ar t pour l'ar t—art for art's sake—has often been interpreted as a rebellion against the notion that art must serve a moral purpose or improve humanity. This phrase essentially declares, "Let morality go to hell!" Yet, even in this rejection, we see how deeply entrenched the moral bias remains. The act of opposing morality in art still acknowledges its overwhelming influence. If art is stripped of its role as a preacher of morals or a tool for human betterment, this does not mean it is left entirely without purpose or meaning. To say that art has no purpose, no point, no sense—this is what l'art pour l'art suggests. It is like a snake biting its own tail: a pure passion insisting, "No purpose at all is better than a moral purpose."

But a psychologist must question this: What does art actually do? Does it not praise? Does it not elevate certain ideas while diminishing others? Does it not highlight and amplify? In doing so, art reinforces or diminishes certain values. Can this be dismissed as an incidental outcome or a mere accident, independent of the artist's intentions? Or is it, rather, a fundamental instinct of the artist to shape and serve life through art? Is the artist's true drive concerned with art itself, or does it instead lie in the aim of art—to enrich and enhance life, to advocate for a specific way of living? Art is a tremendous stimulus to life; how, then, can it be seen as pointless or purposeless? It is not simply l'art pour l'art.

And what of the dark and unsettling aspects that art sometimes reveals? When art exposes what is ugly, harsh, or deeply troubling, does it not risk making life unbearable? Some philosophers have thought so. For example, Schopenhauer argued that the purpose of art, especially tragedy, was to free us from the relentless desires of the will and to lead us toward resignation. Tragedy, for him, was valuable because it made us more willing to renounce life. But this view reflects a pessimistic perspective—a deeply negative outlook. To understand art, we must consult the artist, not the pessimist. What does the tragic artist convey to us? Surely it is not resignation but rather a fearless embrace of life's terrors and uncertainties. The artist shows us how to face profound suffering with courage and strength. This attitude is a triumph in itself, and those who have experienced it know it is something to be revered. The artist must share this perspective. A true artist and a genius in communication cannot help but share it.

The tragic artist exalts a heroic spirit, one that confronts overwhelming challenges, sublime catastrophes, and terrifying mysteries with dignity and resolve. This spirit celebrates itself in tragedy, finding joy even in suffering. The tragic artist extends this "cup of sweetest cruelty" to those who are attuned to hardship, who seek it out and embrace it as a defining aspect of life. Tragedy is not about giving up; it is about finding meaning and affirmation in struggle.

A related notion is the idea of hospitality in one's soul. To welcome anyone and everyone into one's inner world may seem generous, but it lacks discernment. A truly noble heart holds its finest chambers in reserve, waiting for worthy guests—guests who are not merely anybody but rather individuals of real substance. Such hearts are rich in depth, with shutters closed and windows veiled, not out of fear or selfishness, but in anticipation of those who merit their best.

Too often, we undervalue ourselves when we attempt to articulate the deepest contents of our souls. Our most profound experiences are not verbose; they are beyond words and would resist even the most earnest attempts at expression. The very act of finding words for something suggests that it has already been overcome or rendered less significant. Speech itself diminishes, for in speaking, we simplify and vulgarize. Words are the currency of the average, the mundane, the communicable. To speak is to betray the depth of what one truly feels, revealing instead only a shadow of the truth. This recognition might well serve as a moral guide for philosophers and others who value the unspoken.

And what of those who strive for objectivity, who pride themselves on their detached and impartial perspectives? Their wisdom, patience, and tolerance may seem impressive, even virtuous, but it often comes at the cost of passion and genuine self-control. Such individuals, drenched in their indulgence and sympathy, should occasionally permit themselves a dose of raw emotion, even a small emotional vice. It may feel uncomfortable, even ridiculous, to them, but it serves as a form of self-discipline—a kind of asceticism for those who have mastered detachment but risk losing touch with their own humanity.

In becoming personal, the so-called "objective" individuals reveal their own virtues, for objectivity often masks a deeper desire: the need to feel above the fray, detached from the common lot. Yet true nobility lies not in keeping oneself apart but in knowing when and how to connect with others authentically. The virtues of objectivity are limited without the courage to embrace and engage with life's messy, subjective truths.

Excerpt from a doctor's exam paper: "What is the ultimate goal of all advanced education?" To transform a human being into a machine. "What methods are employed to achieve this?" Teaching the individual how to endure boredom. "And how is this boredom instilled?" Through the concept of duty. "What model of duty is presented to the student?" The philologist, who embodies the art of relentless, uninspired diligence. "Who, then, is the ideal human being?" The government official. "And which philosophy provides the definitive framework for this ideal?" Kant's philosophy: envisioning the government official as the ultimate abstraction—the thing- in-itself— presiding over his worldly role as mere appearance.

The Right to Stupidity: Picture the exhausted worker, his breath measured, his demeanor mild, his actions guided by inertia rather than intent. This archetype, a product of our era of relentless labor (and "Empire"), now inhabits every class. This weary figure seeks escape and leisure, claiming even Art for himself—books,

newspapers, and, most notably, beautiful landscapes like Italy. This man of the evening, with his "wild instincts lulled," as Faust might say, requires his summer holidays, his coastal retreats, his alpine glaciers, and his pilgrimage to Bayreuth. In times like these, Art gains the right to be utterly frivolous—a playful retreat for wit, spirit, and emotion. Wagner, of course, understood this well. Pure silliness becomes a form of refreshment, a tonic for the fatigued.

A Further Question of Discipline: Consider the methods Julius Caesar used to safeguard himself against illness and headaches: grueling marches, a life stripped to its simplest essentials, constant exposure to the elements, and enduring hardships without respite. These strategies represent the necessary defenses and survival tactics for those intricate, high-performing organisms called geniuses. Such lives, always teetering at the edge of their capacity, demand such rigorous measures to maintain their vitality.

The Immoralist Speaks: Nothing is more repugnant to true philosophers than observing man in the act of wishing. When they see man purely in his actions—this most fearless, cunning, and resilient of animals, navigating life's calamities with remarkable ingenuity—he earns their admiration. They may even encourage him. Yet the moment man begins to wish or pursue "ideals," he becomes contemptible in their eyes. They reject not only the man of desires but also the very concept of "desirability" and all the ideals and aspirations that humans project upon the world.

Were a true philosopher inclined to nihilism, it would not be because of the absence of meaning but because every human ideal reveals not grandeur but something base: futility, absurdity, frailty, cowardice, fatigue, and the residue left over from life's excesses. Why is it that man, so admirable in his tangible existence, becomes unworthy of respect the moment he begins to desire? Is it some kind of cosmic balancing act? Must the heights of his reality be counterbalanced by the lowliness of his imagination and aspirations? Humanity's history of desires has always been its most shameful chapter; one would be wise not to delve too deeply into it.

What redeems mankind is not its dreams or ideals but its tangible reality. This reality justifies humanity—now and forever. A real man, living and acting in the world, is infinitely more valuable than the mere shadow of a man shaped by desires, fantasies, and delusions. Any ideal man, no matter how elevated he may seem, pales in comparison to the flesh-and-blood individual who embodies the truth of existence. And it is precisely the "ideal man"—the product of abstractions, longings, and lies—that a philosopher finds most insufferable.

The Natural Value of Egoism: The worth of selfishness depends entirely on the inherent value of the individual who practices it. This value may be immense, or it may be insignificant and even contemptible. Every person can be evaluated based on whether they represent the ascending or descending trajectory of life. Once this determination is made, it becomes possible to measure the value of their egoism. If a person embodies the upward movement of life—its growth, strength, and vitality—then their worth is extraordinary. For the collective progress of humanity, which advances through such individuals, it is essential to focus on ensuring their well-being and creating the optimal conditions for them to thrive. These individuals are not isolated entities, mere atoms, or passive inheritors of history; instead, they represent the entire trajectory of humanity culminating in their existence.

Conversely, if an individual represents decline, degeneration, or chronic decay, their value diminishes significantly. Sickness, for instance, is often the result, rather than the cause, of such decline. In such cases, it would be most equitable if these individuals took as little as possible from those who are nature's fortunate creations. These declining individuals become parasitic, drawing from the vitality of others without contributing to life's upward momentum.

The Christian and the Anarchist: When the anarchist, as the voice of the decaying elements in society, cries out for "rights," "justice," or "equality," it is not an enlightened demand but a symptom of their deeper ignorance. They do not understand the true source of their suffering: a poverty not of material possessions but of life itself. An instinct for finding blame is at work here; someone must bear responsibility for their discomfort and unease. Their anger, their dramatic indignation, serves as a fleeting relief—a kind of temporary intoxication that offers them a sense of power, however small. To complain, to bewail one's condition, even to hurl accusations, is a twisted consolation. It allows them to endure their existence by adding a layer of satisfaction to their misery.

There is always an element of revenge in lamentation. In every complaint lies the unspoken accusation: "Because I suffer, you ought to suffer too." This logic, though bitter, is the foundation of revolutions. To grumble about one's plight, however, is always degrading. It stems from weakness, whether one blames others or oneself for one's suffering. The socialist blames society; the Christian, by contrast, blames themselves. But both share a common flaw—the need to identify a scapegoat for their pain. This shared instinct, ignoble in both cases, is driven by the desire to alleviate suffering with the sweet, temporary balm of revenge.

The targets of this vengeful instinct are often incidental, chosen simply because they offer a convenient outlet. The Christian turns their blame inward, condemning their own sinfulness, while the anarchist directs their anger outward, railing against society and its perceived injustices. Yet, both are products of decline, symptoms of decadence. Even the Christian, in their acts of condemnation, slander, and defamation, mirrors the same instinct that drives the socialist worker to vilify society. The ultimate Christian fantasy— the Last Judgment—is nothing more than a dramatic extension of this need for vengeance, a cosmic reckoning that satisfies their desire to see wrongs avenged on the grandest scale.

In this way, the Christian's idea of the "Beyond" serves as nothing more than a tool to defame the "Here." It is not born out of a genuine belief in transcendence but from the need to disparage and denigrate this world. Similarly, the anarchist's dream of revolution is merely a more immediate expression of the same instinct—a wish for upheaval to punish those they blame for their suffering. Whether through the promise of an apocalyptic reckoning or the hope for societal collapse, both use these fantasies to lash out at life, unable to embrace its reality or its challenges.

An "altruistic" morality, one that causes selfishness to weaken and fade away, is always a troubling sign. This holds true not only for individuals but especially for nations. When selfishness starts to diminish, it signals the absence of the best and strongest qualities. To instinctively choose what harms oneself or to be drawn to so-called "selfless" motives is nearly a definition of decadence. The idea of "not prioritizing one's own interests" is nothing more than a moral disguise for a deeper problem, a physiological one: the person no longer knows what truly benefits them. This is the collapse of instincts, the breakdown of life's natural guidance system. A person who becomes overly altruistic is on a dangerous path. Instead of admitting honestly, "I am no longer any good," the lie that decadents tell themselves through morality is, "Nothing is any good— life itself is worthless."

This kind of judgment is deeply harmful, as it can spread like a poison, infecting others. On the polluted soil of society, such ideas grow wildly and take root, appearing now as religion, like Christianity, or as philosophy, like Schopenhauer's worldview. In some cases, even the faintest trace of such toxic ideas, sprouting as they do from the decay of life itself, can harm humanity for thousands of years.

The sick man, in this context, becomes a parasite to society. There are times when continuing to live becomes indecent. When life's meaning and one's right to live have been lost, clinging to existence through doctors and treatments should be viewed with disdain. Doctors themselves should be the ones to instill this sense of contempt; instead of prolonging such lives with prescriptions, they should daily serve their patients a dose of disgust. A new duty should fall upon the doctor—to mercilessly prevent and eliminate degenerate life in cases where the higher interests of life demand it. This would include defending the right to be born, the right to live, and even the right to procreate. One should embrace death proudly when living proudly is no longer possible. Death should be a conscious choice, welcomed at the right time, with clarity and joy, and shared with loved ones in a way that allows a proper farewell. A person should remain fully themselves, able to reflect on their achievements and measure the value of life itself before departing.

This vision is the complete opposite of the grotesque drama that Christianity has turned the moment of death into. Christianity has abused the vulnerability of dying people, violating their conscience and exploiting their final moments as a way of judging them and their lives. For this, Christianity deserves no forgiveness. It is our duty to restore the dignity of death, reclaiming it as a natural, physiological process, even though "natural death" is often nothing more than a euphemism for suicide. No one perishes because of someone else; one dies only because of their own nature. Yet the kind of death that happens by chance, at the wrong time, or under cowardly circumstances, is the most disgraceful. Out of love for life itself, one should strive for a death that is deliberate and free, neither accidental nor unexpected.

Let me offer some advice to the pessimists and other decadents among us. We cannot undo the fact of our birth—that mistake, if it was one—but we can choose to correct it if we wish. The act of taking one's own life can be the most honorable deed. In fact, the person who ends their life almost earns the right to live for having had the strength to do so. Such an act benefits society—and life itself—far more than a life wasted in weakness, self-denial, or other so-called virtues. At the very least, the one who takes their own life spares others the burden of their existence and removes one more objection to the value of life.

Pure pessimism can only truly be proven by the actions of pessimists themselves. They must go further in their logic. To merely deny life in theory, as Schopenhauer did in The World as Will and Idea, is not enough; the next step is to deny Schopenhauer himself. Incidentally, pessimism, no matter how contagious it might appear, does not actually increase the decay of an era or a species. It merely reflects the decay that already exists. Like cholera, it only afflicts those who are already susceptible. Pessimism does not add a single person to the ranks of the world's degenerates. Let me remind you of an important fact: during years when cholera rages, the overall number of deaths does not exceed those of other years.

Have we really become more moral? Many insist that we have, yet I find this belief itself to be grounds for skepticism. In Germany, for instance, the entire force of moral indignation—the kind that passes for morality—was directed against my idea of "Beyond Good and Evil." People argued passionately that modern moral sentiment demonstrates our progress, claiming that compared to us, a figure like Cæsar Borgia could not be seen as a "higher man" or the kind of "superman" I described him to be. One editor even congratulated me for my boldness while accusing me of aiming to abolish all decency. A curious compliment indeed! But I pose this question in return: Have we truly become more moral?

We modern people like to imagine our heightened sensitivity and mutual consideration as evidence of moral advancement. This collective sense of care and support, this avoidance of harm or offense, seems to us a significant step forward—proof that we surpass the brutal and daring men of the Renaissance. Yet every era believes itself superior in such ways; it is inevitable.

One thing is certain: we could not survive the raw reality of the Renaissance, nor could we imagine enduring its conditions. Our nerves and constitutions are simply too frail. But this does not signify progress. It only reflects the weakened, more delicate nature of our current state, a kind of physiological aging that has given rise to a morality of tenderness and caution.

If we strip away this frailty and delicateness, our so-called morality of "humanization" loses all meaning. In such a context, it might even appear contemptible. Let us also consider how our humanitarian virtues would have seemed to Renaissance men— those accustomed to a richer, bolder, and more overflowing vitality. They would have laughed themselves to death at our modern notions of virtue. Unwittingly, we have become laughable. Our supposed "progress" in reducing suspicion and hostility is simply a byproduct of our dwindling vitality. Living in such dependency and fragility requires endless caution and cooperation. In this environment, we become a society of mutual invalids and caregivers, calling this arrangement "virtue."

To men of a fuller, more daring era, our lifestyle might be seen as cowardice, weakness, or the morality of the old and infirm. What I call our softening of morals is not progress but evidence of decline. By contrast, a harder, fiercer moral code often arises in times of surplus vitality. When life overflows with energy, people take risks, embrace challenges, and even waste their strength freely. What once added zest to life might now poison us. Even indifference—a form of strength— is beyond our reach because we are too sensitive, too frail. Our morality of pity, which I was the first to criticize, reflects the hyper-irritability that marks all decadence. Attempts to give this morality a scientific foundation, as Schopenhauer's morality of pity sought to do, are fundamentally decadent and closely aligned with Christian ethics.

Strong ages and noble cultures regarded pity, neighborly love, and self- denial as contemptible traits. They measured their worth by their positive forces, their creative tension, and their ability to stand apart. By this measure, the Renaissance stands as the last great age, while we moderns—obsessed with self- preservation, neighborly love, and cautious virtues like industry and equity— represent a weak one. Our virtues arise from our frailty. The modern idea of "equality" and the process of leveling everyone to the same standard are hallmarks of a declining culture. Strong ages celebrated the differences between people, the "pathos of distance," the instinct to distinguish oneself, and the courage to embrace hierarchy. These qualities are eroding. The gap between extremes is closing, and society is flattening into sameness.

All our political theories, including the structure of "The German Empire," reflect this decline. Even the ideals of modern science are unconsciously shaped by the forces of decadence. My critique of

English and French sociology remains the same: it takes the symptoms of societal decline—its frailty and leveling instincts— and mistakes them for universal norms. Sociology today idealizes descending life, the decay of all organizing power, and the erosion of rank and distinction. This is what our socialists champion as progress. But it is not only socialists who are guilty of this error. Herbert Spencer, with his vision of altruism's triumph, was equally a decadent. To him, and to many others, this collapse of vitality appeared as an ideal to be pursued.

My Concept of Freedom.—The value of something is not always found in what it helps us achieve but often in what it demands from us—the price we must pay. Liberal institutions, for example, lose their essence of freedom the moment they become securely established. Once they are no longer contested, they turn into oppressive forces that stifle true freedom. These institutions undermine the Will to Power, promoting mediocrity as a virtue. They encourage conformity, making people timid, complacent, and fixated on comfort. Under them, the herd instinct triumphs, and humanity is reduced to a collective of obedient cattle. Liberalism, stripped of its idealism, becomes nothing more than the domestication of mankind.

However, the same liberal institutions, when fought for and not yet fully realized, can inspire the very opposite. Struggle for their creation and survival fosters freedom because it involves conflict. And it is war—war for freedom— that preserves the untamed, illiberal instincts essential for liberty. War trains individuals to be free. So, what is freedom? Freedom is the will to take responsibility for oneself. It is the capacity to maintain the distance that distinguishes you from others, to embrace hardship, endure privation, and remain indifferent even to life itself when necessary. It is the willingness to sacrifice, not only others but also yourself, for a cause you believe in. Freedom is the triumph of warrior instincts—those that revel in challenge and victory— over the instincts that crave mere comfort and happiness.

The truly free man despises the shallow comfort idolized by merchants, Christians, cattle, women, Englishmen, and democrats. For him, comfort is contemptible. The free man is a warrior. The measure of freedom, whether in individuals or nations, is determined by the resistance they have to overcome and the effort it takes to stay above it all. True freedom is greatest where the challenge is fiercest— just steps away from tyranny, on the threshold of being overpowered. Psychologically, tyranny represents the inner, powerful instincts that demand the utmost discipline to subdue. Julius Caesar is the finest example of such a free spirit, a man who mastered his instincts with an iron will. Politically, the same holds true: history shows that nations worth admiring were never formed under liberal institutions. It was great danger that shaped them into something worthy of reverence. Danger reveals our hidden strengths, awakens our virtues, and compels us to innovate and defend ourselves. It forces us to become resourceful and discover our inner genius.

The first principle of freedom is this: strength is born of necessity. Without the need to be strong, no one becomes strong. The greatest incubators of strength, the strongest individuals and societies to ever exist, emerged from aristocratic communities like Rome and Venice. These societies understood freedom as I do—not as a given, but as something that must be seized, something you either have or do not have, something you will for yourself and take by force.

A Criticism of Modernity.—We all agree on one thing: our institutions are failing. Yet the fault does not lie with these institutions themselves but with us. We no longer possess the instincts that once gave rise to institutions and sustained them. Without those instincts, the institutions themselves are crumbling and disappearing because we are no longer capable of upholding them. Democracy has always marked the decline of organizational power. I pointed this out as early as "Human,

All Too Human," where I described modern democracy, along with its half-measures like the "German Empire," as forms of a decaying State.

For institutions to exist and thrive, a particular kind of will is necessary—a will that is instinctive, commanding, and even harshly anti-liberal. This will demands allegiance to tradition, authority, and a responsibility that spans generations, stretching infinitely backward and forward in time. When such a will is present, empires with lasting power emerge, like the imperium Romanum or, in our era, Russia. Russia is the only nation today that demonstrates the endurance, strength, and patience required for genuine stability, a nation that can afford to wait, that can still promise a future. Russia stands as the antithesis of the petty- statism, fragility, and nervous exhaustion that plague Europe, particularly brought to the forefront by the foundation of the German Empire.

The modern Western world no longer harbors the instincts that produce institutions or the future. These instincts are fundamentally at odds with what is called the "modern spirit." People live recklessly in the moment, at breakneck speed, with little thought for long-term responsibility. And yet, this is celebrated and called "freedom." But all the qualities that make institutions enduring and meaningful are now despised, ridiculed, and rejected. Even the faintest whisper of authority sends people into a panic about a potential new slavery. In our politics and political parties, the instinct to value and preserve what is solid has decayed so deeply that people instinctively prefer what dissolves, what speeds up the collapse of everything.

Take modern marriage as an example. Its original rationality has vanished completely, but this is not a criticism of marriage itself— it is a criticism of modernity. Marriage once had a clear, rational foundation. It rested on the exclusive legal responsibility of the husband, which acted as a stabilizing force within the union. This stability gave marriage a weight and seriousness that countered the fleeting impulses of sentiment, passion, or momentary desires.

Marriage also relied on the absolute indissolubility of the bond, which instilled it with permanence, regardless of the accidents of emotion. Additionally, the responsibility of choosing marriage partners fell to the family, which ensured a certain strategic and long-term coherence in these unions.

The increasing preference for love marriages, however, has undermined the very foundation of matrimony. No institution can ever be built upon a fleeting idiosyncrasy such as "love." Love is too transitory, too unstable to bear the weight of a lasting structure. Marriage can be based on more enduring forces: sexual desire, the instinct of property (with the wife and children seen as possessions), or the instinct of dominion. The latter is particularly vital, as it drives the creation of the smallest yet enduring unit of governance—the family. The family requires children and heirs to carry forward its acquired power, wealth, and influence, ensuring a continuity of purpose and solidarity in instincts from one generation to the next.

Marriage, as an institution, assumes a commitment to the greatest and most enduring forms of organization. It presupposes that society as a whole is willing to secure its own continuity into the distant future. Without this shared commitment, marriage loses its meaning. And this is exactly what has happened to modern marriage: it has lost its meaning, and as a result, it is gradually being abolished.

The question of the working man arises from a combination of foolishness and the underlying degenerate instincts that fuel the intellectual confusion of modern times. There are matters so basic and essential to the order of things that they should never even be questioned. This principle, rooted in instinct, serves as the foundation for survival and continuity. Yet here we are, asking what we should do about the European working class, having transformed their existence into a "question." What is expected now? These workers have been made too aware of their position, their situation framed as an issue, and their sense of entitlement has grown. They question more and more, with increasing boldness, and why wouldn't they? They know they have the numbers on their side.

There's no chance now of cultivating a humble, contented worker like the kind found in China—a course that would have been both reasonable and necessary. Instead, thoughtless and shortsighted decisions have destroyed the very instincts required for the existence of a functional and stable working class. By declaring the working man fit for military service, granting him the right to unionize, and giving him a vote, society has made his discontent inevitable. What did people expect? These concessions have led him to see his position not as a fact of life but as a moral outrage, as an injustice. And yet I ask again, what is the goal here? If people desire a certain outcome, they must also desire the means to achieve it. If society wants workers, it is madness to educate them into believing they are masters.

The kind of freedom being clamored for today is not the kind I mean when I speak of freedom. In our era, leaving individuals to their instincts only leads to chaos. These instincts often contradict and destroy one another, tearing individuals apart from within. Modern life itself can be described as a state of physiological self-contradiction. A rational system of education would seek to suppress some instincts with rigorous discipline, allowing others to grow strong and dominant. This pruning would make individuals coherent and capable. Instead, what we see today is the opposite. The loudest calls for independence, for unchecked development, and for "letting go" come from those who most desperately need restraint. This phenomenon extends to politics and even art. It is a sign of decline, another proof of our instincts faltering. The modern understanding of "freedom" is not a triumph; it is evidence of our degeneration.

When faith becomes necessary, honesty among moralists and saints becomes exceedingly rare. They may claim to value honesty; they may even believe they practice it. But when belief is more effective, more convincing, and ultimately more useful than deliberate hypocrisy, instinct makes that hypocrisy innocent. This principle is key to understanding the behavior of great saints. The same can be said for philosophers, who are their own kind of saint. Their role requires them to uphold certain truths, truths that bolster their craft and grant it public approval. To borrow from Kant, these are the truths of "practical reason." Philosophers know what they must prove. This is their pragmatism, their trade secret. They recognize one another by their shared adherence to these "essential truths." The commandment "Thou shalt not lie" is, for the philosopher, merely a warning: Do not dare, dear philosopher, to speak the entire truth.

A quiet reminder to conservatives: What we have learned—or should have learned—is that regression is impossible. Reverting to a previous state, whether biologically, culturally, or morally, is a fantasy. As physiologists, we know this for a fact. Yet priests and moralists have always believed otherwise. They have tried to bend and force humanity back into older molds of virtue, imposing the rigid standards of morality as if humanity could fit back into them. Even modern politicians mimic these moralists. Today, some political movements aim to force the world into a backward march, longing for an imagined past where everything supposedly worked. But not everyone is suited to move backward like a crab.

The truth is, humanity must move forward, even if this means deeper descent into decadence. This is how I define modern "progress": each step forward is another step further into decay. We cannot halt this trajectory entirely. At best, we might delay it, creating bottlenecks of degeneration that will only result in more violent and catastrophic outbursts later on. But we cannot turn back the tide. Progress, as we conceive of it today, is no more than the managed advance of decline.

My concept of genius begins with the idea that great men and great eras are like explosive forces, holding within them a tremendous amount of stored energy. Their very existence depends on both historical and physiological conditions. They arise only when energy has been conserved, hoarded, and preserved over long periods without any premature release. Once the tension has built to an extreme, even the slightest trigger can ignite the force, giving rise to genius, extraordinary deeds, and monumental changes in the world.

What, then, is the significance of external factors like environment, historical periods, or the so-called "spirit of the age"? Consider Napoleon as an example. Revolutionary France, and even more so the years preceding the Revolution, cultivated values and produced types of people entirely contrary to what Napoleon represented. Yet Napoleon emerged not as a product of that age, but as a legacy of a stronger, older, and more enduring civilization—a civilization whose vitality France was busy dismantling. Precisely because he was different, because he drew from a deeper reservoir of power and tradition, Napoleon became the uncontested master of his time. His strength surpassed that of his contemporaries, allowing him to dominate them.

Great individuals are essential, yet the era in which they appear is largely a matter of chance. Their near-inevitable mastery of their time stems from their greater strength, maturity, and the longer duration for which power has been stored within them. The relationship between genius and its era is like that between strength and weakness, or maturity and immaturity. A genius always towers above his age, which is comparatively youthful, feeble, indecisive, and naive.

Today, however, many people hold a different view, especially in France, where the idea that the "environment" or "zeitgeist" shapes genius has gained almost scientific credibility, even among physiologists. This belief—a sort of nervous disorder disguised as intellectual insight—is a troubling and disheartening sign. England, too, subscribes to this view, but this is hardly surprising. The English tend to interpret genius in only two ways: either through a democratic lens, as exemplified by Buckle, or through a religious perspective, as Carlyle does.

Great individuals and great ages bring with them immense danger. They exhaust what came before and often leave sterility in their wake.

A great man signifies an ending, just as a great age—take the Renaissance, for instance— marks the conclusion of a long buildup of energy. Genius, in both action and creation, is inherently extravagant. Its greatness lies in its uncontainable outpouring of energy. The instinct for self-preservation is overridden in such figures; their overwhelming energy compels them to give and expend themselves completely, without restraint. This process is not calculated or deliberate—it is as inevitable as a river bursting through its dams.

People often misinterpret this self-expenditure, labeling it "self-sacrifice" or admiring it as "heroism." They speak of the genius's disregard for personal well- being, their unwavering dedication to an idea, a cause, or a nation. But these are misconceptions. A genius does not act out of deliberate self-sacrifice; they overflow naturally, consuming themselves in the process. They cannot help but give everything—they are compelled by their very nature to do so, just as a river must flow.

Humanity, having reaped countless benefits from such explosive forces, has responded with a peculiar kind of gratitude. It has attributed to these figures a higher morality, seeing in them ideals of selflessness and devotion. Yet this, too, is a misunderstanding. It is not morality that drives the genius; it is the sheer necessity of their nature. Humanity thanks its benefactors in the only way it knows—by misinterpreting them.

The criminal and those like him represent the strong man placed in conditions that do not suit him—a strong nature forced into sickness. He is a man who thrives in wild and untamed environments, where freedom and danger shape life, where the instincts of strength—his shield and sword—find their rightful place. But within society, these very virtues are outlawed. His natural instincts are immediately entangled with emotions like fear, suspicion, and shame. Such a conflict is nearly a formula for physical and psychological decline. When a person must carry out what he is best at—what he most loves—not openly but in secrecy, with constant caution, restraint, and craftiness, it saps his vitality. The repeated necessity of paying for his instincts through danger, persecution, or punishment causes him to turn against those very instincts. He comes to see them as his curse.

This process unfolds most severely in our society, which is tame, average, and emasculated. A natural man, one unshaped by civilization, coming from the mountains or the open seas, is almost certain to decay into a criminal in such an environment. Yet, not always: there are cases where the natural man is stronger than society itself. Napoleon, the Corsican, stands as the most famous example of this triumph.

To explore this further, we can turn to Dostoevsky, a witness of singular importance on this issue. Dostoevsky—incidentally the only psychologist from whom I have learned anything—was among the great discoveries of my life, even more rewarding than Stendhal. This deeply insightful man, who had every reason to hold the shallow Germans in contempt, found among the Siberian convicts he lived with for years—those utterly hopeless criminals with no chance of returning to society—a type of humanity very different from what he had anticipated. These convicts were made of the hardest and most valuable material to be found in Russian society, carved from a superior stock.

Now let us generalize the case of the criminal. Let us think of all individuals who, for whatever reason, fail to gain society's approval. These are people who know they are not seen as beneficial or respectable. They exist with the feelings of outcasts, akin to the Chandala, aware that they are not treated as equals but as untouchables, proscribed, or polluted. Their thoughts and actions are shaped by this awareness, marked by a certain shadowy, subterranean quality. Their inner world becomes dimmed compared to those who live in the sunlight of public favor.

Interestingly, many of the figures we now admire and respect once lived under such conditions. The scientist, the artist, the genius, the independent thinker, the actor, the entrepreneur, and the great adventurer—all of these lived lives that were once disdained. As long as the priest stood as the highest type of man, all others of value were diminished, seen as less worthy. However, the time is coming—this I assert with certainty—when the priest will be regarded as the lowest type of man, as our Chandala, the most dishonest and disreputable among us.

Even now, under the most lenient and humane customs ever known in Europe, any life that stands apart, that is prolonged in obscurity or strangeness, begins to resemble the criminal type. All pioneers of the spirit bear for a time the grim and fateful mark of the Chandala. It is not because they are directly seen as such by others, but because they themselves feel the enormous gulf that separates them from what is accepted and honored in tradition. Nearly every genius experiences this phase of the "Catilinarian life"—a stage filled with hatred, revenge, and rebellion against everything stagnant and established. Catiline—the early form of every future Caesar.

Here the outlook is free. When a philosopher chooses silence, it can signify the greatness of his soul; when he contradicts himself, it might stem from love; and when he lies, it may well be the courtesy of a knight of knowledge. As someone aptly remarked, "It is unworthy of great hearts to spread the turmoil they feel." Yet, it is equally true that there can be greatness in not avoiding what seems undignified. A woman in love may sacrifice her honor, a knight of knowledge who "loves" may sacrifice his humanity, and a god who loved became a Jew.

Beauty is no accident. Even the beauty of a race or family, the grace and perfection of all its movements, does not come easily. Like genius, it is the culmination of generations of effort. Great sacrifices have always been made on the altar of good taste, and much has been deliberately left undone. The 17th century in France serves as a prime example of this, a time when both action and restraint worked hand in hand to elevate aesthetics. A principle of selection was applied to everything—company, environment, clothing, and even the expression of sexual desire. Beauty was prioritized over profit, habit, public opinion, and laziness. The first rule was simple: no one should "let themselves go," not even in private.

Good things are exceedingly expensive. This is true not only in monetary terms but in the discipline required to acquire them.

Whoever possesses beauty or refinement is different from someone still striving for it. Everything good is an inheritance, something passed down and refined over time. What isn't inherited is incomplete; it is only a beginning. In ancient Athens, during Cicero's time, men and boys were more beautiful than women. But this was the result of centuries of rigorous effort and self-discipline devoted to male beauty. Let us not be deceived: refining feelings and thoughts alone is insufficient. This is the great failing of German culture, which emphasizes abstract ideals but neglects the body.

The body must be persuaded first. Maintaining a refined and tasteful demeanor, associating only with others who do the same, shapes one's entire being over a few generations. The destiny of a people or humanity is determined by where they begin their cultural efforts. The starting point must be the body, behavior, diet, and physiology—not the "soul," as priests and moralists insist. The Greeks understood this foundational truth and acted upon it, which is why they remain the first true creators of culture. Christianity, with its disdain for the body, has been the greatest misfortune to ever befall humanity.

Progress, as I see it, is not about returning to a primal state but ascending into a more profound and untamed naturalness. It is about reaching a height where one can grapple with grand challenges, even play with them. Take Napoleon as an example of what I mean by a "return to nature." In his tactics and strategy, he exemplified this ascent. But Rousseau? Where did he wish to return? Rousseau, that first modern man, was both an idealist and a scoundrel. Needing moral dignity to endure his own reflection, he was a creature of vanity and self-loathing. He camped on the threshold of modernity, calling for a "return to nature." But what kind of nature did he envision? I detest Rousseau even in the Revolution. The Revolution's bloody spectacle does not disturb me as much as its Rousseau-inspired morality. It was the morality of mediocrity masquerading as justice.

The doctrine of equality is the deadliest poison of all, for it pretends to speak in the name of justice while veiling true justice. Justice would say, "To equals, equality; to unequals, inequality." Never should unequal things be made equal. The horrors and bloodshed associated with this doctrine have granted it an undeserved aura of sanctity. The Revolution, as a drama, has deceived even noble minds. Only Goethe, as far as I can see, viewed it as it should be seen— with utter disdain.

Goethe was not merely a German figure but a European one. He was a bold attempt to overcome the 18th century by reclaiming the naturalness of the Renaissance. In Goethe, the instincts of his century—its sentimentality, its idolization of nature, and its anti-historical spirit—were transformed. He was a realist who embraced life rather than shrinking from it. Goethe sought wholeness, uniting reason, feeling, sensuality, and will, in opposition to the fragmented doctrines of Kant. He disciplined himself into a harmonious whole and became a master of himself.

Goethe dreamed of a complete human being: cultured, physically skilled, self-respecting, and capable of indulging in life's richness without being destroyed by it. He was tolerant not from weakness but from strength, turning adversity to his advantage.

He embodied a cheerful fatalism, embracing the universe with confidence. Such faith, the highest of all, is what I have called Dionysian—a celebration of life that affirms all existence.

In some ways, the 19th century aspired to Goethe's ideals: broad understanding, bold realism, and reverence for life's facts. Yet, the result was chaos, fatigue, and a retreat into the sentimental mediocrity of the 18th century—romanticism, socialism, and altruism. This century, especially in its later years, became an intensified version of its predecessor: a period of decline. Goethe, despite his greatness, was merely an episode—a magnificent but futile effort.

Great men should not be judged by their immediate utility. Humanity often misunderstands its benefactors, attributing to them motives they never had. Goethe is the last German I respect. He understood the cross, as I understand it, and shared my disdain for what it symbolizes. People often ask why I write in German when I am so little read in Germany. My aim is not immediate recognition but to create works that time itself cannot erode. Both in form and content, I strive for a degree of immortality. The aphorism and the concise sentence, forms in which I am a master, are eternal. My ambition is to say in ten sentences what others cannot say in a whole book.

With Thus Spoke Zarathustra, I have given humanity its deepest book.

Soon, I will give it its most independent one.

Chapter 10
Things I owe to The Ancients

In conclusion, I want to say a few words about that world to which I have sought new ways of access and for which I may have discovered a new passage—the ancient world. My taste, which is perhaps the opposite of tolerant, does not wholeheartedly embrace even this world. In general, I am not eager to say Yes to things. I would rather say No, or, better yet, say nothing at all. This is true of entire cultures; it is true of books; and it is true of places and landscapes.

To be honest, there are very few ancient books that hold a special place in my life, and the most famous ones are not included among them.

My sense of style, particularly for the epigram as a form of expression, seemed to awaken almost instantly when I first encountered Sallust. I still recall the astonishment of my respected teacher Corssen when he was compelled to give his worst Latin student the highest marks. Suddenly, and all at once, I understood everything there was to learn. The condensed and austere language, packed with meaning and with an almost mischievous indifference to "beautiful words" and "beautiful feelings"—in these I found my own inclination. In my writings leading up to Thus Spoke Zarathustra, you will notice a serious effort to achieve a Roman style—a style that aspires to the permanence of "more enduring than bronze."

The same thing occurred when I first read Horace. No poet, even to this day, has given me the same intense artistic pleasure as an ode by Horace did from the very beginning. In some languages, it would be ridiculous to even attempt what Horace achieves. His writing is like a mosaic where every word radiates its influence both to the left and the right. Its placement, sound, and meaning all work together to create an extraordinary effect. This economy of words—where the least amount of signs produces the maximum energy—is distinctly Roman. And, if you trust my judgment, it is the very definition of noble excellence. Compared to this, all other poetry seems almost crude, like meaningless, sentimental rambling.

I cannot say that I owe the Greeks anything resembling the profound impressions I have received from the Romans. To be frank, the Greeks can never hold the same significance for us as the Romans do. The Greeks are not teachers in the same way. Their style is too peculiar, too fluid, to impose itself as a model or to attain the weight of a true classic. Who has ever truly learned how to write from a Greek? It is impossible to imagine anyone mastering writing without the Romans. They are our true instructors. And do not suggest Plato to me—I remain fundamentally skeptical of him. I have never been able to align myself with the tradition among scholars of admiring Plato as an artist.

Even in antiquity, the most refined critics of taste were not taken by Plato as we are led to believe. To my mind, Plato jumbles all the forms of style into a chaotic mix. In this sense, he is one of the earliest examples of stylistic decadence. He shares this fault with the Cynics, who created the satura Menippea. The Platonic dialogue—a smug, almost juvenile form of dialectics—could only charm someone who has never read good French writers, such as Fontenelle. Plato, I must confess, bores me. At heart, my distrust of him is fundamental. I see him as profoundly removed from the essential instincts of the Hellenes, steeped in moral prejudices, and, in some respects, as a precursor to Christianity. For Plato, the idea of "good" is already the supreme value—a concept that foreshadows the Christian morality to come. If I had to give Plato's philosophy a blunt name, I might call it "lofty nonsense," or, if preferred, "idealism."

Humanity has paid a high price for this Athenian's education among the Egyptians—or perhaps among the Jews in Egypt? Plato, with his double-edged charm—the so-called "ideal"— became the bridge by which the nobler spirits of antiquity were led to misunderstand themselves and cross into the ideology that culminated in the Christian cross. And even now, how much Plato remains entrenched in the concepts of the "church," in its architecture, its system, and its practices!

For me, the cure, the antidote, and the reprieve from all this Platonism has always been Thucydides. His work represents my ideal of clarity and realism.

Perhaps Machiavelli's The Prince is his closest relative in spirit. Both refuse to delude themselves. They seek reason in reality, not in abstract rationality or morality. Thucydides is the antithesis of the sugary, romanticised vision of the Greeks that modern "classical education" instills in young minds. His writings should be read with great care, each line scrutinised, and his unspoken ideas considered just as seriously as his explicit words. Few thinkers possess so much depth in what they leave unsaid.

Thucydides is the consummate expression of the Sophist tradition, that movement grounded in realism which resisted the idealistic pretensions and moral posturing of Socratic thought as it spread in all directions. For me, Greek philosophy represents the decline of Greek instincts, whereas Thucydides encapsulates the unflinching, rigorous realism of the ancient Hellene.

The distinction between Thucydides and Plato is ultimately one of courage versus fear. Thucydides confronts reality with bravery and clarity, while Plato shrinks from it, retreating into the comforting arms of ideals. Thucydides is a master of his own mind and therefore a master of life. Plato, on the other hand, flees from life into the shadows of abstract ideals. This makes Thucydides not just a historian, but a thinker of unyielding power and strength, unmatched in his affirmation of reality.

To unearth examples of "beautiful souls," "golden means," or other supposed perfections among the Greeks, to admire their serene grandeur, their so-called ideal attitudes, or their exalted simplicity— this "exalted simplicity," which in truth is nothing more than a piece of German naivety, was something from which my inner psychologist always saved me. What I saw instead was their most powerful instinct: the relentless Will to Power. I saw them driven by the fierce and untamed force of this will, trembling with its violence. I recognized that their institutions were not built on harmony but on strategies of containment, created to protect every individual from the volatile, explosive energy simmering within their neighbor.

This immense internal tension found its outlet in violent and ruthless aggression directed outward, toward other states. Their cities tore at one another in brutal conflict, each striving to maintain peace within by externalizing the chaos. Strength became an absolute necessity in this environment, for danger was constant and ever-present, lurking at every corner. The extraordinary grace and flexibility of their bodies, the bold realism, and even the characteristic amorality of the Hellenes—these were not innate attributes but rather survival mechanisms. These traits were forged under the pressures of their circumstances, not gifts they were born with.

Even their festivals and artistic achievements were not mere expressions of joy or creativity but instruments of self-assertion and self-glorification. These were deliberate efforts to heighten their sense of superiority, to project it outward, and sometimes to inspire terror in those who observed them. Imagine judging the Greeks through a lens shaped by German interpretations—seeing them through the narrow focus of their philosophers. Worse yet, imagine using the staid, suburban respectability of the Socratic schools as the key to understanding the essence of what is truly Hellenic!

The truth is that the philosophers were the decadent offshoots of Hellas, a counter-movement that ran against the grain of their original and noble values. They opposed the agonal instinct, the competitive drive that defined the Hellenic spirit; they rejected the spirit of the polis, the pride in racial excellence, and the authority of deep-rooted traditions. Socratic virtues were only preached to the Greeks because the Greeks had already begun to lose their virtue. Irritable, cowardly, unsteady, and increasingly prone to theatricality, they were a people in decline, desperate for the moral sermons directed at them.

But these moral prescriptions did not save them. They could not. Instead, these grand gestures and lofty words were little more than adornments for a society in decay. Decadents are always drawn to such displays, for they cling to the illusion of greatness even as it slips further from their grasp. Morality, as the Greeks came to know it through their philosophers, was not a cure but a symptom—a symptom of a people who had already lost their way.

I was the first to take the phenomenon of Dionysus seriously in order to understand the ancient, vibrant, and abundantly rich Hellenic instinct. This phenomenon, remarkable in its essence, can only be interpreted as an expression of overflowing energy. Whoever has studied the Greeks as profoundly as Jakob Burckhardt of Basel, one of the finest connoisseurs of their culture, would immediately recognize that this interpretation opened a new path of understanding. In his Cultur der Griechen, Burckhardt even dedicated a special chapter to this subject, acknowledging its significance. On the other hand, consider the almost laughable deficiency of instinct displayed by German philologists when they approach the question of Dionysus. The famous Lobeck, for example, burrowed into this mysterious realm with the assuredness of a dried-up bookworm, convinced he was being scientific when, in truth, his approach was painfully superficial and immature.

With all the pomp of erudition, Lobeck reduced the mysteries to trivialities, suggesting that the orgies merely taught participants banal facts like how wine stirs desire or that plants bloom and fade with the seasons. He explained away the immense wealth of rites, symbols, and myths rooted in these rituals—which permeate the entirety of antiquity—with the dismissive notion that the Greeks merely invented festivals and myths as idle diversions. His conclusion, that celebratory behaviors like laughing, weeping, and dancing formed the basis of elaborate traditions, is nothing short of absurd. This reductionist nonsense, presented as scholarship, deserves no serious consideration.

Contrast this with the more profound vision of the Greeks as seen by figures like Winckelmann and Goethe. Yet even they misunderstood something essential. Their idealized image of the Greeks—one of calm grandeur, rational simplicity, and harmonious beauty—could not accommodate the Dionysian essence. Goethe, for instance, likely dismissed the ecstatic fervor of Dionysian rites, failing to recognize that these mysteries revealed the core of the Greek soul. This core was their "will to life," expressed most powerfully in the Dionysian state. Through these mysteries, the Greeks secured for themselves a profound connection to life eternal, embracing its cyclical nature and celebrating the continuity of existence through procreation and renewal.

To the Greeks, the mysteries of sexuality symbolized the sacred foundation of life itself. Every aspect of birth, creation, and renewal was steeped in reverence and seen as divine. Even pain, particularly the pain of childbirth, was sanctified, as it was inseparable from creation and growth. This sanctification of pain carried a deeper message: to ensure the endless joy of creation, the "pains of childbirth" must be eternal. Such is the symbolism of Dionysus, the affirmation of life in all its fullness, including its suffering, its ecstasy, and its inexhaustible capacity for renewal.

Christianity later distorted this profound connection, branding sexuality as impure and casting filth upon the very foundation of existence. In doing so, it severed humanity from the instinctual reverence for life that the Greeks held sacred. Yet it was the psychology of orgiasm—this experience of overwhelming vitality, where even pain becomes a stimulant—that gave me the key to understanding the concept of tragic feeling. Aristotle and the pessimists misunderstood tragedy entirely. Far from being an expression of Greek pessimism, as Schopenhauer claimed, tragedy represents the ultimate rejection of such a worldview. It is a triumphant affirmation of life, embracing even its most perplexing and terrifying aspects.

The essence of tragedy lies in its exultation of life's inexhaustible energy, even in the sacrifice of its highest forms. This is the Dionysian spirit, the bridge to the psychology of the tragic poet. It does not aim to escape terror and pity or to purge dangerous passions through catharsis, as Aristotle supposed. Instead, it transcends terror and pity, rejoicing in the eternal cycle of creation and destruction, the endless becoming that is life itself. This lust for life, which includes a love for destruction as part of creation, is at the heart of the Dionysian worldview.

With this understanding, I return to the foundation of my philosophy, to the starting point of my intellectual journey. The Birth of Tragedy was my first attempt to reevaluate all values, and here, once again, I stand upon the same ground from which my will and power originate. I am the last disciple of the philosopher Dionysus, the prophet of eternal recurrence.

The End

Thank You for Reading

Dear Reader,

We hope this timeless classic has sparked your imagination and enriched your literary journey. Now that you've turned the final page, we want to share a vision for the future of reading—one where every classic you've ever wanted to explore is at your fingertips, in a format that best suits your life.

We'd like to invite you to gain immediate, unlimited digital & audiobook access to hundreds of the most treasured literary classics ever written—along with the option to secure deluxe paperback, hardcover & box set editions at printing cost. Together, we can spark a new global literary renaissance alongside our small, independent publishing house called "The Library of Alexandria."

Thousands of years ago, the Library of Alexandria stood as a beacon of knowledge—until it was lost to history. We aim to reignite that spirit of preservation and discovery right now, in the modern age—only this time, it's accessible to all, in every language and every format.

Picture a world where every timeless classic, novel, poem, or philosophical treatise is not only available to read but also updated for today's readers—modernized, translated into any language or dialect, and ready to enjoy in any format you choose, whether that is in an eBook, audiobook, paperback, or deluxe hardcover & box set version a printing cost.

By joining our movement to rebuild the modern Library of Alexandria, you become part of an unprecedented mission to offer:

- **Unlimited Audiobook & eBook Access to the Greatest Classics of All Time**

    Instantly explore thousands of legendary works, from Plato and Shakespeare to Jane Austen and Leo Tolstoy. All are instantly ready to read or listen to, giving you a complete literary universe at your fingertips.

- **Paperback & Deluxe Editions at Printing Costs:**

  Purchase any title in a paperback, deluxe hardbound, or deluxe boxset edition at printing costs, shipped right to your doorstep. Curate your personal library of Alexandria with editions worthy of display—crafted to last, designed to captivate, and delivered straight to your door.

- **Modern translations for Contemporary Readers in all languages and dialects**

  Discover a vast selection of classics reimagined in clear, current language—no more struggling with outdated phrases or obscure references. Next to the original versions, we aim to offer translations in as many languages and dialects as possible.

  As we continue our translation efforts and add new languages, readers everywhere can connect with these works as if they were written today. By bridging linguistic divides, you're contributing to ensuring that these timeless stories become more meaningful, accessible, and inspiring for people across the globe.

- **Your Personal Library of Alexandria:**

  Over the months and years, you'll curate a unique physical archive of classics—each volume a testament to your taste, curiosity, and love of knowledge. It's not just about owning books—it's about curating a cultural legacy you'll cherish and pass down for generations to come.

- **Join a Global Literary Renaissance:**

  Your support fuels an ongoing mission: allowing us to reinvest in offering deluxe print editions (including special boxsets) at their true cost, broaden the range of available formats and translations, and extend the reach of these works to new audiences worldwide. By joining today, you're not just preserving a legacy of masterpieces; you set in motion a powerful wave of literary accessibility.

We are more than a publisher—we're a movement, and we can't do it alone. Your support lets us scale our mission, preserving and reimagining history's greatest works for tomorrow's readers.

Become a Torchbearer of knowledge.

Thank you for picking up this book and allowing us into your literary journey. As you turn the pages, know that you're part of something larger: a global effort to keep these stories alive, share their wisdom across borders and generations, and spark a true cultural revival for the modern era.

If this resonates with you—please consider taking the next step by visiting:

www.libraryofalexandria.com

With gratitude and a shared love of knowledge,

The Modern Library of Alexandria Team

Visit:

www.libraryofalexandria.com

Or scan the code below:

www.ingramcontent.com/pod-product-compliance
Lightning Source LLC
Chambersburg PA
CBHW011959050726
47499CB00010BA/3213